The Accidental Prophet

Quin Hillyer

A Conservatarian Press Publication

ISBN: 978-1-957586-26-7

The Accidental Prophet

(Previously published in three parts as Mad Jones, Heretic; Mad Jones, Hero; and Mad Jones, Agonistes)

Copyright 2023 Quin Hillyer

All Rights Reserved

This book is a work of fiction. People, places, events, and situations are the product of the writer's imagination.

No part of this book may be reproduced, stored in a retrieval system, or transmitted by any means without the written permission of the author and publisher.

In memory of **Dorothy Lill**, the best school librarian ever, who re-instilled my love of reading back in 1973.

Contents

Genesis 7

    Chapter One 9

    Chapter 1(a) 23

    Chapter Two 25

    Chapter Three 41

Exodus 51

    Chapter One 53

    Chapter Two 57

    Chapter Three 75

    Chapter Four 87

    Chapter Five 113

    Chapter 5(a) 127

    Chapter Six 129

    Chapter Seven 147

    Chapter Eight 165

Chronicles 193

    Chapter One 195

    Chapter Two 211

    Chapter Three 241

    Chapter Four 263

    Chapter Five 277

    Chapter Six 307

Chapter Seven 323

Chapter Eight 341

Chapter Nine 355

Psalms 389

Second Chronicles 395

Chapter One 397

Chapter Two 413

Chapter Three 443

Lamentations 455

Chapter One 457

Chapter Two 469

Chapter Three 483

Chapter Four 497

Chapter Five 513

Chapter Six 543

Chapter Seven 555

Chapter Eight 567

Chapter Nine 579

Chapter Ten 597

Chapter Eleven 611

Chapter Twelve 621

Revelation 629

Appendix A 659

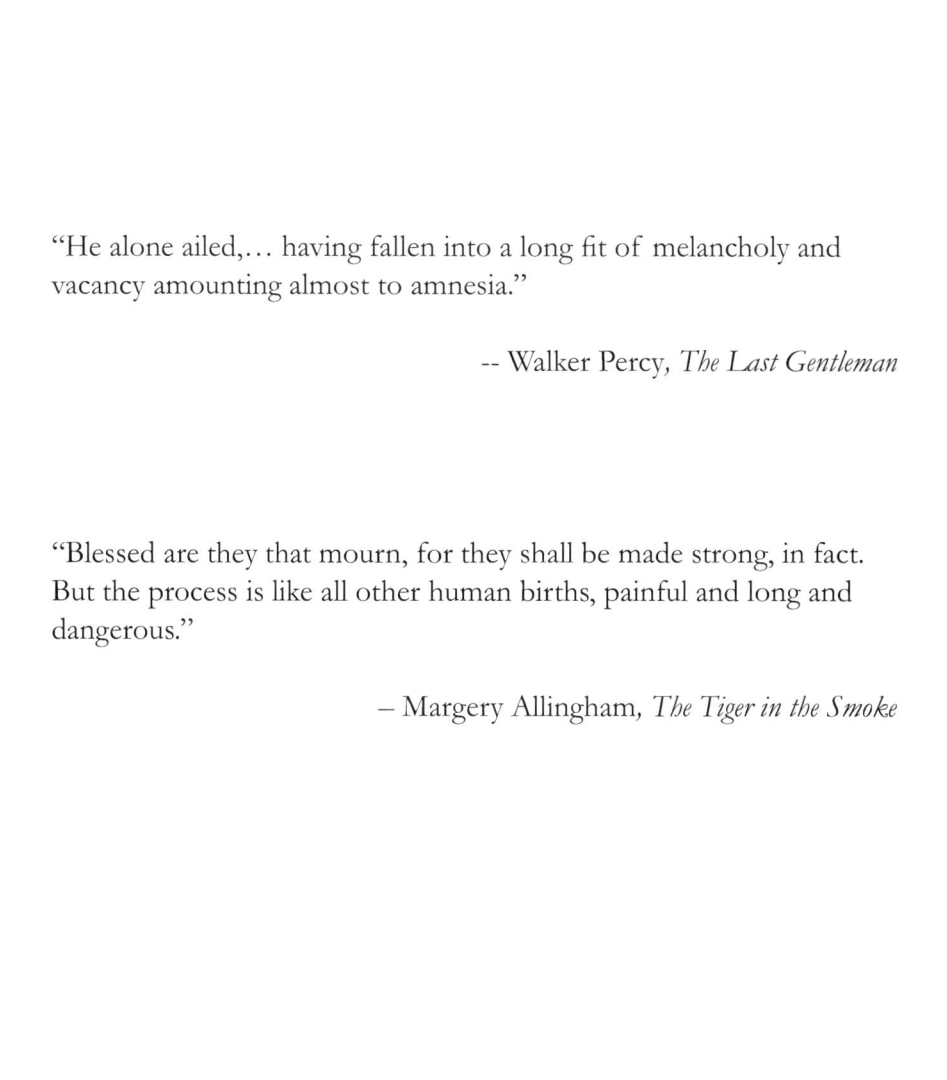

"He alone ailed,… having fallen into a long fit of melancholy and vacancy amounting almost to amnesia."

-- Walker Percy, *The Last Gentleman*

"Blessed are they that mourn, for they shall be made strong, in fact. But the process is like all other human births, painful and long and dangerous."

– Margery Allingham, *The Tiger in the Smoke*

Genesis

Chapter One

"Would you believe?…" began Maxwell Smart from the TV screen, and young Mad Jones began to laugh out loud from his hospital bed. Mad buzzed the nurse and asked for a legal pad. A half hour later, when the nurse finally entered his room to deliver a few odd sheets of looseleaf paper, she found Mad curled into a fetal position, sobbing.

So much for discharge from the medical center tomorrow.

The nurse quietly set the papers on the small, round bedside table, and then found herself leaning over and kissing Mad on the forehead, as a middle-aged daughter would tenderly kiss a senile dad. Mad didn't respond, and the nurse hurried back to her station, wondering why her face suddenly felt flushed.

It wasn't until nearly an hour later that Mad sat up, reached for the loose-leaf and a soft purple Marks-A-Lot that rested atop a Bible, and scrawled:

Theses
By Mad Jones

Would you believe ...

1. God is a flawed sonuvabitch, just like the humans he created.

* * *

In the stillest part of the night – 1:43 a.m. according to the neon digital clock, above the door, which kept the room from ever reaching pitch black – Mad awoke, clammy and chilled, from a restless sleep troubled by dead people. His mind turned to the oft-told story of how his father met his mother in The Tombs…

Ben Jones, intermittently devout Episcopalian from the once-Catholic Spanish decrepit historic mosquito-filled town of Mobile, Alabama, was a graduate student in history at the Jefferson-haunted University of Virginia in May of 1970. At age 24, just two years after graduating magna cum laude (disappointed it wasn't summa) also from U.Va., he had just handed in his Masters thesis on the overlooked virtues of the mostly ineffectual Articles of Confederation. He and a friend called Buzz had driven the two hours up to D.C. to celebrate Ben's accomplishment. They had decided to start their night at The Tombs, an old-style basement tavern loosely affiliated with Georgetown University, and then to go wherever Jefferson's spirit moved them.

Jefferson didn't move them for hours. Lee kept them occupied instead.

Ben Jones, an Oxfords-and-khaki stalwart, usually had no use for the beads and jeans his generation made popular. He dated Southern belles who maintained at least the semblance of refinement. But there at the bar at The Tombs that night was a bead-and-jean clad, flaxen-haired lovely whose eyes alone out-smiled the Cheshire Cat. From the angle of his table, she was directly in Ben's line of sight – and, despite himself, he couldn't stop staring at her. It wasn't that she was stunningly beautiful, but just refreshingly pretty – and her eyes danced. Four other guys surrounded her barstool.

The waitress was clearing away Buzz' and Ben's appetizer plates when Miss Flaxen-Hair walked over, sat down at their table uninvited, looked directly at Ben, and said: "Your stare could embarrass the Queen of Sheba. Now I know what an amoeba feels like under a microscope. Do I have spinach in my teeth, or what?"

To which Ben responded: "Huh?"

With such suave sophistication, the story went, did Ben Jones win the heart of his ladylove. Her name was Mel, which actually was an acronym for Mary Elizabeth Lee. She was of the Virginia Lees, though not descended directly from Robert E., but rather from a cousin. Her great-granddaddy had married a committed Catholic and converted to the One True Faith, and each succeeding Lee son dated only within the faith. Her mother was so devout, she was saved from the convent only by a night of wholly unanticipated passion with a Lee boy. In hopes that the resulting daughter would prove worthier and holier than she, the mother named her after both the Blessed Virgin and Mary's cousin Elizabeth, the mother of John the Baptist. But Daddy Lee, whose blood carried the memory of Lighthorse Harry, called the girl Mel and took her fox-hunting and adventuring throughout the Shenandoah.

Mel was now finishing her sophomore year at the School of Nursing at Georgetown, which pleased her mother because the Jesuits ran the place and pleased her father because it was both a historic and a patriotic American institution and also because it meant his tall slender Little Girl remained just a couple of hours from home. Mel's mom was a Pax-above-all, turn-the-other cheek type of Catholic, so Mel hated the war in 'Nam; but because Mel was a Lee, she admired and honored the American soldiers. Mel believed in Peace, Love, and the Beatles, never touched illegal drugs, drank only brandy or single-malt scotch on the rocks, and idolized Hemingway and Katherine Hepburn. She quite openly lusted after Redskin quarterback Sonny Jurgensen (whom she had never met), and the only times she ever cried were when Lassie or Flipper got in danger on TV.

And she liked to flirt with some of the Jesuits, just to see them blush and squirm.

Mel remained at Ben's table for five solid hours, until the tavern's closing time. (In the meantime, Buzz had time to begin and end three woulda-been-lifelong relationships with other girls at The Tombs, and even managed to escort one across the street to the top of the spooky cliffside stairway that would become famous two years later in the Exorcist – but all he got for his trouble was a girl getting nauseous from a combination of beer and vertigo.) When Ben and Mel finally parted after he walked her back to campus, Ben said, "You know, I already love you madly."

And that was that.

In essence, it was already settled.

Twenty-five months later, just after Mel graduated from Georgetown and three months before Ben's breakneck academic schedule earned him a Ph.D. in history (dissertation: "The Unacknowledged Roots of James Madison's Political Philosophy"), Ben and Mel married in Old Richmond and honeymooned on the Isle of Wight. After their first meeting, not a day went by without him telling her, by phone or post or personal greeting, that he loved her madly.

At U.Va., a proud Daddy Lee arranged to have Ben admitted into the prestigious, mysterious, philanthropic Crazy Eights Society; at Georgetown, Mel prevailed upon her favorite Jesuit, a sprightly young 70-year-old named Joe Durkin, to arrange a professorship for Ben at the Jesuit-run Spring Hill College in Ben's hometown of Mobile. Spring Hill's chairman of the history department had been a seminarian with Father Durkin 50 years before and considered any young man recommended by Joe Durkin to be a golden find.

So Ben and Mel, now three months pregnant with a Wight-conceived bundle, moved down to Mobile just in time for Fall classes at Spring Hill. Mel was disappointed to find that Mobile had no fox-hunting clubs, but she enthusiastically took up fishing and wrote anti-war letters to the editor of the Mobile Press. She also quickly made room for Bear Bryant in her pantheon of heroes.

On March 3 of 1973, as Ben nervously and proudly paced the hospital hallways, Mel gave one last mighty push and expelled from her womb a healthy eight-pound baby boy. Ten seconds later, before Mel ever knew what hit her, she died instantly from the most sudden and massive hemorrhage her obstetrician had ever witnessed....

Twenty-five years later, in the room of the psychiatric ward to which Mad had admitted himself two days earlier, Mad suddenly yelled out at a frightening decibel level: "I was born of a hemorrhage and now I've died of a hemorrhage!!!"

Down the hall, the night-shift nurse – a different one from the evening before, 50ish and plumper – was startled awake by the scream and rushed to Mad's room to see what was up. She too found Mad in a fetal position, this time sucking his thumb. Gently, she asked if he was okay. No response. She asked if he wanted anything. No response. Tears forming in her eyes, she leaned over him. "What can I do for you?" No response.

Even in such a pathetic state, there was something about this young man. She briefly envisioned herself crawling onto on the hospital bed with Mad, spooning him from behind as he continued to squeeze his eyes tight and suck his thumb. But she didn't. Instead, full of compassion but with legs oddly wobbling, the nurse pulled away and shuffled back to her station.

Mad awoke six hours later, grabbed his purple marker and the paper and, regularly consulting the Bible, he spent the next half-hour writing – this time in the small, neat handwriting that was his norm:

2. "So God created man in his own image, in the image of God created He him; male and female created He them." Genesis 1:27

3. "I, the Lord thy God, am a jealous God, visiting the iniquity of the fathers upon the children unto the third and fourth generation." Exodus 20:5
"For the Lord thy God is a consuming fire, even a jealous God." Deuteronomy 4:24

4. "For thus saith the Lord God of Israel unto me: 'Take from my hand this cup filled with the wine of my wrath, and cause all the nations, to whom I send thee, to drink it. And they shall drink, and be moved, and be mad, because of the sword that I will send among them." Jeremiah 25:15-16

5. God is arrogant, and mad with power, as when he tortures Job. God says: "Who then is able to stand before me? Who hath prevented me, that I should repay him? Whatsoever is under the whole heaven is mine." Job 41:10-11

Mad looked over what he had written. He thought he might be making headway towards some important ideas, but he really didn't know what, and his mind was too disturbed right now, his heart too pained, for him to really care much where this was leading. All he knew was that after he wrote each thesis, he knew approximately where to look in the Bible, through some trial and error, to make the next thesis follow at least a semi-logical pattern. And that somehow the logic of writing helped mask the pain of grief. After some disjointed thoughts, he continued:

> 6. Christ said: "And his lord was wroth, and delivered him to the tormentors, till he should pay all that was due unto him. So likewise shall my heavenly Father do also unto you, if ye from your hearts forgive not every one his brother their trespasses." Matthew 18:34-35

> 7. It therefore follows that when God created man in God's image, or "likeness" (Genesis 5:1), it was a spiritual and emotional likeness — an interior image — intended, not a physical likeness (which is abundantly made clear throughout the Bible). So we see that God is jealous and wrathful and unfair (as He was to Job), and arrogant and prone to going mad with His own power, and that He punishes mankind overly harshly, even unto torture, when man acts imperfectly, even though it was He, God, who created man as an imperfect being because man is in God's own image — which, of necessity, means that God Himself is imperfect. QED.

Mad was proud of himself now, although he wasn't sure why. He was on a roll, and didn't even need the Bible's help to make the next points that insinuated themselves into his adrenalized brain. Rocking back and forth with nervous energy, he continued:

> 8. As God is imperfect, therefore He is inconsistent — yea, even mercurial.
>
> 9. As God is mercurial, therefore His mercy, at least here on earth, is dependent on God's mood swings, or, i.e., contingent rather than unconditional.
>
> 10. As God's mercy is contingent, and as God is imperfect, so therefore may His mercy be contingent on something other than man's own merit, but rather, at times, on circumstances beyond the ken of man.
>
> 11. God's mercy is therefore entirely unpredictable and unreliable, at least within man's temporal existence.

Finally, seized by a sudden anger that flared up inside him with near-dangerous (and unaccustomed) intensity, Mad wrote in increasingly large print:

> 12. For all intents and purposes, then, to man's way of knowing, **God Is A Jerk.**

* * *

Ben never openly wept for Mel. But his eyes were at least moist every time he held his son in the next few days. He named the boy after his dissertation subject, James Madison, and after his wife's family. Thus, for all anyone else knew, did Madison Lee Jones come to be. But there was another reason, too, for the name. Ben could look at his son, call him Mad (short for Madison) Lee, and remember his wife every time. "I love you, Mad Lee," he would say to his infant, over and over – and in so doing, repeat what he had always told Mel: that he loved her "madly." And it was true, he did love Mad Lee madly, as he loved Mel, but he also loved his son sadly and wistfully and, as the years wore on, somewhat fearfully, as if young Mad Lee were a phantom who might disappear at any moment if Ben tried to hold on to him too tightly.

Ben became a popular professor at Spring Hill – dapper, brilliant, wry, and kind. His students even found it amusing that he gave off a faint air of distraction, as if he were aware he had forgotten something that he was supposed to remember by the string around his finger, only there was no string and, even if there was, he would have forgotten to notice it anyway.

Child care at first was no problem: Mel's mother and Daddy Lee moved down to Mobile and doted on Madison. But when Mrs. Lee ate herself right into a fatal heart attack just 18 months later, Daddy Lee moved back to Virginia to gallivant around the Shenandoah, chasing pretty divorcees. Ben's own parents had both died abnormally young, of rather mysterious sudden ailments, and Ben had no other relatives to call on.

That's when Ben devised a unique plan for the daytime care of little Mad Lee. He wanted to ensure that Mad wouldn't suffer from lack of female influence, so he advertised on the Spring Hill campus for nannies to look after the boy from 9:45 to 5:15 every weekday. He set up a rotating system of up to five student-nannies per semester, with the following special criteria in addition to the girls being responsible and good with kids: 1) They could not be students in his classes, and must pledge never to take his classes (to protect against him being tempted to show them favoritism), and 2) they must have their own transportation (to protect against him being tempted romantically in the course of giving them rides home). Ben paid the girls minimum wage plus free soft drinks, and he expected them to love Mad Lee madly and read to him and play with him and show him what girls liked in their men.

And if they wanted to bring along their boyfriends to play ballgames with the growing boy, that was fine as long as the boyfriends never went inside the house at the same time as the girls (to protect against carnal knowledge). Thus did Mad grow up with a father who returned home from campus promptly by 5:15 each day and, if light permitted, threw and hit the baseball with him to the point of joyous exhaustion. After ball each night, Ben put together a nutritious but exceedingly simple bachelor's dinner, during which he told Mad stories from the only sources he knew intimately: the history books. By age 9, Mad knew more of Presidents Jefferson and Madison – and of William the Conqueror and Martin Luther and Joan of Arc – than most high school graduates. That was Mad's childhood: baseball and history lessons with a kindly but semi-clueless dad, and doting female day-sitters at home (all day before he was school age, or after school once he was old enough for classes). And every summer he would visit Daddy Lee in the Shenandoah for a month and help him gallivant after chic-naughty-cultured wanna-be step-grandmoms whom Daddy Lee kept in endless and rapidly revolving supply.

At school Mad seemed effortlessly clever, effortlessly blond-haired, blue-eyed popular, effortlessly good at baseball (and at most other sports when he tried them), and studiously wry and laconic. He was the kind of boy whom all his schoolmates admired, the kind so easily accepted that he developed no sharp edges. Giving no offense, he made no enemies. Making no enemies, he was the kind of boy whose friendship everyone else coveted, and whose favor everybody else, in their own minds, assumed they had earned. He was not his own Tabula Rasa, but everyone else's – and in his effortlessly popular way, Mad let everyone else imagine him to be whomever they wanted him to be.

Teachers, too, seemed to admire him – although two of the more observant of them, one in kindergarten and one in third grade, mentioned to Ben that Mad skated along with so little apparent effort that he seemed to lack some emotional *depth*. The few setbacks Mad did experience, the teachers noted, he seemed to ignore with an odd detachment.

"That's my boy!" Ben would answer them, proudly. "Won't let *anything* get him down. Sounds like a winner to me!"

And then Ben would wander off, distractedly, as if the conversation were over.

The boy grew tall for his age, and by 11, he respectfully told Ben he didn't need sitters after school any more – to which Ben, again distractedly, replied that he'd cut Mad loose on Mad's 13th birthday.

"But Dad, I'm tired of having these college chicks tell me I'm 'such a cute little boy,'" Mad said – to which Ben responded with a seemingly pointless story culled from the history books about a French Dauphin with a retinue of comely governesses.

* * *

In his hospital room, Mad buzzed the nurse – yet a third one, just come for the beginning of her shift – and pleasantly asked for a whole pad of paper and a ballpoint pen to replace his purple marker.

"Really, I'm not gonna stab myself with a pen," he said to her, winking. "I just want to write you a love letter, that's all."

The nurse, fighting off a strange tingling sensation near her navel, crossed off the "Possibly Suicidal" notation that some doctor had written on Mad's chart and complied with his requests before scurrying back to the nurses' station.

Mad re-copied, word for word, his 12 so-called theses (still with extra size and emphasis on "God is a jerk!"), and then added in his usual neat handwriting:

> 13.   Because God is a jerk, mankind cannot count on God for comfort during this life.

> 14.   Therefore, men and women must rely on other men and women for comfort on earth. (For what it's worth, safe sex can be heap big comfort.)

And then Mad lay back down and thought about a particular day when he was just beginning Seventh Grade…

* * *

Actually, there was someone else who also still remembered that day well. She was Grace Feinstein – so named because her mother was a fan of a certain actress-turned-princess. At the time Mad was starting Seventh Grade, Grace was just beginning her freshman year at Spring Hill, where she was one of the very few Jews at the Jesuit University. She had chosen Spring Hill so as to be with her Catholic boyfriend, who was to play soccer for the NAIA Badgers. Both were from New Orleans, her education gleaned from an elite private school and his from Jesuit High. Grace was a petite (5'1") blonde who was simultaneously lithe and buxom – and she was more than worldly, at one time having quickly secured an abortion without a speck of remorse, and without her boyfriend ever knowing he had made her pregnant.

The day she and Mad both remembered was early September, when she was still a month shy of her 18th birthday. Grace was Professor Jones' most recent hire as a sitter, a job which by now merely entailed picking Mad up at St. James Episcopal School, driving him home to the Jones' mid-town house, and being available in case of emergency for the 1½ hours until Professor Jones got home from work. Mad usually spent the time perfunctorily doing homework, so he'd be free when Ben got home for their ritualized hours (it was still daylight savings time) of baseball.

On this day, the phone was ringing just as Grace and Mad got home, so Mad flung his book-bag on the floor in his race to reach the phone. The bag's contents flew out, and Grace was amused to see that what flew out farthest from between the books was the September issue of "Playboy." When Mad returned from his too-late dash for the phone, he found Grace holding the magazine aloft and smiling.

"So, I bet you like the articles?" she teased, and winked, and then laughed as young Mad's face turned crimson. "Which do you like best – the interviews, or the fiction?"

Flustered, Mad Lee stammered, and Grace took a step towards him. "It's okay," she said, still teasing. "A big, strong boy like you – you look like you've matured early – I bet you're already making out with all your little classmates."

Then, stepping even closer and laying on a thick faux-breathless accent, she murmured: "You big stud, you."

Mad's discomfort showed no signs of abating, and Grace was enjoying herself immensely. Then, hoping to see Mad really squirm, Grace said: "I bet your little girlfriends can't kiss as good as this" – and she closed the remaining gap between them to put her mouth on his, for just a brief hemi-second, just to enjoy her power, just to leave Mad thoroughly flummoxed.

Except … except that as she put her mouth to Mad's, she realized he was already taller than she was … and that his eyes were a particularly deep shade of blue… and that something about his proximity, maybe something about his smell, sent a peculiar sensation from her sinuses through her scalp and down her spine, which began to tremble at its base where it attached to her pelvic region. And without any intention of lingering, she did *not* withdraw her mouth from his, did *not* draw back immediately from his adolescent, frightened, inexpert kiss.

Struggling with her composure, she eventually pulled away for a breath and, attempting to regain her posture of power, said: "See, I *thought* you'd need a lesson, young man: Your technique is all wrong."

And then Grace was kissing Mad again, moving his now-spastic right hand to her high, firm, left breast, and – again trying to sound both in control and only mockingly feral – she purred and rubbed herself against his crotch and tried to say, "You wanna show me whatcha got, Big Boy?"

But all that came out before she lip-locked again was: "wanna (breath) … big."

There was something happening that the worldly Grace couldn't understand, and that a now-writhing Mad certainly didn't understand, and that would have turned Grace's boyfriend violent had he known. And within five minutes, Grace was desperately reaching for one of the ever-ready condoms she kept in her purse…

Two condoms later, Grace's eyes happened upon the clock on the wall, and she screamed: "Ohmygod, we gotta get dressed!"

Which they both managed less than a minute before they heard Ben's car pull into the driveway.

The next day, Grace left a note on Ben's office door saying her schedule had changed and she wouldn't be able to continue sitting for Ben's adorable young Mad and she hoped this wouldn't leave him in the lurch. She and Mad had not seen each other since.

Mad, having discovered through Grace an odd power over female companions, proceeded to deflower three of his classmates before they even reached high school. He always used condoms, and the girls remained curiously devoted to him even as he good-naturedly moved on to other girls without the slightest compunction or depth of feeling.

Because everything came so easily to him, depth of feeling was not a quality Mad had ever really needed to develop. Or so he would have thought, it he had ever thought about it at all – which he hadn't.

* * *

Now, though, in the psych ward, Mad was feeling more than he could bear. Soul-black grief held him in a death-vise. He felt like one does after a bout with the dry-heaves, except that the emptiness and pain seemed to have no one particular source, seemed to plague him from both the outside-in and the inside-out.

He tried to compose himself. As had always been his wont on those rare occasions when he did begin to feel too strongly, he tried to reason instead. Mad added the fifteenth "thesis" to his list:

> 15. When human turns to human for comfort, which man often does because God cannot be counted on to provide it, God may become jealous (for He is a jealous God), and in His jealousy God may deliberately cause discomfort to man — for no good reason, not even for good reason according to the unknowable lights of God.

Chapter 1(a)

"Would you believe," a middle-aged Jesuit asked his college theology class, "that God created this same world in two different ways? Well, unless you understand that the Bible was actually recorded by many different people at different times, you'll be very confused at the very start, at Genesis, in which there are two creation stories entirely distinct from each other. In one version, for instance, God created the animals before creating man; in the other, He created man before the animals. And in the second story, God tells man what future awaits him, namely a life of toil. …"

This Jesuit with an Italian surname had no way of knowing that only a few miles from him, a young man lay in a psychiatric ward, a young man with and for whom he would toil, in the not-too-distant future. The Jesuit was a man of great faith, and the young man would be in need of great faith. For the young man would come to know great fame, yea, and great controversy too. With politicians and preachers would the young man be oft-loved and also oft-reviled, and lo, the media would raise him up and cut him down, and raise him and cut him, as in the cycles of the seasons of the earth. And the Jesuit would come to see the young man as his ward and keep, and the Jesuit would try mightily to hold the young man up so the young man might not lose sight of the love and the glory of his Lord.

The Jesuit was a sage, but verily he was no prophet, and thus the Jesuit did not know that this was so.

Chapter Two

In his hospital bed, Mad lay back and, feeling slightly purged of his anger, continued his reverie....

When Mad was sixteen and just beginning his junior year of high school, he and Ben found themselves of a late afternoon almost ready to put steaks on the grill for their annual father-son Labor Day barbeque, just the two of them, marking the end of summer.

"So, Dad, I've never really asked you, but why didn't you ever even date anybody since, you know, my mom died?"

Ben smiled his wry wistful sardonic smile and mumbled: "Wouldna been fair."

"Huh?"

"It would not have been right, Son. I mean not fair to anybody I'd have dated. I would always have compared them to your mother, and they could never have measured up in my mind, and they'd sense that they couldn't, and… it just would not have been fair."

"Oh." Then, looking at the charcoals, Mad said: "I think these are ready for the steaks. I'll go get'em."

At the door from the patio to the kitchen, Mad turned back to Ben.

"Yeah, Dad, but what about fair to *you*? Didn't you ever want to have somebody else? Didn't you get, like, lonely?"

Another smile from Ben, suffused with warmth. "I had you around, Son, and that's all I needed."

Then, knowing it would embarrass Mad a little, Ben added, chuckling: "And you know I love you mad-ly."

Hurrying inside to hide his embarrassment, Mad then took his time grabbing the steaks (on their marinade plate) and then returned with them to the patio … to find Ben slouched over in an odd sideways position in his lawn chair, a wryly satisfied smile on his face – not breathing.

Ben had died immediately, of a burst aneurysm in his brain's occipital lobe. He was only 43.

*　*　*

Sitting in his hospital bed, Mad's thoughts turned from his father's death nine years ago to what had happened less than four days ago that had led him to the hospital. An increasingly uneasy ache began to corkscrew in his gut.

"No, I will *not* think about it," Mad muttered to himself. Picking up paper, pen, and Bible, Mad went back to his theses. Looking at number 15, about a jealous God causing discomfort to man, he picked up the thread with these:

> 16. This reality helps explain the words of Jesus to the crowd of wailing women, as Jesus was led on his march of death to Golgotha: "Daughters of Jerusalem, weep not for me, but weep for yourselves, and for your children. For behold, the days are coming in which they shall say, Blessed are the barren, and the wombs that never bore and the breasts which never gave suck." Luke 23:28-29

> 17. Yea, verily do I ask of you: What kind of God, except a fallible God who is a jerk, would curse innocent women whose wombs become with child according to the life-creating union sanctified by God himself through Holy Matrimony?

> 18.   "For we know that the whole creation groaneth and travaileth in pain together until now." Romans 8:22
>
> 19.   "As it is written, For thy sake we are killed all the day long; we are accounted as sheep for the slaughter." Romans 8:36

A while later, Nurse No. 1 peeked into Mad's room. He wasn't in a fetal position, but he stared glassy-eyed, apparently uncomprehendingly, at the TV.

"Do you need anything, Honey?" she asked.

No response. Mad still stared vacantly at the TV.

The nurse went over and sat on the foot of Mad's bed.

"Honey?"

Mad finally focused on her, then turned away. She was pretty. She moved closer. He buried his face in his pillow. She patted his leg through the bedsheet. She felt his pain. She felt her own inexplicable longing. She patted his upper thigh. She felt she was losing control – and she was a girl who liked to be *in* control. Then she noticed the Bible still clutched in his hands, and she thought it condemned her. She left the room feeling guilty for touching Mad's upper thigh through the bedsheet.

* * *

Mad was flooded with letters after Ben's death, letters from all over the country written by students whose lives Ben had touched. He even received a note from Grace Feinstein, whom he hadn't seen since she robbed him from the cradle four years before. She wrote that she would never be able to explain why she did what she did, or why she had then disappeared – but that she wanted him to know how sorry she felt for him when she heard of Ben's death, and that she wished him well. Mad thought it a rather odd letter.

Mad's godfather Buzz, whom Mad barely knew even though Ben had talked about him frequently, came down and helped Daddy Lee oversee the funeral arrangements. Between his Masters and his Ph.D., Buzz had honorably served a six-month rotation in 'Nam before Nixon signed the peace accord, and Buzz had ended up a professor teaching military history at The American University in Washington, D.C. Buzz' hero was Robert E. Lee, and he and Daddy Lee had over the years developed a cross-generational friendship consisting mostly of warm correspondence. The night after the funeral, Buzz and Daddy Lee and the 16 year-old Mad got mildly, oddly happily drunk at a topless bar in the Mobile County boondocks; and Buzz, whose own brief marriage had ended childless, told Mad that any son of good ol' Ben was a son of his – and could Mad *believe* the treasure that dancer had for a chest?

As it turned out, Ben had taken out an unusually large life insurance policy which easily paid the small remainder of his house mortgage, with plenty enough left to generously cover Mad's living expenses for the last two years of high school. Daddy Lee, who by then had begun a fairly comfortable retirement, agreed to move to Mobile to serve as Mad's legal guardian so as not to move Mad from his home, his friends, St. James School, and his baseball team. (Daddy Lee, being firmly of the opinion that young Madison could take care of himself, arranged to sneak away for weeks at a time to gallivant in the Shenandoah, leaving his car behind in Mad's driveway for cover in case somebody from Social Services checked in. Mad's constantly changing supply of girlfriends all found Mad a charming overnight host.)

When it became time for Mad to start applying to college, Daddy Lee informed his grandson that, much as he wanted young Madison to attend *the family college* (Washington & Lee, his *alma mater*), he felt compelled to advise Mad to attend Jefferson's University of Virginia. Letting Mad in on the secret that Ben, along with Daddy Lee's long-deceased brother Jackson, had been somehow affiliated with Virginia's mysterious, philanthropic Crazy Eights Society, Daddy Lee said he had been given an $88,888 check from the Eights which was to be used at U.Va. for the orphan Mad's college tuition, room, board, and expenses. Mad gladly concurred.

In April, however, out of the blue, Mad was offered one of Georgetown's few full baseball scholarships if he chose to attend his mother's *alma mater*. Being an upstanding young man who always honored his commitments, Mad was ready to turn Georgetown down when Daddy Lee phoned from the Shenandoah with amazing news: The Eights, knowing Mad's love for baseball, and knowing that Virginia's coach had oddly shown no interest in having Mad on his team, had sent word that Mad could accept the scholarship to G.U. *and* keep the $88,888 anyway, in a trust fund for after college. The only condition would be that each semester Mad lead a pilgrimage of eight different Georgetown students to Jefferson's famous home, Monticello – plus another 16 either during the summers or within one year of graduation, for a total of 80 – and transmit to the Society, through Daddy Lee, the visitors' names plus at least one comment from each.

So Mad, feeling blessed beyond belief, went off to become a Georgetown Hoya.

In his heart, however, Mad made a private oath to one day do honor to both U.Va. and Jefferson – and to his much-missed father, who had been the one constant in his life, the one person for whom Mad had felt so close that he secretly had to struggle to maintain his usual air of emotional detachment. Mad dearly loved his father, but had never let himself properly grieve Ben's death. *Honor* his late father, though – that, young Mad was determined to do.

* * *

Remembering all this in his hospital room, Mad began to feel a little stronger, a little more solid. Consulting his Bible again, he began to write.

> 20. If we are in pain, and are counted as sheep for the slaughter, shall we then bleat like sheep? Nay, we are sheep only insofar as we acquiesce to sheep-hood.
>
> 21. To acquiesce in sheep-hood is to sin greatly, for it puts us in the position of trying to become Christ, who is the only Lamb of God. Christ Himself commanded us, not to be lambs, but rather to consume Him, the only Lamb, by partaking of the Eucharist. Lambs do not eat Lamb; lions do.

22.   Therefore, Christ calls us all to be lions.

23.   No wonder, then, that the first of God's worshipful seraphim was like a lion (Revelation 4:7) and that the being found worthy to open the book of God was "the Lion of the tribe of Judah" (Revelation 5:5).

24.   As we are called to be lions, and to honor the Lamb by consuming the Lamb, therefore let us also devour life with both reverence and gusto, or else God's great but imperfect creation will devour us who are unworthy, timid souls whose existence rebukes God by reminding Him that what He created can be weak.

25.   "For we are made partakers of Christ, if we hold the beginning of our confidence steadfast unto the end." Hebrews 3:1

Mad particularly liked that quote, so he began to write in larger letters.

26.   "Cast not away therefore your confidence, which hath great recompense of reward... but if any man draw back, my soul shall have no pleasure in him. But we are not of them who draw back unto perdition, but of them that believe to the saving of the soul." Hebrews 10:35, 38-39.

Mad was interrupted by Nurse #2 – the 50ish plump one – who brought in his tray of food (with an extra Jell-O serving as a sign of affection).

"You're looking so much better," she said, again not knowing why her heart raced. "You'll be able to check out of here in no time."

Mad smiled wickedly.

"Cast not away therefore your confidence, which hath great recompense of reward!" he yelled out in a curious, sing-song fashion. "And tonight, you can be my reward!"

Nurse No. 2, frightened, backed quickly out of the room. Mad smiled, and turned on the TV. A couple of good old movies were on, back to back. One was about an upturned ocean liner. Another, very loosely based on a real incident, starred Sean Connery as a sheikh and Candice Bergen as the widow Perdicaris, rescued with the help of a famous ultimatum from Teddy Roosevelt.

Movies over, Mad again began to write on his pad of theses (unknowingly making a slight misquotation in the first).

27. "The Lord loves winners." Gene Hackman, in The Poseidon Adventure.

28. Winners and lions. The Wind and the Lion. Perdicaris alive. And God said: Yes, we can survive even in the desert of our souls. Yes.

29. Jesus survived the wilderness of the desert for 40 days, and withstood the temptations of Satan, all on God's account; yet God repaid Jesus' loyalty by requiring that Jesus suffer on the cross. Jesus did not forsake God, yet Jesus on the cross was moved to ask, and ask rightly, "Eloi, Eloi, lama sabachthani?" — which means "My God, my God, why have you forsaken me?" (Matthew 27:46; Mark 15:34) They were his last words.

30. Christ, God the Son, was forsaken by God the Father. It is said that Christ suffered in order to take upon himself the sins of the world — but God the Father created the world, and created it flawed, so the world had sin.

> Therefore, God is the original author of the sins of the world, sins which we, mankind, who are not omnipotent, have therefore not only committed but also suffered from due to the sins not of our own commission, but of God's.
>
> 31. As in: "Hath not the potter power over the clay, of the same lump to make one vessel unto honour, and another unto dishonour?" Romans 9:21
>
> 32. Christ's suffering therefore not only redeemed us, for our sins against God, but also redeemed God for his sins against we humans who mightily suffer.
>
> 33. Christ died, and was raised through the ultimate grace and glory of God, to save sinners; so, therefore, Christ died to save God, whose mercy grew in strength because Christ allowed Himself to be forsaken and thus gave God a new birth in man's hearts just as he gave man a new birth in the Holy Spirit.

Mad looked at that one; thought to himself that it was a little too rambling and run-on; but then decided that he would have to come back and touch it up later. He continued (and this next was one of which he later would be particularly proud):

> 34. In prayer we call Jesus Christ "our only mediator and advocate." A mediator, by nature, mediates between two (or more) entities, and so therefore both entities are equally beneficiaries of the mediation. God, therefore, is a beneficiary of Christ's mediation with us just as we are beneficiaries of Christ's mediation with God.

> 35.　"As it is written, There is none righteous, no not one." Romans 3:10
>
> 36.　God, too, is among those who aren't righteous. Jesus withstood Satan's temptation, but God did not withstand Satan's temptation when Satan challenged God to prove His power over Job. "Then Satan answered the Lord, and said, Doth Job fear God for nought?" Job 1:9

He had been at his task for hours. Mad finally put down his pen, and slept. He dreamed of a clear Victory.

*　*　*

In early March of 1995, in Madison Jones' last semester as a Georgetown undergraduate, the young history major took his last group of fellow students to Monticello. Among the group was a young woman he didn't know, a sophomore from New Orleans named Claire Victory who had signed up for the Monticello tour at the urging of the now-91-year-old Jesuit, Joe Durkin, whom she knew through the campus Right-to-Life group. Claire was a slender brunette with a mischievous smile, a laughingly lilting voice, and greenish eyes which had the aspect of windows into a rapidly whirring mind. She was a theology major and a borderline member of the Georgetown women's tennis team. And, wow, could she ever carry on a conversation! Books, movies, politics, quantum theory, shoe styles, penguin mating habits: On seemingly any subject under any sun, Claire could sound intelligent and interesting, yet find a way to make everyone else in the conversation feel as if *they* were the ones making the most clever comments. Before the group was halfway from D.C. to Charlottesville, Mad wanted to devour her.

Mad wasn't real familiar with this urge to devour; he was more accustomed to being the object of others' devouring passions. Mad had become a legendary Lothario on the Catholic campus, casually and kindly "hooking up" with a couple dozen Hoya women during the course of his studies, yet somehow leaving not a single one bitter over the shortness of her tenure in Mad's favor.

But Claire – Claire was different. Claire seemed a double major in class and charm, a Phi Beta Kappa in capital fun. At Monticello she smartened the dumb-waiter, gusted through the covered breezeway from the kitchen, and made Mr. James Madison's simple, private entrance seem all dolleyed up.

The tour over and the return trip to Georgetown accomplished, Mad treated all eight of his charges to a night at The Tombs, having secured permission (through Daddy Lee) to draw down his trust fund in celebration of fully honoring his commitment to the Crazy Eights. As the night wore on, one by one the seven other group members wandered off, until only a slightly tipsy Claire remained with Mad. (She was still below the senseless drinking age of 21, but Mad had long ago developed the clout with management to sneak her any drink she wanted.) Mad knew exactly where this night was going.

"I'll walk you home," he finally said, having determined that Claire lived clear across campus in the Henle Village apartments.

"I *should* hold out for a winged chariot ride," she slurred. Next thing she knew, Claire was clinging to Mad's neck as she rode his back up 36th Street and then up 'O' Street to campus. Mad somehow spun Claire up onto the lap of the statue of school founder John Carroll – patriot, priest, prelate – and then clambered up after her with a remarkable surety. And, sure enough, as he fully expected, within seconds he was kissing her while she responded with the enthusiasm to which he had grown accustomed.

Down off John Carroll, across more of the campus, to the archway past the familiar Red Square. Behind the archway they kissed again, madly, and Mad Lee put a well-practiced hand to Claire's breast.

She laughed, and pushed his hand away.

Mad didn't expect that. It made him only further intrigued as she broke from his lip-lock, skittered away, and yelled "Catch me if you can!"

Surprisingly, it took him nearly two hundred yards to do so – after which she kissed him again, pushed away his hand again and, turning, led him up to her apartment door.

There, turning towards Mad again, her mouth attacked his with unbounded passion. Mad knew then, in the marrow of his bones, that Victory would be his that very night.

When she finally opened her door and began to back inside, Mad began with an easy confidence to step in with her.

"Unh-uh," said Claire, shaking her head "no," clearly and firmly.

Mad, puzzled, said "Huh?" In all his young life, Mad had never once been denied after the kissing became so passionate.

"Mad, this was great – please let's go out again?" she said.

"Absolutely," he said, quite madly. Then, brightly: "Once I come in for a minute, we can figure out which day this week is best for both of us."

Kindly, green eyes flashing the promise of things to come, Claire answered: "Never once has a young man crossed my threshold at the end of a first date – and this wasn't even really a date!" She smiled, and shut the door.

* * *

Mad buzzed, and Nurse No. 3 appeared in the doorway. He hadn't noticed before, but she was shapely, in her 30s, and without a ring.

"Kiss me," he said to her – and somehow, it wasn't ridiculous that she seemed to have an enraptured look in her eye, and seemed to be – well, maybe – leaning over as if, yes, perhaps, to kiss him, as his hand reached up toward one of her breasts.

As if from a trance, Mad suddenly started, and pulled back.

"Oh, Esmerelda," he shouted (though her name was Sue), "Fit me a wagon to your starry bowl of soup." The kindest way he knew to get rid of her before things went any farther was to pretend to be truly mad.

Back at her nurse's station, Sue beeped the psychiatrist on call. "We've got a live one," she told the doctor, though she wasn't sure exactly why her knees were trembling.

* * *

"So, nothing was ever the same for me after that," Mad was telling the psychiatrist.

"You mean, because Claire wouldn't immediately go to bed with you?" asked the shrink.

"No, no, no, that's not it," Mad said. "I mean, yeah, for some reason I've always been able to have girls sleep with me, so yeah, I was surprised she wouldn't let me in. But you're missing the point: The point is that nobody had ever touched my heart so much. I was, like, lost in her before we ever left the Tombs. But look, lemme tell you…"

"She also was the first girl who ever turned you down, or so you say. It's a common syndrome: People often fall in love with what they can't quite so easily have. And sex denied is an incredibly powerful aphrodisiac. Freud said…"

"Look, screw Freud. He was a pervert. You're not even letting me get to the important part of my story. I mean, the only reason I went into so much detail is because you insisted you wanted every freakin' detail of when I first met Claire. But that's not even what I wanna talk about. For that matter, dammit, I didn't even ask you in here – you insisted on coming. I just want to be left alone."

"Sorry, Mr. Jones, I know it can be hard facing these feelings. But with all due respect, you *did* check into this psych ward, which means we are responsible for your care. Now I am doing this psychiatric examination, and I will determine what's relevant to your case. I'm perfectly aware that your wife and mother-in-law have both just died, but even so, your behavior is far from a normal clinical expression of grief."

Then, shifting his bifocals and consulting his notes: "Now tell me, when did you first meet your mother-in-law, and were you sexually attracted to her as well?"

Mad's eyes narrowed. He looked at the doctor as if the doctor were fly-bait in a stable.

"Yes, doctor – how'd you know? And I assume you know as well that I also like to perform fellatio on dromedaries and rhinoceri."

The psychiatrist wrote "belligerent" in his notebook, stood up, and left the room. Mad's anger morphed into something else entirely as soon as its object, the shrink, left the room. Mad curled into a fetal position, and began to cry.

*　*　*

The hospital staff left Mad alone for several hours. At some point his inner hellstorm began to dissipate, its fury becoming focused and understandable. Finally he uncurled, pulled out his Bible and his writings, and, in the course of time, after much thumbing through the Book, he added:

> 37. God also cruelly tested Abraham: "And He said, Take now thine only son Isaac, whom thou lovest, and ... offer him thee for a burnt offering." Genesis 22:2
>
> 38. What kind of God is it who requires that his chosen patriarch be willing to sacrifice the son who is most dear to him, and that his righteous follower Job suffer, and that His only Son be crucified, all to demonstrate His own power and glory (Amen)?
>
> 39. Yes, until Christ Jesus transcended the Law so that man might be justified by faith in God's grace, God was consistently a jerk — and He continues frequently in such jerkiness, which is part of His flawed nature, with the distinction that, post-Christ, God allows us eventual union with God's better self, by means of our spiritual resurrection after death, which is given us through our faith by means of God's grace.
>
> 40. Because God sent Christ to redeem man to God and God to man, and because God's ultimate will is grace (even when his temporal will is inconstant and jealous and wrathful, and causes us to suffer for no good reason),

therefore "whatsoever ye do, do all to the glory of God (Corinthians 10:31)."

Q: How, then, does one do glory to a fallible, jealous, and wrathful God who nevertheless wills to us, by way of his better self, a merciful life everlasting?

Looking up at the TV, Madison noticed Maxwell Smart was on Nick at Nite again. He wrote:

Would you believe?

41. Abide by the Ten Commandments, as Christ explained.

42. Abide by the two Great Commandments identified by Christ Jesus. (Love the Lord with all thy heart, etc., and the second is like unto it, etc.)

43. Ignore (if you must) all those other rules in Leviticus, which were for a particular people at a particular time, for Paul said (in effect) that the Law was superseded by Christ — although those who keep the rules still are to be honored for keeping their faith through the centuries.

44. All, of all faiths, should honor the Jews, "chiefly, because that unto them were committed the oracles of God." Romans 3:2

45. Do all such good works as the Lord hast prepared for us to walk in.

> 46. It is very meet, right, and our bounden duty that we should at all times, and in all places, give thanks unto… Everlasting God.

The last few words were barely legible. Mad fell asleep with his pen still in his hand.

Chapter Three

What had happened between Mad and Claire was that Claire had effortlessly punctured, invaded, penetrated Mad's lifelong psychic exoskeleton, the exoskeleton that was effortlessly clever and effortlessly blond-haired blue-eyed popular. With Claire, Mad always felt deliciously off balance, beautifully challenged, and exhaustingly, comfortably exhilarated. They played tennis at odd hours, they watched movies, they laughed, they kissed, they debated the relative merits of Shakespeare, Spielberg, Springsteen and Spinoza, and once they even awoke before the crack of dawn to volunteer at a downtown soup kitchen for the homeless. And all this was all just in the last two months of Mad's undergraduate career at Georgetown, while Mad was deep into his last season of Hoya baseball and Claire was holding on to her tenuous position on the tennis team.

It was because of Claire that Mad turned down a chance for grad school at Princeton, choosing instead to remain at Georgetown for a Master's degree in History. It was because of Claire that he chose a thesis topic that mirrored her own major subject focus of Reformation-era Theology: She, a strict Catholic, sympathized with Erasmus' defense of the Church; he, a nominal Episcopalian, wrote his thesis on the salutary historical effects of Luther's revolt.

It was because of Claire that Mad deigned to listen to classical music, because of Claire that Mad got hooked on the novels of Walker Percy, because of Claire that he took up volunteerism, C.S. Lewis, the encyclicals of Pope John Paul II, an appreciation for the Dutch Masters, and a habit of questioning every old habit he ever had. It was also because of Claire that Mad gave up sex – because in her mind, only the bad died stupid, and not enough Catholic girls started late enough, which meant never before one's wedding night. For more than two long years Mad agonized over Claire's abrupt line of demarcation between a passionate, almost lusty physical abandon above the waist and a strict enforcement of discipline below.

It was only much later that Mad learned that often, when they finally parted for the night during those two years, Claire would sob herself to sleep, racked by the effort of denying herself to the young man she loved so madly. She was no ice princess, as Mad to his delight confirmed on their wedding night – for yes, they were indeed married, in the July after she graduated *magna cum laude* and he from his Masters curriculum – but rather one of that rare breed who abided all the more strongly by her own standards of virtue the more those standards were tested.

She took Mad's breath away.

Yet more than the new interests to which Claire introduced Mad, more than the odd excitement of anticipation engendered by the new celibacy, more than any other outward manifestation of changes in Mad's outlook, Claire began to rearrange something deeper in Mad, something more profound. Mad, who had glided through life, or even above it, above its depths and undertows as if on skis, now began to dive into life, fathoms deep. He began to discover that he had a whole soul to explore (his), and another soul (Claire's) to cherish and take wonder in. He began to let himself feel – really *feel* – and, to a degree previously unknown, to love.

Back at Claire's home in New Orleans, Claire's widowed mother – born Marcelle Rideau, of one of the old New Orleans families, before marrying the dashing Lyons Victory – had readily welcomed Mad as the son she never had. Mad had come down with mononucleosis early in the summer after he first met Claire, and Marcelle, having met Mad only twice, had driven to Mobile for a full week to help mother him back to health during a time when Daddy Lee was obligated to a certain Shenandoah divorcee who was sponsoring a charitable shindig. Upon Daddy Lee's return to Mobile to check on his ailing grandson, Marcelle politely rebuffed his Cavalier advances while cooking up several more gallons of hearty soup to leave behind for Mad's continued convalescence.

"If Claire cooks as well as you," Mad had said as Marcelle prepared to drive back home to New Orleans, "I'll have to marry her on the spot."

"You're in luck; She does," said Marcelle with a smile. "But the wedding will have to wait until you can kiss the bride without giving my daughter the plague of mono." Then, winking: "Because of course you wouldn't have *caught* it from my charming daughter in the first place, now would you have?"

Which was how the subject of Mad's and Claire's marriage first came up, two years before it actually happened – giving Mad in one fell swoop the perfect wife and the most wonderful surrogate mother imaginable.

So they became a family in July of 1997, and moved back to Mobile for Mad to teach history at his high school *alma mater* while Claire took a job next door doing academic research for the Jesuit community at Spring Hill College. On Halloween Day, Claire found out she was five weeks pregnant, and for Thanksgiving they invited Buzz down from Washington in hopes (unrealized) of fomenting a romance with Marcelle, and at Christmas they visited Daddy Lee in Virginia to celebrate his first holiday as a newly remarried man. Yes, at age 76 going on 55, after more than 22 years of bachelorhood, Daddy Lee had tied the knot again with a woman three decades his junior. "It'll keep me from stealing young Claire from my grandson," he told anyone who would listen.

Three weeks later, Daddy Lee was killed when thrown from a horse during a fox hunt in which his new wife had ordered him not to participate. Claire, her belly just starting to noticeably thicken with its growing package inside, held Mad close as he sobbed all night long. It was the first time he had ever let himself feel grief.

For Valentine's Day of 1998, Mad gave Claire a love poem he had written to her, secretly working on it for nearly two months. That night, for the very first time, he thought he felt his baby move in her belly.

Two weeks later, at 3:16 a.m. on a Saturday, he was awakened by Claire screaming in agony, their bed already a pool of blood. The ambulance arrived in eight minutes. Claire and the baby were already dead.

* * *

Mad awoke in mid-sob to find his sterile hospital pillow drenched, presumably by his own tears. Just barely aloud, Mad muttered: "Why, God – why?"

Then, again, louder: "Why-y-y-y-eye?!?"

Then, suddenly at a full-rasping-hacking-burning-throated bellow: "**WHY!?!?!?!?**"

Shaking uncontrollably, Mad bit the pillow to silence himself. Amazingly, no nurse came sprinting down the hall to check on the patient. Then, trying to gather himself, trying to sound firm and stern and fearless, speaking to the empty room in a low but menacing voice, Mad said: "God, you're an asshole. That's it: a rotten stinking futher-mucking asshole. Asshole, do you hear? You go straight to Hell, because I'm already there, you understand? Come down here and take my place." Now, slightly louder, bolder: "Asshole! Asshole!!" Then, sobbing again: "Ass/(gasp)/hole."

Mad's body, so convulsed by sobs that he could no longer speak, no longer control itself, seemed to fold in on itself like an accordion made of raw nerve endings. Mad tried to stop the sobs, tried (but failed) to gather himself to yell the word "Rectum" loud enough to burst eardrums, tried to summon all the anger and pain of an Earth gone haywire to direct the anger at God in a punishment that was meet, right, and Mad's bounden duty to inflict.

Instead, something else, something spine-bendingly unexpected, happened. Yes, it *happened*: Mad did not cause nor wish it; it happened to him but nevertheless seemed to come from somewhereeven more than fathoms-deep inside him. What happened was that Mad felt, was sure he felt, God laugh. God laughed from deep inside of Mad. God didn't laugh *at* Mad, but through him, through his sobs and his pains with a deep, pre-primal, joyous, uncontrollable belly laugh. And Mad, still trying to curse God, found himself laughing, too – laughing loudly and uncontrollably, against his will and better judgment. Mad laughed the deep rolling belly laugh with God until he felt he could no longer breathe, yet he laughed more.

And then, finally, peace.

Fifteen minutes later, as if awakening from a not-unpleasant trance, Mad shook his head and reached for pen and paper.

47.   Yet the greatest thanks we can give God is our honesty, which means we should curse him mightily (though fearfully and with love-not-hate) when he does us wrong.

48.   <u>God respects and ultimately blesses those who wrestle with him honestly, as Jacob did at Penuel.</u> Wrestle with God for that which is good, however, not to give license for sin.

(Mad particularly liked that first part, so he underlined it.)

49.   The Twelve Commandments are to be observed because they are right and just and good in and of themselves, not because we want to gain God's favor.

50.   Just as the Law (12 Commandments) condemns us when we break it (though we are not eternally condemned if we accept God's grace), so too does the Law condemn God when we faithfully observe the Law and God does not reward us in this life for our doing so.

51.   God is condemned by the Saints who He allows or forces to suffer even though they abide by the 12 Commandments.

52.   God is redeemed by offering the grace of eternal life in propitiation for the sins He and we commit against each other.

Mad slept.

* * *

After a day that passed without incident in which he acted smilingly proper and polite to the nurses, he found himself again watching TV. For some reason, "Touched by an Angel" was being aired in a special, one-time, Friday night time slot. Mad watched intently as the angels taught another human in crisis that God's will and essence were truth and love. When it ended he again grabbed his pen and paper and, thinking of Claire, he wrote:

> 53. There is a special place in Heaven for the saints, who become Guardian Angels and thus find the special joys of helping future generations abide and find some triumph over the pains of earthly life. (For reference, see angels throughout the Bible.)
>
> 54. "Blessed are they that do his commandments, that they may have right to the tree of life." Revelation 22:14
>
> 55. Despite his temporal jerkiness, "For God so loved the world, that he gave his only begotten Son, that whosoever believeth in him should not perish, but have everlasting life." John 3:16
>
> 56. Said Jesus Christ: "Come unto me, all ye that travail and are heavy laden, and I will refresh you." Matthew 11:28
>
> 57. Forgive God the Father, take comfort and joy in God the Son, and honor both by striving to be lions and winners.

> 58.   Therefore, hold fast to that which is good; be strong and of good courage.

Finally, finishing with a large and exuberant flourish, Mad wrote:

> 59.   As Paul wrote (Romans 5:3-4): "Suffering produces endurance, and endurance produces character, and character produces hope, and hope does not disappoint us, because God's love has been poured into our hearts through the Holy Spirit which has been given to us."
>
> Amen.
> Here I shout; I cannot do otherwise.
> Madison Lee Jones

It was past 11 when he finally finished. Again, Mad slept.

* * *

The next morning, a Saturday at 9 a.m., Mad asked to meet with a different psychiatrist who had ward duty for the day. With every sign of perfect rationality, crying softly at the appropriate times but otherwise demonstrating a stoic though pained self-control, Mad told this far wiser doctor the whole story: first Daddy Lee's death, and then Claire's with his unborn baby. Then how, upon hearing the news, Marcelle in New Orleans had jumped in her car and sped all too fast toward Mobile, losing control on the I-10 bridge over the Pascagoula River and crashing gruesomely to her own death. How, when *that* word reached Mad on that god-awful Saturday night, he had called Buzz in D.C. and, speaking with an eerie calm, told Buzz of the three deaths within the previous 12 hours. "Here's what I want you to do," he had told, indeed ordered, his dad's old friend. "Come down here as soon as you can, get the key from its hiding place, and go into my kitchen. In the knife drawer, under a false bottom, you will find $8,000. Use that to pay for all of the arrangements, or at least as down payment. You'll be handling every single thing with the funerals. Everything. Please, don't argue. Just tell everyone I'm incapacitated with grief. I'm going to disappear for a while. Don't try to find me. I'll be okay. Sorry I'm laying all this on you, but that's the way it's gotta be. No, Buzz, don't argue. I'm just gonna disappear. I'll be back eventually. Just handle it. Thanks. Bye."

With that, Mad had hung up, taken the 8K from its safe and put it in the knife drawer, carefully packed a suitcase, slept, awoken at the crack of Sunday dawn, driven to the hospital, handed over a VISA Platinum Card with a $100,000 credit limit, and checked himself into the psych ward with explicit written instructions not to be disturbed by anyone other than medical personnel. No one outside the hospital was to know he was there. He flashed another $800 in cash – like the $8,000, it came from his original grant from the Crazy Eights – to convince the oddly enraptured admitting woman to waive all hospital policies to the contrary.

He asked for total darkness in his room that first day, but was told it was unbendable policy that the digital phosphorescent clock above his door was never to be turned off. "Well, then, only as far as that clock goes," Mad had said, "let there be light."

Mad had slept 20 hours straight. The next day he had made no noise, ate what was put before him, and stared blankly at the TV screen until Maxwell Smart appeared to 86 his reverie.

Now, 111 hours after starting to Get Smart, at 11 a.m., this new psychiatrist signed Mad's release papers with great empathy and understanding. The doctor wrote a lengthy report on Mad's case. Among his findings:

> "Mr. Jones is suffering a reasonably normal response to a highly abnormal situation...The loss of four significant persons within such a short period of time would naturally result in shock, emotional overload, and an inability to deal with things. Shock, horror, disbelief, and an inability to grasp consensual reality are normal reactions to sudden, major, or horrific loss. These reactions can encompass the mental, emotional, spiritual and physical aspects of one's life. In this case, Jones seems to have been overwhelmed in all four aspects.... But Jones shows no cognitive impairment. He is aware of his circumstances and their abnormaility. However, he is obsessed

with the religious aspects of this loss, and focuses maniacally on this topic. This behavior, while not normal in his daily life, is an appropriate response to his trauma and quite probably an excellent outlet for his overactive thoughts. Concentration on this topic may persist for some time. Assimilation of his loss may take months to years. If, as I believe, he had interruption of the attachment and bonding process in childhood, loss of all the key people in his life will likely not be assimilated without a great deal of searching and adaptation.

Circumstances and luck will play a key role in this process. … Jones' emotional responses are within the range of normal for severe trauma. He has flattened affect, with the exception of his sudden religious interests, on which he shows fervor. But he has no wish to associate with others and… this withdrawal is a normal emotional response…

Summary: Jones suffers from a severe case of Adult Adjustment Reaction, almost as if it were post-traumatic stress. His prognosis is guarded and will depend on his resiliency, his circumstances, his determination to allow healing, and his future relationships. But no further medical intervention is warranted at this time, other than some anti-depressants which I have prescribed and a strong recommendation for future counseling. I believe that there is a good possibility that, over time, he will return to what he seems to have been before his trauma -- a thoroughly charming young man, bereaved but neither beaten nor bereft of his full faculties."

Mad didn't leave the hospital until nightfall; the remainder of the daylight hours of his hospital stay's seventh day, he rested.

Exodus

Chapter One

Freshly showered and dressed, Mad gathered his suitcase, pen, paper, Bible, and purple marker, and made his way down the hall to the nurse's station. A new one was on weekend duty, and she felt a charge go through her as he flashed a grin. He asked if he could have the Saturday Mobile Register behind her counter (Weekend Nurse gladly complied) and then, whistling the tune "There's Got to be a Morning After," walked jauntily out of the Psych Ward, down to the hospital entrance, and out the electric-sensor doors which parted as if on his command and then closed up after him with a strange hydraulic hissing sound, like that of a tide rapidly reclaiming lost bottomland.

Thence to his Saturn, out the lot, and down the road to a nearby Kinko's Copies. At Kinko's, he stood over a copier counting the churches listed in the directory in the Religion section of the Mobile Register. One hundred and thirty-four. Painstakingly, then, he made 144 copies – ("ten extra for such a *gross* job," he punned to himself) – of each page of his handwritten Theses, and sorted and stapled them by hand. (A technological ignoramus, he didn't realize the machine could do that for him.) At the counter, he bought three packs of 50 thumbtacks.

Thence, to a nearby coffee house called, perhaps appropriately, Carpe Diem. (Since the hour was nearing 8 p.m., a more precise name for his purposes might have been Carpe Nocturne, for it was the dark hours he would seize.) He needed to map his route to all the churches. Which, while sipping a dark South American blend and eating a chicken salad sandwich, he proceeded to do, plotting addresses from the paper's church directory onto the city map taken from his car's glove compartment.

In the course of doing so, his eyes fell upon the column by religion reporter Kristin Campbell: "A bunch of Saturdays ago, I drove hundreds of miles on an errand. ... I'd just spent a day looking for things I couldn't find. ... [People] find new and old ways to celebrate that which is sacred. They ask more questions. ... Their journey leads some to celebrate different faiths, within different denominations. Often, it means people discover a more authentic faith."

Right now, Mad was mad for authenticity.

At 9 p.m. he emerged and walked across the street to his own St. James Episcopal Church – sponsoring parish of the school where he taught history – walked to the white-painted, wooden front doors, and thumb-tacked a copy of his Theses at eye level. Admiringly, he perused his handiwork as if it was the work of a sage of the ages, totally and eye-openingly new to him. Then, suddenly, he turned and ran. Sprinted, rather, back across the street to his Saturn. Almost diving in the driver's door, he didn't need to consult his map to know where the next church on his list was. He peeled off, tires screeching. At church number two, the same routine ensued: forcefully pressing the thumb-tacked Theses into the door, briefly admiring the copy with childlike eyes, then a sprint back to his car and a screech-out towards his next destination. On it went throughout the night, Mad fully mobile in Mobile, with a Dire Straits cassette playing on his Saturn stereo, occasionally alternating it with Springsteen's *Born to Run* or just with the radio.

The hours passed. Mad's spirits sagged. His feet and eyes grew tired; his thumb grew sore. But still he drove and tacked and admired and drove again, though his energy fell well below the intensity of the barbaric yawp expressed in his Xeroxed Theses. Past suburban strip malls, crisscrossing Interstate 65, through decrepit black neighborhoods as well as oak-lined, mansion-strewn enclaves, Mad carried out his self-appointed rounds like an old-fashioned doctor on house-call. He covered every kind of church he could find – Baptist, Catholic, Christian Science, Mennonite. Some church doors had no wood; Mad madly made do whatever way he could by using door jambs, mail slots, or whatever else looked receptive for his papers, his Theses, his prescriptions for spiritual relief.

For some reason, visions of Daddy Lee kept riding through his mind. Daddy Lee, horsebound and fox-flushed, gallivanting. Then

Daddy Lee at the strip club after Ben's funeral, cracking wise at the gyrating talent on stage. And again and again the same scene, as if on a jammed VCR: Daddy Lee turning half towards Mad, so a bosom-besotted Buzz wouldn't hear, saying, "No matter where we are, Madison, people are always watching; we're always on stage, and when we're on stage we're always naked. So you damn well better show them something good worth looking at, or else all they'll see is the grief inside."

And then, rasping lasciviously at a passing waitress: "Serve up another bourbon, my love; I need to get more blurry-eyed so your beauty won't blind me."

What this recurring scene had to do with 134 church doors, Mad could not fathom. But Mad was no more in control of the movie reel in his mind than his car was in charge of its destination, and like his car, his mind was an insensate vehicle for directions he didn't understand.

Finally, mercifully, at the very heart of downtown Mobile, at the very foot of, yes, Church Street, Mad trudged on painful feet up the front steps of the magnificent Christ Episcopal Church, founded 1823, and on its massive doors tacked up his duty to the Lord. Christ Church, according to its newspaper listing, was "Where History and The Holy Spirit Meet." Back in his car, the radio DJ played Springsteen's "Blinded by the Light." But Mad, made sleepy by the dark, nevertheless hopped right onto Interstate 10 and headed west – west past Theodore, west past Tillman's Corner, past the Alabama state line and the Pascagoula River, the Tchoutacabouffa River, west into the night two hours towards New Orleans, the City That Care Forgot.

Once there, off the Interstate at Elysian Fields, toward the Mississippi, toward the Quarter, a few zigs and turns to the back of Pirate's Alley. Leaving his hazard lights flashing, Mad stumbled up the alley, around the corner past the Cabildo, to the front door of old historic Catholic St. Louis Cathedral, on which he affixed one more stapled, thumb-tacked sheaf of Theses-bearing pages.

Back in his car, up Royal and St. Charles, up to the grand old Pontchartrain Hotel, where he flashed his cash and a room was made available. Suitcase in hand, up the elevator, down a curiously narrow hallway, into an old-fashioned room that was spare yet elegant, flopped onto a bed without even covers drawn, and immediately the sleep of angels. Dawn was just breaking.

Chapter Two

Church doors, all shapes and sizes, chased Madison Lee Jones off a cliff, down, down, down onto a bed full of blood. On the pillow, his father's head atop a barbeque grill mouthed "I love you madly," and then rolled onto the bed full of blood. Mad's pulse quickened as a short blonde co-ed opened Playboy magazine to show a picture of a bed full of blood. A clock in the distance flashed 3:16, and a baby cried behind the church doors and Mad tried to reach it by climbing onto the lap of a patriot, priest, and prelate, only to find that the lap of the stone-cold Jesuit was a bed full of blood. In the distance a horse stumbled, and Daddy Lee fell through the church doors onto a bed full of blood as the clock held by a rainbow-colored-Afro'd man flashed 3:16, illuminating the car skidding off the bridge onto a bed full of warm pooling dark screaming agony blood.

Screaming, shrieking, Mad scrambled furiously to escape the drowning pools of red red… and found himself hitting his head on the floor as he fell off the hotel bed. Dimming light eked through the window. Sweat ran down his forehead as his heart pounded a hard-rock drumbeat against his pain-wracked rib cage. The clock didn't say 3:16, but 4:57 p.m., and there was no blood but only a finely appointed old New Orleans hotel room. Mad turned on the TV, too loudly, and stumbled to the bathroom. With trembling hands, he slowly undressed, leaning against the wash basin, then turned on the shower full blast, lukewarm, and stepped under the cleansing gusher.

As the water washed away his nightmare, certain practicalities entered his consciousness for the first time. He figured he would have some explaining to do. Such as how he could have missed the funerals of his own wife, unborn child, and mother-in-law. Such as how he could have failed even to check in with St. James School for a week, not even to make sure they had a substitute for him and assignments for his students. Such as how he could have disappeared, incommunicado, while friends doubtless had tried desperately to find him to offer comfort. And such as how he could possibly have dumped all the funereal and other responsibilities into the lap of Buzz, without any follow-up or explanation. Poor Buzz was probably worried half-past-sick about him.

In slow motion, Mad lathered up, spaced out, scrubbed, spaced out, rinsed off, and then absent-mindedly repeated the whole process. Finally turning off the lukewarm stream nearly half an hour later, he focused his mind again and said, out loud, to the semi-fogged mirror above the washbasin: "Yeah, I'll have to give Buzz a buzz – let him know I'm alive." Then, this time silently, he thought to himself: "I wonder if he's at my house in Mobile, or if he's gone back to D.C.?"

Drying off, he tried to re-focus, after his week's hiatus, on practicalities, on the everyday existence to which he must return.

Stepping nudely from the bathroom, however, he was disabused of his notions of normalcy by the sound of a TV newscast returning from a commercial break.

"And now, our final story of the evening," said the female anchor, "Stephanie Riegel looks into the mystery of a missing man who says God is a jerk. Stephanie?"

There on camera, in front of the St. Louis Cathedral, stood a pretty, slender brunette, surrounded by a small phantasmagoria of Crescent City characters. An old man in a wizard's hat. A mime with angry fist raised heavenward. A female bag of bones, of indeterminate age, petting a baby iguana with a bonnet on its head. And, among others, a man with a purple double-breasted suit and slicked-back, jet-black hair, holding aloft a sign that read "BLasPHeMers REPENT!"

"… where at the crack of dawn this morning," the reporter was saying, "a pedestrian noticed a sheaf of papers thumb-tacked to the cathedral doors. On them were written 59 religious theses, or propositions, outlining what seems to be a whole new theology. Though the theses end with a message of hope, what has people here all atwitter is Thesis 12, which says 'God is a Jerk.'"

From the crowd behind her a man stuck out a sign: "Worship the Jerk: It's important!"

"Before long a crowd gathered," the reporter continued, "and someone with a portable computer apparently got word on the Internet that the same theses were posted at dozens of churches 150 miles to the East, in Mobile." (Footage of St. James Episcopal Church in Mobile, and other Mobile churches in a rapid montage, flashed across the TV screen.) "The theses are signed by a man named Madison Lee Jones, who we have confirmed is a Mobile high school teacher who has been missing for eight days, ever since his pregnant wife and unborn child died of a massive hemorrhage. The apparently grief-stricken Mr. Jones is still nowhere to be found, but all across the Central Gulf Coast, people are talking about these religious theses he's posted. It's all a big mystery. This is Stephanie Riegel reporting."

Suddenly, the mime behind Ms. Riegel turned to the camera and, face in a spasm, yelled aloud "God is a Jerk!," just before the picture switched back to the news studio anchors.

In his hotel room, Mad's head felt light, like it does upside down on a roller-coaster loop-de-loop, and his legs buckled. He half-sat, half-fell, at a funny sideways angle, his butt grazing but failing to alight on the corner of the bed. For the second time in an hour, he thudded to the floor – side and shoulder first, but with his head slamming after it, hard enough to send a jolt of pain in a screaming of nerves throughout his body. A few seconds later he found himself groggily trying to sit up, one hand using the side of the bed for leverage, the other pressed against the rear right side of his cranium. That hand he pulled down and checked. No blood. He again placed it on his head, to a spot that was already starting to throb. Yes, a lump was already forming.

How could this happen? How could his theses be on the news? He hadn't thought of that. He hadn't really thought of anything. If he *had* thought, he would have thought that 135 church custodians would have thrown 135 copies of his theses into 135 trash cans – but he definitely had not even thought that far at all. All Mad had wanted to do was vent, and now all he wanted to do was go home. Instead, he had angry mimes and bonneted iguanas and who-knows-how-many Internet freaks all presumably looking for him, all afire with the notion that God is a jerk.

"That pretty reporter, she'll understand," he thought. "She was fair enough to report that I ended with hope. … Damn, my head hurts! … Yeah, she'll understand."

Gingerly, slowly, Mad crawled to the phone, found a phone book, looked up WWL-TV, and called the newsroom.

"No, Ms. Riegel isn't coming back to the station tonight," said a fresh-sounding voice – the third voice of the call, after transfers through two receptionists – on the other end of the line. "But I'm an assistant producer for the newscast. Can I help you?"

Head throbbing even more, Mad felt panic, triggered by all the unexpected attention, rise up his sternum. Taking a deep breath, he mentally rolled the dice.

"I'm Madison Jones – the guy who wrote those theses she reported on."

"Oh really?" The voice laughed. "You're already the second Mr. Jones to call. I just hung up on a guy who said he was God's houseguest on the planet Zebulon."

"Wait! Please don't hang up on me." Mad's panic crept up his torso again, this time almost to his Adam's apple. "I can prove I'm me. I… uh … Okay, you can check on this. That Riegel woman didn't report this part of the story: My mother-in-law just died too. She's from New Orleans. She died a week ago. Her name's Marcelle Rideau Victory. She lived in a white frame house, with Doric columns, on Sixth Street off Coliseum. She liked to cook shrimp ettouffee for me. She drove off the bridge over the Pascagoula River. My nickname is Mad, but she always called me Madison. …"

Suddenly he felt a sob rising from some unknown place under his right collarbone. "This is really me; you've got to believe me."

After a week cloistered in a hospital, Mad was starved for a human connection. He desperately wanted to be believed. He felt like he was in a confessional – although, as an Episcopalian, he had never been in one – but the priest was not accepting his tale. He felt like he was admitting that he *did* deliberately peek into an opponent's poker hand, thereby winning an ill-gotten pot, but that the priest thought he was just looking for attention. He felt bizarrely racked, twisted, spaghetti-wilted by guilt of an indeterminate source, and he needed this fresh-voiced assistant to absolve him of it.

"Did you say your nickname is *Mad*?" said the fresh voice. "We didn't report that on the air, but the top of the theses was signed 'Mad' instead of Madison, and Stephanie and I discussed which identifier she should use in her report. And I knew Mrs. Victory; she lived next door to my godmother. But I didn't even hear that she died."

"Well, she did; she drove her car off the bridge and she's gone and so are Claire and my baby and I can't get them back!"

"Wow – I think this really *is* you," said the fresh voice. "I'm Laura Green. As I said, Stephanie's not available, but you can talk to me."

"It's just that she got it right, but the crowd got it wrong," Mad said. "That crowd behind her was saying God's a jerk. I mean, he is a jerk, or he can be a jerk, but that's not the point. I mean, well, I don't know what I mean; I mean I know what I mean but can't explain it, at least right now, I mean, and well, I didn't think anybody would read them and, I mean… damn, I just can't explain it on the phone."

"That's okay," said fresh-sounding Laura. "Really, it's okay. This sounds real complicated, and I'm on your side. It's just that you wouldn't believe how many people are talking about it all over town already, and we understand the Mobile TV stations are going nuts with the story. You wanna come by the studio and tell it to me? I'll stay here for you."

Again, panic.

"No! Not the studio! Not on TV!" Mad was surprised by the vehement sound of his own voice. Then, more calmly: "Sorry; I didn't mean to yell. I don't want any cameras; I don't want all that attention. I just want y'all to get the story out so it's out there right, out there the way I meant it, not out there like God's only a jerk and some nutcases in wizards' hats are his jerky apostles."

"We can meet somewhere else, dear." Damn, her voice wasn't just fresh, but soothing as aloe. "No cameras. No tricks. Just me and a notepad; maybe a tape recorder so my boss can hear your voice."

"No tapes. Please, no tapes." Mad was adamant. He didn't want his own voice, or picture, coming back to haunt him.

"Okay, no tapes. But it's got to be somewhere safe, like some restaurant easy to get to. I can't go meet some stranger in a back alley, you know."

Mad remembered driving past a Houston's on St. Charles Avenue just before he reached the Pontchartrain Hotel early that morning. That seemed as good a place as any.

"How will I know you?" he asked.

"Well, my name is Green and tonight I happen to be wearing green. It's a light green blouse, with a blue skirt. I'm 25, dark brunette, about 5'5". My hair's long; I'll put it in a ponytail once I get there as a signal that it's me. I can be there in about 20 minutes. How's that sound?"

So Mad pulled on an Oxford shirt and some khakis, combed his hair very lightly so as to disturb his throbbing lump as little as possible, took the elevator to the lobby, got the valet to bring him his car, and drove off to Houston's restaurant. Buzz, he thought, would have to wait a few more hours for a phone call.

Mad was seated at the bar when a lovely young green-clad woman with a runner's build walked in and, while saying something to the hostess inside the door, began to put her long dark hair into a ponytail. Mad sprang up, ignoring a wave of pain from his injured head. "You must be Laura. I'm me."

"Well, hello Mr. 'Me.' Wow, you're handsome! I was just asking the hostess for the most private table she's got. I assume that will be to your liking?"

Mad liked this girl. He felt he might trust her. She had an air about her, not of a hard-edged newswoman, but of a cherished older sister (even though she and Mad were the same age) – a confidante, a wise advice-giver, a female shaman for troubled souls. Maybe it was just his aching head playing tricks on his brain, but Laura Green seemed, even more than had the reporter on TV, to be the kind of woman who would understand him, fully understand him, more than well enough to set the record straight. He didn't want people saying God was a jerk; a jerky God might blame him and punish him even more – as if, he thought to himself, that were even remotely possible.

"But that's not how God works, anyway," he reminded himself as they sat down at the table to which the waitress had led them.

He *thought* he had just thought those words to himself – but a moment later he realized that he had spoken them aloud, for they hung in the air like an off-key bell.

"What?" asked Laura, sounding amused, at the same time that the college-aged waitress said, "Ex-CUSE me? Hunh?"

Maybe, Mad thought, he was insane. Maybe he really belonged in a psychiatric ward. Turning to the waitress, he smiled: "Oh, I was just rehearsing lines in my mind for a community theatre play I'm in; I didn't mean to say them out loud. Ignore what I just said. But could you bring me a Michelob? I could really use a good cold beer."

Looking a little perplexed, the waitress scurried off. And Laura, bless her heart, reached across the table, caressed his hand like it was a piece of solid but intricately textured pottery, and said: "You've had a rough time, haven't you?"

Floodgates opened in the corners of Mad's eyes; a torrent of words spilled from his mouth and heart. He didn't really notice what he ordered, or what he ate or how much he drank; he only knew that he had to keep talking, and that this lovely green person across the table took pages and pages of notes without once seeming to establish a reporter's distance of objectivity from him. No, Laura Green did not seem like a prying adversary, but like a joyfully rediscovered friend of his deepest soul. In his eagerness to have her hear him, he even forgot the pounding from the lump on his head.

Somewhere along the line, Laura began looking blurry to him. Somewhere along the line, she began to appear velveteen. Some way or other, her voice became music, a flute played by a well-meaning sorceress that cast a spell on his id. Somehow in a thoroughly dreamy state, he didn't see any reason to object when, after she paid the bill with a company credit card, she insisted on accompanying him back to the Pontchartrain to get a hand-signed copy of one of his remaining nine sets of theses, as one final proof for her news director that she had indeed found the right man. And somehow it seemed normal and right to him when, like all the other girls but Claire, Laura Green responded to his proximity as if subject to a deep-seated and inescapable genetic imperative to procreate right then and there.

Some time after 2 a.m., thoroughly flummoxed by her own unexpected behavior, Laura Green extricated herself from a sleeping Mad's embrace and crept from his room, notes and signed theses in hand, like a thief escaping a crime scene. Something was truly different about this man, she thought, something wonderful and scary and unforgivably erotic. Because of what her genes forced her to do, she had forgotten to call her exclusive story in for last evening's 10 o'clock news. But she'd be damned if she didn't scoop all the other local stations on WWL's morning show with a full report on this Mad man who wrote that God was a jerk but really was worth worshipping anyhow. She didn't even begin to understand his theological point – truth be told, it didn't interest her at all – nor was she sure that Madison Jones knew what he himself was trying to say. But she felt thoroughly sympathetic towards his palpable grief, thoroughly enraptured (if not quite sure why) by what they had done in his hotel bedroom – and, most important of all, thoroughly sure that, minus the bit about the bedroom, she had one hell of a "human interest" story on her hands.

Laura rushed home just long enough to rinse off, change clothes, and apply enough makeup to mask her lack of sleep, then drove through the still-dark streets back to the station where, her mind already whirring with ways to approach her story, she planned to insist that she herself be put on the air to make the report. It wasn't every day that some grief-stricken history teacher came up with an entirely new theology so different that, overnight, it galvanized loons and fruitcakes throughout a whole 150-mile region of the Gulf Coast.

A bit before 6 a.m., light pouring into his uncurtained windows woke Mad with a headache so pounding it made him nauseous. He half-crawled, half-slithered to the bathroom just in time to fill the commode with vomit. With each heave, his head pounded more, and with each pound, he became more ill. Lord, when would all his misery stop?

Maybe, he thought a few minutes later when it finally seemed to be over, the fall from his fainting spell last night had given him a concussion. Didn't concussions often cause nausea? He was not one of those self-diagnosticians who memorized just enough medical facts and wives' tales to make him dangerous. Truth be known, he had always just gone about his business unless he felt so bad he had to lie down, and then stayed down until somebody came to nurse him back to health. Other than that, he didn't worry. So who was it that had told him concussions caused nausea? Some girlfriend biology major, probably. ...

No, it was Claire. How she knew, he wasn't sure. Yes, it was Claire.

And then it hit him: Claire was dead – what, just nine days? – and what the hell had he done last night? What the sonuvabitching hell?!?!

"Ohmygod, Claire, I'm SORRY!!!!!"

A wave of guilt so strong it seemed to buckle his rib cage joined more pounding in his head, and his nausea returned, long past the point where his stomach was empty, past where dry heaves turned to pain-wracked sobs, until his body had nothing left with which to heave or sob or even tremble. For the first time in his life, it occurred to him that his inexplicable erotic power over women was not a blessing but a curse, a sick joke, a punishment for some unknown sins. The sins of a father's father's father, perhaps, passed down through three or four or forty generations. But wherever the original sin came from, he was sure he had compounded it – not a sin against God, whoever or whatever God was, but against Claire's memory, which was now far more sacred than any god under or over the sun. He had shown no shame, no forbearance. Forget God; Mad damned himself, and then shrank into the hole of his own damnation.

Eventually, Mad dragged himself into the shower and, having haphazardly turned the knobs, let some too-cool water wash over him for God knows how long, while he just prayed for the pain to stop.

Which, amazingly, it did, or at least abated. Cleaner, he wobbled back to his bed and turned on the TV. It was 7 a.m. on the dot.

"To begin this hour," a pert morning anchor was saying, "in her first-ever stint on this side of the camera, assistant producer Laura Green gives the exclusive report on the mystery man who, in just 24 hours, has the Gulf Coast in an uproar over some religious writings he posted on church doors all the way from Mobile to New Orleans. ... Laura?"

And there was an amazingly fresh-faced Laura, this time with green only as trim around a milky white blouse, looking so poised and commanding that it seemed she must have always lived inside the camera frame.

"Yes, I interviewed Mr. Jones last night at length," Laura said. "It's a remarkable story, and remarkably poignant. Just nine days ago in his hometown of Mobile, Madison Jones' wife and unborn baby died of a sudden hemorrhage, and then his mother-in-law, New Orleans socialite Marcelle Victory, died in a car wreck while rushing over to Mobile to join him. He was so grief-stricken, he skipped the funerals and spent the next week in a personal hideaway, 'wrestling with a silent God,' as he told me.

"Mr. Jones is a history teacher with a special interest in the revolt that Martin Luther led against the Catholic Church in the 1500s. So, just as Luther did, Mr. Jones wrote out a list of theses, or religious propositions, to question the common understanding of the Christian faith. It is these modern theses, posted in Mobile and New Orleans the night before last, that have caused such an uproar."

Laura's visage was replaced with more footage of crowds of wackos demonstrating outside the St. Louis Cathedral and also outside the Catholic Cathedral in downtown Mobile. Many of those in New Orleans were holding those signs saying, "Worship the Jerk: It's important," which was a takeoff on a local political slogan seven years earlier. And one man, painted red and wearing a devil's costume, held a sign saying, "My Triumph is at hand!"

(Only in New Orleans!)

"In my exclusive interview with Mr. Jones," Laura's voice continued, "who is now resting in a secret place in Louisiana, he said, and I quote: 'Really, I was just venting. I never thought anybody would pay any attention.'

"But when your theses call God a 'flawed SOB' and a 'Jerk,' as Mr. Jones' did, people tend to notice.

"Mr. Jones refused, for now, to go on camera. But in our interview, he insisted that his theses reflect a state of grace he has now reached, and indeed they close with a famous Bible passage about how suffering ends up producing strength and then hope and a reaffirmation of God's loving presence.

"He said, finally, that he intends to return soon to Mobile, to the high-school history class that he teaches – and that he expects all of yesterday's hoo-rah to simmer down."

By this time, the camera was back on Laura, who then turned to the perky morning anchor and said: "But I'll leave you with his thought – maybe it won't simmer down so soon. Because as our interview ended, I asked Mr. Jones if he still thinks God is a jerk. And he laughed, and said, and again I quote, 'Well, he sure as hell can be.' Which, especially in this city which thrives on offbeat stories, leads me to believe this controversy might continue for quite some time."

That was it: just over two minutes of airtime. But, sitting naked on his bed, Mad felt like the world was closing in on him, was too much with him, late and soon. Why did Laura have to end with him saying again that God is a jerk? Why her insistence that the story wasn't over? His whole point last night, he thought, was to get somebody on the news to tell the world not to bother, that what he wrote was really nothing, that it was all just a momentary rant. He really thought she understood. Why'd she have to keep the story going?

Baffled, perhaps still in the grips of the spell that Laura seemed to have cast on him last night, Mad switched the channel.

"… courtesy of our sister station in Mobile, here's Mr. Jones' long-time family friend, Myron 'Buzz' Buskirk, with a message for the young man who has caused such a stir."

And then Buzz' broad-featured face was on the screen, still topped after all these years by nearly crew-cut hair.

"If somebody knows where Mad is, and can get the message to him," Buzz said, voice obviously strained, "please tell him to come home, that we're worried sick about him… that we'll make it all alright if he just comes home. I don't know anything about all of this stuff about God and lions and lambs; me and his friends just want to know that he's okay."

Mad clicked off the TV with an agitated vehemence. His eyes fell on the room phone. Yes, that was it: He'd call Buzz. 1-334-….

Damn weird dial tone. 1-334-…. Damn tone again. Oh, yeah, he probably had to dial 8 or something to call out of the hotel. Yeah –

reading the instructions on the phone – that was it. So Mad Lee phoned home – and it was busy. He dialed again. Busy again. And, after a wait of only 5 or 10 seconds, still busy.

Oh, of course. His number was listed; with all the news coverage, everybody would be trying to get through to his house. But he HAD to talk to Buzz.

Cell phone! Didn't Buzz have a cell phone? Yes, of course: His little address book would have Buzz's cell number, too. (Oddly, as Mad thought these thoughts to himself, he seemed to hear him himself think them – or, rather, seemed to hear a narrator reporting to him that he was thinking them. "Mad thought," the narrator told Mad, "that Mad was thinking how odd it was to be hearing himself think what he was thinking about Buzz' cell number." It was like a damned echo chamber, a not-so-Funhouse hall of mirrors of silent sound, in his brain.) Some not-quite-sensible thumbing through little pocket pages (why was he looking for "Buskirk" in the "M" section?), an eventual discovery of the right digits, some button pressing and re-pressing when his fingers went the wrong way, a few odd rings, and then Buzz' thoroughly flustered voice was saying "Hello, who's this?"

"I'm coming home today," Mad answered, without introduction. "Can you meet me at Carpe Diem at 1 o'clock?"

* * *

In an Uptown New Orleans kitchen, meanwhile, a buxom blonde divorcee, 30, was having trouble concentrating. Her seven-year-old son and six-year-old daughter, both rambunctious little demons, were giving her their usual before-school trouble. But that, she could handle. What had her off-kilter was what she had just seen on the morning news. Poor, poor Mad. Tall young handsome baffled tragedy-wracked Mad. Mad, whom she had known for only a few afternoons, one of which neither of them would forget – he for the sheer wonder and excitement of it, she for the soul-disrupting embarrassment of her losing control so utterly to a teeny-bopper. She still didn't understand it, still couldn't forgive herself for it, not even 12 years later. A few years afterwards, she had felt almost-hysterically sorrowful, sorrowful for Mad's sake, when Professor Jones had died. And now, again, she felt utterly discombobulated by this news of someone who in all but one sense she barely knew at all. She didn't even know what he would look like now, but she wanted to reach out to him, to hold him, to make everything okay for him. Something about Madison Lee Jones, Grace Feinstein Martin thought to herself, just flat-out broke her heart. There in her mind was a tall but still-young boy turning beet-red about a Playboy magazine, and there was a big, school-paper obituary for his suddenly dead father, and here was word that an already death-haunted young man had written that God is a Jerk – a God that she, Grace, relegated to the realm of myths and legends, of Sasquatches and unicorns and Scottish lake monsters.

And two little children threw milk-soaked Cheerios at each other across the breakfast counter, and she still was wearing a bathrobe just that morning stained anew by spilt café au lait, and she wasn't sure, even if she could throw on some old jeans in time to take the kids to school, whether she had left enough gas in the car to get there without stopping at the Shell station on State and Magazine. And that gas stop, of course, would make them even more late, and none of it seemed the remotest bit fair, especially this news story indicating that Mad sounded mad with a depth of grief she could hardly imagine.

Grace wept.

* * *

A little after 8:30, Mad emerged from the hotel elevator into the lobby… to find Laura waiting for him there.

"Sweetheart, are you going home?"

"Uh, yeah. … Weren't you just at the TV station?"

Mad, distracted, shoved several hundred-dollar bills at the girl behind the registration counter.

"They're re-running my report on tape," Laura said, "but they wanted me to come find you."

"Well, uh, let me get the valet to get my car. I'm leaving. Why'd you keep the story alive – I thought you were gonna do a story saying there is no more story?"

"Sweetheart," she said, this time back in that tone of voice that mesmerized him so much the previous night. "I've got a camera waiting outside. You look great this morning, sweetheart. Just stop for the camera and tell everybody you're okay. You can even say you believe in redemption, or something like that. Tell'em you accept God's ultimate plan. That's it: Tell'em that life goes on and so will you."

Still sensing his hesitation, Laura revved up her thought processes even further.

"It'll be easy, sweetheart," she stalled. "You'll do great."

Then, suddenly, brightly: "Tell everybody you're gonna work with God to do all the good that Claire would have wanted you to do. You'll be honoring Claire's memory. Claire would want you to do this, sweetheart."

Mad's guilt-ridden button perfectly punched, he allowed Laura to push him through the lobby doors to the sidewalk. A camera rushed to greet him, and somebody handed Laura a microphone.

"Laura Green reporting here, with the man of the hour, Madison Lee Jones. Mr. Jones, you had something you wanted to tell everybody?"

"Uh… well…."

"Something about God's plan for all of us, right?" Laura prompted.

"Yes, everybody should try to be one with God's plan," he said, seeking Laura's approval as a substitute for the certitude he himself didn't feel. "My wife, Claire, she loved God. I think she wants me to work with God to do something good with my life. I think that's what we're all supposed to do."

"So there you have it," Laura segued, turning back to the camera. "Out of grief, a new prophet of good works. This is Laura Green reporting."

As the camera light faded out, the valet pulled Mad's car up to the curb. Laura gave Mad's hand a squeeze, whispered "Call me," into his ear, and released him to the valet. Within two minutes, Mad was doing a U-Turn on St. Charles Avenue, back towards Interstate 10, back towards home.

First, though, he zigged around Lee Circle to the Exxon Station, where he gassed up and bought a cinnamon roll, a large orange juice and a big, too-weak coffee, all of which he balanced in his lap as he drove up the ramp and navigated the semi-loop to I-10 East. One hand on the wheel, the other wiping splashed OJ from his pants, Mad wished his mind could find some equilibrium. One moment he felt panicked, another he felt resolute and in control, and the next he felt both numb and empty. He kept trying to eliminate from his mind all memory of his tryst with Laura Green the previous night, only to then try to make sense of this morning's little interlude before the cameras and to try to remember exactly what he had said under Laura's prodding. He wasn't exactly sure what he had mumbled – but the more he tried to remember it, the more he remembered the tryst instead, and the guiltier he felt for it. And Mad was not a young man at all accustomed to feeling guilt. The guiltier he felt, the more quickly he tried to swallow the coffee, juice and pastry. By the time he reached the marshland between New Orleans East and Lake Pontchartrain, he was finished with all three, but only at the cost of annoyingly sticky hands and mouth that begged to be wiped off with napkins he didn't have.

"My kingdom for a napkin!" he yelled out the window to the passing swamp grass.

Hearing himself yell it, Mad wondered again, as he had in Houston's restaurant last night, if he really were insane after all. He was bouncing back and forth so fast between different moods, acting so spontaneously and illogically, that he didn't even recognize himself. But grief, as the Mobile psychiatrist had written, can manifest itself in many ways.

Mad clicked on the radio. WWOZ, the local jazz and heritage station. Louis Armstrong was singing that he's "got the heebie jeebies." Yep, that was it. Mad had to have the heebies. And as his tires played a rhythmic back-beat on the expansion grids of the long bridge above the choppy lake, he wondered if the heebie jeebies would ever go away.

By the first main Slidell exit, another annoyance had arisen. His bladder had begun making its presence known. By the Mississippi state line atop the East Pearl River Bridge, the bladder became more insistent. Still, he didn't want to pull over. He had bought gas just 35 minutes ago, and wanted to put New Orleans farther in the past – or, rather, to feel that home and Mobile were coming far closer. His urge, intensely, was to be home again. Just home.

More than that, he hated using a gas station bathroom without buying something. It made him feel like a freeloader. So he kept on going.

Past the Stennis space center, past a few more exits advertising gas stations. His other urge, his bladder's urge, got stronger. And his sticky hands had created a sticky wheel, and he was overwhelmingly miserable yet again. His mind was turning everything into a crisis, and he damn well needed a respite.

Ahh, there was a "Rest Area" sign. Just what he needed. It looked sort of desolate, but what the heck. Bladder now screaming for relief, sticky hands eager for a napkin, off the highway he pulled.

Desolate wasn't the word for it. More like butt-ugly. The rest area was just that – an area, not a building. No bathroom, no nothing but a road through a scraggly grass field, with one loop marked off for big-rig trucks. From the car-park area (unmarked by parking lines, with just some dirt and gravel instead) it was a 50-yard trek across soggy lowland to the truck-lane, and then another 40 yards through even soggier ground covered with high, itching weeds to the edge of the line of bushes that bordered the brownish, unkempt woods. Not that any of the truck drivers would have paid attention if he just unzipped right by the side of the asphalt. But Mad, out of habit, sloshed on towards more privacy. Finally, his shoes soaked by lowland ooze, he figured he was far enough out of sight to be decent, and he began easing his bladder's furious pressure.

"HIISS-SSSS-SSS" – and a breath-stopping rustling at his feet.

Damn, he was so startled that he wet his own shoes and lower pants legs even more than the marsh had. Three feet away, a blackish snake lurched and then slithered away.

Crazily, Mad aimed his stream at the retreating reptile. "Fie on you, Serpent!" he yelled. "Crawl on your belly, you pathetic Satan!"

"Yes," he thought, "I am insane."

Mad turned, still half unzipped, and stumbled back to his car. Inside, with the door closed, he pulled the lever and let the seat-back recline as far as possible. He already was dog-tired again, even though it was still only mid-morning.

He just had to get a grip on himself. Dammit, other people lost loved ones all the time. Yes, he had loved Claire with an ardor so deep it swallowed him, and already loved his unborn child, and both loved and idolized Daddy Lee – oh, and loved Marcelle with an almost child-like quality, as if she were the mother he had never known. But this was pathetic. His behavior was pathetic. His weakness was pathetic. His pathetic-ness was pitiful. And then the sex with Laura last night – that was the worst of all. It was as if Mad had reverted, by force of insufficiently buried habit, to his pre-Claire self: the self who breezed along the surface of life without feeling deeply, the self that treated the world casually and treated intimacy casually too, as if it weren't really intimacy at all, but only skin-deep pleasure at less than skin-deep emotional risk. Claire had made Mad better than that – or so Mad had thought, until he blew it all last night. Mad wanted to be a better person than that. Mad wanted to be worthier than that. Now, in his grief, Mad turned his anger on himself….

And what about those theses he had written? In his self-loathing, he now pronounced those theses idiotic, the rantings of an unwell mind. *What* had he been thinking?!? What was his point? Damned if he knew. He just needed to get a grip, to return to normalcy, to go back to living a life of routine, a life of students and pop-quizzes and grading papers and assisting the baseball coach after school. Yes, that was the thing… baseball. There was a freshman already on the varsity who seemed very promising…

Fitfully for a few minutes, and then fully (if only briefly), Mad dozed.

Mad eventually was stirred by the sound of an 18-wheeler firing back to life and rumbling past his car. Turning on his own ignition, he realized that he felt calmer. His thoughts seemed clear. His spine felt straight. His chest no longer felt the weight of three or four gravities. At least for now, in short, he felt more-or-less normal.

Before he put the car into "Drive," he went through a checklist in his mind. 1. Meet Buzz at Carpe Diem, the coffee shop. 2. Beg forgiveness. Discuss practicalities of what Buzz had handled for him while he was gone; who needed thank-you notes, what bills (if any) still needed paying – that kind of thing. 3. Get Buzz to accompany him to the St.

James campus, where he could ask forgiveness from the headmaster and, he hoped, schedule a return to work within the week. 4. Go for a run, for his first real exercise (tryst aside) in 10 days. Hope that some endorphins kicked in and boosted his mood. 5. Take Buzz out to Ruth's Chris Steak House.

Oh… damn. Somewhere in there, if the New Orleans news coverage were an indicator of what Mobile's would be like, he'd probably have to do a few interviews. So… 6. *Do the blasted interviews and put this stupid story to rest*. Everybody would surely forget his theses in a few days, wouldn't they?

Yes, Madison was in control again. He had a plan. He had his senses back. He shifted the car into drive and pulled back onto I-10. This time he really was on the way home.

Chapter Three

Arriving ahead of schedule, Mad killed time by meandering around some Mobile neighborhoods before he pulled into the parking lot of Carpe Diem at 1 o'clock sharp. The coffee shop, located in an old, tree-shaded, wood-frame house across the street from an entrance to Spring Hill College, had a neighborhood-y feel and was permeated, even more than most coffee houses, with a rich and enticing coffee aroma. Mad used it as a favorite haunt for grading papers and for quick, light lunches away from the St. James school grounds. This day he entered and, not seeing Buzz up front, went into the fireplace-and-sofa-graced back room. Sure enough, there sat his godfather – along with, of all people, Justin Luke.

Justin was an old friend or, more accurately, Mad's foremost disciple. Always a shrimp – now a wiry 5'3" – Justin had latched onto Mad way back in Fourth Grade like a super-friendly remora to a shark. Earnest, intense, and nervous, Justin was smart without genius, mildly witty without superior humor, and consciously empathetic without any real psychological insight. All the other kids had treated him like he was an annoyingly yappy Yorkshire terrier; but Mad, even though somewhat distractedly, had always shown Justin at least the semblance of respect. And Justin, utterly hopeless at other sports, shared Mad's passion for baseball and, by dint of sheer will, turned himself into a high school player with highly specialized skills just valuable enough for a seat on the varsity bench. Seriously lacking in basic arm strength and hitting power, Justin nevertheless saw limited action as a late-inning defensive replacement out in left field and as an uncannily talented situational bunter.

Mad could not remember Justin ever making a fielding error, not one, not even in practice. Most memorably, Justin had a whole-body throwing motion that used his entire small frame like a bullwhip, transferring every bit of stored kinetic energy in his muscles from his feet through his hips and pelvis, back and shoulders, with his arm finally snapping around and towards his target in a peculiar, snake-strike lunge. The result was always the same: a baseball thrown at a tolerably decent pace, with remarkably unerring precision. The play made, Justin would return to his position with a jaunty skip-step, his bare fist excitedly pounding his glove, his carrot-colored hair poking haphazardly from under his cap.

A Vanderbilt graduate in kinesiology (the study of human movement), Justin had recently returned to Mobile. He had parlayed his degree (with honors) into a job as a physical trainer for bored 40-ish women at a swanky workout gym. In the few months that both he and Mad had been back in Mobile, Mad had mostly dodged Justin's phone calls, although they and Claire had twice grabbed beers together at a neighborhood bar while Justin prattled on about some dreamgirl in Pensacola who he was just sure would be the one for him. Even Claire, who saw the best in everybody, couldn't help finding Justin a bit annoying. Nevertheless, she was touched by Justin's earnest manner and by his obvious devotion to her husband and, through Mad, to her as well.

"Beneath it all, that guy's a treasure of a friend for you," she had said to Mad just three weeks earlier. "Bless his hyper little heart."

Even so, Mad thought now, why did Justin, of all people, have to be there with Buzz at this moment, when the last thing Mad needed was a bunch of frenzied, orange-headed vibes to re-disturb Mad's short-lived equilibrium?

Sure enough, Justin was already running at the mouth before Mad or Buzz could even say hello.

"Madison, this is like James Bond super-spy stuff we've been playing today. You wouldn't believe what Mr. Buskirk and I had to do to escape all the TV cameras when we left your house. We had to take two cars and go in different directions – the TV trucks all followed Mr. Buskirk, cuz he's been the spokesman – and then go to the Dew Drop Inn, and Mr. Buskirk went in through the front and out to the back lot where I was waiting, and then hauled ass to my house and ditched my Corvette for my old pick-up, and then we...."

Tuning Justin out, Mad stole a glance at Buzz, who shrugged his shoulders and nodded his head as if to say that, well, yeah, this little carrot-top's story was pretty much on target.

"Justin, Buzz ..." Mad interrupted. "Y'all are saints for putting up with all this mess. I didn't intend for all this to happen. How can I just make it all go away?"

Buzz looked more than slightly annoyed.

"Shit, Mad, I don't know. I've gotta get back to D.C., soon, like last Friday or something. Thank goodness that American U. was on spring break last week, or the history department chairman would be having a conniption fit at me by now."

Then, a tear forming in one of his tough-guy eyes, his tone changed: "I'm really sorry, Mad. I can't imagine what you've been through. I'm crushed by all that happened, even though you and Claire and Marcelle aren't technically even family. I'm always here for you, young buddy, always here."

Then, wearily rubbing his forehead, Buzz continued: "I wish I could stay longer, but I'm outta here tomorrow. I don't understand any of these religious messages you've been posting, but I just wanna know you're okay before I skip town."

Over a meal of soup, salad, jumbo muffin, and herbal iced tea, in the interregnums between Justin's good-hearted yammering, Mad and Buzz tried to figure out the mundane particulars of how to get Mad's life back on track. Secretly relieved when Justin suddenly announced that he had an appointment back at his gym, Mad waited until Justin was out the door before asking, "How'd *he* get to be your right-hand man while I was gone?"

"Shoot, Mad, I was gonna ask you where you came up with such a goofy best friend."

"*Best?*" said Mad, incredulously. "Poor guy – is that what he told you? Justin's okay, but he can be, totally unintentionally, the world's single biggest pain in the backside since, I don't know, probably since hemorrhoids were invented."

"He just showed up at your door the day before the funeral," Buzz said, "and, when he found out you weren't around, he insisted on pitching in with arrangements and wouldn't leave. When he started quoting all your exact baseball stats from your Georgetown career, and then kept telling stories about your glory days together on the diamond in high school, I figured you guys had to be tight. He's really not a bad sort."

Lunch over, Mad and Buzz walked down the road towards St. James school, where Mad was greeted by the front office staff like he was the most beloved of all prodigal sons. But the headmaster, who was particularly fond of Mad, had a serious problem at hand.

"My phone's been ringing off the hook," he explained. "A lot of parents are so irate over this 'God's a jerk' thing that they're threatening to pull their kids out of school if you come back here to teach. You've had an incredibly traumatic experience, Madison. I think you should take some more time off, maybe a couple of weeks, until all this craziness blows over."

"But I really miss the kids, miss my teaching, miss helping coach the baseball team," Mad protested.

"Just take a little time, Madison, and give me some time to mollify the parents," the headmaster repeated, kindly but firmly. "By Easter, we'll be past all this, and then we can see about getting back to normal."

But normal was far from what was in the offing. After leaving Carpe Diem, swinging by the Dew Drop for Buzz to pick up his rental, and driving in their separate cars to Mad's midtown house, Buzz and Mad were each hard-pressed even to turn into Mad's driveway, which was almost utterly blocked by news trucks. At the far end of the block, a crowd of perhaps three dozen onlookers and protesters was held at bay by four uniformed policemen. With Buzz emerging first and running interference, Mad was able to scurry into his patio and through his kitchen door without acknowledging the news hounds – but, crowding around his shuttered windows, the cameramen showed every sign of becoming permanent fixtures if that's what was required of them.

"I told you this had already gotten just insane," Buzz said, once the two were safely inside. "Those religious proclamations of yours have only been out, what, less than two days, and yet it's like you were Billy Graham, Elvis Presley, and the Phantom of the Opera, all wrapped into one. I took your home phone off the hook last night, but this morning I found a note dropped through the mail slot with what claims to be the number of Larry King's top assistant. I don't know how this foolishness could already have interested folks at CNN, but this is obviously your time for 15 minutes of fame."

Mad, looking somewhat frazzled, merely grunted in acknowledgement.

Opening the fridge, he pulled out a bottled water. His mind started moving more quickly, and practically, than it had since Claire died. He figured that the best way to get rid of the media was to meet them head-on.

"Okay, how's this sound?..." he asked Buzz. "How 'bout you tell them that a half-hour from now – what would that be: 4 o'clock? – I'll come out and do one long interview with all of them, almost like a press conference, where I try to answer all their questions. But only on the condition that, once it's done, they leave me in peace to go for a run, and promise not to come back to my house again without calling first? Tell them I'll remember anybody who breaks this agreement, and that I'll make sure there will be hell to pay."

As if following a sergeant's orders, Buzz marched out through the front door to relay the message to the media. For some reason, it struck neither Buzz nor his godson as odd that Buzz, the age of Mad's father, should so readily jump as if at the younger man's command. Buzz was a square-jawed sort not likely to strike anyone as a "yes man." But here he was, with every reason to be furious at Mad for disappearing for eight days, acting as his godson's aide-de-camp. But the media accepted Buzz as a kind of press secretary, and this after only one day on the story.

At the appointed time, Mad stepped through his front door, and without looking at the faces of any of the news people, began reading from some scribbles he had written on a couple of sheets of kitchen-phone message paper.

"I am Madison Jones. As I gather has been widely reported, I lost my wife, my unborn child, and my mother-in-law just over a week ago, all within a few hours. In response, trying to work out a host of emotions so strong I cannot even describe them, I wrote out the list of religious theses that, apparently, has caused quite a stir.

"I posted the theses all over Mobile, and at St. Louis Cathedral in New Orleans, as a way, I think, to purge my system. I never figured anybody would pay much attention.

"I am not a theologian. I am a history teacher specializing in the Reformation Era, which also happened to be the college major concentration of my wife Claire, who was a theology major. But I claim no special insight. Everything I wrote was my desperate attempt to deal with pain.

"To set the record straight, the news coverage I have seen and the crowd reactions I have seen have focused, wrongly, on just one of my theses. Yes, I did write that God is a jerk, and I meant it when I wrote it. But that was not my point. In writing the theses, I was writing for myself, and my message to myself was what I ended with, that somehow I had to force myself to believe that suffering produces endurance, and then character and then hope. I'm still not sure what I'm supposed to hope for, because my whole world seems dead. But I wish everybody would leave me in peace to figure that out for myself.

"Please, people: Pretend I never posted those theses. I never intended to upset anybody. I have no authority, especially on matters of religion. I'm just trying to find my own way in a very confusing time. Please. Let's just let this go.

"Thank you."

Mad's voice had been strong and clear throughout his statement. Maybe too strong and clear. If it had cracked a little, maybe the reporters would have been moved by his distress and let things rest. But, in an effort to keep from breaking down, Mad had overcompensated. Even as he professed no authority, he spoke with an authoritative air.

So, as he turned to re-enter his house, a TV reporter – some tall white guy – shouted out. "But how do you put the genie back in the bottle, Madison?" Seeing Mad half-turn back towards him, the reporter continued: "As of an hour ago, there is already a web site up, called

'Mad religion,' and its chat room has entries that claim to be from as far away as Hawaii, Saskatchewan, and Scotland. You've touched a nerve, Mr. Jones."

He paused and, then, thinking quickly and cleverly: "How do you get the neurons to stop firing?"

Mad was stunned. "A web site?!? A chat room? You've gotta be kidding?!"

"No, Mr. Jones – you're a celebrity," said another reporter.

"I can't be! I'm just a guy who lost his wife." Panic started setting in, and Mad's voice went up half an octave. "Can't you guys tell them to stop?"

A young female reporter with a kind face stepped forward just a tad. Maybe she was with the paper; she didn't seem attached to any TV camera. "Mr. Jones…" Her voice, less insistent than the others, less controlling, was full of empathy. "Maybe people are finding comfort in what you wrote. You've got some interesting ideas there; you seem to be reaffirming a Christ-centered faith; you say that through Christ, God makes amends even for his own mistakes. That's not orthodox, but maybe people think it makes God more approachable."

Pause for breath. Ignoring the stares from other reporters, who looked at her as if she spoke a foreign tongue, she continued: "If you find that what you wrote is somehow doing good for some people, would you still want all this attention just to go away?"

Mad knew not what to say. How could *he* comfort anybody? All he himself could feel was pain.

"I dunno," he said, almost pleadingly, with his hands upturned in supplication. "Maybe people these days are desperate for prophets wherever they can find one. If somebody finds some truth in what I wrote, then I guess that's good. But I don't have anything else to add, not right now. That's a really good question you asked… but, please, I don't have any answers. I just want my life back."

Buzz, sensing Mad's distress, tried to pull his godson back through the door, back into the house.

"*Prophet?*" shouted another reporter. "Are you a prophet, then?"

"I don't feel smart enough right now to be a prophet." Mad, unused to the media, was too polite to let a question go unanswered. He kept talking, thinking aloud, utterly transparent, without any filter. "All I know is I hurt enough right now that I feel like a martyr must feel. I don't know what sins I'm suffering for, but I just want all those sins and all the suffering to go away. My world doesn't deserve this grief. Nobody's world does. I'm just trying to make the grief bearable."

Buzz, sensing that Mad was feeding the fire rather than dousing it, stepped forward and more forcefully guided Mad inside.

"That's enough, everybody," he said over his shoulder. "You've got your story; now leave this poor boy alone!"

Which, as the door shut behind him, the media actually did – but not, in most cases, due to any innate or abundant decency. The TV folks, especially, had deadlines to meet in very short order.

Inside, Mad announced that he needed a run, and soon. But, after changing into T-shirt and shorts, he didn't get far beyond his front door. On the sidewalk in front of his house, a couple dozen loons were holding a vigil. (The cops who had held them at bay had apparently left when the media did.) Seeing Mad, some began to rush him, a few yelling epithets; others, praise. Before they could reach him, Mad retreated again behind his door.

"Dammit, Buzz, there are some freaks outside. I really need some exercise; can you help me ditch'em and gimme a ride back up to campus? Maybe I can run in peace up there."

Seconds later, from the side driveway, Buzz was obliging, with peeling tires that left the crowd no time to find their own vehicles and follow.

At Spring Hill a few minutes later, Buzz dropped Mad off, but not before telling Mad that he would wait for him to finish his run and then hustle him home in time to watch the 6 o'clock local news.

Then Mad, like John Updike's Rabbit, ran. Ran like a hound-chased hare. Ran so fast his lungs screamed in agony. Agony so bad he cut his intended loop short. Slowed to a jog, then a bare stumble-paced shuffle, he made his way back to a waiting Buzz. The whole ride home, Mad's lungs craved oxygen so badly that he was nearly hyperventilating.

Hyperventilation was as nothing compared to his response when back home (no loons in sight, thank goodness), Gatorade- and water-cooled, he watched the news on three TV sets Buzz arranged side-by-side. One station even led off with his story.

"We start tonight with the story everybody's been talking about for the last two days, about young history teacher Madison Jones, who lost his wife and then wrote 59 religious propositions that he attached to church doors all over Mobile. Back in town today, Mr. Jones repeated the offbeat message that has drawn so much attention." (A cut to footage of Mad on his front porch.) "Yes, I did write that God is a jerk, and I meant it," Mad's picture was saying – and then, almost seamlessly, with virtually no visual evidence that the videotape had been spliced: "I'm still not sure what I'm supposed to hope for, because my whole world seems dead."

Anchor's voiceover: "Later, young Mr. Jones elaborated on his new-found role." (Video still rolling, Mad's voice again came through.) "I feel like a martyr." Then, again with little noticeable sign of splicing: "My world doesn't deserve this grief. Nobody's world does. I'm just trying to make the grief bearable."

(The visual returned to the studio anchor.) "Apparently, there are lots of people out there who agree with Mr. Jones that calling God a jerk is a good way to get rid of grief. There's already a web site up called 'Mad religion' – and, as an Arizonan all the way from Phoenix, wrote on the site's chat room: 'This is really cool stuff. You wrestle with God, and then you rise from the ashes.'

"There's no word yet on the next steps Madison Jones wants to take, to spread his ministry of encouraging anger at God."

Just as that station's take on the story was ending, another newscast picked it up.

"… Mr. Jones said he wasn't a prophet, but that he might be a martyr assuming a host of unknown sins. 'My world doesn't deserve this grief. Nobody's world does. I'm just trying to make the grief bearable.' Instead, though, he seems to be *causing* some grief, at least to his neighbors.

(Footage of some of the angrier loons at the end of Mad's block, kept at bay by a few Mobile policemen.)

"As somebody from the City of Angels, Los Angeles, wrote on a new web site that has already sprung up: 'This is heresy, pure and simple, and it's dangerous. What this guy really needs to do is make a thorough confession, and then say about 5,000 Hail Marys to boot.'"

In his den, Mad began pacing madly. Hadn't those TV idiots *heard* anything he said?!? Too agitated to continue watching, Mad literally ran up his stairs to take a shower. Shaking almost uncontrollably under the gusher, he didn't emerge for 30 minutes. Only Buzz was watching, then, when the third station, the one with the highest ratings, finally did its piece as the last story of its newscast, after first running 'teasers' on it three different times earlier in the program. Instead of the 75-second treatment given by the other stations, this one went into more depth, for a solid four minutes of airtime.

This version portrayed Mad as a bereaved young widower, much loved by his students – one of whom, a senior girl, said on camera, giggling a little, that all her classmates had a crush on him.

"He's had a rough blow," said a Presbyterian minister into the camera. "But the truly admirable thing about this young man is that, if you read his theses closely, you discover that his ultimate message is redemptive. He has taken his pain and is trying to find something good on the other side."

Cut to Mad on his front porch: "I had to force myself to believe that suffering produces endurance, and then character and then hope."

Then, back to the anchor: "Mr. Jones was paraphrasing a passage from St. Paul's letter to the Romans, a passage which ends by saying, quote, 'hope does not disappoint us, because God's love has been poured into our hearts through the Holy Spirit which has been given to us.' On that note, let's all wish comfort to this young local history teacher who has caused such commotion. If you'll allow some editorializing, all of us at the station would like all *his* good hopes to be fulfilled."

Later, when Buzz tried to tell Mad about that station's sympathetic treatment of him, Mad remained unconsolable. All he could think of was the other anchor talking about him causing grief for his neighbors, and about the person from Los Angeles writing "heresy" and "dangerous." Buzz and Mad scrapped the plans to go out for a good steak, and ordered a pizza instead. Mad slept only fitfully that night, and awoke in the morning feeling like a deflated inner tube.

Buzz, still full of worry about his young friend, insisting that Mad call him at a moment's notice if things began going too badly, reluctantly embarked mid-morning for the airport and his flight back to D.C. As he pulled out of Mad's driveway, he resisted an urge to run over the few protesters who had returned shortly after dawn. Two held aloft a big sign, in fluorescent orange lettering, that said: "If you're Mad – hell, you don't have to take it any more!"

Chapter Four

Only after Buzz left did Mad read the morning *Mobile Register*. Its story on him ran on the front page, just below the fold. He was surprised, and gratified, to see that the article was thorough, accurate, fair, and even nuanced. Still gun-shy, however, he kept the phone off the hook after just one call from somebody purporting to be – and who may well have been – from MSNBC, the cable news outfit.

Justin, mouth running nonstop, appeared in the early afternoon and stayed for two hours, driving Mad crazy with talk of how Mad could capitalize on his fame and do a world of good, by organizing a lecture tour to spread the word that tragedies and everyday life could be conquered by those who are lionhearted enough to try.

"I tell you, Mad, you're onto something! People eat this stuff up. And that's what this country needs, anyway, is a little more toughness. We're too soft! That's what my whole business, my workout training, is all about. Self-improvement not through some namby-pamby New Age stuff, but by hard work! Courage! This is big, Mad, really big!"

The rector of his church showed up at his door, just to say his office would always be open if Mad wanted to talk. But, not wanting to be overbearing, he didn't stay long.

Others rang his bell, too: several folks saying they were freelance writers (Mad turned them away); two fellow St. James teachers with a six-pack of Michelob in hand (Mad drank one beer, then pled exhaustion, and they left); five members, still sweaty from practice, of the school's baseball team he helped coach (somehow they ended up talking with each other about their girlfriends and how much they did or didn't "put out," and failed to notice when Mad's eyes glazed over). The kind-faced female newspaper reporter showed up, too. She was young, with a warm smile. Mad thanked her for her coverage and took her card, but said he was in no shape to talk any more right then, and could he call her back another time?

At 8 p.m., noticing that the protesters had given up for the day, Mad drove to the grocery so as to re-stock his refrigerator. A few of the other customers pointed at him in recognition – some seemingly approvingly, some muttering imprecations. One old lady called him a "poor sweet boy" and patted his head. The checkout girl asked for his autograph; Mad, embarrassed, complied.

Finally home again, groceries put away, Mad fell quickly asleep. In his dreams, Justin threw out a runner at home plate – on target, as always – Claire (serving at love) double-faulted to his father, his house's walls closed in and the furniture disappeared, and a stranger chased him through the empty rooms while wielding a Bible like a machete. Laura showed up and said everything would be okay; but when she started taking off her clothes, a hidden microphone fell out, so Buzz and Justin picked it up to unscrew its top and see if a Fortune-cookie message was inside.

Mad forced himself awake, refused to look at the clock, and soon was back asleep again, this time the sleep of angels.

* * *

Awaking on Wednesday morning, Mad was determined to get out of the house. Maybe a round of golf would do. But, peering through his front upstairs curtains, he was surprised to see perhaps 50 protesters milling around his front porch. Then he heard a familiar, oddly pitched voice above the crowd's regular murmur.

"Let me through! Let me through! I'm his best friend. Let me through right now!"

Justin, again.

Then there was the sound of a key turning in his front lock, and as Mad came down his stairs, there was Justin squeezing through the door while obviously trying forcibly to keep somebody else outside.

Slamming the door behind him, Justin turned to see Mad on the bottom stair, looking at him with a puzzled impression.

"Hey, Justin – where'd you get a key?"

"Mr. Buskirk gave me one last week, Mad. Good thing; I thought you might be asleep and didn't want to wake you. This is all gonna be bad enough without you having to wake up before you're ready. This is just so bad!" Even by Justin's standards, the little guy was unusually agitated. His eyes kept darting around as if he expected somebody to ambush him from behind.

"Huh? What's so bad? I thought maybe this would all die down…."

"The sidewalk, Mad, the sidewalk! You can't see it now because of the crowd, but the sidewalk is just awful! The morning news was full of the story. How dare somebody? This is awful!"

Mad still had no idea what Justin was talking about.

"Slow down, Justin. Why is this morning any different from yesterday or the day before?"

"The sidewalk, Mad, the sidewalk! It's written all over the sidewalk!"

"*What's* written on the sidewalk, dammit? What are you talking about?"

Justin tried, not fully successfully, to take a deep breath. "HERETIC! DEMON! In big, bold letters, somebody spray-painted HERETIC and DEMON on the walk in front of your house! I rushed right over as soon as I saw the news. Some nutcase out there hates you, buddy. But they'll have to come through me first if they want to get at you." (Justin was talking too fast again; a few drops of spray were chasing the words from his mouth.) "I know I'm not big, but I'm a physical trainer. I'm in good enough shape to hold off anybody for a while. Just let'em try! Just let'em!"

Somehow, Justin's protective rage made Mad oddly calm – as if the house had only enough room for a specified amount of nervousness or anger, and Justin was already providing the full limit. Mad smiled reassuringly at his annoying, endearing little friend.

"You won't have to stand alone, Justin. Probably half those people out there are praising me, not hating me. Any psycho who wants a piece of me will have to deal with them, too, in addition to you. But I appreciate your coming over."

The doorbell rang, immediately followed by a pounding on the door.

"It's the police, Mr. Jones: Open up!"

Sure enough, two policemen were on Mad's porch. One was a young, powerfully built black guy; another was a seriously overweight, late-ish-middle-aged white.

"Officer Williams, here, Mr. Jones," said the white one, extending his hand. "And this here is Officer Jones. No problem keeping up with the Joneses on this detail!"

"Mr. Jones, these protesters have become a public nuisance," said black Officer Jones, stepping forward with an air of dignified authority. "We're gonna move them on out; try to give you a little space and a little peace."

"And those TV cameras," interrupted Officer Williams, "we're gonna keep them away, too. Nobody's got the right to trespass against your home, no matter what kind of stupid things you say."

"Oh, well, uh…" Mad didn't know exactly how to take all this, and he was taken aback at the word "stupid." Hell, he hadn't even had breakfast yet. He at least needed coffee so his brain could process these developments.

But Justin had already jumped in. "It's not stupid, Mr. Policeman. What my friend here is saying isn't stupid at all!" He looked about to burst out of his skin – and fat Officer Williams gave him the kind of look Southern good-ol-boys give to male interior decorators.

It was left to Officer Jones to provide a measure of calm, which he did merely with a further straightening of his broad shoulders, a hand gesture at once placating and strong, and a polite clearing of his throat.

"Do you have a kitchen table, Mr. Jones?" he asked. "Our chief wants us to sit down with you and try to work out some security arrangement until this all blows over."

Which, over the next half hour, they proceeded to do, with Justin scurrying around fixing coffee and, after a little kitchen foraging, heating up some danishes Mad had bought the night before. At least through the weekend, Officers Jones and Williams and a female cop named Sellers, not yet on the scene, would alternate 8-hour shifts, around the clock, on Mad's front porch. As it turned out, some crank had called in to police headquarters a veiled threat against Mad – and that, combined with the graffiti and the disturbance that the crowds were causing for Mad's neighbors, had convinced the police chief to put out word that all bystanders were to be dispersed. The police had first tried calling Mad, but his phone was still, by design, off the hook.

"I just want this all to end," Mad kept saying. "I'll do whatever you tell me to make it all end."

Finally, all details worked out, Officer Jones told Mad to go ahead and go play golf. He, Officer Jones, would keep an eye on things at the house.

So Justin bustled off to an appointment and Mad drove out to Magnolia Grove, home of two of the Robert Trent Jones Trail golf courses that graced the whole state of Alabama. Finding the Crossings course strangely empty, Mad teed off alone – walking, not riding a cart – and proceeded to knock his second shot on the first hole a foot from the pin for an easy birdie. But concentration soon failed him and, four bogeys, a double-bogey and a triple-bogey later – he was a 9 handicap, so this was unusually bad play for him – he again found himself well into the woods off the 8th green. Not that any of this seemed to bother him. His score didn't seem to matter. Stepping through a thicket to where he thought his ball was, Mad became distracted by the antics of a baby squirrel and its mother. He sat down to watch. His mind wandered. He watched a sparrow. He listened to some other rustlings in the woods. He forgot about his ball. He wondered who would win the National League pennant this year. He wondered who would win the Masters next month. He watched the interplay of leaves, shadows, and narrow rays of sun on the forest floor. The dappled light looked like it was straight from a painting by Joan White-Spunner, a local artist.

Eventually, he slept – or at least it was something like sleep, perhaps more of a trance than anything else.

At some point in his nap/trance, he dreamed of Claire holding him in her arms, and a full two hours later he woke up crying. Picking up his golf bag, he trudged back to the clubhouse.

"Mr. Jones, Mr. Jones!" From a perch on the bottom of the clubhouse steps, the tall white reporter from the other day came running, a cameraman hustling after him. Mad's mind flashed back to a sideways glance that another golfer had given him in the pro shop as he had paid his green fee before the round. Had that guy recognized him and alerted the dadgummed TV station?

"What do you have to say about the HERETIC message in front of your house this morning? What about being called a DEMON?"

These guys just never quit, did they? This was getting to be more than he could take. And the reporter was still yelling:

"Wouldn't you say that it takes a high degree of arrogance to question God like you do?!?"

As they had been ever since Claire's death, Mad's moods still were volatile. Equilibrium was a long way away. Just as the camera's red light came on, Mad was hit by a sudden burst of rage. The rage boiled from inside as if he were a Saudi oil well newly uncapped. Why couldn't they *leave – him -- ALONE?!*

Dropping his bag, he grabbed his titanium driver and began shaking it menacingly at his two tormentors.

"Just get away from me, I tell you…. Just get away!"

The tall reporter backed up a few steps, but the camera kept rolling.

Mad, wild-eyed, kept advancing. "This golf course is supposed to be my sanctuary! Get out, I tell you, *get out!*"

Two golf shop employees and a just-paid late foursome had by now rushed out to the balcony to watch.

"*A plague on both your houses!*" Mad yelled and, twirling the driver, his rod, about his head, let it fly in the general direction of the camera. Whereupon, watching the titanium instrument clatter onto the cartpath, Mad let cross his face a look of horror at his own action. Grabbing up his golf bag again, Mad ran at a full sprint, clubs bouncing painfully on his shoulders, around the clubhouse and into the parking lot where, throwing the remaining clubs through his unlocked back door, he jammed his keys into the ignition and roared out of the driveway.

Back on the other side of the clubhouse, an alert caddy grabbed Mad's driver and hustled it back inside.

The next day, oddly enough, the tall reporter came down with chicken pox that kept him ill for nearly four weeks. The same day, the cameraman's refrigerator/freezer failed, and all the food in it spoiled.

* * *

Turning onto his block and then, waving to Officer Jones on the front porch, into his driveway, Mad was pleased to see that neither protesters nor media were present. The police obviously had done their job. He knew, however, that he was in for a bumpy ride. When would his mood swings end? When would life get back to normal – or, at least as normal as it could ever get again without Claire? And when would the damned media stop hounding him, when would the cameras go away, when would people stop paying attention to what he had written or what he would say, as if he were a prophet or major theologian instead of a high school teacher who wanted nothing more than to sit undisturbed in the bleachers of the local minor league stadium?

Not just the local news that night, but the national network with which the tall reporter's station was affiliated, ran the footage of Mad hurling his golf club like an oversized tomahawk. The network played it as a humorous and picaresque slice of Southern life, but made it sound as if Mad were the long-established leader of a large local cult.

Justin returned shortly afterwards to fuss and fidget; Buzz tracked down Mad by way of Justin's cell phone (Mad himself did not own one) and urged him to go to a priest for counseling; reporter after reporter showed up and tried, unsuccessfully, to talk their way past Officer Sellers (aged 45, chunky, with a permanent scowl on her face).

At least eight of Mad's former girlfriends (or, at least, sexual conquests) had seen the newscast; two of them – one in St. Louis, the other in Houston – packed up their cars that very night and started driving to Mobile. In New Orleans, as her children threw butterbeans across the table at each other, Grace saw the coverage and wept again. And at the home of the headmaster of St. James school, concerned parents kept the phone ringing off the hook.

Mad, having finally shooed Justin away, holed up in his bedroom, alternating between mindlessly flipping through cable channels on his TV set and doing sets of 25 pushups until his whole upper body ached with fatigue.

Finally, mercifully, sometime past midnight, he fell asleep.

* * *

The next morning, still groggy, Mad made his way down to his kitchen and began rooting around for some coffee. The more he shuffled around, for some reason, the more his nerves seemed to be rat-a-tat-tatting. Finally, coffee finally ready, he sat at the kitchen table and began to sip. Only then did he realize that the incessant tapping wasn't coming from inside him, from his nerves, but from the pane of glass in the door leading to his side patio. Then he realized that there was a face in the door windowpane, a lovely face.

It was Laura.

"What the …?"

"Shhhhh…." she said, finger to her lips, as she entered the door he had opened for her. "I don't want anyone to know I'm here – at least, not yet."

She was in a slightly dirt-smudged T-shirt and blue jeans, but the clothes emphasized the lithe quality that helped make her look appealing. Her explanation was just wild enough to be believable. Thursdays and Fridays were her days off and, seeing the national newscast the night before, Laura had determined to come update Mad's story herself, on her own time, and do it right. (She already had been trying since early Monday afternoon to reach Mad on the phone but, of course, his phone had been off the hook.) So at 4 a.m. she had roused herself and driven the two hours to Mobile and, with a gas station map in hand, tracked down Mad's house. Fat Officer Williams, now on duty on the porch, had shooed her away despite all her protestations. But Laura wasn't one to give up easily. Circling the block, she had parked around the corner, sneaked up somebody's driveway, and scaled a wooden fence and then onto the roof of somebody's back shed – the other corner of which formed one boundary of the small patio where Ben had died near the barbeque grill nine years earlier. She had carefully lowered herself into the patio. There, hidden from Officer Williams' view, she had found a spot from which she could see into Mad's kitchen, and waited the 45 minutes until Mad shuffled down.

Mad didn't know whether to be angry or flattered. He had felt a little used by Laura on Monday morning. But, on the other hand, she had this way of making him feel like she was on his side. By this time, they were eating some eggs he had scrambled for both of them, along with some toast and jelly. She had this way of making herself at home, as if she just belonged there by natural right.

"My news director just loved the way I handled myself on camera," she was saying. "We're meeting tomorrow afternoon to negotiate a new contract for me as an on-air reporter. But before I did that, I just couldn't leave you in the lurch. The network news made you look like a crazy cult leader or something. I want to try to get you in a good interview, a fair interview, sweetheart, for my national network. I want to get your story out the right way, sweetheart. That's why I came on my own time when I couldn't reach you on the phone."

Mad's expression indicated that this sounded, perhaps, a little dubious.

"Don't you see?" Laura continued. "The beauty of this is that I'm here without anybody knowing it, and we can practice what you'll say. I mean, that's not normally good journalism, but I want people to understand you, sweetheart, the way *I* understand you. I mean, you've got the phone off the hook, you've got cops out front, you've got the curtains closed. Oh, the media will be back outside today – you may not have heard this, but somebody got a court injunction telling the police they couldn't keep TV trucks off of a public street, as long as they don't trespass on private property or interfere with your neighbors' rights; and they'll probably have a horde of us media folks setting up outside again real soon. But I figure you have a room their zoom lenses can't find – we'll go over what you'll say, again and again, until you get it down the way you like it."

She caressed his hand again, the way she had back at Houston's on Sunday night. Her voice had again taken on the tone that mesmerized him.

"Don't you see, sweetheart?" She was changing tack. "No matter what anybody says about you being a heretic, you've obviously touched people. What you wrote was really brilliant. It can help people. You have a gift that can help people."

Laura struggled to remember something specific he had written, but her face betrayed no sign that she was anything other than fully conversant with every word of his theses. One phrase came to mind, and she didn't miss a beat.

"I mean, that stuff about wrestling with God, how God appreciates us wrestling with him. That's good, sweetheart, really good."

Pause. Then… brilliance:

"Maybe God's calling to you a ministry, Mad. Maybe that's why he had both you and Claire study aspects of that Luther guy. God must want you to give modern Americans a message they can relate to. You've been chosen for this, Mad, and maybe *I* was sent to help you get your message out."

Laura's verbal caress was becoming even more effective. By now, she was leaning in real close, invading Mad's space in a tender way that made it welcome.

"You can do it, sweetheart. You really can."

Her own nether regions, meanwhile, were uncomfortably warm. What was it about this guy that eroticized her so?

Mad was totally taken in. "Well… I guess so, I mean… I don't know, maybe you're right. If it'll make Claire's life mean something…"

Then, unexpectedly, panic and horror. "Claire! Ohmygod, Claire! I can't believe I did that to Claire."

Laura, utterly confused, gripped Mad's hand more tightly. "You didn't do anything to Claire, sweetheart." Sensing that she was losing him, she spoke through clenched teeth, less empathetically than she had meant to sound.

Mad's eyes focused hard, suddenly boring into her own. "NO SEX!" He spoke loudly enough that he would have attracted Officer Williams' attention, if the policeman weren't just that minute handling a situation of his own.

Laura dropped Mad's hand. "Okay, sweetheart," she tried to purr. She still wasn't sure what had gone wrong, why he was so agitated. "I'm here to help you tell your story, sweetheart, that's all." Regaining, by force of will, her tone that had been so effective earlier, she added: "Trust me, sweetheart. I'm here for you however you want me."

Mad relaxed.

"It's just that we shouldn't have done that the other night," he tried to explain, his voice cracking. "It was like I dishonored Claire's memory. I don't know what came over me."

"It's okay, Mad, it's okay." Laura leaned into Mad again, put her arm around his shoulder, pulled his head into the crook of her own shoulder, hugged him like a mother hugging a toddler with a newly scraped knee. "You didn't do anything wrong. You were just being sweet to me, that's all. You were just being a big old sweetheart."

Mad let his tall frame relax into Laura's embrace.

"Do you really think my theses can do some good for people?" he asked.

"Of course, Mad… Of course they can."

Mad semi-surrendered. "Okay, I'll probably do it."

Just then, the doorbell rang with a three-peated pattern that was the signal the officers had told him they would use if they who needed to talk to him.

"Can I make it upstairs without anybody seeing me through the window?" Laura asked, and Mad nodded affirmatively. Once she had made it upstairs, he opened his front door.

Officer Williams hulk-waddled through the door, closing it behind him. "You've got a real persistent little piece of ass out there, says she's a friend of yours, says you would let her in if you knew she was here, but she ain't on the list you gave me. I took her cell phone number and sent her away, told her you'd call if you wanted her. Damn cameras and everything are starting to set up – court says we can't stop'em – so I didn't want to waste too much more time with her. Sorta reddish-blonde hair, hot as a firecracker, says her name's Becky. Becky Matthews. Sounds like she's from Texas, acts like one o'them debutantes who done turned feminist and then can't remember if she's supposed to hate us men or love us, or both at the same time. Real piece of work. Here's her number. If she comes back, should I let her in, or what?"

Mad remembered Becky. Sophomore year at Georgetown, lasted three weeks with him. In the business school. All she ever wanted to do was talk about making money and then go have sex. In fact, he met her in a class called "Theology and Sexuality." Real aggressive. More aggressive than he wanted to deal with right now.

As he considered how he wanted Officer Williams to handle her, the key turned in the lock and Justin burst in again, highly agitated.

"Oh, there you are, there you are," he said to the officer. "Why'd you let all those cameras back here? Who let them back on Mad's street? (Then, to Mad:) D'ya want me to go run'em off for you?"

As Officer Williams explained about the court case, Mad got an idea.

"Hey Justin, take this phone number and call it. Girl named Becky Matthews. Might be your dream girl, buddy. Tell her I'm not feeling well. Go take her to get some coffee or something. Humor her, romance her, whatever it takes, but get her off my case. I don't want to deal with her right now, but she's a real pistol. Just the kind of woman you're looking for."

Before Justin could answer, the doorbell rang again. Mad retreated to the kitchen while the officer and Justin opened the door.

"Hi, I'm Mary McGuire. I'm a friend of Mad's. Is he here?"

Damn, they were coming out of the woodwork now. Mad remembered Mary. Freshman year, sorta plain looking, real sweet, also a history major, had wanted to go to law school. He had actually sorta cared about her, but she got too cling-y too fast. He stepped out of the kitchen to see the same girl he remembered: average height, average build, nondescript face, but with a shy smile that made her look perpetually friendly.

"C'mon in, Mary. What brings you here?"

She took a few running steps and gave him a hug so impassioned it almost hurt.

"You poor thing, Mad, you poor thing. I saw you on the news. What can I do to help?"

The circus was getting to be too much for Officer Williams, so he let himself back out to the porch. Good lookin' fella, he thought to himself about Mad, seemed nice enough, but had some real bad luck and then wrote somethin' up that got all this unwanted attention. But he sure attracted some wackos. This Justin guy was a little nerd, and then there were these two women this morning who both talked like they were educated more than women had a right to be, and of course all the demonstrators he and his police colleagues had sent away. Made him feel real proud that he himself never messed with all that intellectual shit; he just carried a gun and did his job keeping those shit-ass criminals at bay. Four more years and he could retire with a nice pension. Four more years of probably having to share a detail with a nigger – although, as niggers went, his young partner Jones-y wasn't bad. He musta had a momma who used a belt on him or something, to keep him on the straight and narrow and turn him into the kind of nigger who made a good, honest cop. Good thing Jones-y would be here within the hour to take his turn on the porch. Officer Williams had had enough of this shit for one day.

Inside, Mad tried to politely negotiate his way back into solitude – well, not exactly solitude, because Laura was still hiding upstairs – by finding a reason for both Justin and Mary to leave. Mary looked worn out; she had driven all night from St. Louis.

"Becky Matthews?" Mary said when she heard Justin asking Mad for more instructions about what to say when he called her. "I knew her a little bit. I didn't like her at all when I first met her during freshman year, so I never spent much time with her. I thought she was just a little slut, to tell the truth. But I ended up drinking with her at a party during senior week, and I really liked her. Damn, it sounds like I just missed her by a minute or two, right out front of your house this morning."

Mad had a brainstorm.

"Okay, here's how you both can help me the most. Justin, you call Becky and tell her I'm ill. Mary, you get on the phone, too, and tell her that you got past the cop by following Justin into my house as if you were with him. Tell her I came down the stairs looking like death warmed over. Yeah, that's it. Then all three of you can go out for coffee; Justin, take'em both to Carpe Diem, on me. I'll go upstairs and get some money for y'all.

"Mary, I'm really flattered, really touched, that you came all the way from St. Louis when you saw me on the news throwing my golf club. You've always been so sweet to me, even when I didn't deserve it. I'll tell you what: When y'all go for coffee, you get decaf, and then take a nap. Come back at, say, 4 – I'll tell the police to let you in – and we can visit. Maybe even have dinner, but I can't plan anything else … (Mad's brain scrambled for a good excuse) … There's no telling what other disaster the media has in store for me today, and I also just don't have enough energy to do much more than just eat and sleep. Besides, Lord only knows what's gonna happen next."

Mary reached out, a bit clumsily, to grab Mad's hands. Her voice was full of the kind of empathy born in part from one's own neediness. "I packed enough clothes to last through the weekend, Mad. I'm here for you for whatever you need me to do."

It was another 20 minutes before Mad finally herded both of them out his door in a way that made them feel as if they were on an important mission for him. Mad was at least happy to know that Justin wouldn't be back for the rest of the day because he had physical training appointments that began again at around 11 and lasted straight through until 8 that night.

Retreating up his stairs, he found Laura in a little side work-room, where Claire had set up a computer. How Laura had signed on to the Internet from a machine that wasn't hers, Mad didn't know, because he was a techno-tard. But she was intently reading the chat room of the "Mad religion" site.

"I was starting to think you had called a convention down there, sweetheart," she said. "But whoever those people were who you were talking to, I bet none of them realized just how much greatness they were in the presence of. This chat room has some really thoughtful comments on it, and some of them say you're a genius."

"Huh? Me? Everything I wrote was probably wrong. It made sense to me when I wrote it, but I'm not even sure I could explain all of it now, not even to myself."

"Heck, I don't understand it all, either, sweetheart," Laura said. "I guess I'm supposed to be a Methodist, but I never really paid much attention to religion. But listen to what this one says: 'Mr. Jones has a brilliant thesis about how a mediator must mediate BETWEEN two parties, not on behalf of just one of them. His idea that Christ therefore mediates not just on behalf of man to reconcile us to God, but to reconcile God to man as well, is just great.' And here's another: 'It might be heretical to say that God makes mistakes, but look around you at the world! I say that God made lots of mistakes! He screwed up big time, and we're paying the price! I say Go, Mad Jones, Go! Right on!'"

"You've gotta be kidding…" Mad said.

"Wait, there's more. One guy says you are going to rot in Hell because of what you've written, and quotes some Bible passages about being aware of false prophets during the 'end times' that we're in. But here's the answer from somebody calling herself 'M. Magdalene': 'Oh, ye of little understanding! These are NOT the end times. It's only the end of the line for you morons who think the whole world's history has been building toward the opportunity for you to prove yourself holier than the rest of us. What Mr. Jones is saying is that if we persevere through pain and keep believing in God even when God screws up, then God will match his grace to our faith and make things right in the long run. That's not heretical; it's just a new way of understanding the same important point about God's ultimate grace. This is all about accepting the empowerment God offers to us – not about quoting back some crackpot lines about Armageddon!'

"Wow!" Laura commented at what she had just read. "I don't know who this chick is who's pretending to be Mary Magdalene, but she kicks ass. You go, girl!"

Mad peered over Laura's shoulder at the screen in wonderment.

"I'm telling you, Mad," she said, slipping skillfully back into her mesmerizing tone, "you're on to something here. If you let me set up an interview for you the right way, you could go really far with this! I can make you famous in a way that looks good, Mad. And it'll do some good for lots of people. I *really* think you should go for it."

Under Laura's spell, Mad had no will of his own. For a young man who always had effortlessly skated through life – or, rather, above it – it was easier, especially in a time of despair, to just flow with whatever current was momentarily strongest. It was a tendency Mad would show time again in the coming months.

"Okay," he said, still nervously unsure of what he was getting into. "What do we do? Where do we start?"

Laura smiled like a kid who just won a game of Capture the Flag.

"Well, first you promise me that no matter what you do, you won't talk to any of those TV cameras out there. Not a one of them. If you have to go outside on an errand, just keep your car window rolled up and don't say a word. Now, let's find a couple of chairs, and put a TV behind me as if it's a camera. And let's get out those religious thingbobbies of yours, those thesis things, to look at them. We'll just keep on going over questions and answers, questions and answers, until we're both totally comfortable with how this interview is gonna go."

Which is what they did for most of the next six hours, stopping only for lunch, with Laura constantly interrupting Mad, taking notes, asking for background about theology and Luther and even the Poseidon Adventure. Every so often Mad would peer out the front window, and see that the TV trucks were still there, and sigh. And every so often, Laura would catch herself leaning in too closely, and feeling an unwelcome heat, and force herself to back off.

"Who the hell is Perdicaris? ... What's this 'heap big comfort' stuff? Won't that offend Native Americans? ... Do you really believe in angels? ... Is it really a good idea to curse God? Isn't that what's known as blasphemy?" Nothing, no matter how silly or inconsequential, ponderous or potentially momentous, missed her scrutiny.

Finally, Mad said he had had enough, and needed to lie down. Laura, who had been on the go since 4 a.m., needed to do likewise – but, fearing to do anything that would scare Mad off from doing an interview, she crawled, alone, onto the bed in Ben's old room.

But it didn't seem like too much longer when all hell broke loose.

The doorbell rang in three-peat fashion. Laura closed the door to Ben's room, where she could hide. Mad, realizing that he was still unshowered and unshaven, strode embarrassedly down the stairs to open the door. There, Officer Jones stood, imperturbable as Johnny Unitas in the face of a blitz.

"You've got those two young ladies there, with that redhead talking to that TV guy over there. The other one's name was on my list to let in at 4, but they say you know they're together. I told them both to stay off the porch until I could clear this with you, but meanwhile those camera folks started yelling questions at them, and…."

At that moment, one of the camera crews began advancing from the street onto Mad's small front lawn, towards the porch, ignoring the rules laid down by the court.

"Mr. Jones, Mr. Jones, is it true what these women are saying? Are you really going to start a ministry? What are your next…."

Mary and Becky rushed around the cameraman, Becky giving the attached reporter a little shove as they did, only to be met by Officer Jones' solid mass at the top of the front steps. Other reporters rushed behind them; the 65-year-old neighbor lady came scooting across her own lawn, shaking her fist at the trespassers; the mime from New Orleans – this time *sans* mime outfit – having somehow mingled in with the reporters, stepped forward and began yelling that God is a jerk.

Officer Jones, still outwardly unruffled, changed his mind and said: "Ladies: Inside, now." Stepping past them down to the bottom steps, he met the media and put his hands up in a "stop" motion, scowling sternly but otherwise silent. The man had a real presence. The media, two of them getting tangled in their own lines, halted as if they were kids suddenly realizing that nobody had told them "Simon says."

Mad didn't see or hear the rest. Mary and Becky scooted through the door, and he slammed it shut.

"HOLYMOTHEROFCHRISTALMIGHTY! What pricks those guys are!"

That was Becky, by way of introduction. Then, focusing her eyes on Mad's face: "Christ, Mad, you look like shit."

With Mary hanging back and only rarely interjecting with empathetic murmurs, Becky explained that the two of them had worked out a plan with Justin – "By the way, I think your funny little friend is trying to hit on me already, but I wouldn't screw him even if he were hung with 15 inches" – and that they wouldn't take 'no' for an answer. (She ignored Mary's weak protestations that, well, they only wanted what was *best* for Mad, and if he *really* thought this was a bad idea….)

"Mad, you can't stop the momentum now," she said, "so you better get ahead of the curve and do it right, before those media pricks make you out to be some kind of lunatic cult creep."

"Do *what* right?" Mad had tried to listen to Becky for the last five minutes, but somehow what she said hadn't fully registered.

"Dammit, Mad, I told you: this ministry you've gotta start. I've just been checking out the web site, and you've already got followers all over the place. We can make a ton of money and (sensing Mad's disapproval) help a lot of people feel healed and even start a charity, call it 'Aid for the Lionhearted,' or something like that. I'll run the Houston chapter and Mary will open one in St. Louis. That Justin dude can help you organize it here; he's weird but he's honest and he's devoted to you and has enough energy and intelligence to make it all work. And he says there's some guy named Buskirk that might help up in D.C. This is a great opportunity, loverboy."

(Mad now remembered how she used to call him that, at least for the three weeks they were together, and he *hated* it.)

Mary, hesitantly, spoke up. "We thought we'd both stay here through the weekend to help you plan – if you think this is a good idea, of course, honey – and then we can both go back home and get started."

"Yeah, you can be bigger than Billy Graham ever was," Becky broke in again.

Just then, Becky's cell phone rang. It was Justin, on a break between clients, demanding to talk to Mad.

"Well, buddy, whaddya think, buddy? I told you two days ago, this is big, Mad, really big! Mary and Becky agree with what I said: You're onto something. Oh, and you're right about Becky; I think she's hot for me. Babe city, buddy. But anyway, as I was saying, this is big; this can really work!"

Mad's heart began pounding. This was all just *way* too much.

"Justin, please, I don't know. You're all going too fast for me even to think. I need to think, Justin. I *need* to think."

"Great, buddy, think all you want. Of course you need to think, buddy. You can think, and we can do all the rest of the work. This is gonna be great buddy, just great! I gotta run to train my next client, buddy, but I'll swing by there just after 8 for more planning with you and the girls. Be sure to keep Becky around for me. She's hot-a-licious. Bye!"

Hot-a-licious? Where *did* Justin come up with these things? As Mad hung up, he thought again, for the umpteenth time, that poor Justin was just totally clueless.

* * *

From that point on, out of sheer necessity, Mad had pulled himself together enough to take charge, or at least partial charge. No, the girls couldn't stay at his house overnight; the media would use that for all *kinds* of innuendo. (He didn't mention to them, of course, that them staying would make it exceedingly difficult to smuggle Laura back out.) No, he wouldn't authorize some kind of nationwide ministry, at least not yet, but yes, he wouldn't rule it out, because he was too overwhelmed by all the events of the past five days to know *what* he was supposed to do. Yes, he wouldn't mind if the girls stayed in town through the weekend – mainly because he had not enough will of his own to stop them – as long as they found somewhere else to stay. (He insisted he would pay for their motel room, out of his Crazy Eights money).

Before he did anything else, though, he felt he had to get an unbiased viewpoint.

"I really like that Officer Jones out there; would you mind going out and asking him if he would mind visiting with us in here when his shift on the porch ends? I think Officer Sellers is due to relieve him in, like, 20 minutes or so."

Becky and Mary were both unhappy that they couldn't stay – Becky openly so, Mary only inwardly – because both thought he needed… uh, comforting. Neither, of course, wanted the other one to stay, but Becky didn't really care who else was around while she was operating. Besides, Becky's active mind was already working out business plans and marketing strategies, so she took more than a little solace in the knowledge that she would have three more full days to work Mad over enough to give her permission to run with her idea. Poor Mad's world had clearly been knocked off its axis, and he was uncharacteristically malleable as a result. That was fine with her; she lived for chances to perform malleation.

Becky had never seen a phenomenon like the overnight reaction to Mad's theses, but she knew a gold mine when she saw it. She also had already convinced herself that Mad needed help, and she was willing to forgive him for having jettisoned her so quickly six years ago. Even though he was acting like a whipped puppy right now, she remembered all too well that under ordinary circumstances there was just *something* about him that no other guy had – and she was sure she was the one who could best enjoy it *and* return his affections measure for measure.

Such were her thoughts as she poked her head out the door to invite Officer Jones inside. Officer Sellers having arrived a few minutes early, Officer Jones agreed to come in.

"What can I do for you, Mr. Jones?" The officer was very dignified, businesslike.

"To start with, you can call me Madison, or Mad. With us both being Joneses, I think we oughtta go by first names – especially since you're not much younger than I am."

"Thank you, Mr. Jones, but as long as I'm working, I need to keep calling you 'Mr.' It's a sign of respect for the citizens we serve. What can I do for you?"

"You're off duty now, right?" Seeing the officer's nod, Mad continued, "I assume if you're off duty, you can give me your honest thoughts on something…"

Seeing where this was going, Mary leaned forward as if to hear better. She really wanted to know what the officer thought. Becky, though, blanched. She could just envision how one negative word from a cop could throw off all her newly hatched plans.

"What I'd really like," Mad was saying, "if you're willing, is to get your reaction to these things I wrote that caused all those TV cameras to camp out in the street there. Just judging from the way you handle the crowd, you seem to have your head on real straight: Is there anything I wrote that's worth paying attention to?"

"I can't really say, Mr. Jones. I haven't read them, to tell the truth. All I know is that I'm told there's something in them that says God is a jerk, and I'll tell you straight out that I don't believe that at all. But you seem to be a good sort of man, Mr. Jones, so I figured there must be more to it than just that."

"Will you read them now, and tell me what you think?" Mad found that he was almost desperately intent on this officer's answer.

"Mr. Jones, I might be willing to do that, and maybe I'd be interested. Yes, maybe I would. I'd like to see what's in there that makes up for you saying God's a jerk. But I can't do that right now; my wife and baby are waiting for me to come home. I'm slightly dyslexic, Mr. Jones: I'm a good reader, did okay in school, but it takes me a little longer than most. I just wouldn't have time to read them all now."

"How about overnight? As a favor, would you read them overnight?"

Officer Jones smiled. "I'd be honored to give you my thoughts, Mr. Jones. Yes, I'll read them tonight. There must be something pretty special in there, to have so many folks so excited." Then, wanting to make himself clear, he added: "But if I don't like them, Mr. Jones, I'll tell you I don't like'em. God's important to me, Mr. Jones, and I won't tell any falsehoods, especially when *He's* the subject – not even to make somebody feel good, not even somebody who has had some real rough luck."

Now it was Mad's turn to smile. "That's exactly what I want, Officer: a totally honest opinion. You seem so solid that I feel I can count on you. I think your opinion on this would be really valuable." Mad handed him one of his copies of the theses.

They arranged, then, for the officer to come a little early for his shift the next morning. Mad would set his alarm so as to be sure to be awake and caffeinated enough to fully appreciate the officer's reactions.

As Officer Jones left the house, quiet Mary looked at her watch. "Hey, do y'all have a 5 o'clock local newscast here? Shouldn't we look to see what the stations have come up with today?"

Just as on the other afternoon, Mad used three TVs, this time flipping back and forth to keep tabs on all four stations (one from Pensacola). Sure enough, all four aired another story on Mad – two of them as their lead piece, with one of the leads and one of the others featuring live standups in front of Mad's house. Two of the stations continued to portray Mad as an anti-God crusader who now was garnering even more national attention. One pictured Mad as a curiosity piece, highlighting the footage of Becky and Mary rushing inside as Officer Jones played stone wall against the media. All four newscasts mentioned prominently the report that Mad had female "apostles" in from Houston and St. Louis, planning to start a national "ministry." Two of them actually had Becky being interviewed on camera (one up close, one from more of a distance):

"Yes, we're old friends of Mad's. We know his heart. We think he's put out a great message for this modern world, a message of strength in the face of adversity, and, uh, we're ready to take that message all over the country in the coming months."

The anchor on one newscast said: "It remains to be seen whether the whole country is ready for the message that God is a jerk." (Becky caught Mad shooting her a dirty look as he watched, and she made a mental note that she still had some work to do on him, probably with a little more subtlety than she had used so far.)

Another station closed by repeating the footage of Mad hurling his golf club the day before, as the anchor smirked that nobody yet knew whether Mad's theories would really "take flight." A third anchor, in a monotone and looking plastic, made an abrupt transition to the next story, with no commentary on Mad at all.

The fourth station, however – the one with the less close-up shot of Becky, but with the exact same quote – played the story later in the telecast, without anything edited in a way that either sensationalized or belittled it. But it put Becky's comments in the context of the debate taking place on the "Mad religion" web site. Mad was fascinated to see that it, too, picked out the same "M. Magdalene" entry that Laura had showed him: "What Mr. Jones is saying is that if we persevere through pain, and keep believing in God even when God screws up, then God will match his grace to our faith and make things right in the long run."

The on-site reporter was left to sum up, live, as Officer Sellers looked down off the porch in the background: "Mr. Jones remained inside his house all day, with nothing to say in public about the interest swirling around him. But it's clear that, no matter how uncomfortable he seems to be with the attention, his theses are being taken seriously by a growing number of people. Where it all goes from here, perhaps only God knows."

At 5:30, another of the national network newscasts ran footage of Mad throwing his driver, followed by the scene of Becky and Mary pushing their way to his front porch, in a 45-second "lighter side" close to its newscast.

Using the same words the tall white reporter had used two days before, Mary quietly said: "Mad, I don't think you can put the genie back in the bottle." The way she said it, so soft, so empathetic, had the effect of making it not a challenge to anything Mad might be thinking, but a simple statement of reality. When Mad didn't argue, Becky took note. Maybe it really *would* prove to be a good thing that Mary was there, too, Becky thought. When Becky came on too strong, Mary's softness gave Mad a reassurance he seemed to need. Without planning it – and mainly because Mary was so sincerely and obviously infatuated with Mad that all she could think about was making him feel comfortable – the two of them, Becky and Mary, were making an effective tag team. So the calculator in Becky's head kept whirring on.

Both young women stayed for a spaghetti dinner that the three of them rustled up together from the groceries Mad had bought two nights earlier. (Mad desperately wanted to get rid of them – especially with poor Laura still hiding upstairs after all this time – but he felt that keeping them around for dinner was the least he could do, considering how far they had each driven on his behalf.) And just as they were finishing (both women by now showing serious signs of fatigue), Justin showed up again, mouth running two million miles a minute and eyes too often fixated on Becky's chest. Thank goodness, at least, that he declined to eat the rest of the food they had cooked. (It didn't comport with the strict turbo-energy diet he maintained as part of his physical training regimen.) Mad knew Laura must be famished, and he had carefully and quietly saved enough for her.

It was after 9 before Mad could politely make all three feel it was their idea to leave. Apologizing for his request, he asked all not to come back the next day until after lunch. It was crucial, he explained, that he be able both to meet with Officer Jones alone, and to make some private phone calls, and to have time by himself to think about their proposals for a national ministry. (He didn't tell them so, but he still thought the idea absurd.)

Finally, mercifully, he made his way upstairs where, before he could even reach the top, Laura was bursting through the door of Ben's room and throwing her arms around him in an emphatic hug. "HOLYMOTH-EROFCHRISTALMIGHTY, *Loverboy*," she said, imitating Becky, "I thought they would NEVER leave!"

Her confinement, though, had not put her in a bad mood. She was laughing gaily. "Thank goodness I had my cell phone with me. I closed the bedroom door, took it into the closet, closed that door, too, so y'all wouldn't be able to hear me… and worked out absolutely everything with not only my news director, but with a producer for the network's alternative news magazine show, 'Acute Vision.' You may not even have heard of it; it's the network's third-string news mag, a mid-season filler. They're gonna let ME conduct the interview, at my insistence! Their ratings are struggling, and their marketing surveys say that religion is really selling right now – so they are *so* desperate to be the first with your story, a story that is just starting to creep into national news and may not stay there long, that they agreed to let me be the one! Since your phone has been off the hook, I'm the *only* one who has access to you – and they want to run this next Thursday night. If they don't have a high-rated episode soon, they'll be cancelled. I have them eating out of the palm of my hand."

"You told them you were in my house?" Mad was confused.

"No, don't be silly! But I made up this cock-and-bull story about how I had set up a back phone line to you through your normal computer line. Anyway, they are sending one of our camera crews from New Orleans – our Mobile affiliate is really pissed off, but my news director drove a hard bargain – tomorrow. We're taping at 10:30 a.m., on your patio! We're gonna be big! I mean, this isn't one of those established, high-rated news magazine shows, not yet anyway, but it's *national*, Mad, it's *national!* We've only been at this for five days now, and we're already going coast to coast on TV!"

A nervous, sick feeling grew in the pit of Mad's stomach, but he tried to ignore it. Laura's euphoria was contagious enough that he let it overwhelm what might have been better judgment. As usual, she was in control.

"Hey, do you have that 'Counting Crows' CD, the one with 'Round Here' on it, and… uh…" (she had started to say something else), "'Rain King,' and their other big hits?"

"Uhmm… yeah." This was all going too fast for Mad; he couldn't follow Laura's thought processes. "Why?"

"Do you have a CD player upstairs? Can I play something for you? Even with all the negotiations from my cell phone in the closet, I had plenty of time to think of other things, and this popped into my mind. If you have something downstairs I can eat, cuz I'm famished, I want to play Counting Crows for you right after."

Less than an hour later, fed and at least somewhat freshened up, Laura set Mad down on the edge of his bed, told him to listen closely, and turned on the music on a portable jam box Mad produced from a closet.

Mad had to laugh as it dawned on him what Laura's point was. She danced around his room, in a sort of slow, sensual shimmy, as Laura mouthed the words along with Adam Duritz: "I want to be a lion/ Everybody wants to pass as cats/ We all want to be big big stars, but we got different reasons for that/ Believe in me because I don't believe in anything and I want to be someone to believe/ Mr. Jones and me…"

Laura sang the "Mr. Jones" part aloud, pointing at Mad while writhing close to him. "Mis-ter Jones and me… Mis-ter Jones and me, staring at the video/When I look at the television, I want to see me staring right back at me…. Mis-ter Jones and me, we're gonna be big stars."

Mad had no desire to be a big star, but Laura's attitude was infectious. He was enjoying her performance.

And that song wasn't the end of Laura's show.

"Pretend my name's Maria," she said, while pushing the buttons on the jam box to find the desired song.

The music from "Round Here" played halfway through before Laura said: "Here's the part from your theses, Mad!," just before Duritz sang "Round here we talk just like lions/ But we sacrifice like lambs…"

Song over, she pushed the buttons to play it again, still doing a little sultry dance with her torso. Mad was captivated, and Laura began acting out the verses. The words rolled on:

"Maria came from … (Laura sang loudly: "New Orleans") … with a suitcase in her hand/ She said she'd like to meet a boy who looks like Elvis/ She walks along the edge… (Laura, doing a tiptoe routine, began untucking her T-shirt from her jeans) … of where the ocean meets the land/ Just like she's walking on a wire in the circus…"

For some reason, she was unbuttoning her jeans. "She parks her car outside of my house/ Takes her clothes off/ Says she's close to understanding Jesus…"

Mad didn't hear the rest. Laura was magically naked, wrapped around him, her hands pulling at his clothes. He did not, could not, resist….

…. Or maybe he could resist. Because, unbidden, a vision of Claire flickered through his mind. It was all he needed.

"*NO!!*" he yelled.

Despite the look of surprise and confusion on Laura's face, Mad pushed her away. He would *not* dishonor Claire again. But as he tried to explain this to Laura, her face turned stonily impassive. Icily, she made her way back to Ben's old room for the remainder of the night.

Chapter Five

By the next morning, very early, Laura was mentally flogging herself. She had had everything under control, and now… *this*. She knew he was weirded out about his wife. Hell, she couldn't blame him. She *knew* he'd regret sleeping with her if she seduced him again. Hell, he had *told* her so. But she just hadn't been able to resist trying – there was just *something* overwhelmingly erotic about him.

Laura pulled on her day-old clothes and entered Mad's room.

"Sweetheart, I'm sorry about that scene last night," she said. "It was unprofessional of me. But it sure as heck shows I like you." Mad didn't respond, so she continued, "It shows I want to make you like me. It shows I have a reason to make you look good in our interview – now doesn't it?"

"Uh-huh." Mad's voice was monotone, but at least he had finally spoken.

Laura kneeled back onto the bed, leaned over Mad, brushed a lock of his hair off his forehead, and kissed him on the cheek. "Mad, I'm so proud of you. You're gonna do great on this interview today. And come next Thursday night, when this thing airs coast to coast, you'll have influenced lots of lives for the better. This is all in God's plan for you, sweetheart. Trust me. Will you trust me, sweetheart?"

"I guess so."

"I've gotta go sneak out the way I came," Laura explained. "My suitcase and good clothes are in my car. I've gotta go find a motel to shower in, to show on my expense account that I got a room – cuz they know I wasn't in town in New Orleans. I'll be back around 10, to help my camera crew set up."

She kissed him again on the cheek, said "I'll see you in a few hours," and disappeared down the steps. Out the patio door she went, quietly moved a patio chair over to the corner where the neighbor's shed was and used it to boost herself up on top. Good thing she was young and in shape, she thought. She felt very feline – and if anyone had watched her, they would have said she looked it, too. With great stealth, she reversed her route from the morning before, and snuck up the neighbor's driveway to her car.

*　*　*

Mad's alarm rang at 8, waking him again. He was surprised that he actually felt refreshed.

He hustled through his shower, dressed in a nice, pale blue, Oxford button-down shirt and navy dress slacks, and quickly brewed some coffee. At 8:30 sharp, the bell rang the cops' three-peat signal, and he let Officer Jones in.

Officer Williams, tired from his night on porch duty, gave them both an odd look. Maybe this Madison Jones guy really was cracked, he thought. Nice young fella; but why was he asking this uppity nigger in, even a polite uppity nigger like Jones-y, to ask *his* opinion about those goofy religious sayings? Who cared what some dumb-ass nigger thought?

Jones brought a *Mobile Register* in with him. Friday the Thirteenth of March, it was. It figured: Mad's one real phobia was of Friday the Thirteenth. It always meant bad news.

But there on the front page, beneath the latest headlines about the Lewinsky scandal, was a smaller headline: "Jones keeps up," and a subhead: "Mobilian's 'God' message garners more response."

"Good story in here, Mr. Jones," said the young black officer. "I woke up real early to think more about your writings, and there was the story on you on the front page. I had some time, so I read that, too. Made you look okay, it did. There's even some minister, I think it said he's a Methodist, who says that with a little touching up, you might be onto something. Whole thing sure don't make you look bad, not at all."

Hmmm… Mad would have to read it for himself later. It couldn't be a good, fair story – not on Friday the Thirteenth. Then again, it was by that kind-faced young reporter woman who seemed to be conscientious, so maybe it really would turn out to be okay.

Anyway, the two Joneses sat down at Mad's kitchen table.

"Well, what did YOU think of what I wrote? Did you get the chance to read it overnight?" Mad's heart was poundly oddly in his chest. He was nervous, like he was a high diving competitor getting judged on his form.

"Well, Mr. Jones, at first I didn't like it, not what you said at first. It made me angry at first, Mr. Jones. But then when I worked through the whole thing, it made me think a lot. It raised lots of questions for me, Mr. Jones. Lots of questions. Enough questions so that I'd want to sit and talk to you about it for hours, Mr. Jones, not just a few minutes here before work. There could be something good in there, Mr. Jones. But on some of those thesis things, I just couldn't really understand what you were getting at."

Mad felt a rush of unexpected excitement flow through his nerve endings. "Really? You thought some of it was valuable? Which parts?"

Officer Jones pulled out a copy of the theses and began pointing to certain passages. "Well, Mr. Jones, my God isn't a jerk. He's my Lord and savior, Mr. Jones. He's blessed me through all my troubles. But I started liking it right here, at number 21. I think too many people think that God asks them to be a sacrifice, that they use that as an excuse for all the bad things in this life. I don't think God acts that way; I think Jesus Christ Almighty died on the Cross so that we wouldn't have to be sacrifices ourselves. I think you're right that we're not supposed to be lambs. We're supposed to be lions. That's part of why I like police work, because it means standing up for what's right instead of lying down like sheep."

He took a breath. Seeing that Mad seemed to be listening very intently, with great respect, he looked back at the theses and continued: "I also like 26, about not casting away our confidence, but instead believing that God can save our souls. And, um… To tell the truth, I don't know what Perdicaris is, on 28 – and then you get into stuff that doesn't sound right again, Mr. Jones. You're awfully hard on God, Mr. Jones. You're lucky He's a forgiving God because you say some awful bad things against Him."

"Go on," Mad said, eagerly. "Go on. Don't worry about Perdicaris; that's a guy who Teddy Roosevelt saved from a kidnapper a hundred years ago. When it ended, did you like it again, or did you still think I was off base?"

"Oh, I think I really liked it at the end," the officer said. "Almost everything from number 40 on sounded really good, except… lemme see… oh yeah, number 51, about God being condemned. But the rest is right up my alley, Mr. Jones. It's just that I'm not sure I understand how you got where you got. That's why I have so many more questions – because I like where you got, but I'm confused on how you got there. It seems like an awful roundabout way to say that our God is a loving God. And that's what I believe with all my heart: God loves us, and he blesses us always."

"Except for those times, of course, when we aren't seeming to be blessed at all," Mad said quietly.

"That's kinda what my wife said, too," Officer Jones said. "She didn't have any problems with the parts I had problems with. She said she agrees with you. She said that if God was always blessing us, then her father would not be in jail and her mother wouldn't be on drugs. But I told her that those bad circumstances allowed her to be raised by her grandparents, who are some of the finest people I know. But for some reason that just made her mad, so I dropped the subject and volunteered to go change our baby before we put her to bed."

These personal details, spoken just in passing, were for some reason fascinating to Mad. He asked the officer to tell him more about the officer's family and his background. The officer said his parents were both hard-working custodians at a local elementary school, that he had one older sister who learned to type well enough to get a job as a banker's secretary right out of high school, and that he had wanted to please his parents by outdoing her and going to college. He had been a promising linebacker in high school football, with realistic dreams of a college scholarship, until he tore up his knee in the last quarter of the last game of his junior year.

He worked hard enough at his studies – hard enough that, despite his dyslexia, he had earned a C+ average. That would have been good enough to get him into a local college, but not at all good enough to earn a decent scholarship. And with his family needing financial help to provide for his two diabetic grandparents, who had moved in with his parents the year before, he had put his dreams on hold and joined the police force instead. That was more than four years ago, and he had told himself he would only stay on the force for five years. But he had gotten married a year and a half ago, and now had a six-month-old daughter, and college was beginning to look farther away than ever. (Not that he didn't like police work, he hastened to add. He was a good cop, and he took pride in upholding the laws and keeping society safe. His superior officers had told him he showed promise, and that he would almost certainly be chosen for an advanced career track if he stayed on the force.)

By the time Mad had elicited these details, Officer Williams was three-peat ringing on the front door. It was time for his shift to end, and for Officer Jones to begin his porch duty. Mad was sorry the conversation had to end and made Officer Jones promise to continue it later. It was a promise the officer seemed just as eager to make as Mad was eager to hear it.

Officer Williams, meanwhile, was visibly muttering to himself as he walked away from his post. Mad thought he heard the words "shit-ass goofy," but he couldn't be sure.

The good news was that there were no cameras out there this morning – only the occasional gawker or protester to be shooed away. Thank goodness the media has a short attention span: Just one day with nothing new happening, and their focus turns elsewhere. To Mad, this was a promising sign – and it brought into question whether he was wise to do this interview with Laura. If he did the interview, wouldn't that be throwing fuel on a fire that otherwise might finally be burning itself out?

Oh, well.... He had promised her he'd do it. Too late to change his mind now.

Retreating to his kitchen, Mad plugged the phone back in for the first time in days. He had to call his headmaster, to get everything straight for his return to the classroom (and the baseball diamond!) on

Monday. When he thought about it, he was surprised to discover just how eager he was to return to work, just what a relief it would seem.

As it turned out, though, Mad had another "think" coming. The headmaster had bad news.

"Madison," he said, voice full of sincere concern, "this thing you're doing, this religious soothsaying, is getting out of hand. I want – *everybody* here at school wants – to do everything possible to help you out. You're one of our own, Madison. We're all hurting for you, with everything you've been through. But you're so controversial, your return would be treated by those TV people like a freak show. Everything you've been doing looks like a freak show. Our kids, our classes, can't be put in that kind of situation, Madison. And some of our parents – actually, more than just some of them – are up in arms about what you've said. I've seen your theses, Madison: I don't agree with everything, but I see that you end up on a redemptive note. But not everybody sees that. All they see is you saying that God is a jerk; and frankly, Madison, some of them are not at all happy about it. Not at all happy. More like 'furious.' They don't want their kids anywhere near you, Madison – even some of the ones who remember you from when you were a student here and who used to think the world of you. They will think highly of you again, I'm sure, one day, but right now with all the news coverage they are just really insistent that you would be a bad influence on their children. There's nothing I can do, Madison, nothing I can do."

It was a longish speech, sounding semi-rehearsed, and Mad had not been able to get a word in at all. But even when Mad finally tried to explain, the headmaster was unmoved. The solution, the headmaster went on to say, quite sympathetically, was for Mad to take off the rest of the school year, at full pay, and meanwhile to try to get some counseling (the school would pay for that, too) and, above all, stay out of the limelight. In May, Mad should come back in for a meeting, with the thought that there might be a good chance for him to return to teaching next fall. But for that to happen, he would really have to tone down his act.

Told that Mad was about to do an interview for a national TV program to run next Thursday, the headmaster sighed heavily.

"Well, Madison, try to wrap it all up, then. Use the interview to throw cold water on all the hype. I don't know how, Madison, but just tell the TV audience that you're no expert on all this theological stuff and make them believe your thoughts on religion are not worth getting too bothered about."

Mad was crushed. What *had* he been thinking? Why had he posted those blasted theses? All he knew now was that he must put an end to all those crazy plans that Becky, Mary and Justin were hatching. National ministry, his rear end. Who the heck was he to do a national ministry? He wasn't even ordained; he wasn't even very devout. All he was, was hurting. All he had done was just venting. Why was anybody taking him seriously at all? And why were mimes and iguana ladies and cameramen and oversexed brunette reporters all hounding him? Okay, maybe he understood Laura; she seemed to really want to help him, especially if it helped her own career at the same time – but what about all those other freakazoids? This was all backwards: *he* thought of himself as the normal guy, so why was *he* like a circus freak act being ogled by everybody else, while it was the real freaks who were doing the ogling? Lord-oh-Lord, what would Daddy Lee say about all this? A Lee could get away with being a bit of a rake, but never with losing his dignity, much less losing his job. This was all very unbecoming. How had he managed to turn into such a screw-up?

Whatever good mood Mad had developed while talking to Officer Jones was now more than gone. He tried reading the newspaper – avoiding the article on himself but trying to pore over the sports statistics and the comics especially – but nothing really would register in his brain. He found himself reading the same lines or the same comic strip panels over and over again. When Dennis the Menace blew the bugle at Mr. Wilson for the eighth time that morning, Mad realized it was hopeless. All he could do was sit and wait for Laura to arrive, and to try to practice the lines the two had worked out the previous afternoon.

At 10:00 sharp, Laura arrived with several TV cameras in tow. With the practiced voice of an interviewer familiar to, but no-more-than-politely friendly with, the subject, she introduced Mad to the cameramen, to the sound men, and to a producer the national network had sent down to oversee the project. The weather was perfect, with bright sunshine and not even the remotest chance of rain in the forecast of a high of 75 degrees, so they set up in Mad's patio, unfurling extension wires and all kinds of other electronic equipment with a ruthless efficiency. As this was happening, the producer made small talk with Mad, in a tone meant to sound soothing but still slightly condescending. Only the furtive, reassuring glances from Laura kept Mad from a visible aggravation at the producer, the wires, and the whole pre-interview process.

Then Mad found himself being stage-directed, almost manhandled, into a patio chair, and there was Laura sitting in a similar chair facing him, and somebody was saying something like "roll, tape," and Laura was asking him something that sounded vaguely familiar but which didn't register in his brain.

"Madison Jones," she repeated. "Some people are already saying you're a heretic, and some are saying you are a modern prophet, and yet you say you're just a young man in mourning for his beautiful young bride. But what's undeniable is that you've somehow struck a big response, very quickly, with a lot of people. What is it about what you wrote that you think is new or different enough to have caused such a fuss?"

Mad recognized the question. They had practiced the answer the day before. But she wasn't supposed to lead off with it; this was one that she said she would use further along in the interview. Disconcerted, he stammered a little until the rehearsed answer seeped back, at least partly, into his brain.

"Uh, well, it's all been a surprise to me. I think maybe people are just empathizing with the idea of struggling with God, struggling with a sense that some things that happen are just too bad or sad or unfair for a loving God to even allow them to happen, much less include them in some kind of cosmic plan. …"

Mad had rehearsed another sentence, but Laura cut him off: "But the problem of pain, of bad things happening to good people, is nothing new," she said. "What makes your take on it so special?"

This was another question Mad expected, but only after an intervening query that Laura had now failed to ask. Again, he had to fast-forward his mental audiotape in order to scramble for an answer.

And the whole interview went like that. Laura stayed mostly with familiar questions, but in different orders and with different emphases. Three times, she completely blindsided him: twice with questions asking him to apply his "new theology," as she called it, to aspects of the Clinton/Lewinsky scandal that was dominating the headlines; and once with a totally offbeat suggestion, with an interrogatory inflection of her voice, that somehow a few of his theses were re-statements of themes from the still record-setting movie "Titanic."

A couple of times, she asked if he would repeat an answer while a camera moved in for a different angle. She also asked several times for something called "a two shot," where he answered the same question over again while one of the cameras moved in for more of a close-up of her. Funny: It seemed to him that even though she said his repeated answer wouldn't really matter (because the object of the two-shot was to focus on *her*), he still thought one of the other cameras aimed at him was diligently recording his words and expression.

Every chance he got, Mad tried to downplay the whole mini phenomenon that he had caused. Mindful of the headmaster's words, he kept trying to say that nothing he had written was anything really special. Every time he thought he was beginning to make that point effectively, though, Laura interrupted with another question, whether rehearsed or not, that made him delve more deeply into what some would call his unorthodoxy. The whole thing took an hour, by the end of which Mad realized his forehead was sweating profusely despite the temperate weather. And then Laura was unhooking her microphone and clasping his hands and saying, "Mr. Jones, thank you so much for your time," and the cameramen and technicians were unplugging things and furling up wire and pushing away their equipment. When nobody was looking, Laura did manage to whisper in Mad's ear – this time familiarly calling him "Mad" – that he had just done so beautifully, and to be sure to watch next Thursday night. Soon the producer was dismissing him, like he was a schoolchild, from his own patio, telling him that he was perfectly free (read: expected) to go back into his house while the technicians finished their clean-up work.

As Mad shut his kitchen door behind him, he thought he heard somebody out there say something about "a real pigeon," but he couldn't be sure.

* * *

Before the TV folks left for good, Laura rang his doorbell and handed him a cell phone. "Keep it for now," she said. "I'll tell the station that I lost it somewhere. But this way I'll be able to reach you even when your phone is off the hook. You know, you really oughtta get a cell phone for yourself, and an unlisted home number – which you'll give to me, of course – so that people you *want* to reach you can do so."

Not much later, the threesome of Justin, Becky and Mary arrived, brimming with energy. Justin, of course, was also overflowing with a geiser of words.

"Oh buddy, oh boy oh boy, we're just kicking major A with our ideas, buddy. I cancelled all my training appointments for the rest of the day; we're onto a gold mine of spiritual/physical self-improvement here!"

Mary hung back, but Becky was purring something about how Mad was the perfect person to meld together a new "God-message" and sex appeal. And then Justin – "Mr. Luke, here" was what Becky had taken to calling him, presumably to help ward off any romantic ideas he might be having – was off on another torrential tangent of verbosity about marketing rights and broadcast options and so much other seemingly foolish data that Mad totally tuned him out. At times like these, when his normally high enthusiasm became even more hypercaffeinated, Justin's very presence became nothing more than bright orange noise with no "off" button. Even if Mad had kept listening, he would not have understood half of what Justin was talking about.

It was left to Mary to notice that the more Justin (and occasionally Becky) talked, the more uncomfortable Mad became.

"Are you okay, honey?" she asked, quietly.

Without knowing why, Mad realized that he was fighting back tears.

"I don't *want* any of this," he was saying. "I just want to go back to teaching, and now I've been ordered not to go back to school until next fall. My headmaster wants all this to end, and I don't even know what it's all about. Hell, sometimes I can't even remember what it was that I wrote, even though I just wrote it last week."

Justin looked like he had been kicked in the stomach. Becky looked like she had just propositioned somebody and been turned down flat.

"I know that you all have put a lot of thought into this – into helping me – these last few days," Mad continued. "But I just can't go ahead with any of this."

"But, but, but…" Justin was spluttering. Becky looked like she was trying to rouse herself into a convincing rejoinder but hadn't found the right words yet. Ever so calmly, though, Mary spoke in a soothing near whisper.

"Of course this is hard for you, Mad," she said. "That's why we're here: to be your friends to make all this a little more bearable." She was now standing behind Mad, massaging his shoulders. "You just did a TV interview, honey, and it won't run until next Thursday. You can't stop the amusement park ride, so you might as well try to direct it instead. We're here for you, Mad. We're gonna help you make something good out of all of this."

For Mary, that was an epic-length speech.

It had the effect not of deciding anything, but of stopping Mad's tears and of keeping all options open. But even then, Mary wasn't finished.

"You just need to grieve, Mad. Go ahead and grieve and leave everything to us. You know you can trust us. You just relax, and we'll wait for the show on Thursday, and we'll play it by ear and take it from there."

Mad found he couldn't speak, but he nodded. Heck, he didn't know what he was supposed to do. But Mary was a good sort; he *could* trust her.

Mad hadn't noticed before, but Mary had a briefcase with her. "Just sign these papers," she said, "so we can stop anybody else from profiting off your name and ideas. We're lucky that that 'Mad religion' site hasn't already tried copyrighting anything or selling ads or something."

Mad, still as malleable as he had been ever since Claire's death, signed what Mary put in front of him. He didn't notice that Becky flashed Mary a look that spoke of surprise bordering on awe.

Soon thereafter, all three of his friends were, mysteriously, gone. He must've zoned out because he didn't remember much else of what they had said. Oh, okay… he did remember that Becky had given him a lip-brushing goodbye kiss, and that Justin had said something about how he needed to go show these "babe-ettes" – yes, he said "babe-ettes" – a "night on the rip-roaring town."

As for Mad, he now needed some exercise. Peeking out a front window, he saw no crowd or cameras. He opened the front door a crack, told Officer Jones he was leaving, and then exited through his kitchen door and patio. He drove out to school, to the gym, and worked out alone (all the sports teams were still outside, practicing) until his muscles hurt like hell.

* * *

Becky showed up again that night, alone. Mad had to admit she was awfully attractive. Strawberry blonde, medium-high cheekbones, sly and bewitching smile, very nice figure. But there was something just too aggressive about her. She wanted sex. He said no and wouldn't yield. She wasn't very happy when she left.

Laura called on the cell phone she had left him. Yes, she got a great contract for an on-air job at the New Orleans station, but with an easy-out clause if the network wanted to hire her to go national. Five days ago, she was an assistant producer; now she was already "talent" who had the upper hand over management.

Justin showed up, looking for Becky. He just couldn't understand how she could have disappeared like that; he thought they had plans for a wild night out at a dance club in West Mobile. Satisfied that she wasn't at Mad's house, he soon left to continue trying to track her down.

Officer Sellers knocked on the door. "Nobody's been out here all day or evening," she said. "Mind if I come in for a minute to use your bathroom?" Mad had already told all three of the rotating cops, of course, that they could use his bathroom whenever they needed. He had even given them a key, so he wasn't sure why she had knocked. He was tired, he wanted to go to bed, and he told her to make herself at home.

Bad choice of words. She started unbuttoning her uniform shirt. She was large, in every way. Not attractive. Sour personality, too. And now she, too, was trying to come on to him. Damn! Why couldn't women ever leave him alone?

He played dumb, and like a half-addled psycho, and managed to shoo her back out his front door. He had had enough, and tried to go upstairs to bed. Taking the stairs two at a time, he stubbed his toe on the third-highest step and took a tumble, jarring his elbow on the funny-bone in the process. It hurt like mad. Yep, this was Friday the Thirteenth all right. As he finally crawled into bed, he thought that he would be lucky to avoid a nightmare so bad that it gave him a heart attack. Fridays the Thirteenth just sucked.

* * *

Saturday was weird. Everybody just left him alone. Mad did yard work and housework and watched some sports on TV. No protesters or gawkers came by his house. Justin, Becky and Mary all stayed away. Mad tried calling Buzz in D.C., got an answering machine, and left a message with his cell phone number. When Officer Jones' shift ended at 5, Mad insisted that the cop come in for a Coke and more conversation. The officer said he reckoned his wife would let him get away with being 15 minutes late, but no more. Besides, his wife had said she was intrigued with Mad's notion of Christ mediating not just on behalf of mankind, for God's blessing, but mediating between men and God because both needed to reconcile with the other (Thesis 34). She wanted her husband to get Mad to explain that one a little more.

"She said to me, 'Shiloh, I think that guy is right about that one. Ask him for me how he thinks that works.'"

So "Shiloh" was the officer's first name?

"Oh, yeah," the cop said. "My mother went to the Baptist church a lot, and she liked that idea of that Hebrew sanctuary named Shiloh. And then she found out that Shiloh was a place where the Yankee army, who were trying to free all the black folk, won a big Civil War battle. So she figured Shiloh was a name full of luck and goodness, and that's what she named me."

That led to a discussion of how Mad had gotten *his* name, and soon the 15 minutes were up without them having discussed at all the question from young Mrs. Jones about Thesis 34.

When Shiloh Jones left the house, Officer Sellers sneered sourly at Mad.

Bored after dinner, Mad turned on the computer and called up the "Mad religion" web site. Its chat room was still going fairly strong, with 56 new entries that day. An anonymous somebody even reported the "rumor" that one of the network news outfits was going to do a "special" show on Mad. In response, M. Magdalene chimed in that she had "sources" somewhere on the Gulf Coast and so she thought she could soon find out if the rumor were true. Meanwhile, she suggested that all Mad's fans on the web site should call the networks and ask that they all give Mad more attention. "Make it sound like a real grassroots uprising of interest," she wrote.

That message had been typed in at 3 p.m. As Mad finished reading the chat entries, around 7:30, he pushed the "Refresh" button before signing off. He was amused to see a new message had come in from M. Magdalene just in the previous 5 minutes.

"Confirmed!" it read. "My sources tell me that a TV truck was set up outside Madison's house yesterday. It had the name of a New Orleans station painted on the side – but the back window had a sign in it that said, 'Acute Vision.' That's the spring fill-in news show for the network, the one that's way down at the bottom of the Nielsens. It runs on Thursday nights. Do you think Mad might be on it as early as next week?"

Mad himself started to enter an anonymous message confirming that yes, indeed, he had network sources who confirmed that Thursday's show would feature Madison Jones. But then he decided maybe it wasn't such a good idea to hype the show, so he never pushed the "Send" button.

Turning off the computer, Mad tried phoning Buzz again, but again just reached the machine. He read two issues of Sports Illustrated instead and drifted off to sleep. He dreamed of Claire in a garden near a rocky hillside, peering into a little cave with a big stone beside it. She was dressed in old-time Middle Eastern garb. Nobody was inside the cave, and she left to go spread the news. But his headmaster didn't believe her, and Mad's father Ben had to leave the Spring Hill/Georgetown campus while Cleon Jones, a Mobile native, ran down baseballs in the Mets outfield in the background. The Sports Illustrated photographer was there to capture the scene, but when the photographer turned around, he was Laura. The cock crowed but Buzz still wasn't there.

Chapter 5(a)

Verily did Madison Jones stumble into the limelight, for he understood the limelight not. For the American news cycle finds one serious political topic at a time, and one topic of human interest, and only the one of politics and the one of the other shall grab the limelight at any one time. Verily the short attention span of the modern American doth make it so. And Madison Jones, who looked like the famed Redford of the silver screen, and who inspired others to feats of great travel on his behalf, was, yea, a human-interest story for relief from talk of presidential impeachment. And no middle-aged Jesuit had yet come to him to offer guidance, no Jesuit with an Italian surname, so Madison did stumble into greater glory and greater realms of acrimony, knowing not what he did nor what the limelight held. Neither Madison nor the Jesuit was a prophet, so neither knew the power of the limelight. And a new day dawned, the evening and the morning of the seventh day of Exodus, and Madison awoke.

Chapter Six

Sunday morning Mad decided to go to church. He was only a semi-haphazardly regular churchgoer, but he figured that if he ever needed divine guidance, this was surely the time. His fellow parishioners greeted him warmly and sympathetically, but with typical Episcopalian reserve. Or, at least, most of them did. Mad thought that one or two looked at him with condescension or disgust, or maybe with anger. Many more, though, smiled broadly and nodded at him. And when the rector gave him communion, it was with a warmth nobody could miss.

Mad had a hard time concentrating on the service. If he had thought he would find some deep meaning there, some explanation for everything he had been through in the past weeks, he had been wrong. He didn't know what to pray for or about, and he certainly didn't hear any messages *from* God, either. The service just seemed like the same old litany of nice, familiar words that felt rather comfortable to repeat, in this case rather mindlessly. Our Father who art in heaven… We believe in one God, Father almighty… one catholic and apostolic church … The Blood of Christ, the Cup of Salvation. None of it really registered with Mad that morning, but something about it all felt pretty good anyway.

But the good feelings didn't last. When the service was over, the congregation was greeted by TV cameras at the front exit. It was the local affiliate of Laura's network, wanting footage of Mad actually at church. Mad ducked the cameras, as did most of the congregation, but a few parishioners eagerly spoke to the reporter.

Mad, agitated, sped home. Justin, Becky, and Mary were all waiting for him. Both women reported that they had to drive back to their home cities but wanted to make sure they had a way to get in touch with Mad. Reluctantly, he gave them his cell phone number. They assured him that they had "everything" under control – whatever "everything" meant. He still wasn't sure what he had agreed to. He just hadn't been focusing on Friday. As Justin held back, Mary gave him a hug, and then Becky called him "Loverboy" again and assaulted him with a lip-lock that lingered longer than Mad found comfortable. Apparently she had overcome her disappointment at being rebuffed the other night. The two women hugged each other, too, and Mary hugged Justin. But Justin had to chase Becky down just to get a goodbye handshake.

As Shiloh Jones watched from the porch, smiling broadly, Becky turned around at her car door and again yelled at Mad: "Bye, Loverboy! Talk soon!"

Why such a highly attractive woman had to be so aggressive, when men would chase her without her even trying, Mad couldn't understand.

Justin followed Mad into the house. "Those are some smart women who just left here!" he was saying. "And holy hot potatoes, Becky's hot as a hot plate. She's playing hard to get, but I've got her phone number, so I think she really digs me, Mad, dontcha think?"

This was just as Mad was closing the door. As he did, he and Shiloh Jones exchanged rolling-eyeball glances, and Shiloh had to cover his mouth to keep from laughing aloud.

Poor Justin.

But poor Justin was also loquacious Justin, and he kept babbling on about God-only-knows-what. Mad kept nodding at him, but tuned him out as surely as if he, Mad, were wearing ear plugs. One of these days he might miss Justin say something that was actually important, but Mad seriously doubted it. Mad continued to make encouraging noises, but his mind was occupied with thoughts ranging from brief memories of Claire, just as quickly suppressed, to wonderings about how he would fill his time without any classes to teach for the next several months.

A good 45 minutes later, as Justin finally left, Mad tuned back in as the little guy was saying "… will call us when she has the contract in hand. Anyway, see'ya, buddy!"

What contract? *Who* would call back? Mad had no idea what Justin was talking about.

With Justin finally out of his hair, and still no nutty onlookers in sight (maybe this really was all blowing over!), Mad joined Shiloh on the porch. Because Shiloh insisted on still calling him "Mr. Jones," Mad reciprocated by calling Shiloh "Officer," but he already felt like Shiloh was a friend.

"You know, this is our last day guarding your house," Shiloh said. "The chief's original order went only through Sunday night, and with everybody leaving you alone, now, that's what he's sticking to. But I'll tell you what: If I can convince my partner to do so, we'll try to make sure our patrol takes us past this place as often as possible. Williams has been in sorta a bad mood for the last couple of days, but I think he feels sorry for you anyway, and I think he'll agree to do that."

Mad said that was really nice of them, and he was happy for them to do it, but that they would probably find after a few days that it wasn't at all necessary. He said he was clearly a one-week wonder as far as these religious theses were concerned, and he was darn glad it was all quieting down.

"I dunno about that, Mr. Jones," said the officer. "My wife and I really do think you are saying something important. She thinks that everything you wrote is important, and I think it's important that you end up back with God even after straying so far away from Him. It's like that song: You once were lost, but now am found, was blind but now you see. That's what I think, anyway."

"But Officer, I'm not even a minister, or a Doctor of Theology, or anything. I was mad, and still am mad, that Claire and my baby and Claire's mom were all taken away from me. But that's it. I swear I'm not even sure if I even remember half of what I wrote."

"But that's how God works, Mr. Jones. He can take anybody he wants and make a prophet out of them, or a king. Look at King David. All he was, was a sheep-boy, or something like that. And St. Paul was persecuting Christians until God flashed his light at him, and made him change his name, and then he became the one who spread the Word all over. People are responding to what you wrote like it's something powerful. How do you know that God didn't put it into your mind, or at least put part of it into your mind once you started getting angry at Him? Maybe he found you down and out and on the ropes and writing a bunch of blasphemy, and then chose to turn your blasphemy around to something good and use you to reach people that have been running away from him. They say that God works in mysterious ways, Mr. Jones. Maybe you're one of those mysterious ways."

"You really know your Bible, don't you?" said Mad in admiration.

"That's what you gotta do if you love God," answered Shiloh. "You've gotta read his Word every day, or at least most days. That's what I always try to do."

The two men grew silent. Another question was forming in Mad's mind, but he couldn't quite get a hold on it. Then he lost his train of thought completely, because of the sudden ringing of Laura's cell phone, which he was wearing on his belt.

It was Buzz, finally returning his calls.

"Hello, young friend," he said. "You've got some nice-sounding girlfriends there working with little Justin. And they sound pretty damned smart, if you ask me."

"Huh? You mean you've talked to them?"

"Hell yeah, of course I talked to them. Lotsa times, these last few days. They've got a really good plan worked up."

"Huh? What kind of plan?"

There were a few seconds of silence from Buzz's end, and then Buzz started laughing.

"Damn, Mad, that's a good one. You had me going there for a second. 'What kind of plan?' That's pretty funny. Man, if you keep that deadpan humor to go with your theology, you'll have an act that'll sell not just in churches but in comedy clubs. I'll tell you, I was really getting worried about you when I saw you throw that golf club on the news. That's why I said you really oughtta get counseling. But I shoulda known that there's a method to your Madness. *MADness*, get it? Damn, this is just too rich for words!"

Mad truly didn't know what was going on, so he just kept making some "uh-huh" noises while his mind tried to figure out what Buzz was talking about. It seemed like everybody knew something about his own plans that he didn't know. His *own* plans, ferChrissakes! The odd thought popped into his mind that maybe this was what it was like to be President, with a strong chief of staff who controlled the schedule and told you what you were supposed to do next in your own administration. Like Ronald Reagan with James Baker, or Bush with that Sununu guy, or Ike with… hell, his dad was the American historian, not him. Mad taught old European stuff. All he could remember with Ike was Mamie and those Dulles guys the airport was named after, but they were foreign policy, not…. Anyway, what was Buzz saying now?

"… the show Thursday night and then we'll really know if we can make this a big-time thing. It's after the show that I'll get with that PR guy from your Georgetown class, that whathisname guy who's already sick of the California jackass he works for in Congress, and he'll decide if this is worth him leaving Mr. California and trying to make this work."

"*What* PR guy?" Mad just had no clue.

"Oh, you know, young whats-his-face. The guy with the preppy kiss-ass attitude. Ron? Don? Something like that. Anyway, he says he's not only good with the regular news guys, but he's got some kind of tabloid contacts he can hype this with. We're on a roll, Mad, on a roll."

Mad didn't know where his mind was, or where his own will was, but he knew that whatever Buzz was talking about, and that Justin had been talking about earlier, was too much for him to contemplate now. If his choices were between thinking hard enough to make decisions about something he didn't know anything about, or just tuning out, he again would choose tuning out. He was having a good conversation with Shiloh Jones, so why not just get back to it?

"That's good, Buzz. Yes, sounds good. Okay, I'll be talking to you soon, Buzz. I'm gonna get an unlisted number tomorrow, and when I know what it is, I'll letcha know. You just tell old Don or Ron or whoever that I said surf's up. Thanks, Buzz. Bye."

When Mad got off the phone, the officer was out at his car talking on the police radio.

"Mr. Jones," he said, coming back up to the porch, "I gotta go. Chief says our time here is done, that you're in no danger anymore. He wants me back at the office to fill in some paperwork."

Both men felt a bit saddened by this news. They shook hands warmly, and then Mad found himself sitting on his front steps, alone, looking out at an empty street.

After a few minutes he roused himself. NCAA basketball was on; he might as well go watch it.

A few hours later, Mad drove to a nearby Taco Bell for dinner. He left the TV on. When he returned, its noise drew him back to it. Nothing much good was on, so he decided to turn the dratted thing off. But before he could, a commercial came on that chilled him.

There again was the footage of himself running like a banshee towards the camera, yelling, and hurling his driver like an oversized tomahawk. It was followed by a quick shot of the mime in New Orleans, angry fist raised heavenward, and then of Mad exiting his church that very morning, with the camera's focus such that it looked like a large crowd of worshippers was devotedly following his footsteps. A narrator said: "Madison Jones is angry – angry at God, and, we found out, angry at President Clinton too. Two weeks ago, he was a total unknown. But is he now the exemplar and prophet of a new, 'New South' theology, a theology of angry young white men? He has a surprisingly large following already. Find out why on Thursday, on 'Acute Vision.' 9 p.m. Eastern time."

Mad started shaking, and his stomach felt almost queasy enough to vomit. What in God's name had Laura gotten him into?

Quiveringly, he tried calling her, but to no avail. She didn't answer any of the numbers he had for her. He tried calling Mary on her cell phone; by now, she should be nearly to Memphis, en route back to St. Louis. She didn't answer, either. He couldn't bear the thought of calling Becky or Justin, and he was afraid to talk to Buzz because he thought it would become clear in the course of any new conversation just how poorly he had listened to whatever Buzz had said earlier in the day. He thought of an old high-school friend named David with whom, along with David's wife, Jennifer, he and Claire had gone out to dinner a few times. But Mad felt really weak; he didn't want to sound weak to David.

Jason was a slightly older teacher at his school, maybe 32 or so and still single, although probably soon to be engaged. He taught math and coached the soccer team. Mad tried to call him… but got another stupid machine.

Mad felt very alone.

Although it was already dark out, Mad decided he needed to go for a road run. Wearing a bright yellow shirt that he hoped would be visible to motorists, he ran in a straight line down Emogene Street, one mile, two miles, more, until his thighs started to ache. Turning around, he slightly twisted an ankle. At one point a car looked wholly unwilling to give him any room – or maybe the driver just didn't see him – and Mad was forced to jump quickly sideways onto the curb. A few blocks from his house, he got a stitch in his side. That was enough. He walked the rest of the way home, cursing himself for wimpiness.

Outside his front door, this time on the porch itself, the chalk-artist had struck again.

"Heretic," said the big letters. "Heathen!"

Mad rushed inside, turned out all the lights and, still sweaty, dove into bed. He wouldn't sleep well, but at least he could hide under his covers.

* * *

The next four days were something of a blur. Probably spurred by repeated commercials hyping Mad's upcoming appearance on "Acute Vision," occasional gawkers and a few picketers coalesced and dispersed at odd intervals outside Mad's house. The mime from New Orleans, wearing different outfits at different times, was such a frequent bystander that it almost seemed as if he were a ringleader for the others. None of them seemed at all dangerous, but Officers Williams and Jones drove by occasionally to make sure they remained peaceful.

Mad tried to stay busy with books, magazines, TV, errands (including arranging for an unlisted phone number), and fierce bursts of exercise, but he had trouble concentrating long on much of anything. He learned quickly not to put the TV on the network that sponsored "Acute Vision," because the promos consistently made him either nervous or angry. One short promo went like this:

"Madison Jones' dreams have sunk like the Titanic, but Mr. Jones still says, 'the heart does go on.' But did he also find God in the depths? Find out about America's newest religious sensation: Thursday, on 'Acute Vision.'"

Mad fielded several phone calls each from Becky, Buzz, and Mary, and an annoying amount of calls from Justin. He didn't really want to know what they were doing, and he thought it was a waste of time, but he had too much kindness and too little willpower to stop them. As the psychiatrist had written on his release form, Mad had a "flattened affect." It means he was too numbed to exert great effort; he would choose the path of least resistance.

It seemed as if his friends were all working to set up some kind of national conglomerate based on him and his theses. He thought they were crazy. They were talking about a fund-generating web site, a lecture tour, a self-help book and even a syndicated newspaper advice column like Billy Graham's. (Where they found the time, in the midst of their jobs or classes in Houston, St. Louis, D.C., and Mobile, Mad didn't even begin to know.) All their scheming, of course, depended on the idea that interest in him would multiply as a result of Thursday's TV feature.

Mad humored them by feigning interest. What else *could* he do? He felt utterly out of control of his own life, as if his whole existence were a runaway train while he, its only passenger, was stuck in the caboose. Ideas and plans rushed past him like trees and fields past a train's window; the mime and his cohorts were the landscape's indigenous fauna.

Laura called him just once, to tell him she had nothing to do with scripting the promos and, not to worry, the show with her edited interview of him should be just fine. "Mr. Jones and me, we're gonna be big stars," she said laughingly, again quoting Counting Crows, in closing.

On the original "Mad religion" web site, M. Magdalene kept hyping the upcoming TV program while engaging in ever-wilder speculation on how Mad would be portrayed.

"Have you ever even met the man?" asked one chat room participant, self-dubbed "Doubting Thomas."

"No, but I think he looks like a hunk, and he's obviously brilliant, and I just feel a real spiritual link with him," was M. Magdalene's response.

The Accidental Prophet | 137

Then she added: "Tell all your friends to watch! Mad's a prophet, and we can be his pride of lions!"

Mad didn't see it, but one last promo for the show superimposed that very e-mail exchange on the TV screen, right after the now-familiar scene of Mad leaving his church at the head of a throng of fellow-worshippers.

"Is young Madison Jones a new American prophet?" intoned the narrator. "He already has cyberspace disciples called M. Magdalene and Doubting Thomas. Can he resurrect your faith as well? Find out Thursday, on 'Acute Vision.'"

Obviously, the network had decided to give its latest tabloid TV show one massive final promotional boost in one last chance to move up the Nielson ratings before, if it failed, being cancelled.

On Thursday, Mad visited Carpe Diem with his teacher friend, Jason, just after Jason's school day ended. Mad returned home at the same time the two patrolmen motored down his oak-shaded street. Officer Williams, driving, quickly pulled over. "Mr. Jones," he said, "I know this is highly irregular, but can I run in and use yer crapper?"

When Mad nodded assent, Williams turned to his partner and said: "Jones-y, you wait here in the car: I'll be out faster'n you can count your fingers ten times."

Two minutes later, Williams emerged in his corpulent way from Mad's downstairs bathroom.

"Look here, son, I been meanin' to say sumthin to ya fer a coupla days now." The officer was drawling, more like a stereotypical redneck than he normally sounded. "You seem like a nice young fella, but I don't like the way you're taking advantage of Jones-y. I mean at first I thought maybe you was just cracked enough to actually take seriously what some nigger would say about your crazy-assed religious thingamajigs, just cuz Jones-y is a little on the smart side as far as niggers go. But I been watching you: You may be a little strange, but you ain't no lunatic and you ain't no dummy. So I says to myself, 'Buster Williams, that rich white boy is just trying to use your partner Jones-y for some kind of profit or other.' Yes, son, I see you are objecting, but you can't fool me. You probably figure you can use Jones-y for some kind of intro to all the black religious folk, so you can sell them on your crackpot ideas and make a big wad of money."

Officer Williams had waddled within inches of Mad by now, close enough for Mad to smell something bad on his breath.

"But lemme tell you a thing or two, son. Jones-y is a nigger, so maybe he ain't worth much, but he's a good nigger and keeps his nose clean. If I find out you do anything that makes him get hurt, I'm gonna make your life hell. I don't think you would, cuz I think you're basically a good kid, too. But I don't want you messing up my partner's mind, cuz if he gets all screwy and the Chief takes him away from me, Chief'll probably make me finish my career with a much dumber nigger than Jones-y riding shotgun. So: You mess with Jones-y, you're messing with me."

Mad was speechless.

The officer swiveled around like a walrus trying to be agile and swayed out the door and back to the patrol car where Officer Jones waited, unaware of what had just transpired. As their car pulled around the corner, the mime appeared from behind an SUV in a neighbor's driveway. He was dressed this time like a drunken frat boy. The mime turned his backside to the disappearing vehicle, lowered his pants a little and mooned the cops just as they turned far enough around the bend that they could not see him.

* * *

Mad really wanted to be not alone for the program that night, but he also felt nervous enough that he didn't trust what his own reactions to it would be. He didn't want to break down in front of any friends, so he didn't call any to join him. It dawned on him that the person he did trust was Officer Jones. He sent a message through the police switchboard to the cop's home and was gratified when Jones rang back.

"Oh, yes, me and my wife are going to watch it, sure enough," he said. "And to tell the truth, I want her to meet you. I'd love for us to come watch it with you. But we can't go out on such short notice, not at night. Gotta put baby to bed. But I'd sure be glad to give you a call tomorrow or something to tell you what we thought.

"Oh… and here's my home number. Call it any time. And if you want, you can call me 'Shiloh.'"

Justin, of course, showed up at Mad's door five minutes before the program began. By now, Mad was really sick of the little guy, but Mad couldn't politely ditch him. At least he was carrying a big notebook and a pen, so maybe he would pay such close attention to Laura's report that he'd keep his mouth more-or-less shut.

And then Mad's face, dappled with soft patio sunlight, was filling the screen.

"The only thing I know for sure," he was saying, "is that there *is* a God. But whether He's a jerk or not, or pure love or pure power or anything else some religion might say He is: Well, your guess is as good as mine."

Then there was a hostess' face saying that 'Acute Vision' would be right back, with "special correspondent Laura Green" reporting the first of its two stories for the night. What followed for Mad were fourteen minutes (three of them for commercials) of pure torture, full of what he considered to be unfairly spliced quotes, out of context and out of the order they were asked. It went like this:

(Laura's voice came on above photos, which she must have stolen from Mad's house while she hid upstairs, of Mad, Claire, Daddy Lee, and Marcelle. Those pictures were later replaced with footage of the crowd from that first morning outside of St. Louis Cathedral.)

"Until this year, young history teacher Madison Lee Jones, known to friends as 'Mad Jones,' seemed to have everything going his way. A sweet young wife with their first child on the way, a privileged background including a larger-than-life grandfather, a doting mother-in-law to whom he was especially close. Then it all went bad. Two months ago, his grandfather died from a fall off a horse. Less than three weeks ago, Mad's wife died of a massive hemorrhage, and their unborn child with her. Then his mother-in-law, speeding to join Mad in their mutual grief, died in a car wreck. Mr. Jones has no other relatives. It was more than he could take. In hiding for a week at an undisclosed location, young Jones produced a set of 59 religious propositions that he posted at churches throughout his hometown of Mobile, Alabama, and also at historic St. Louis Cathedral in New Orleans. Literally overnight, he became a sensation. So bold were some of his propositions, known as theses, so challenging to religious orthodoxy, that they drew both angry protesters and devoted followers to come out in force. The thesis drawing the most attention, and the one Mr. Jones says is the most misunderstood, is Number 12, which ends by asserting that 'God is a jerk.'

"A web site sprung up, it's chat room featuring a furious debate involving participants calling themselves names such as 'M. Magdalene' and 'Doubting Thomas.' And in the center of a storm he says he never really meant to inspire, Madison Jones still tries to deal with his grief while claiming that he's neither heretic nor prophet. Last week I sat down with Mr. Jones in the patio of his Mobile home. Here's what he had to say."

"Some things that happen are just too bad or sad or unfair for a loving God to even allow them to happen, much less include them in some kind of cosmic plan...."

"But the problem of pain, of bad things happening to good people, is nothing new," Laura said. "What makes your take on it so special?"

"It's really no big deal," said Mad's face on the screen. "I was angry, so I wrote that God is a jerk...."

"Well, is He a jerk?"

"Only part of the time, but that's not my point."

"What is your point, then, Mr. Jones?"

"Maybe God messes up sometimes. Maybe He's flawed like the rest of us. Maybe He gets jealous, or absent-minded, or some other frame of mind we don't understand."

(Mad remembered this part. His next sentence in person had been something about how the "ultimate will of God" was forgiving and loving and generous, if we have faith that, in the long run, it will be so. But that's not what the next sentence was on camera. Instead, the camera angle switched, but in a way that made it look like, despite the new angle, what came next was a continuation of the same thought.)

"What I know is that God lets suffering occur that is so deep, so awful, that if the suffering is at all a part of His will, then it amounts to unspeakable cruelty. Our choice is whether to surrender to that suffering, or to try to overcome it."

(Another splice, this time with a close-up of an intent-looking Laura seeming as if she wasn't about to let her subject off the hook:)

"But who are you to question God?"

(Mad had said: "I'm no one special, but…" That sentence fragment, though, ended on the cutting room floor.)

"… I think we *all* should question God. I think God wants us to wrestle with Him. That's what Jacob did, wrestle with God, and hurt his leg in the process, but God blessed Jacob for it afterwards."

"So are we humans as good as God, then? Are we even better than Him? If we wrestle with Him, can we beat Him? And would the world be better off if we pinned God to the mat and made him cry 'Uncle'?"

(Mad's answer wasn't presented. Instead, the show cut to footage of an elderly lady outside of Mad's church, with Mad visible walking past in the background. Laura said: "Not even every member of Mr. Jones' home church seems to agree.")

The old lady said: "I've watched this Madison boy grow up ever since his momma died in childbirth. I always thought he was a nice boy, but something obviously went wrong with him not having a momma to raise him. Now I see he's just an arrogant young man. How dare he question God? How dare he call God a jerk? And somebody told me he even wrote something encouraging 'safe sex' in the same breath that he's talking about God Almighty. That kind of immorality is just not acceptable. It's exactly what's wrong with our country today: Everybody acts like they are better than God is, like they can ignore His commandments. How dare they?"

"On the other hand," said Laura's voice-over, "some people are so excited by the boldness of Mr. Jones that even mimes have been moved to yell out their assent."

There followed the scene from outside the cathedral, just as Stephanie Riegel of New Orleans was signing off from the first news report on the controversy that Mad had watched from the Pontchartrain Hotel, in which the mime stepped forward and yelled "God is a jerk!"

"When we come back," said Laura, "we'll delve more deeply into Mr. Jones' new theology, and to the controversy it has caused. Also, Mr. Jones applies his theology to current events, such as the Lewinsky matter and the movie 'Titanic.'"

The commercial break was only 30-seconds long – just long enough for Mad to angrily say to Justin: "What is it with all this Clinton and Titanic stuff? Laura had to ask me about ten times to comment on either of them and they have nothing to do with anything, dammit."

(Commercial over, camera again to Laura, in a studio with the show's hostess.)

"When we left," Laura was saying, "a fellow parishioner of Mr. Jones made reference to perhaps the oddest entry of all the 59 theses in the Jones theology. In Thesis Number 14, he writes that, quote, 'men and women must rely on other men and women for comfort on earth. (For what it's worth, safe sex can be heap big comfort.)' Unquote. It seems out of place among the rest of his writings. And he said he definitely did NOT mean it to excuse the alleged adultery between President Clinton and Monica Lewinsky."

"Yes, I'm angry at the president," said Mad from his patio. "I mean, I think it's obvious that he lied, under oath, and somebody will find a way to prove he lied. I just think that destroys trust in our whole system...."

"In Mr. Jones' writings," narrated Laura into the camera from the TV studio, "the Ten Commandments are so important that he devotes thesis 41 to reminding everybody that abiding by them, and by the two great commandments to love God and thy neighbor, is the most important duty of a Christian even *after* God has let us down and allowed us to suffer. In essence, it almost sounds like Madison Jones says we should abide by the Commandments as a way to show God up, as it were, because, as Jones writes in Thesis 36, God, quote, 'is among those who isn't righteous.'"

(Then the program cut back to tape of Laura interviewing Mad in his patio.)

"Some would say you are overtly committing blasphemy, Mr. Jones. How do you respond?"

(Here came the most egregious splice of all. Mad originally said: "I'm not trying to offend anybody. I was just writing these for myself. I claim no special ability to interpret God or religion or anything. I just wrote those lines because it seems like a God who lets children starve to death in Africa, or who asks His greatest Saints to suffer as martyrs, or any of the other horrible things that happen that He could stop if He truly is all-powerful, is anything but a righteous God. I think everybody has the right to feel the human emotion of anger when senseless suffering happens; after all, it was God who gave us the emotion of anger in the first place.")

But all the TV screen showed was: "A God who lets children starve to death in Africa, or who asks His greatest saints to suffer as martyrs, or any of the other horrible things that happen that He could stop if He truly is all-powerful, is anything but a righteous God."

(Back to Laura and the hostess in studio.)

"Mr. Jones' theses seem full of anger," said the hostess. "Yet already he seems to have a big following. Is being in touch with anger one of the Signs of the Modern Age? Or is it that he's from the Heart of Dixie, Alabama. Is this just an 'angry Southern white man' thing?"

"Well," said Laura, "I talked to several of his supporters off camera. I don't think it's a Southern thing, but I think that the willingness to be angry is indeed what some find so appealing. When you're told all your life, they say, that God is love, and then you can't find love yourself, they say if there's a God at all then we have to have a new understanding with God that makes us not so subservient, because we're all taught in this culture, from the Declaration of Independence on, that we have a right to happiness – and God hasn't given us the happiness that is our right."

"So is Mr. Jones just a voice of protest against whatever we call 'God,' or fate, or 'holy Nature,' or 'Gaia' or 'Mother Earth' or whatever we choose to believe in?"

"In different words, I asked him that," Laura said. *("No you didn't!" yelled Mad at his home TV screen.)*

"You know, people are going to worship however they want to," said the patio Mad from the TV. "All I'm trying to do is find a way to endure and to heal my heart. I think if God can forgive outright disobedience, he can certainly forgive us for protesting our fate."

"We'll be right back," said the hostess, "to see how Mr. Jones reconciles his anger with what he claims is still an unyielding faith."

This time there followed two minutes of commercials, during which Mad rocked back and forth, holding his knees, unspeakably upset, while Justin babbled on with a big smile on his face, telling Mad that "this is just so great, so great, buddy, this is just perfect, buddy, yes indeed-y-oh, just perfect!"

(Break over, the camera came back to the hostess in the studio.)

"Back to the story about the newest New South, New Age theologian, Madison Jones. His writings show a particular fondness for two movies. Roll tape!"

(The movie title of "The Wind and the Lion" filled the screen, followed by a clip of Sean Connery riding across the desert. Then came the title shot from "The Poseidon Adventure," followed by a clip of Gene Hackman preaching on deck that God wants everybody to be winners and that He loves those who never stop trying.)

"In his increasingly famous 59 Theses, Mad Jones made mention of those two movies," said Laura from the studio. "Mr. Jones wrote, and I quote, that 'The Lord loves winners,' and also, quote, that 'we can survive constantly in the deserts of our souls.' End quote. Mr. Jones said that Christ was sent to Earth by God in order to teach us to be winners, to survive all the adversity that God allows to come our way. Therefore, writes Mr. Jones, and again I quote, 'hold fast to that which is good; be strong and of good courage.' And he quotes St. Paul, that 'suffering produces endurance, and endurance produces character, and character produces hope, and hope does not disappoint us.' End quote, from the last of Mad's 59 theses.

"Of course, another movie that right now is breaking all the records is also about endurance and about character producing hope. Here's what Mr. Jones had to say:

"The Titanic story does fit in to what I'm saying." *(Cut out was what Mad had said before that sentence: "Yes, I guess, if you really insist, you could argue that the Titanic....")* "You could think about it this way: that even when we are sinking, there is art and love and beauty to sustain us, even if it's only the memory of art and love and beauty. How does the song put it? 'The heart does go on.' *(on cutting room floor: If I wanted people to take me as a sage or a prophet, which is not at all what I want, of course…*) … what I would want for people reading my theses is the sense that no matter what happens, God keeps coming back to try to do right by us in the end."

"So your faith is still strong?" asked the patio Laura.

"It's a different faith now because I was a believer earlier but not real devout. But in some ways, it is stronger than ever. I can't explain it, because I'm still so hurt and angry, but there are times in these last few weeks when I still have felt God was there. And it was better for Him to be there, than not to be there."

Then the studio Laura was back on camera. "Sure enough, despite all the tragedy in Mad Jones' life, he wrote this quote from the Bible: 'We are not of them who draw back unto perdition, but of them that believe to the saving of the soul.' End quote.

"And, judging by the growing following, the web sites, the rumors of a national ministry in Mad Jones's name, there are lots of people out there more than willing to follow Madison Jones's unique lead as their means to God's salvation."

Chapter Seven

Mad was in shock. No amount of effusions from Justin could overcome his feeling of having been used. He had spent an hour-long interview trying to downplay his theses, but the program had not aired a single one of his demurrals. Every self-abnegation had been ignored in favor of another line tending towards hype.

When Becky, Mary, Buzz, and Don the PR guy called together through some sort of conference-call set-up, Mad refused to talk about their plans. (Mad still couldn't remember from his Georgetown days exactly who Don was, but Don sure seemed to know him.) Becky said that Mad had come across with a compelling presence – attractive, interesting, and just edgy enough to be riveting without being overly threatening. Mad wouldn't listen. He just wanted to get them off the phone so he could call his headmaster. Mad wanted his job back and was sure that Laura's report had not helped that cause. But the others were so enthusiastic that they paid little heed to his protestations. Even Mary's usually quiet voice came across at an uncharacteristically high decibel level.

"Okay, okay," Mad finally agreed. "On Saturday we'll all do another conference call, and then we can put all this business to rest once and for all."

* * *

The headmaster, however, was hard to reach. His phone was constantly busy for the next two hours. Irate parents said that this young Jones guy better not come back and teach their children. Some objected on religious grounds; others just thought all the commotion was tacky. The school's mostly upper-crust clientele wasn't comfortable with this kind of tabloid-ish attention.

* * *

In Los Angeles, the editor of a true tabloid, *The Zodiac*, saw potential for a story worth following. This Jones guy from Mobile had almost-movie-star looks and might hit it big. If Jones went Hollywood, thought the editor, *The Zodiac* would be ready for him. He called a reporter at home. "There's no huge rush on this, Jock," the editor said, "but whenever you get a lull in trying to find something interesting on Kate Winslet, I want you to start making some inquiries into the Mad Jones guy from Mobile.… Oh, you didn't see it. Well, 'Acute Vision' just did a feature on him. He's some new young religious prophet down on the Gulf Coast. Looks sorta like a young Robert Redford but comes across like *The Accidental Tourist*: not much apparent personality, but for some reason he's utterly captivating.… Yeah, anyway, I think he's gonna be a big pop-culture hit. His wife died, and he went into hiding and wrote a bunch of religious claptrap blaming God, or something like that. Anyway, it struck me that it seems like kind of a mystery where it was that he went into hiding. Maybe there's an angle there; see if you can find out. And also all the usual: sex scandals, criminal record, dark family secrets, whatever you can find. It may be a waste of time because this guy may never get enough star power to make it worth it. But I do have a feeling about him, Jock. I think he *will* hit it big. And when he does, you and I will be waiting for him."

* * *

At an aggressively growing publishing house in New York, a rising star in the editing ranks made a mental note to track down this Jones guy. Maybe he could put together a quick book deal. Religion was hot right now and getting hotter. And now all the evangelical types were starting to make noise about the coming millennium and Armageddon. Maybe Jones could be persuaded to chime in from that angle.

* * *

In New Orleans, Grace F. Martin lay alone in her bed, relieved that, for once, both her children seemed to be sleeping soundly rather than finding novel ways to cause trouble from their respective little bedrooms. That TV feature on young Mad had moved Grace in a way she found entirely unexpected. It wasn't physical; it was, if she had dared say it, spiritual. She didn't even believe in God, but what Mad said had struck a chord with her. The God she had been raised on, the idea of God she had rejected as being so out of touch with reality that it made the whole notion of a God seem absurd, was a God who was a stern taskmaster meting out a harsh but unimpeachable justice. This God had supposedly promised that her people were his chosen people, fated to enjoy great rewards for their steadfast obedience. Instead, they had suffered the Holocaust. Instead, nothing in life seemed fair at all. Instead, life always seemed to favor the strong, and enjoyment came to those who grabbed it for themselves the way she had always done as an adolescent and as a younger woman.

And then the one person she had *not* hurt through her own selfishness, the one she had always treated the best, the one she had dated for six years and then wedded, had abandoned her after only five years of marriage, with no satisfactory explanation, leaving her two years ago with bratty kids aged five and four. She loved those kids dearly but was still struggling with how to raise them on her own. And now she had a boring job as a paralegal, working for an SOB of a hotshot-lawyer boss. She also hated that the 20 pounds she had not lost after her pregnancies were hard to hide on her short frame – although, thank goodness, her large chest still drew enough attention to embolden idiot guys to salve her ego by occasionally trying to hit on her, on the rare occasions she escaped her kids for a night out with friends. (It was curiously liberating to be hit on and then to shoot down the idiots with a wholly feigned haughtiness.)

No, she didn't now believe, and never had believed, in God, who was obviously just a fairy-tale for the weak. But if God did exist, it did seem as if he could be one hell of a jerk. And now here was Mad acknowledging that God is a jerk, yet saying God is still worth paying homage to, anyway. This was something new and paradoxical and interesting. And it came from a young man she had known. Known, she thought, explicitly in the Biblical sense, much to her everlasting shame. Actually, it had been the first time she remembered ever feeling shame of any kind. She wondered if Mad's theses dealt with shame. Tomorrow, she thought, she would look up those theses on the internet.

* * *

In Atlanta, a powerful televangelist named Rob Patterson found himself both angry and elated at the same time. Angry, or actually furious, because here were those blasted godless liberal networks giving airtime to a young punk who says that God is a jerk. The young creep looked like one of those vapid pretty boys who thinks the whole world owes him an easy life and who never worries about any of the sins he commits. Young creep probably smokes dope, too, thought Patterson. All those pretty boys smoke dope, or worse. He clearly was a bad influence, but he had enough charisma to develop a following if he weren't stopped. Patterson decided that he needed to crush this young Jones guy, crush him like a bug.

But Patterson was also thrilled. This Jones kid was exactly the type he had been warning people about. Jones proved that he, Patterson, had been right all along. As the millennium reached its end, more and more of Jones' type, more and more false prophets, would be coming out of the woodwork and crawling out from under rocks. And as they did, Patterson's warnings against them would ring more and more true, and draw more and more adherents to Patterson's ministry. Patterson's empire would grow bigger because of fear of Jones and his ilk, and Patterson could lead more people to having their souls saved by Jesus Christ the Lord Almighty, and God would look down on Patterson with even more favor and multiply his holdings and his investment values so Patterson's blessed ministry and influence would become larger and larger still. God was truly good, to have given Patterson a new enemy to fight and exploit so that he could build his flock in the face of the ultimate enemy, Satan himself, who even now was on the march.

* * *

In Jefferson Parish, Louisiana, just West of New Orleans, another preacher had a different take on the program he had just watched. Pierre Hebert, loosely affiliated with Patterson's religious movement, made up for being somewhat dimwitted by having a kind and generous heart. His wife Angelina was the bright one in the family, and she agreed with Pierre that Madison Jones showed great potential. "You can hear the pain and the sincerity in his voice when he talks, the poor dear boy," she observed. "But he speaks forcefully, and he says that even after all he's been through, he thinks God is worth coming home to. I think our congregation will love him. Maybe he should be our guest preacher one day. And I'd like to fix him up with a nice home-cooked meal, and maybe introduce him to one of those cute girls right out of college who run our singles group. Maybe Rhonda might be good for him, or maybe even Tonya. They're both looking for a nice godly young beau."

* * *

In Charlottesville, Virginia, meanwhile, a gentleman known merely as "The Colonel" was apoplectic. After all the extraordinary lengths he and his cohorts had gone to, to help the Lee grandson fulfill his potential in the face of tragedy, this was the thanks they got. A certain arrogance had always run in that particular branch of the Lee tree, but not this kind of unseemly showboating. And the sheer gall of an Eight fomenting religious controversy! The gall of it! He wondered if he should call an emergency phone conference first thing in the morning.

* * *

The headmaster, agitated and by now exhausted, decided to answer the blasted phone one more time before he turned out the lights, despite his wife's request that they just let the answering machine do its work. The caller was Mad. His voice was shaky. He swore that he had tried to tamp down the controversy, but that 'Acute Vision' had changed the whole context of what he said.

But the headmaster felt he had few options. He thought he knew Mad well enough to know Mad wouldn't lie, but by now it almost didn't matter. He, the headmaster, would have to sleep on the whole matter. But he doubted things would change much in the morning. He said as of right now, he thought it unlikely Mad would be welcomed back next fall. Oh, sure, they could still have their meeting in May to come to a final resolution of the situation, and maybe things would have calmed down by then. He wasn't ruling out the possibility of Mad returning. But the likelihood of that had certainly diminished.

Yes, in just over half a year, Mad had shown himself to be a very promising young teacher and a solid assistant coach. That's why all these developments were so upsetting: The headmaster was very fond of Mad and had indeed been fond of him all those years when Mad was a student at the school. The headmaster had high hopes for Mad. Now, though, Mad was making things very difficult – difficult for his fellow teachers, difficult for the headmaster, difficult for Mad himself.

The headmaster was very sorry. But that was the way matters looked right now.

* * *

Ever since leaving the psych ward, Mad had been able to experience, or at least to acknowledge or express, very little anger (except, of course, for the golf-course incident). Temperamentally, neither he nor Ben had been much prone to anger anyway. As he hung up with the headmaster, however, the dam burst. Mad was furious. And it was all Laura's fault.

It took several phone calls, but he tracked her down on a new cell phone number. (Mad still had Laura's cell phone from the TV station.) He had a hard time hearing her because there was lots of background noise. She said she was out with media friends at some bar in the French Quarter called Molly's at the Market, celebrating her successful network debut. (Mad didn't understand how she could be in New Orleans. Hadn't she been in the network studio in New York? Mad didn't realize that the studio portions with Laura in them had been taped the day before.)

"Wasn't it just great, Mad? Wasn't that just fantastic?!?"

"Fantastic" was hardly the word Mad was thinking. But there was too much background noise for them to really hear each other. Frustrated, Mad said he'd call back the next day.

* * *

The next morning didn't start very well, either. Mad was trying to sleep late after suffering insomnia half the night but was awakened at 9 by a ringing phone. (How the caller found the number was a mystery.) The voice on the other end sounded like the *basso profundo* of Foghorn Leghorn, that rooster from the Warner Bros. cartoons.

"I say, I say, I say, son, you're causin' some mighty big consternation in these parts. You can call me 'The Colonel,' son, I say, you can jes call me 'The Colonel.' Even my old buddy Armbrister – you knew him as 'Daddy Lee,' I believe – even ol' Bris called me 'Colonel' back when we was jes whippersnappers raisin' hell with the ladies. Anyway, I say, you're making us have some serious stomach-churnin', if you know what I mean, son."

Mad's mind was reeling. Was he supposed to know who this was?

"Uh, sir, I, uh …well, not really, sir."

"Madison, son, I say, where's your brain, son? This is The Colonel, from Virginia. Surely ol' Bris mentioned me when he was handing over the money we sent you every year? Or maybe your Daddy Lee was even better at keepin' secrets than I thought he was, and maybe he didn't even let my moniker out. I say, son, is that what happened? Did ol' Bris never tell you that it was The Colonel who was lookin' out fer you?"

"Excuse me, sir, but he never did. So you're from … well, from The Society, then?"

"I say, son, now you're catchin' on. You bet yer old Virginny blood that I'm from The Society. We've got one life less than a cat, son, if you know what I mean, but right now you're putting either yourself or us right behind that old 8-ball. *Eight*-ball: Get it, son?"

"Yes, sir. *Eight*. Now I understand, sir. Did I do something wrong, sir?"

"Something wrong? I say, I say, that's rich, son. Something wrong? I grant you that I've never seen a young man with such a bad run of luck, son, but yes, indeedy, by the sacred honor of Jefferson himself, I promise you that you have indeed done something wrong. You're blaspheming the name of the Almighty, and making a spectacle of yourself, and bringing disrepute on the house of an old Virginia name, and you ask if you've done something wrong? Well, son, you must not have picked up enough common sense from Daddy Lee even with all those summer days you spent fox-hunting with him in the Shenandoah. I say, son, what happened to your couth?"

"Couth, sir?"

"You been UNcouth, son, that's what I'm sayin'. Uncouth. Unseemly. And, for that matter, flat-out unwise. And son, we don't like it, not one bit. Now we can't rightly do nothin' about it, son, because our money was a gift to you, free and clear. And we only do good, son, we never do harm to anybody, so you got no reason to fear us. But I'm telling you, son, I say, I say, son, you damn well ought to know that a group of Virginia's finest gentlemen all talked this morning, and they are mighty displeased with you. Mighty displeased. And we hope you stop all this nonsense and go back to teaching history and doing justice to your family name."

Mad was flabbergasted. He felt smaller than a mustard seed.

"Sir, I'm very sorry, sir. That's not what I was trying to do, sir. I was trying to put a lid on all this, sir, but they edited out everything I said about how nobody should take their theology from a high school history teacher. Those TV folks changed all my context, sir, and that's the truth."

"Well, son, I say, you jes better be careful. Because if all those news people start digging around in your past, they gonna find us in your past, and we want to be left alone. We just do good things for the University of Virginia, and for the memory of old Tom Jefferson, and we don't want nobody digging around in our charity work. The good book says you ain't supposed to do good works for the sake of the credit, but for the sake of the works themselves. If some of those news folk dig around our good works, the attention will pollute all our good intentions."

"I understand, sir. I'm trying to stop all this, sir; really, I am."

"Well, that's a good boy, son, I say, that's a good boy. You jes be careful, okay?"

"Yes, Mr. Colonel – I mean, yes, sir, Colonel."

The line went dead.

* * *

Now Mad was agitated. Nearly chair-tossing agitated. And he tried to take it out on Laura when he tracked her down at the New Orleans TV office. Barely keeping his voice within reasonable decibel range, Mad told Laura that she had made him look like a self-promoter even though he had wanted all the attention to just die down. But she was nursing a bad hangover, and she wasn't yet in her usual mode of self-control.

"Christ almighty, you're such a freak," she said in response to his strong complaint. "I don't have to put up with any more of your soul-twisted self-pity. I made you a star, and now you're angry that you're in the limelight? Get a grip."

"Made me a star?! This whole thing was about you using me so you can be the next Barbara Walters, or something. You couldn't care less what I was trying to say!"

"Oh, stuff it!" she said, with her pounding head unable to rein in a streak of bitchiness she usually kept well hidden. "Geez, Mad, I'll admit you're a great lay, but what else did I think I saw in you? You're just a confused, self-absorbed big old baby. Why don't you just go mourn your wife some more, and leave me alone?"

That last sentence went way too far, and Laura knew it instantly. But she didn't know how to take it back. The damage was done. There was dead silence on the other end of the line. Then, what sounded like a muffled sob. And then the sound of a phone rattling a little on the hook before it came to rest. Only the dial tone answered as Laura desperately yelled: "God, I'm sorry, Mad, please, I'm sorry!" She stared at the wall of her office, trying to figure out what it was about Mad that had made her lose control.

Out of nowhere, a tune from *Jesus Christ, Superstar* sounded through her brain. Yvonne Elliman was singing: "… I don't know how to ta-ake this/ I don't know why he moo-ooves me…"

For the first time she could ever remember, Laura Green allowed herself to question her own motives. A remarkably self-assured young woman, certain that the world owed her whatever good she could wring from it without any malice, she no longer felt so self-assured.

* * *

Mad knelt down and prayed for God to make his nightmare go away. He wanted to wake up and find that Claire was still alive and with him. He wanted to see her smile again. He wanted to be near enough to her again that he could feel overwhelmed by the sheer goodness, the lovingness, of her aura. "Please don't let her actually be gone," he cried aloud. "Why isn't she here with me, God…. Why?"

The answer he received, of course, was silence.

* * *

Actually, the silence was only inside Mad's house. In the absence of the police presence on Mad's porch, and with the new national attention from the previous night's TV program, a crowd had re-formed outside. It was at that moment that Mad first noticed its chanting. "HER-E-TIC! HER-E-TIC! HER-E-TIC!!!" This was an angry crowd. If Mad had any supporters out there, they were too few, or too cowed, to make their presence known.

Shakily, Mad pushed aside a curtain just an inch and peered through. Maybe 40 people were on the sidewalk and on his small front lawn, with a few up against his front steps. Some held insulting signs; some just brandished crosses. They looked as if they were working themselves into a frenzy, a few of them almost as if they wanted nothing better than to storm Mad's house in a frontal assault.

But then there was a commotion from the street behind them. Through his narrow opening, Mad couldn't see exactly what was going on. Soon enough, though, he recognized a stern rednecky voice.

"Back away, now, you better just back away!" It was Officer Williams. "If y'all don't disperse right this minute, I'll give every one of you good reason to get your pansy asses far away from here! Now move it!" The crowd parted a little, and Mad could then see the officer. He was sort of shifting back and forth on his feet, his corpulence literally adding weight to his words. His right hand rested quite prominently on a gun no less menacing for being still holstered.

"Move it, or I'll arrest every last one of you for disturbing the peace!"

The crowd scattered like tenpins. Now Mad could see all the way through to the street. Shiloh sat in the driver's seat of the patrol car, smiling so broadly he looked as if he were about to laugh.

Officer Williams turned back to face Officer Jones. "I told you, Jones-y, that nobody messes with ol'Buster when I get my back up! I'm still the toughest-ass cop in the business, Jones-y, and don't you fergit it! Hey, d'ya think we oughtta rouse Mr. Jones and tell him what's been happening? He's a goofy-assed kid, but he don't deserve a bunch of wackos yelling outside his front door."

Mad didn't want to face either policeman, so he backed away from the curtain and slunk up the stairs. The officers never did ring his bell.

* * *

All Mad did the rest of that day was watch TV and perform multiple sets of pushups. Mid-afternoon, the headmaster called to say that everybody in the school administration agreed, for now, with his tentative decision that they ought to begin looking for a full-time replacement for Mad for next fall. Mad was too wrung-out to argue.

Some time in the evening, Mad decided to try to remember how to access the 'Mad religion' site on the Internet. He felt an urgent need to get some feedback from the previous night's show. As he fiddled inexpertly with the search engines, he wondered if he were some kind of masochist. Judging from the protesters who had been outside his door, he must have come across really badly on Laura's program. He expected more of the same vituperation from the chat room denizens.

What he found, instead, was a revelation.

"… a nuanced new understanding…," wrote somebody shortly after the program ended. "… from pain, a paean," wrote another, who went by the moniker "Theo Professor."

Later, "Theo Prof" added: "There is nothing more central to the Christian story than is paradox. Madison Jones has captured that sense of paradox, and quite brilliantly."

The few-but-persistent critics – "a big baby," one wrote of Mad, and another wrote that Mad was "confused to the point of evil" – were easily outnumbered by those bearing praise, or at least serious and respectful questions and challenging follow-ups.

On Friday morning, M. Magdalene had chimed in: "Mad came across well. And his most important ideas were highlighted superbly by reporter Laura Green. She has a real future and TV journalism needs more bright and balanced reporters like her. She really found a way to let Mad's resiliency come through, and for it to inspire others. She and Mad were both fantastic!"

"Formerly Doubting Thomas," later shortened to "FD Thom," entered a number of comments, each one enthusiastic about Mad's ideas. Somebody else wrote that "Mad makes me want to try to believe again, makes my faith reaffirmed and restored" – and signed it "Affirmed."

"Affirmed is a horse, you dolt," answered one of the critics, "and even that is a stretch for you Mad-heads, because you don't even have enough basic horse-sense to know a fool from a prophet."

Affirmed fired back: "Best I remember, Affirmed won the Triple Crown. After watching Mad, I'm rededicating myself to the Triple Crown of the Father, Son, and Holy Ghost. And I'm back in the running for salvation!"

"You're not Affirmed; you're just a Sham!" wrote another critic, apparently referring to Secretariat's frequent also-ran. To which more than a few angry chat-roomers suggested that if the critics didn't see the value in Mad's approach, they should just get off the site and stop bothering the believers.

And so the debates and comments had gone on all day, some silly, some thoughtful, some inane, and some even profound. Hundreds of comments. Often passionate comments. Evidence that, whatever else had happened, the one thing certain was that Mad somehow had touched a nerve.

But a late-afternoon entry brought Mad up short.

"Hi, everybody, I'm the reporter Laura Green. I was very touched and flattered by M. Magdalene's compliments for me this morning, and by a few of the other nice remarks. Whoever you are, I thank you. But this note is for Mad. I hope he reads it. When I spoke with him for a follow-up this morning, I said something really nasty that I didn't mean at all. I am very very very sorry I said it; he'll know what I'm talking about and, so he'll know this is really me on this chat room, I'll mention that off the air we talked about Counting Crows. I hope he believes how sorry I am. Anyway, for everybody else out there, you should know that in my interviews with Mad Jones I found him to be a good man and a very sweet man. I am honored that he let me interview him for my first national spot. I wish him the best of luck."

Mad didn't know what to feel.

"Hear, hear for Ms. Green!" wrote FD Thom.

"Sounds like Mad even made a believer out of a reporter, and those media types are notoriously cynical," wrote somebody called "Perdicaris." The writer added: "If so, she's right to believe, because the way I feel, Mad Jones rescued me. I was captive to my own pain, and Mad made me see that I could be angry at God without it meaning that I lost my faith forever."

"Hey, did anybody out there think that Laura Green looked pretty hot? Laura, are you single?" That one came from "Mr. Mississippi." (Laura didn't respond.)

Mad kept scrolling through the entries. He was amazed at the outpouring of people who, in one way or another, had been moved by his story. Maybe Justin and the girls were right, and maybe Shiloh Jones was right. Maybe he was indeed supposed to allow his message, such as it was, to be spread.

He decided to press the "Refresh" button one more time before he turned off his machine, to see if anybody had written anything new while he had been reading the earlier ones. Yes, there was one new entry. And it blew him away.

"Hi, everybody," it said. "I've been coming back to this site again and again all day, trying to decide what if anything I should say. I've read and re-read all the theses, and I taped last night's show and watched it again twice more tonight. I've actually met Mad before. I think he's a wonderful guy. But I never had any use for God, not before now, and when I heard that Mad was on some kind of God kick, I just felt sorry for him. I don't think God exists. Or at least I didn't think so. Now I don't know what to think. I don't understand all this theology stuff. I don't understand the concept of a person being 'redeemed.' And I'm a long, long way from being ready to worship any entity on heaven or on Earth, much less a God who, as Mad pointed out, supposedly put Abraham and Job both cruelly to the test, just for the sake of testing them. None of this makes any sense. Live and let live is what I always believed. However, now it seems that letting live isn't by itself enough.

"Please forgive this message for being so long, but I really need to get this off my chest. I'm not even sure where I'm going with this message, not even after thinking about it all day. But if there's anyone out there who is an atheist, but who now for the first time is feeling that atheism amounts to hiding from some kind of truth you were always afraid to know, then please answer me. What I see is a boy I once knew who suffered great pain and yet still writes, in No. 45, that we should do all such good works as the Lord has prepared for us to walk in. I've never gone out of my way to do good works. How does one go so fast from pain to feeling a need to do good works? That sure wouldn't be my response to being shocked by a bunch of sudden deaths. It must take something powerful to turn pain into good works. It must take something powerful to hold on to what is good and to be strong and courageous. Something as powerful as a god. And Mad is just so cute and nice, but he isn't a god. So does that mean that there really is a 'God' who is working through Mad Jones? I don't know why these questions are running through my mind, why they affect me so much. But I know my life is missing something, and I only realized that something was missing when I saw Mad in the news. I want to know more. Can anybody out there help me?"

The message was signed "Jezebel?" The question mark made the moniker look especially odd. Mad had no clue who "Jezebel?" was.

A strange calm settled over Mad. He turned off the machine. He had a lot of thinking to do.

* * *

After drinking some coffee the next morning, Mad re-entered the web site. He wrote the following note:

> "Hi, everybody, this is Mad. I want to thank all of you for responding so well, and in many cases with such thoughtfulness, to my theses. I had no idea they would cause such a stir. Your comments, especially your compliments, have been a great source of comfort for me during some very difficult days. And whoever 'Jezebel?' is, I especially thank her. Her message last night helped me decide what to do next. I'll probably have an announcement soon. Thanks again,
>
> Mad."

He had considered also adding a note for Laura, but he couldn't figure out what to say. He didn't know what to think of her. He didn't know whether to believe that she was sorry or not for her snide remark about him needing to mourn his wife some more. And he was still angry at how the show had come out – if perhaps not as angry as before.

In the end, he decided not to mention her in his chat-room comment.

He then sat down and wrote notes to himself for points to bring up during the phone conference. His friends had said they would call at 10.

The call came promptly. On the line were Becky, Justin, Mary, Buzz, and Don the congressional PR guy. They said that also waiting to join them telephonically, as soon as Mad agreed, was some guy from a publishing house in New York. Mad didn't quite catch his name when Don (whoever *he* was) mentioned it.

"Here's the deal, Mad," Becky began. "You've started something that with a little guidance could become the next cultural phenomenon. You just need to give us the go-ahead, and…"

Mad interrupted. "Yes," he said.

Becky, not sure what she had heard, repeated: "Give us the go-ahead, and we'll…"

"Yes," said Mad, more loudly and clearly. "Yes. Go ahead."

Excitedly, everybody started trying to talk at once. Mad couldn't make heads or tails of what they were saying. Too much information, too many voices. He interrupted again.

"Okay, everybody, this is my turn to talk. Everybody listen up. This is how it's gonna be."

He told them he still didn't comprehend the response he'd been getting, but he couldn't fight it anymore. He said it had probably cost him his job as a teacher, and it had made some of his grandfather's friends very angry to boot, but he couldn't turn back the clock. People really thought he had something to say that was worth heeding. And apparently a lot of people even found some weird comfort in it. His new friend Shiloh Jones had said that maybe God was using him for something good, and while Mad had a hard time believing it, he kept finding that every time he tried to put a lid on the story, he somehow further fanned the flames. So now he was just going to go with the flow.

"All of these big plans y'all have, I think they're crazy. And I don't want to know any details. It just makes me nervous. But go ahead and do them. But these are the conditions. First, any substance comes from me. Nobody writes anything in my name, nobody interprets theology in my name. If you want me to go speak somewhere, I'll go speak. But I'll decide what I say; nobody else will. If you want me to write answers to people's questions, do some kind of newspaper advice column, or whatever all these ideas are, then I'll do it. But I'll do it myself; nobody does it for me.

"Second, this all has to be a non-profit. Becky, I know you have an MBA; I know you have some kind of complicated business plan worked up. I don't want to know the details. I just want to insist that nobody uses this to get rich. Nobody uses me to get rich. I don't see how there's any money in this anyhow, but if there is, then anything over and above a reasonable reimbursement for your efforts – anything over some salary you want to pay yourselves that's not out of line – it must go to charity. And if that time comes, I'll pick the charity.

"Third, I won't talk to the press unless I decide to talk to them. If they ask if I'll talk, the answer is no. If I have something to say to them, I'll let y'all know, and then you can tell them I'm ready to talk. But otherwise, no interviews. They're all a pack of hyenas.

"There, that's it. Three conditions: I do the substance. We do this non-profit. And no interviews without my permission. Understand?"

This was not the pliant Mad of the previous few weeks. This was not the Mad buffeted all akimbo by even the slightest breeze. Emboldened by the chat-room compliments, this was a Madison Lee Jones who knew what he wanted. It was a Mad who barked out orders. It was a Mad who was decisive. This was the Mad whose longstanding self-confidence had helped make him effortlessly popular.

In the previous weeks, this face of Mad had shown itself only once, when he told Buzz what to say to the media horde on Mad's first afternoon back in Mobile. But now this Mad, the confident, pre-tragedy Mad, was back, at least for a short while. He was still cycling through various stages of grief. But in this take-charge mode, the others on the conference call – just as Buzz had done that earlier day – accepted Mad's commands as gospel.

"Oh, and one more thing," he added. "I'm not ready to talk to some publishing guy today, not somebody I don't even know. If there really is a book deal here, you work out the details of a proposal and let me know. I'll say yes or no once you lay it all out for me. But keep this guy off the line right now."

There was a yammer of voices, and Mad interrupted again.

"Like the coffee klatsch woman says on Saturday Night Live, 'Talk amongst yourselves.' I'm hanging up now. Justin, you come over on Monday morning and tell me what's next. I'm gonna spend all weekend watching the NCAA basketball tournament, and I don't want to be bothered. Thank y'all; y'all are good friends. I don't know what we're getting into, but I trust y'all. Thanks again. Bye."

Chapter Eight

Becky Matthews had plenty of family money to fall back on. She quit her job to become Chief Operating Officer for the new company called "Mad, Mad World." The still-mysterious Don would milk Congress for another four or six weeks of paychecks, and then come on board MMW Corp. as a salaried PR guy. Mary McGuire would finish law school in little more than a month, take the bar in the summer, and immediately take MMW as her first client for the small St. Louis firm she expected to join. Buzz would keep his professorship but serve a partly remunerated position as company vice-president. Justin was listed as a "consultant," with details and pay (if any) to be worked out later, but with the rights to use MMW themes and the name in a private business he would launch (called "Justin Time") to promote holistic, body-and-spirit healthfulness. And Mad would, at least nominally, be Chairman of the Board and CEO, but had already signed (without really paying it much heed) a form transferring CEO duties and powers to Becky (powers he could revoke at any time), with Mary delegated as Becky's alternate in case of any incapacity on Becky's part. And the new company would be incorporated under one of the non-profit parts of the tax code, with all "excess" revenues (above those specifically dedicated for salaries of listed officers) to be assigned to charities to be determined later.

Mad paid close attention to none of this. Business affairs didn't interest him.

What he agreed to, when Justin visited on Monday, was to sign off on a press release announcing that a press conference would be held a week from the upcoming Friday (which would be two days before Palm Sunday) to announce the official launching of Mad, Mad World.

Somehow or other, the new company had arranged to take over the "Mad Religion" web site (paying a fee to its founder, who lived in Oxford, Mississippi), and add advertising to it to generate revenue. Mad would do a spiritual advice column, to be distributed by a national syndicate. He also would go on a (reasonably priced) paid speaking tour. And his theses, his speeches, and some of his advice columns eventually would be collected, edited, and anthologized into book form, to be published by the company of this guy in New York whose name Mad never quite caught.

In the interim before the press conference, Mad would try to play lots of golf and tennis and set up a meeting with the rector of his church for some spiritual counseling to help him deal with his grief. He would try to catch up, and spend time, with his various friends in Mobile whom he had been avoiding since Claire's death.

He also would monitor the web site once a day to keep tabs on what all the anonymous web surfers were saying.

The demonstrators, both pro and con, continued intermittently to gather outside Mad's house – with the mime often in attendance, with a different costume almost every day, to show support for Mad and anger at God. They never stayed very long, however, because patrolling officers Jones and Williams invariably appearing in their car, as if out of nowhere, to chase them away. Officer Williams didn't know it and would not have liked it if he knew, but Mad phoned Shiloh on two different evenings in order to probe the officer for more detailed responses to Mad's theses. Shiloh continued to have mixed feelings thoughts about what Mad had written, but he insisted that he thought Mad was doing the Lord's work merely by spurring people to talk about God in a serious fashion. Shiloh's wife, LaShauna, joined them for just five minutes once to urge Mad to continue his preaching, because she thought he was right on target.

Meanwhile, controversy continued to swirl. The first MMW press release had gone out on Tuesday, at about the same time the Nielsen ratings were released. The Nielsens showed that "Acute Vision" the previous Thursday had moved up from 77th in the rankings all the way to 11th. The network's hype had paid off, and Mad and Laura had received a huge audience.

The combination of MMW and the Nielsens was too much for Rob Patterson, who called a press conference for the very next day to answer what he saw as a serious threat.

"I see by press release that this young pretty-boy from Mobile is planning to announce the launch of a company to promote his dangerous, his truly dangerous, ideas," said Patterson to the cameras assembled at his Atlanta headquarters. "This is surely the kind of thing the good Lord Jesus Christ, and all his apostles, warned us about when they said we should beware of false prophets! By their fruits ye shall know them, sayeth the Lord, and the fruits intended by this pretty-boy Jones clearly involve profiteering from the spread of godless ideas. A multimedia company, exploiting the Beast's modern communication tools, to spread the word that the good and bless-ed Lord Almighty is a jerk! The very idea of it sickens me. It truly does, it sickens me. And this is coming from not a minister of the Lord, not a Doctor or even Master of Theology, not even one of our well-meaning brethren in the Catholic priesthood, but from a man with no formal training in The Word. This is a blasphemer, a heretic, and a profiteer of the rankest New Age variety. And he must be stopped! He must be stopped for the good of our nation. He must be stopped for the good of the faithful worldwide. I have no doubt that if he is successful, his success will encourage other false prophets to capitalize on the coming end of the millennium by spreading a false gospel, by encouraging sinful attitudes and actions, and by exploiting the most vulnerable among us for their own secular-humanist ends.

"I therefore call upon all believers, especially all the true and holy believers of the confederated evangelistic churches associated with Rob Patterson Ministries, to fight Mr. Jones' mad heresies with every ounce of strength and resistance in their souls. This is not the last battle against the powers of darkness, but it may well be the first of a coming series of important skirmishes that culminate in the final defeat, if we are so fortunate and if we are so faithful, yea, the defeat of the Lord of Darkness and all his minions on the final Judgment Day.

"Bless-ed is the Lord Jesus! Amen!

"Are there any questions?"

The day after that, televangelist Larry Falstaff, operating out of Washington, D.C., joined the fray while a guest on a CNN talk show.

"You can never tell what's in a young man's heart until you've spoken to him at length or watched him for a long time," Falstaff said, sounding oh-so-reasonable. "And truly my heart goes out to him for the grievous losses he has suffered. And I'll even acknowledge that his so-called theses end on a note apparently meant to inspire bravery and a renewed kind of faith."

But then came the whammy.

"*Never*-the-*less*!" Falstaff said with odd syllabic emphases, mixing metaphors liberally as he went. "We must beware a wolf in sheep's clothing, or in this case beware a serpent trying to pose as a lion. Mr. Jones seems to want to claim a new faith rebuilt on the ashes of the old one. But that new faith, like the seed sown on rocky ground, is built on a foundation that will not hold water. What kind of foundation is it to claim that God is a jerk, and that He sent Christ not to save us but to save Himself? I hope the young man is merely misguided, rather than deliberately conniving, because the real heart of what he is saying certainly tends toward evil with a great big capital 'E.' Those theses amount to 'false witness,' pure and simple, and Mr. Jones ought to withdraw them and end his ill-motivated plans for a new corporate ministry. If you're watching, Mr. Jones, I say to you that forgiveness is still available to you, but right now you are treading on thin ice above an inferno you won't be able to put back into the jack-in-a-box. Cease and desist now, Mr. Jones, cease and desist."

* * *

On Thursday night, Mad received another call from The Colonel. "Sir, I tried and failed to put the genie back in the bottle," Mad said, repeating the metaphor somebody else had used a few weeks earlier. "And I lost my job as a teacher, I think. So I figured the best thing I can do is to try to control my own message, to try to set the record straight and not let other people define what my message is, so that maybe I can make something good come out of this after all…. Yes, sir, I'm aware that you and The Society are displeased with me…. Yes, sir, I'm aware that Daddy Lee would probably not be happy with me right now. But you have to believe me, Colonel, sir, that I am trying to make things right by letting this new enterprise go forward. I don't want to embarrass The Society, Colonel. I would do whatever I can, eight times over, sir, to make The Society proud of me. I owe so very much to you, and I will try hard not to let you down."

"I say, son, I say," said The Colonel. "I'm not sure you know what you are doing, son. But I think you are a good boy, I do, I say. Just try to tone it down, son. I say, jes' try to tone it down."

Again abruptly, the line then went dead.

* * *

That night Mad checked the web site again for reassurance before the morrow's scheduled press conference. All week long the most active participant had been FD Thom, who seemed to grow more and more enthusiastic with each day. "I can't wait for Friday's divine Mad-ness," was one his typical exclamations.

Until Mad saw an entry from that afternoon, though, he hadn't noticed that M. Magdalene had been strangely silent. But that afternoon she had finally chimed in.

"Good luck tomorrow, Mad," was all she said.

"Hey, Magdalene, where you been all week?" asked Affirmed. But there was no response.

Mad desperately scrolled up and down the entries looking for something new from Jezebel?, but found nothing. "Hey, Jezebel?, this is Mad, believe it or not. I miss you. Any words of advice for tomorrow?"

The chat room had gone nuts after that entry, with a fierce running debate about whether that had truly been Mad, or just somebody using his name. But Jezebel? herself never answered. It was left to Perdicaris to offer something close to the kind of encouragement Mad needed: "I understand that Fox News may carry part of Mad's press conference live. I only wish they could interview some of us who have found courage from his theses. The story's not complete unless people hear the responses from us believers. Because of Mad, I'm in from the desert, looking at what might be greener pastures ahead."

"You give me too much credit," Mad wrote, knowing that many of those reading would not believe they were really his words. "If you've escaped a desert spot, it's because you found the energy to escape. Congratulations!"

* * *

At 10:30 the next morning, Mad entered a room at the Adams Mark Hotel in downtown Mobile that his associates had reserved for the press conference. He was amazed to see that that room was jam-packed. Don (whoever he was) still had a few weeks left working for the California congressman, making him unavailable, so some local PR person was just finishing handing out media packets when Mad stepped to the microphone-heavy podium. The top sheet in the packet contained a few soundbites, supposedly quotes from Mad, that Mad himself would never quite get around to saying aloud. "All of us pilgrims are trying to make a mad world sane." "Even in faith, there is room for doubt and questions." "This is the start of a new national movement. But I'm not the mover; I'm the one being moved by a heart-warming response."

Mad's mouth felt a little dry.

"Hello, everybody, I'm Madison Jones," he began. "As you know by now, I'm here to announce the formation of a new, national, non-profit enterprise, called 'Mad, Mad World,' or MMW for short. Let me make clear what this is, and what it isn't. This is NOT a vehicle for me to get rich. I have set a maximum salary for myself of $44,000. And frankly, I doubt this enterprise will even be lucrative enough for me personally to make that much."

(In the back of the room, Becky, in from Houston, cringed at that remark. Justin, standing beside her, fidgeted nervously.)

"On top of that," Mad continued, "this is a non-profit corporation. All proceeds above staff salaries and reimbursement will go to charity.

"Now, with that out of the way, here's what MMW actually is. It's a way for people to find spiritual comfort in a crazy world, a mad mad world. It's a way for those who, for reasons I still can't fathom, find my words of value…" (Mad realized he was lost in an odd syntax) … "anyway, for those people to take my very imperfect wisdom and hold it before God – not as truth, but as a question, as a hypothesis for God to either approve or correct, in their own lives and in their hearts. God knows that we on Earth are of little understanding, but He recognizes, I believe, that the very effort to understand is itself an act of faith."

The assembled media looked at him blankly, as if he were speaking Greek or Hebrew.

"Maybe I'm getting a little esoteric here," Mad continued. "What I mean is that I claim no special insight, and I certainly am neither ordained nor properly credentialed to be preaching the Gospel. All I have is a historian's knowledge of some of the issues, combined with a willingness to speak from the heart. I truly believe that the future of faith lies in lay ministry, in the acts and voices of everyday people without benefit of seminary who nevertheless witness their faith to one another. All I'm doing with Mad, Mad World is providing a forum for that lay ministry to find a voice."

Mad took a deep breath, looked out over the still befuddled media, cleared his throat, and continued:

"Anyway... I, um... I know you all have received packets outlining the specific plans for MMW, the web site and newspaper column and lecture tour and all that – assuming, of course, this all comes to pass like it's s'posed to – and so I won't really say much about those things. The main thing I want to stress is that I'm on a venture here that is not top-down, not hierarchical, but instead on a joint quest where all of us struggling with God can both teach other and learn from each other. ... Oh, yeah, I guess I'm supposed to say some quote that's in your press packets. Something like how I'm not a prime mover, but I'm the one being moved by how kind and strong the response of the public has been. And it's true. So if this works at all, it will work because we're all in this together.

"Any questions?"

As usual, the most aggressive questioner was also the one who was the most banal and clueless.

"Mr. Jones, Mr. Jones!" yelled some young gun Mad vaguely recognized from network news reports. "What makes you think you can get away with saying that God is a jerk? Won't that be offensive to people who really believe in all this Christian stuff?"

Mad felt his bile rising. Here he was trying to explain himself, and this guy was still stuck on the "jerk" line. Some atavistic impulse, probably honed during his experiences with competitive sports, gave him the urge to go for the jugular.

"*All this Christian stuff?!?* What kind of condescending BS is that? You sound like religion is an alien creature or something. Are you one of those overeducated nimrods who thinks all believers are just *idiots*? You media types are all alike. I remember a couple of years ago in *Time* or *Newsweek* or somewhere, seeing a headline about, and I quote from memory, 'The surprising unsecularity of the American public.' What kind of word is 'unsecularity'? For that matter, what kind of word is 'secularity'? You media idiots all act as if atheism is the norm and faith is a quaint relic that's an opiate for morons. Why is 'unsecularity'— or, in a better word, 'faith' – why is faith a surprise? Maybe if *you* really believed in what you call 'all this Christian stuff,' you wouldn't be hung up on such an easy target as my use of the word 'jerk.' Maybe then you'd have a clue what I'm talking about.

"Now, does anybody here have an *intelligent* question?"

Ever since Claire's death, Mad had been off-kilter, or at least what for him was not on kilter. All his life, Mad had floated effortlessly, popular and accomplished without even straining, thus allowing him always to ape his late father's courteousness. Now, though, he never knew what mood or state of mind would force itself to the fore. He was emoting straight from the gut, and he found it strangely refreshing.

An agitated and uneasy murmur that swept the room. The first reporter, accustomed to being on the attack instead of to being the object of attack, slunk back without a further word. That gave an opportunity for a voice that Mad recognized to fill the void. It was the kind-faced young woman from the local paper. Mad felt horrible that he had not yet given her a personal interview; she was the only reporter who really seemed to wrestle with the real questions his theses had inexpertly grappled with.

"Madison, I mean Mr. Jones, I intend this question entirely respectfully. I'm trying to get to the heart of what you're really saying. I, um… I'll try to put this delicately. As the story has been told, you wrote your theses in response to what anybody would consider an awful tragedy. And what's radically new about what you wrote is that you say God makes mistakes, and that it was Christ who was God's atonement for those mistakes at the same time that He, Christ, helps us humans atone for our own sins. But here's the question if you'll bear with me. Other people, every day, suffer horrible tragedies, and even more others just go on day to day with lives of despair. But they don't say that God is fallible. Mr. Jones, they don't say that God's a jerk.

"Okay, really, I promise, *this* is the question: What is different about your grief that led you to write something so radical? And what can your ministry offer to all those people who deal with even worse grief in more orthodox ways?"

More murmuring from the network guys. It was clear they were wondering what kind of pathetic, roundabout question was that?

Mad brought them up short. "That's a really good question, or two questions," he said, with his equanimity restored. "I'll be the first to admit that as much as I have been hurting – as much as it seems just too cruel to lose my wife and child the same way I lost the mother I never knew, by a hemorrhage at childbirth, and also to have lost my father and grandfather and mother-in-law – even with all that, I still have my health and friends and a nice place to live and all the rest. Some people, dying of AIDS in Africa or suffering horrid physical torture for political reasons in dictatorships around the world, or whatever, would sneer at my suffering as being not worth the word 'suffering' itself…"

(Becky thought this was turning into a fiasco and tried to wave at him from the back of the room to tell him to get back on track about MMW. But Mad didn't see her.)

"Earlier this week I went to the rector of my church for some grief counseling. I've never done that before. What I ended up discovering was that none of the questions in my theses were particularly novel, but that I just took the time to both write them down and to try to find some Biblical basis for what I was feeling. I don't think there really is an 'orthodox' way to deal with grief; I just think that some people eventually are attracted to orthodox answers. They may be right, and my unorthodox answers may be wrong. I don't know. I have total respect for the orthodox answers. But what Mad, Mad World will attempt to do is to provide a forum for exploring these issues and making sense of them, and in doing so, to see if there's a way for those explorations to lead us to a peace with God rather than away from Him."

Pause.

"There, I hope that made at least a little sense. I hope it answered your question… (Kind-faced reporter nodded.) And I hope that anybody who is watching this live out there in TV-land will understand that I have no simple, cookie-cutter answers. All I have are questions, and semi-informed gut responses. That's all that MMW can offer. I hope it's an offer that people find worthwhile. Thanks so much for your interest."

Mad then turned around and walked out of the room, ignoring the frustrated shouts from the rest of the media who had come armed with questions far less esoteric, far more aimed at 'hard news' subjects like dollars and sense, schedules, staffing details, and the like. More than one reporter yelled out questions seeking a response to the criticisms from televangelists Rob Patterson and Larry Falstaff. But Mad ducked into a semi-secret freight elevator and sped back to his Midtown house.

* * *

Becky had real work to do on site to help the hired local PR person mollify the press, and she was apoplectic (at Mad) by the time she and Justin left the Adams Mark well past a half-hour later. When they reached Mad's block, she was amazed to see that a gathering crowd contained no angry faces. The mime was there in front, silently waving poster-board flashcards to some 50 enthusiasts all yelling in unison, at his silent direction, "WE … LOVE …MAD! WE … LOVE … MAD!!" The throng was crowded right up to Mad's front porch, but the mime recognized Becky and Justin and waved them through to Mad's door, where Justin used his own key to let them in. The kitchen TV was turned up more loudly than usual, and that's where they found Mad with a flabbergasted look on his face.

"I'm a hit on Fox's insta-poll," he said to them in wonderment, by way of greeting. "Eighty-two percent of callers thought I came across well, only twelve percent said I looked bad, and the rest aren't sure. And the few voices they have actually put on the air all say the same thing. They say it's high time somebody stood up to the arrogant media like that. One guy said I'm a hero – his exact word, a 'hero' – for telling off that network guy. I don't believe this: I keep thinking I've written or said something dumb, and every time I do, people love it."

Justin, repeatedly punching one fist into his other open palm, began smiling so hard at this news that for once he was speechless. And Becky, who lad left the hotel loaded for bear, had to take a minute to re-process her business brain with this new information. From the street in front of Mad's house, the chants of "WE-LOVE-MAD" still echoed.

The phone rang. It was Buzz calling from D.C. "You did it, Madison, you did it! You're not gonna believe this, and I need your permission first, of course, but I just got a call from the host of that cable show, 'Gut Check.' Yeah, that hard ass named Matheson from Chicago. He's a friend of a friend of mine, was grabbing a beer with my friend the other night who told him that *his* friend, meaning me, was the godfather of this religious upstart from Mobile who has Patterson and Falstaff all hot and bothered. Anyway, Matheson watched you on Fox – he was ticked off that his own cable network didn't carry you live – and he loved the way you went after that reporter. He tracked me down and said your attitude was perfect for 'Gut Check,' and he wanted to take a break for just one night from his all-Lewinsky, all-the-time focus. Long story short, Mad, he wants you on the show at some point, but for a short segment tonight he wants to air a clip of your outburst and then wants me on with him to comment. If you say okay, Madison, I'm gonna be on 'Gut Check' tonight!"

Mad relayed this to Justin and Becky. Becky, her mind whirring with the mushrooming possibilities afforded by all the exposure, said *yes, yes, YES!*, by all means he should tell Buzz to go ahead. Justin just looked giddy.

"Aw, hell, alright," Mad told Buzz. "But try not to get into the theology; just tell him as best you can where you think I'm coming from."

"WE …LOVE … MAD!!!" The throng outside still hadn't quit. Becky walked to the front and peered through a curtain.

"Hey, loverboy, there's another TV camera out there now as well. Why don't you go give your fans something to hold onto, and give the camera a good show as well? Go out to the porch and thank them, why don't you?"

"Do it, Mad, do it!" said Justin, grabbing Mad's arm and pulling him forward just after Mad hung up the phone. "Becky's right, buddy! Do it!"

Without really making a decision to do so, Mad found himself being pushed by his friends through his own front door. A roar went up from the crowd, now numbering probably 75 or 80.

"Hey, everybody!" Mad spoke loudly, holding his hands up for silence. "Thank you so much. Thank you very, very much!"

"WE ... LOVE ... MAD!"

From the corner of his eye, Mad saw the police cruiser coming down the street behind the crowd.

"Lookahere!" he shouted over the din, again holding up his hands for silence. "I'm more grateful than you can know for your support. I've had a tough time, but your response makes me feel like I've done something worthwhile, even though I don't know what...."

"We ... Love ... Mad," began a few in the crowd, but the mime in front motioned for them to shut up and listen. Mad had no idea in advance what he was saying, so he just let the words flow from instinct:

"But I've got to ask a favor of you. I don't think it's fair to my neighbors to subject them to these crowds and this noise. And I believe what Christ said, that I should love my neighbor. Now that my friends have founded Mad, Mad World, there will be plenty of chances to hear me in public. Is there any way, then, that you could leave my house alone?"

"But we love you, Mad; you really told off that reporter!" yelled one middle-aged woman.

"I love you too!" Mad smiled as a few women put their hands to their hearts and feigned swoons, while a couple of men raised their fists and pumped them high with triumph. "But this isn't fair to my neighbors. ... [Mad paused to think of what to say next.] ... Hey, ya'll, we can all be lions together, just not on my block. How's that sound? You can be my first pride of lions!"

By this time, the mime had seen Officer Jones step from his car. The mime jumped to the stairs up to Mad's porch, did a leaping pirouette and made a big roundhouse motion with his arms for attention. Then, still silently, he somehow communicated to the crowd that they should all disperse. Amazingly, they did, virtually in marching order, all the while chanting – at the mime's flash-card directions again – "WE ... LOVE ... MAD!!!"

Watching their retreating backs, Shiloh laughed aloud. He turned back to Mad (and to Becky and Justin, who had joined him on the porch, Becky hugging Mad from the side with both arms).

"Well, Mr. Jones," said the officer. "Looks like you just did an excellent job of keeping the peace. And you know what our Lord said: Bless-ed are the peacemakers. You're a good man, Mr. Jones, a real good man."

From the car behind him, Officer Williams looked out his window with an expression that he seemed to want to turn into a scowl. Somehow, the scowl never came to full fruition, and a sort of fleshy smile showed through instead.

* * *

On 'Gut Check' that night, host Steve Matheson saved Buzz for the last segment.

"Moving from politics for a minute, we'll end tonight with just a fantastic little taste of how Joe Blow out there sees us media types," Matheson told his audience with relish. "And frankly, I think we probably deserve it. You may have seen stories about this young guy down in Mobile, name of Madison Jones, or Mad Jones for short, who wrote a bunch of religious propositions that have lots of folks in a tizzy. One of the propositions – this is beautiful, it's just such a great gut-check kind of statement – one of the propositions is that God is a jerk. That's not young Jones' point, of course. I've read his propositions, and he ends up saying that God's not such a jerk in the long run, and we've gotta be brave in the meantime, and stuff like that. But anyway, he's got some folks with their panties in a wad, and now my old sparring partners Rob Patterson and Larry Falstaff, both sometimes guests on this show, have both denounced Mad Jones in no uncertain terms. So Jones has a press conference today, and the first question out of the box is just great, just a perfect microcosm of something or other out there in Joe Blow land. This is great! Roll tape."

There was the network reporter again asking about "all this Christian stuff," and there was Mad blasting him in response. The tape over, Matheson continued:

"Dontcha just love it? I mean, I love this guy. I don't think many people would have picked up on the underlying assumption of the question, which seemed to be that 'all this Christian stuff' is just some fairy tale anyway. But not only does this Jones guy catch the reporter's assumption, but he just rolls over the reporter. I mean, this is perfect gut-check stuff.

"I have only another minute or so here, but with me tonight is Buzz Buskirk, a history professor at American University here in Washington and, more to the point, the godfather of young Mad Jones. So, Buzz, I think there's this line from Jesus Christ Superstar that I'll use: What's the Buzz; tell me what's-a-happening? I mean, what's the deal with your godson? I see there's a web site already up full of admirers, and a snapshot unscientific poll said his performance today was boffo. This guy just fires away. What can you tell us about him?"

"Well," Buzz said, trying to catch up with Matheson's loud torrent of words. "He's a great young guy with a good mind and a good heart, and he's almost embarrassingly honest. His father, my good friend, really raised him right, and…"

"That's great, that's great, Buzz, I hate to say we ran overtime over on some earlier segments, and we're just about out of time. But tell us, does Mad have what it takes to stare down the Reverends Patterson and Falstaff the way he took on that network reporter?"

"I don't think Mad wants to pick a fight with anybody, Steve, but I think he'll always tell it like he sees it. But the important thing…"

"Thanks Buzz, that's it, gotta go, but I just love this guy's attitude," said Matheson. "This is the end of the Gut-Check for tonight, so thanks everybody for joining us. Man, I get a kick out of this Mad Jones guy. Bye, everyone."

* * *

So now Mad was certifiably a growing star of the cable ranks. On Palm Sunday, there was a noticeable buzz from his fellow parishioners when he entered his church, and a TV truck ostentatiously taped the scene from a parking lot across the street. But a few of the stalwart members, looking worried, whispered plans to each other to meet about nipping in the bud all of the unseemly attention that Mad was bringing to their congregation.

* * *

Meanwhile, anticipation was high in Jefferson Parish, Louisiana, for Mad's first-ever scheduled appearance as a speaker, which was set for the next Friday. *Good Friday.* At 3 p.m., Pierre Hebert's nondenominational charismatic church, "Apostles of the Word," had set up a special service to commemorate the exact moment when Christ was supposed to have breathed his last. Who better to mark this instant of despair, this instant when Jesus had asked God why He had forsaken his own son, than the young man who had written that God is a jerk, only later to again pledge fealty to the Father? The Rev. Hebert was truly excited at the thought of hosting this young guest lay preacher, especially as the very first stop for Mad's national tour of ministry. He usually respected the Rev. Rob Patterson's judgment, but was convinced that Patterson was wrong about Mad. Despite Patterson's warnings, Hebert was sure that Mad was a good and godly young man. (Despite an infamous description in a top national newspaper, the religious followers of the Rev. Patterson were far from automatons who were "easily led.") And Hebert's wife Angelina looked forward to playing matchmaker. She had arranged for her two young favorites, Tonya and Rhonda, to be part of the official greeting party.

But Mad had been having some troubles. Twice already that week he had gone into one of those spaced-out zones like the one he had experienced that day near the 8th green of the golf course. His mind got distracted, and the world seemed to get sort of hazy, and tiny little things seemed to take on a significance that, if he had tried to describe the impression, he would have said was either cosmic or Zen-like – he wasn't sure which – maybe it was both. He sat in his patio and started noticing the patterns of the cracks in the individual bricks. Or he drove to campus intending to run three or four miles but, while stretching under a tree, got distracted by the shapes of the roots and a strong compulsion to have some scientist check the quality of the soil.

Becky, who had moved to Mobile from Houston and set up a West Mobile office for MMW Enterprises, told Mad that these episodes really worried her. "You need somebody to stay overnight with you, loverboy, to make sure you don't get freaked out by the darkness or something," she said, in a suggestive tone of voice. But Mad wanted none of that and, as politely as he could, declined the offer.

Becky also wanted to drive him to his engagement at Apostles of the Word, but he convinced her he would be fine. He said that since she had hired a cameraman to tape his preaching for later promotional purposes, she should go to the Louisiana church early in order to make sure everything was set up properly.

As for himself, Mad had a little excursion planned. The church was a 2½ hour drive via Interstate 10, but Mad had always wanted to drive the whole way to New Orleans on old U.S. Highway 90. No particular reason; just curiosity. To give himself plenty of time, he left his Mobile house at 9:30 a.m.

The first part of the drive was familiar to Mad, and thus uninteresting. In downtown Mobile, U.S. 90 was1 also known as Government Street, a beautiful oak-lined avenue full of big, elegant historic houses. But Government Street quickly turned into a nondescript and even ugly stretch of seedy motels, fast-food joints, run-down strip malls and a few "adult-entertainment" spots. Traffic lights slowed his progress enough to have seriously annoyed him if he had been in a hurry. Then U.S. 90 became a two-lane road, alongside some railroad tracks, through nondescript rural flatlands which also were far from interesting. All the way through Mobile County, Mad paid little attention to his surroundings. But Mississippi was another matter.

For one thing, Mad made better time because the highway widened to two lanes each way. Mad ignored the sameness of the strip malls in Pascagoula, anticipating better scenery in Ocean Springs. That little seaside town, home to the late naturalist artist Walter Anderson, has a reputation as an artists' mecca. But Mad was to be disappointed. He thought U.S. 90 went alongside the beach, and near the galleries, in Ocean Springs, but he was mistaken. He probably should have taken one of the turns. As it was… still more strip malls. And then as he crossed Biloxi Bay, he was greeted by the atrocious ugliness of the comparatively towering casinos – Casino Magic, Isle of Capri, the Grand – that brought fast cash to the area but badly tainted its charm. Through Biloxi and Gulfport, what should have been a nice view of a wide white sand beach gently lapped by tiny waves instead was a monument to gaudiness. The only part that brought a smile was when he passed Fun Time USA, a combination miniature golf/ arcade/ bumper boats/ and other "kiddie-attraction" spot that had been the site of what was probably Mad's single most embarrassing moment....

Shortly after Mad had recovered from his mononucleosis that first summer that he and Claire dated, the two of them had chosen to spend a day on the Mississippi Coast to be capped by a rock concert that night at the coast's "Coliseum." Claire drove from New Orleans, Mad from Mobile (both using the interstate), and they met in the middle. With time to kill in early evening, tired of the beach but too early for the concert, they decided as a lark to try out the bumper boats. At the far end of the boat pond, a decorative fountain provided a nice backdrop for the action.

Mad and Claire bumped each other a few times, and then Mad determined to make a large, wide turn to build up momentum for a big final assault. At the farthest point of his turn, though, his boat ran out of power and left him adrift. He tried to wave to the attendants, but they weren't looking. And then he realized that a current was pulling him farther and farther from the boat dock.

Right towards the fountain. The pumps that fed the fountain apparently created a suction strong enough to create the current. And there Mad was, caught in the current, drifting slowly towards the cascade.

"Mad, what are you doing?!?" Claire yelled from her boat. Helplessly, Mad just shrugged his shoulders. Shrugging was all he could do. Soon his boat was right under the spot where the fountain's shower splashed down, and he was getting drenched. Even worse, his boat was caught in a small whirlpool, turning it in tight circles directly under the torrent. Within about 10 seconds he looked like a drowned rat – and Claire was laughing so uncontrollably at the sight that she almost fell out of her boat.

Mad, dripping from head to thoroughly bedraggled toe, had eventually been rescued by a 16-year-old attendant. And without any other change of clean clothes, he had attended the concert in the same thoroughly drenched knit shirt and jeans. And Claire, full of good-humored mirth, had kidded Mad about the experience ever since. In fact, the story had been the source of much merriment at the rehearsal dinner for their wedding two years later....

Anyway, his memories of Fun Time USA kept him from being too depressed by the over-development of once-lovely coastline. Finally, blessedly, he reached first Long Beach and then, most welcome, the little town of Pass Christian, which had refused to approve casinos. This was what the coast should look like. Graceful homes, many shaded by old oaks and towering pines, overlooked the highway that ran right along the beach. Very peaceful, very pretty.

Thence around the curve away from the beach, and onto the two-mile bridge across Bay St. Louis. Mad thought it would be a challenging and worthwhile excursion one day to swim all the way across the bay, with a friend floating alongside in a skiff with an ice chest full of bottled water and Gatorade. On the other side of the bay, the town of Bay St. Louis had grown noticeably since the casinos came, and again Mad didn't like the ambiance. And that was where U.S. 90 (joined by state highway 607) would move inland, away from the beach. Again, not very scenic.

So far, the drive had been so slow that more than two hours had elapsed for a journey that by interstate would have taken only a little over half that time. Mad figured that he better grab lunch, so he pulled into a fast-food burger place. The line wasn't too bad, but the servers were slow. That was okay; it was only around noon, so Mad still had time. As he chewed his meal, he mentally reviewed what he intended to say in his homily to the Rev. Hebert's congregation....

Back in his car, Mad was glad when, 15 minutes later, U.S. 90 pulled off to the left of 607. He knew that 90 went over some bayous; maybe there would be something quaint or otherwise interesting to see. But then, as he veered left, he remembered a story Marcelle had told him about an old family tradition of hers, one she regretted having not passed down to Claire.

Marcelle had said that every year on Mother's Day, her family had taken a day-long excursion on U.S. 90 from New Orleans to Pass Christian, stopping at a number of spots along the way to pick blackberries which grew wild, in abundance, on their thorny vines along the unkempt roadside. It was hot, itchy work: The thorns and mosquitoes were highly bothersome, and Marcelle said she always had to be on the lookout for snakes, especially water moccasins which sometimes inhabited the ditches and low-lying wetlands that were prime blackberry spots. But if they were diligent, the payoff was huge: sometimes as many as several gallons of blackberries which her family baked into pies, or ate over ice cream or cereal, or gave away to friends, or froze for later use.

Mad wondered if the blackberry vines still grew, or if modern roadside maintenance had made them a thing of the past. It was still a month before Mother's Day, so the fruit themselves might not even have ripened yet – but it had been an unusually warm winter, and spring had come early, so maybe the blackberries had sprung out early as well. No other cars seemed to be behind him, so Mad drove slowly while peering intently out the window for signs of blackberry life. A few times, most notably near one of the series of tiny bridges that traversed some bayous, he even pulled off the two-lane roadway and looked into what seemed like promising underbrush – but to no avail.

After a half hour, he had almost given up. He crossed a slightly larger bridge, a narrow drawbridge, into Louisiana. There! There over in a ditch, Mad saw two huge blackberries amidst a plethora of brambles. He pulled onto the roadside. Lucky for him, he thought to himself, that he always carried a small Styrofoam ice chest in his trunk. If there were more berries where he had spied those two, he would collect them in the chest.

His clothes were a problem, though. He was wearing a coat and tie for his church appearance… Oh, good. He had a clean, spare T-shirt in the trunk. He changed into it, leaving the tie and Oxford shirt on his back seat. He still had his dress pants on, but… what the heck. Over to the ditch, reaching out to the berries …. Ouch! Those thorns were nasty. More carefully now … yes, he had the first one. And then the second. And yes, there were more. He ate one. Nice and sweet….

Reaching gingerly, stepping carefully, Mad worked his way along the ditch. Many of the berries were still small and green, but some had already ripened enough to be worth picking. Actually, this was kind of fun. It took a kind of concentration, a kind of precise small-muscle control, to pluck the berries without getting scratched by the thorns. Especially tough was when a mosquito bit his hand: The natural reaction was to jerk the hand away in response, but if his hand was already amidst the thorns, that was the exact-worst reaction. Thank goodness, at least, today's temperature was mild.

There! He scored a particularly plump and juicy berry. And there! he collected another one. Wow …. These blackberry bushes extended across the ditch, back towards the wetlands. Mad, stepping ever-so-cautiously through the weeds and brambles, lost himself in his endeavor. He found that he could concentrate on his task with half his mind, while at the same time the other half wandered. He wondered how Jack Nicklaus was doing that day in the Masters golf tournament. The tournament had dedicated a plaque in the Golden Bear's memory earlier that week; wouldn't it be cool if he turned back the clock and contended again?

Yes, there was another good blackberry…. And what about poor, fate-beleaguered Greg Norman? Would he ever win a Masters? Norman was from Australia; Mad had always wanted to go to Australia…. There was another good berry …. Yeah, Australia. Nice beaches, odd animal-life, the barrier reef. That would be a nice trip. And he also wanted to go to Greece. That was another dream vacation. Greek isles. Great history. Olympian and Odyssean myths. Mad loved the Odyssey. … Another berry …. Mad found a clear, dry, shaded spot, and sat down to rest. His mind continued wandering. He fell into another of those trance-like states, the third one that week. He noticed that his lower pants legs were dirt smudged. The dirt on the fabric formed a fascinating design……

A long time later, Mad's reverie was broken by raindrops. Ohmygosh! He didn't want to be soaked when he arrived at the church. Church! What time was it? When Mad checked his watch, the panic rose so fast that he almost became nauseously sick on the spot. It was already 2:16. He was due at Apostles church in 14 minutes, and the service would start in 44 minutes – and he still was, he estimated, an hour away, even if he flagrantly ignored the speed limits.

Nervously, Mad stumbled and sloshed back through the thorny vines and over the ditch, further tearing and discoloring his lower pants legs as he did. He was careful, however, not to spill any of the blackberries from his ¾-full little ice chest. Back in his car, he sped off… only to come upon a line of stopped cars at the bridge over the Rigolets, which was the local name for the pass between Lakes Borne and Pontchartrain. A tall pleasure boat was entering Lake Pontchartrain, and the drawbridge had to be raised to accommodate it. The only good news was that the drizzle had stopped; the thunderstorm was passing to the North.

Nearly ten minutes later, Mad was back on his way, madly passing cars on the two-lane road every time ongoing traffic allowed him the chance. Past the ramshackle fishing camps with names such as Camp Comfey, Paw Paw's Dream, and By "U" Self Plantation; onto four-lanes again past Textron Marine Services and through an area that, based on the signage, obviously was a Vietnamese fishing community; through old working-class residential areas and one small stretch of newer, finer homes; past more strip malls, and finally back to Interstate 10 where it crossed U.S. 90 just east of downtown New Orleans, Mad sped at a rate just short of flat-out dangerous. On I-10, Mad ignored the speed limit of 60 and wove through medium traffic at nearly 80 miles-per-hour, praying that no troopers were on patrol. He veered onto I-610 to escape the downtown traffic, joined back to I-10 at the Jefferson Parish line, and had to slow for some heavier traffic. It was already past 3 p.m.

Finally, near the airport exit, Mad found his turn off the interstate. Checking directions that the Rev. Hebert had faxed him, Mad made his way through generic suburbia to where Apostles of the Word, looking like nothing so much as a large warehouse with a 20-foot cross on top, sprawled in the midst of a large asphalt parking lot. Mad realized he still was wearing the T-shirt, so he parked at the far end of the lot, pulled his dress shirt from the back seat and roughly put it on. Fumblingly, not very artfully, he re-knotted his tie, then somehow found the armholes for his suit jacket and wriggled into it as well. Mad was sweating profusely and accomplished little by mopping his brow. It was just about 3:30 and this whole situation was an utter disaster. Mad sprinted across the lot.

Becky, looking both pale and furious, emerged from the building to meet him 10 yards outside the entrance. "You son of a bitch!" she hissed through clenched teeth as she grabbed his arm and yanked him inside.

In stentorian tones, through a loudspeaker, the Rev. Hebert's voice reverberated throughout the building above the insistent, repetitive chords of a simple refrain played on a loud electric keyboard. Row after row after row of worshippers stood or kneeled in front of folding chairs, swaying and chanting. On each row, some of worshippers were calling out in strange, unintelligible, Arabic-sounding words. They were speaking in tongues.

"THE LORD HAS DIED!" yelled the preacher. "LONG LIVE THE LORD! THE LORD HAS DIED! LONG LIVE THE LORD!"

In the back rows, some of the congregation noticed and recognized Mad. They stopped their chanting, turned and pointed. A murmur began and worked its way forward. Two attractive-but-overly-mascara-painted women in their early 20s, followed by Angelina Hebert, began to scurry over from a side enclave. The Rev. Hebert, mid-sentence, noticed the interruption. Looking out over his flock, he spied an extremely flustered-looking Mad and Becky at the very back of the middle aisle. With a dramatic arm movement, he waved for all the chanting to stop. "SILENCE!" he shouted. "OUR HONORED GUEST HAS ARRIVED! COME FORWARD, MR. JONES!"

Trembling, Mad approached the microphone stand. The Rev. Hebert, seeming untroubled by Mad's tardiness, embraced him in an overly hearty bear hug.

"People of the Lord!" Hebert said into the mike once Mad had extricated himself. "Just in time for the preaching, the Lord Jesus has delivered our guest safe and sound! Bless-ed be the Lord!"

An excited buzz came from the congregation. "Mr. Jones," Hebert said, "The lead microphone is yours. What is your godly message for us today?"

The Rev. Hebert moved to the side, where another, wireless microphone was produced for him by an assistant. Mad, heart still racing in distress at his lateness, overwhelmed by the size and energy of the congregation, desperately wanted to make amends for his terribly belated arrival.

"Rev. Hebert, and all you good people, you apostles of the word, I thank you for your patience, and I apologize profusely for being so late," Mad began. "Actually, I was so eager to get here that I left Mobile early, hours and hours ago. But because I had so much time, I decided to take old Highway 90 all the way from Mobile. I thought somehow the old route would give me inspiration."

"HEAR WHAT HE SAYS, PEOPLE!" interrupted the reverend. "HE SAYS THE OLD WAYS ARE BETTER. THE TRIED-AND-TRUE WAYS, THE PROVEN WAYS. PREACH IT TO US, BROTHER JONES!"

Mad thought that maybe the reverend was making fun of him. He figured he needed to explain himself further. "In Ocean Springs, Mississippi, I wanted to take a little break, because I had heard great things about some art galleries there, where the naturalist paintings are supposed to be just so beautiful…."

"HEAR HIM, PEOPLE! HE SAYS THE WORKS OF GOD IN NATURE ARE A DELIGHT TO THE SENSES! PRAISE THE LORD!"

Mad didn't know what else to say, so he continued. "But I also was so intent on not getting off the main Highway 90, and thus being late for here, that I must have missed the turn to where the galleries were, and…."

"GOD'S TIME KNOWS NO MAN-MADE CLOCK! TAKE THE TIME, PEOPLE, TO EXPERIENCE THE FULLNESS OF GOD'S CREATION!"

"Well, I kept on going, past all those horrible casinos…."

"HEAR HIM PEOPLE! GAMBLING AWAY GOD'S BLESSINGS IS A SIN!"

"…. And then I crossed Bay St. Louis and pulled off the main strip there to follow the old route to New Orleans…"

"STILL THE OLD WAY, BLESS THE LORD!"

"… I remembered how my mother-in-law told me about great amounts of blackberry bushes along that part of Highway 90. She just died six weeks ago, and I miss her greatly…."

"LISTEN TO HOW HE HONORS HIS FAMILY TIES! FAITH AND FAMILY, FAMILY AND FAITH! THAT'S THE TICKET TO SALVATION!"

By now Mad had no idea where he was going with this apology. Every time the Rev. Hebert interrupted, it flustered Mad even more and made him feel that much more determined to explain his tardiness.

"Uh…, I just feel so bad for being late, but what happened was that, sure enough, I saw some luscious blackberries in a ditch by the highway."

"THE FRUITS OF THE LORD ARE WORTH GATHERING!" shouted Hebert.

"The berries were hard to get to, because they grow on some very thorny vines…"

"HEAR WHAT HE SAYS! THE FRUITS OF THE SPIRIT ARE NOT EASY TO ATTAIN! THE DEVIL LAYS SNARES FOR US ALWAYS!"

"… But these berries looked just so good, so I persisted. And where I had seen the first two bushes, I discovered that more and more awaited further up in the weeds and brambles…."

"PERSISTENCE! THAT'S A KEY TO FAITHFULNESS: PERSISTENCE AMIDST THE THORNS OF LIFE! TELL THEM HOW IT IS, MR. JONES, YOU JUST KEEP TELLING'EM HOW IT IS!"

"So I kept working my way further in, collecting more and more of the berries. Of course, it is early for blackberries yet, and many more were too green and unripe to pick…"

"IT IS STILL TO EARLY FOR THE LORD'S FINAL HARVEST! WE CAN GATHER SOME FRUITS OF THE SPIRIT, THROUGH GRACE BY FAITH, AS WE LIVE THIS LIFE! BUT MOST OF THE FRUITS OF THE SPIRIT, AND SALVATION ITSELF, WILL COME ONLY IN GOD'S OWN GOOD TIME!"

"Well, umm, anyway, I, umm, I don't know exactly how to explain this, but in picking the berries, I somehow became distracted. I began thinking of other things, and it was warm and I had recently eaten lunch and I think my blood sugar dropped or something, and I just… I guess I went into a sort of trance, or maybe fell asleep, and just lost track of where I was. I'm really, really sorry, but…"

"HEAR HIS LESSON, PEOPLE! MR. JONES IS TELLING A WONDERFUL PARABLE HERE! THIS IS TERRIFIC! HE SAYS THAT THE FRUITS OF THE SPIRIT REQUIRE CONCENTRATION! THE PATH TO THE LORD HAS DETOURS. LOSE YOUR WAY, LOSE YOUR DIRECTION, LOSE YOUR SENSE

OF URGENCY, AND YOU MIGHT BE LATE FOR THE LORD'S BLESSINGS. SATAN CAN TAKE HOLD OF YOUR MIND, PEOPLE! THE DEVIL WILL WAYLAY YOU ANY CHANCE HE GETS. THAT OLD EVIL SATAN WILL TRY TO PUT YOU INTO HIS TRANCE EVEN AMIDST THE VERY FRUITS OF THE LORD, EVEN AMIDST THE LORD'S HARVEST ITSELF. BEWARE, CITIZENS OF THE LORD! BEWARE, YOU PEOPLE OF THE SPIRIT!"

The Rev. Hebert, looking radiant, nodded for Mad to continue. Mad had no choice except to do so.

"It was only when it rained a little that I came out of my trance and realized that the hour was late."

"THE LORD SENDS US REMINDERS FROM HEAVEN ITSELF. WHEN THE HOUR IS LATE, HE SENDS US NOURISHMENT FROM ABOVE!"

The congregation was now yelling, too. "You tell us, Reverend! You tell us, Mr. Jones! Praise the Lord!"

"So then," said Mad, having no idea how to extricate himself from his explanation so he could start the homily he had actually prepared, "I hustled back to my car and tried as hard as I could to reach you here at this terrific house of worship. I am just amazed, and gratified, and touched and humbled that you have received me so warmly despite my tremendous tardiness…"

"HUMILITY! DILIGENCE ON THE WAY ONCE ONE'S OWN ERROR HAS BEEN ACKNOWLEDGED! AND A PEOPLE OF FAITH STILL WELCOMING THE ONE WHO ONLY TEMPORARILY LOST HIS WAY! THIS YOUNG MAN SPEAKS TRULY! A GODLY PEOPLE WILL ALWAYS WELCOME BACK HOME A PRODIGAL SON!

"BUT…," and here the reverend finally lowered his voice a few decibels. "Don't let me interrupt. I'm sure this parable has a lesson that Mr. Jones can explain for himself better than my poor understanding can translate. Tell us, young Brother Jones!"

"*Preach* to us, Mr. Jones!" repeated one member of the congregation in a loud voice. "Lead us to salvation!"

The rest of the congregation began to chant, more and more loudly, PRAISE THE LORD, PRAISE THE LORD!

Mad was thoroughly flummoxed by now. Off the top of his head, he threw out a line:

"Well, Reverend Hebert, this is Good Friday. There is no hour darker than this, yet we have the advantage of knowing that Easter is just two days away. And on my way here, thank goodness, the rain went away, and the dark storm clouds dissipated, and at least I was able to get here before it was too late entirely, and now this truly is seeming like a good Friday after all, and I am already full of anticipation for Easter's joy…."

Mad was then going to try to a segue into a version of his intended homily, collapsed into just about one paragraph, something about how in these last few months he had been come through the darkness and been blessed by God, and how that was in truth the message of Holy Week itself. But he was not given the opportunity. For a final time, the Rev. Hebert interrupted:

"PRAISE THE LORD! PRAISE THE LORD! PRAISE THE LORD! THIS IS INDEED A GOOD FRIDAY, AND OUR GUEST HAS DESCRIBED FOR US THE TRUE WAY TO THE LORD, AND EASTER DAY AWAITS. THANK YOU SO MUCH FOR YOUR BRILLIANT PARABLE, MR. JONES, AND FOR MAKING IT SO MUCH MORE REAL AND DRAMATIC BY ACTING IT OUT WITH YOUR MID-SERVICE ENTRANCE. BRILLIANT, MR. JONES, BRILLIANT! PRAISE THE LORD AND MAY ALL OF US FIND EASTER JOY TOGETHER!"

And then Hebert was motioning Mad towards a seat, and his wife Angelina was taking his arm and leading him there, and the congregation was applauding wildly and yelling GLORY BE and PRAISE THE LORD, and even as unfamiliar as every bit of this was for Mad, he found himself swept away by their sincere and spirited expressions of happiness and love… and for the very first time since Claire died, and almost against his better judgment, Mad experienced a deep and utter joy. The rest of the service was a blur. All Mad knew was that his very soul was experiencing a boundless optimism.

It had been exactly 40 days since he checked himself into the psychiatric ward. He felt that he was leaving a wilderness, and that a Promised Land awaited.

Chronicles

Chapter One

The Heberts had prevailed upon Mad to stay for dinner with some of the congregation's leaders after the service. (The same invitation was not extended to Becky, who couldn't help radiating a disdain for the brand of religion they practiced.) Mad wasn't there long before he realized that the dinner was matchmaker Angelina's set-up for him to meet Tonya and Rhonda, two of the most devout young adults at the church. Both wore sequined, body-hugging outfits; both had highly styled shoulder-length hair, Tonya's jet-black and Rhonda's bleached blonde. Rhonda, a 20-year-old waitress, seemed genuinely sweet and demure. But Tonya, 21, a student at the University of New Orleans, kept finding ways to put her hand on Mad's butt, and kept licking her lips at him and winking when she thought nobody else could see. Mad had been relieved to finally escape and made the drive back to Mobile in just over two hours.

He found Becky waiting for him on his front porch. She was in a foul mood. She said the video taken that day would be a disaster if shown to any Catholic or mainline Protestant audience; she said she was surprised Mad hadn't stayed overnight with "one of those little holy-roller tarts" (apparently referring to Tonya and Rhonda); she said Mad's tardiness was inexcusably unprofessional; and she said she had put too much work in the new venture to see Mad screw it all up – "especially when I'm not getting laid while I'm at it." She was some kind of ticked off. Mad felt thoroughly chastened.

Two days later, Mad repaired immediately from Easter services to join the headmaster's family for dinner. The headmaster wanted Mad to know that even though his teaching job was lost for now, he still was considered part of the school family and still was afforded everybody's love and sympathy. Mad appreciated the gesture.

By Monday night, Becky's attitude had changed entirely. The office phone had rung all day, with charismatic churches all across the country calling to schedule Mad. Word had gone out all weekend from Apostles of the Word that Mad was the real deal, despite what the highly respected Rev. Rob Patterson had thought and said. But except for a few Gulf Coast-area engagements (at which Becky agreed to let Mad speak for less than what would be his usual fee), Mad's first real speaking tour would not begin for about another month. It was being set up quite carefully to best use the board members' strengths and to appeal to carefully targeted demographics.

Also on Monday, Mad's first daily, self-syndicated, spiritual-advice newspaper column – called "Madison Avenue" – had run in 11 morning papers ranging from Florida to Oregon. It was packaged to run only 300 words each day, letter-writer's question included. The first question had been picked by Mad from submissions to the web site: "Dear Madison: I want to be devout, but I can't stand my pastor, and I can't leave my church because my family has gone to the same church for three generations and it would break my mother's heart if I did. What should I do? Sincerely, Stuck in Wrong Flock"

"Dear Stuck," answered Mad. "Your note didn't say why you are not happy with your pastor, but the way I see it, faith isn't for the fainthearted. Only the faint-hearted would let a poor pastor be an obstacle for a spiritual life.

"Even though the Bible says that the way to God the Father is through the Son, it still leaves open the possibility that there are many ways to the Son. A church is more than its pastor or priest. A church is made up of a whole community of believers. Find people in your church with whom you share interests or values, and work with them to house the homeless or feed the hungry, or to start a spiritual discussion group, or whatever else floats your religious boat so it can sail towards Jesus. Christ did not say (Thesis 56) 'come unto thy pastor… and he will refresh you.' He said to go unto Him, unto Jesus. Meanwhile, though, try to get to know your pastor more deeply. Maybe you are missing something good in him. We're all flawed, and the important thing is to look past what you see as flaws and find the good in someone. That's how it is with approaching God, as well. Even if God seems to have acquiesced to something that seems unfair to us, we need to keep going back to Him and back to Him and back to Him. That's what faith is all about."

Mad meant every word of it but, frankly, he thought it nevertheless was pablum. "What the heck do I know about this stuff?" he kept saying to Becky and Justin. "I've never been profound about anything, so why should anyone take me seriously?"

"Oh, just shut up and write, loverboy," was Becky's invariable answer, once adding that "there's gold in your lack of profundity."

Mad reacted angrily to that; he didn't care about gold, but about helping people find faith.

Amazingly to him, it seemed that lots and lots of people wanted Mad to help them find it. In addition to strong demand for Mad to take speaking engagements (usually at $1,000, plus bare-minimum travel expenses, per appearance), letters were flooding in to Madison Avenue – and the Mad Religion website was already attracting a fair number of advertisers and loads of web-surfer "hits." Part of the appeal was that Mad promised to write at least one entry each day for the chat room. (Becky had set up a special electronic identifier, triggered only by Mad's special password, that let other chat participants know that it was indeed Mad, not some impostor from Timbuktu or somewhere.)

By week's end, six more papers had signed up to start running Mad's advice column within the month. Arrangements had been made, too, by the aggressive young New York book publisher to send down a ghostwriter in the near future who would spend hours talking to and taping Mad, so the writer and publisher could start figuring out how best to present Mad's ideas into a marketable book format.

Mad didn't really know what to make of all this. He just followed whatever schedule Becky gave him each day. He did as much as he could from home, so as to avoid Becky's unceasing sexual innuendoes whenever he joined her and the new (grandmotherly) part-time secretary at the office. Staying away from the office also meant he was blessedly able to see less of Justin, who kept finding excuses between physical training sessions to drop in at the office unannounced. Justin's motive was as obvious as it was seemingly hopeless: He desperately wanted romance with Becky. To discourage him, Becky still insisted calling him "Mr. Luke," even though they were contemporaries.

("Mad," Becky complained late that first week, "If that little fruitcake doesn't find somebody else to dream about humping, and find her soon, I'm gonna personally castrate his little things and throw them to the fishes in Mobile Bay!" Then, as an afterthought: "On the other hand, Mad, if *you* do *not* start humping me, I'll castrate you, too, and make you the modern world's first gelded prophet.")

Despite all her inexplicable crassness, Mad had to admit to himself that Becky was enormously talented at the business side. He had doubted that Mad, Mad World, Inc. could attract enough money to pay the salaries and fees for Mad, Becky, Justin, Mary, Buzz, Don, and the part-time secretary, much less generate a cash flow big enough to have some left over for charity. But Becky was a whiz. He had no clue how it all worked; he only knew that Becky announced four days after Easter that he should already start thinking about which charitable causes he wanted to support with MMW's first grant.

* * *

In the chat room, FD Thom, Affirmed, and Perdicaris had become the most frequent participants, along with a new, bitter critic calling himself "Defender of the Faith" (later shortened to just "Defender"). M. Magdalene, oddly, had dropped completely from the picture.

Late in the week, Mad was happy to see Jezebel? finally show up again, even for only one quick comment. It was in response to a particularly venomous entry from Defender, part of which said that Mad ought to "stop polluting his family name with his idiotic blatherings."

"Hey, Defender, lay off," wrote Jezebel?. "I knew Mad's father, and I think he'd be proud that his son is inspiring atheists like me to consider whether there really might be a God after all. You may think you have all the answers, but I don't think you even understand the questions some of us have. Mad does, and I thank him for it."

Mad was dying to know who Jezebel? was. He figured that if she had known Ben, she must be somebody from Mobile. Maybe one of those liberal English or Sociology professors from Spring Hill, he thought.

Maybe one of those intelligent women who always wished that Ben would let go of Mel's memory and begin dating again.

"Hello, Jezebel?," Mad wrote, his entry highlighted on the screen with the purple border Becky had created. "Thanks for being so nice. I really wish I knew who you are. Please let me know. If not on the chatroom, then call my office."

But Jezebel? neither answered nor called, and Affirmed and Perdicaris picked up the cudgel against Defender for several more hours of sometimes vitriolic debate. Affirmed, thought Mad when reviewing the messages later that night, was starting to go a little overboard, at one point writing that Mad might even be "a new Moses."

The lines that Mad liked best, however, came from "Cowardly Lion," who was apparently a new participant. "I can't believe how intense and angry all you folks are getting," he wrote. "Some of you Mad-vocates sound like you have no brains, and Defender sounds like you have no heart. If I had enough courage, I'd tell the whole lot of you to get off this yellow-brick Internet and go get high in the poppy fields. Every one of you needs to just chill out, dudes, or else the great Wizard will never let you reach the Emerald City in the sky."

It was a bizarre entry, thought Mad, but something about it really tickled him.

* * *

MMW kept growing, and Mad actually became somewhat accustomed to the routine of monitoring the web site, writing his newspaper column, reading a host of books on theology and spirituality, exercising nearly daily, and writing notes to himself for things he wanted to include in future discussions with his book ghostwriter. He also wrote and re-wrote notes for his upcoming lecture tour, and repeatedly practiced his delivery in front of a mirror. He still had trouble ginning up consistent enthusiasm for the whole enterprise but figured that he darn well ought to live up to the responsibilities he had assumed. He told himself that, in a roundabout way, he was doing it to honor Claire's memory – and also because he knew Daddy Lee would be disappointed if he ever failed to deliver on an obligation.

Fortunately, ever since his post-press conference plea to the demonstrators for them to vacate his block for the sake of his neighbors – which, amazingly, they honored – Mad no longer felt under siege. The mime and a small, hardy band of enthusiasts did occasionally show up outside the charmless office building that MMW shared with a small realty firm and a three-person law partnership, almost always with some new, clever chant or posterboard sign, but they never stayed more than an hour or so and never really got in anybody's way. Once Mad had tried to approach the mime to express appreciation (feigned) for the mime's support, but the mime arched his back, hissed, and ran away like a skittish kitten.

* * *

Towards the end of April, Steve Matheson had the Rev. Patterson as a guest on "Gut Check." Patterson was railing against President Clinton about the Lewinsky situation. With a few minutes left in the show, Matheson deftly switched gears.

"Okay, Rob, lemme move on to a slightly different topic. You know, I've been fascinated by this guy Madison Jones, down in Mobile, who wrote up 59 religious propositions where he says God isn't always perfect, but in the long run God does offer salvation and should therefore still be worshipped. That's not exactly it, but as I see it, that's the gist of what Jones is saying. What I love about this young guy – and he's only 25, I think – what I love is that he doesn't take any guff from anybody. He held a press conference a few weeks back, and one of those arrogant network reporters asked a question that seemed to belittle Christian faith as a fairy-tale or something, and this Jones guy just ripped him to shreds. It was beautiful, just beautiful."

Patterson, anticipating where Matheson's monologue was going, had tried to interrupt, but Matheson's word flow was like a river too big to dam.

"Anyway," continued Matheson, "I've watched re-runs of a feature on Jones that the 'Acute Vision' show did, and in it Jones was asked about the Lewinsky situation, and he was critical of the president just like you are, although really not very stridently. Still, he's on your side on this, Reverend. But you have been very critical of this young man. You've called him a 'false prophet' and a 'pretty boy,' and you said he is 'a blasphemer, a heretic, and a profiteer of the rankest New Age variety.' That's really harsh, Rob, really harsh. What I want to know is, if this young man is inspiring skeptics to become Christians, and if he's on your side of the culture wars, or at least of the Clinton Wars, then why are you blasting him from here to Kingdom Come?"

Finally, Patterson spoke up, voice oozing with Georgia peachiness. "Well, Steve, I'm just not sure you unduh-sta-uhnd. Anybody with a lick of clev-uh-ness can position himself against the lies and moral de-PRAV-uh-tee of Bill Clinton, especially if he's in the South where such de-PRAV-uh-tee is especially detested. The Boy is trying to fool devout God-fearing people into buying his snake oil to make him rich. But the Scripture says…"

Matheson interrupted: "But Rob, here's a guy who took on the demon 'elite media' that you are always warning against! And he says that even if we interpret God as having done us wrong, we should still remain faithful! And he says Clinton's lying! Isn't this Jones guy a horse out of your own barn?"

"Steve, this Jones guy even goes by the name of Mad. That's what he truly is, he's mad. I think the young man is unstable. He says God is a jerk, and…."

"And he says," broke in Matheson, looking down at some notes, "Be strong and of good courage, uh… da-dum-da-dum-da-dum, some other stuff along those lines, quote, 'because God's love has been poured into our hearts through the Holy Spirit which has been given to us.' That's right up your alley, Reverend, and then, this is what I love about this guy, just a real gut-check kinda guy, he closes by writing 'Here I shout; I cannot do otherwise.'"

"But Steve…."

"He's paraphrasing your Protestant founder, Reverend, he's paraphrasing Martin Luther, who of course all urban Catholics like me were taught was almost akin to Lucifer, but he's your idol, and Luther said, 'here I stand,' and now this Jones guy says 'here I shout!' Nothing reticent about this guy, Reverend, and he's right from your Protestant tradition. You should love him! Anyway, time's run out, we gotta go, I thank the Reverend Patterson and my other guests; this has been Gut Check, and we'll have more gut checks same time tomorrow night. G-bye!"

* * *

Laura Green's life had become a whirlwind. Her work on "Acute Vision," which had boosted the ratings enough to earn the show a renewal for next fall, had so impressed the network majordomos that they had twice again requested she be pulled from her new duties at the New Orleans station to do special assignments for them. Rumor had it, they were considering a full-time contract offer for her as the ace reporter, second only to the show's hostess. The honchos had always liked a male-female balance; but their market research showed that tabloid-ish news magazine shows were seen as more believable, and drew larger audiences, when the reports were made by women. So the new schtick for "Acute Vision," to distinguish it from all the other similar shows, would be for women to do almost all the on-camera work. And Laura supposedly was at the top of their list.

Not only that, but a New York-based network reporter, a fast-rising young star, had shown some major extracurricular interest in Laura. He flew her up to the Big Apple each of the last three weekends of April, wined and dined her and, by the third weekend, bedded her as well. (Obviously, she knew how and when to use sex for her benefit. Besides, this guy *really* was a hunk, even if a little shallow and vain for her tastes.)

Still, she couldn't get Mad out of her mind. On that first weekend visiting the New York hunk, her flight out of New Orleans left Friday evening. She knew that Mad's first speaking engagement would be that afternoon at Apostles of the Word, which wasn't too far from the airport. The timing was just right. Out of sheer curiosity (so she told herself), she had attended. Within two minutes of her arrival, she had felt like Charlton Heston on the Planet of the Apes, visiting territory that looked familiar but that had a distinctly alien feel. Everything seemed out of kilter. This wasn't Uptown or even Mid-City New Orleans, or even the Jefferson Parish suburbs that she knew. Surrounded by enthusiasts quickly enraptured by every mention of "The Lord" or "Jesus," her senses assaulted by loud, repetitive music, Laura had had no idea how to behave. And she couldn't understand why, during the first half-hour, Mad was nowhere to be seen. On either side of her, people had begun speaking in tongues. But she had stood there, towards the back of the far-right row, stiff-legged and uncomfortable.

When Mad made his dramatic entrance and tried to explain his lateness, only to have his whole story treated as a parable by the Rev. Hebert, Laura had first been offended by Hebert's interruptions and then amazed that everybody around her accepted it as part of the normal order of things. "Poor, poor Mad," she had thought. "He's become a one-man freak show, and this is all my fault."

Yet just as she felt the most out of place and out of sorts, she had glimpsed a few rows away one other young woman, a buxom and slightly thick-hipped blonde maybe 30 years old, who looked as uncomfortable as she, Laura, felt. Ms. Buxom had not spoken in tongues, had not joined the chants, had not participated at all. She had just stared way up to where Mad stood in front of the congregation, looked decidedly perplexed and troubled, and occasionally wiped her eyes. Like Laura, she was dressed in a slightly more muted, more classic blouse and skirt, unlike the gaudier clothes of most of the female Apostles worshippers. Laura had felt the blonde was a kindred spirit, and had determined to speak her when the service was over. But when it finally did end, the blonde disappeared quickly from the crush of people, and Laura missed her.

Now, three weeks later, some wild hair had led Laura to watch "Gut Check," and there she had seen host Steve Matheson take the unctuous Rev. Patterson to task. And out of the blue, a picture of the buxom blonde flashed across her mind again. Whoever she was, she had seemed moved by Mad in a similar way to Laura.

And it was only in thinking *that*, that Laura first acknowledged to herself that she indeed had been moved. It wasn't the sex; it was the faith. Something about Mad's earnestness had moved her. Something about his pain-deepened courage. Somehow, it radiated. *He* radiated. Or, rather, something radiated that was both from within him and yet greater than he and working through him, taking on Mad's essence as it did.

Laura shook her head to clear it. Damn, what was she thinking? What was all of this esoteric crap?

* * *

From the Mad Religion chat room:

"Hey, did you all see the way Steve Matheson blew away Rob Patterson last night?" wrote FD Thom. "Matheson made a monkey of him!"

From Cowardly Lion: "Yeah, but some monkeys can fly, and they'll swoop down and snatch you from the Yellow Brick Road and put you in the witch's castle!"

To which somebody writing anonymously said: "Hey Coward, your act is getting old and it always was pointless. Why don't you just shut up already with your Oz sh**?"

* * *

On April 30, a few days before he was to begin his first extensive speaking tour, Mad pulled out of his large stack of mail a hand-addressed envelope with a Spring Hill College logo. Inside was a multi-paged, hand-written letter:

"Dear Madison,

I don't know if you would remember meeting me, although we have met once or twice, but through my prayers I have felt an increasing impulse to contact you. I can't seem to reach you by phone, because your home number is unlisted and the messages I've left at your office are probably lost among who-knows-how-many others. Anyway, we have a number of connections, you and I. I am (semi-) retiring next month from 36 years on the Theology faculty here at Spring Hill. Your father Ben, over in the history department, was a younger colleague of mine whom I respected and liked although age and differing interests played a role in keeping us from a true friendship. But my uncle was the chairman of the history department who hired Ben. In fact, Ben was his very last hire before my uncle retired. Also, you and I share another kinship: I also attended Georgetown (nearly 40 years or so before you), where Father Joe Durkin, my uncle's very good friend, was probably my most important mentor, just as he had been a mentor for Ben's wife, your late mother, Mel. And, from what dear Claire told me, old Father Durkin still was active enough when you two both attended the Hilltop that he had been important to her experience there as well – and indeed, she told me, Father D. was the one who arranged for her to go on some excursion down Virginia-way somewhere which provided her the opportunity to meet you.

Ah, Claire. I was not really her boss, but I was one of those Jesuits she performed work for here at the college. She was a lovely young woman, bright and kind and devout and true, and I mourn her passing very greatly, and I send my deepest condolences to you for her loss.

All this is prologue, Madison, for the real point of my letter. When I attended the memorial services for Claire and for the child who surely would have graced both your lives, I was so very disheartened to find that you were not there – that you were apparently too distraught to receive the hundreds of condolences that might have been of comfort to you. Ever since then, I have followed your saga closely.

It might surprise you to know that although I am as orthodox a Catholic as you will meet, I nevertheless find much of value in your theses. (As a Catholic, and an ordained Jesuit at that, the very idea of theses on church doors, with their evocation of Luther's crusade that split the church, might have been enough, when I was younger, to dangerously raise my blood pressure – but age has a way of mellowing a person.) I think that you have touched on an age-old, almost insoluble paradox of the Christian faith, namely the problem of evil and of wholly undeserved bad fortune, in a way that is so fresh and raw that it piques my interest. A very Jesuitical thing, it is, this desire to welcome and be challenged by fresh ideas, even if only to respond by exposing the errors therein. Not that all of your ideas are wrong. In fact, I find them worthy of discussion, of intellectual inquiry, of serious philosophical and theological discourse.

But more than that, I have been emphatically moved by your saga, by your struggle to come to grips with, to articulate, and to hold true to, your innermost emotions, in a way that is both intellectually honest and that somehow finds a path back to faith in Our Heavenly Father. I watch you, and I ache with you, and, though you are ever so much younger than I am, I admire you. And, as a man facing retirement and thus obviously on the verge of leaving 'middle-aged' for 'old' (how hard that is to admit!), I have the aging man's egotistical notion that I have accumulated enough wisdom and discernment and maybe empathetic abilities as well so that what I say and do may be of service or of succor to you. In short, Madison, I am offering myself as a sounding board, a confidant, a spiritual adviser if needed (although I certainly do not want to infer that your own priest – I understand you are Episcopalian – is unsuited for that task), or just as an older friend, if you should ever find yourself feeling lost or overwhelmed by this new task you have taken on. I will certainly not be offended should you decline my offer, but just keep it at hand in case you feel the need for the counsel of a rather cranky Jesuit who doesn't really know what he's going to do with his time now that he is leaving full-time professorship duties. (I'll still teach a seminar or two.)

All my best to you, and for your new endeavors.

In the Lord's name, yours truly,

Peter Vignelli, S.J.

Mad read and re-read the letter several times. The words anchored themselves in his heart. He thought he knew which one Vignelli was – balding, mid-60s, but still athletic-looking. If it were indeed Vignelli he was picturing in his mind's eye, the Jesuit had the look and air of somebody solid and strong and admirable. Yes, Mad would call him. Soon. Take him to lunch, maybe. This was a man he should know.

* * *

Two days later, just before midnight on a Saturday, Becky Matthews lay in her bed in the small unit she rented in a West Mobile apartment complex. Her head rested in the narrow, partial valley between two pillows. Her knees hugged another pillow, and her arms were tightly wrapped around yet a fourth. Silent tears streamed down her face.

Becky had now lived in Mobile for more than a month, and she was miserable. Soul-black miserable. She had left her promising (though boring) job at the Houston oil company, left the near environs of her family (which had made clear its strong disagreement with her unconventional career choice), left the fun and familiar social life surrounding so many of her high-school friends who had moved back to Houston after college, left all the big-city offerings, not just because she had always longed for an entrepreneurial enterprise, but also because she really believed in Mad. Not in his message (such as it was), actually, but in Mad himself. She believed there was something special about him. In fact, she thought she loved him. She loved him for the ease with which he seemed to moved through life, and for his utter lack of meanness – and, of course, for the way, when they were together, that he made her nerve-endings jump and her mind and heart float in an ecstatic trance-like state. She had loved him ever since their first night together during their all-too-stunningly-brief romance at Georgetown. Unlike most of the other girls who seemed oddly contented to have enjoyed Mad's attentions for just a little while and not overly upset (just sort of happily wistful) when he moved on, Becky had taken the "break-up" hard. Not that she showed it, of course. But it had eaten at her for months, and she had never understood why he had not wanted to continue the relationship. And she didn't understand now why he wouldn't renew it.

Becky knew she was hot looking. All the guys told her that. Guys tried to hit on her all the time. She had a body well endowed by nature and well maintained through her own hard work at staying in shape. She had a pretty face, and luscious hair that was a natural strawberry-blonde with no artificial coloring required. And she didn't play games about sex: She liked sex, and made it known she liked it – and after all, wasn't that what men wanted, anyway? No games, no hassle, just honest enjoyment of mutual attraction.

Yet with all that to offer him, Mad acted as if she was part of the furniture. She had come to this godforsaken town that the rednecks and social elite alike in Alabama actually considered a big city, and she knew nobody except Mad and had found nothing fun to do and not enough people she considered intelligent, and she had done a remarkable job in creating MMW from scratch … and yet Mad seemed, if anything, annoyed by her labors and perhaps by her very presence. His attitude broke her heart.

And it was a real heart she had, a heart as tender as everybody else's, even though she did her best to hide it behind her unhidden sexuality and her unyielding modern-woman toughness.

Then, tonight, she had found herself so mind-numbingly, god-forsakingly bored that she had finally consented to join that twerp Justin for a night out at what she considered those two-bit bars and dance clubs that made up a few-block strip on Lower Dauphin Street in downtown Mobile. The whole situation sucked. Justin kept insisting on dancing, even though he looked as goofy as Dudley Moore's character in that old Goldie Hawn movie, *Foul Play*. Idiot rednecky guys or sophomoric college guys kept trying to hit on her when Justin either wasn't looking or had excused himself to the restroom. Then, the only time all night when she saw two young men who had the look and air of Becky's "type," Justin noticed their interest and moved in close to her as if he owned her. Those two guys had turned away, laughing at some private joke that Becky was sure must have expressed contempt for her own taste or self-worth on the basis that she allowed herself to be seen with such a runt.

Appalled that she had sunk to such a low, all in service of a guy named Mad – MAD, indeed! – who paid her no respect, she had pleaded a headache long before Justin was ready to call it a night.

But Justin's disappointment was so palpable as he drove her home that she felt a twinge of remorse, for the first time, at treating him so shabbily.

"Holy mother of God!" her brain had screamed. On top of all the rest of it, on top of being a total loser who had given up a good life for a dumb pursuit in a town that (compared to Houston) was just Podunksville, USA, "you're also a bitch of the first order," she told herself contemptuously. "Who the hell are you to look down on that well-meaning little twerp?"

Becky squeezed her pillows even more tightly and cried still harder. Tomorrow was supposed to be a triumphant day for her, and instead it promised nothing but disaster.

* * *

The next day, Sunday, Mad would embark on his first real mini-tour as a speaker. Becky had arranged the whole thing, using her hometown of Houston as a point of embarkation. They would fly to Houston; meet Don the P.R. guy from Washington (his resignation from the staff of the California congressman had become official on Friday); have a late lunch with her wealthy parents (at *their* insistence; she feared it would be a disaster); and then have Mad speak at the Sunday night service of a large Methodist church. The next morning, they would drive down to Galveston for the breakfast meeting of a prominent civic club, back up to Houston for a luncheon sponsored by a major women's auxiliary, and then all the way over to San Antonio for the monthly Monday night forum of a large young professionals' group. The next day would feature another luncheon, this one in Austin, followed by a flight home (plane change in Dallas) to Mobile that evening.

Mad was as nervous as a caged blue jay in a cat kennel. He could barely sleep that night, and when he did sleep (fitfully) he kept having variations of one particular dream.

It always started the same. Mad was in the bumper boat, the fountain splashing down on his head, the boat turning lazy circles in the weak whirlpool beneath it. But the whole situation was wonderfully funny and lighthearted: Claire drove her little boat 30 yards away, pointing at him and laughing merrily. Even at that distance, her laughter was so infectious that Mad had to laugh, too, almost entirely unembarrassed by the jeers and laughter of bystanders at the boat-pool's edge.

But then the dream always started going wrong. The gentle whirlpool became stronger, and then stronger still. Rather than holding his bumper boat in a lazy circular pattern under the gusher, the whirlpool started spinning him faster and faster. Soon Mad was spinning like a passenger on one of those crazy amusement-park rides, and then being sucked into the whirlpool's vortex. He no longer was in the boat, but instead in the insane clutches of Becky and Justin and Buzz and Mary. And it wasn't Claire laughing merrily that he heard, but a green-clad Laura Green talking into a microphone like a play-by-play announcer, describing Mad's whirlpool plight as if he were the athlete in a spectator sport. Then Laura turned into Rob Patterson telling Mad that the whirlpool would carry him straight down to Hell, and then Patterson turned into the kind Rev. Hebert yelling helplessly that Mad had left his blackberries at the side of the pool. And just as Mad seemed about to be sucked under for good, he awoke.

When Mad finally fell into the next sleep, he had the dream again, and this time it was the mime and the iguana lady and the tall white Mobile TV reporter guy who had him in their clutches. And another time as he sank into the vortex, he grabbed for a lifeline somebody had thrown him – only to have it yanked away by Officer Williams on account of Mad being a "nigger lover." Still another time Mad actually grabbed the lifeline and pulled himself to apparent safety – only to be so startled, as he finally stood at poolside, by the feel of black-haired Tonya's hand on his buttocks that he fell back into the water and began to be sucked under....

This time, before drowning, Mad awoke to see his clock showing a bit past 6 a.m., and he decided he might as well get up and start prepping for his 9 o'clock flight. The only thing that kept his jitters from being unbearable for the rest of that morning was that when he checked the web site, he found a late-night entry from M. Magdalene. Unless he had missed one somewhere along the way, this was her first appearance on the site since the night before MMW's opening press conference. Just as on that earlier night, her message here was as brief as could be.

"Hey, Mad," she wrote. "Good luck with your Texas speeches."

That was it – but it was enough, somehow, to calm Mad down. Calmed him enough, in fact, to allow him to notice that when he picked Becky up on the way to the airport, she looked unusually pale and drawn and uncharacteristically despondent. She was surprised, pleasantly, when he gave her shoulders a reassuring squeeze before she got into his car.

"I know you've put a lot of work into this, Becky," he said. "I appreciate it, and I won't let you down."

Becky sighed and managed a wan half-smile.

Chapter Two

If Mad had been familiar with Washington's Capitol Hill, he might have recognized Don the PR guy as a typical representative of one of the Hill's several subspecies. Blow-dried and buffed and too immaculately dressed; blandly well-meaning and with an intelligence just enough above average for him to excel at conventional wisdom but to shrink from original thought, Don was trim, proper and dark-haired handsome. Yet when he met Mad's and Becky's plane at the Houston airport, Mad *still* didn't remember him from his Georgetown days. Maybe Don had been one of those boring sorts who always told the professor exactly what Don thought the professor wanted to hear. Mad had never paid attention to those people. But Don greeted him like a long-lost friend from the cradle. And he kept flashing towards Becky those knowing, sideways glances that Mad assumed meant they had, at least once, "hooked up" on campus.

For whatever reason, Becky perked up to about four-fifths of her normal energy level. Four-fifths, Mad thought, was just about right: rather than loud and attention-hogging, and refinedly crass in the way some debutantes try to show they aren't porcelain princesses, Becky at four-fifths energy was vibrant and attention-earning and just edgy enough to be exciting. For the first time since she had shown up uninvited at his door some seven weeks earlier, she evoked in Mad the libidinous sensations that had briefly attracted him at Georgetown.

Mad's focus was re-directed quickly, though, by Don, who had morphed seamlessly from old-friend pleasantries to what could only be described as an aide's "briefing" to a boss. Such and such a number of people were expected that night in Houston, compared to "X" number in Galveston the next morning. Podiums were set up at all locations, but the P.A. system could be switched to a portable microphone if Mad wanted. The press probably would be at a few of the events, but he didn't have to take their questions if he didn't want to, and it was best to limit media access at least somewhat. Don hadn't done press releases because Mad had not been ready to tell Don what he planned to say.

And so mind-numbingly they moved on, down to baggage claim (past two people who recognized Mad and asked for an autograph), over to the rental car, and onto the highway, with Becky driving, towards the home of Becky's parents. Finally, mainly to put an end to Don's officious chatter, Mad changed the subject.

"Hey, Don, are any of those congressmen decent people, or are they all just a bunch of self-important jackasses?"

"You got all types, Mad, all types. My boss was a raging tyrant – the stories I could tell you about him! A lot of them are basically well-meaning, but a little aloof. Staffers know which ones are which. And some of 'em are real great guys. For instance, Bob Livingston, from Louisiana, all his staffers think he's terrific. And everybody was bummed when Sonny Bono died; he was nice to everybody. And …."

Mad listened with half an ear. With the rest of his brain, he again tried to remember what class or activity at Georgetown had been the one he and Don had in common. It was like trying to remember what the campus cafeteria had served the day the Hoyas lost to U. Mass in the Elite Eight round of the NCAA tourney: Don had made no impression at all.

What soon *did* make an impression on Mad was the neighborhood into which Becky had turned. Huge mansions, widely spaced, lined the streets. Large grassy medians, dotted with small trees, divided the sides of a boulevard. Ancient and majestic trees shaded the mansions themselves. Front yards were spacious, driveways and garages decidedly ample, and front porticos semi-tastefully ornate.

"Here we are, homey-home-home of the parental magnates," said Becky, rather sneeringly, as she pulled into a brick drive encircling a stone fountain, a good seven feet in diameter, with a stone Cupid and two small stone nymphs adorning its center. "The place where black gold and greenbacks turn into cold white marble. The finest place money can buy, except of course for the chalet in the Alps and the 5,000 square foot 'cottage' on Monterey. The place where Daddy Dearest hangs his slippers and the Mommy with the Mostest hosts her ring of amazing gossip! Welcome, welcome, and try not to run away too soon!"

Mad was taken aback by Becky's bitterness. But Don entirely missed her sarcasm.

"Oh, is your mom a good conversationalist?" he asked with an almost creepy earnestness. "I can't wait to meet her."

By the time all three of them had climbed out of the rental car, a Hispanic maid in a perfectly starched white uniform had emerged from a wooden door so thick and heavy it looked like the entrance to a church crypt. "Miss Becky, Miss Becky, you still looking bue-tee-foll, just as bue-tee-foll as ever!!!"

"Yeah, whatever," Becky mumbled, sidestepping her impatiently… and then, as if suddenly stricken with a conscience, she stopped and turned back to face the maid. "Oh, Gloria," she said, giving the woman a semi-formal half-hug, "you're always so sweet to me. It's good to see you. Gloria, this is Madison and this is Don; you all, this is Gloria. She's my fave, my heart. … Now c'mon inside to face the firing squad!"

* * *

Back in Mobile, Justin sat in his upscale condo, fidgeting and nervously punching the TV remote control. The final round of a golf tournament was on, and a tennis match, and an NBA game, and a Braves game with Greg Maddux pitching. None of them meant much to him, although later in the season he would pay more attention to the Braves. For now, though, he just didn't know what to do with himself. He really had wanted to travel to Houston with Becky and Mad, but he had to admit there was no role for him there. He just hated that Becky had been feeling ill last night; he knew that her headache last night was probably a tension headache, and as a trainer he knew exactly the right pressure points to relieve tension headaches.

And what bad luck! Just when Becky had finally agreed to come out with him and was obviously having a good time, that headache of hers had to strike! He knew she wasn't overwhelmed with him, but he was sure there was at least a little spark somewhere, and just give him a chance, and he'd show her! Yes indeed he would!

But then she had gotten that headache, and now she was in Houston with Mad, whom she obviously had a crush on, and one of these days Mad would wake up and grab her and then he, Justin, would be out of luck. And with all the attention he had paid to Becky, he had tried less often to reach that girl in Pensacola who had seemed so promising, and whenever he DID try, he got her answering machine – and he didn't think *it* worked right, because she had never called him back.

Then those thoughts, those thoughts that he hated, started creeping into his mind. Those thoughts told him that Becky wasn't even the slightest bit interested. And that the machine in Pensacola did work, but that the girl had no desire to call back. And that all those 40-somethings at the gym who were so impressed by his knowledge and approach as a trainer were the only women who would ever pay him any heed – and that while they all liked him, not a single one had any romantic inclinations towards him of the Mrs. Robinson-to-Dustin Hoffman variety. Maybe all they saw was the inches of air above his 5'3" height, those inches where the men they wanted had strong faces to look up to rather than a clever little face like his that was at their own eye level or even below.

Justin didn't want to admit, not even to himself, how lonely he was. Heck, if it weren't for his good buddy Mad, he would have hardly any social life at all. And now Mad was on the road with that exquisitely sexy and intelligent creature, Becky, and Justin was stuck at home watching the Braves lose and feeling like a total loser himself. He knew he wasn't a loser, he told himself, but sometimes he sure as hell felt like one.

Damn, if only Becky could see the real him!

* * *

Becky led Mad and Don through an ornate hallway and a very unlived-in "living room" full of antique furniture and porcelain figurines, to a cold and spacious room dominated by a huge ebony table five paces long. Rising from a stiff chair at one end, a hearty-looking rock of a man, maybe 50ish, was telling them all welcome, extending a hand of introduction to Mad and Don, and then trying awkwardly to hug a resentful-looking Becky. Chet Matthews was a third-generation oil magnate who had shown a solid ability to take a minor fortune and turn it into a sextupled one. He exuded an aura of somebody trying desperately and sincerely to come across with warmth but succeeding only in projecting a heightened territoriality.

At the other end of the table, a perfectly coiffed, tight-skinned, thin-boned woman sat frigidly in a cushioned armchair. She had a once-natural prettiness now marred by a store-bought beauty and a mouth whose smile muscles seemed to have atrophied.

"Becky, dear, are you going to present these two young gentlemen to your mother?" Ginger Matthews spoke without even shifting in her armchair. Don walked towards her with the practiced ease of a trained courtier. "Mrs. Matthews, I'm honored," he said, taking her limply extended hand as if it were silk-lined taffeta. "So gracious of you to invite us into your home."

Ginger Matthews nodded assent.

"And you," she said, turning to Mad, "you're the young man who has taken Becky on this fool's errand. Tell me, is my lovely daughter shacking up with you yet?"

There was an awkward silence. Chet chewed sternly on his lower lip while his eyes shot angry lasers at his wife. Ginger paid him no heed but stared stonily at Mad. Don smiled nervously. Becky shut her eyes tightly and clenched her teeth. Mad looked down at his feet, shifting his weight uneasily back and forth.

"Oh, come now," Ginger said, now half-smiling. "I *do* have a lovely and talented daughter of whom I'm very proud, I'm sure. I figured it would take a young man like you, who looks like Robert Redford, to snare her. You should be proud of your looks, young Madison. With the right kind of training, you could put them to worthwhile use. I know some divorcees my age who could really use a good boy-toy."

That was enough for Chet.

"Don't mind my wife," he interrupted, looking at Mad with what he hoped was male camaraderie. "She's just upset that her daughter moved away."

Then an odd thing happened. Becky sprung to her mother's defense. Here was her father trying (if not entirely successfully) to be friendly, and yet it was at her father that Becky flashed her fury – as if, Mad thought, it was a subconscious transference of her rage from the offending object, her mother, to the one, her father, who had been inoffensive. "Well at least Mother shows some concern about my pursuits, Daddy Dearest," she said, voice icy enough to sink the Titanic. "Whatever I do is just fine with you, since nothing a little girlie can do will amount to a hill o'beans anyway, compared to what a mythical son of yours could have done if he had played for the Longhorns."

Becky's inflections and accents, while never losing their iciness, alternated oddly between Texas-cowboy and Houston-debutante, with a touch of oil-bidnessman thrown in for a word or two. And Chet, looking as if he had been winged by a sniper but wanted to tough-out the pain, turned on his heel towards the kitchen mumbling something about "making sure Buster knows when to baste the prime rib." Mad and Don, each struggling with discomfort, silently found a tableside seat.

The rest of their visit – a hearty four-course lunch with apparently mandatory Heinekens for the men and a 1977 white wine for the women followed by three quick games of pool in the billiards room (Mad and Chet versus Don and Becky, with Ginger having excused herself) – was less awkward only in comparison to that rocky beginning. As most women did, Ginger warmed (or at least thawed) toward Mad, even to the point of flirting. She continued to treat Becky almost disdainfully, but when she did acknowledge Becky's existence without an unambiguous insult, Becky hung upon each word as if it were the tender cooing of a long-lost true love. Conversely, on the repeated occasions that Chet inexpertly and almost desperately tried to show a real fondness for his daughter, Becky reacted as if he had spoken to her like an ogre to a captive young duchess. The psychology of it all was rather strange.

"No, Daddy Dearest," she said sarcastically at one point, as she connected on a 2-ball-to-6-ball combination to a corner pocket, "I haven't found a nice neighborhood yet where your little girlie can be safey-wafey; I'm in a little condo where I can hear the upstairs neighbors boink each other at 3 a.m. every other night."

When she excused herself once to go to the restroom, and Don went to return his beer glass to the kitchen in order to save the maid the trouble, Chet looked at Mad with as pained as an expression could be from a man of such otherwise aggressive solidity.

"Mad," he said, in a muted tone, "my daughter doesn't like me, and I don't know why. And while I was dead set against her leaving her job here and going to Mobile to run your preachin' bidness, I've changed my mind today. I like you, son. Somethin' tells me you got integrity and prob'ly some goodness as well. Maybe you can rub off on her. Becky's not a happy person. And I'd do anything I could to make her happy. She doesn't understand that I respect her, much less that I love her. But if you can help her find somethin' inside herself that makes her more content, then I say more power to you. I want my daughter back, Mad, I want her back in this big dumb old father's heart of mine. You help bring her back to me, son, and I'll be forever in your debt."

Becky and Don both re-entered the room from different doorways, and Chet lined up and perfectly executed three shots in a row.

"Game, set, and match, kids," he said as the 8-ball disappeared in the appropriate pocket. "Nobody beats Chet Matthews in my own damn house."

* * *

At six Eastern time that evening, Buzz met TV host Steve Matheson for dinner at the Tombs in Georgetown. The two had hit it off well when Buzz served as a stand-in guest on Mad's behalf. Matheson had told Buzz he would call soon to grab a bite, and now several weeks later proved true to his word. Matheson was not only a political junkie but an amateur military history buff, and he thought that a meal with a military-history professor would be a pretty interesting way to spend an evening since his wife was out of town visiting relatives. And Buzz, who liked Matheson's take-no-prisoners on-air persona, was flattered that a big TV guy was paying attention to him.

All Buzz's life, he had played the sturdy second fiddle. In high-school football in south-central Pennsylvania he had been an All-District guard, a basically anonymous position, at a mid-sized school. But that still left him nowhere near good enough to play college football except at a small school that didn't give scholarships, and he opted instead for an ROTC partial scholarship to the University of Maryland. There he avoided the student protests, kept his nose clean except for drinking lots of beer, and through sheer hard work earned grades high enough to make him a candidate for a decent grad school – but just six one-hundredths of a point too low to be *cum laude*. The University of Virginia at first indicated he would not be admitted to its Master's history program, and Buzz was all ready to serve his ROTC obligation in 'Nam when U.Va. accepted him as a replacement for another graduate candidate (who deferred admission at the last moment for family reasons).

At Virginia he had made a fast friend in Ben Jones, but always came off a bit dull in comparison to Ben's quiet panache.

After graduate school and his rotation in Vietnam (away from the front lines, thank goodness), Buzz came home eager to settle down with a sweet all-American girl. Instead, he lost his heart to Suzy Wilson, a vivacious little sprite who looked far sweeter than she turned out to be. They divorced after just two years when he caught her in an affair with a rich Chevy Chase doctor. For the next two decades, he had put on the public face of one of those beefy he-men who chose bachelorhood because it gave him more options to play the field. But the truth was that nothing much ever really clicked for him on that front.

Professionally, his reputation as a professor was that of an unremarkable workman who neither bored his students nor greatly inspired them, and whose scholarship was steady but far from original.

So having a recognizable TV guy like Matheson take a liking to him was a highly welcome development.

"So, Buzz," Matheson was saying between swallows of Killian's Red, "what's the over-under on how long your godson keeps this religious thing going? Eight months? Year-and-a-half?"

Buzz didn't really want to talk about Mad. When he was around Mad or even on the phone with him, it was true, he did for some reason fall into the habit of deferring to the younger man. The second-fiddle role was just too ingrained. But he didn't want to waste a meal with Matheson on Mad's stuff, when he could be talking politics or the military or women or something fun. (Not that he wasn't enthusiastic about MMW; he truly did want Mad to succeed. Mad was a good kid; besides, he felt a duty to his late friend Ben to be there for Ben's son.) But Buzz wanted to talk to Matheson, who was about Buzz's age, as a peer – not as a shill for somebody else.

"Well, Steve, I'd say Mad will still get attention at least as long as this Lewinsky mess continues, if only because I think the whole scandal brings 'values issues' to the core, so there's a market for people talking about subjects like religion. Speaking of which …" (and it was here that he tried to segue away from the subject of Mad) … "how do you see this Lewinsky stuff playing in the elections six months from now? Do Clinton's troubles mean death to the Democrats, or what?"

Since Matheson could never resist a conversation about politics, even when he was not working, Buzz's segue had the desired effect. And politics morphed into foreign policy, and from thence into military affairs and then (over dessert even more libations) into military history, and the subject of Mad's endeavors was pushed well aside. Matheson eventually cabbed it home thinking that this Buzz guy was a pretty decent "Average Joe," not at all like most of the high-falutin' pointy-heads usually associated with academia.

* * *

One time zone behind Buzz and Matheson, 537 people packed the Methodist church for an evening service that usually drew only 125. Two TV cameras stood watch outside the building, but the minister and ushers had refused them admittance to the service itself. A newspaper guy and a radio lady, however, both smuggled tape recorders into pews near the front.

The service proceeded in its normal manner until time for the sermon. The lead minister took the pulpit as he ordinarily would, but said: "Tonight, as you all know, we will not have a sermon by me or another ordained minister, but a homily instead by a new lay leader whose thoughtful Christian theses have challenged both the faith and the intellect of a rapidly growing number of adherents and critics alike. Tonight, we welcome him to our pulpit neither to endorse his views nor to dispute them, but instead to be provoked and prodded into reflections on our own faith. He quite rightly claims no particular authority to interpret Scripture, but after reading his work and speaking to him on the phone and meeting with him for a half-hour before this service, I'm convinced he possesses a heart honestly engaged in the struggle and the duty to know God and to love Him. Tonight, we welcome Mr. Madison Lee Jones. Mr. Jones, the pulpit is yours."

Mad was quite nervous as he took the pulpit. Something had gone very wrong. He had pulled out his Episcopal prayer book weeks earlier, in anticipation of this event, and looked up the readings for this Sunday. His whole homily was based on those readings. But the readings – the two lessons and the Gospel – that they had just finished hearing were *not* the same ones he had prepared for. Maybe the Methodists used a different lectionary than Episcopalians did. He hadn't thought of that.

He licked his lips. He cleared his throat. He licked his lips again. He took a deep breath. Finally, he managed to begin.

"To you good people of this vibrant church, I thank you for your hospitality. I pray that nothing I say makes you regret it. I come not to offend, nor to teach, for I have no formal authority on matters of faith. I come only to facilitate discussion by speaking from the heart, from a wounded heart and its particular point of view that is concerned not with being orthodox or with overthrowing orthodoxy, but only with being heard and understood on that particular heart's own terms.

"But, good people, be forewarned: That heart's terms, *my* heart's terms, are the terms of a heart that is hurt and angry and frightened. As most of you may have heard, I have had an odd and ugly relationship with childbirth and with death. My mother died while birthing me. My father died when I was young. My grandfather, who was my friend and mentor and larger than life, fell off his horse earlier this year and died. And two months ago, my young wife and unborn child both died, as had my mother, of a massive hemorrhage. And my wife's mother, who had become like a mother to me, died in a car wreck while rushing to join me in mutual commiseration.

"Good people: I have never been good at dealing with pain. I have never been good at dealing with deep feelings. And when all this happened, I was not only *not* good; I was very bad. I wrote my theses to channel my grief. No more reason than that, and no less. Yet today I find myself giving you a homily, from the pulpit, as if I'm an expert or a man of God. I am neither. In fact, so limited is my knowledge in most areas that I somehow prepared for different lessons and a different Gospel than the ones we have heard tonight. I thought all mainline Protestants used the same lectionary, but I am obviously mistaken. I prepared for the Episcopal readings today. So please bear with me."

There was a nervous fidgeting from some of the pews. Mad continued:

"Regardless of the proper readings, the problem of spiritual pain will not go away, especially from a layman too confused to focus on the correct Gospel passage for your lovely church. All I am is a young man to whom much of the teaching of the modern churches does not make sense. It does not square with the reality I've experienced. And, if you are honest with yourself, I dare say that it might not square with your experience either.

"Take today's Psalm. By sheer coincidence of the calendars of both the Episcopal church and the Methodist one, today's Psalm for both denominations is the most famous and comforting one in the whole Bible. At one point children learned it by heart by the time they were five or six years old; even today, it is part of the warp and woof of our most spiritual hearts. You all know the 23rd Psalm; we just recited it: 'The Lord is my shepherd, I shall not want, etcetera, etcetera... Even though I walk through the valley of the shadows of death, I shall fear no evil; for thou art with me, etcetera... Surely goodness and mercy shall follow me all the days of my life.'

"To all of which, good people, I say this: 'Yada yada yada, B.S. and yada some more.'"

From multiple places in the congregation arose an audible intake of breath, followed by a disturbed and perhaps angry buzz. Mad continued:

"People, this is baby food; this is a comforting fairy tale to tell us that all will be right with the world because nice kind Daddy in heaven will protect us. *Yeah, right.* Some protection.

"The first lesson that I prepared for today is from Acts. It is the story of Stephen, the pure and devoted disciple, a man described, as being, quote, 'full of faith and of the Holy Spirit.' And for his troubles, what kind of mercy did Stephen receive? He was stoned to death for preaching the Gospel.

"And then, in what I thought was supposed to be today's second lesson, there is the First Letter of Peter. Peter, or the anonymous author writing in Peter's name, recognizes how often those who do right are nevertheless forced to suffer, or at least allowed to suffer. 'For one is approved,' Peter writes, 'if, mindful of God, he endures pain while suffering unjustly ... But if when you do right and suffer for it you take it patiently, you have God's approval. For to this you have been called, because Christ also suffered for you, leaving you an example, that you should follow in his steps.' And so on and so forth, until Peter writes that by Christ's wounds 'you have been healed.'

"Well, good people, I don't know about healing. I don't know when the magic moment occurs when somebody unjustly victimized becomes more healed than he is suffering. But I do know this: The Bible is full of unmerited suffering. So are the stories of the Christian saints. And the Old Testament especially is full of stories of suffering not just allowed by God – which would be bad enough – but caused directly by God. God caused Job to suffer merely so He, God, could prove a point to his evil counterpart. God demanded of Abraham that Abe be willing to sacrifice his own son, the pride and love of his life, just to prove Abraham's own obedience to God. And God did not lift a finger when I lost my mother and my father and my grandfather and my wife and my child and my mother-in-law, each of them well before their time.

"And God allows innocent children in sub-Saharan Africa to suffer and starve and bloat and die. He allows innocent children in our inner cities to be terrorized by crack-addicted parents. And this suffering is so very unwarranted.

"And you out there in the fourth pew: Yes, you in the navy-blue dress. Have you never suffered, not from your own mistakes nor from the cruelty of other people, but from seemingly random acts of fate? I bet you have. And you two rows further back, in the tan suit with the flowered tie: Haven't you at times felt like the world, God's world, did you harm you did not deserve?

"Conversely, to all of you, I ask: Do you really fear no evil when you walk or hobble or even crawl through the valley? Do you have a table prepared for you in the sight of your enemies?

"Of course not. Not if you are honest. More likely, there have been times in all your lives, dark times, when as in the letter to the Romans – in a passage that became my 18th thesis, from the King James version – 'We know that the whole creation groaneth and travaileth in pain together until now.' And later in Romans, also quoted in my theses, for God's sake 'we are killed all the day long; we are accounted as sheep for the slaughter.'

"Yes, people, this is the God that we worship. Does He sound much like one worth worshipping?"

One couple about three-quarters of the way back in the congregation gathered up their three young children and ostentatiously walked out of the church. A clearly unhappy murmur spread through many of the other pews. Mad could feel a nervous sweat trickling down the back of his neck. But he knew he was ready to turn the theme around, and so he pressed forward.

"And yet… and yet and yet and yet. Yet in all this pain and all this suffering, suffering that an all-powerful God surely could alleviate if he chose, still we believers have an ace in the hole. Still, we believers have hope, and still we believers have life. Our faiths, our hopes, our very lives, find their redemption in the Gospel. They find their redemption in the person of Jesus of Nazareth, whom we call the Christ. In what I thought was today's Gospel, John chapter 10 a few verses before our own readings today actually begin, Jesus says it concisely. 'I am the door of the sheep,' he says. 'I am the door; if anyone enters by me, he will be saved, and will go in and out and find pasture. … I came that they may have life, and have it abundantly.'

"Yes, suffering does occur. God allows or sometimes forces suffering to occur. And some of that suffering is decidedly undeserved. Some of us, probably all of us at times, are victims, pure and simple. But the same God who so messed up his own creation, and who still so messes it up, has sent us a Christ to represent God's own ultimate will: His ultimate will that, in the end, regardless of our own many many egregious mistakes and of God's own failings as well, we will all be reconciled together, we and God, if we have faith, through the mediation of the Christ who is God's only perfect creation. Our suffering will continue, but with Christ we now have everlasting life, with the 23rd Psalm's clear still waters, to look forward to. That everlasting life in Christ's love may be exceedingly small comfort now, but it is all the comfort we have, and it might just be enough comfort for us, to know that some time in what seems the far-too-distant future, some time when life is done, a better and more comforting and more loving life awaits. Christ is our door to that life, and it is toward that door we must always aim our steps.

"Finally, I dare say that our steps will lead us to that door more readily, more surely and unambiguously, if we walk in love with the world around us, with the people around us, each one of us lending a shoulder, each one of us there to pick another off the ground if one falls.

"This is the message of the Gospel; this is the message of our hope. And while it may sometimes seem paltry indeed in times of pain and trouble, it may still be message enough if we trust enough and believe enough and pray enough to let it be so.

"Therefore, in all our anger and all our pain and all our weak humanity, let us nevertheless praise the Father for giving us his Son, and praise the Son for giving us our hope, world without end, Amen."

As Mad walked back to his seat, the church was engulfed in utter silence that lasted a good 15 seconds. But when the celebrant audibly gulped and then began the prayer that continued the service, the two reporters clicked off their tape recorders, grabbed their notebooks, and walked purposefully down the aisles to the church entrance and from thence back to their respective haunts. Both had latched onto the same segment of Mad's homily that they were sure would get their reports decent attention….

After the service, a number of the congregation exited quickly, many with pursed lips and angry glares. The cameras outside caught their expressions. But a couple hundred stayed for a reception with Mad in the church's meeting hall, and dozens crowded around him excitedly wanting to shake his hand and thank him for inspiring them. Even though both Don and especially Becky tried to stay right by Mad's side, three women in their 20s each managed to slip phone numbers into Mad's pockets. An intense 17-year-old boy tried to argue with Mad, but his mother pulled him away. An older man, who could only be described as elegant, briefly monopolized Mad's attention; he kept calling Mad 'my dear boy' and alternately praising and refuting various of Mad's homiletics. And the lead minister stood fairly close by, perfectly gracious but with a decidedly uncomfortable smile painted, with great effort, on his face.

* * *

At nine Central time, the Rev. Bill White opened his nationally broadcast radio program with a sorrowful warning against "a new, sinful voice of anger." He meant Mad. The Rev. White was a nominal Southern Baptist, both ally and rival of the Rev. Rob Patterson and a onetime lieutenant of the Rev. Larry Falstaff before branching off and making a name for himself. Pudgy and wholly unimpressive in person, he had a perfect voice for radio and a knack for using deliberate understatement in a kind of reverse-psychological way that made his points all the stronger for sounding so reasonable. The radio reporter in the Methodist church was White's top assistant.

"I don't want to unduly prejudice the opinions of you, my faithful listeners, against this poor confused young man who calls himself 'Mad,'" White said. "I'll let you decide for yourselves. Here's what Mad Jones, speaking right here in Houston less than three miles from my ministry office, had to say about our beloved 23rd Psalm."

A tape of Mad's voice began to roll: "You all know the 23rd Psalm; we just recited it: 'The Lord is my shepherd, I shall not want, etcetera, etcetera… Even though I walk through the valley of the shadows of death, I shall fear no evil; for thou art with me, etcetera… Surely goodness and mercy shall follow me all the days of my life.'

"To all of which, good people, I say this: 'Yada yada yada, B.S. and yada some more.' People, this is baby food; this is a comforting fairy tale to tell us that all will be right with the world because nice kind Daddy in heaven will protect us. *Yeah, right.* Some protection."

The Rev. White continued: "But that's not all this poor, deluded boy had to say. Later in his sermonette, he continued his shall-we-say 'unique' version of witnessing to the Lord's works."

Tape again: "More likely, there have been times in all your lives, dark times, when as in the letter to the Romans – in a passage that became my 18th thesis, quoting from the King James version – 'We know that the whole creation groaneth and travaileth in pain together until now.' And later in Romans, also quoted in my theses, for God's sake 'we are killed all the day long; we are accounted as sheep for the slaughter.'

"Yes, people, this is the God that we worship. Does He sound much like one worth worshipping?"

Again the Rev. White: "Okay, listeners, you have heard the words of Mr. Jones. Some would say they sound immoderate. Some would say they sound impudent. Some would say they even sound blasphemous.

Yes, I dare say many would say they sound blasphemous, but who am I to judge? Let he who has not sinned cast the first stone. But I myself, I the sinner, feel confident in saying at least this much. I say that Madison Jones is not spreading a message that godly people will agree with. I say that the pain of some devastating losses – and yes, people, you should all know in this young man's defense that he has suffered the untimely death of a number of loved ones – I say the pain of his losses has led him at least a little bit astray.

"I am not angered by his words. Who am I, a sinner, to be angry? But some of you listeners may be angry. And if you are, it is undoubtedly a righteous anger. There is sinful anger, the anger of improperly challenging God, the anger displayed so prominently by Madison Jones. And then there is righteous anger, the anger of those who proclaim the Gospel and those who seek the truth, the anger of the Elect company of believers. And I know many of you fall into that company, and I will not dissuade you from your anger. God may indeed forgive this boy, but forgiveness is God's to grant; forgiveness of egregious sin is not our province. Our province – or rather, your province, dear godly listeners who are not guilty of my own sins of false pride – yes, I say, your province is to decide for yourselves whether the words of Madison Jones will go uncontested, or instead whether you will warn your flocks against what you know in your hearts is the dangerous and heretical notion that God is not to be worshipped and loved and praised.

"The choice is up to you. You can stand up for God, or you can stand silently by and let sinfully angry words go unchallenged. I am not one to say what is sinful, for I am a sinner. But if you yourselves recognize sin, then call a spade a spade and identify the sin for what it is and go ahead and denounce it.

"In sum, Madison Jones makes me sorrowful at the same time he seems to insult those of you who have been born again in the Spirit. May God show mercy upon his sinful soul. ... Now, I'll be back after these brief commercial messages."

* * *

Mad's web site was sleepy on Sunday night; not many of the true "regulars" listened to the Rev. White's show, so they were unaware of his commentary. But Defender was a White devotee, and he blistered Mad in three lengthy entries. In addition to ripping Mad on substance, he also noted that not only had Mad used the Episcopal lectionary instead of the Methodist one, but that he had also used the readings from the wrong year in the three-year Episcopal cycle. "Not only is he obnoxious," Defender wrote of Mad in his final comment of the night, "but he doesn't know enough about his faith to fill a chalice even halfway. Somebody needs to muzzle this guy, and soon."

* * *

Also that night, Shiloh Jones paced back and forth across his bedroom floor, quite upset, while LaShauna sat propped up in bed with a romance novel. Shiloh often listened to the Rev. White, and tonight he had been stunned by what he had heard.

"I just can't believe Mad said that!" Shiloh repeated for about the fifth time. "I mean, that's just wrong, calling the Lord's word 'yada yada and BS.' And especially in the 23rd Psalm! My mother always made me recite that one when I was growing up. Mad just *couldn't* have meant it! There must be more to what he said!"

LaShauna put down her book. "Honey, I got two things to say," she said, with some exasperation. "First, I think he's got a point. That Psalm sounds all pretty, but it ain't reality. Reality ain't so pretty. That ain't God's word; that Psalm is the words of some Hebrew way back then who wanted his world to seem nicer than it was."

Shiloh hated when LaShauna got like this, so he pretended he hadn't heard it. If he really had to acknowledge to himself that that was how she saw the world, it would have upset him too much.

"Mad MUST have said more than that," he continued. "I've seen it happen for weeks now: The press only reports part of what he says, the part that sounds most controversial, and they don't do justice to the whole man. I don't agree with everything he says, but his heart is in the right place – and now even Rev. White isn't giving the whole picture!"

"Honey, you're getting too upset, especially over a white man." Now LaShauna was going places Shiloh really couldn't abide. "That's the second thing I wanted to say. He might've been nice to you, made you think your opinion's important or something. But you know damn well that when it really comes down to it, Mad Jones just thinks of your opinion as an interesting little sideshow. He still sees you as a BLACK man; ain't no white guy gonna put your opinion above what white power says to him."

"That's ENOUGH, LaShauna! That's just not true! This man is a friend of mine."

"Ain't no white man really your friend, honey, not even one who I think makes lotsa sense. You just be careful now."

Her tone was less sympathetic than it was hectoring. Shiloh didn't answer. He clenched his fists, walked out of the bedroom, and out his front door. He sat on the curbside for nearly an hour, staring into the night.

* * *

The next morning, Houstonians who turned to the first page of the local-news section of the Houston paper were greeted by a headline just below the fold: "Homilist Pans 23rd Psalm." The longer subhead read: "Jones Calls Psalm 'Baby Food,' 'Fairy Tale.'/ Says God Allows Too Much Suffering."

A sleepy Mad read it en route to Galveston, as Becky chauffered in icy silence and Don, in the back seat, dutifully made a list of the benefits and drawbacks of the coverage thus far. Mad was pleased to see that one member of the congregegation, a woman identified as Diana Evans, was quoted saying that "You had to listen to his whole homily to get his message, which was that Christ makes everything right and offers us hope. I thought Jones was inspiring."

But another man, who wouldn't give his name, said he was "greatly offended, not only by Jones' message, but also because he didn't even do his homework. He based his whole offensive homily on the wrong Gospel passage and the wrong lessons. It showed a great disrespect for our congregation, and it shows he's too uninformed to pay any attention to at all. He doesn't need to preach; he just needs therapy."

"Help me, Claire," Mad silently said to the heavens. "If you can hear me, please help me."

A vision flashed into his mind. A green-eyed brunette looked down at him, laughingly, from the lap of a statue of a priest, patriot, and prelate, and he began to clamber up after her, knowing that a first kiss would be his prize.

* * *

Outside the civic club meeting in Galveston, a bearded man with wild eyes shouted epithets as he ran up, shaking his fist angrily, to where Mad was climbing out of the rental car. A security guard intercepted him and led him away.

Mad's speech there followed the same lines as his homily the evening before, but today Mad somehow found the grace and humor to make fun of himself for having used the Episcopal reading schedule instead of the Methodist one. He added an awful pun: "I guess my preparations weren't Method-ical, or maybe not Methodistical, enough."

Also, at Don's suggestion, "yada yada yada B.S." became "and so on and so on," and "fairy tale" became "a reassuring story."

In short, Mad took some of the edge off. And unlike in the church, today's breakfast meeting allowed about 10 minutes for post-speech Q&A. Somehow Mad had touched the good side of most of the audience, so the Q&A actually produced some lighthearted banter.

"Mad, I understand that last night you called the 23rd Psalm a fairy tale," said one 40ish businessman, obviously the club's resident wag, trying ineffectually to be funny. "Are you talking Brothers Grimm here, or more like Mother Goose?"

Mad said the first thing that popped into his head. "Well, the Psalm talks about a shepherd, so maybe it's more along the lines of Little Bo Peep," he said. Some people chuckled at the inanity of the exchange, but others looked offended, so Mad quickly added: "Seriously, the Psalm is lovely poetry. I'm not trying to put down the people who build their faiths around its imagery. It just doesn't work for me, at least not now." Then, not wanting to lose the lighthearted mood that had developed, he added: "Maybe that makes me a 'Baa Baa Blacksheep' for questioning the Psalm at all, but last I checked, God still offers forgiveness even to black sheep, so maybe there's hope for me yet."

* * *

In the ride back to Houston, Becky showed at least a smidgen of life and decent humor for the first time this entire trip.

"Hey, Loverboy, maybe I won't murder you after all," she said. "You actually charmed some of those people."

"Charmed" became an understatement at the next meeting – the women's auxiliary meeting in Houston. Most of the women were old enough to be his mother, a few old enough to be his grandmother – and Mad flirted shamelessly with them all. Before, during and after his speech, he made lots of eye contact, winked a few times, smiled a lot, and made wryly, ever-so-slightly risqué comments every chance he could. He didn't really know why, but he was on a roll.

Also, even more than in Galveston, the bitter edges fell from his speech, the angry tone softened to a mere sorrowful one, and the redemptive elements took on more life and more power.

"So therefore, in all our anger and all our pain and all our weak humanity," Mad began to sum up, "let us all nevertheless praise the Father for giving us his Son, and praise the Son for giving us our hope – and praise our mothers and sisters and wives and daughters for keeping us civilized enough and loved enough and inspired enough to latch on to the hope for everything we're worth, world without end, Amen."

"Madison, can I adopt you?" asked the first woman, age 60-or-so, to reach the microphone after his speech.

"Forget adoption; will you marry me?" shouted another one, in her early 40s, to peals of laughter.

"Hell, Marge, forgit marriage!" yelled still a third. "How 'bout just a nice little torrid affair?"

The room broke up.

Only problem was, TV cameras and microphones, attracted by that morning's headlines, were there recording the whole thing. The mood in the banquet hall was warm and light, but the electronic media couldn't capture the atmosphere. What the newscasts would show that night was a seeming non-sequitur of cropped footage with a young man saying that God allows innocent children to suffer, and then clearly winking at an unseen audience member, and then laughing as a clearly fading former beauty yelled out that she wanted to marry him – all punctuated by the shallow narration of hair-sprayed news anchors reading scripts written by uncomprehending producers. The impression created was that of a bizarre cult-like gathering.

Leaving the banquet hall, Mad and Becky were startled to see the mime waiting for them, with yet another camera recording the scene. This time he was dressed to impressively detailed effect as a rampant lion, fully maned, holding aloft a banner saying, "Hear God's Mad roar!"

"That guy's *everywhere!*" whispered Mad to Becky as they walked out of earshot. "New Orleans, Mobile, and now all the way over here in Houston!"

"Geez, doesn't he have a *life?*" Becky responded.

* * *

By the time they reached San Antonio after an afternoon's drive, the internet, radio, and news wires had all ginned up further interest in Mad's appearance. Word was out that the guy who had called God a jerk was now saying that the 23rd Psalm was baby food and a fairy tale; yet somehow, he was attracting a bigger and bigger following that included women so devoted they were calling out marriage proposals to him. Further, Mad's disciples included a mime most recently dressed up as a lion, while national conservative religious leaders took highly public shots at him and a heated web-site debate raged between characters known as Formerly Doubting Thomas, Defender, and Cowardly Lion, the latter of whom was clearly a loose cannon. This was a freak show, soap opera and religious dispute all wrapped up into one, and it made great theater.

More media, protesters, supporters, and curious onlookers greeted Mad, Becky and Don as they arrived at the hotel where the young professional club had rented a meeting room. Don tried to run interference with the reporters and cameramen, but the rest of the crowd, maybe 50 strong, was unwieldy and security was either nonexistent or so weak as to be wholly ineffective. Pushing through the crowd, even the friendly component, was a decidedly unpleasant experience, and Becky was sure that some moisture she felt on one of her arms was the result of somebody spitting on them.

Mad was already tired from the long day. Public speaking, especially with lots of travel involved, can be exhausting. As a new experience it can be downright draining. Now, with the added element of an unruly crowd, Mad felt shaken and very "off his game."

Also, even though the day's two meetings had gone fairly well, Don had strongly advised him to alter his approach to the Yuppies and make it less sermon-like, less overtly religious, somehow more of a generic exhortation to personal growth and hope through self-sufficiency. The instructions, and what he thought was an implicit criticism of his approach, perplexed him. How could he make a religious topic less religious?

Being tired, frazzled and confused also made Mad nervous. As he hobnobbed with Yuppie strangers sipping wines and beers in the pre-meeting reception, he felt a fiasco brewing. Then when the official program started, the club president introduced him in a sort of smirking fashion (although, on the surface, entirely politely), as if this month's meeting represented a break from serious topics in favor of what amounted to a curiosity piece just for fun. One of those super-serious, break-the-glass-ceiling types of young women, the president seemed oblivious to any reason why Mad's message should prove attractive.

On the other hand, Becky's fine looks were attracting serious attention from some of the young men, including three with wedding rings on their fingers who appeared to be imbibing heavily. The ring-wearers she tried to ignore, but two others were very handsome, confident, and quite obviously successful. They were just the type she would like to disappear with for a while if she didn't feel the need to nursemaid Mad for the sake of her nascent business venture. The result was that when an out-of-sorts Mad tried to catch her eye for a reassuring glance, she greeted him instead with a kind of resentful indifference before returning her focus to the Yuppies vying for her attention.

So, by the time Mad took the microphone, he felt utterly lost.

"Hello, everybody, and thank you for having me here," he began, uninspiringly. "I come tonight as a rather befuddled participant in a growing enterprise that I began without intending to do so. I'm a high school history teacher at heart, not a preacher or a theologian.

"But I bet my kind of story isn't new to many of you. I bet many of you left college certain you were on track for a particular job, only to find that you have not only changed jobs but entire careers for reasons you never would have imagined even a few short years before. The old orthodoxy of climbing the corporate ladder, rung by rung, just doesn't apply any more. Similarly, I've found in the past few months that a religious orthodoxy I had neither questioned nor particularly thought much about has turned out not to fit my life or my experiences or my heart."

Then Mad segued into lines from his sermon of the night before.

"*My* heart's terms, I must admit, are now the terms of a heart that is hurt and angry and frightened. As most of you may have heard, I have had an odd and ugly relationship with childbirth and with death...." Mad went into hisw litany of woe. But this time, Mad's delivery was flat. He sounded not at all compelling, but whiny. No decent response, no positive energy, came his way from the audience. Mad began to sweat.

"Anyway, you all probably know the story. As a way to cope, I wrote a bunch of religious propositions, more to work through my own grief than for any other reason. Then, in an almost catatonic state of grief, I posted them at a bunch of churches, and that caused a bunch of trouble, and now here I am making a bunch of speeches."

Mad had little idea where he was going with this, and his whole demeanor showed it. He saw a number of people fidgeting in their chairs as if trying to force themselves to pay attention, perhaps even to keep from dozing off. The room was a little too warm.

Still, he went on: "And I guess there is a point to what I've been saying, but some TV and media reports would make you think my whole point is that God's a jerk or that the 23rd Psalm is nonsense or that, I don't know, maybe even that we're better than God Himself is. People hear me complaining about how I've suffered or how Job suffered in the Bible or how life is unfair or whatever, and … and… and, well, they miss the point, or at least what I think my point is…. when I'm thinking at all, which some people may say I'm not doing."

Mad was trying vaguely to be self-deprecatingly funny, trying vaguely to find the thread of a message, and trying haphazardly to give his audience a reason to show some life. He was floundering badly, and he knew it. Desperate, he threw up a Hail Mary pass.

"So let's cut to the chase," he said, still not knowing exactly what his next sentence would be. Stalling, he interjected: "I love saying that: cut to the chase. It makes me think of Meg Ryan saying that line, I think it was in that movie *The Presidio*. Let's cut to the chase. Here's what the chase is. … The chase is this. …"

Something, something angry, frustrated, wild and irrepressible clicked in Mad's brain, and he just let fly:

"The chase is the quest to make some sense of our lives by getting ahead in business, or getting laid, or getting some notoriety, or by doing any number of things to make ourselves feel important.

"And you know what? It's all crap. It's all a bunch of self-aggrandizing, onanistic crap!

"Because you know what really matters? What really matters is the integrity that shows itself in doing good for its own sake, whether anybody notices or not and whether there is a God to reward us or not. What matters is the wholeness that comes from loving people and loving this world for the sake of those people and the sake of this world.

"And what does God have to do with any of this? Why is it that what I've said and written has anything to do with God? Because that's how I believe God loves us and loves this world. Just as, even with the best of intentions, we make others suffer; and just as our own actions or failure to act can force or allow suffering to happen in a way that, we tell ourselves, we have no control over, so too I think that a not-quite-perfect God allows suffering and even causes it, but in his heart of hearts He would rather that we not suffer. In my own view, Jesus is his emissary to tell us and show us that suffering is not necessarily eternal and that redemption is always possible.

"And our petty, onanistic concerns can get in the way of recognizing and grabbing hold of those redemptive possibilities. Our striving to get ahead for any reason other than to improve our deepest selves, to improve our wholeness and integrity … that kind of striving, for reasons other than these, is just crap!

"So go out and love somebody today. Go out and love the world today. And while you're at it, go out and love God today, because in the course of loving we find small but wonderful redemptions all along the way."

Mad paused and considered whether to say any more. He couldn't think of anything else. He was spent.

"Anyway, that's all I have to say right now. I don't know if it made any sense to you all, and if it didn't then I guess I'm outta luck. Thanks for listening to me rant."

With that, he turned from the podium. He felt claustrophobic and dizzy, and he had to leave. With applause, angry shouts, questions, reverent compliments, and offended glances all surrounding him in a great big jumble, Mad hurried from the meeting room without another word. He and Becky and Don were all staying in separate rooms at that very hotel, and he hustled to the elevator and up to his room without waiting for Becky and Don to catch up. Pushing through his door, he roughly slung the "Do Not Disturb" sign onto the outer doorknob and fell into a bed and waited for his heart to slow down and his head to stop spinning. What in the Lord's name had he gotten himself into?

* * *

In the crowd at the young professional meeting, some were clearly inspired by Mad's sudden intensity and by his challenge to them to seek redemptive possibilities. Others, perhaps a majority, were deeply angered by his message and his attitude, and furious at his abrupt departure. Don dutifully went to work trying to spin the media and soothe the fury of the club president. Becky decided Mad was so maddening that he wasn't even worth worrying about, at least not for that night. Of the two young men she was most interested in that evening, she made a hard choice and slowly (and expertly) blew one off while signaling the other that she was open to his company. Even if it just led to a nice one-night stand, well ... she was a *Sex in the City* aficionado. She had been working hard and deserved a chance to play.

The guy she chose, name of Brad, was stereotypically tall, dark, and handsome. He sold her on a jazz club on San Antonio's famous riverfront called Jim Cullum's Landing. Nice place. Great photographs of old-time jazz musicians graced the walls. Lots of people having fun, enjoying the music. But Becky had anticipated that the music would be Charlie-Parker-like, or Miles Davis. This, though, was something she wasn't used to; it was the *really* old stuff, the stuff that came out of New Orleans in like the 1920s or something. She could vaguely understand its appeal, but it just wasn't her thing. As it turned out, neither was Brad. She had been attracted by his obvious physical attributes, and by his apparent wealth. She thought he might be a good lay. But as they sat in the jazz club, his vanity overwhelmed her. He was interested in Brad, Bradself, and Bradley, and secondarily interested in how lucky Becky would feel if she gave herself to Brad, Bradself and Bradley. As frustrated as Becky was, as much in need of a little diversion to work out her frustrations from these last few months and from her uncomfortable visit back home the day before, Bradley wasn't the answer by a long shot. By 10:30, she convinced him to escort her back to the hotel, where she left him in the lobby without a backward glance. Once finally in bed, she wanted to cry, but mercifully and quickly fell asleep instead.

Her sleep was a good thing, too. As was Mad's. Both needed the sleep in order to face the newspaper and radio stories the next morning. The newspaper helpfully pointed out that "onanistic" meant "masturbatory," and a regional radio talk show was having a field day with Mad's remarks. Phone-in lines at the station were so busy that the technician thought the system might crash. Some callers were thrilled that Mad had "told it like it was," and seemed to revel in the idea of somebody speaking bluntly to a bunch of "stuffed shirt" Yuppies. Many others were offended beyond belief that a speaker on a religious topic had used language as coarse as "onanistic crap."

Not only that, but word was also out, even in areas whose daily papers did not carry Mad's advice column, that his column that morning had dealt with sex. In answer to a writer's question, Mad had written that, as far as he could tell, pre-marital sex among never-married people did not qualify as "adultery," and that it was not his role to either encourage or discourage it for consenting adults. His point was that "this is a matter of morality and ethics to be determined within and through the web of relationships that may include family and priest, pastor or rabbi. The potentially important faith considerations make it a question that should, in theory at least, be considered prayerfully. No one knows with certainty what God thinks about this issue (or any other), but it is a certainty that sins of the flesh have the potential to put up barriers between man and God."

At one of the 17 papers carrying the column, a headline writer who was either less-than-careful or else a deliberate muck-stirrer had titled that column thusly: "God May Not Frown/ On Pre-Marital Sex." The radio talk show host, alerted via e-mail, was naturally all over that one.

By the time the now-sullen MMW threesome reached Austin for their luncheon, all Hades seemed ready to break as loose as a runaway barge down the mighty Mississippi.

Amazingly, the mime had somehow managed to make his way to Austin, still in his lion suit, and he was using hand-signals to lead a group of maybe 60 or 70 supporters in cheers of "Mad is good! Mad is good!" A number of the supporters looked college age or else immediate-post-college Bohemian types.

But even in the "hip" town of Austin, they were mostly drowned out by unhappy protesters, some business-suited, some conservative at-home-mom attired, some grandmotherly, and some of the righteously-well-groomed-but-intensely-angry-young-man variety. One hundred strong had gathered to denounce Mad's dangerously libertine and profane messages. Security was reasonably tight, but nevertheless someone managed, unseen by officers, to hurl over the crowd several stones, one of which missed Becky's forehead by inches and another of which actually grazed the shoulder of Mad's suit jacket. So it was a frightened Becky and an angrily befuddled Mad that entered the country club restaurant. Even Don, whose whole persona and professional conceit relied on an air of unflappability, seemed for once not only flappable but positively flapped.

The country clubbers in attendance had signed up for what had been marketed as an interesting talk on religion by a nice-but-galvanizing young man who was becoming "all the rage" for in-the-know people to talk about if they wanted a "serious" topic other than Lewinsky. What they got instead was this rabble outside, and a speaker whose mood was better suited for a fight, rather than a speech.

Unintroduced, Mad took the microphone even before the waiters had finished filling the water and iced-tea glasses.

"Hello, everybody, I'm obviously Madison Jones," he said. "Look, every time I give a speech or write something down or give an interview, some media muckraker takes my points out of context and turns what I hope are nuanced thoughts into a controversial caricature. So today I'm scrapping the nuance, and I'm scrapping any set speech. All I'm gonna say is that life can be something other than a beach, and that I think an omnipotent God who is also all-loving could, if he wanted to, and probably should, ease some of the suffering – but that even with all the suffering that God unreasonably allows, we are still better off, still better people, still more whole and still more fully human in the best sense and, yes, still more blessed, if we are in relationship with God than we are without Him. That's it. Pretty simple, really. Any questions?"

The floodgates opened. Questions flowed in from front, left, back, and right. Some were approving, some comforting in tone, some angry, some challenging, some searching, some excited, some flustered, some confused. With no holds barred, Mad answered every one with penetrating directness. Take it or leave it, his whole demeanor said. This is how I think, and for some odd reason people are paying attention to what and how I think, so let'er rip. Love, sex, death, time, God, redemption, intellectual and spiritual rebellion, subservience to greater goods and higher understandings, and the ceaseless human quest – quoting Tennyson – "to strive, to seek, to find, and not to yield": All of these and more were topics over and through which Mad roamed for the next solid hour and a half. Agree or disagree with what he said, or even whether able or unable to follow the logic (or, arguably, lack thereof), it was a tour de force. At the end, the enraged and the enthused alike gave Mad a roaring and vociferous ovation more fit for a union hall than a country club ballroom.

The MMW threesome flew home that evening as if in the thralls of an epiphany. And the "buzz" about Mad, that he was a young man to behold, grew and grew and spread and spread. Among the many dozens of participants that night in a web site debate that raged on past midnight, it was an exchange between the Cowardly Lion, Perdicaris, and some new guys called "The Scot" and "Ever Faithful" that caught the mood the best.

"I think Mad is showing great courage," wrote the Lion. "And as you know, I'm an expert on the need for courage, since it took the

Wizard to help me find my own. If he keeps his courage up, he'll be able to overcome the flying monkeys. If he doesn't – watch out!"

"Aye, but ye'll soon be in trouble beyond your ken if ye have nought but courage without some sense of how the world works and how ye need to pick your spots," wrote The Scot. "I'm all for what the young man is saying, but there's a time to charge like William Wallace and a time to plan and plot your moves. 'Hidden bunkers' aren't hidden if ye walk the course beforehand to plan your approach. That's what Jones must do if he's to survive and keep doing good work."

Ever Faithful shot back: "I think my man Defender has gone to bed, so I'm carrying this argument alone right now, but I have enough of that idiot lion's courage to say that you all are a bunch of fools. Jones isn't avoiding bunkers; he IS a bunker. The only way to God's green is to follow the way, the truth, and the light, and what this nincompoop Jones is preaching is nothing but a hazard. Follow Christ, my friends, and sin no more."

Perdicaris responded: "Sin, schmin. You worry about sin, I'll take redemption any day. Mad makes me feel able to be redeemed. That's good enough for me."

(Cowardly Lion, offended, also made a retort. "I resent being called an idiot. It wasn't me without a brain; that was the scarecrow. Get your story straight!")

Chapter Three

"Young Alabama preacher causes stir," read the headline of a small story buried on page B-7 of the next morning's *New Orleans Times-Picayune*. The story identified Mad as the young man who first came to prominence by posting his theses at the Crescent City's St. Louis Cathedral, and then briefly summarized the controversy he had fomented during his Texas stops and in the previous day's spiritual advice column. Grace rarely got that far into the morning paper before taking her kids to school; but she saw the headline when that particular page fell out in the course of her using the paper to swat at a mosquito that found its way into her Uptown house. Taken from an Associated Press wire account that ran in dozens of papers across the country, the article described the growing unruliness of the crowds that greeted Mad's appearances. It reported Mad's dismissal of the 23rd Psalm, his use of the words "crap" and "onanism," and his refusal to condemn premarital sex. Then, as if he had used "sex" and "love" interchangeably, it quoted the penultimate lines from his "onanism speech" in San Antonio: "Go out and love somebody today. Go out and love the world today. And while you're at it, go out and love God today, because in the course of loving we find small but wonderful redemptions all along the way." The effect made him sound like a late 1960s "free love" enthusiast.

But for Grace, the apparent sexual context was background noise. Something in those lines struck her the way Mad had meant them, in a way that spoke of attitudes of the spirit. As she hustled her ever-squabbling kids off to school and, later, herself to work, the last two phrases reverberated in her consciousness. "Go out and love God today, because in the course of loving we find small but wonderful redemptions along the way." Grace felt again what she had lately begun to realize, namely that she had never developed a full understanding of what love is. She had thought she loved her ex-husband, but in retrospect, something vital was always missing. She knew she loved her kids, unruly as they were, with a love that ached and consumed her. But even that wasn't what Mad seemed to be talking about; her love for her kids was like loving two extensions of herself that she could advise and direct but could not control.

Somehow, though, she sensed from those few short newspaper lines that Mad was talking about something different. Something so different it unnerved her and inspired her simultaneously.

But how could someone love an amorphous entity like God, especially one for which, unicorn-like, there was no empirical evidence of existence? Grace had major difficulties with the whole "God" concept.

And what did "redemption" really mean? What events, what occurrences, qualified as "redemptions"? And why did these questions nag at her so insistently? Why were they so compelling? Her occasional childhood visits to a synagogue had meant almost nothing to her; no majesty or mystery impressed itself upon her psyche. And her visit last month to Apostles of the Word was like being beamed onto an alien planet. People writhing and speaking in tongues, and a loud-voiced preacher interpreting Mad's blackberry story as if it were a wise and thoughtful parable: Was this what the Christian religion was all about?

Thanks, but no thanks.

And yet… and yet. Every single time during these past few months that she had seen reports of Mad's doings, something about his words or his actions had moved her. And she was sure that it wasn't exclusively Mad himself, but rather his message. If Mad stood before a crowd and extolled the majesty of the game of baseball, Grace was sure she would *not* have been so moved.

God…. Redemption…. Love…. Why did these considerations, these ill-defined concepts, bother her so much? Grace just could not let go of them.

As she entered the elevator of the downtown office building where she worked, she shuddered to see that the only person inside was the recently divorced partner in her boss's firm who was always making suggestive remarks to her – remarks that were just barely on the safe side of legally actionable as sexual harassment. *Sleazebag*. If she could invent a God, she thought, He would give this lawyer a severe case of excruciatingly itchy hives every time he even thought about a woman.

* * *

For Mad, the next several months roared by like a Gulf-fed squall, with unpredictable elements so stark and sudden they were frightening – yet, at the same time, strangely invigorating. Mad and Don were traveling four or five days of every other week, with Mad making speeches or homilies to a variety of cultural and civic groups, faith-based charities and Christian churches of virtually every denomination. (Becky always stayed back in the Mobile office; she had accompanied them on the first trip only because it was based out of her hometown of Houston.) Each trip was a roller coaster of highs and lows, of support and rejection, of well-crafted remarks that sometimes soared and sometimes fell utterly flat, and also of off-the-cuff rants that sometimes enraged the audience but more often won its awestruck allegiance by virtue of Mad's raw honesty and passion. Everywhere they went, Mad unintentionally found some new way to generate controversy. Everywhere they went, at least some in the crowds were angry enough to seem scary. Everywhere they went, a few of the media accounts were fair and accurate – but more accounts were sensationalized or hopelessly out of context. To believe some of the accounts, Mad was a stereotypical Southern white guy in unfocused revolt against a world he could not control; by other accounts he was the voice of a radical assault against traditional virtue.

He repeatedly earned the opprobrium either of the Rev. Rob Patterson or of the Rev. Bill White or, less caustically, of the Rev. Larry Falstaff. A number of charismatic churches organized noisy protests against his appearances. But Mad also found that among his heartiest admirers were ministers in still other charismatic churches who were thrilled, as the Rev. Hebert had been, by Mad's emphasis on redemption and ultimate reconciliation with God. At the four appearances Mad made at such churches in the next two months, Mad found that many of the worshippers were among the most warm and genuine he encountered anywhere, and also among the least cynical. And they certainly were generous: Three of the four insisted that as part of his visit, he devote some time or attention to one of the vast social-service ministries the churches oversaw. As for the Rev. Hebert, he repeatedly and politely pestered Becky to schedule a return visit by Mad and won assurances that one would be arranged soon.

As for Don, Mad never was exactly sure what he did, because the press' agenda always seemed impervious to Don's influence. But Becky insisted that Don was an integral part of the operation, and his personality was so generic and studiously inoffensive as to make him an acceptable traveling companion.

Don joined Becky (and Justin and, by phone, Buzz and Mary) in growing concern over the unruliness and near-violence of some of the mobs that greeted Mad on the road, but Mad learned to tune most of it out. Amazingly, the mime managed to show up for at least one stop of each bi-weekly excursion, once in San Diego, once in Columbus, Ohio, and once in Jacksonville, Florida.

Mad's daily column picked up seven more papers as subscribers as of June 1 – for a total now of 24 – and Steve Matheson took to quoting from it on "Gut Check" at least once a week. "And before I leave the air tonight," he'd say after a whole hour of Lewinsky talk, "my favorite young social commentator has done it again, with the kind of straight talk that I wish our politicians would emulate. This is a line from his column this morning, this one in response to one of those whiny letter writers who wants spiritual cover for having committed some unspecified indiscretion. I quote: 'God's not to blame, and neither is anybody else but you, if your suffering is self-inflicted.' Isn't that great? I mean, Mad Jones wasn't talking about anything having to do with politics, but I'd like to leave that as a parting thought for Bill Clinton tonight. The president's troubles right now are self-inflicted, and I say he needs to stop whining. That's 'Gut Check' for tonight. G'bye!"

Mad got a kick out of Matheson's enthusiastic support but was far less enthused by the attention he began receiving from renegade Catholic priests and sex-crazed, left-wing, mainline Protestant ministers. Just as the likes of Patterson, White, and sometimes Falstaff were demonizing Mad for their own purposes, so too were these leftist yahoos using random sentences from Mad to push their radical re-creation of Christianity in their own image. One said, quite approvingly, that Mad's ultimate message was that Jesus was a homosexual activist. Another, equally approvingly, somehow found in Mad's speeches support for the argument that Christ was a Marxist feminist vegetarian. A third interpreted a Mad column as a theologically sound call to arms against American hegemonism.

Mad, of course, had said and written nothing of the sort. Don dutifully put out press releases denouncing these misrepresentations, but few media outlets paid attention to them.

Meanwhile, a nationally renowned black activist, commonly referred to simply as "The Rev," ran with some otherwise forgettable, passing remark Mad had made in criticism of white racism.

"Here's a white mouth of the South," said The Rev, "who sees through the trees. Here's a man of the hour who speaks truth to power. The first Madison wrote the Constitution; today's Madison offers a solution. Follow the logic of his declaration, and it leads to reparations. America, the home of the brave, must do justice to the descendants of the slaves. The Lord is like a mighty river, and it's time for his people to deliver. Justice for African-Americans! Homage paid to African-Americans! Reparations for African-Americans! Justice now! Justice now! Justice now!"

It was enough to make Mad nauseous.

What sustained him were the times he spent, when not on the road, with friends back in Mobile. When he could escape Justin, he hung out and went for runs or golf games with his friend Jason, the math teacher and soccer coach. When Becky wasn't riding herd on him to prepare speeches and his newspaper columns, he sometimes vegged out in front of the TV tuned to ESPN. And he made time at least once a week to grab cups of coffee, always at Carpe Diem, while engaging in long discussions either with Shiloh Jones (with whom a genuine friendship had developed despite LaShauna's warnings) or with the semi-retired Jesuit, Peter Vignelli. Mad had called Vignelli the day after returning from his Texas tour and found in the priest the mentor he desperately needed.

One Saturday afternoon, Mad managed to get Shiloh and Father Vignelli to Carpe Diem at the same time.

"Look, Mad," Shiloh was saying, "I just watched *The Poseidon Adventure* on cable last night. And the way I see it, Gene Hackman's character made the same mistake you make in your theses. At the beginning of the movie, he's there preaching on the deck of the boat, and he goes on and on about how God loves winners and God wants you to be strong and self-reliant, and stuff about how we need to worship the part of God that is in ourselves, not the God up in heaven. And then the whole way up to where they're gonna get rescued, Hackman is yelling at God and acting like he, Hackman, is the one saving everybody while God tries to put roadblocks in their path. Well, look who dies: It's Hackman. Mr. Self-Reliant, Mr. God-inside-myself, is the one who dies. And where does he die? He falls into the fire, like he's falling into Hell. That's what worries me, Mad – I think you're a good man, but you're always talking about challenging God rather than obeying him, just like Gene Hackman did, and that's a sure way to let the devil pull you down to Hell. I don't want that to happen to you, Mad. And I think Father here probably agrees with me."

Mad started to protest, but Peter Vignelli responded first:

"Shiloh's basically right, Mad. One of the most major sins, a sin of the spirit more serious than many sins of the flesh, is pride so overblown that it puts the self above God and says, in effect, that we are responsible for our own salvation. You're right in your theses when you say that God wants us to try to be strong – to 'be lions,' as you put it – but that comes only after we acknowledge the far more difficult thing for us prideful humans to admit, which is that we are creatures who are very, very weak, especially spiritually weak. We lean on God to forgive our weakness and make us strong, and then with God's help we lend our own effort to living life.

"Maybe that wasn't clear enough. What I mean, and what the church has always taught, is that if we just give up, then won't be able to draw upon the strength that God gives us. So there is a sense that how we live depends on our own will and our own effort. But even with our own will and effort, our strength doesn't come from within ourselves; our strength comes from God, and our choice is whether to accept that strength and do something good with it, or to reject God's strength and live a life devoid of effort and meaning."

"But what if God is working against us?" Mad asked. "That's what Gene Hackman said at the end, that God was working against them. That's why Hackman had to die, as one more sacrifice that God either demanded or else sat back and let fate demand from the group Hackman was leading."

"God doesn't work against us," said Shiloh. "Satan does. Hackman was wrong to blame God for the work of Satan."

"Look, let's forget fiction for a moment," said Vignelli. "Mad, if this gets too uncomfortable, please stop me, and I'll use another example. But we've talked several times in the past few weeks about what happened in your life, and Shiloh here knows your basic story. Can I talk about Claire?"

Mad felt a chill and a shudder pass through him. But he nodded for the Jesuit to continue.

"I've told you how fond I was of Claire," said Vignelli. "Although you haven't explicitly said so, your logic in your theses seems to say you believe that God either caused what happened to Claire or else that he was at least indifferent to it – indifferent to her extreme sudden suffering and indifferent to the suffering that her death caused you to experience. Now I've grown fond of you just as I was fond of Claire, and I wouldn't worship a God who was indifferent to the suffering of a lovely girl like Claire or of a good and decent young man like you. The God I believe in is not indifferent to that suffering. He suffers with you, and …."

"But then you've got to say He's not omnipotent, then," Mad broke in. "Either He is omnipotent, in which case He can stop the suffering if the suffering is not part of His will, or else he's not all-powerful after all."

"That's the classic argument and the classic dilemma," the priest said. "But can't you see a third way? Can't you see that a God who neither desires our suffering nor is indifferent to it, nevertheless must allow it to occur, while He suffers along with us, if He is going to deal honestly with this world He has created?"

"Honestly?!?" Mad was perplexed and a little angry at Vignelli's words. "What does honesty have to do with it? Are you saying that God sort of sets the rules in advance, and that it wouldn't be right for Him to change them mid-course – that it would somehow break the rules for Him to step in every time or at least some of the time in order to stop sinless suffering from occurring? If God wanted to, couldn't he have created a world where He didn't face that kind of choice? Couldn't He have created a world where unmerited suffering didn't happen at all?

And if He could have done so, but didn't do so, then in some sense He is the original cause of the suffering and is responsible for it."

"But you're forgetting Satan," Shiloh broke in. "What if Satan is the one who introduced suffering into the world, and if Satan is so nearly as powerful as God is that God can't help but lose a lot of individual battles to Satan, little battles of suffering, even if God by the very nature of good over evil is destined to win out in the end because love is more powerful than hate. Am I making any sense to you?"

Round and round the three of them went on the selfsame topic that millions have debated, over dinner and over wine and in prisons and in churches and in other places of both horror and beauty, over the course of thousands of years. After a while their conversation went off on tangents, and at one point, strong Shiloh got teary-eyed when recounting something unintentionally hurtful that LaShauna had said to him that week, and at another point Peter Vignelli felt a deep ache when telling of the young woman whose love he had to abjure some four decades ago when he entered Catholic seminary and took a vow to wed himself to God and the church.

After well more than two hours the conversation hit a lull and a silence intruded in a way that begged its own removal.

"So…" Mad said, looking for a relief from the weight of their discussion, "…. How'bout that Mike Ditka? D'y'all think he's really got the Saints going in the right direction this year?"

Fifteen minutes later, all three were on their respective ways back home.

* * *

Becky wasn't able to enjoy any such interpersonal communion. She was working too hard running MMW, the work broken only by daily trips to a health club at odd hours that didn't afford her the chance to meet anybody interesting. Mad took her to lunch a couple of times a week, but otherwise left her to her own devices – and managed to evade being around her in any circumstances, especially at night, that might suggest any romantic possibilities.

Justin constantly found new excuses to ask her out, new "can't miss" events around Mobile or at the Gulf Shores beach an hour away – but she usually found excuses of her own for why she couldn't join him. To her big-city mind, "can't miss" in Mobile was usually very miss-able indeed, especially when a companion got on her nerves the way Justin did. One time, though, she did consent to joining Justin for a dinner with one of his potential "clients" for his MMW/physical training spinoff business, and Becky actually found the evening enjoyable. They and the client's husband went to dinner at a little place in West Mobile called "Guido's" that was carved out of a small wood-frame house, and she was surprised to find the meal to be of admirably high quality. For quite a reasonable price, Becky had a broiled fish smothered in some luscious lemon sauce, with a nice salad and fresh vegetables and two glasses of an exquisite white wine. The client, a 42-year-old trying hard, but only partially successfully, to maintain her figure, and her husband, a balding lawyer, both turned out to be excellent conversationalists. But what was most amazing was that Justin somehow managed, not only to contain his usual goofiness, but to contribute a few wry, perfectly timed lines that were actually quite funny. And she was touched when he said to the other couple, in all earnestness and without any sense of false flattery, that Mobile should feel lucky Becky had moved there because she brought with her a "radiance that can enlighten us all."

Sweet goofy annoying little Justin. He truly had a good heart.

For his part, Justin too was consumed with work. Using the "lion-hearted" themes from Mad's theses, Justin was trying to market (first regionally and then, hopefully, nationally) a body-and-spirit training regimen that he hoped would earn a fortune while spreading health and happiness to its adherents.

Not that he himself was really happy, if he had allowed himself to assess his own state of mind. Something was missing in his life. Something important. He missed, profoundly, the sense of being in a relationship with anybody else – romantic or friendly – who cared about him in any deep or meaningful way. Sure, there was his "good buddy" Mad, who had never pushed Justin away the way so many others (for some reason) seemed to do. But Mad these days was distracted, only intermittently "present" in the everyday world. When Mad wasn't on the road or working on MMW tasks, he would disappear to points unknown

(unknown at least to Justin). In any case, Mad certainly wasn't available for the kind of social bonding that Justin profoundly needed.

But that was okay, Justin kept telling himself. He, Justin Luke, knew that he was a winner. He knew he had a lionhearted attitude. And he knew that lovely sexy Becky would eventually see and be impressed by that attitude. He knew it, he told himself. He just knew it.

* * *

On June 26, a front-page story in the *New York Times* proclaimed "Vatican Settles a Historic Issue With Lutherans." The story went to the heart of Mad's main area of expertise as a historian, namely the dispute that had led Martin Luther to begin splitting from the Catholic Church in 1517. Mad's focus had always been less on the theology of the dispute (that was Claire's big interest) than on the societal and political changes that had exploded out of Luther's challenge. Still, he considered the apparent new accord a momentous development – and, as one who, like Luther, had posted theses on church doors, he was immediately besieged by the media for a response.

The argument, 481 years old, concerned the route to salvation. Luther's careful study of the Bible, especially the letters of Paul, led him to believe that salvation came not as a result of any works of man – not something earned, like brownie points – but only through grace from a God of mercy. Those who had faith in God's grace were saved *in spite of* the inevitable failure of their attempts to live sinless lives.

The Catholic Church, on the other hand, believed that although grace was the foremost cause of man's salvation, the grace became manifest only through good works, without which the grace almost always lay dormant and unredeemed. The Catholic Church feared that Luther's way would lead to a wholesale abandonment of good works, making society less orderly, more brutish and, what's worse, more licentious.

Luther, in increasingly intemperate language, insisted that the church was mistaken: that good works would not only continue, but be of purer motivation, if they were undertaken not in hopes of "earning" salvation but, instead, as a response to the salvation that had already been offered. Righteous lives and selfless action, said Luther, would multiply among men and women in gratitude for the grace they had received.

Luther also objected to the church's practice, growing from the church's theological idea of "works righteousness," of encouraging even its poorer adherents to buy "indulgences" (official pardons for their sins) from the church. In effect, Luther thought, the church profited from the poor while also harming their souls by leading them to believe that the act of paying money for indulgences could itself represent a "good work" that would help them find salvation.

And so the matter stood until 1965, when the Vatican and the Lutheran World Federation began allowing groups of scholars to re-study the issue and try to reach accommodation. In 1983, the 500th anniversary of Luther's birth, the scholars achieved an initial consensus. But it took another 15 years for the two denominations to announce they had achieved (tentatively) an agreement. While reserving the right to differ on emphases and other peripheral issues of some import, reported the Times, the churches agreed on a carefully worded, 44-point statement.

The statement's most important passage was elegant: "Together we confess: By grace alone, in faith in Christ's saving work and not by any merit on our part, we are accepted by God and receive the Holy Spirit, who renews our hearts while equipping us and calling us to good works."

When fully parsed, the statement certainly looked to Mad as if it were, effectively, a victory for Luther's interpretation of Scripture.

The first person to call Mad for his reaction to the story was an enterprising reporter for *The Metropolitan Daily* (motto: "The newspaper of record"). His full-time news 'beat' was religion. "You imitated Luther when you posted your theses on all those church doors," the reporter said to Mad, as Don listened in on a separate phone extension. "You must have some reaction to this development."

"Well, I'm not in total agreement with Luther's take on everything – in fact, I think some of Luther's ideas ought to be turned on their heads – but as far as this new accord goes, I think Luther's position pretty much kicked butt."

From his perch on the other line, Don cringed and covered his eyes. Mad continued: "What I mean is that anybody who reads the letters of Paul with an open mind has to admit that, objectively speaking, Luther interpreted Paul correctly. If Paul is the authority, then the Papists were clearly wrong. This accord looks to me like a dignified way for the Catholic Church to yield on this one very important point: that salvation occurs not because of our actions but through faith alone."

The reporter was a real pro, with an excellent grasp of his subject. He immediately homed in on the three focal points of Mad's answer.

"Okay, from what I can see, you've raised three different issues," he said. "I'll throw all three out right now, and we can then take them one at a time if you want.

"First, why is this such a victory for Luther? All of the official statements and all the expert analysis I've seen so far indicates that this is a pretty darn good 50-50 compromise. Why do you think differently?

"Second, what is it about Luther's teachings that you personally disagree with? How is it that his ideas should be turned on their heads?

"And third, you included a qualifier in your answer. You said *IF* Paul is the authority. That's a pretty big 'if.' Are you suggesting that Paul should *not* be the authority?"

After all his experiences with clueless journalists, Mad was delighted to be confronted with a reporter who really knew his stuff. Mad dropped all his defenses and launched into a broad intellectual discussion of the issues involved.

"Well, let me pull out my Luther book …. Yes, that's where I thought this was. You obviously don't have this right in front of you, but after I saw today's story I was in the process of pulling this out when you called. I'm looking at Luther's theses for the Heidelberg Disputation, thesis number 25. It says, quote, 'the one who does much "work" is not the righteous one, but the one who, without "work," has much faith in Christ.' The new Catholic-Lutheran accord uses almost the exact same words: 'in faith in Christ's saving work and not by any merit on our part, we are accepted by God and receive the Holy Spirit.' And lemme see, I've got a note cross-referenced here in my book. Gimme a second to look it up …. Yeah, here's from Luther's Preface to the New Testament: 'It is not by our own works, but by His work, His passion and death, that He makes us righteous, and gives us life and salvation.'

"That's why I say Luther kicked butt: because this accord tracks Luther's position almost exactly.

"Now, let me take your questions out of order. I think it was your third question that asked whether Paul was the correct authority. I mean, Luther identified explicitly with Paul, and his writings clearly track Paul's own. The Catholic Church was spitting in the wind by trying to deny that. But what made Paul the be-all and end-all, anyway? Paul spread the Gospel, but does that mean that the words of Paul himself should be taken as Gospel? The way I see it, the Gospel is the Gospel, and Paul's epistles are Paul's epistles, his letters – and the two should not be confused with each other. The ultimate authority shouldn't be Paul; the ultimate authority is Jesus Christ. Who's to say that Paul didn't misinterpret Jesus? I mean, Luther could have been right about Paul, but that doesn't mean that Paul was always right about Christ."

The reporter was intrigued. "Well, is there any example you can give where you think Paul and Jesus were at odds?"

Mad thought a moment. "Hmmmm…. Okay, try this. Now this is sorta off the top of my head; I mean, I've thought of this before, but haven't really thought it all the way through, but just use this for the sake of argument of what I mean *could* be an example…."

"Okay, okay," said the reporter. "Enough of the disclaimers. I get it; I get it: We're talking hypothetically. Go ahead and spill the beans already."

"Okay, think about probably the most famous parable of all, the one about the Good Samaritan," Mad said. "In the verses just before the parable itself, what was the question the guy asked, the one that Jesus' parable responded to? I'll tell you what the question was; the question was precisely the one at issue in this dispute between the Catholic Church and Luther. The question was, 'Teacher, what shall I do to inherit eternal life?'

"Now look closely at Jesus' answer. He said there were two things the man could do. First, he should love the Lord, etcetera. Basically, that's faith. That could be taken to support Luther's position of salvation through faith alone. But then there's the second thing: Love thy neighbor. The man specifically was told to love his neighbor – and then Jesus went on to explain what it meant to love a neighbor. That's when

He told this parable about the Samaritan, and the Samaritan's good works to help the injured man along the roadside...."

"Yeah, yeah, I know the story," said the reporter impatiently. His willingness to explore the issues did not translate into a desire to sit around for the equivalent of a dorm-room bull session: He had work to do. "What's the point?"

"Okay, I'm getting there," said Mad, a little taken aback by the reporter's East Coast brusqueness. "Don't you see? Jesus was talking about reaching salvation by loving one's neighbor, and he specifically equated loving one's neighbor with doing the kinds of acts that demonstrate love. The man asked Jesus what to do to inherit eternal life; Jesus answered, in effect, by telling him to go do works of love. And that's the centuries-old Catholic position, that through our good works we can earn, or at least help ourselves earn, salvation. But it's not Paul's position: Luther was right that Paul said we are 'justified,' or saved, by grace alone, not by our own works. So Paul and Jesus seem to be at odds, and while Luther was right on the scholarship, it might make more sense to use Jesus as the authority, not Paul – dontcha think?"

The reporter's head was spinning a little, but he was able to get the gist of Mad's logic, such as it was.

"Okay, then, what you're saying is," the reporter summarized, "that this week's accord is a capitulation by the Catholics to the effect that Luther was right about what Paul said, and therefore that Luther was right about the way to salvation – but that even though the Catholics are admitting defeat, as well they should if the answer is to be based solely on a correct interpretation of Paul, that the Catholics might actually be correct on the larger issue of salvation; because Paul himself is wrong because *his* teachings don't track Jesus'. Is that what you're saying?"

Now it was Mad's turn to try to follow the other person's logic. In this case, Mad had to think a few seconds to try to figure out the reporter's logic in the reporter's effort to follow Mad's own logic on a set of abstract concepts. It had the potential to degenerate into one of those vaudeville routines where one guy says to the other that he said that the second one said that the first one said that the second one said that ..., *ad infinitum*.

"Well," Mad said, tentatively. "Yes, that sounds like what I'm saying."

"So, in a nutshell," the reporter said, now trying for something more concise that he could use in his story, "you say the accord shows that the Catholics were wrong even though the Catholics are actually right."

"Yes," said Mad. "More or less. Maybe."

"Okay, now that we've got *that* settled," said the reporter, stifling a chuckle that showed he actually did have a sense of humor, "there's the third question I asked, or actually the second question, but you've left it as the third one to answer. What is it about Luther's teachings that you personally disagree with? How is it that his ideas should be turned on their heads? Is it just that Luther was wrong to give primacy to Paul when we should actually all give primacy to Jesus' own teachings, or is there something more?"

"Well, there's that, yes, but there's also more. The whole upshot of Luther's message was that only God is good and that man is never truly good, and that God is by his very nature nothing *but* good, all the time, world without end, Amen. Here, since I've got Luther's Heidelberg Disputation theses open, here's thesis number 4, in Luther's own words. Luther said, quote, 'The works of God may always appear to be unattractive and seemingly bad. They are nevertheless truly immortal merits.' End quote. But that's the opposite of what I wrote in my 59 theses that landed me into this whole public mess that makes people like you act as if I'm worth asking about any of this. I wrote that God Himself is imperfect, and that He sent Jesus to reconcile His own, God-the-Father's, imperfections with man's own imperfections, to mediate and achieve an ultimate perfection or state of grace from the mire of two separate sets of imperfection.

"Luther wrote that everything God does is actually an immortal merit, while I wrote that 'God is jealous and wrathful and unfair, and arrogant and prone to going mad with his own power, and that he punishes mankind overly harshly.' That's a polar opposite of Luther's message. In the short run at least, I guess it turns Luther on his head – even though, in the end, we both come back to the goodness of God's ultimate will and the need to have faith in God's grace even when faith is severely tested."

Something in what Mad said struck the reporter in a way that for some reason seemed sort of funny. Stupid-funny, but funny nonetheless.

"You said you wrote 59 theses?" he asked. "Somehow that number never registered with me before now. You posted 59 theses on church doors, and Luther posted 95 theses on the church door at Wittenberg. And now you say you are turning Luther on his head. Luther, 95, you, 59. 95-59. On his head. Get it? Turn 95 over, you get 59. I don't know why, but that seems really funny to me. What a riot: '*On his head.*' That's just too rich."

Mad had never thought of this before, and it struck him, too, as being funny. For some reason the numerical pun put him in a good mood. He ended the interview and hung up the phone feeling certain he finally had found a reporter (in addition to the kind-faced young woman in Mobile) who would neither twist nor sensationalize what Mad was saying. This guy was really conversant with the issues, such as they were, and so this guy's story could help Mad avoid another round of bitter controversy.

Don wasn't so sure. Don, trained media ear that he was, thought he recognized a host of potential pitfalls – a bevy of fires lit by Mad that MMW Corp. might have to douse.

Don was correct.

It was the Sunday *Metropolitan Daily*, invariably a top seller nationwide, that ran the reporter's story as a lengthy in-depth feature. The article itself was a remarkably well-done piece on the tentative accord, with a thorough and readily understandable history of the centuries-old dispute and a nuanced explanation of the issues, combined with a broad range of reactions to the accord from experts across the theological spectrum. Mad's responses, appropriately enough, were afforded just five paragraphs halfway through a 75-paragraph story. The text itself was unexceptional:

> One commentator, a historian and scholar and imitator of Luther, took issue with the prevailing opinion that the accord's central statement represented equal concessions from both sides. Madison Jones, the young man from Mobile, Alabama, who in the past few months has launched a growing nationwide ministry, said that Catholic theologians gave far more ground because they acknowledged for the first time the

undisputed primacy of "faith" over "works" in the quest for eternal salvation.

"I think Luther pretty much kicked butt," Jones said, before launching into a lengthy and far more measured explanation. "The Papists were clearly wrong."

To support his contention, Jones quoted the following passage from Luther's writings: "It is not by our own works, but by His work, His passion and death, that He makes us righteous, and gives us life and salvation." Jones compared that to the new accord's passage that salvation comes "in faith in Christ's saving work and not because of any merit on our part."

But Jones, who has quickly established a reputation for unconventional interpretations, said that despite his own Protestantism he thinks the former Catholic position might actually be the stronger one. He said that the new accord more accurately represents the views expressed in the letters of the apostle Paul, but that the question shouldn't end there.

"The ultimate authority shouldn't be Paul," Jones said. "The ultimate authority is Jesus Christ. Who's to say that Paul didn't misinterpret Jesus?"

And Jesus, Jones said, consistently preached a message that emphasized the necessity of good works.

Leaders of other mainline Protestant denominations, meanwhile, ……

Fair and accurate as the article was, however, it was the sub-*sub*-headline that raised a ruckus. The story was headlined "Harmonic convergence?" with a slightly smaller-type sub-head saying, "Faith accord strikes 'grace' notes". But then came the kicker sub-head: "But one observer says 'Luther … kicked butt.'"

It was enough to send some Catholics into apoplexy. A national hyper-traditionalist Catholic organization, *Pulchra Maria* ("Beautiful Mary") denounced both the accord and Mad in scathing terms. "The reaction of Mr. Jones is evidence of a disrespect, bordering on dangerous bias, against the Catholic faithful," said its press release. "Triumphalist reactions like his also show the folly of any efforts by Rome to yield, even on semantics, to any psychological need for 'validation' on the part of Protestants in expiation for their mistake of abandoning the One True Faith. We urge the Holy See to reject this tentative accord rather than signing it, as scheduled, this fall. Protestants should always be welcome to return to the fold, but it is they, not Catholics, who must undertake the journey."

A few Archbishops also responded negatively, albeit in language more gentle and politic, to Mad's "kicked butt" line.

And then there was the legendary, conservative Catholic, political activist out of Chicago, Gladys Phillpott. Mrs. Phillpott, now well into her 70s, had wielded a conservative cudgel in national politics since the days of Robert Taft's battles against Thomas Dewey for Republican supremacy in the mid-1940s. Feminists despised her and ridiculed her as an embittered but cowering housewife. During the abortion battles of the 1970s and 1980s, they even made a pun from her name for a silly chant with which they greeted each of her public appearances: "Fill-pots, and fill pans, and kiss the feet of your man!"

But for all that, Mrs. Phillpott was a formidable and indefatigable trench fighter. And nothing, no Reagan nor Helms nor Buchanan, was more important to her than her faith. Through her national conservative woman's organization, "The 'Old Glory' Chorus," she released the following personal statement:

"I usually would not deign to respond to an upstart young man who enjoys neither ecclesiastical authority from any church nor any elective office. But the remarks of Madison Jones (if reported accurately by the liberal *Metropolitan Daily*) demand careful scrutiny. Like many other committed Catholics, I was insulted by Mr. Jones' comment that Martin Luther has now effectively 'kicked butt' against the Catholic Church. But a closer reading caused me a momentary double-take. It is important that, in other remarks, Mr. Jones acknowledged the primacy of Our Lord Jesus Christ whenever the Lord's own words seem in apparent contradiction with other parts of the Bible – and that he credited Catholics, in passing at least, for our fealty to Christ's words. Clearly, Mr. Jones is a young man able to recognize, at least on an intellectual level, the nuances of our faith.

"Nevertheless, I must in the end denounce Mr. Jones in the strongest terms – not because he is a danger to a faith too strong to be easily wounded, but because he is a danger to our politics. The danger was buried in the text of yesterday's feature article. What he said was, and I quote, that 'The Papists were clearly wrong' about how the letters of Paul should be interpreted. The problem is in the word 'Papists.' I'm not usually one for political correctness based on hurt feelings over word use. But the term 'Papist' long has been used as a perjorative, especially in the South, to indicate a wholly unjustified fear that Catholics were loyal to the Pope rather than to our nation, even on matters of purely secular authority. In short, it questions our patriotism. And it gives voice to the anti-Catholic prejudices that ruled this nation's politics for some 175 years.

"For conservative and patriotic Catholic Americans such as myself, therefore, this indication of hostility to our faith, no matter how well disguised by other, purely intellectual concessions, represents a serious threat if it is goes unchallenged. I call on all the media of this country, therefore, to no longer provide a forum for Madison Jones – who, after all, has no church authority, no Ph.D., no elective office and, in short, no legitimacy other than a talent for self-promotion."

Mad was stunned. He had meant no slur against Catholics. "Papists" was a word Luther himself often used, in his debates with Erasmus and others, to distinguish those who backed the Pope on central issues from those who agreed with Luther's interpretation of Scripture. Mad had used the term as an academician would, in effect paying homage to his subject by using his subject's own language.

Mad therefore asked MMW's grandmotherly secretary to track down Mrs. Phillpott's phone number, and he placed a call to the conservative movement's doyenne. He wanted to apologize, and to explain his word choice. Gladys Phillpott, though, was brusque and skeptical.

"You're a very cheeky young man," she finally said. "If this call is sincere, then I appreciate it. But I'll be watching you. You're playing in the big leagues now, and I've seen plenty of ambitious youngsters like you over the last half-century who caused harm to our society before being deservedly hoisted on their own petards. So you be careful. You don't want to make an enemy out of me."

Somehow, the lady's harshness did not make Mad angry, but chastened. It was like being lectured to by a venerable great-aunt, too mean to truly love but who nevertheless had lived a life of such unbending principle that she commanded respect.

"Mrs. Phillpott," he responded. "Please don't judge me too soon or too harshly. In more ways than not, I'm basically on your side."

Mrs. Phillpott harrumphed. "We'll see about that. Goodbye."

Two hours later, Mad was rocked from both sides of the religio-political spectrum for his challenge to the authority of St. Paul. From the Rev. Larry Falstaff: "Jones denigrates the Word of God, which cannot contradict itself. Paul's letters may have been physically penned by Paul's hand, but the words are the Lord's, which is why they are Scripture. And Scripture is infallible. Mad Jones is therefore as wrong as he can be, and he risks mightily the just and majestic wrath of God."

And he also came under attack from "The Rev," part of whose shtick in his preachings to black congregations was that he, like St. Paul, had experienced a similar white-light-and-booming-voice conversion experience. Not only did The Rev identify with St. Paul, but he also fancied himself a diplomat of the first order who claimed a special ability to negotiate with Syria.

Referring to Mad, The Rev had this to say: "He should come and ask us who have been to Damascus. St. Paul's words are strong and can never be wrong. Jones is picking a fight, but he can't see the light. His nice comments on race have made him my brother, but on Scriptural word there can be no other – no other than me, The Rev, because like Paul I know, what it's like when God's favor sets me aglow. Praise the Lord – The Rev will lead you! Praise the Lord – The Rev will lead you! Praise the Lord!"

* * *

"I SAY, I say, I mean I say," said the booming Southern voice of the Colonel, through the phone line to Mad's house late at night. "Every time I turn around, son, you are causing another tempest in a teapot, and your teapots keep getting bigger and bigger. I say, son, don't you realize you're embarrassing yourself?"

The phone call had woken Mad from the first stages of an REM sleep. His mind was foggy and a little scrambled. "I'm not trying to be an embassment … a barament… I mean, sir, I'm not trying to be an em-barr-assment. Everything I say just gets all twusted, ip, uhh, twisted up."

"Sounds to me like your brain's all twisted up, son. I say, have you been drinking? Don't you know how to hold your bourbon, son?"

"No, sir, I'm sorry, sir, I just woke up."

"Well, son, I say, speaking of sorry, you've got $80,000 of our money, son, and some of us are feeling mighty sorry that we gave it to you. You're not doing us proud, son, I say, you're not doing us proud at all."

The phone line went dead.

* * *

While it seemed to Mad as if all kinds of people he had never meant to offend were furious at him, his advocates in the chat room were now more than ever in his corner, one of them to an extent that actually had become uncomfortable.

From Affirmed: "Let all the false idolators fulminate! I still say Mad is our new Moses and Luther all wrapped into one! You know the man speaks truth when the harpies of the right and the demagogues of the left both criticize him. GO MAD GO! GO MAD GO! GO MAD GO!"

To which Defender acidly responded: "Straight to perdition, you doofus, straight to perdition."

Chapter Four

In late July Mad received in the mail an announcement from the St. Louis law firm of Zimlich, Shanahan and Woods to the effect that recent Washington University (of St. Louis) law school graduate Mary McWyre would be joining the firm. Mad had not spoken much with Mary in the past few months; he knew she was finishing school and studying for the bar exam, and Becky had been diligent in relaying the few messages Mary sent his way. Mad also knew that a week hence, Mary and Buzz were both to fly down to Mobile from their respective cities for the first official MMW board meeting. But the mailed announcement somehow made Mad especially proud of his soft-spoken friend, so he decided not to wait until the next week to congratulate her.

"Hey Mary, this is Mad," he said into the phone. "I got the announcement from the Zimlich law firm. Many congrats!"

Mary was more than a little surprised to hear from him. Mad had broken her heart back in college, abandoning her almost cavalierly, and now all these years later he had seemed utterly ungrateful for her work (or Becky's or anybody else's) in launching MMW. And, of course, he had again shown no interest whatsoever in resuming any kind of romantic relationship – not that she had made a real obvious play for one, unlike Becky.

Mary was from a huge family, the sixth of ten kids, seven of whom were girls. Plain and quiet and shy and earnest, she was accustomed to being lost in the shuffle. But that didn't mean she liked it. By two one-hundredths of a point, she had finished third in her class at her Catholic high school, and thus had been missed being recognized as either the valedictorian or the salutatorian. She had been decent but not spectacular at field hockey, for which she was named Honorable Mention all-district – but the local paper did not print the Honorable Mentions. She tried her hand at high school theatre, for which she once was named the lead's understudy (and never made it on stage) and three times was given "fifth business" parts where her dialogue consisted of "straight" lines that provided material for the other actors to play off for either laughs or high drama.

Accepted to Georgetown off its "wait list," she missed Phi Beta Kappa solely because of a disputed 'C' in an Economics elective, and otherwise floated through her four years while causing nary a ripple. Sure, she made some decent friends, two of whom would likely be friends for life. And she had one other boyfriend, who actually lasted most of her senior year, but neither was truly enamored with the other and they just sort of drifted apart. And she took a Capitol Hill internship one semester, and she spent half her junior year abroad at the University of Limerick in Ireland, and she was always dutiful and kind and people referred to her (when they referred to her at all) as "good ol' Mary."

Law school was more of the same: hard work, good grades, one more blah boyfriend for five months during the three-year school ride, and little notice from most of her professors or classmates.

And for some reason a few months ago she found herself driving all night from St. Louis to Mobile to comfort a guy who had treated her like a short-term fling, and then worked feverishly (using her developing legal knowledge in the process) to help set up a nationwide enterprise for him. Yet until this phone call, she wasn't even sure that the guy ever thought of her or valued her in the slightest.

"Oh, well, thanks a lot, Mad. It's good to hear from you."

"Well, I'm not as good as I should be about keeping in touch, but I wanted you to know I'm impressed. I'm told that Zimlich, Shanahan is one of the most respected firms in all of Missouri."

"They're okay," said Mary.

"Hey, listen, I've also got to apologize. All along I thought your name was spelled M-c-G-u-i-r-e, but I see from this announcement that it's spelled with a 'W' and a 'Y.' I've never seen it spelled that way."

"Nothing to apologize for. I just changed it from McGuire-with-a-'G' last month. When I spent my junior year in Ireland, I started researching my genealogy, and kept up with the research sporadically since then. I found that my ancestors had actually lived in Wales in the 1100s, and the 'WY' is a more accurate rendition of their name than 'GUI' is. I figured it was distinctive, too, and might help me stand out in the legal profession – so I went ahead and had the spelling legally changed. How's that for an example of thorough research? I'm actually sorta hoping the story gets out, because it might impress potential clients with the quality and persistence of my researching abilities. If I can find some Welsh-Irish peasants back in the 12th Century, maybe my potential clients will think I'll be able to find the buried legal clause or piece of evidence that wins their case for them."

Mad had to laugh. Mary was so quiet, but she never, ever missed her mark. She was pretty damned sharp.

"That's damned good, Mary, damn good. Hey, look, anyway, Becky's after me to get my column for three weeks from now written and transmitted off to the syndicate that distributes it, so I gotta run. But I just wanted to congratulate you. I'll see you next week, and we can catch up more then."

* * *

At noon on Saturday August 1, all six of MMW's principals gathered in Mad's living room. It was the first time that Buzz had met Becky and Mary in person. Becky had insisted that a summer Saturday in Mobile was too hot, even with air conditioning available, for anything but casual clothes, and she arrived wearing a shorts-and-sleeveless-chemise outfit that well highlighted her physical assets. Even though her attitude was all business, Buzz had a hard time trying not to leer at her. Mary, meanwhile, in shapeless shorts and T-shirt, seemed at first to fade into the background. Don was as efficient and colorless as always, and Justin, of course, couldn't shut up. Mad, for his part, just wanted to get the whole thing over with.

Becky reported that MMW's balance sheet was already getting very close to, yes, balance. She explained that an operating deficit so small after such a short time was a very impressive performance. She also explained that the unique deal she had worked out with the book publisher in New York had called for a two-part advance: a smaller sum at the beginning of the interview process by the ghostwriter – a process now complete – and a larger sum once Mad had signed off on the final version of the book, which was supposed to be by mid-October so the publisher could rush it into print for the official day-after-Thanksgiving start to the Christmas season. Her point was that with the larger part of the advance still coming – and, if things went very well, with a royalty-escalator clause that would begin to kick in if more than 20,000 of the books were sold – there was a chance for MMW to reach or even surpass break-even by year's end. And if the company was turning a "profit" by the next regularly scheduled board meeting in February of 1999, it would be time for Mad (with the board's input) to begin deciding which charities would get the proceeds.

Justin reported that his spinoff business was growing, too. In fact, he reported it in great detail (despite it having no legal connection with MMW) and with such a superabundance of enthusiasm that Buzz tuned out completely in favor of daydreaming about disrobing Becky, who of course was young enough to be his daughter.

But it was Mary who, by incremental degrees, took over the meeting without anybody being aware that she was doing so. She kept asking probing questions, usually involving legal angles, that showed deep insights of a mind both analytic and creative. After a while, even Buzz was impressed enough to stop sneaking glances at Becky's cleavage. Mary was plain-looking, but as Buzz became ever more impressed by the acuity of her intelligence, he began to look at her more than he stared at Becky.

Mad, for his part, was struck by how lucky he was to have talented friends like these who had re-arranged their own lives out of a fondness for him and a belief in his potential.

Then Becky and Don brought them all up short. They reported there was still one serious problem that was not being addressed. Mad's propensity to shoot from the hip, his talent for creating unintended controversy, was engendering an increasingly volatile atmosphere at his public appearances. Don reported a situation that Mad had become somewhat oblivious to, namely that some protesters seemed ripe for violence. In addition to the occasion on the Texas trip, there had been two other incidents of rock-throwing, and almost every appearance was now marred at least by some fairly aggressive pushing and shoving. Then Becky lowered the boom: In the past ten days, MMW's offices had received two anonymous threats of violence to Mad's person, one by letter and the other by phone, the latter of which sounded like a thinly veiled death threat. She had reported the threats to the Mobile police, which put her in touch with the FBI, which was now investigating. Both agencies were sympathetic, Becky said, but indicated there was little to offer Mad for his physical protection.

"We'll keep investigating, and we hope to track down these cowards," they had told her, "but meanwhile, your company might want to hire a bodyguard for Mr. Jones."

"Now Mad, I know you're not going to like this," Becky said, "but I totally agree. There are obviously some real nutcases out there. I think you are in danger. I think you need protection."

"Aw, hell, Becky, I'm just some two-bit history teacher," Mad said. "Nobody would seriously want to hurt me."

Don broke in: "Those rocks weren't aimed at thin air, Mad, they were aimed at you. It's not just that some people are so offended by you and so crazy that they *want* to hurt you; it's that some have already *tried* to hurt you. And frankly, since I'm always right by you on the road, I'm just as unsafe as you are, and I demand protection."

"Yes, Mad, I demand it too, for both your sakes," said Becky, to general agreement from all the others assembled. "The only problem is that a bodyguard will cost us a whole other salary, plus raise our travel expenses substantially, and that will throw off the numbers of the rosy financial scenario I've laid out."

Back and forth, around and around they went, but it eventually became clear to Mad that this was an argument he would not win.

Just as Mad began to bow to the inevitable, his phone rang. It was Shiloh, saying that both LaShauna and their baby were taking a nap and that therefore he wanted to get out of the house – and would Mad be interested in meeting him at Carpe Diem, or maybe even going somewhere to throw around a football for the heck of it?

Shiloh! Bingo! That was it!

"Hey, Shiloh, talk about timing! How would you like to be my bodyguard?"

Long story short, Shiloh eventually agreed. But it took some doing, and the details weren't all worked out for nearly a month. Shiloh still had more than three months to go to reach five years on the Mobile police force and thus become vested in its retirement plan. Until then, he would travel with Mad and Don as his police force schedule permitted – moonlighting, as it were. (For other times until Shiloh could come on board full-time, Becky would insist that their hosts provide heightened security.)

As it turned out, the police department was so high on Shiloh that it set up a part-time schedule for him even after he joined MMW full-time. The brass thought he had major leadership potential; they also figured MMW was a flash in the pan and that Shiloh would soon want to come back on board full-time with the force.

As further inducement (other than friendship) for Shiloh to join MMW for a salary only slightly higher than the one from the Mobile force, Mad offered him a side-deal bonus that Shiloh thought (mistakenly) was coming from MMW funds. Mad took $20,000 from his remaining Crazy Eights money and put it in a high-yield investment fund from which Shiloh could eventually draw, for one purpose and one purpose only: college tuition. In a few years, Mad told him, Shiloh could finally achieve his dream of attending college.

MMW Corp., meanwhile, would partially recoup the cost of Shiloh's salary by raising the appearance fees it charged for Mad's appearances (demand was high enough by now to support that anyway), and its principals would have to accept the fact that earning a surplus for charities might not happen as early as next February.

* * *

When the board meeting ended, Justin took everybody down to his health club for a workout, sauna, and free massage by the club's in-house specialist. (He charged it all to the corporate account of his spinoff business.) From there, after a rest and some showers, all six, joined (at Mad's insistence) by Father Vignelli, went to dinner at The Pillars, a fine-dining establishment in a grand old mansion on Mobile's historic

Government Street. Becky again was sleeveless, this time in pink satin that would have been modest except for a teardrop opening at the very top of her bust line. But the real revelation was Mary, who had for once used makeup judiciously, even expertly, to go along with a shimmery, light-blue dress so well cut that it provided excellent lines for her otherwise unremarkable figure. All the others (except for the collared Father Vignelli) wore sharp business suits, though Justin's bright purple tie was far too loud, especially when contrasted with his shock of mis-cut orange hair.

Problem was, Becky proceeded to drink far too much white wine. She had for months been so stressed and unhappy that, with the board meeting over, she was "letting herself go" for the first time since she moved to Mobile. Father Vignelli, a marvelous storyteller, was in the midst of a sweetly humorous tale about Eugene Walter (the recently late Mobile literary personality and *bon vivant*) when Becky interrupted.

"You say he was wearing a pnurp, I mean a purple, striped shirt at this formal event?" she repeated in reference to a passing detail in Vignelli's story. "Was it as bwight as Justin's gwow-in-da-dark tie?" Justin looked hurt and nobody else laughed, but Becky didn't notice. She was having trouble not laughing at her own (what-she-thought-was) humor. "Was it a purpowe-peopo-eater shirt, or was this guy fat enuff to be a purpowe-cow?"

Even Buzz, who rarely turned down an opportunity to imbibe, was embarrassed for her. Here was this incredibly sexy and intelligent woman who had done such a good job launching a company and running today's board meeting, and now she was an embarrassing drunk. Mary, sitting next to Buzz, leaned over, and whispered in his ear. "Now's your chance, Buzz," she said, teasingly. Buzz turned and looked at Mary in mock-confusion.

"I saw her this way one night during senior week at Georgetown," Mary continued, "and she started running a dice game to see which of ten guys would get to go to bed with her. But Mad won't touch her and she won't touch Justin and Father Vignelli is a Catholic priest. Tonight, honey, she's all yours." (She didn't even think to mention Don, who was so bland that he had disappeared into the background.)

Buzz rolled his eyes as if pained. He leaned over and whispered back: "Sorry, but I prefer that my women be at least semi-conscious."

Mary just smiled. The truth was that she had seen no such thing during senior week, although she *had* once seen a drunken Becky ostentatiously grab a then-boyfriend's butt. But after all, what was a little exaggeration among friendly business associates?

Soon enough, Becky's drunken voice, spewing inanities, became embarrassing for all assembled. It was not a good closing note for what otherwise had been a fairly upbeat day. Justin, hurt as he was (Becky had by this time referred to his tie in jest more than a dozen times), gallantly insisted on being the one who hustled her out of the Pillars and drove her home to her condo. There, she rushed stumblingly to the bathroom, became violently ill, and soon passed out on the linoleum floor.

As she had not closed the door, Justin eventually tiptoed in there to check on her. He found a clean towel and, without her stirring at all, he gently cleaned her mouth and chin. He lifted her head enough to slip underneath it another clean towel, carefully multi-folded into a soft makeshift pillow. She didn't wake.

Justin noticed the bathroom was cold. Exiting the bathroom again temporarily, he looked for a thermostat, but didn't find one. So he entered her bedroom, pulled the blanket and bedspread from her bed, pulled a quilt that he noticed peeking from underneath the bed, and brought all three back to the bathroom. Draping the first two of those covers over Becky's prone body, Justin then sat back against the side of the bathtub and wrapped the quilt around himself. He then just sat staring at her. Even in a crumpled heap, she was beautiful. Her features were exquisite.

After about an hour, he drifted off to sleep. At around six the next morning, Becky's head throbbing unbearably and her mouth so cottony-dry that it hurt even to part her lips, she opened her eyes to see the little guy slumped over, half-sitting, half-sideways against the tub. Bless his little heart.

* * *

Just over two weeks later, on Monday August 17, President Bill Clinton went before Independent Counsel Kenneth Starr and admitted, for the first time, that he had had intimate sexual contact with intern Monica Lewinsky. And in a fit of pique that night, the president went on national TV with a disastrously defiant attack on Mr. Starr's team. Three days earlier, a local Mobile columnist had already written that the president should resign, not just because of the Lewinsky mess, but because of a litany of "abuses of power so great that the precedents he has set are not just disturbing but dangerous." The column ran in many papers, including the *Atlanta Constitution* and the *Houston Chronicle*. Flying back to New Orleans from another trysting three-day weekend in New York, Laura Green picked up a *Constitution* during her plane's stopover in Atlanta. Seeing the Mobilian's byline gave her an idea.

"Mad, you've just *got* to do this," she said to Mad when he finally (reluctantly and only at Becky's urging) agreed to accept a phone call from Laura. "This is a great opportunity for you; there's nothing in it for me: I'm just trying to be helpful."

Laura suggested that she use her newfound contacts at the network to get Mad included among the list of religious leaders asked to comment on camera about the president's predicament. Southern Baptists were already on record blasting Clinton; some liberal Protestants (including the president's personal "spiritual advisor," named Tony Campolo) were noisily demanding that the nation afford Clinton full "forgiveness"; and the other usual religio-political suspects were taking their own predictable positions. But the network, which noticed ratings improvements whenever it reported on matters religious, planned to go beyond the Bible-waving professional talking heads and ask influential-but-less-famous religious experts about the spiritual aspects of the scandal. Laura thought this was yet another opportunity for Mad to boost his own profile, and Becky agreed.

"I don't do politics," Mad responded. "Sorry, but I just don't do politics."

Mad's tone of voice was more than a little edgy. He still didn't know how to feel about Laura. Frankly, he thought she had used him, and misrepresented and more than slightly sensationalized his positions, in order to climb the network star ladder. And he was still ticked off at her nasty phone comment berating him for mourning his wife. Yes, she had apologized on the web site, but he just couldn't be sure she meant it. And now his mind was whirring, trying to figure what her angle was this time.

"Dammit, Mad, I just don't understand you!" said Laura. "All I've ever wanted to do is help you, and you act like I'm some sort of Jezebel. I really worked hard on the 'Acute Vision' feature on you, and you turned around and cursed me for it. Now you're not only acting suspicious of me, but your tone of voice says I'm just some piece of shit. Damn you! Damn you! Just God-freakin'-damn you to hell."

She hung up the phone.

Mad was stunned. Laura had sounded genuinely hurt. It sounded like she had no ulterior motive. She sounded like she really cared.

But more than all that, a revelation came to him like a flash. Laura had said he treated her like a "Jezebel." Could she be the "Jezebel?" from the chat room? It made sense. Her own professed ignorance of matters religious, her strong and kind good wishes for him, her use of the question mark in the chat room name to indicate that she may or may not be internally conflicted by ulterior motives: Everything seemed to fit together nicely. And wasn't Jezebel in the Bible a seductress, possibly a seductress and a betrayer at the same time? Mad was no expert on the Old Testament. He'd have to look up the story check all the details. But Laura certainly had seduced him – and until now, he felt she had betrayed him as well.

Yes, Laura just had to be "Jezebel?". And Jezebel?'s chat room comments about him had been so full of feeling, so kind, they had moved him greatly.

But hadn't Jezebel? written that she had known him for a long time, and that she had known his father, too? He wouldn't put it past Laura to have thrown those details in as false clues, as red herrings. Yes, that was certainly it. Laura and Jezebel? were obviously the same.

Mad dialed Laura's phone number. Dadgummed voice mail. Mad wasn't ready for that, so he hung up. Five minutes later, he called again. Voice mail again. But this time Mad was ready.

"Laura, this is Mad. Look, this time it's *my* turn to give *you* an apology. I'm really sorry if I hurt you. Maybe I've misjudged you. In person, you've never been anything but extremely sweet to me. I feel like a jerk. Anyway, I still think it's a bad idea for me to comment on Clinton; it's true I just don't want to get involved in politics, cuz all it does it get me more unwanted controversy. So I'm still not gonna accept your offer, your suggestion. But after thinking about it all, I really, truly, absolutely appreciate your thinking of me. I am touched you are still trying to help me. I think maybe we should be friends. And I wish you luck with the fall TV season. You deserve all the success in the world. Okay, that's it. I guess. Sorry for such a long message. Again, thanks, and please forgive me."

She didn't call back.

* * *

The "Mad Religion" chat room was humming. Mad himself may not have wanted to discuss the Lewinsky mess, but the cyberspace aficionados certainly did. While Mad was quietly disdainful of President Clinton, some of his strongest supporters were jumping to the president's defense.

From Perdicaris: "I feel sure that Mad is probably with me on this. Mad's all about forgiveness and moving on with our lives, and that's what we need to do as a nation. Clinton might have acted like a scumbag, but he's got all these ministers saying that he truly repents. Heck, if even God can screw up – which is what Mad says – then certainly we can forgive Bill C. for screwing up, too."

From Cowardly Lion: "Damn, Perd, pay attention: He wasn't screwing up, or screwing down; he wasn't screwing at all; he was just getting some big BJs from an intern chick who saw the president as her personal yellow-brick road. But except for you having your facts wrong on the screwing part, you're probably right. Mad is sure to come to the president's defense. Don't forget that Mad himself wrote that sex can be 'heap big comfort.' Which reminds me: I've always wondered if the Tin Man was oiling up Dorothy when the rest of us weren't paying attention. Anybody have any thoughts on that?"

From FD Thom: "Stupid Lion's act is getting way way way way old but, yeah, I say stick it to all those hypocritical moralists like Patterson and Falstaff. Both of them are calling for Clinton to resign. They're both persecuting Clinton just like they've persecuted Mad. But I say that if those two are against Clinton, then I'm damn well for him, and I bet Mad is, too!"

Defender, of course, disagreed. "This is all typical relativistic bullhockey from all you moronic liberal excuse-makers. Slick Willie's been committing adultery with a girl less than half his age who, as an intern, was supposed to be under his protection. And he committed perjury and obstruction of justice, sure as can be. And that's not all; he's a liar and cheater and scam artist from all the way back to his draft-dodging days, and he's abused all kinds of laws with the FBI files and Travelgate and all the rest. In fact, the only thing Mad has said that I've ever liked was when he criticized Clinton during that TV feature on him by that dumb news magazine show. He's been awfully silent on the subject in recent months, but I bet even Mad, who is your hero, disagrees with you still. I bet he thinks Clinton should go. As for you guys, if you don't like the rule of law, go found an anarchy somewhere and leave us good Americans alone."

And Affirmed broke ranks with his fellow Mad supporters. "I hate to say it," he wrote, "but for once I agree with Defender. Clinton is denigrating the presidency, and he really needs to resign."

Finally, this comment came from Jezebel?, in her first entry in many months: "Look, I don't care for Clinton either way. But I do care about Monica. She's the one really getting a raw deal out of this. She's the one who gave her heart the only way she knew how, which was by giving her body. If that's all she knows, you can't blame her. And now this Ken Starr guy keeps dragging her name all through the mud. The way I see it, Mad is always for the victim, and Monica's the victim here. I'm still not straight with all the God stuff, but I feel sure that if there is a God, then He's gotta be trying to make this poor girl feel better about herself. There are a whole lot of us women out here who have made sexual mistakes but aren't bad people, and who sure as hell are glad we don't have our behavior scrutinized by hundreds of millions of people like Monica's has been. Clinton can go to Hell, and when he does, he'll find some of those prosecutors already roasting there!

"P.S. to Mad if he's reading this: I'm glad you liked my earlier messages. Thanks for being a great guy!"

Reading this around 10 at night, Mad became even more certain that Jezebel? was Laura. It sounded just like her, and this was probably her way of acknowledging his apology without having to call him back. The "sexual mistakes" line also was probably intended for him, Mad thought, as a reference to and apology for seducing him when he was grieving so desperately for Claire.

The phone rang. It was Shiloh, speaking quietly so as not to wake his wife or baby.

"Mad, I've just gotta know, because I feel strongly about this. Now that Clinton has admitted that he and Lewinsky had sexual contact, what do you think should happen?"

"Well, Shiloh, what do *you* think?"

"The man's gotta go, Mad. He obviously lied under oath, and it's pretty clear he got others to lie as well. That's obstruction of justice, Mad. I'm law enforcement, Mad. I take the law seriously. That's my life is making sure that the laws are followed so that everybody can have their rights protected. We can't have one set of laws for the rest of us and another easier set of laws for a president. Clinton's gotta resign. Or else impeach him. He's bad for this country, Mad."

"Well, Shiloh, I'm staying out of this in public. But I'll tell you the truth: I'm inclined to agree with you. Yes, I do. I agree."

Chapter Five

"Hey, Pretty Boy, you been messing where I told you not to mess."

It was Officer Williams, on the Saturday of Labor Day weekend. Off duty and in civilian clothes, he had driven to Mad's house and rung the doorbell. He was mad as a hornet that was far too fat to fly. He had just found out about Mad's deal with Shiloh. Shiloh had arranged some vacation days so he could take a first-time trip as Mad's bodyguard beginning the next morning and running through Wednesday. That's how Officer Williams found out that Shiloh would later that year be leaving the full-time employ of the police department.

Officer Williams turned his head and unleashed a huge wad of spit onto Mad's lawn. "Way back all those months ago, Pretty Boy, I told you not to mess with my partner Jones-y. Didn't I tell you not to go messing with his head? Didn't I tell you I was watching you? He's just a dumb nigger, but he's a good nigger and he has a good future in front of him in the police – and now you've filled his head with all this bodyguard crap for a dumb-ass fake-religious business that ain't gonna last, and you told him you'll put money aside for him for college, as if a nigger like that who can't no longer play football has any business in college anyway."

Officer Williams' words, drawled as they were, nevertheless were coming in a torrent. "You know as well as I know, Pretty Boy, that you just using my partner for your own reasons. You're messing with his head, Pretty Boy, and I don't like it!"

Mad had been watching college football on TV, and the two teams were within a few points of each other late in the fourth quarter. He didn't have time for this racist garbage. He slammed the door in the officer's face.

* * *

Early the next morning, at about the same time that Mad, Shiloh and Don were leaving Mobile via rental car, Pierre and Angelina Hebert sat at their breakfast counter in Kenner, Louisiana. Pierre, as was his custom on Sundays so he would be well fortified for his energetic preaching, was working his way through a feast. Scrambled eggs. Three large whole wheat-and-apple muffins. A grapefruit. Whole milk. A 32-ounce mega-glass of orange juice. Two oxymoronically "low-fat" sausage patties. A barely ripe banana. This was a meal that was supposed to last him until dinner.

"My good woman, do you realize what an honor this is?" Pierre asked. "Of all the churches in this country, Madison Jones has picked ours to be the site of his first repeat appearance! What an endorsement! It shows this congregation is full of the welcoming Holy Spirit!"

What he didn't say, but of course Angelina knew, was that he had hounded Becky with phone call after phone call, letter after letter, begging for this "honor." Frankly, he was peeved that his indirect spiritual mentor, The Rev. Rob Patterson, was continually and harshly criticizing such a nice young man as Madison Jones. Mad's return visit would serve to show that not all churches loosely affiliated with the Rev. Patterson marched in lockstep to his drumbeat.

Angelina responded with only a small smile. She liked Mad, too, and she appreciated her husband's enthusiasm. But she had been disappointed that Mad had not "taken a cotton" to either of the two young women, Tonya and Rhonda, whom she had taken under her wing. She also was fairly certain her husband had misinterpreted Mad's story about picking blackberries. She didn't think Mad had meant to tell a parable. She thought he was just trying to be a polite by making a sincere apology for being late.

"And the congregation is so excited, too!" Pierre continued. "What a powerful preacher this young man is!"

"DearHeart," said Angelina, softly. "You know what I think would be a good idea?"

"I always want your input, good woman," he said. "You're full of good ideas."

"Well, DearHeart, I think the young man is such a good speaker that he's one of those rare preachers who doesn't even need a translator. I think you should let him preach on his own, rather than in tandem with you. I think you can wait until he's finished for you to sum up what he has said, if that's even needed."

Seeing her husband's dubious facial expression, one perhaps tinged with hurt on the grounds that his own preaching was being gently criticized, Angelina hurriedly went for a rescue. "Two preachers as powerful as the two of you," she said, "are probably more than our congregation can absorb. If Madison gets their spirits aloft, your passion will probably send them deep into the galaxy, so far that they won't come down to earth again. And I don't think the good Lord wants his flock to leave this Earth yet; I don't think he wants a Rapture before its time."

"You are such a good woman," said the appeased husband. "You have so much common sense. Of course you're right. What would I do without you to keep me focused?" He scootched his chair part-way around the counter, leaned over while still sitting, and gave Angelina's shoulders a grateful squeeze.

So it was that, three hours later, Mad was surprised to find that the Rev. Hebert was *not* interrupting his homily. Mad had worked hard at crafting a message specifically for Apostles of the Word that was so clear and direct that it only lent itself to one interpretation – so that Hebert's expected running commentary would lend itself to the point Mad was trying to make, not confuse it. In fact, Mad was so expecting Hebert's amplifications that he deliberately kept his own words low-key.

Too low-key. He sensed the audience fidgeting, their minds wandering.

"… and so, on this weekend that we celebrate the good honest labor that the Lord has commanded us to undertake, …." Mad paused. He looked over at the Rev. Hebert, who himself was looking pleadingly at his wife with the appearance of a not-fully-broken horse champing at the bit, ready to explode into action. But Angelina was looking not at her husband, but at Mad. He wasn't hitting on all cylinders today, she thought, but what a nice young man. She wished she had a son like him.

Mad liked the Heberts. Their style of worship wasn't his own, but they clearly meant well. He wanted to please them. He didn't know why Pierre Hebert was being so reticent, but Mad felt compelled to do something grand so as to wake up the congregation and redeem the faith the Heberts had put in his preaching ability. Not only that, but by now, more than three months into his full-time "ministry," Mad had developed a performer's urgent need to please his audience. The worshippers had come in eager anticipation of a boffo homily, and by God, he wasn't going to let them down. He saw Shiloh out of the corner of his eye and remembered their conversation from a few weeks back.

Mad began raising the tempo and volume of his words and began to ad-lib.

"… as I said, on this weekend of celebrating labor, let us not be unwilling to bear the even heavier yoke that is being put on this country by the scandals that are paralyzing our nation's capital. Let us not allow ourselves to become mere voyeurs into the brothel that our elected leader has turned the Oval Office into. Let us not forget that his own adultery and lies and perjury and obstruction of justice, and …" as Mad paused to find words to end the sentence, he felt an approving, excited stir spread through the congregation. "… and his venality and false pride and his unseemly anger against law enforcement officials who are just doing their jobs – let us not forget that all of these failings of Bill Clinton *not only* do *not* excuse our own failings, but they require that we ourselves labor even harder to keep this country from being paralyzed by voyeurism. They require that we make our economy continue to hum so as to keep poverty away from God's people. We are too strong to be paralyzed! We are better than that! We're worthier than that! We're more lion-hearted than that! In fact, we just won't put up with that!"

"Praise the Lord!" yelled somebody from the congregation. Then several more: "Praise the Lord!!"

"Yes, praise the Lord!" shouted Mad, playing thoroughly to his audience. "Praise the Lord for making us a better people than to be brought down by one man turning our Oval Office into an Oral Office! Praise the Lord! Praise the Lord for giving us the sense to go about our lives! Praise the Lord!"

The congregation, aroused almost to a frenzy, began chanting, again and again: "PRAISE… THE… LORD!! PRAISE… THE LORD!!!!!"

Angelina had a mile-wide smile across her face, and Pierre was lifting his hands heavenward while yelling the same chant into his microphone. But in the very back row of the congregation, an unobtrusive Don had buried his head in his hands. Earlier, he had seen a reporter with a microphone, trying to find a front-row seat. Don knew this meant more controversy coming his way.

Meanwhile, nobody had noticed the mime standing just inside the back doors of the great hall. He had snuck in late, wearing an extremely baggy but spiffy-clean sweatsuit. Now a look of extreme triumph covered his countenance. He had guessed right! The mime pulled off his sweat suit to reveal, underneath, a navy-blue cocktail dress with an ugly, blotchy white stain (created with Campbell's clam chowder), low cut to reveal an illusion of cleavage created with different shades of skin-toned body paint. Somehow, he also produced a wig of thick, semi-long black hair and, to top it all off, a stylish woman's beret-hat. In the midst of the chanting, worshipping congregation members, the mime ran, leaping, down one aisle and up the next, down another, across the platform up front, and right up to the microphone stand where a stunned Mad watched in horror. Throwing himself to his knees a few feet in front of Mad's waist, the mime proceeded, without actually touching Mad, to perform a perfect thin-air rendition of fellatio.

Many in the congregation thought this was part of Mad's planned act, and they howled with laughter until they realized that Mad, horrified, had yelled to Shiloh for assistance. But as Shiloh reached the platform, looking ready to manhandle the mime, the mime looked up at the bodyguard, smiled and winked, and then hopped up and sprinted out a side door before Shiloh could catch him.

Angelina, seeing all hell ready to take over the aroused and confused congregation, took to the electric organ and began playing a loud and insistent version of "Amazing Grace." And as the congregation ever-so-slowly settled down, nobody much noticed a curious little man, with a hidden mini-camera stashed inside what looked like a large Bible, as he eased his way out of the church.

*   *   *

That afternoon, Mad and his traveling companions arrived a bit ahead of schedule for a huge outdoor worship-service and picnic that was the annual Labor-Sunday tradition of the Holy Pentecostal Methodist American Church of Our Lord and Savior (known colloquially as the "American Savior" church) – a 100% black congregation outside of Canton, Miss., a little north of Jackson. There had been some confusion about the fees involved for this appearance. Becky usually demanded Mad's speaking fee up front, but she was eager for Mad to make inroads into the super-active black congregations of the South. And the American Savior church, run by the legendary Preacher McGee, was the top-of-the-line of Southern black churches. That's why, when negotiation with Preacher McGee kept going around in nonconcentric circles, Becky didn't pull the plug on the whole deal. For some reason Preacher wanted to write a check from one account for twice Mad's usual fee, then have Becky send with Mad a check for half that amount from MMW Corp., made payable to "HPMA Church, c/o P.McGee." Preacher, who on the phone sounded warm and wonderful and gracious and big-hearted, said something about how the ceremony of a check from a guest preacher spurred the generosity of the congregation when it came time to pass the offering plate. He said that generosity was the linchpin around which the American Savior church carried out its unparalleled abundance of rural social services.

The account Preacher wanted to write his check on, payable to MMW Corp., had run out of checks, and Preacher expected the new checkbooks to arrive from the bank a few days before Labor Day weekend. "I'll just give your man his check then, little lady," Preacher said with a reassuring warmth.

"Aw, what the hell," Becky had finally said to MMW's part-time secretary. "It's pretty much a shell game with the money, but we'll end up with the same amount either way, so what do I care?"

Anyway, none of that seemed to matter when Mad, Don and Shiloh arrived at the huge fallow farm field, bordered by and dotted with pecan trees and adorned on one side with a massive, fan-cooled tent, that served as the picnic grounds. Preacher, a strapping, smiling man in his mid-50s, welcomed them with a delight and effervescence that put all three immediately at ease. The only discordant notes were the diamond rings that Preacher wore on each pinky finger, and what looked like a ruby set in what was certainly a sterling silver belt buckle attached to a braided-rope belt around Preacher's contentedly ample girth.

After some pleasantries and a quick male-bonding radio check-up on the latest NFL scores, Preacher excused himself. "We'll have plenty of time to visit and to go over our plan for the service," he said. "It's just 4 now, and we don't start until 5:30 – so why don't y'all go mingle and get to know my wonderful people and fill your bellies with good barbeque, and come back to this corner of the tent at, say, 5:15 or maybe a few minutes before that, and we'll get all our plans straight then?"

That was more than fine with Shiloh. Except that it was so rural, this was his kind of crowd, 3,000-strong. Kids in cutoffs ran around playing tag and throwing footballs and climbing trees and splashing through the tiny brook that ran along one edge of the picnic grounds. Men lounged around and drank RC Colas while happily debating the merits of Jackson State football, the size of the coming harvest, and the worthiness of their respective women's backsides. Women congregated on picnic blankets, gossiped and ladled out cold lemonade to their kids when the young ones ran, panting, back from their play.

Despite the rampant good will, Don nervously kept to himself. He had never been around so many black people in one place in his life. But Mad wandered happily through the crowd and joined every bit of merriment and jaunty argument that he could make himself part of. Everybody treated him like a long-time member of the community, as if he too were black, semi-rural and a Mississippian. Kids threw balls to him; women of all ages flirted with him with mock-propositions; men invited him to share their off-color jokes. These were good people.

The only sign of tension was a heated debate raging throughout the grounds about the Lewinsky scandal. A clear majority backed the president to the hilt, but a fairly sizeable minority felt he had disgraced the office and lost all the moral authority needed to govern.

Mad managed to wander off to another group whenever the subject came up.

At 5:15, the three white visitors met up with Preacher and Mrs. McGee, a surprisingly meek little woman who said next to nothing at all. At lickedy-split speed, Preacher explained the format of the upcoming prayer service. "And don't think I've forgotten the money," he said. "I've got everything all ready."

Deftly, Preacher made a show of producing the check from his church account, for the agreed-upon amount, and even more deftly took possession of the check made out to his care from the MMW Corp. account. Then the checks were handed back and forth one more time for some reason – some kind of dual-endorsement procedure that Mad didn't really understand. And then a fat teenager was blowing a bugle and a loud-voiced man was yelling through a jury-rigged microphone for everybody to gather at the worship tent, which had magically been cleared of the many tables.

Soon enough the service started, and the singing was heartfelt and spirited and loud and heavenly and moving, and Preacher's introduction of Mad was warm and generous and inspiring; and when Mad took the portable microphone, he was so inspired that he began ad-libbing his in a way but it was so on-target and backed by so much energy, with Mad pacing back and forth like a leopard, that the crowd responded and responded and responded some more with a genuine and deep and content-filled love for their Creator, their God Jehovah. And when Preacher produced the check Mad had given him and announced how generous it was, the love that flowed from the 3,000 in attendance enveloped Mad like a warm cocoon. Rarely in his adult life, except on his wedding day, had Mad's very soul felt so triumphant.

It was well past dark when Mad, Don and Shiloh exchanged their final hugs and handshakes with Preacher McGee and the remaining elders of the American Savior church. Driving happily back towards Jackson, where motel rooms awaited, Shiloh remembered something he had promised to do.

"Hey, Mad, Becky told me to be sure to get that check that Preacher gave you. She said you're so absent-minded that you'd lose it somewhere along the roadside."

Mad absent-mindedly replied that he didn't have the check; Preacher surely gave the check to Shiloh, didn't he?

But nobody in the car had the check. They didn't know it, but the check was torn into about 60 pieces that rested at the bottom of a huge barbequed-rib-filled garbage barrel back at the picnic grounds. But on Tuesday, the check from MMW Corp., made payable to "HPMA Church, c/o P.McGee," was cleared and deposited into the McGee bank account, which was rapidly growing large enough to cover the cost of another ruby-encrusted belt.

* * *

The reporter at the Hebert's church was with one of the big wire services, and his account ran the next day in many dozens of papers, including the one in Jackson. Obviously, he thought the mime was a planned part of Mad's act, and the article reflected that misperception. Making matters worse, the reporter had mis-heard Mad's line about the White House now having an "Oral Office." Read one headline: "Oval Office now an 'Oral Orifice'?" Another paper wrote: "Lay preacher mimics Clinton's sex act." And so the headlines went, most of them accurately reflecting that same mistaken report. The story described Mad's words as "perhaps the harshest comments yet by an American religious leader." The third paragraph quoted Mad's remark about "the brothel that our elected leader has turned the Oval Office into." He also quoted Mad accusing the president of "venality and false pride" and of "adultery and lies and perjury and obstruction of justice." And then came the mis-quotation of Mad supposedly saying "Praise the Lord for making us a better people than to be brought down by one man turning our Oval Office into an Oral Orifice!," juxtaposed with a description of the mime-dressed-as-Lewinsky pretending to perform oral sex on Mad.

Somehow a Jackson TV station had word that Mad was staying at a motel in town, and Mad was greeted aggressively by its camera when he walked out of his motel door that morning. Shiloh, trying to interpose himself between Mad and the camera, made matters worse – not because he made any contact with the latter, or even betrayed any anger, but because the camera angle, combined with the picture jiggling as the cameraman retreated, made it appear as if Mad had a big black goon who assaulted the reporter. Hard-up for any solid stories on Labor Day, the station ran with the footage on its noon newscast.

Mad's schedule that day began with a private brunch (unpaid) invitation that his church rector in Mobile had asked him to set up, outside of which another unruly mob scene greeted the travelers. From there, the drive North was mostly silent. For Mad and Shiloh, too much was happening, too quickly. They both just cogitated.

Don sat in the back seat, wearing out his cell phone with soft but hectic conversations with "contacts" all over the country reporting how their local papers were playing the story of this young "religious leader" who had so crudely taken President Clinton to task. He desperately wanted to put out a press release clarifying Mad's remarks from the day before, but Becky was back home in Houston for the long weekend and there was nobody else in Mobile he trusted with the job. Finally, Don found a buddy on Capitol Hill who owed him a favor and convinced the guy to sneak into his Hill office and put together a press release on plain white paper and distribute it by blast e-mail from a nearby Kinko's. Don was nothing if not diligent. For his efforts, the wire service put out a brief one-line correction noting that Mad had said "Oral Office," not "Oral Orifice." (As if it made much difference.) Exactly three papers bothered with the correction the next day.

The next stop on Mad's speaking tour was Oxford, Mississippi. It was the home of Ole Miss University, of William Faulkner's house, and of Square Books, which (along with Maple Street Book Shop in New Orleans) was certainly one of the two most personality-filled bookstores in the South. Oxford also was the hometown, as Becky's research had discovered, of a man named Mark Mariasson who had first set up the "Mad Religion" website. (MMW Corp. had bought the web site from Mariasson for a $5,000 price tag.)

Mad was expected for a courtesy call at Square Books at 4:30 that afternoon. The New York publisher had arranged it. Square Books was a "must stop" on the national book-signing circuit; the publisher wanted Mad to charm the store owners. That way, they'd be eager to invite him for a signing that Fall or Winter, when Mad's book was due out.

First, though, Mad was dying to see Rowan Oak, the home of famed author William Faulkner. They arrived in Oxford at 2:30, so he had plenty of time to spare.

Rowan Oak's front walkway, a gently winding footpath under a canopy of cedar trees, was peaceful and lovely. It was a perfect welcome to a stately white antebellum-looking mini-mansion. It had the look, if not the size, of an old plantation house. Mad wasn't a particularly visual person, certainly not an architecture buff, but he was impressed with the writerly aura that oozed from every nook and cranny. Most fascinating was the back room in which Faulkner had written the outline for his last novel in a sequence on the walls themselves. On Monday, in the novel, such and such was to happen; and then the next wall-space listed Tuesday's events, and so on, alongside the adjoining wall, through the book's climax on Sunday. Something about Faulkner's wall-scribblings, covering one week's time, reminded Mad of his own week-long sojourn in the psychiatric ward writing his theses.

"Hey, Shiloh," Mad said as he finished the house tour, "You and Don take a break and go explore the campus or something. I need to do some thinking, and I'd like to hike through Faulkner's woods. Would you just come back and pick me up at 4:15?"

The suggestion was agreeable to them, so Mad wandered onto the path through a wooded area adjoining the house. The path was maintained, and kept open to the public, by the university. This was nice. Summer's heat still lay heavy on Labor Day, but the shade of the woods provided ample relief. Dappled sunlight played on the leaf-strewn ground the same way it had done in the woods at the golf course where he'd napped while looking for his errant ball. Mad's mind was suffused with looking-glass memories of that weird week in the psych ward whose fruits had somehow transformed him from a high school history teacher into a nationally controversial religious theorist.

As Mad walked – bearing right, over a little bridge, circling even farther right, up a hill, still on a narrow sundappled footpath through the peaceful woods – he kept searching his memory. Faulkner's room, Faulkner's walls, and now Faulkner's woods were talking to him, urging him to remember something important from the psych ward, something he now had forgotten.

The path split. Mad chose the upper, leftward option. Before long, however, it led out of the woods, onto a semi-ugly hillside overlooking cement tennis courts and towered over by massive power lines. This was not where he wanted to be. He wandered back down to the split, tried the other direction – and found the path faded out into underbrush too thick to walk through. The path had a lovely beginning but no such end; it was not a loop but an enticingly blind alley. Back at the split, Mad sat down on his haunches. He KNEW there was something else he was supposed to remember.

He pulled his legs up to his chest, wrapped his arms around them tightly, and rocked back and forth. It was like a fetal position but sitting upright rather than lying on his side. He recalled curling into a fetal position several times during the psych-ward week. He remembered how much pain he had been in. Odd, the pain came back now very rarely, and far less searingly. He remembered when it had been the worst, when he yelled out and cursed God and … and then had felt folded up like an accordion and then had felt wracked not with sobs but with a laughter he could not control.

That was it! God had laughed through him. He was sure of it: God had laughed! In the midst of his pain, along with the gritty endurance, there had been an actual laughburst of joy!

That's what had been missing from Mad's message! Joy! At its best, Mad's message was life-affirming and unwilling to yield to harsh circumstance, insistent that a winning attitude and a willful love for even a flawed God would eventually produce rich rewards. But the message contained no joy. Endurance, but no joy. Hope, but no joy. Life, but no joy.

But God had laughed! LAUGHED! Through him, through Mad, God had laughed.

Mad's revelation was overpowering. He needed to add joy and laughter to his message. Adrenaline suddenly pumping through his veins, Mad leapt up and ran back along the path to its source. A few minutes later, he emerged from the forest, panting happily. Though not quite yet 4:15, Don and Shiloh already were there waiting for him.

* * *

Square Books is located on one corner of the town square of Oxford. Two stories high, with a tiny coffee bar upstairs and a nice long balcony overlooking the shops and restaurants and traffic circle of a truly bustling little town, the shop is such an Oxford landmark that, three years after Mad's visit, its owner was elected mayor of the town. A few doors down, the same owner ran another shop for used and otherwise discounted books, with room enough to host lectures or book readings for crowds well upwards of 100. In order to get Mad invited back there in a few months' time for a reading, Mad's publisher just wanted Mad to schmooze.

But with all the press coverage of Mad's new controversies, word had gotten around town that he was coming to the book shop. About a dozen curious Ole Miss students pretended to browse casually through the stacks, but obviously were there to see Mad. All of them, guys and gals alike, pointed and whispered and giggled, with the former doing so dismissively while the girls seemed a little starstruck. A few diffident professor types managed to screw up the courage to address Mad, three from the political left and two from the right. Mad, radiating joy, managed in ten minutes of conversation to leave all of them feeling as if their shy-but-deeply-held opinions were valuable.

One of the co-eds left the radius of her giggling friends and approached Mad while twirling the ends of her long blond hair around a ball point pen. "You're Mad Jones, aren't you?" she asked, although she already knew the answer. "My name's Mindy and … well, my girlfriends over there and I, we all think you're cute."

Mindy was a slight bit heavyset, but still shapely and sort of cute. Something about her gave Mad a rush below his beltline of the kind he had consciously tried to avoid in the months since his night-time encounter with Laura. Against his better judgment, he flashed a warm and wicked smile her way. He was saved, though, by the appearance at his elbow of a pushy late-middle-aged matron on a mission to save Mad's soul.

As if Mindy weren't even there, the matron started right in with a voice one part honey to five parts Brillo pad. "Madison, I'm Lola Jennings, and I've been reading about you for months now. You've got some potential, young man, but you've also got a penchant for real outlandish behavior. You need to calm down, young man, and get rid of your anger. What you need is a spiritual mentor who can channel your energy toward the good rather than toward some of the imbecilic places your mouth wants to take you. You're fortunate to come to Oxford, though, because we have just the man for you here. He's the rector at the church just two blocks from here – a nice young minister who's probably goin' to be bishop of this state one day…."

Mrs. Jennings was obviously just warming up for what could turn into a Castro-length diatribe that she had been waiting for months to unleash. But Mindy wasn't to be deterred so easily by some old battle-axe.

"Oh, Mrs. Jenkins here" [carelessly getting the name wrong] "is just so right about our rector," Mindy said, touching Mad's arm to draw his attention back to her. "He is just such a sweetheart of a man. But really, Mad" [segueing back into the point of her initial approach] "I think you need to concentrate, like, on people just a little younger than you are, like me and my friends, like, because I think your message can really, uh, influence with us, you know?"

Mrs. Jennings eyes flashed switchblades at Mindy. As if Mindy were a fly to be waved at but not worth swatting, Mrs. Jennings picked up her monologue right where she left off.

"You can learn something from a good priest, one who has a real spiritual center that I think you lack...."

Mindy had a competitive nature. She brushed Mad's arm again, jumping right back in. "Yeah, Mad, Mrs. Jenkins is very very wise in telling you to go see our priest; he gives great sermons that really speak to young people like me. But you can reach us even better because you're almost exactly our generation, you know, and it's like you can just, like, talk to us where we really live. That's why I think you should come to get a pizza with us right down the street, 'cuz your calling really is with college people, you know?"

"I didn't catch your name, Miss, but I can see that you might be better off dining with Miss Manners than with confused young Mr. Jones here." As she spoke, Mrs. Jennings told herself she was not to be easily outgunned by some little college tart. "I think both of you young people should keep your traps shut a little more often and really listen to what our clergy have to say and learn from it."

Mad felt like a mouse in the midst of a closed-arena catfight. But he still was riding high on his rediscovery of the importance of joyfulness. He forced himself into a broad smile and an expansively welcoming dual arm gesture. "Ladies, it sounds like both of you agree that I should meet this local minister, and I think that sounds like a good idea. I've already got a dinner engagement for tonight, Mindy, but how'bout I give you a rain check and promise that the next time I'm in Oxford I'll set up a function with this minister that BOTH of you ladies can come to?"

Mad's charisma level had risen just high enough for him to pull it off. Leaving both Mindy and Mrs. Jennings a little nonplussed, he managed to escape the premises. But only after Mindy had succeeded in pressing into his hand a scrap of paper with her phone number scrawled thereon. (He put it in his pocket.)

"I don't know if I'll ever get to meet this minister," he said to Shiloh and Don back in the car, "but whoever he is, I want to learn his secret. How any one human being can be spoken of so highly by two such different women is beyond me! All I seem to do is divide people and cause controversy; I need to find a way to bring people together instead."

"Amen to that," said the risk-averse Don, under his breath.

* * *

Dinner was scheduled with Mark Mariasson, the web-site creator. Mariasson was a 40-year-old divorced math professor who six months earlier had been spending a random weekend in New Orleans when he noticed, just before dawn, a young man affixing a sheaf of papers to the front of the St. Louis Cathedral. (Mark had been returning to his French Quarter bed-and-breakfast from an all-nighter capped by a sober-up visit to Café du Monde for beignets and café au lait.) Something about the theses, or maybe something about all the Pat O'Brien's hurricanes sloshing through his veins, had moved him so greatly that he had returned to his B&B room to grab his portable laptop and bring it back with him to the Cathedral. With a few intrigued passers-by also taking a look, Mariasson had typed in all 59 theses, lurched again back to the B&B, and e-mailed them to some friends around the country. He had then tried to sleep but, with so much coffee-and-chicory in his system, had been unable to do so. Blearyeyed but caffeined up, partly hung over and partly still drunk, Mark Mariasson had then gone about setting up a crude web site just for the hell of it.

After a short afternoon nap that finally, blessedly came, he had begun the four-plus-hour drive back to Oxford. His body wasn't really up to the drive. With frequent stops for dizziness, it took him more than six hours, until nearly midnight. Still in recovery the day after that, he had asked his department to post a note on his door canceling classes, and in early afternoon, bored, he finished enough work on the web site to launch it into cyber space. He called it "Mad Religion," and he did it as a lark. Instead, it helped create a ministry.

Now, six months later, the visit to Mark's house was nothing more than a casual courtesy call over take-out pizza and beer. Mad wanted to know this guy who had started his web site, and Mark wanted to meet the guy whose writings had inspired his site. Truth was, Mark had been going through quite a transformation in his life. When his wife left him just over a year before, he found himself bereft in a universe of numbers and postulates, devoid of meaning, full of a randomness that "probability theory" made only more stark and fearsome. He thought Einstein's famous assertion that "God does not play dice with the universe" was true, not because there is actually order or purposiveness in the universe (he thought there wasn't), but because no God existed at all. If God does not exist, He cannot play dice. If <not 'A'>, then <not 'B'>.

But in the midst of a black hole labeled "depression," while desperately hoping to find a wrinkle in time that would help him speed more quickly through his miserable existence so that to the Earth's elements he could return, Mark had somehow stumbled across the writings of one Arthur Peacocke. Dr. Peacocke was a dual-Ph.D., first having established a superb international reputation as a physical biochemist and then, while trying to unlock the mysteries of DNA, coming to be so convinced that God was in the sub-atomic details that he earned a doctorate in theology as well and was eventually ordained an Anglican priest. Mark had wondered how this could be. How could an eminent scientist, especially one in the math-physico-chemical realm where randomness was so conspicuous, possibly buy into the myth called "God"?

But Peacocke wasn't alone. As Mark Mariasson discovered when he did more research, Peacocke was part of a growing movement of eminent scientists, especially highly theoretical physicists, who became awed by the *improbability* of having random chance combine all the elements and atoms and quarks in just the right way to create the universe as we know it. Behind the randomness, they came to believe, lay intelligent design. Others of influence, he discovered, included physicist Freeman J. Dyson and physicist/theologian Ian Barbour.

Through Mark's explorations of Peacocke, he found an Internet cross-reference to a Georgetown theology professor named John Haught, who approached the same subject from the other side of the science/religion divide and ended up on similar ground as Peacocke. From there Mark had been off on a journey through the works of

1920s Harvard professor Alfred North Whitehead and of naturalist/anthropologist/poet Loren Eiseley, and of the Jesuit anthropologist Pierre Teilhard de Chardin, among others, towards a growing realization that distinguished thinkers for decades had been reconciling science and religion, the immanent and the transcendent, the physical with the spiritual.

Mark had not been long embarked on this journey on that morning when he stumbled upon Mad posting his theses at the St. Louis Cathedral. Mark saw Mad as another man who had lost his wife (although, unlike Mariasson, Mad had not been cuckolded), who was dealing with grief – and who in his grief found not the absence of God, not the randomness of subatomic particles bouncing hither and yon for no good reason, but instead the absolute presence and ultimate love of a God who Himself wanted a reconciliation with mankind. It was his astonishment at such a discovery that led Mark first to create the web site, then to maintain it for months even while almost never himself joining the chat room discussions – and those few times only anonymously. It had taken some clever sleuthing on Becky's part to track him down so she could buy the site from him, but then he became so flattered by her interest that he begged almost pitifully for a visit sometime by Mad. So it was that Becky had effectively built an entire trip for Mad around a pizza dinner from which MMW (and, eventually, its charitable beneficiaries) would reap exactly zero dollars. (Don, seeing no media potential in the visit, had begged off in favor of trolling the local bars for co-eds.)

Mark lived in a small, two-bedroom house on an attractive dead-end street near both the town square and the campus, and less than two blocks from Rowan Oak. It wasn't long after Mad and Shiloh arrived that Mad was struck by the overwhelming fact of Mark's loneliness. This was a man with such a combination of introversion and a wounded heart, Mad sensed, that easy laughter would seem so foreign to Mark as to frighten him. It was almost as if Mark the mathematician had searched so hard to find the nonexistent square root of negative-one that he himself had subconsciously tried to shrivel up into $-i$. Immediately upon opening the door to his visitors, for instance, Mark had shrunk back into his living room like a lame, stray puppy cornered by two alley cats.

"Yer-awf'ly-kind-ter-cum-here," he mumbled as he retreated. "Pizza's-cumming'-beer-in-fridge."

Mad and Shiloh, exchanging glances that bespoke great sympathy for their meek-souled host, helped themselves to a couple of Michelobs.

"So you must be a real computer whiz, to have set up the web site in just one day," Mad said, trying to break the ice. "I'm impressed."

"Really-nuthin'-toit.   Not-much-brains-needed.   Ennybody-coulda-dunnnit."

It took some serious effort from Mad and Shiloh to make Mark feel at home in his own house. But Mad had been so energized by that day's revelation, by his rediscovery of the principle of joyfulness, that he felt especially commissioned for the task of helping Mariasson find his Mark. So open was Mad, so at ease, so kind, that he slowly began producing the desired effect. Shiloh was a big help, too, his solidity and palpable decency so reassuring that Mark started feeling, well, *safe* in the company of others.

An hour later, then, pizza delivered and mostly consumed, with each man into his third lager, Mark was coaxed into enthusiastic discussion of his newfound passion.

"Look, here's a favorite passage of mine from the writings of Albert Einstein," Mark said, thumbing through one of a dozen books he had laid out on his dining room table. "It's from something called 'The Religious Spirit of Science,' in 1934. Listen: Quote:

"'The religious feeling [of a scientist] takes the form of a rapturous amazement at the harmony of natural law, which reveals an intelligence of such superiority that, compared with it, all the systematic thinking and acting of human beings is an utterly insignificant reflection.' And in another essay he wrote for the *New York Times Magazine* in 1930, he said that 'in this materialistic age of ours the serious scientific workers are the only profoundly religious people.' And here, from an address at Princeton in 1939, he famously said that 'science without religion is lame, religion without science is blind.'

"And then there's this guy John Polkinghorne, a professor of mathematical physics so distinguished that he was actually once president of Queens College, Cambridge. He's also an ordained priest in the church of England and was knighted by the queen last year. Anyway, he says that 'a universe capable of evolving carbon-based life is a very particular universe indeed, *finely tuned* in the character of its basic physical processes, one might say.' And then he takes a while to get to the point, but he pretty much says – here, let me quote again – he says that to understand how everything works so perfectly, it is almost an absolute necessity to, quote, 'look beyond science to some other ground of belief in order to provide an explanation.'"

Like many introverts whose defenses are finally overcome, Mark was so encouraged by finding that he was actually being listened to, and that he actually was in communion with other people, that now his words couldn't be stopped. They gushed forth like a (controlled) nuclear chain reaction, both creating and feeding off their own unleashed energy.

"You see what I'm getting at?" he asked. "Do you get it? God is in the atom. God is in the workings of *pi*. All of which was a revelation to me, until I realized that if God was in everything, it means that God is in evil as well. And that's exactly the point I had reached when I saw you put up those theorems that said 'God is a jerk' – but that in the end, He doesn't really mean to be a jerk. He's got all these semi-random scientific processes going on all the time, and He's trying to catch up with all of them because He's set things up a little cockeyed so that some things get out of hand, so then He sends Christ as His mediator to reconcile all the good with the bad, the weak with the spiritually strong, etcetera etcetera – and it all ends up fitting together, the way you've explained it combined with the way all these pro-religious scientists explain it, to describe a God I can finally relate to. Not only that, but a God I *want* to relate to.

"I mean, it's just all so cool."

Mad was no scientist, and he was having a little trouble following all the quantum leaps in Mark's logic. But he at least understood the gist of it.

"So you're saying that science is actually proving, or at least giving strong credence, to the fact that God exists?" Mad asked.

"Well, it's the kind of thing that's not prove-able, but what quantum physics is suggesting is that arriving at the likelihood that God exists isn't too big an ontological leap."

(Neither Mad nor Shiloh was quite sure what 'ontological' meant, but both let it pass.)

And so the discussion went (with, of course, a host of digressions), through another beer or two and then some semi-decaf coffee, for upwards of two more hours. At one point Shiloh made perhaps the most sensible point of the evening.

"But see here," he said, "what it boils down to is that we each find a different way, all based on how our particular minds work, to reach an understanding of God. But no matter how we get there, we all end up with a God who ultimately loves us. Well, I say that that's an incredibly powerful and incredibly *good* God who can take all of our weird minds and find a way to lead them all to Him."

"Praise the Lord!" said Mad, laughing. "And pass some more of that quantum coffee!"

* * *

That night, Mark Mariasson went to bed feeling like a man reborn, with the new confidence that comes from having one's ideas validated by others. Meanwhile, the Michelob and coffee both were working just enough on Mad's mind that he arrived at his motel still raring to go. And it really wasn't that late: just 10:30 or so. Emptying his pockets, he came across the phone number Mindy had pressed into his hand at the book shop. A vision of a cute, blonde-framed smile and shapely chest flashed into his mind. A charge again ran below his beltline. It had been months since he had succumbed to Laura. Temptation ran so high it was barely bearable. It would be so easy to call her now. It wouldn't be too late; all college girls were still up at 10:30, weren't they?

Mad picked up the phone. He started to dial her number. But after just three digits, the phone rang and Shiloh, of all people, answered.

Mad had forgotten to dial '9' to exit the motel's internal phone system. By pure coincidence, the first three digits of Mindy's number were the same as Shiloh's room number. (More proof, perhaps, Mad thought, of intelligent causation behind seemingly random chance?)

"Oh, God, Shiloh, you've got to save me from myself. Remember that blonde college girl at the book shop? She gave me her number, and I was just about to call her and go get myself laid."

Suddenly Shiloh was formal again, for the first time in months.

"Mr. Jones," he said, "that ain't any of my business. Telling you whether to go around fornicating or not ain't in my job description. And the Bible ain't a hundred percent clear on what a man is supposed to do if his wife up-and-dies on him. I know what I think are the right morals for your situation, but that's just not for me to say to you."

"Aw, Shiloh, cut out this 'Mr. Jones' crap. It's just that…"

Mad had been instantly annoyed with Shiloh's formality, but as he responded to his new friend, Mad's brain began parsing Shiloh's words. The phrase "wife up-and-dies on him" brought Mad short. In mid-sentence, a vision of Claire filled his head. The vision overwhelmed his male desires and his pre-Claire habit of easily taking advantage of what was freely offered to him.

Mad's voice had trailed off, but Shiloh didn't break the silence.

"… Oh, never mind," Mad said, while trying to figure out his own emotions. Mad sighed, stuffed the scrap of paper back into his pants pocket, mumbled good night, and hung up the phone. Not too much later, he fell asleep – but it was a sleep full of disturbing dreams.

* * *

Tuesday was again an early morning. They had to be in Memphis, more than an hour north, for a major 8 a.m. breakfast meeting. About 200 people were expected. But the *Memphis Commercial Appeal* had carried a story about Mad's Sunday comments on the Lewinsky scandal (and the mime's lewd antics) and mentioned that he was making a stop in Memphis. More than 200 outsiders, wholly unconnected with the convention, showed up and demanded admission. Noting that their rented meeting room was plenty big enough and seeing a way to recoup some of their costs, the convention organizers on the spur of the moment decided to let in anyone from the general public who was willing to pay $10 for the privilege. More than a few reporters squeezed in, too.

Some 400 people, therefore, crowded into a convention room, all wanting to hear, and either applaud or contest, Mad's explanation for why both God and Bill Clinton were jerks.

Again jettisoning his prepared notes, Mad spoke about neither.

"One of the very next books on my reading list is called *Surprised by Joy* by C.S. Lewis," he told them. "I haven't read it yet, but I love the title, and now I can't wait to get started. You see, yesterday I myself was surprised by joy. And the experience reminded me that God intends, in his deepest and truest longings, to provide for each of us a joy that surpasseth human understanding. Let me tell you about that experience, and about other tastes of joy I've experienced in my life, and about how the promise of the joy of God's love is the precisely desired end result of the process described in the letter to the Romans, in the passage that ends – and with which my own infamous theses end – with the certainty that, quote, 'God's love has been poured into our hearts through the Holy Spirit which has been given to us.'…."

And Mad was off on a happy and rambunctious tour of memories of Faulkner's woods, and of kisses garnered on the lap of Jesuit statues, and of scampering to home plate just ahead of a catcher's tag. And somehow he pulled numerous strands together in a way that inspired the vast bulk of his audience to a standing ovation. And when, in the Q&A session afterwards, several people asked about the Lewinsky scandal, Mad repeatedly declined to answer – and by the fourth time he declined, the vast majority of the audience gave him rousing applause. There were huge smiles on faces and rich psychic warmth throughout most of the room, and Mad felt for the first time as if he knew exactly what his mission was and exactly why he had been called into the life of a traveling preacher.

His job was not only to explain why God's jerkiness was not the end of the story, but also to proactively spread the news that the rest of the story was joy.

* * *

From Memphis it was more than a five-hour drive straight up I-55 to St. Louis. (Don spent almost the whole time on his cell phone, because interest in Mad had continued to snowball since his harsh words and the mime's performance at Apostles of the Word church on Sunday.) Events at the "Gateway to the West" were to be Mary's production, first to last. Because her law firm saw great potential in the business she was bringing its way from MMW, the firm had avoided dumping (yet) the huge "new associate's" load on her that it otherwise would have, instead giving her a bit more leeway to drum up interest in Mad's appearances. And what Mary had done had at first seemed a bit of a risk from the standpoints of both public relations and finance: There was no guaranteed fee for Mad's big lecture that night. Mary had rented a hall that could hold up to 2,000 people, and she was charging $5 admission to the lecture. Up-front costs, for the hall and for publicity, etcetera, ran around $1,000, so 200 people would have to show just to avoid break even (not even counting travel expenses for Mad, Shiloh and Don, nor counting the usual fee that MMW charged for each of Mad's appearances).

Mary was already confident her event would succeed, anyway – but with Mad's remarks vis-à-vis Clinton, anticipation had surged. When Mad walked on stage at 6:30 that evening, he was met by an almost-raucous crowd which not only filled every seat, but also featured perhaps 250 more people standing in the back and in parts of the aisles, and even spilling a bit into the rear foyer. The throng was probably large enough to violate the fire code.

Mad was raring to go. He had spent much of the ride from Memphis completely re-writing his prepared text, and once in St. Louis had had time for a two-hour nap. So it was with neither hesitation nor any pleasing introductory niceties that he leapt right into his speech.

"'God does not play dice with the universe.'

"That's what Albert Einstein once said. And although Einstein's theology was not exactly conventional, he was nevertheless a deeply religious man. So if the world's greatest genius says, first, that there is indeed a God, and, second, that God does not leave his creation to random chance, then I think we all at least ought to take those opinions seriously.

"Don't you?

"Of course, a little background is in order. What Einstein was talking about, and what a whole host of advanced physicists and other scientists are also now saying, is that the odds against life having developed, and indeed this universe having developed, exactly as it has, are positively astronomical – literally astronomical, because it all began with the energy of a gazillion stars. So astronomical, in fact, that pure randomness just cannot account for it all. One little change in one little atom at one specific time, and maybe the Big Bang would have been a Big Fizzle instead.

"Or something like that. I'm not only not a scientist, I'm an absolute techno-tard, so don't take my scientific terminology as, well, *Gospel*."

Mad's timing and inflection were right on target, and he was rewarded with an appreciative chuckle from a number of audience members.

"But anyway, here's the deal: If order was unlikely to arise from chaos due to random chance, then – many scientists believe – something must have *caused* the atoms to line up the way they did, and for the quarks to line up inside the atoms the way they did, and so on and so on. In short, some outside agency loaded Einstein's cosmic dice so that they would add up to something rather than crap-out into nothingness. However you or I or anybody understands that outside agency, that cosmic dice-loader, the entity to which we refer is known commonly by the name of 'God.'

"And out of disorder, God created a universe of meaning – just as all the atoms and molecules in the ink in today's newspaper have no intrinsic meaning, but nevertheless are imbued with meaning by the writer, for the reader. In the ink, and in the universe, there is an order and an intelligence and a thoughtfulness that is provided not by the ink itself, but by the outside agent, in this case the human, who puts the ink on the paper – and in the universe there is a meaning assigned to it by the God who lined up the atoms in just the way they were lined up.

"Are you following me so far? I see a lot of heads nodding; that's a good sign. Okay, here's where all this gets both more interesting and more challenging – and even more than that, more maddening.

"Here's the problem: If God loaded the dice in order to create order of out chaos, then He is responsible for the form the order has taken. And if what we call 'God' is the sole source of the order, then He is as responsible for the problems in the order as He is for the good parts of the order. He is just as responsible for the pain as he is for the happiness.

"And this holds true whether you are a Deist like Thomas Jefferson, who basically thought of God as a cosmic watchmaker who set things going at the beginning and then stood back for eternity to watch, never again interfering with His own creation; or it holds true if you believe that God acts within history at specific times, through miracles and through answers to prayers and through any number of other means. Either way, God set things up in such a way that some things go wrong. Either way, God is therefore either cruel or else less-than-perfectly skilled.

"And even if there is an agent of evil, a Satan loose in the world, then that is God's own fault, too. For if God is indeed the Alpha and the Omega, the first cause and the end result of all first causes and end results, then God Himself created Satan *him*self.

"It's like the Snickers bar where no matter how you slice it, it comes up peanuts. In this case, no matter how you slice it, it comes up God's ultimate fault and God's ultimate glory all at the same time, and forever and forever and world without end. And if the world seems nutty, then no matter how you slice it, it comes up that God is the original nut."

By now, Mad's listeners were demonstrating a number of different reactions. A small minority looked bored, and some looked intrigued but puzzled – but most were beginning to show signs of significant reactions to what Mad was saying. Many were chuckling, a few were nodding strong assent. But some were frowning, a few looking angry and a subset of those muttering angrily aloud.

Mad took a sip of water, and plunged ahead: "That's sort of where I came in. My world very quickly turned nutty, and horrifyingly painful. Having lost both parents when I was young, my life was horrendously uprooted this year. I lost the grandfather I idolized earlier this year and then, just weeks later, my wife and unborn child died; and then, later that same day, my wife's mother, who had become my surrogate mother as well, died in a car crash. It was pain I didn't know how to deal with, even though it was perhaps less pain even than many others in the world deal with every day. I mean, toddlers with distended bellies or whose mothers are dying of AIDS – those toddlers have known nothing but a pain that puts my own pain to shame.

"So I got mad at God. I got mad at the Alpha nut, the first cause, the universe's dice loader, the one who created the particular order we know out of chaos, the one who created atoms and waves and particles and who created a mind like Einstein's to find sense and meaning in those atoms and waves. What He gave me, what God gave me, seemed to be nothing but pain. And so I wrote that God is a flawed SOB, and that God is a jerk. And I meant it then, and in some ways I still mean it today, still believe today that it is true. If we feel pain, then God's a jerk, because God is the original author of that pain. It's that simple. God's a jerk."

By now, the audience was showing all the signs of a Sybil-like multi-personality disorder. Mad's whole manner was more than engaging tonight; it was galvanizing. But the listeners were being galvanized, quite predictably, in different directions. Unlike at previous speeches and homilies over the past six months, though, Mad this time was *not* perfectly happy to see people react angrily, so long as they reacted at all. This time his goal was to bring everybody together, to bring them along with him to a more fulfilling spiritual place. He did not want to leave even a single sheep behind.

So he hurried on:

"But that is NOT the end of the story. In fact, as Winston Churchill said in another context, it is not even the beginning of the end. Instead, the true story about God being a jerk is only the end of the beginning.

"You must understand that what I'm referring to as 'the beginning' is in the *Old* Testament. In many parts of the Old Testament, God is a jerk. I'll be the first to admit that I'm glad I wasn't a Jew during all those times when God was alternately rewarding them for goodness and then punishing them in an absolutely draconian fashion when they strayed. I mean, yes, they strayed, if you are to take the Bible literally – but God's response to their sins makes the current criminal justice system in Singapore look utterly wimpy by comparison. Floods! Capture! Torture and banishment! Death and destruction! And even the thoroughly innocent Job was treated horrendously for years until God finally repented of God's own cruelty.

"But then…. BUT THEN …. Hear me out, people. *BUT THEN*, we Christians believe, God sent Christ, his very son, the living Word, to make things right. He sent Jesus Christ to teach, and to live the example of, the new Covenant. And the New Covenant was and is and evermore shalt be that our God is ultimately a God less of judgment than of mercy, less a God jealous for our obedience than a God solicitous of our love. Our God is now a God who, despite all His mistakes and despite His own tendencies towards jerkiness, and despite our own manifold wickedness, still and always offers us redemption if we are courageous enough to have faith enough to accept the immeasurable grace that is the wondrous means of that redemption.

"God calls us to be strong – not solely because we need that strength to overcome His own jerkiness, but because He wants us to delight in the strength He gave us as a free gift.

"God calls us to be brave – not solely to overcome the pain that God forces or allows us to suffer, but because He gave us our bravery as part and parcel of our better selves.

"Mostly, God calls us to joy. Yes, joy.

"I'll get back to joy in a minute. But first, please understand what is my favorite passage in the Bible. It's the passage I ended my theses with, the passage that represents the goal towards which we can turn all our pain and sorrow and transform it. It's from St. Paul's letter to the Romans, chapter 5. It says that 'suffering produces endurance, and endurance produces character, and character produces hope, and hope does not disappoint us, because God's love has been poured into our hearts through the Holy Spirit which has been given to us.'"

"Until yesterday, I thought that with that passage I had come not just to the end of the beginning, but the be-all and end-all of faith. Until yesterday, that's where my message stopped.

"But now there's more. Now I recognize that passage not as the end of the end, but only as the beginning of the end. Because that passage leaves unanswered, leaves undescribed and unfleshed-out, the nature of God's love which has been poured into our hearts.

"As of yesterday, I think I now have an inkling of the nature of that love of God's. That love has a name, and its name is *joy*. And joy is so wonderful that it's a wonder that I ever forgot it.

"I was reminded of that joy yesterday, in Oxford, Mississippi, as I sat in the woods on land once owned by the great writer William Faulkner. Faulkner, bless his heart, was in his writings a celebrant of many types of unexpected revelations. And so I found a revelation in Faulkner's woods, on what I thought was a dead-end path. And so you, too, can find revelation in unfamiliar places, even on a path that seems to have petered out.

"And the revelation I had was a memory … a memory of the time when I was in my deepest pain. It was a memory of the time I was in hiding, in the week after my tragedies struck. It was a time when I was literally cursing God, cursing Him aloud, cursing Him for being a jerk – and 'jerk' is a much milder word than I was using.

"And as I was yelling at God, God laughed. I still can't find the right words to describe it, but God laughed.

"And He didn't laugh at me; God laughed through me and with me, and He turned all my anger into laughter and somehow made me laugh too. The laugh made no sense and the laugh had no reason. But it was a laugh of pure, unmitigated, unadulterated joy. In the midst of pain, there suddenly was joy, and the joy made no sense and the joy had no reason, other than the only reason joy ever needs, which is that joy is sent from God. And if the joy is sent by God, then that's all the reason you will ever need. God sends joy. That's what God does. Joy is God's will. And since God's will created everything, God's will is everything, and God's will is joy. And our task is merely to rejoice – to RE-joice, to make the joice, or joys, REverberate as many times as we can.

"You've had joy. All of you. I know you have. Some of you have known joy in holding the hands of your children. Some of you have known joy in a glance from your spouse. Some have known joy in physical achievement, in an expression of your art, your music, your writing. Some have known joy in the company of a friend, and sometimes even in the company of strangers who turn out not to be so strange after all.

"And yes, we know that God planned this joy. He sent this joy by way of Christ, and His sending of Christ was long in the planning. This may be a little abstruse but bear with me. Remember how I said that the God of the Old Testament was often the God who was most noticeably a jerk? But even by the end of the Old Testament period, God was beginning to turn. God was beginning to make the way for the Christ of hope and redemption and joy.

"There's a book in the Bible, from the part of the Bible known as the Apocrypha, which contains writings that some officially accept as part of God's word and others don't. Many of those writings were produced after the final, fully accepted part of the Old Testament – far closer to the birth of Christ. And one of those books, called Baruch, may be the book written most closely to the time before God sent His Son, his joy, to Bethlehem. Baruch supposedly lived 500 years before Jesus did, but scholars say the book itself took final form much later, perhaps as late as 60 B.C. So for those reasons, I choose to read Baruch as God's final words before Christ. Baruch showed where God was going.

"And here is how Baruch begins to end. It says to Jerusalem, quote, to 'see the joy that is coming to you from God! Behold, your sons are coming, whom you sent away; they are coming, gathered from east and west, at the word of the Holy One, rejoicing in the glory of God. Take off the garment of your sorrow and affliction, O Jerusalem, and put on for ever the beauty of the glory from God.'

"And then a few verses later comes the very end of the book of Baruch, the end of what perhaps was the last word from God before He sent His Son. Hear the word, and I quote: 'God has ordered … to make level ground, so that Israel may walk safely in the glory of God. The woods and every fragrant tree have shaded Israel at God's command. For God will lead Israel with joy, in the light of His glory, with the mercy and righteousness that come from Him.'"

"End quote.

"Again, it says that God will lead Israel with joy —WITH JOY! – and that mercy and righteousness come from God. God is a God of mercy and love, even when He began as a God who seemed to be a jerk… and God's love has been poured into our hearts through the Holy Spirit which he has given us, just as mercy and righteousness have been given us, just as joy has been given us.

"Endure, and you will find joy! Show character, and you will find joy! Hold onto hope, and hope will find joy! God's joy through Christ is the Alpha and Omega, world without end. God's joy is our everlasting Amen!"

And then, a pause, and much much softer, and all the more powerful because it was, Mad said simply: "The dice are loaded in your favor, so Joy and Amen to you all."

Applause and cheers washed over him like an updraft from the wings of angels. People were crying and stomping and sobbing and clapping and just flat-out being joyful. Mad's words might have fallen flat, might have sounded trite and syrupy and sickly sweet, if he did not possessed a charisma surpassing most men. But Mad had that charisma, had always had that charisma, and it gave his words the power to move minds and hearts. And so they were moved, minds 2,200 strong and hearts 2,200 strong. Minds and hearts full of joy.

Chapter Six

Mad was spent. But this was Mary's show as much as Houston had been Becky's show, and Mary had arranged for a fancy-restaurant, post-forum dinner (*sans* Don and Shiloh, insensitively) with the managing partner of the Zimlich, Shanahan firm and his wife, and a high-school friend of Mary's named Julie who now was a computer-graphic artist – and, in a big surprise, with Buzz. It seemed as if Buzz had long been promising to visit an old college buddy of his who now lived in St. Louis and had decided to turn the visit into a 4½-day weekend so he could see Mad in action.

All five of the other diners said that Mad's address that evening had been spectacular. The Zimlich partner opined that Mad had a persuasive ability that would have served him well in a courtroom if he had gone into law. His wife said Mad should go into politics. (Mad winced.) Mary didn't say much at all, but somehow seemed to be the unseen force guiding the conversation's entire direction. And Julie kept insisting that Mad ought to go into acting, both on Broadway and in Hollywood, because, speaking purely objectively (of course), he had the right "sex appeal" to be a big star. She said it very matter-of-factly, but did so only while modestly avoiding eye contact with Mad as she twirled and untwirled the ends of her shoulder-length hair around her right index finger.

But it was Buzz who was the most effusive, reiterating in a number of different ways how his "young buddy" had "done the memory of his old man proud."

"You shoulda known Mad's old man," Buzz said at one point, very intently, across the table to Mary. "A great man, ol' Ben was, a great

great friend to have. Of course ol' Buzz here, yours truly, had to teach him a few things about the ways of women, but ol' Ben was just the kind of good and decent man to have such a good and decent son."

Mary smiled, but she was most interested in how the confusing handling of checks at Preacher McGee's gathering would have left MMW Corp. in arrears on this trip if it had not been for the huge turnout at tonight's fee-for-admission speech.

"Sounds to me like you guys got snookered by Preacher McGee," she said. "You know, I think there's a legal way to protect against con artists by instituting a kind of dual-signature requirement for company checks." Turning to the managing partner, she asked, "Isn't that right, Augustus? Isn't there some way to require a countersignature for certain corporate checks?"

Mad was too tired, and too little interested in the money, to pay much attention, but he gathered that Augustus Whats-his-name agreed and that Mary would follow up on the subject with Becky.

"Looks like Mary here has all the bases covered," said Buzz approvingly at one point. "And speaking of covering all the bases, that reminds me of what my good pal Steve Matheson, the TV guy, said over a beer the other night. Steve said that…."

Gab, gab, gab: It was all a blur to Mad. He just kept nodding politely while secretly pining for his hotel bed and, on the morrow, a return flight to Mobile and a day of rest.

* * *

But the next day brought no rest. First came a cancelled flight out of St. Louis, then a big layover at the Atlanta airport once the replacement flight deposited the three travelers there. It was already fairly late in the afternoon when the pre-boarding announcements began. Just as the voice on the loudspeakers was saying something about "medallion-level customers," Don jumped up like a jack-in-a-box.

"Geez, Don, cool it," Mad said lightly. "We won't be called for a while; we're on Row 14."

But Don was already out of earshot – and he wasn't moving toward the boarding line. Instead, he was running like O.J. across the way to a news stand where a deliveryman was dropping off a new load of some magazine or other. Mad couldn't see from his angle what the fuss was about, but he saw Don grab the very first publication off the top of the new stack, before it was even off the man's handtruck. Mad had never seen Don so agitated. He saw Don pull out some money and virtually throw it across the counter and then, thumbing quickly through the pages, slowly stagger back across the concourse. He had the stunned, blank look of somebody stumbling through the immediate wreckage from a tornado in a trailer park. But Mad still couldn't see what periodical it was that Don was holding.

Still more oddly, Don tucked the publication under his arm when he neared the boarding line. The loudspeaker voice was still looking for "Rows 20 and above," but Don got in line anyway while determinedly looking away from Mad and Shiloh. The ticket-taker didn't check his seat number closely, so Don was also able to board earlier than his two traveling companions. So it was still another six or seven minutes before Mad finally sat down next to Don on Row 14 and said, "So, man, what's up? Why so glum?"

"Mad, I'm sorry; it's all my fault. I'm supposed to know these things are coming out, and I just hadn't heard a word about this. I'm responsible for your image, and somehow this one got by me." Don was actually shaking.

Mad still didn't know what Don was talking about, but for the very first time he felt a pang of real human concern for the press aide Becky had hired all those months before. Don was just so blandly polite, so unobtrusive, and such a preening-Yuppie lackey that Mad had just sort of accepted his presence but given him almost no individual thought. But now Mad was moved by how deeply Don obviously cared about his job, just how much personal responsibility he took for every single bit of publicity that came Mad's way. Mad considered Don a vacuous drudge – but now he finally realized that Don was a *deeply well-intentioned* vacuous drudge. And that made all the difference.

"It's okay, Don, whatever it is can't be your fault. I'm the one who keeps putting my foot either in dog piles or in my mouth, one of the two. Now whatcha got there for me?"

Wordlessly, Don handed over the folded-up copy of *The Zodiac*. On the cover of the Los Angeles-based tabloid was a striking photograph.

Until now, only a reporter's words had described Sunday's performance by the mime-*cum*-Lewinsky. But now here was a large color photo shot from an angle behind the mime's right ear that, combined with the distortion of a zoom lens, made it impossible to tell that the mime's head never had come closer than four or five feet from Mad's body. All the reader could see was a Lewinsky-wigged figure on its knees, head bent forward, mouth directly at the level of Mad's groin. On Mad's face was an oddly contorted grimace – in reality the result of his shock at the mime's actions, but in the context of this cover photo appearing to be the expression of a man deliberately faking orgasm.

Screaming across one side of the cover, in big letters, was this headline: "Clinton's Opponents Suck!"

Nobody in Mad's entourage knew it, but the reporter for *The Zodiac* tabloid had been occasionally trailing Mad, off and on, for some five months, in between devastating exposés on the sex lives of various Hollywood stars. By now he had quite a dossier on Mad, but his editor was waiting for the right moment to publish a hit on the young Mobilian. Even with all the intermittent publicity, the editor thought (correctly) that Mad wasn't known well enough by the general public to be an attention-grabber on *The Zodiac*'s pages.

But now the time had come. The reporter always carried a device straight out of a James Bond movie: a large faux-Bible with a camera hidden inside. When his editor saw the photo of the mime feigning fellatio, he knew he had struck gold.

"Jock," he had said, "you're the man; oh yes, you're the man! Now here's what I want you to do: Put together a short article on this Mad Jones guy, real quick, that I can use along with this picture as the cover photo. But don't use all your best stuff. This photo will sell the next issue big-time, and introduce most of our readers to Mad. Then, once everybody knows who he is, we can follow up with another devastating exposé, using whatever else you've found on the guy – his sex life, some financial shenanigans, or whatever it is that he's got hidden in his closet that you've found out."

So Jock had dutifully thrown together a fairly vapid article that just barely covered the bases of Mad's sudden rise to prominence, with the slant that Mad was just another faker using religion as a platform for right-wing politics. And now, with the help of *The Zodiac*, Mad would become the face of the "politics of hate" that supposedly was arrayed against President Clinton.

Studying the publication in their row on the airplane, Mad, Don and Shiloh were dumbfounded. Everything having anything to do with Mad's life seemed like a massive yo-yo ride. Here they were coming off a trip that, after the mime/Lewinsky incident, had gone phenomenally well, and here was Mad feeling high on a newfound, exuberant peacefulness – but everywhere they turned, the reaction to the mime's event got worse and worse. In just three days Mad's preaching had moved a thematic light year, from an emphasis on a fierce resistance to life's unfairness to a new focus on life's God-given joys. But the news cycle portraying Mad as a divisive political actor was only just beginning, and each day it became more exaggerated.

And the Lord only knew how the intensely beleaguered Becky would be back in the MMW offices in Mobile.

Before their plane landed, in fact, a phalanx of Democratic congressmen had already descended on the House and Senate TV galleries to denounce the president's opponents, suddenly embodied by Madison Lee Jones, for the supposedly increasing crudity of their viciousness.

"Nothing Mr. Clinton has done, no matter how strongly I condemn his unwise behavior, could possibly defame the presidency to even a fraction of the degree to which his persecutors are defaming it," said the unctuous "Gentleman" from Michigan. "Our Republican colleagues have succumbed entirely to the hateful theocracy of the Religious Right – represented in this disgusting photo by angry white Southerner Madison Jones – and they don't care if their hatred rips apart the sanctity of our sacred institutions."

The lugubrious "Gentleman" from Vermont chimed in: "Have they no shame?!? Oh, I ask you, have they no shame? I cry for our country when a president's few moments of weakness are turned by his political enemies into an occasion for calumny, for callousness, and for cruelty. We must fight off the ravages of these savage assaults! These attacks are un-American! We must rally around our flag by rallying around our president!"

And the oh-so-rectitudinous "Gentle Lady" from California used a handkerchief to dab moisture from the corner of her eyes. "Look at this photo," she said, head turned aside while holding *The Zodiac* at arm's length as if it were a pooper-scooper. "It makes me just so sad that our country has come to this. I want nothing more than to work with my Republican colleagues to find common ground, but their supposedly religious allies continue to sow discord among us. It makes my heart just weep, and then weep further still. So sad. It's just so sad."

One of the "Big Three" networks even led their evening news with the story, with the anchor's tone of voice and facial expression saying clearly that this was a new low for American politics.

Even the national Episcopal Church got into the act. The national church office put out a statement denouncing Mad's actions. (Oddly, there was no particular name, such as the Presiding Bishop's, attached to the statement; instead, it was just a nameless screed that had the effect of seeming to be the official, corporate position of the whole denomination.) "Madison Jones may have been baptized and confirmed an Episcopalian, but he has never attended seminary, much less even been *considered* for ordination," it said. "He therefore speaks and acts with no ecclesiastical authority, and by presuming to pass judgment on our President in the President's time of need, Mr. Jones shows himself unfamiliar with the notion of Christian charity and thus unworthy of respect as a theologian, preacher or religious sage. The Episcopal Church should not be seen in any way as being associated with Mr. Jones' enterprises or his un-Christian viewpoint."

By 6:30 that evening, somebody had thrown rotten eggs and toilet paper at the MMW offices.

So it was that when Don was informed of these developments by cell phone as soon as he, Mad and Shiloh deplaned, he was possessed by a primitive desire for revenge unlike any emotion he had let himself feel since at least early adolescence.

"I know how to turn this story around," he told Mad through clenched teeth. "I know how to neutralize all this. Will you trust me to get it taken care of?"

Since Mad neither understood the press, nor cared to understand it, he just nodded. "Sure, Don, whatever you think is right. I don't think we can undo the damage any time quickly; I just have to stay away from politics for a long enough time that eventually this'll be forgotten. But, yeah, whatever you want to do. I trust your judgment."

Truth was, Mad had never before given a thought to Don's judgment, or to his job. But he was touched by how deeply Don obviously felt about all this, touched by how much Don seemed to care what happened to Mad's image. So, sure, whatever Don wanted to do was fine by him. He, Mad, just wanted to hole up in his own home for the night.

As for Shiloh, he knew he would have LaShauna to deal with. LaShauna and he didn't agree about Bill Clinton. And she would have had four straight days now of handling the baby by herself. He didn't expect a particularly warm homecoming. But she was a fine woman, he told himself, and he loved her dearly.

* * *

The Mad Religion chat room had been broiling for three days. Thousands of notes had made the site so jammed up as to be almost inaccessible. There was no way Mad could read all the messages, so he just perused some of them at random while keeping an eye out for entries from his "regulars."

"A cheap publicity stunt!" said one entry.

"A brilliant parody," read another.

"These religious people should just shut up about politics," said a third about Mad. "What an a$$h0le!"

Feelings ran very intensely. Very few of the comments could be qualified as thoughtful. Mad was impressed, however, with one from "Intrigued in Idaho": "I'll admit to being as offended by Clinton as anyone," she wrote. "His politics make me ill, and his immorality offends me. But this isn't about Clinton, it's about Madison Jones. I had never heard of him until today, when I saw a tiny news account of his anti-Clinton comments and pantomime at that church outside New Orleans. But I've spent the last solid hour reading and trying to makes sense of his theses posted on this web site. I'm pretty strict in my faith, in fact very traditionalist, but when I take the theses as a whole, they don't offend me at all. I mean, here's a guy who was in real pain, and you can just see him working through his pain as he wrote them. Even on all those parts of the theses I don't agree with (and some I just don't understand), I am fascinated by his thought processes. If you take him on his own terms, rather than with any pre-conceived beliefs (such as my own, which I've been trying to set aside for the last hour so I could follow Jones' own arguments), then he's really found an original way to arrive at an understanding of God's grace. And now that I know he agrees with me on Clinton, I feel a kinship with him. I'll be paying a lot closer attention to him from now on!"

(To which some lunk had written: "Who unearthed the Idaho potato? It's obviously rotten. What a load of fertilizer!")

Skimming through the comments, Mad realized just what a mistake he had made by spouting off about Clinton. Mad's entire message, such as it was, was being lost in the political sniper fire. Already, he saw that by Tuesday afternoon he had lost one of his most devoted adherents.

"Dam Mad! [sic] Dam him! Just when I was starting to believe in somebody, he goes and joins the Pattersons and Falstaffs of the world and takes a cheap shot at my president. My soul is back in the desert again! I have nobody to believe in anymore. You'll never see me in this chat room again. All of you can just go to He**!!!"

It was signed "Perdicaris."

The entry broke Mad's heart. He felt guilty. He wished he knew how to reach Perdicaris, so he could explain what had happened. Mad didn't care that *he* had lost a believer, but it just killed him to think of this guy's soul being back in a "desert," especially when he had seemed so close to opening up to God.

But back to the chat room. "Mad's turned into the Scarecrow!" wrote Cowardly Lion. "He doesn't have a brain! But don't worry, because I've found enough courage to help him find the wizard and get his senses back. Unlike Perdicaris, I ain't leaving!"

Defender was delighted with Mad's criticism of Clinton and said maybe Mad wasn't totally misguided after all. Affirmed was more than delighted; he was ecstatic.

"So far I'm with Mad on everything!!!" he wrote. "I'm with him on religion and I'm with him on Clinton. I told you guys I understand him! That's why you guys should believe me when I say he's Moses and

Luther all at once. Or maybe he's Elijah. But he's definitely one of the great prophets come back for another visit. Hear his words, people, and heed his words!"

On the other hand, there was FD Thom, who wrote with great sorrow: "I'm not ready to give up on Mad entirely, at least not just yet, but this wounds me to the heart. Mad's criticism of Clinton is inconsistent with his whole message. I'll stick around for a while guys, but I'm again dropping the 'Formerly' from my name. From henceforth, I again am Doubting Thomas. Over and out – D Thom."

And then there was this from Jezebel?, added that night after the evening news: "Look, guys, I've been biting my tongue, but I can't keep quiet anymore after watching how the media is playing this story. I wish I had some real clout with the networks, because then I'd set them all straight! You see, they are all getting all this all wrong. The reason I know is because I was there Sunday morning at Apostles of the Word Church. I was there and I saw it all. That guy in the Lewinsky suit was as much of a surprise to Mad as he was to all the rest of us. You could tell by looking at Mad's face that he was horrified and shocked. The guy just came running up the aisle out of nowhere, and totally took all the power from what Mad was trying to say!

"Now I don't like Clinton, and I don't like his Republican critics either, and I didn't like Mad using Clinton in his speech at church, but you could tell he was ad-libbing. It wasn't planned at all. I could tell he was just hitting on notes that were in the tune of the audience, so he could get his bigger message across to them. I'm still not up on all this God stuff, but I was there and I tell you Mad didn't mean it to come out the way all the reports have made it seem. And I still think that if there is anybody who can make me understand more about God, if there even is a God, then it's Mad."

Mad felt goosebumps up and down his arms. Bless that Laura! After all the suspicion he had shown her, here she was setting the record straight and defending him. And of course it was Laura; now there was no doubt. Who else would have been in the New Orleans area, and with the interest to go all the way out to Apostles of the Word even when she wasn't sure there was a God, just to hear what Mad had to say?

"Jezebel? has it right again, and I thank her for it," he wrote (with the appropriate electronic identifier). "I had no idea the mime was gonna pull that Lewinsky act, or even that he was there on Sunday morning. He's around me a lot, and he's talented and sometimes he's really funny, but this time I thought he was not in good taste. Anyway, Jez is also right that I didn't plan even to talk about Clinton. But I wasn't hitting on all cylinders that morning, and I was losing my audience, so I just started to spout off on the spur of the moment about what I really thought about Clinton, since that's on everybody's minds. But I promise y'all I'll try real hard NOT to talk politics anymore. That's not what I'm about. In fact, I already told Jez (hint hint) that I wouldn't talk politics, way back a couple of weeks ago, and I just slipped up.

"Oh, and if Idaho is still there, I liked and appreciated your comments. And if Perdicaris is reading this, or if anybody knows how to reach him, please tell him to forgive me and come back. Just because he doesn't agree with me on Clinton doesn't mean I don't care what he thinks. His comments are always so constructive, he's a real valuable member of this web site.

"Now, what I really want to say is, I've had a revelation in the last three days. From now on, you all will hear me talking a lot less about overcoming God's mistakes, and more about celebrating God's joy. More on that later. Thanks, as always, for reading. *Mad*."

Mad turned off his computer too soon to see M. Magdalene's first "Mad Religion" comment in ages. "I hope Mad's not confused about something," she wrote. "But Mad should know he has just as much right as anybody else to talk about politics, and if it's done right, without any surprises from a mime, it can give him some good publicity for the rest of his message. And every time he goes on TV he'll get more women followers. For instance, even in *The Zodiac* cover photo, I still think he looks like a hunk. I wish I could meet him some day!"

As for Perdicaris, he never returned.

* * *

On Thursday morning in New York, famed TV news guy Spike Walters looked at the summary review folder, prepared by his personal assistant, of the previous day's news from a host of sources. Among the items inside were the front page and Jock's story from *The Zodiac*, along with the criticisms from the Democratic congressmen and the transcript of his own network news' lead story on the subject from the night before. Walters wasn't just any news guy; he was the septuagenarian host of the granddaddy of all TV news magazines, "Hour of Truth." In his own mind at least, he was more responsible for exposing the crookedness, hypocrisy and other forms of venality of more skinflints, scoundrels, and scofflaws than was any other living journalist. A regular crusader for justice, he was, and also so wise as to be the definer of what was and wasn't just in the first place.

And now here was some upstart Christian hatemonger bringing the presidency of the United States down into the gutter, at a time when the nation obviously needed to forgive and forget (and punish Ken Starr for prosecutorial abuse). This was more than right-thinking people should have to bear.

He buzzed his personal assistant. "Start up a file on this Madison Jones guy," Walters said. "Find out all the usual stuff. Check his finances; get Bishop Pringle and Rabbi Heintz to poke holes in his theology. I don't just want an Achilles' heel on this guy; I want his Achilles' gonads being used to feed the fishes. Let's see how fast we can build a dossier and decide whether he's worth a segment on our show. If he's worth going after at all, we'll want to do it before the Republican jihad against Clinton plays itself out. Oh – and see if we can get that aggressive producer on this. Whatshername, Martina? Yeah, Martina Bigtitsky, or whatever it is."

And so it was that the assistant, Al Bobbitt, and young producer Martina Beritzky began their pursuit of Mad Jones.

* * *

That same morning, the Rev. Larry Falstaff released a statement distancing himself from the Mad/mime antics: "It is unfair to paint all conservative Christians with the brush of a crude charlatan whom I have already personally denounced at every turn for months on end."

The Rev. Rob Patterson remained silent, but he personally thought the mime had performed a useful service. The more the godless liberals held up *The Zodiac* front page and the more they denounced Mad, the more the image would get planted in American minds of just how vile was the president's behavior that the mime was mocking. Patterson was surprised by how strongly Mad himself was reported to have denounced Clinton, but he figured that Mad was merely seeking publicity and hoping to piggyback on the strongly anti-Clinton sentiment the polls had shown in the first two weeks after his mid-August deposition. In Patterson's mind, it showed that the young upstart was desperate for attention – which meant that Mad's ministry must not be going well. When a man is imploding, Patterson thought, there's no need to help him do so. Just stand back and enjoy the spectacle.

As for Gladys Phillpott, the doyenne of the conservative movement, she just watched and wondered. She couldn't yet ascertain whether the young man would be a boon or a challenging enemy for her causes. He certainly had a talent for publicity. He merited close scrutiny.

* * *

Mad slept late on Thursday morning. But when he finally forced himself out of bed, he decided to take care of something that had been bugging him for more than four days. He called the police headquarters and left a message for Officer Williams to call him when he went off duty.

A dispatcher relayed the message to Williams in his patrol car (he was alone this morning, because Shiloh had desk duty until mid-afternoon), and since it was a slow day, Williams drove right over. He figured it was time he taught this young pissant a lesson.

Mad was shocked, first, to hear his doorbell ring, and second, to find Officer Williams there on his porch, belly thrusting angrily forward like an aggravated hippo.

"Whachu-want, a-ess-hole?" said the officer. "You mighta been an ath-uh-lete in high school, but if I wudn't in uniform right now, I'd kick yer pansy faggot ass until it was as black'n'blue as a nigger's toothache."

Mad immediately felt his bile rising, but by dint of supreme effort he kept a temperate countenance.

"I didn't expect you so soon," he said, opening the door more widely and making a gesture of welcome. "Can you come in for a minute?"

The officer looked at him suspiciously. "Last time I was here, you shut the door in my face, a-ess-hole. What makes ya think I want to contaminate my uniform by entering yer pansy-ass premises?"

Mad stared into the officer's jowl-dominated face. He felt his fists clenching and unclenching of their own accord. He forced himself into a half-smile.

"A good cup of coffee, perhaps? It might make my apology easier to swallow."

Still scowling, but also looking a little confused, the officer lumbered inside while saying, "Ya better damn well apologize, ya two-bit punk, or else I'll be forcin' an apol'gy down yer gullet so far that ya shit it out with yer breakfast."

By now, Mad was grinding his teeth enough to give hope to a den of dentists. But he walked Williams back to the kitchen and poured him a cup.

"Here's the deal," he said, finally. "You've been making me mighty angry by the way you've been talking about Shiloh Jones, and by the way you call him a 'nigger' and warn me away from him as if you own him or something…."

The officer sneered and started to say something, but Mad put up his hand to stop him and continued his thought: "… But that's no excuse for me slamming the door in your face. That's why I apologize. I think you and I need to reach some kind of understanding."

The officer was still suspicious, but slightly less belligerent. "I'll tell ya what ya need ta understand, punk, is that ya shouldn't be messing with the head of Jones-y. Yer leadin'im in the wrong die-reckshun, and ya damn well know it." Williams was poking his finger near Mad's chest for emphasis. "And fillin' his head with all that college garbage, as if a nigger who cain't play sports no longer has any business thinkin' about college!"

Mad tried one more time. "Officer, why don't we try something here? Here's what I want to try. Why don't you let Shiloh make his own decisions, and why don't you give me the courtesy of not offending me by calling him a nigger – and in return, I'll lay a promise on you. In return, I give you my word of honor that if college doesn't work for Shiloh – and I know it WILL work for him, but I'll pledge this anyway – then I will personally repay Shiloh for the amount of police pension he'll be losing by coming to work for me. And not only that, but …

[Mad searched his mind for something else to say]… but, uh, if you just give ME a chance, I'll, uh, I'll even…"

Officer Williams cut him off. "You better not be trying to bribe me, boy. You better not be about to offer me some cash to keep me from kickin' yer ass. But I'll tell you what. I'll tell you this. Maybe you're actually sincere about this. Maybe you're one of those goody-two-shoes dreamers who really think that nigg – I mean that our Negro friends have some mental abilities. I'll tell ya what: You promise never to shut a door in my face again, and I'll take ya up on yer offer to make up the money in Jones-y's pension. And I'll accept yer apology, fer now, and we'll both stay out of each other's way. You jes go about preachin' yer nonsense interpretation of religion, and I'll jes go about protectin' the citizens of Mobile. And I'll even tell everybody that asks that you're a good kid at heart, even if you're a little cracked. How's that? We got a deal?"

Mad forced himself to reach out his hand for a handshake. "The joy of the Lord be with you, Officer," he said.

* * *

That afternoon, Mad received a phone call from The Colonel.

"I say, I say, I say, Son, you been kickin' up a mighty big fuss, Son, you been kickin' up a fuss. Our Society had another phone conference about it, Son, yes we did, I say, we had a conference."

"Sir, I'm sorry, sir, it's just that…"

"Hear me out, now, Son, I say, hear me out. I'm not finished talkin', Son."

Mad sighed. "Yes, sir."

"You gotta understand, Son, that our Society isn't threatening you with anything. All we do is good for the University, Son; we never do anybody harm. But, I say, Son, I say, you're not behaving like a Gentleman, Son. We have a big investment in you, Son, and we want you to live up to its standards. All we can do is appeal to your conscience, Son, but we ARE appealing to it, and we're appealing to it RIGHT NOW. If you're gonna go around doing this preaching and meddling, Son, at least do it with dignity. Please at least promise me that, Son. And if you don't promise it for the sake of the Society, Son, then do it for the memory of your Daddy Lee. Am I making myself clear?"

"Yes, sir, I promise this time that I'm really going to watch myself. The Society has been very good to me, sir, and I am very sorry if I am letting you down."

"Well, that's good, Son, that's very good. Now I don't want to have to call you again, Son, I say, I don't want to have to chastise you again."

"Yes, sir." Mad's politeness had its limits, and they were fast approaching, but he managed to still stay within its bounds. Besides, he was sure this conversation was about to end.

"Oh, Son, and between just you and me, Son, I say, just one more thing."

"Yes, sir?"

For the first time on any of these phone calls, The Colonel chuckled. "Every one of us on the conference this morning, every one of us who know the power of Eight, we all like the fact that you're against that draft-dodging drug-using womanizing piece of trash. Frankly, if anybody else but one of our own had pulled that stunt with the guy looking like Lewinsky, our whole Society would be laughing about it over cocktails and loving every bit of it.

"But that's jes between you and me, Son. You just keep up your dignity, and you'll be okay."

The phone went dead.

* * *

The next day, the fruits of Don's damage-control labors became evident. Personally, Mad didn't really like the counteroffensive when he saw it, but for this week at least he was beyond worrying too much about what was in print. No matter what he did, the media seemed out of control, so he tried to just ignore it all.

Don's ploy was to call in some old chits he had with the other major national tabloid, *The Investigator*, produced from an office in the Hollywood hills and delivered at all newsstands first thing every Friday morning. True to form, *The Investigator* was vicious. "Soiled White

House, Dirty Tricks," read the headline. The gist of the article was not just that the mime's Lewinsky impersonation was a surprise to Mad and everybody else at Apostles of the Word (the Rev. Hebert was quoted saying that "that nice young Jones boy was obviously horrified"), but that the whole thing had been a set-up by the Clinton White House so as to make their opponents look sleazier than the president did. It quoted Mad's chatroom comment that he thought the mime "was not in good taste." And it quoted "an observer in the church that day" (Don, speaking anonymously) to the effect that "that mime is obviously just a nutball."

"And sources say," concluded the article, "that proof will soon be forthcoming that the White House made him a nutball for hire."

In his tiny (500 square-foot) French Quarter apartment, the mime read the tabloid and fumed. He wasn't a nutball, he was an artist. And he didn't know a soul at the White House, and he would never sacrifice his artistic talent for dirty lucre regardless. He wished he could find out who in the church had called him a "nutball." Whoever it was should pay a price.

Chapter Seven

The tabloid publicity boosted Mad from mid-level stardom to certifiable national phenomenon. Even when Congress released the videotape of President Clinton's Lewinsky testimony, and Mad studiously avoided all requests for comment, his very refusal drew attention. In some ways he had achieved that uniquely American status of being "famous for being famous." Becky was able to jack up Mad's appearance fees, and even began following Mary's lead by charging admission to some of his speeches, and yet ever-larger throngs crowded each event. It quickly became clear that at MMW Corp.'s next semi-annual board meeting, the company would have plenty of "profit" on hand to donate to charities. Quietly, Becky began sending out word through the non-profit network that MMW would begin taking applications for grants.

But Mad was taking only intermittent pleasure in his "success." He was lonely. He still missed Claire so much, sometimes, that his insides felt twisted in Gordian knots not only too tangled to untie, but also too hard and unyielding for any knife known to man to cut through. But when he wasn't missing Claire, he increasingly was cognizant again of the bodily desires that had tempted him with the co-ed Mindy at Ole Miss. He had not yet succumbed (other than, months ago, to Laura), but the temptations were becoming more and more difficult to ignore. And when Hurricane Georges battered southern Alabama on Sept. 27 and 28, Mad had an odd reaction. Rather then fret much about whether his house would suffer damage, and rather than become agitated when his section of town lost power for nearly a day, all Mad could think about was how frustrated he was that he was holed up in the darkness without an intelligent woman to keep him company.

The first weekend of October, Justin and Becky and a few others dragged Mad out (in dark glasses) to Mobile's downtown street music festival known as Bayfest. A mix of local and national acts performing at stages spread over about 25 square blocks, Bayfest is a perfect event – busy, but not overcrowded – at which to relax and just have fun. There, at one of the stages in the very early Sunday afternoon, Mad found himself entranced by a singer out of New Orleans of whom he had never heard before. Leslie Smith was a fit, long-legged, dark-haired beauty with a voice so rich and expressive that even in broad daylight it evoked the deepest tragedies and triumphs of the most dramatic of love stories played out in the best of dark, smoky, post-midnight jazz joints. Mad had never seen and heard anything like her. She looked perhaps a few years older (at most) than his 25, but he wouldn't let that deter him. *This* was a woman he just had to meet.

So Mad stayed after her act, hoping he could catch her mingling afterwards with the crowd so he could make an approach. Sure enough, she came right off the stage to a holding area just across a small police barricade from where Mad and Justin stood. But before he could try to get her attention, she was whisked away by a vibrant short-haired woman who seemed to be a good friend of the singer's and a wavy-dark-haired man with a mustache who seemed to be a friend of the short-haired woman.

"Damn, Justin," Mad said. "That woman has it all. I gotta find a way to hear her sing again."

For once, Justin was speechless. He, too, was enthralled.

Only later did Mad realize that this was the first time since Claire's death that he had even considered taking the initiative to meet a woman, for any reason. It was like breaking through an invisible electric fence. Henceforth, he might just begin – he might just consider – he might occasionally find himself in a mood – to actively look for female companionship.

But still he didn't act on those thoughts. Mad, the ghostwriter and their publisher approved a final version of their book (like the web site, to be called *Mad Religion*), and Mad kept writing his newspaper columns and taking three-to-four-day speaking tours every other week, constantly updating and modifying his basic message of Creator/Dice-loading-God as jerk-turned-joygiver. The fall elections came and went, and Speaker Newt Gingrich was deposed, and the *Mobile Register* bragged that it had the only columnist in America who correctly predicted the electoral outcomes – but Mad's life seemed to just spin along of its own accord. (*The Zodiac* and "Hour of Truth" quietly continued to investigate Mad's life for potential use in future "hit pieces," but Mad was unaware of their efforts.)

But on Friday morning, November 20, Justin gave Mad's life a jolt. He called Mad from New Orleans, where Justin was attending some seminar or other for athletic trainers.

"Hey, buddy, I'm here in New Orleans, buddy, and I'm checking out their 'Lagniappe' section of the paper, which is where they list all the musical acts and stuff. And buddy, guess what? This is your day, buddy, this is your day! Guess who's singing tonight? Just guess. No, don't guess, I'll tell you: It's that girl Leslie Smith, that gorgeous singer from Bayfest. Yeah, buddy, here's your chance. She's with some group with a weird name called 'The Cleminists,' whatever that means, and she's at this place called Carrollton Station. Why don't you come over to New Orleans tonight? I know you got nothing going on in Mobile. Come on over here, crash in my hotel room, and come out with me to hear your dream girl."

Mad protested feebly, but Justin knew that the protests would fade. So by 4 p.m. Mad was on the road to New Orleans, and by 7:30 he and Justin and were finally seated (after a lengthy Friday-night wait) at the Houston's on St. Charles Avenue. Snippets from more than a few overheard conversations made clear that lots of people in New Orleans were excited that its native son and congressman, Bob Livingston, was about to become Speaker of the U.S. House of Representatives. Judging from the comments, he seemed to be an unusually well-liked politician. People sounded genuinely proud of him.

But as for Justin, he didn't look very good, and he kept sniffling. "I don't know what it is, Mad, cuz I felt great this morning, but since mid-afternoon I've been sneezing and getting all congested and my eyes are itchy and it's just driving me crazy."

"Hmmm... Allergy attack," Mad mumbled.

"I dunno, Mad, I've never had allergies before – but you know what, come to think of it, last time I was in New Orleans, the same dad-gummed thing happened."

Anyway, Justin's sinus problem didn't stop him from talking a light-year a minute, and by dinner's end the monologue combined with the sniffling was getting on Mad's nerves. They drove on over to the riverbend neighborhood of small shops and modest houses where the Carrollton Station bar competed with two other nearby music clubs, with Justin insisting all the way that of course he felt good enough to stay out and listen to "that Smith babe" play. But he was wrong. Even before the music started shortly after 10, the little guy had developed a pounding sinus headache to go along with his watery nose and itchy eyes.

"Look, friend," Mad said. "You go on back to the hotel room and sleep it off. You've already given me an extra room key; I'll just catch a cab when I'm ready to call it quits for the night. Yes, I'm serious: Go on. I'll be fine here by myself. Go get some sleep, Justin."

Which was how Mad got to hear Leslie Smith and the Cleminists without having to endure Justin's running commentary. Again, he was entranced. Smith was sultry and soulful and obviously highly intelligent, all at once, with a voice that could move even a statue's emotions. She was joined by two other attractive and talented women – one on piano and the other, who looked barely out of high school, on bass. They were terrific. And Leslie Smith was a woman Mad told himself he just had to meet.

So it was that Mad's hunting instincts were re-awakened for good. Problem was, when the first set was over and Mad made his way up to try to speak to the singer, two other guys got there first. One was a skinny dark-haired guy with a beard, the other was more heavy-set and curly-haired, like a less hefty Norm from "Cheers." Ms. Smith greeted the former like a long-lost friend, so Mad hung back to wait for a less intrusive opportunity.

Which was when he heard a voice, a fresh and soothing voice, that he recognized.

"Ohmygod, it's Mad! Gosh, Mad, what are you doing here?" It was Laura Green, and she sounded genuinely delighted to see him. And Mad was destined to never meet Leslie Smith.

Which was how, as Mad reflected much later, life seemed always to work. Led by a chance phone call from a friend, you finally decide to go after one thing, and something else entirely comes up instead that would never have arisen if you hadn't responded to the possibility of the first.

Mad could have been home in Mobile, staying out of trouble and perhaps enjoying a quick bite with Father Vignelli, or maybe with his friend Jason and Jason's fiancée, Vicki. Or Mad might just have been sofa-bound in front of a silly rental movie like *Scream 2*. Hell, he thought Neve Campbell was cute. He would have been perfectly safe at home watching her escape a deranged killer again. But no, not Mad. He had to drive all the way to New Orleans to try to introduce himself to a singer he had heard only once in his life, and then he had to go and virtually order back to the hotel the annoying little buddy who would otherwise have kept him from doing anything he later regretted. And, Mad being Mad, he had to do it all *not* in order to meet this entrancing singer, but instead to find himself soothed again by Laura's fresh-sounding voice that always seemed to have an odd power over him. It was all as if fate was the scriptwriter for an inane TV sitcom called "Mad Life" – one of those sitcoms where the joke was always on the main character. Which, of course, was Mad.

Before Mad really knew what was happening, he and Laura were deep in conversation. She was telling him how she had moved up to New York to work full-time for "Acute Vision," and how the show was still languishing slightly below the middle of the ratings list, but well above where it had been when she and he made their debuts on it last spring. It was still, therefore, on the network's "bubble" of shows that may or may not be cancelled at any minute. But the good news was that the network execs were happy with her work on the show and had already begun talking with her about changing her contract so that she would be tied not to "Acute Vision" specifically but to the overall network news operation. In other words, if the show were cancelled, she would still have a job. She was back in New Orleans only because her show's whole crew had Thanksgiving week off; she had flown into town just that evening. But she wasn't staying at her parents' small house; she was "house-sitting" at the apartment of a friend who hhad flown out that night to spend the week with family back in the Atlanta suburbs. Laura was supposed to meet some other friends at Carrollton Station, but so far they hadn't shown up.

The conversation continued even when another band called "Twangorama," this one all men, took the stage. (Apparently Leslie and the Cleminists were only doing one set.) Laura forgave Mad for mistrusting her; Mad forgave Laura for failing to emphasize, in her national report on him, how reluctant he had been to be a public figure. A few times he pointedly, but laughingly, called her "Jezebel," and she always shrugged off the reference with what looked like a slightly quizzical smile. "You don't mind me calling you 'Jezebel'?" he asked at one point. "Sweetheart, you can call me just about anything you want to," she said, leaning in close to him. "Besides, wasn't Jezebel a powerful woman? I like being thought of as a powerful woman, sweetheart. And if Jezebel was bad… well, I can be bad, too, if ya'know what I mean."

She was practically purring.

What she didn't tell Mad about was her network boyfriend up in New York. He hadn't proposed to her yet, so certainly she was free for a little play on the side while on vacation – wasn't she?

Mad couldn't resist. As before, Laura did have a power over him. Not only that, but this time he was on the prowl anyway. She offered to drive him back to his hotel. At her car around the corner from the music club, he found himself kissing her. Kissing her with abandon.

They never made it to Justin's hotel. They went back to her friend's apartment instead. And the next morning, Mad didn't cry. He smiled.

* * *

What they didn't notice was the young woman who had several times tried to get their attention at Carrollton Station, and who had even begun to follow them around the corner in hopes of getting a few words with them. She was a reporter for the local paper. She wrote the weekly "seen-about-town" social gossip column called "Hip Chick's Picks." The column was the "cool" younger version of the society page, and Yuppies and chic *artistes* alike usually got a kick out of being recognized in it. The Hip Chick had been out for a non-working night on the town when she recognized both Mad and Laura. As a matter of fact, she had seen and heard their surprise at running into each other and, knowing of how they had effectively helped each other reach public stardom, she had figured a few comments from each about their chance meeting might liven up her next column. But after she pulled a tiny notebook out of her purse, she could never catch their eyes. Both of them obviously were aware only of each other.

Now *this*, thought the Hip Chick, was even more interesting. Juicy stuff for her column, perhaps.

And so it was that, six days later, a special Thanksgiving Day version of Hip Chick's Picks contained these lines near the top of its rollicking survey of the New Orleans social scene:

> "The pre-holiday weekend got off to a Mad, Mad start last Friday night at Carrollton Station, where young religious phenom **Mad Jones** was seen canoodling with local-girl-made-network-newsie **Laura Green**, whose up-close reporting helped launch Jones' career back last March. But her reporting then was nothing near as 'up-close' as the, uh, rapt attention she was paying to Mr. Jones on Friday night. … And speaking of rapt, 'It's a wrap.' That's what the word is from the director of the latest movie to use the Crescent City as a backdrop…."

The ensuing firestorm didn't exactly erupt; to mix metaphors oxymoronically, the firestorm snowballed. It started small but grew as it rolled along. Laura was at her parents' house early to help prepare Thanksgiving dinner and had not even thought of reading the paper. Until, that is, her mom casually asked, "Darling, what does 'canoodling' mean?" She handed the paper to her daughter and watched as her normally composed baby Laura began to blush.

The news director for the local affiliate of a competing network did know what canoodling was. Truth be told, he was less interested in knowing whether the canoodling had led anywhere that night than he was in knowing if the canoodling was the continuation of similar activity from as far back as March. He remembered when Mad's theses first were discovered, and remembered the race among the news shows to try to track Mad down – and he remembered thinking then how odd it was that a second-rate assistant producer had been the one to get the scoop. "So who is this Laura Green girl?" he had asked his news staff back then.

"Oh, I've run across her before," said one of his cub reporters. "She's a little vamp on the make. I wouldn't put it past her to screw her way into a scoop." (The cub reporter hadn't mentioned that she had turned him down cold when he had asked her for a date.)

The news director didn't like getting scooped, not on anything, and he had the hubris to think that the only way he could get scooped was through a violation of journalistic ethics by his competitors. And sleeping with a source isn't exactly kosher. Heck, if he could bring this Green girl down, her former bosses at his competitor's newscast would surely be tarred with guilt by association. So he made a few phone calls.

Phone calls were also on the mind of Nurse Number 3, Sue, from the Mobile psychiatric ward. Driving that morning from Mobile to her family's Baton Rouge home for Thanksgiving dinner, the nurse picked up a paper in New Orleans when she stopped for gas. That afternoon, while all the family men were in one room watching football, she escaped dishwashing duty by sneaking into her old childhood bedroom with the paper. The column entitled "Hip Chick's Picks" caught her eye. She thought it sounded like a fun read. And when she saw the item about Mad and Laura, it made her think back to that weird incident in the hospital room when Mad had grabbed her breast. (Okay, she had actually taken the initiative in placing his hand there, but nobody would ever know that.) She pulled out a scrap of paper she had carried in her wallet for two months now. It was a parenthetical note, including a contact phone number, that ran at the bottom of Jock's story in *The Zodiac*: "*The Zodiac* is offering a $50,000 reward for anybody with information, and proof, of where Mad Jones spent his week in hiding after his wife's tragic death."

Hospital records were, of course, confidential. She could lose her job if she released them without permission. To her, $50,000 was a lot of money, but not enough to make it worth losing her job. But these tabloids loved stories with a sexual angle. This "canoodling" stuff with Laura gave her an idea. Maybe if she played her cards right, she could get *The Zodiac* to jack up its reward money. For $100,000, she probably would be willing to give up her job. Heck, she figured she was smart enough to parlay a nest egg that large into something really special.

She called an old high-school friend of hers, now a lawyer, and he used three-way dial so together they could call the number listed in the tabloid.

Their call would make Jock the reporter very happy.

* * *

On the day after Thanksgiving, otherwise universally known as "the busiest shopping day of the year," bookstore browsers nationwide were greeted with stacks of quickly produced hardbacks titled *Mad Religion*. The cover photo showed a Redford-like 25-year-old with an engaging smile, against the backdrop of a medieval scroll with the word "Theses" barely discernible in larger type than the rest of the scroll's faded calligraphy.

Inside was a book that was an amalgam of a short (20-page) biography of Mad and a "popular religion" manifesto that "unpacked" Mad's unique, controversial and somewhat complicated theology in a way that could be understood by an educated 9th Grader. (For mass sales to the American reading public, that's about as demanding a comprehension level as could be risked.)

Five pages had been devoted to an explanation of the history behind Martin Luther's original 95 theses in 1517. Exactly 1½ pages had been devoted to each of Mad's 59 theses. His St. Louis speech, in which Mad first combined his highly individual explication of the Einstein/science/religion background with his new message of God's joy, was printed in its entirety. So were reprints, each on its own page, of the 50 of Mad's daily advice columns (out of more than 200 published so far) that Mad and the ghostwriter and the publisher had determined were probably the most popular or memorable.

Padded with a series of lists ("Mad's suggested reading list of religious-themed books"; "Mad's top 20 Heroes of the 20th Century"; "Mad's favorite movies," etc.), along with a concluding 1,500-word essay by Mad, the whole thing barely stretched to 200 pages. It was intended by the publisher to be a mass-marketed quick read for the spiritually challenged – that year's winning Christmas entry in the "dumbed-down, self-help way to spiritual wholeness" sweepstakes.

Mad (along with Shiloh, in his inaugural service on MMW's full-time payroll) was scheduled for a brutal three-week book, cross-country book tour. The publishing house would handle all the publicity, so Don would not be shadowing Mad to do whatever mysterious alchemy it is that PR folks are supposed to do. (In what should have been a blow to Don's ego, part of his duties in Mobile during those three weeks would be to run errands for LaShauna, who was not at all happy that her husband's new job would take him away from sharing parenting duties with her for three whole weeks.)

The tour was to begin in New York on Friday evening. In what was a harbinger of how controversy would dog its every step, the very first event was graced with the re-appearance, for the first time since Labor Day, of the mime. Shiloh eyed him warily, but as the mime was on his best behavior and causing no actionable disturbance, nobody could figure out reasonable grounds to ask him to leave. He was dressed like Santa Claus, with the one difference being that rather than wearing Santa's red cap he was wearing a Lewinsky beret. He obviously wanted people to know that he was the same guy whose back had graced the photo on *The Zodiac*'s cover. (Of course, when a reporter tried to interview him, the mime wouldn't make even a sound. He was, after all, a mime.) But what his presence mainly accomplished was to change the whole focus of the event from Mad's intended message to Mad's views of the ongoing impeachment drama. The more Mad declined to comment, the more people (especially the reporters) tried to find clever ways to lure him into at least an indirect reference to the scandal. The way the elite media works, any and every story has a better chance of garnering attention if it is somehow tied in to the day's dominant story or theme.

"Listen to me!" an exasperated Mad finally said in response to the sixth or seventh question relating to President Clinton. "I'm not here to talk about politics, but about faith. Faith is what's important. In fact, maybe if people paid more attention to their faith, then our politics wouldn't be so polluted with these kinds of stories. Now, as I was saying about how God respects those who wrestle with him,...."

Mad went right back to his theological themes. But one of the New York papers the next day ran a small story, but well placed at the top of an inside page, headlined thusly: "'Polluted' politics." The sub-head read: "Religious author says faithlessness at root of scandal."

Other than the short new quote from Mad, the rest of the story was a re-hash of the Labor Day weekend controversy, along with a passing mention that Mad was in town to plug his new book. Alongside the story ran a photo of the mime as beret-clad Santa.

That same morning, Mad's advice column, now running in 71 papers, added more grist for the unintentional-publicity mill. The letter writer had asked a question concerning divorce. Mad responded that, although he didn't personally condemn those who got divorced, the Bible and especially Christ himself spoke rather explicitly against the practice.

"I think it's safe to say," Mad wrote, "that there are three absolutely legitimate grounds for divorce: abuse, adultery and abandonment. Beyond that, divorce is hard for me to justify, based on my understanding both of my faith and of my moral belief that a promise made should be a promise kept. And he or she who is not faithful to that promise will have to answer, in some way, to God – who may well forgive, but that's for God alone to know. As for third-party witnesses to an act of faithlessness, such as adultery, I think our vows as members of a Christian community require that we quietly but firmly let it be known, in private conversations with the adulterer, that we urge him or her not to forget that he (or she) made a vow before God's altar. Nobody should ever give the impression that adultery is acceptable, or that abandonment or abuse is acceptable either. And if believers abjure all three of those betrayals, divorce should diminish as well."

It was a fairly orthodox Anglo-Catholic response. But in coming days it would be juxtaposed with the New York paper's sub-head – both spoke of a condemnation of "faithlessness" – in a way that made it seem, during such a mono-maniacal news focus on the Lewinsky scandal, as if Mad were taking another shot at the president.

And then there was a slowly-but-surely growing buzz, fueled both by the Internet and by quiet efforts of the New Orleans news director, about the report of Mad canoodling with the very reporter who helped make him famous. His book, marketed brilliantly by the publishing house, was already flying off the shelves. The sense that Mad was controversial further fueled its success. And as his book tour moved from New York to Philadelphia to Washington, D.C., he was met everywhere by excitedly burbling crowds.

Then, Wednesday afternoon rolled around, and *The Zodiac* hit the news stands.

It was the kind of story that, if its subject survived it, would guarantee the subject's ensconcement into the realm of superstardom. But survival of such a story would be a decidedly dicey proposition.

Here was the headline:

Clinton Hater: Nutty, slutty, rich men's putty

It ran across the cover, bracketing a photo of Mad from one of his appearances months earlier, when Jock the reporter caught him with an odd and highly unflattering expression.

The story inside, a massive one, ran as follows:

> Mad Jones, the newest religion phenomenon and fakir who grabbed some free publicity several months back by jumping on what then seemed like an anti-Clinton bandwagon – with a vile mock act of fellatio in a right-wing "church," no less – is now revealed, in a Zodiac exclusive, to be not just "Mad" by nickname but actually mentally unstable.
>
> Mr. Jones also has a history as a sex addict – possibly turning that to his advantage by using sex to help launch his so-called "ministry" in the first place – and, in another twist worthy of suspicion, may have long benefited from the support of a shadowy cabal, a "secret society," based at the University of Virginia.
>
> Put all these strands together, and it may well be that Mad Jones is at the vanguard of the actual "vast right-wing conspiracy" that Hillary Clinton was ridiculed for warning the nation about late last winter.
>
> These revelations come courtesy of an exhaustive eight-month investigation by *The Zodiac*.
>
> First things first: Three new developments in the past week have again put Jones in the spotlight. First, *The Zodiac* has discovered that Jones has a history of mental illness (see related story beginning on this same page). Second, a "social scene"

column in a New Orleans paper reported on Thanksgiving Day that Jones had been seen "canoodling" the weekend before with Laura Green, one of the top reporters for the network news show "Acute Vision." Green was a mere assistant producer at a local New Orleans TV station when Jones first posted his religious "theses," or propositions, around which he has built his entire ministry. But, with no prior experience as an investigative reporter, Green somehow beat a host of other reporters trying to track down Jones, who had been in hiding for more than a week after his wife died unexpectedly of a mysterious "hemhorrage."

The question naturally arises, if Jones was "canoodling" with Green two weekends ago, is there a history there? Did Jones and Green mutually sleep their way to stardom? *The Zodiac* has uncovered evidence that makes this speculation sound less farfetched.

But more on that in a moment.

The third new development in the growing brouhaha over Jones occurred last weekend, when, as the *New York Informer* reported, Jones began a new book tour by accusing President Clinton of "faithlessness," on the same day that his syndicated newspaper column equated marital "faithlessness" with spousal abuse (otherwise known as "wife beating").

Jones' Clinton-bashing is in line with his earlier remarks at a right-wing New Orleans-area "church," when he said the president had turned the White House into a "brothel" and that the Oval Office had become an "Oral Orifice." Right after he said so, an accomplice wearing a Lewinsky wig and blue dress rushed the platform and simulated oral sex on Mr. Jones as a way to dramatize the president's supposed transgressions.

And as early as the interview Ms. Green did with Mr. Jones for her "Acute Vision" debut last March, Mr. Jones was criticizing Mr. Clinton.

All of which, *The Zodiac* has learned, leaves Jones wide open to potential charges of rank hypocrisy. Not only is his relationship with Laura Green in question – after all, this is still less than nine months after his supposedly beloved wife suddenly died, and his original interview liaison with Green was barely more than a week after the mysterious and tragic demise – but, as *The Zodiac*'s investigations long ago discovered, Jones has a history as a "lady's man" that Bill Clinton could only hope to emulate.

Ironically, Jones is a graduate of Clinton's own *alma mater*, Georgetown University. A former Georgetown classmate of Jones', now a Democratic staffer on Capitol Hill who asked to remain unnamed, said that Jones' sexual exploits were legendary on the campus.

"Mad wasn't a one-night stand guy," said the classmate, "but he was the king of the three-night stands. Find a girl and con her into bed on the very first night; jump her bones again a few nights later, then give her the old horizontal mambo one more night for good measure – and then, after the girl was hopelessly in love with him, dump her like a ton of bricks."

And Jake Murphy, a teammate of Jones' on the Georgetown baseball team, called Jones "a regular babe magnet. I mean, most of the guys on the team did okay with the ladies, if you know what I mean, but Mad was the kind who got so much action that we were all in awe of him."

Also, the Chief Operating Officer of "Mad Mad World" (Jones' supposedly non-profit corporation), Becky Matthews, has been identified by several former Georgetown classmates as an old flame of Jones'. "She's a slut through and through," said one former classmate who wished to remain unidentified. "I remember when she and Mad hooked up in the first place. She couldn't stop bragging about it."

Matthews, still single, is now living in Mobile, Alabama, just a few miles from where the also-single Jones maintains his bachelor pad.

And in the crowning blow to Jones' standing as a legitimate critic on sexual issues, he was reported for sexual misconduct while a patient at a Mobile hospital (see related story).

Finally, there is the matter of the secret cabal that may have been financing Jones' efforts as early as his days as an undergraduate at Georgetown. Oddly, the shadowy organization at issue is not affiliated with Georgetown, but with the University of Virginia, which has numerous "secret societies" running around on campus. Most of them are known for pulling harmless, funny pranks, but the granddaddy of them all, the "Crazy Eights," are more serious.

While nobody has ever offered proof of any nefarious doing by the "Eights," as they are commonly known, they have an aura of mystery and power. The Eights are known for donating large gifts to the university, making them obviously a gathering of the wealthy elite of Virginia society. But on a more sinister note, powerful secret societies have long been associated with elitist tendencies and sometimes bizarre, even Satanic, rituals, and those in the South have sometimes been suspected of virulently racist activities. Few doubt that such cabals are a hotbed of right-wing thought and action.

Two factors make it likely that Jones has some connection with the Eights. First is his family history. As a member of the famous Lee family of Virginia (on his mother's side), Jones had a great uncle, Jackson Lee, who was a prominent financier and graduate of U.Va. who was widely suspected of being a member of the Eights. And Jones' late father, Ben, received not one but three different degrees from Virginia.

The second factor was an odd ritual Jones performed each semester while at Georgetown. Once per semester, Jones would recruit eight new Georgetown students to make a pilgrimage two hours South from Washington D.C. to Monticello, the home of U.Va. founder Thomas Jefferson.

Yes, eight students. A crazy eight, perhaps?

On each of those trips, Jones paid for all the gasoline and for light snacks for the ride. In fact, fellow classmates said Jones always seemed to be (by student standards) "rolling in dough," in the words of one Hoya – which was odd considering that Jones had been orphaned by his middle-class father when Jones was only 16.

Apprised of all these facts, U.S. Rep. Rusty O'Sullivan (D-Mass.) said he was not surprised.

"It all adds up," he said. "This is just more evidence that the forces arrayed against our president are both reactionary and dangerous. This young man appears to me to be a hater of the first order – and, if what you say of his sex life is true, he's also a hypocrite of the first order as well. Of course, the right-wing elite has long been known for wanting to apply draconian standards to others while allowing themselves to behave like Mount Olympians in heat."

And Democratic consultant Carney "The Gorgeous Georgian" James had this to say: "It just goes to show that the president's enemies are rotten to the core. But the war this Jones guy is fighting along with all his right-wing nutcake friends is a war that will turn against them and obliterate them all."

Along with that article ran this shorter sidebar, headlined "Jones' secret psychiatric retreat".

A nurse at a prominent Mobile hospital has finally cleared up the mystery of Mad Jones' whereabouts during the first week after his wife, Claire, died, immediately after which interlude Jones posted the 59 religious propositions that first made him famous.

The nurse showed *The Zodiac* copies of hospital records that prove that Jones spent the week in a psychiatric ward. There, not only was Jones prone to "insane-sounding outbursts," as the nurse put it (and as the records confirm), but he was recorded as having made aggressive, inappropriate sexual advances against the nurses.

(The nurse who is *The Zodiac*'s source asked to remain nameless, for fear of losing her job – and because of the same possibility, was reimbursed by this newspaper for her cooperation with our investigation.)

According to the hospital records, the nurse reported an incident in which Jones suddenly placed his hand under her uniform and grabbed her breast.

"Not only that," she told *The Zodiac*, "but as he did it, he said one of the most insane things I've ever heard – and since I work on a psychiatric ward, I've heard some crazy stuff. He almost shouted it. He called me 'Esmerelda,' even though he was looking right at my name tag that showed my name to be nothing like that, and then he said, 'Esmerelda, your eyes are like stars in a chuck wagon soup.' It was so bizarre it scared me. I felt lucky to have escaped his room without any further harm."

The nurse said that she had good reason, based on cryptic comments from two of her colleagues, to believe that at least those two other nurses also experienced uncomfortable, sexually charged incidents with Mr. Jones.

The records show that Mr. Jones checked himself into the psychiatric ward on the morning of Sunday, March 1 of this year – just one day after the mysterious death of his wife. He checked himself out during the evening of Saturday, March 7. In the interim, he was diagnosed with severe depression bordering on dementia, highly passive-aggressive behavior, and sexual dysfunction, and he was reported to see imaginary visions and to carry on loud "conversations with God" in his empty room.

Nevertheless, a psychiatrist on duty the next weekend, Dr. Theodore Theodore – who had not overseen Jones' care at all during the week – signed Jones' release papers. Four days later, Jones was videotaped hurling a golf club at a TV reporter and a cameraman while yelling: "A plague on both your houses!"

Since that incident, Mr. Jones has not been seen in public engaged in behavior that, according to several psychiatrists consulted by *The Zodiac*, could be characterized as psychotic. But he has at times seemed to experience what observers have called "somewhat volatile mood swings."

Mr. Jones could not be reached for comments on these reports.

Chapter Eight

Late that afternoon, all the usual suspects in Congress paraded before the microphones. The unctuous Democratic "Gentleman from Michigan" said this was just one more case where "the president's accusers are themselves unclean. Mr. Clinton's sins are a speck compared to the mote in his accusers' eyes. Can any of them stand the scrutiny? Let those who have not sinned cast stones, but let the rest of these hypocrites be warned that they have opened themselves up for stoning." He paused, as if thinking deep thoughts. Then he added: "Let it be clear that the mentally ill are to be pitied and not condemned, but I do think it's instructive to learn that some of this anti-Clinton hysteria and hate comes straight out of the loony bin."

Added the rectitudinous Democratic "Gentle Lady from California": "This is all so sad. Rather than wallowing in the mire of hate and lunacy that our Republican colleagues have been sucked into, I think we need to elevate our conversation and go back to doing the nation's business."

Shortly afterwards, the four most prominent "moderate" Republicans on Capitol Hill issued a joint statement. Hailing from Maine, Connecticut, Illinois and Oregon, the three male representatives and one female senator were widely known by the moniker "The Mod Squad."

"We have long been troubled by the intemperate tendencies of some of our more conservative Republican colleagues," they said. "Now we see that they are taking their lead from a charlatan who may well be mentally unstable. Our country needs healing, so this impeachment saga must be stopped. Regretfully, we urge adoption of a resolution of censure for our troubled president – and then we should move on to saving Social Security and providing better health care for all Americans."

On the congressional Right, reactions were mixed. Some immediately distanced themselves from Mad. A mid-level member of the Senate leadership blasted the left-wing media for trying to link all Republicans with "a confused young man who not a single one of us even knows," and said that the latest "tempest in a tabloid" should not stop the House from "doing its duty by the Constitution to see that the laws be faithfully executed." But the libertarian Republican representative from Florida jumped to Mad's defense, urging a full-scale investigation of how Mad's hospital records had been made public. "This is an egregious violation of his civil rights by the nexis of the left-wing media and the allies of the Big Brother in the White House who has done the same thing many times before, ranging from the pilfered FBI files to the threats made against so many of the other women who were victims of Bill Clinton's libidinous exploits."

As a guest on CNN that night, Gladys Phillpott said empathetically that the media should "leave that poor boy [Madison] alone and concentrate on the constitutional crimes of the president." But on MSNBC, the Rev. Larry Patterson said that "the sinner from Mobile should repent, just as our criminally perjurious president must be made to pay the piper. We who favor impeachment as a simple matter of justice do not deserve to be branded with the mark of a sexual deviant we have long condemned. We stand with the Lord against sinners of both the Left and the Right. And by the way, speaking of the Lord's justice, I think it's interesting that the biggest hurricane to strike the United States this year went straight for Mobile, which is Madison Jones' hometown."

* * *

Justin, calling on Mad's cell phone, was apoplectic. "They're not gonna get away with it, buddy! We'll sue them all, buddy, we'll sue! And how dare they say those things about Becky? If I get my hands on that *Zodiac* reporter, I'll rip his nuts off! I swear I'll rip his nuts off!"

For her part, Becky passed out, dead drunk, under her desk at the office.

* * *

That same night, The Colonel somehow tracked down Mad on the road. (How the Colonel always managed to know how to reach Mad was more than a little unnerving to Mad, to say the least.) But this time The Colonel wasn't calling to chew Mad out.

"I say, I say, I say, Son, this is one fine mess we're in. These evil bastards have used you to attack us, and they've used us to attack you, all at the same time. This won't stand, I say, this won't stand. We're in this together, Son, we're in this together."

"But Sir, I thought you would be furious at me," Mad said.

"I say, Son, you are one of our own by adoption, Son, and you've been wronged by those bastards. Our disappointments with you in the past are jes' between you and us, but we stand up for our own. We're like the Crazy Eight Musketeers, Son, 'all for one' and all that good stuff. And I jes' want to make some things clear, Son, before we talk about what we're gwoin tuh do to respond to this outrage.

"First, Son, I say, first I want to reassure you that the Crazy Eights have never done anything to hurt anybody, not in all the long, long history of our organization. We have no Satanic rituals, and while we are proud of the old South, we aren't the slightest bit racist. Not only do we have Negro members, but back when the university was integrated, we played a role in making sure it was integrated without any of the unseemly problems that were seen in places like Mississippi and Alabama and Arkansas. All we ever do is provide anonymous gifts and services to our beloved Jefferson's university, Son, and that's all we will ever do. I say, that's all we'll ever do."

Mad was a bit dumbfounded. He had grown to heartily dislike and even slightly fear The Colonel, even while he was grateful for the financial support the Eights had provided him. But here was The Colonel entirely on his side.

"Aren't you disappointed in me, Sir?"

"I say, Son, now is not the time for us to worry about the past. So you took a little vacation in a hospital when you lost your lovely bride so soon after losing your Daddy Lee: So what? And so you sowed wild oats in college: So what? And even if you're back to your old tricks of playing around with the ladies, well, so what? As long as you keep your vows when you're married, what does the rest of it matter when you're fancy free? If having a way with the ladies were a crime, your Daddy Lee woulda been cut off from contact with the Society ages and ages ago. We sure as heck wouldna' provided all that money to his grandson if we were embarrassed by him doin' what any red-blooded man woulda done once his wife departed this Earth."

The Colonel went on to give Mad "instructions" on how Mad should respond to *The Zodiac* article. Mad should issue a statement, every word of it true, to the effect that he was not now, nor had he ever been, a member of the Crazy Eights. He should say that his MMW Corp. had "never received a dime" in support from the Eights, nor was it affiliated with the Eights in any way. He should say further that he had never knowingly even laid eyes on a living member of the Crazy Eights, and that his father Ben had never even said a word about the Eights to him. And, based on the implication that Mad, his father or his great uncle had any connection with any group that took racist actions or performed Satanic rituals, Mad should say that he was having lawyers investigate the possibility of suing *The Zodiac* for libel.

Meanwhile, The Colonel told Mad that a former governor of Virginia would call a press conference on behalf of the secret society during which the governor would relay the message that the Eights themselves were considering a libel suit against the tabloid. The governor would note that while he wasn't himself a member of the Eights, he knew them to be of excellent character and a "progressive" force in the state. The potential libel suit would be based on the implication that the Eights did harm to people, that they were racist and Satanic, that they were politically active or "right wing," or that they had in any way donated money to MMW Corp. in order to promulgate an anti-Clinton agenda. He also was to relay the message that Madison Jones was not now, nor had he ever been, a member of the Crazy Eights.

"The idea, Son, I say, the idea is to give our message heft and weight by threatening legal action. That'll get the news stories we want. But of course neither of us will actually follow up with a lawsuit, because that would open the Eights up to 'discovery' during depositions. The whole point of doing anonymous good deeds for a university is so that the individuals involved will do the good deeds for the sake of the school and not for public credit and self-aggrandizement. If they do 'discovery,' and publish our membership, then that whole point will be defeated.

"Meanwhile, Son, I got one more message for you: Keep on preaching *your* message that Christ is a redeemer and that God's goal for us is joy. None of us quite understands all your theology, Son, but we've been noticing that you are emphasizing those two constructive ideas. So jes' keep it up, Son. Now that we've been attacked together, we'll make sure you have all the support you need. All for one and one for Eight."

The line went dead.

* * *

The next morning in New York, Spike Walters looked through the packet that assistant Al Bobbitt had prepared for him. It included *The Zodiac*'s hit piece on Mad. Walters buzzed Bobbitt on the intercom.

"Hey, Al, I see where this trashy tabloid took young Mr. Jones to the cleaners. They really did a number on him. Could not have happened to a more deserving little punk. But, look, I don't want 'Hour of Truth' to look like we're following in the footsteps of a trashy tabloid. Besides, as far as the Clinton fight goes, Jones has been totally discredited now, so there's no use for us to go ahead with a show on him. So I know this might disappoint you and Martina, but this project is now on hold. But I'll tell you what: I don't think we've heard the last of this punk, so keep your file on him. Keep it active. We won't blast him now, but if he raises his punk head to cause any more trouble later on, we'll be ready for him."

* * *

Mad's publisher didn't know whether *The Zodiac* story would be a disaster for book sales or a boon. He suspected that, if the publicist did his job right, it would be the latter. Controversy creates buzz, and buzz sells books. He decided to play the story up. Mad was due in Atlanta the next afternoon; the publicist made sure all the appropriate Atlanta radio stations talked up the arrival of the "controversial, sometimes outrageous, and sometimes, yes, *mad*, Mad Jones."

It worked. The crowds in Atlanta that evening were bigger than ever. And Mad, hyped up on angry adrenaline, wowed them all. It took him hours to sign all the books that sold at the bookstore that hosted him.

But when the adrenaline wore off that night, Mad had another of his "episodes." Shiloh found Mad sitting at the base of the ice machine at the end of their hotel hallway. Mad was holding his hands together in a cupped position, staring intently into them. In his hands was a tiny pool of water with a few tiny pieces of not-quite-yet melted ice. Mad's stare was so intense, it looked as if he were trying to divine some mysteries from the melting ice the same way a fortune teller uses a crystal ball.

"Hey Mad, you okay?" Shiloh asked.

Mad stared at him rather blankly. "This, too, shall melt away," he said.

Shiloh reached down and shook Mad gently by the shoulder. This was really weird, he thought.

With the shake, Mad jerked his head a little and his eyes lost their glaze. "Oh, Shiloh, were you saying something? I must've fallen asleep. I better get back to my room and go to bed."

* * *

The next day, Mad's tour took him to Savannah. While the publicist took care of some business, Mad and Shiloh visited some of the city's historic homes, ate lunch at the Pirate's House restaurant and relaxed for a while, unrecognized, in the lovely Trustees' Gardens. It really did seem like a charming place. They saw two plaques there, dedicated to the husband-and-wife team who apparently had started the city's whole historic renovation movement a good half-century earlier. "If only all of us could leave as pleasant a legacy as these two folks…" Mad said to his bodyguard.

Shiloh was happy to see that Mad showed no signs whatsoever of the weirdness he had demonstrated the night before.

When they checked in at their hotel that afternoon before the evening book-signing, Mad was greeted by a FedEx letter along with a copy of the newest weekly *Investigator*, just out on the news stands that morning. Again, Don had planted a hit piece of his own to counter *The Zodiac*'s article. The story in *The Investigator* essentially accused Carney "The Gorgeous Georgian" James of orchestrating the entirety of *The*

Zodiac's coverage of Mad. The press questions that had goaded Mad into the quick veiled reference to "faithlessness" in politics? The Georgian's doing, said the article. The "bribe" paid to the nurse to release records of Mad's psych-ward stay? Financed by Carney James. The false accusation that Mad was a member of the Crazy Eights, and that the Eights were racist and Satanic? Again, a Clinton hit job funneled through Mr. James. And so on and so forth. And the story quoted an "associate of Madison Jones" as saying that "there's every reason to believe the mime is actually a paid political hack."

Inside the FedEx letter were two pieces of paper and a videotape. One paper was a copy of the press release put out the previous afternoon, from Mobile, by Don. Two paragraphs of the release followed The Colonel's instructions (as relayed through Mad) to a 'T,' with the libel suit explicitly threatened but no mention of which law firm was looking into the case. Another paragraph contained a quote from Mad: "Again, a wholly random comment of mine has been blown way out of proportion. Yes – when asked again and again about my opinion on the current impeachment crisis – I reluctantly expressed my disapproval of the president's actions. But I have never tried to emphasize that subject. In fact, I consider myself fairly apolitical. And, far from being right wing, my personal political beliefs (when I even think about politics, which isn't all that often) are only slightly to the right of center: 'moderate' by national standards, and perhaps even 'liberal' by the standards of the average Alabamian."

A final paragraph gave information on the next stops of Mad's book tour and referred all questions concerning it to the publishing house in New York.

The second paper was a letter to Mad from Don. It was Don's resignation from MMW Corp., effective immediately.

"You will see, Mad, that I have responded professionally to the latest controversy. I have followed all your instructions, and I also took the initiative to again plant a story in *The Investigator* to provide cover for you. But I can no longer allow my reputation to be sullied by association with somebody who has spent time in a nuthouse and who has ties to a sinister secret society at a university that is not even our own *alma mater*. You should have told me of these flaws of yours before I agreed to join your employ. Anyway, as a professional I will certainly leave your employment quietly, with no public notice. But I leave, nevertheless, with some bitterness. As a close personal friend of yours, I believe I was owed full disclosure from you before you allowed me to put my own reputation on the line on your behalf. I think I will go back to work on Capitol Hill, where the politicians have more character than you do."

Mad was not overly disturbed to see Don go. "Close personal friend?" Where did that come from? And Mad was distinctly uncomfortable with the retaliatory hit piece in *The Investigator*. That just wasn't Mad's style.

Nevertheless, Mad felt a little guilty. Don was a cipher and a drone, but Mad realized that Don had put himself on the line for Mad, for whatever reason. And Mad had never extended himself in the slightest on Don's behalf. Mad thought of himself as a more considerate person than the one who had taken Don so much for granted. How, he wondered, had he allowed himself to become so oblivious to the feelings of another person?

Finally, there was the videotape. Scotch-taped to the top of it was a hand-written note from Don: "Did you give your approval for this? As your press secretary, I should have known about this. Your failure to inform me about it is just one more example of why I can no longer work for you."

From somewhere or other, the publisher's publicist conjured up a VCR machine. When they plopped in the videotape, Steve Matheson's face and voice filled the screen.

"And as our last guest of the night, we have Buzz Buskirk, distinguished history professor and also godfather of Madison Lee Jones, the young armchair theologian who has caused such a stir not only in the religious community this year but also in politics through his pithy criticisms of our priapic president. Mr. Jones, as some of you know, was recently revealed by *The Zodiac* – if you can believe *The Zodiac*, of course, when it's not writing about Martians landing in Mayberry – anyway, Mr. Jones apparently spent a week in a psychiatric ward earlier this year after his wife died.

"Buzz, you're a military historian: What would Sun Tzu have said in his famous 'Art of War' writings about somebody who takes on the president just a few months after creating a sexual storm with the nurses at a loony bin? I mean, I just love the style of your godson, but isn't there some good advice somewhere about not attacking from a position of weakness?"

"Well, Steve, not even I knew where he had been during that week when he was incommunicado, so I still don't know if the tabloid report is true. But I'll tell you what, Steve, Madison is a fine young man and even if he went haywire there for a week you've gotta understand just what a lovely bride he had just lost. Not only that, but…."

"So you're saying Mad is not mad?" Matheson interrupted. "Not even a little looped? I mean, dontcha have to be a little loopy to take on a president whom critics say is surrounded by thugs who threaten to break the kneecaps of his amorous conquests? I mean, you're a friend of mine, you know I'm just joshing with you a little, but after this *Zodiac* article don't you think your godson oughtta lie low for a while? Or is this his 'Gut Check' time where he stands up for what he believes, no matter how his own past makes him look?"

"Well, uh…"

"I know you'll say, and I believe too, that perjury by a president is worse than a little nookie in a loony bin, but dontcha think Mad is getting into some pretty tough company when he tries to match epithets with Carney James, the 'Gorgeous Georgian' who is so often a guest here on 'Gut Check'?"

"Well, you know Steve that compared to Mad I'm just a wise old owl past my best hooting days, but you know how young people can ignore the advice of their elders. I might advise him to cool it, you know, but when you're young it can be awfully fun to be rash."

"Well," Matheson said, "I say more power to him. If he's got a gripe with the president, good for him for going for it with gusto. But meanwhile, Buzz, if I need any wisdom over a few workingman's brews, I'll turn to you even if your godson won't. Thanks a lot for being on 'Gut Check,' and come back soon. Bye, folks!"

Mad covered his eyes and groaned.

Why had nobody asked him if it was okay for Buzz to go on the air? Mad thought the result of his godfather's appearance was that he, Mad, sounded like a circus freak. Who gave Buzz permission to go on the air?

If it wasn't Don, it must've been Becky. Damn her – how could she do this without asking *him*?

Mad grabbed his cell phone and began to call Becky at the Mobile office, but then changed his mind and instead dialed the number of Buzz' university office. Maybe Buzz would be done with classes for the day.

"Y'ello?" said Buzz.

"Dammit Buzz, this is Mad. Did Becky tell you to go on last night with Steve Matheson? How could you go on the show without checking with me?!?"

"Hey, young buddy, I was just doing you a favor. It was a last-minute thing: Steve had somebody cancel on him, so he called me up and said to go over to the studio. I didn't even think of calling Becky, and I didn't know how to get in touch with you on the road for your book tour, and I figured that *some*body needed to stand up and defend you. What're you so hacked off about?"

"Dammit Buzz, the one thing I insisted on at the very beginning of all this lunacy was that if y'all wanted me to start a so-called ministry, that NOBODY could speak for me without my permission. You made me sound like a clown, Buzz!"

"Jesus, Mad, all I was doing was doing you a favor! But okay, I'll tell you what: Steve'll have me on his show again lots of times, cuz he says he needs an academic expert on military affairs like I am. So from now on when he wants me on his show, I'll be the star instead of making you the star. How's that sound, *young* buddy? You just get somebody else to defend your honor. *If* you can find somebody else. Jesus, you really have let all this attention go to your head, haven't you?"

Mad was therefore not in the best of moods for his book-signing that evening. Even worse, the mime was there. Shiloh really was tempted to give the mime a piece of his mind, but he couldn't bring himself to do so because the mime was actually making him laugh. Dressed like a penitential altar boy, with ashes smeared on his forehead, the mime wore a sign on his back that said:

Mea culpa

…But…

Mad's a Cupid

A local reporter at the book-signing tried to ask the mime a few questions, but the mime covered his own mouth and ran away.

* * *

That same night, Justin convinced Becky to let him take her to a nice dinner at a little restaurant across Mobile Bay in the quaint bayside town of Fairhope. By now, Becky considered Justin a friend, despite how much he unintentionally annoyed her. She referred to him as "my sweet little man," and when he told her that she deserved a nice night out to take her mind off *The Zodiac*'s "hideously unfair slander," she didn't even try to find an excuse to decline.

Still wary of alcohol after her terrible hangover the day before, Becky had to be coaxed even to accept a single glass of wine with dinner. That's why she knew it wasn't drunkenness that led her to actually laugh at some of Justin's oddball jokes that on previous occasions would have made her cringe at his "weirdness." Her "sweet little man" was still a goofball, but at least his heart was good and he made for a loyal friend. She didn't understand why she had not found a boyfriend since moving to Mobile, but a sweet little platonic companion was better than renting a movie alone at home or getting hit on by rednecks or sleazy lawyers in various bars around town.

After dinner she was too tired to go "out on the happenin' town," as Justin put it, but when he dropped her off back at her condo and showily kissed her hand in that silly little way of his, she responded for the first time ever by kissing him on the cheek.

"G'night, Justin," she said. "You're a good guy; you know that?"

* * *

That same Friday night, "Acute Vision" aired in the dead-end time slot to which it had recently been moved in a last attempt to find it a more receptive audience. Laura was the reporter for the show's first segment (an investigation of a $2,311 student loan that a local bank back in 1962 had "inexplicably" forgiven for a now-leading Republican, when the Republican had been an entry-level, 23-year-old corporate sales clerk recovering from a badly broken leg). With the "canoodling report" and then the *Zodiac* article, the "Acute Vision" executives had wondered whether they should garner some publicity by firing Laura for supposedly compromised journalistic ethics. In the end, they decided she was the most glamorous thing going for the struggling show, so they just "called her on the carpet" at a meeting intended primarily to scare her and remind her (for their own ego-gratification) that she served only at their pleasure. She had told them the same lie she told her network boyfriend: She had unexpectedly run into Mad after having about four drinks, and so yes, she had responded to his kiss for about ten seconds when he opened her car door for her – and then they had both laughed and she drove him back to his hotel without further incident. *Of course* there was no history there, especially no romantic history that had anything to do with the story she had done on Mad for the show. (Her boyfriend accepted the story and "forgave" her, but only at the cost of making her "prove" her love for him by performing some new bedroom gymnastics for him.)

Anyway, what neither the network executives nor Laura expected was that the show would jump up 14 spots in the Nielsen ratings that week. The publicity about Laura's possible tryst with Mad had attracted a host of living room TV rubberneckers, eager to see for themselves what this vixen looked like and whether the stress from the attention would cause her to have an on-camera wreck.

But Laura had done fine, and although the show's real investigatory news value was nearly nil, her slim and fresh good looks impressed a segment of the 20-something American male population. The better ratings – still not spectacular, but solidly acceptable to the network – continued the next week, and the week after that, and the week after that. And in the back of her mind, Laura made note of the career advantages that could accrue from canoodling in public.

* * *

The chat room traffic had become so heavy that the server was having trouble handling it all. Critics were having a field day calling Mad a "male slut," a "heretic," and an "orgiastic fornicator," and also a "cracked cultist," a "crazy nutbag," and a "Cuckoo's nester in lust with Nurse Ratched."

Jezebel?, though, had become active again, defending Mad fervently. "He's a young man and he's gorgeous," she wrote in one entry. "Who are any of you to condemn him for doing what comes naturally?" About the psych ward visit, she wrote that "if I were the nurse, I would have jumped his bones and kept my mouth shut about it." And as for the reports about the supposedly evil secret society, she called it "nothing but innuendo that I don't believe for even a moment. But if he's involved in a ritual, I want to be the woman he ravishes. SO THERE! But on a more serious note, what does any of this other stuff matter? What's important is his message of redemption and joy that is making even this non-believer take another look at God."

Ever Faithful responded that Jezebel? obviously was a sinner who needed to repent of her sexual longings, and that Mad had now been proven "nothing more than a crackpot." Defender, despite his happiness at seeing President Clinton criticized, concurred with Ever Faithful. D Thom wrote that he wouldn't pass judgment until a "real newspaper" ("unlike *The Zodiac*") confirmed the reports about Mad.

But Affirmed was as ebullient as ever. "Okay, so maybe I STILL have my Biblical figure wrong," he wrote. "Instead of Moses (or Luther), maybe Mad is the new King David. David still did great things for God and for God's people even though he screwed around all the time on the side. Remember Bathsheba? Even after that episode where David clearly was in the wrong, God blessed him with power for decades more, because David was overall doing God's will and serving God well. Hail King Madison!"

* * *

The book tour continued down to Florida and then across the country to Phoenix, San Diego, Los Angeles, Sacramento and San Francisco, and the House of Representatives impeached Clinton on two counts, and then the tour took nearly three weeks off for Christmas and New Year's. By that time, Mad realized that he had actually been enjoying himself. He was thriving on the attention. His continuing "episodes" of "spacing out" aside, the stress that did accrue gave him an adrenaline rush that was sort of fun. He managed to succeed at sidestepping the constant political questions and was gratified that the majority of his audiences were more interested in asking him how a God who was a jerk could also be a God whose goal for us is that we find joy through the strength He gives us.

On Christmas Eve, Mad was delighted at a request to read the famous Christmas passage from Luke for a national radio broadcast. "Glory to God in the Highest, and on earth peace, good will toward men," he concluded the reading. Then he added, extemporaneously: "And if I may add, at this Christmas celebration, that we should all rejoice that God's love has been poured into our hearts through the Holy Spirit which has been given to us. Have a Mad-ly Merry Christmas."

The next day would be the first Christmas Mad had ever spent without a single family member, but that was okay: Gifts and cards had come in from all over, and Mad spent much of the day at a soup kitchen doling out meals for the homeless, and he arrived back home to find on his side porch an ice chest with some casserole dishes full of turkey-and-stuffing leftovers, along with a kind note, courtesy of LaShauna and Shiloh.

Mad tried not to think about how, just a year ago, he and pregnant Claire celebrated their first Christmas as a married couple, along with Daddy Lee, with a joyfulness full of the hopes of a lifelong bond complete with not just the wondrous child in Claire's belly, but three or four more children to come. But if life was full of pain, so too was it full of the grace he had somehow, mysteriously, begun to know.

Chapter Nine

After the grueling book-tour schedule between Thanksgiving and Christmas, Mad and Shiloh both had insisted upon easing back into things even after the three-week break. (The "break" had still involved plenty of work, because Mad had naturally fallen a bit behind on his column writing and other projects while on the road.) The agenda in early January involved hitting smaller "prestige" stops rather than big media markets. In fact, part of the trip would retrace the steps they had taken on Labor Day weekend. It began at noon on Saturday, January 9 in New Orleans, at the neighborhood Maple Street Book Shop. Maple Street's owner, Rhoda Faust, had been a second-generation friend of the great novelist Walker Percy and also was friendly with a bevy of other New Orleans-area authors. Not much more than a converted one-story house, the book shop featured narrow aisles where books almost seemed to be falling in on visitors – but somehow with such charm that a literate person would welcome such an avalanche. Really, the shop was too small for the crowds that Mad had been drawing – which was why a second lecture/signing was scheduled for mid-afternoon at the student center of nearby Tulane University.

But because the bookshop's caché was so well established, it was a must-stop on his tour – and it was on the porch at Maple Street that Mad felt immediately at home and, having relaxed so much over Christmas break, was so at ease as to charm virtually everybody in attendance. The crowd, about 50 strong, was clustered in the tiny, fenced-in front yard and spilled out onto the sidewalk. A woman in her late 40s, saying she had been a high-school English teacher of Claire's, asked Mad how, if at all, Claire's memory influenced his theology. Mad was surprised that being asked to talk publicly about Claire didn't rattle him. Maybe it was the pretty day and the shop's homey atmosphere, but Mad felt comfortable in being expansive. And in being expansive, he became more eloquent than he thought he could be.

"If anything I ever do is good or right or helpful to somebody, Claire is somewhere in the endeavor," he said. "I know that people have a tendency to idolize loved ones after they are gone, but since you knew Claire, you'll know I'm not exaggerating when I say that Claire was the kindest, purest, most gracious and grace-filled person I've ever known.

"It was in response to Claire's death that I wrote my theses. To have somebody so good, so loving, so bright and pure, suddenly taken away, is to feel like you've been plunged into the deepest darkness imaginable. And I blamed God for taking her. I blamed him with all the anger and sorrow in my soul. I really thought God was a jerk for taking her away, and that's exactly what I wrote in my theses.

"But as you certainly know, Claire herself would never have believed that God is a jerk, no matter what disasters befell or how wrenching a pain that life could inflict. Claire's faith, not just in God's existence but in his deep and unimpeachable goodness, was unmistakable, unshakeable, and unbreakable. And the more I thought of Claire, the more I knew that for the sake of her memory, if for no other reason, I could not rest until I reached a point where God's apparent jerkiness was not the end of the story.

"I remember one time at Georgetown, a good friend of Claire's was jilted by the boy she thought she was going to marry. In fact, she wasn't just dumped; it was worse than that, although the details aren't important. But what happened was that this girl, this friend of Claire's, found a way to climb up on the roof of the Copley Building on campus. And there is no doubt about it: This girl was going to jump. Meanwhile, Claire and I had been at what for us was a huge event, a play at the Kennedy Center. We didn't know that any of this had happened with Claire's friend. But right in the middle of the final act, Claire stiffened next to me and told me we had to leave. She didn't know why, but she just knew she had to get back to campus. And even in the darkness of the theatre, her eyes shown with an intensity and a light I had never seen before. So I didn't even question her. We rushed out of the theatre, and hailed a taxi, and sped back to campus. Claire was just frantic.

"Anyway, when we got to campus Claire ran to the Copley Lawn and started looking around. And something made her look up, and she spotted her friend on the edge of the roof.

"Well, I'm making this story too long, but what happened is that Claire somehow convinced her friend, calling up to her on the roof, to wait there on the roof until she, Claire, could climb up with her. And she sent me to run for help. And by the time I got back with a couple of campus police officers, there was no sign of either one of the girls on the roof. And then, as I started to go nuts with worry, the two of them walked out of the building, Claire's arms around her friend. Apparently Claire had crawled out on the roof with her, and had talked her back to safety. And when I asked her later how she had done it, Claire wouldn't give me many details. But the one thing she kept repeating, and it has stuck with me, is that 'God is good, and if you open your heart and let him in and let him use you, he'll speak through you. I didn't do anything up there on that roof,' she said; 'God did.'

"So at some point in that week after Claire died, as I wrote those theses, I reached a point where I thought of Claire and thought of her goodness and thought of her love for God. And that's when the tenor of my writing began to change. And you'll see that at some point I wrote about Guardian Angels, and I was thinking about Claire when I did. Suddenly I was re-copying all the most comforting passages from the New Testament, or from prayers I had heard in church, and I somehow ended up with God's love being poured into our hearts through the Holy Spirit.

"And, to finally answer your question, there's no way that, in all my grief and pain, there's no way that I would have ended up there without Claire's memory and her example to lead me back to a sense of God's love."

An agitated young man then spoke up.

"So if you end up with God's love, that leaves out in the cold all of us who think God is a jerk. Just when you give us hope because of your message that we don't have to feel guilty about being mad at God, you leave us in the lurch. What do you have to say to that?"

"Look at it this way," Mad answered. "Are you ever a jerk? Do you ever do things, even or especially to people you love, that really aren't very nice? And if you do jerky things, does that mean you don't actually love the person you do them to? Of course not."

The young man was tentatively nodding his head. Mad continued: "If you do jerky things, it doesn't mean you are always a bad person. It just means that you messed up. And if you're like me, you try to make up for messing up by loving that person even more. Well, why can't God do the same thing? Why can't He be a jerk and yet still love you? And, being God, why can't He go back and forth like that several times, all the while finding the power and goodness within Himself to make sure that He finally brings you to a place where his jerkiness is no longer apparent and where all you know, for ever and evermore, is His love? And, being God, His love is so much richer, so much more joy-filled, than any love you've ever known, that when you come to the place where His love is forevermore, it is indeed greater than any heaven you've even imagined. At least, that's what I've come to think. And I feel sure that that is the conclusion that Claire would want me to reach, no matter what circuitous path I took to get there. And my wish for you is that you reach the same conclusion, and the same place, and God's same love that Claire channeled so well into my own life. Good luck."

The young man first looked like he wanted to make some smart-aleck remark. Then he looked a little puzzled. He cocked his head and stared at Mad with a slightly perplexed expression on his face.

And, suddenly, he smiled. And he nodded. And he smiled again, and then turned and walked away and disappeared down the block in the direction of P.J.'s coffee house.

And Claire's former teacher watched the young man, and then looked at Mad, and then back at the back of the young man walking away – and she had big, happy wet tears in her eyes, and a small but heartfelt smile on her countenance.

* * *

At Tulane, Mad was treated almost like a rock star. That night, he checked the paper to see if jazz singer Leslie Smith was playing anywhere, but did not see her listed – and so, at Shiloh's urging, he took it easy instead. The next morning, he and Shiloh together quietly attended Trinity Episcopal Church in New Orleans – a grand old church at the very edge of the Garden District, built in 1851, with one of the most active "social outreach" programs in the South and a reputation for a warm and welcoming congregation. Not only that, but Trinity Episcopal School, on the same grounds as the church, had a reputation as one of the finest elementary schools in the country. In fact, it was from Trinity's school prayer (he had come across it at an Episcopal Schools conference while working at St. James in Mobile) that Mad had stolen the words to his 58th Thesis: "Hold fast to that which is good; be strong and of good courage." At the communion rail, Mad saw that the rector, Hill Riddle, recognized him. When pressing the wafer into Mad's hands, the Rev. Riddle leaned over and whispered: "Welcome, Mr. Jones. I'd love to visit with you some time. Give me a call."

Mad wasn't sure when he would get back Trinity's way, but a warmth and genuineness of Riddle's words made Mad decide on the spot that if he ever moved to New Orleans, Trinity would become his church home.

Straight from church, Mad's entourage (including the publisher's publicist) drove to the airport for a flight to Memphis. Even though Mad thought Sunday night was an odd time for a book signing, Rhodes College was sponsoring one that evening. Everything went fine – except that there were a couple of cute co-eds there who were clearly, uh, impressed with him, and the attention got his blood flowing. He did, however, resist.

The next day featured a return trip to Oxford, for an early evening book signing at Square Books (actually, its sister shop down the street) and then another dinner (this time at a gourmet pizza place) with web site founder Mark Mariasson. The second-hand book shop event, with nice wine and cheese and crackers, featured a standing-room only crowd. Mad went through his usual routine, being sure to credit Mark Mariasson both for starting the web site and for opening his eyes to the science/religion nexis that now was part of Mad's standard remarks. When he finished his reading, he opened the floor for questions – and saw the old battle-axe, Ms. Jennings, with her hand raised high. Immediately he turned his gaze away and recognized another questioner. And that question over, he looked elsewhere again and recognized another. That Jennings lady had left a bad taste in his mouth.

But after he had called on a third questioner and responded to him, Ms. Jennings gave him no chance to pick a fourth. Without waiting to be recognized, she piped in, loudly: "Young Mr. Jones, Lola Jennings here. Last time you came through Oxford I questioned you about your outlandish behavior – and now it looks like I didn't even know HOW outlandish it was. How can you go around the country putting yourself forward as some religious leader when you're tomcatting around with female reporters and God-only-knows who else? Oh, don't look at me like you don't know what I'm talking about, young man. Your reputation precedes you. I want you to respond to the charge that you are nothing but a bad influence on our youth."

Mad was taken aback. The truth was that, in the 10½ months since Claire's death, the only person he had strayed with was Laura. And what business was it of this old witch, anyway? He took a deep breath to try to control himself before replying.

And then he didn't have to reply at all. Another voice jumped in. It was Mindy, the blonde co-ed. And this time she was more attractive: dressed up more nicely (except for the stupid bow in her hair, which he hated), and, it seemed, at least slightly slimmer than she had been four months earlier.

"Mrs. Jenson [as was the case four months earlier, Mindy got the name wrong], I just have to say something about that. Obviously, I'm one of those youth who you are talking about, and, like, I don't think Mad is a bad influence on us at all. I mean, it's like, you know, we go through college and sometimes we're not always up on God, you know, and then Mad comes along and makes it cool again to talk about God. He can, you know, like relate to us. And, like, not only that, but [cattily] how would somebody your age know what kind of influence Mad is on somebody young like me? I mean, you're like so judgmental and all, and what makes you think you even know what you're talking about when it comes to relating to my generation?"

They were the rude words of a girl with a crush, rashly defending the object of her crush from perceived attack. Mad knew he should be appalled at her rudeness but, truth be told, he got a kick out of her outburst. Before he could think of something good to say, Ms. Jennings chimed in again, with righteous indignation.

"Mind your manners, Missy: I don't believe anybody was speaking to you. But I'll say that if you think you've been influenced by Mr. Jones here, then obviously he's not a very good influence, because if he were a good influence you'd know how to behave like a proper young lady and not like a, ... like an inarticulate little street hussy."

An uncomfortable and embarrassed hush fell over the whole gathering. Mad could see Mindy's face turning reddish. She looked like she was about to erupt. But then, suddenly, what seemed like anger turned into a quivering lip, and tears sprang forth, and Mindy ran from the room. Sometimes the brash confidence of youth masks a lack of self-esteem that lurks just beneath the surface.

Two of her co-ed friends followed Mindy out of the book shop, and the audience, agitated, began murmuring.

Mad had conflicting urges: one, to somehow politely smooth things out and try to make the atmosphere more pleasant; and two, to lash out at the battle axe. Sensing that Mindy's tearful exit had earned the sympathy of the crowd, Mad's second instinct won the day.

"Not to be too cliché about it, Ms. Jennings, but aren't you casting stones here? Is there a mote in your own eye? What gives you the right to call that girl a hussy? And what gives you the right to assume that just because some Hollywood tabloid prints something about me, that it makes everything they print the gospel truth? And what kind of influence does it have on our youth for somebody of your apparent social stature to give credence to trash like *The Zodiac*, anyway? You know what, Ms. Jennings? I bet if you and I compared our beliefs, item for item, we might find we agree far more than we disagree. In a lot of ways, I'm pretty damned... uh, pretty *darned* traditionalist. Who are you to assume anything about me? Do you read my newspaper columns? Do you realize how often I refer my correspondents to either Moses' 10 Commandments or Jesus' Two Great Commandments? And who are you to judge Mindy like that? [He didn't even realize that he remembered her name until it sprang from his lips.] All I know is that I struggle with my faith every day, and if I can influence people like Mindy to struggle with their faith, it's a lot better than if they don't even think of their faith at all. Maybe if you struggled some with your own faith, you'd be less judgmental and more generous. I mean, I really don't want to be rude, Ms. Jennings, but darn it, you just made that girl run out of here crying. I just spent a half hour reading from my book and talking about how God's love has been poured into our hearts, and you start talking like you are the very spokesman for the avenging God of the Old Testament."

Mad paused just a split second for breath, and in that instant was seized by an impulse that at once was generous and also tactically sound from the standpoint of cementing most of the audience in his corner:

"I'll tell you what, Ms. Jennings. I think you've turned a very nice evening into a nasty one. But I'll just chalk it up to it being a bad day for you. How 'bout if you just leave now before you hurt anybody else's feelings, and in return I promise that the next time I come through Oxford, I'll treat you to a nice polite lunch where we can talk theology one on one? How's that sound? I think you probably have some valuable wisdom to impart to me; so why don't we give each other another chance, another time? Sound okay?"

The audience burst into applause, and an aghast Ms. Jennings was hustled out of the book shop by two of *her* matronly friends before any more unpleasantness could ensue.

* * *

Over a restaurant dinner that night that was interrupted numerous times by collegiate autograph-seekers, Mad and Shiloh and Mark Mariasson had another conversation as enriching as their first meeting four months earlier. In the intervening four months, Mark seemed to have come a bit out of his shell, seemed to have re-discovered some confidence and some sense of self. And he was absolutely delighted to know that Mad had been making reference, at all his appearances, to the science-religion nexis to which he, Mark, had introduced Mad. Mark had brought with him a book called *The Cosmic Adventure*, by Georgetown theology professor John F. Haught. Oddly, Mad had never taken a course from Professor Haught, although he had heard good things about Haught's classes. With Mark leafing through Haught's pages, showing passage after passage to Mad and Shiloh, time passed quickly indeed. Three passages hit Mad so well that he grabbed some napkins and used them as paper to jot the passages down for future inclusion in his speeches:

"Ethical concerns are an important dimension of Christian life, but they are not the ultimate horizon of faith. The ultimate horizon of faith and hope is a universal beauty."

"Christianity has an important role to play in the future evolution of our planet. ... Christianity is intrinsically open to the possibility of further cosmic emergence. ... Being a Christian is an acceptable way of endorsing and fostering the scientific discoveries of modernity."

"The ultimate context of our lives is a pattern of ever-widening beauty lured forward, held together and felt in its massiveness and intensity by God."

Shiloh particularly liked the third quote, although he said it sounded a little too "newfangled New Age-like" to him if it didn't also note that the original author of that beauty also was God, and that only through God could that beauty be known – and that when it came right down to it, the beauty itself was part of God's very being, non-existent without God Himself.

But Shiloh definitely did *not* like the third part of the second quote, because he said (in essence) that it made Christianity sound like a means to the end of science, whereas he said the proper sequence would be that *science* is an acceptable way to find a path to Christianity.

"The Good Book says that God is the Alpha and the Omega," Shiloh said. "This quote makes it sound like science is the Omega that God is leading us toward. I never did quite get into all those Greek letters and stuff, but my pastor says that nothing should ever come before God in the beginning or after God in the end."

"You got a point there, Shiloh," Mad said. "I think Professor Haught is probably addressing that sentence, though, to more scientifically inclined people, in order to lure them in to the great possibilities of Christianity. I still think it's a great line, and at times I sure will use it."

* * *

Finally back at his motel room that night, Mad took the napkins-with-notes out of his pants pocket. With them came a scrap of paper. Looking at the scrap, it occurred to him that the last time he had worn those same pants was the last time he was in Oxford. The paper had Mindy's phone number on it. Poor girl, he thought. She seemed so upset earlier tonight. Maybe he should call her and thank her for defending him. It would probably cheer her up.

This time Mad remembered to dial '9' for an outside line. Sure enough, Mindy answered. When Mad convinced her that it really was he on the line, she virtually squealed with delight. After a few back-and-forths, she said: "Hey, do you think, I mean, I just thought that, well, like, would you be interested in, like, a cup of coffee or something? I think the coffee shop is still open."

Mad wasn't at all sleepy. Hell, why not; it would probably make her day.

"What the heck," he said. "But coffee will keep me up; how about a beer instead?"

"Ohmygawd, I would *luu—uuvv* a beer," she said. "But I'm only 20 and my stash of it has run out, and the bars won't sell it to me."

"Idiotic drinking age law!" Mad said. "I'll tell you what: If you really want a beer, I'll buy a six-pack and come pick you up and we'll just go sit in the car somewhere and drink it and you can tell me what college life is like here at Ole Miss. I've only been out of grad school for about a year and a half, and I already feel like college was so long ago that I'm like an old man or something."

"Like, AWESOME," Mindy said.

Something in Mad's head told him he was making a mistake, but that's what they did. And in the rural area surrounding tiny Oxford, the drive to a secluded spot for beer and conversation took almost no time at all. And the more Mindy babbled about college, the more Mad's own college days and college habits seeped back into his way of acting. And one of those habits was girls. And sure enough, Mindy went Mad that night with passion – and Mad went Mindy.

And Mad again didn't question why the sex-conquest thing came so, *so* easily to him. Before Claire, he never had been introspective about sex; now he was reverting to bad old habits.

* * *

The next morning featured the hour-long drive back to Memphis, a short flight to Nashville for an afternoon book-signing, and then a flight back to Mobile. The next two days were extremely busy with column-writing and other office work Becky had piled up for him to do. Mad worked very late both nights, until he was bone-weary. (His Monday night antics with Mindy had already put him behind on sleep.)

The point of getting so much work done was to enable Mad to take a four-day weekend for what would be, in effect, a private retreat with Father Vignelli. Mad had not told anybody other than the priest why he had been so insistent that his retreat be that particular weekend, but he had been adamant about it. His private reason was simple: Saturday was a year to the day after Daddy Lee had been killed when unhorsed while on a fox hunt. In Mad's mind, in retrospect, that's when his life had begun so drastically to change. Daddy Lee, dashing and rakish and breezily dauntless, had been Mad's outsized living icon. A dead Daddy Lee was so unimaginable that it was Mad's first sign that the world could be flapjacked. Now, a year later, the basically apolitical, haphazardly Episcopalian Mad had become a nationally recognized religious guru and sometime political lightning rod.

More amazing was that he was starting to like it.

Celebrity could be really a bitch. But at the same time, what frightened Mad was that it was starting also to feel really cool. If he let it be, celebrity could be a 24-hour head rush. A still-wise part of him even worried that it might become addictive. Before he forgot that wisdom, Mad figured, it was probably time to get himself grounded. Hence, a long weekend near a windswept winter beach with a Gibraltar Rock-like, spiritually centered, semi-retired Jesuit.

A friend was letting Mad have use of a comfortable three-bedroom cottage on a hillock, 75 yards off the beach east of Sandestin, Florida. The beaches on that part of the Florida Panhandle are luxuriously soft and brilliantly white, backed by towering, sparsely grassed dunes. The water is almost always a near-translucent blueish green. The houses, very few of them full-time residences, are packed fairly tightly together, but the garish condos and touristy beach establishments are miles to the West. So, while not exactly secluded, the sands there are usually peopled with only a pleasant smattering of quiet beachgoers searching for a respite from busy lives.

The drive from Mobile took about 2½ hours, and Mad and Peter pulled up to the house a little after noon. After dumping their suitcases inside, the two quickly walked down to the beach. The temperature, as it would be all weekend, was mild: in the high 60s at its hottest (with high 40s overnight). On an otherwise overcast and damp (but rarely rainy) weekend, a short-lived gap in the clouds let the winter sun briefly insert its light well beneath the waves. About 20 yards out, odd dark shapes glided through the surf. Mad and Peter stood silently looking out, with Mad intent on those shapes while the Jesuit gazed more toward the horizon.

"Hey, Peter, what are those things in the surf?" Mad said. "They don't exactly look like fish, but they're not just flotsam; they look alive."

Vignelli adjusted his eyes but had trouble seeing what Mad was pointing to.

"There!" Mad said. "Don't you see? Was that a fin? No… What the heck?"

Mad had been watching about three of the shapes, but suddenly they had been joined by nearly a dozen more. A wave crested, limpid green, and then it all became clear. As if they were bodysurfing, their kite-like "wings" spread expertly into the current, a group of sting rays soared just barely sub-surface. The priest, too, now saw them.

"Well I'll be…" he said. "I didn't know sting rays schooled together like that, much less played in the waves. I've always thought of them as dangerous creatures, but they look positively graceful out there."

Mad nodded and kept watching in silence. But then the sun hid again behind the clouds and took with it the light rays necessary to see the sea's rays. And Mad thought there must be a metaphor in there somewhere, but he couldn't figure out what it was.

Anyway, the plan was for a free afternoon for reading or beach lounging or whatever, followed by a homemade pasta-and-wine dinner (Vignelli was an amateur gourmet chef, and insisted on cooking most of the meals for the whole weekend), followed only then by the introduction to a series of contemplative exercises that the Jesuit had designed specially for Mad. The exercises would continue intermittently through the following three days, to be interrupted by nine quick holes of golf at a nearby course beginning mid-morning on Saturday, an all-day visit by Becky on Sunday (Mad had insisted that she come relax a bit), and a tennis match against the Jesuit early Monday afternoon.

The dinner was divine. Angel-hair pasta luxuriated in a creative tomato/basil/secret-ingredient sauce with occasional visits by small pieces of Italian sausage. The wine was a nice chianti of the sort that pleasantly and thoughtfully loosened the tongue.

"So, Madison," said Father Vignelli suddenly, just after a debate about which teams would play their way into the upcoming Super Bowl, "What the hell are you trying to accomplish for the health of your own heartsick soul?"

"Huh?"

"The spiritual exercises have begun, Mad. Answer my question: In the midst of your high-profile new life, what are you doing for your inmost self? How are you trying to enrich your spirit? How is Madison Jones finding inner victory without Claire Victory Jones to help you find it?"

Confrontation with Claire's absence hit Mad like a hard slap in the face. It temporarily shut down his brain and made him unable to focus on the real point of Peter's questions.

"Umm, what do you mean?" Mad was stalling for time and composure.

"C'mon Mad," Peter answered. "I know it's not fair to expect immediate eloquence from you; I don't expect you to *really* be able to even start to answer these questions decently until you've wrestled with them for a whole weekend. But don't give me this 'whaddya-mean?' crap. You know what I mean. You're going all over the country telling other people how to find God or how to wrestle with God, but you're giving yourself a pass. Well, I'm the hall monitor, and I say your pass is revoked. I'm gonna ride your back all weekend, Mad – and I'm also gonna kick your butt in both tennis and golf for that matter, even though you're supposed to be the star athlete who's 40 years younger than me. So get used to it. You aren't gonna relax this weekend, not even if you're physically napping on the beach. Even your dreams are gonna be serious work. I'm gonna work your butt and work your butt, and it starts right now."

Father Vignelli was true to his word. He gave Mad some spiritual reflection exercises that kept Mad up past midnight (during which time Vignelli did two sets of 50 pushups, and read several chapters of a new biography), and then woke Mad up at 7:30 the next morning for a brisk three-mile run that, considering the three glasses of Chianti Mad drank the night before, left the younger man gasping for breath. Then, while the Jesuit whipped up a five-ingredient omelette along with biscuits, juice, coffee *and* hot cereal, Mad ambled down to the beach for 20 minutes – but only with Peter's admonition that he should use the time to start considering whether he had the humility ever to follow instead of lead.

Breakfast over, Peter hustled him to the golf course. "Only nine holes?" Mad asked.

"Yeah, that's all we'll have time for, because the rest of the afternoon is all work," Peter said.

Mad was a fairly long hitter, but the older man belted his drives within 15 yards of Mad on every hole. A nine handicap, Mad ordinarily would have been more than pleased with his performance upon reaching the ninth tee just three over par – but the Jesuit had played Mad all square to that point, and then told Mad that it was *Mad* who would need an extra boost to win the final hole and thus the match. Although the hole (445 yards uphill) was an extra-long par 4, Father Vignelli announced he would hit only a four wood off the tee, while Mad used his driver. Mad promptly pulled his shot into the left rough, behind a small tree, while Vignelli split the fairway. Mad advanced his ball another 125 yards, and Vignelli used a 3-wood to trickle almost to the front edge of the green. Mad, always a clutch performer, played a beautiful long wedge shot to within three feet of the cup; and then, with Vignelli's permission, rammed in that putt for a par. Vignelli faced a 35-foot putt from the fairway, over a ridge, breaking first left and then right, with a severe downslope just on the far side of the cup. A two-putt would keep the match tied, but even a small mistake could spell a three-putt and give the match to Mad.

Vignelli rapped the putt authoritatively, though, without the slightest apprehension, and watched matter-of-factly as the ball disappeared into the hole. Birdie, Vignelli, and victory in the match.

"You can't beat me, Mad, and no matter how much you wrestle with God, He'll beat you every time as well," said the priest. "Let's go grab some lunch."

Mad didn't know what to make of this aggressive attitude from a mentor who, in the nine months Mad had known him, had offered nothing but comfort and an entirely empathetic (although far from fawning) sounding board. He also was confused. Father Vignelli was asking Mad to focus on himself and his own supposedly unmet spiritual needs, but at the same time the Jesuit was trying to break Mad's self-confidence and maybe his will. The first goal was self-centered, the second was self-abnegating.

Lunch was nothing but a stop at Wendy's. Peter passed over a burger for a cheap salad and baked potato.

Back at the cottage, Mad was so tired he wanted a nap. Vignelli said "no way."

"This is where the real work starts, Mad," he said. "Last night was just an introduction."

What the priest wanted Mad to do was to think of the absolute worst thing that had ever happened to him, *aside* from any deaths of loved ones. He gave Mad a half-hour to consider the question, and to come back not only with a brief oral explanation for it, but also a single rhymed couplet that summed it up.

Mad sat, sweatshirt-draped, on the porch. He came back with the story of how, at age 8, his Little League basketball team had been within one point of the league championship as the clock ticked its last seconds and Mad had the ball. He had just faked the guy guarding him out of the guy's socks and was about to put in an easy layup for the victory when the guy stuck out his leg and deliberately tripped him. Somehow, the referee missed the foul and the game ended with Mad sprawled on the ground as if he had stubbed his own toe in a spastic fit. All that effort, and no championship. His couplet:

"A youth's whole world is in the glory of his game/ So my trust in justice would never be the same."

Vignelli looked at him skeptically. "No wonder you're considered a pop-prophet in such shallow times as these," he said, dismissively.

Peter's next assignment was for Mad to decide what was the biggest mistake he had ever made in the first 20 years of his life. Again, he had a half hour, and again he should come up with a rhymed couplet.

This time Mad wandered down to the beach again. Low clouds blocked the sunlight. He saw neither sting rays nor any other sign of aquatic life. Mad came back telling of how, during the summer after his first year of college, he had driven home drunk one night from across the bay. He said it was the one and only time he had ever driven drunk. But, with a date in the car, he had zoomed down a wide street at nearly 50 miles per hour, been knocked off course by one of Mobile's ubiquitous speed bumps, rolled over the curb and grazed a tree, all before fishtailing horribly across to the other side of the road. Both he and his date had at least been wearing seat belts, but she had been so violently jolted that she banged her temple hard enough to give her a mild concussion. He was lucky, in fact, that nothing worse had come from his idiocy.

"Driving drunk could well have caused a death./ I'll ne'er repeat it, not while I draw breath."

Vignelli rolled his eyes. "Profound," he said, in a voice that made it clear he thought Mad's couplet was anything but.

Something in Mad wanted to react with rage. All Peter had done all weekend (other than the delicious food) was put him down. But something else in Mad was deeply hurt. Vignelli had become such a touchstone for him, had been such a mentor, that Mad was crushed by the Jesuit's sneers and aggression.

"Dammit, Peter, what do you want from me?"

Vignelli, standing rock-straight like a Marine, looked back at Mad coldly.

"What if I told you, Mad, that Claire is coming back to you tonight for a visit? What if I told you that she is full of smiles, that she looks beatific, that indeed you can see a soft halo around her head? What if she is clearly so full of joy where she is, so blessed with God's everlasting love, that it would make your spirit soar? Can't you just see her? Can't you feel her warm intelligence? Can't you just be sure that she is so good and so pure and so wonderful that your whole world would be perfect if only you could embrace her again?

"But you can't touch her. If you reach out towards her, she floats further away. And what if, while she is full of joy, she makes clear her disappointment in you? What if she still and always loves you, but says you have gone way off track? What if she says you are too full of yourself? What if she says you have no clue what you are talking about when you talk about God? What if she says you've done nothing for the past 10½ months but screw things up?"

Mad couldn't believe his ears. He almost thought he really could feel Claire's presence, and through Peter's words it was as if she herself really was condemning him. Why she was condemning him, he didn't know, because he thought he had done alright. He wasn't preaching anger; he was preaching God's joy, just as she would have wanted. Why was Peter doing this to him? What more was he supposed to do?

Mad broke down in wordless tears. Peter kept staring coldly.

"Cry, baby, cry," said the priest. So Mad sobbed some more.

"Here's a poem by Sir Thomas Browne," Vignelli said. "I've reversed the order of the verses, because I like it better this way. Listen, and then I'll give it to you on paper for you to keep. (Peter read aloud):

"Thou are all replete with very thou
And hast such shrewd activity
That when He comes He says 'This is enow
Unto itself – 'twere better let it be,
It is so small and full, there is no room for me'

But if thou could'st empty all thyself of self,
Like to a shell dishabited
Then might He find thee on the ocean shelf,
And say, 'This is not dead,'
And fill thee with Himself instead."

Wordlessly, Mad took the paper and stared at the poem rather blankly. But Peter wasn't finished speaking.

"Okay, Mad, now I'm going to give you some passages from C.S. Lewis' book, *A Grief Observed*. You may be familiar with the book. It's a collection of his writings in his personal journals after his wife died of cancer. He waited until very late in life to find a wife, and then he virtually worshipped her, and then, all too soon, she had a relapse of cancer and she died. And he was crushed so badly that the whole world seemed dead. Certainly his faith took a beating. Here I'm giving you just a few passages from what he wrote: The very first ones, and then some from very near the end of his book. Take them to the beach, while there is still a little daylight left on this cloudy day and study them. And then write something for me. Reach way down inside yourself and write something really good. Make it a poem, or an essay, or a song, or whatever. But make it comes from the deepest recesses of that soul of yours whose surface you rarely go beneath. And don't come back until you have something at least halfway worthwhile. Bring a flashlight; it might take you well into darkness.

"Oh, and you can't mention Claire in what you write. And you can't mention Daddy Lee. It has to be written in such a way that it's universal. So that anybody who picked it up and read it could identify with it."

Mad looked at the priest, peered at him, tried to take all this in.

"Now GO!" Vignelli said. "Go."

Mad took the other sheets of paper from Peter, the sheets with the C.S. Lewis passages. Shaken, he grabbed a flashlight and walked to the beach, turned right, and kept on walking. The sun was within an hour of setting, but only rarely did it faintly peek from behind the clouds. A chill wind blew off of the water. Mad's sweatshirt had a hood, so he pulled it over his head for warmth. He passed four or five houses, and then there was nothing but the huge rolling dunes that began about 25 yards inland from where the waves petered out on the shore. Mad absent-mindedly climbed onto the first dunes, down the other wide, and up to the top of another one. Wispy grasses sprang haphazardly from its top. Mad set, and faced the water, and looked to the Southwest horizon to see a few faint sunset-inspired colors that, wind-blown, were beginning shyly to peek from beneath the clouds. Finally, he looked down at the papers, and read from C.S. Lewis:

"No one ever told me that grief felt so like fear. I am not afraid, but the sensation is like being afraid. The same fluttering in the stomach, the same restlessness, the yawning. I keep on swallowing.

"There are moments, most unexpectedly, when something inside me tries to assure me that I don't really mind so much, not so very much, after all. Love is not the whole of a man's life. I was happy before I ever met H. I've plenty of what are called 'resources.' People get over these things. Come, I shan't do so badly. One is ashamed to listen to this voice but it seems for a little to be making out a good case. Then comes a sudden jab of red-hot memory and all this 'commonsense' vanishes like an ant in the mouth of a furnace.

"On the rebound one passes into tears and pathos. Maudlin tears. I almost prefer the moments of agony. These are at least clean and honest. But the bath of self-pity, the wallow, the loathsome sticky-sweet pleasure of indulging it – that disgusts me. And even while I'm doing it I know it leads me to misrepresent H. herself. Give that mood its head and in a few minutes I shall have substituted for the real woman a mere doll to be blubbered over. Thank God the memory of her is still too strong (will it always be to strong?) to let me get away with it.

"For H. wasn't like that at all. Her mind was lithe and quick and muscular as a leopard. Passion, tenderness and pain were all equally unable to disarm it. It scented the first whiff of the cant of slush; then sprang, and knocked you over before you knew what was happening. How many bubbles of mine she pricked! I soon learned not to talk rot to her unless I did it for the sheer pleasure – and there's another red-hot jab – of being exposed and laughed at."

("then, skipping to page 82 of my edition," Peter had written.)

"The fruition of God. Reunion with the dead. These can't figure in my thinking except as counters. Blank checks. My idea – if you can call it an idea – of the first is a huge, risky extrapolation from a very few and short experiences here on earth. Probably not such valuable experiences as I think. Perhaps even of less value than others I take no account of.

My idea of the second is also an extrapolation. The reality of either – the cashing of either check – would probably blow one's ideas about both (how much more one's ideas about their relations to each other) into smithereens.

"The mystical union on the one hand. The resurrection of the body, on the other. I can't reach the ghost of an image, a formula, or even a feeling, that combines them both. But the reality, we are given to understand, does. Reality the iconoclast once more. Heaven will solve our problems, but not, I think, by showing us subtle reconciliations between all our apparently contradictory notions. The notions will all be knocked from under our feet. We shall see that there never was any problem.

"And, more than once, that impression which I can't describe except by saying that it's like the sound of a chuckle in the darkness. The sense that some shattering and disarming simplicity is the real answer.

"It is often thought that the dead see us. And we assume, whether reasonably or not, that if they see us at all they see us more clearly than before. Does H. now see exactly how much froth or tinsel there was in what she called, and I call, my love? So be it. Look your hardest, dear. I wouldn't hide if I could. We didn't idealize each other. We tried to keep no secrets. You knew most of the rotten places in me already. If you now see anything worse, I can take it. So can you. Rebuke, explain, mock, forgive. For this is one of the miracles of love; it gives – to both, but perhaps especially to the woman – a power of seeing through its own enchantments and yet not being disenchanted.

"To see, in some measure, like God. His love and His knowledge are not distinct from one another, nor from Him. We could almost say He sees because he loves, and therefore loves although He sees."

("as a post-script, here's the last line of the second-last chapter of Lewis' book *Surprised by Joy*," Vignelli had written.)

"The hardness of God is kinder than the softness of men, and His compulsion is our liberation."

Mad looked out at what, because of the clouds, was a supremely dim vista. The sun still had about another ten or fifteen minutes before it would set, but the clouds were so thick it might as well have set already. Only a few pale colors painted the horizon. The surf, Mad now heard more than saw, was up. It sounded like the kind of surf that would create a wicked undertow. In the bleakness, it sounded dangerous.

Mad realized that although he had a pen in his pocket, he had brought no paper other than the sheets on which the C.S. Lewis passages were typed and the one with the poem by Browne. Hesitantly, shivering more from a sadness within him than from the southern winter's mild chill, he began to write on the back of one of those sheets. And he wrote, and he stared at the sea, and he wrote some more, and he stared at what was becoming pitch darkness too thick to see the sea through, and he scratched out some lines and, using the flashlight, he wrote still more.

It wasn't until nearly two hours later, when his fingers were cramped and uncomfortably cold, that he finally stood up and made his way back over the dune, along the beach, and back up to the cottage. Wordlessly, he handed his poem to Father Peter Vignelli, S.J. – who, although his mien was now utterly warm and cheerful, took the paper and folded it inside his biography on the coffee table, without even a look.

The whole cottage smelled delicious. Peter had cooked another feast. Chicken breasts simmered in some kind of white-wine-and-butter sauce, with a fine palette of subtle herbs and spices. A rice dish flavored with the chicken's sauce. Perfectly prepared snap beans. A wonderful salad. Italian bread. Ice water, and (between the two of them) a six-pack of ice-cold Michelob. A fudge-brownie pie *a la mode*. A cup of decaf Irish coffee with a touch of Bailey's Irish Cream for added flavor.

During the whole repast, Peter said not one word about the afternoon's exercises. He didn't explain anything, and he certainly didn't apologize for his harshness. But, with the help of the sensory bonanza on the table, he did manage to draw Mad into a conversation that, of its own momentum, somehow moved from classic movies to Tennyson to Arthurian romance to the legend of Lombardi's Green Bay Packers to (Lord-only-knows how) a line Vignelli had memorized from a John

Cheever short story: "Then it is dark; it is a night where kings in golden suits ride elephants over the mountains."

By the time Mad retired for the night, most of the pain and confusion, the bafflement at Peter's earlier criticisms, had dissipated. With a nice buzz going but far from drunk, he quickly fell asleep.

As for the Jesuit, he did not look at Mad's poem until he was sitting, propped up by a pillow and side-lit by a bedside lamp, in bed in his own room. (This was only after his nightly two sets of 50 pushups.) Mad's poem began:

"Waiting, expectant, hopeful, scared,/ searching, determined, unaware…" (SEE PSALMS).

Vignelli read it slowly. And then re-read it. And then read it yet again, and even yet a fourth time. And the rock-hard priest smiled, and then cried like a child.

* * *

The next morning, an early-rising Becky arrived at the cottage, all the way from Mobile, by 9 a.m., while Mad was still sleeping. The priest welcomed her with some homemade honey-bran muffins. Even in torn blue jeans and a baggy sweatshirt, she looked sensual enough to drive a man to distraction, and Father Vignelli didn't hesitate to tell her so.

"Lotta good it does me," said Becky in disgust. "The way my dating life is going, you'd think I was a leper or something."

"Find some peace, my darling," Peter said, "and love will surely follow."

Before Mad arose, Peter warned Becky that Mad might be out of sorts that day. "I was pretty hard on him yesterday, and I know he doesn't know why. Sometimes you have to tear people down a little in order for them to build themselves up in a better way. Mad's been masking a broken spirit. And I spent all of yesterday exposing his brokenness. So please be gentle on him today."

"I'll do even better than that: I'll leave him by his own big-shot self. All I want to do today is nap on the beach with the sound of the surf. Far as I'm concerned you can tear Mad down all you want, as long as you leave him able to function well enough for him not to screw up my company."

"Peace, child," said the Jesuit.

Becky strode purposefully to the beach, glared quickly at the grayish morning tide, threw down a towel and lay on her stomach. For a pillow, she pulled an old sweater out of her bag and placed it atop her *Iacocca* biography.

Forty-five minutes later Mad sat down beside her. Becky was sleeping. "God, she's gorgeous," Mad thought to himself as he looked at her. "No wonder I hooked up with her back at Georgetown." But oddly, his loins didn't give him a pull as he stared at her. And there wasn't any of her in-your-face, I-am-modern-woman-who-does-what-I-want bravado that was one part sexual come-on and another part warning that she might run you over. Instead, the sleeping Becky looked girlish and somewhat frail. And she didn't look sexy; she looked lovely. While Mad didn't exactly feel brotherly towards her at that moment, he did feel the kind of affection that one might for, say, a third or fourth cousin whom one was fond of in an at least partly disinterested way. And he felt sorry for her. He knew she wasn't happy.

She stirred and opened her eyes. "Oh, it's you," she said.

Mad just nodded. Becky closed her eyes again and lay still. Mad looked out at the sea in silence.

A few minutes later: "Becky?"

She still didn't move. "Huh?"

"Why'd you drop everything and come to Mobile last year when you saw me on the news?"

"I guess I was just stupid," she said.

"No, really. I'm serious. I want to know. I was a jerk to you in college – not that I meant to be one. But I just sort of walked away. Why'd you leave a nice life in Houston for an idiot who you only spent a couple of weeks with?"

"I don't know," she said, a bit impatiently. "What do you care, anyway? I guess I had my reasons, but what's it to you?"

Mad was struck by her bitterness.

"Becky, I want you to know I'm sorry. I mean for everything, not just for how I acted at Georgetown. You're doing a phenomenal job here with MMW Corp., and I'm actually starting to think that our enterprise is doing good for some people despite all my screw-ups. But I know you're not happy."

"Look, Mad, if I wanted a confessor, I'd go talk to Peter. But this isn't a retreat for me; it's just a day for me to get away from that godforsaken burg you call home. And even if it was a retreat, you're not my retreat leader. I'm not about to open my soul to you, or whatever it is you're aiming at. So just go blow."

Mad couldn't think of anything to say to that, so he fell silent. After a while he saw Becky shift uncomfortably, do a funny little stretching rotation of her left shoulder and neck, and then reach up with her left hand and rub the back of her neck.

"You sore from something?" Mad asked.

"Yeah. I don't know if it's from all the working out I've been doing, or just from the tension of running the stupid business for you while you run around making embarrassing headlines."

Mad moved closer and turned over to kneel above her. She was still lying on her stomach.

"I bet I can help with that," he said. "I'm not 'hitting on you' or anything, but can I massage that for you? I think I can help." Becky didn't say a word. Tentatively, Mad reached down and gently used two fingers to rub the nape of her neck. She didn't argue, so he used his whole hand and massaged a little harder. She still didn't say anything, so he shifted into a better position and began using both hands to massage her whole upper back, shoulders, and neck.

"MMmmmm," she said.

"That feel good?"

"Yes, good," she answered. So, silently, Mad continued to massage for another 15 minutes. Even through two layers of clothing, her skin felt taut and healthy. But he could feel some knots in her muscles, and he worked those extra hard while she groaned in the combination pain/

pleasure that is the usual response to having somebody working on one's sore spots.

When Mad finally stopped, he said: "Ya'know, Becky, I'm serious: I want you to be happy. And I'm gonna try more often to show that I appreciate everything you've been doing."

Becky almost shot back a typically caustic line. But for once she caught herself in time.

"Well, uhh…." she said. "Thanks, I guess."

There was another uncomfortable silence, so Mad got up to leave.

"Hey, Mad," Becky said suddenly before he was out of earshot.

"Yeah?"

"Thanks for the massage."

* * *

Vignelli had gone for mass at a nearby Catholic Church, and Mad was just as happy. Despite rallying that morning in his attempt to reach out to Becky, he was now feeling a little shaky from the Jesuit's tough treatment of him the previous day. Yes, the dinner and conversation had been delightful, but its effects had worn off while the aftertaste of Peter calling him "shallow" and a "baby" lingered. And why in hell had Peter made him write that poem if Peter wasn't even going to look at it?

Eventually all three mini-vacationers found themselves back at the cottage for a lunch of leftovers from the previous two nights' meals. As they pushed their plates away, Vignelli surprisingly announced: "Alright, folks, we're going fishing."

Through some contacts he had, the Jesuit had lined up the free use of a 27-foot motorboat that was waiting for them at a nearby mini-marina. He vetoed their protests that, with the dampness and the wind on the open water, the 65-degree day would feel too chilly for a boat ride. "You young people are too soft," he said. "If the wind was lower, I'd put on my full-body wet suit and make you pull me around for a while on water skis."

So they anchored about a quarter-mile offshore, and Peter played classical CDs (some Bach concertos, and "Finlandia" by Sibelius, and even some Aaron Copeland, all at a low volume) on a portable jam box (with a combo of CD and cassette players) while showing them both how to play out their live-baited lines.

Nothing seemed to be biting, and as they rocked with the waves there wasn't much to do but carry on an intermittent conversation about nothing in particular. Or at least it seemed to be about nothing in particular. Somehow, over the course of several hours, the Jesuit managed to work in references to a number of poems potentially pregnant with meaning. There was W.E. Henley's poem "Invictus" ("I am the master of my fate; I am the captain of my soul"), which Peter said would have been the right message if it hadn't overshot its target just a little and veered instead into hubris. There was Hamlet's soliloquy (Peter pronounced it the weak rantings of a self-indulgent twerp). And there was a line from Gerard Manley Hopkins: "Grace rides time like a river."

"Grace, my ass," said Becky. "I'll dam up that stupid river and use big old turbines to produce lots of energy from it. If you wait around for grace, the rest of the world's gonna pass you by and leave you sputtering in its wake."

"Maybe so," said the priest, pulling up anchor. "But wakes are for funerals. Unless you want to provide the occasion for a wake, you might be better off waiting for grace to find you instead."

"So we're heading in?" asked Mad, changing the subject with the sullenness of somebody still smarting from a previous day's emotional thrashing. "I told you we wouldn't catch any fish today."

"Oh, so you want to catch some fish," said the priest, gunning the engine. "You shoulda said so earlier."

With that, they roared up the coast and a little farther offshore. By now it was getting dark. Abruptly, the priest killed the engine and swerved the boat into a sharp turn. "Drop anchor here," he ordered. "Now bait your hooks one more time and throw in your lines."

His two young charges, rolling their eyes, did as they were told – and Vignelli pulled out a cassette tape. Totally shocked them, too: It was a mixed Springsteen tape. The Jesuit played it loudly. "The poets, they don't write nothing at all; they just stand back and let it all be," he sang along. "And in the still of the night they reach for their moment and try to make an honest stand. But they wind up wounded, and not even dead. Tonight, in Jun-gle-land."

Suddenly, the lines of both Mad and Becky went taught. Becky squealed as they both started furiously trying to reel in their lines. The priest pushed some buttons and a different song came on, and he threw in his own line while leaving the younger people to fight their own fish. The music blared on, and Peter sang even more loudly: "I believe in the love that you gave me./ I believe in the faith that can save me./ I believe and I hope and I pray that some day it may raise me/ above these badlands!" His own line went taught, and then began to play out away from the boat. As it did, the priest picked up the Springsteen words again: "It ain't no sin to be glad you're alive!"

Mad soon landed his catch: a four-pound speckled trout. Becky was cursing up a storm as she fought her fish and cursed even more when Mad tried to help her. Finally, she landed a whopping five-pound speck. And then both of them watched, stunned, as the Jesuit strained and played out his line and strained and reeled it in and strained some more. And finally what came to the side of the boat, and what Mad scooped up with a net as the Jesuit held his line, was a 12-pound bull red snapper.

Mad and Becky shot looks at each other as if to ask how on earth Father Vignelli managed to seem so in control of everything he put his mind to, even including control of the fish in the Gulf.

" 'Never question the truth of what you fail to understand,' kids," Peter said. "'For the world is full of wonders.' That's a pearl's wisdom from *King Rinkitink in Oz*, and don't you forget it."

Mad rolled his eyes and began to throw his line out again, but the priest stopped him. "We've got our catch for the night," he said. "We're going in."

When they finally returned to the cottage, Peter expertly filleted all three fish, divided up the snapper and the four-pound speck in three equal portions and put them in the freezer, and then worked his culinary magic on the five-pounder that the three of them shared along with some wild rice and broccoli that he conjured up.

"Is there *anything* you don't do well?" Mad asked.

"I can't do math," said the priest. "And I can't fix anything mechanical that breaks down. And I can't paint or draw to save my life. And my ego is too big. And I'm really, really pathetic at convincing young adults that *carpe diem* should take a back seat to letting grace ride time like a river. All you-all ever want to do is run your race like a sprint, sow your oats, and let the devil take the hindmost of all the badly worn metaphorical clichés I can come up with."

After dinner Becky started gathering her things for the drive home. But the priest pocketed her car keys. "Stay the night, Becky. Take tomorrow off; it's a government holiday for MLK Day. Relax here, and sleep late, my darling."

Unable to bend the Jesuit's will, Becky grabbed a blanket and strode down to the nearly pitch-dark beach. Mad washed the dishes and went to his room to read. Peter did two sets of pushups.

A while later, the priest saw the light under Mad's door go out. He knocked and said: "Mad, don't go to sleep quite yet. Mind if I open your door?"

"Whatever."

So the priest cracked the door open just enough to stick his head through. "By the way, Mad," he said. "Your poem yesterday. It was terrific. We have just one more big spiritual exercise tomorrow. You may not know it, but you've turned a corner."

Then the priest walked to the beach. Becky was curled up in her blanket. He stood about ten feet behind her. He could see that she was shivering a little.

"Becky." His voice was avuncular but strong, like Ronald Reagan's at his best. "Becky, my child. You're a Catholic, but I know you haven't been going to church. God can't give you a break unless you give yourself one. You're a remarkable young lady, brilliant and beautiful and with a heart much bigger and more vulnerable than you let on — and you deserve to be loved. You don't have to be miserable if you don't want to be. I love you, my child. Come on back to the house and go to sleep. Let grace ride, my child. And let yourself ride on grace's back. You'll be loved if you do; I promise you that."

The Jesuit turned and walked back to the cottage, and five minutes later Becky quietly followed.

* * *

The next morning, early, Becky and Mad awoke in their respective rooms to the smell of *huevos rancheros*. Peter had already run a hard mile and a half, showered, and begun to cook.

"You guys run down to the beach real quick," he told them. "The sun is out and bright, but the clouds are supposed to come in again soon. Go take a look at the pretty water for five minutes; your eggs'll stay warm until then."

By now they were both used to following Peter's orders. And it was a good thing, too. They stood on a dune and were amazed. Where the sting rays had played on Friday afternoon, 20 yards offshore, six or maybe even seven porpoises now frolicked in the surf. Neither one of them had seen porpoises quite that close to shore before – and the mammals looked like they were having a high old time. Neither Mad nor Becky could avoid smiling. Then, suddenly, the porpoises turned tail and swam straight away from shore to deeper water.

Back at the cottage, a leisurely and delicious breakfast over, Becky finally gathered her belongings. There was an ease about her, or at least what for her passed for an ease, that Mad had never seen before.

Before she walked out the door, she turned to them both. She was trying not to show it, but her eyes glistened with moisture. "Thank you both," she said. And then she smiled so uncharacteristically and brightly that it would have made the hardest heart go pitter-pat. "I mean it: Really, thank you both."

Once the two men let their breakfasts settle, Peter announced it was time for the tennis match then, rather than after lunch. "You're going to have to dig deep to beat me," he said as they drove to the courts on which they had made arrangements to play. "You'll need to get rid of all your worst instincts, use your brain and your heart, and then work like hell."

Sure enough, the Jesuit began the match by frustrating his companion at every turn. Vignelli belted the ball on every shot with a fierce and slashing power. As the far younger man, Mad couldn't bear the thought of being overpowered. But with so much pace on the ball, he couldn't keep it in control. Sure, the Jesuit missed his fair share of shots, too, but far fewer than Mad did. And Mad kept trying to rush the net, trying to be the aggressor, only to see Peter's shots whiz past him with regularity. Before Mad knew what hit him, Peter closed out the first set, 6-2 and jumped to a 2-0 lead in the second set. Mad felt his equilibrium spinning out of control.

More from disgust than anything else, he tried a drop shot all the way from the baseline on the first point of the next game. Almost by sheer luck, it came off the racket just right. Peter did manage to barely reach it, but his resulting return poofed over the net with lots of airtime and no power at all. Mad, moving in, easily flicked a half-lob over Peter's head for a winner. Peter just smiled.

Something clicked in Mad's mind. Forget his pride. Forget trying to overpower his opponent. Show some humility and use some guile. On the next point, he didn't try a drop shot, but he took pace off the ball and angled it wide. Peter hit it well and hard on the run, but Mad pushed it back, again at half pace, towards the other corner. Again, Peter managed to reach it, but he was out of position. Without using more than half his power, Mad was able to put the next shot away. And then he was off to the races. As fit as the older man was, Peter still couldn't cover as much ground as Mad could. Mad's young legs stretched more quickly and easily. Mixing his shots, using his head, he pulled even and then ahead, and eventually closed out that set 6-4.

Mad also had the advantage in that the Jesuit had run a brisk mile and a half while Mad slept. Mad's legs were not only younger but fresher. In the third set, Mad jumped to a 4-1 lead, and he was serving. The match seemed in the bag. But in that game, Mad got sloppy. After a double-fault and two unforced errors by Mad, Peter hit a winner to take the game at love and close to 4-2. Then Peter held his own serve. 4-3. Mad did manage to hold his serve for a 5-3 lead, but in the next game Peter came up with some viciously effective serves and pulled within 5 to 4. By now both men were breathing heavily between each shot. Mad made a couple of errors, but so did Peter. Mad built a 40-30 lead – *match point*. Mad reared back and belted a zinger of a serve right down the middle. It should have been an ace – but Peter had started moving early, on a pure guess. He flung out his racket, clipped the ball on the frame, and watched as the ball fluttered to the net cord and rolled gently over it, far too short for Mad to reach. Deuce. Mad promptly double-faulted, and then Peter ripped a winner to break serve and pull even at 5 games all.

Peter held serve easily, and Mad, frantic now, fell behind 15-40 on his own serve. Double-match point for Peter. And Mad was gasping for breath. He stalled and paced around the baseline for a minute. He came up with a strategy for the point. Instead of a big serve, he put extra spin on it and the ball, landing just inside the service box, kicked out wide. Peter, stretching, got it back, but he was out of position. Mad easily put it away. Peter's shoulders sagged a little. On the next point, Mad hit another drop shot for a winner. Rejuvenated, Mad held the next two points as well, and it was tiebreaker time. The first one to seven points, with at least a two-point advantage, would win.

Peter had no legs left. Mad jumped out to a seemingly insurmountable 6-2 lead. Two sloppy errors later it was 6-4. Then Peter, grunting, smashed two straight winners. All tied again, and Mad felt like panicking. This blasted Jesuit just seemed to have an undefeatable will. And then Peter served an ace for a lead of 7 points to 6.

Mad tried to collect his thoughts. Peter's pre-match words came back to him: "Use your brain and your heart." Blowing a 6-2 tie-breaker lead would be his most embarrassing defeat since the one time he truly failed in the clutch in baseball, when he struck out for Georgetown once with two outs and the tying run on third base. The opposing pitcher, a fastball specialist, had surprisingly come in at Mad with a screwball, and he whiffed at it helplessly. A screwball. *Hmmmm.*

Mad decided, for the first time in his life, to try the tennis equivalent of a screwball. Rather than curve right-to-left, as most of his serves did, he would try to make it kick out to the right by twisting his wrist and shoulder counter-clockwise on the service motion. He had no idea if it would work.

It did. Perfectly. It landed just inside the service box and kicked out wide past the startled Jesuit's reach. Ace. 7-7. Next point, decent first serve, Peter hit his return low, into the net. Now Peter would be serving, down a match point again. For some reason, this tennis match had taken on a furious importance for Mad. Win it here, and the whole crazy past 10½ months would somehow make sense.

Well, not really, but that's how Mad felt. And he thought of Claire, and wished she were there watching him. She was the real tennis player, not him. He was a baseball player who used his natural athleticism to win at other sports without any particularly practiced skill. In tennis, she had been the technician. What did she always say? "When it's clutch time in a match, I don't try to do too much. I let the point come to me and just take what it offers."

He looked across the net. This time it was Peter, looking physically whipped, who was stalling for time before serving. Mad almost decided to forget Claire's strategy. Peter was weakened; Mad could finally overpower him. That's what the pride of male ego told him to do. But then Peter, bouncing the ball before his serve, mishandled it and it rolled away. That gave Made another few seconds extra to think some more. That provided time for a line from Saturday's C.S. Lewis reading to come, unbidden, to Mad's mind. "The sense that some shattering and disarming simplicity is the real answer."

"Let the point come to me. … Shattering and disarming simplicity. …"

Now the idea came to him. Mad knew what to do. Peter's first serve, hard but safe in the center of the service box, gave Mad the chance to try the shot he wanted. It wasn't a special shot at all. He didn't swing hard, and he didn't try an acute angle, and he didn't try a drop shot, and he didn't do much of anything. Instead, he just stuck out his racket and softly blocked it back at Peter, right to the center-back of the court, with a short pushing motion. Peter, long past being too tired to follow his serve to the net, had been expecting more pace on the ball. He had begun to swing too early – and then in the act of slowing his stroke to wait on the bounce, Peter himself had to push it back weakly towards Mad. With the extra second to prepare, Mad's brain was able to process the court's geometry – and Mad was able to angle a ball short to Peter's backhand. Peter, hustling, scooped it up, but again was unable to do much with it. Scrambling, he tried to return towards the center of the court – and Mad lightly pushed the next shot behind Peter to the spot the priest had just vacated. Vignelli tried to twist around and lunge backwards again, but to no avail. Winner for Mad. Game, set and match for Mad.

Take what life offers, let life come to him, keep things in play with disarming simplicity. And, another line from Peter, from a conversation over coffee months ago with Peter and Shiloh: We must avoid a "pride so overblown that it puts ourselves above God and says, in effect, that we are responsible for our own salvation." Forget ego; keep the ball in play and wait for opportunity to alight.

Against all his instincts, that's what Mad had done.

Mad looked up and Peter was smiling broadly, almost laughing, as he made his way slowly, breathing heavily, to the net to shake Mad's hand.

"Well done, young friend," Peter said, with no sign whatsoever of disappointment that he had lost. "Very well done."

On the drive back to the cottage, Peter gave Mad his last assignment of the retreat. "Write one more poem for me," he said. "I'll give you no direction, but it's gotta be at least as good as the one you wrote Saturday night. Whatever topic strikes your heart. But make it good."

That afternoon, after a ham sandwich and a shower, Mad sat down on the porch to write. It took him three hours. Finally, almost shyly, he handed the paper to Peter. Peter put it down on the coffee table right next to the first poem. He began to read, and as he did so, his smile grew and grew. He finished, and his countenance was bright as the sun. He then read the first poem and smiled some more. And then again he read the new one. It began:

"I crave the limelight, the fine light, the big life. ..."

Psalms

(written on a windswept beach at twilight)

Lost at sea

Waiting, expectant, hopeful, scared,
Searching, determined, unaware
Of how to get from here to --- to where?

Tell me God, how to ride this wave.
From the breakers keep me safe.
I feel the wave is riding me.
If so, I might get lost at sea.

Loves I've lost or never had;
Goals I've set that have gone bad;
Dreams slip-slide away – I'm glad
They came so close, yet mad.

Tell me God, how to ride this wave.
From the breakers keep me safe.
I feel the wave is riding me.
If so, I might get lost at sea.

Every day and every hour,
Every precious we/us/our,
Every struggle side by side:
Will they help us turn the tide?

Tell me God, how to ride this wave.
From the breakers keep me safe.
I feel the wave is riding me.
If so, I might get lost at sea.

Still, friendships, care, abiding love:
They lift me, Lord.
They keep me going, conscious of

A mystic chord
Of memories of future things,
Of times when grace on sea-wind wings
Alights, and of the joy it brings.

Tell me God, how to ride this wave.
From the breakers keep me safe.
I feel the wave is riding me.
If so, I might get lo—
No, might get found at sea
By your harsh peace, which sets me free.

(written on a sunlit porch)

Good works

I crave the limelight, the fine light, the big life.
I want the attention, the dimension of tension
Which, I must mention,
Lets me know that I'm known
As the one
Who alone
Got the task done.

Look at me: Can't you see
That I really, freely, have chosen to be
So noble, so giving, so loving and living
That I set an example
For others to sample?

Of course,
It's a farce.

Not my giving or loving, nor my coming or going,
Nor the fact that God's showing
My way every day – if I pray.
No, I say, none of that's play.

None of that fake, false, or futile.
For that done for God's sake, in his name, for his fame,
If actually helpful – delightful, not frightful –
To those affected, connected
In some sense to the deeds
I hope lead –
If only
Incidentally –
To praise for me too – Whew! –
That good cannot be done in vain.

The farce is in thinking that I am alone in doing God's work.

Or that I am special.

Or that God, who works through me and so many others –
Through lovers, and preachers, and teachers, and creatures,
Through friends and relations
In all of the nations –
With such a God, it's a farce to believe,
He's not the one worthy of praise and of fame.

The limelight shines not on me, but through me,
To God, who works in me and for me, despite me.

But I should not grieve, nor shoulder the blame,
For God has redeemed me – in Jesus' name.

Second Chronicles

Chapter One

Grace Feinstein Martin was worn out. Her son had celebrated his eighth birthday the previous weekend, and what had begun as a roller-skating party had turned into a fight when her son pushed another kid into the railing. The other kid sprained a wrist and bruised some ribs in the process, and his irate parents, even though they were rich as Croesus, had not only threatened to sue Grace but had even commissioned a lawyer to call her at home and repeat the threat. Saturday night, while her ex-husband kept her kids, she had met a man for a rare blind date. He was a total loser. He drank like a fish, and kept touching her without invitation, and then (although they had arrived at the restaurant in separate cars) insisted on following her home – "to make sure you make it safe and sound," he said. She tried to ditch him at a stoplight that was changing, but he ran the red light. And when she got home, he screeched to a halt behind her and rushed to escort her to her door. He even made a move to follow her inside, uninvited, but she finally had had enough.

"You are *not* coming in," she said. "I did *not* invite you in. Good night." At which point he laughed and put a foot inside the door jamb, as if it were a game. All she could think of to do was to kick his shin, hard, and then when he withdrew his leg, howling, she slammed the door and ran to her room, ignoring his yells through the door that she was a "bitch." That night she could barely sleep, and the next day her washing machine went on the fritz while full of clothes and soap and water. And when her ex brought her kids back that night, her daughter was whining incessantly because the son had been the center of attention all weekend.

And so hellishly it had gone through the first two days of Grace's workweek as well. The lawyers she worked for were stressed and ornery, and a client kept doing things to screw up his own case, and she spilled coffee all over her "billable hours" time sheets. Tuesday was February 2, Groundhog Day, and in light of the Bill Murray movie of the same name she thought it sickeningly appropriate that she would have to re-do the record-keeping work she had already completed. So today, Wednesday, she was so depressed that she called in sick and lay in bed watching pointless daytime TV. Something in her life had to change, and soon.

Grace glanced at a scrap of paper she had looked at a number of times before. On it was the phone number for MMW Corp. in Mobile. Some incessant urge had been telling her for months that she should talk to Mad. Oddly enough, she thought he could give her some good counseling.

Grace had already gone a long way on an inner odyssey that began when she first saw the news about Mad's theses nearly 11 months earlier. She didn't know it, but she also had a long way yet to go.

Out of sheer curiosity, Grace had been in the Apostles of the Word church on that Good Friday morning when Mad told the story of the blackberries and the Rev. Hebert had tried to turn it into a profound metaphor. She could tell Mad hadn't meant the story metaphorically, but she was impressed with the graciousness with which he played along with the minister's interruptions. Moreover, she had seen that the grown-up Mad was a remarkably handsome young man. The attractiveness was only heightened by her sense that in some ways he seemed like an innocent, swept along by events and interpretations that he had neither planned nor anticipated. And yet, something emanated from him, something intangible, that had seemed to her that day to suggest a transcendence of sorts.

Considering how bizarre she felt just to be in that church, it was a wonder that anything could make her conscious of transcendence. There she had been, an atheistic Jew divorced from a lapsed Catholic, standing amidst a throng of tongue-speaking worshippers in an evangelical Christian church. If the people around her had not been so genuinely friendly, she might even have been a little frightened. She had felt like a white girl in Harlem.

Grace didn't understand this Jesus thing, though. It made no sense that someone could be fully human and fully divine at the same time. It made no sense that he could be born of a virgin. It made no sense that his death could make up for the sins of all mankind. And so on. And this bit about the "Living Word"? What was that all about? Why would a human, much less a god, be happy to be reduced to a single word, or even a capital-W "Word" as the case may be? For that matter, which Word? The whole Christian story seemed to her just like so much mumbo jumbo.

Yet Grace knew that she felt a void inside her. Maybe it was just a cultural thing. Maybe, having been born into the Jewish culture without ever seriously observing Jewish customs – much less taken any stock in the Jewish faith – what she might be missing was the sense of community that had enabled Jews to remain an identifiable people through three millennia of wars, diaspora, pogroms and Holocaust. Maybe her Jewishness cried out subconsciously for obeisance, for respect, or maybe even for celebration. Or so she had concluded one sleepless night late last summer. In the next few weeks, she had done a little cursory reading about Christianity and a slightly more intensive primer on her own Jewish faith. Or to be more accurate, not her Jewish faith, because she was still faithless, but the Jewish faith of her family. Maybe, she thought, if she took part in some important Jewish ceremonies, the faith might come to her of its own accord.

She was encouraged in that direction by Mad's almost gratuitous inclusion in his theses (No.44) of an exhortation that "all, of all faiths, should honor the Jews." Rosh Hashanah and Yom Kippur were coming soon, and Grace had decided on that summer night to observe both holidays not just nominally, but with a seriousness she had never before afforded them.

Her family had been shocked. Her parents, nominal Jews at best, had taken it as a sign that Grace was so unhappy as to be desperate; her aunt and cousins, far more serious about their faith and culture, welcomed her participation warmly but secretly wondered if she had some ulterior motive.

On one level, everything had gone well for Grace on both of those September holidays. "Leshanah tovah tiktavi vetichtami," she had said, ritually wishing all her family a good new year. Something about all the rituals at Rosh Hashanah – the bread and apple dipped in honey, the recitation of Psalms, the blowing of the shofar (ram's horn) at the synagogue – had the feel of being so right, so appropriate, so full of a solemn-but-joyful hope that Grace wondered why she had ever taken the day for granted. And Yom Kippur, the Day of Atonement marked by fasting and repentance and communal confession of sins, might seem to an outsider to be a grim observance. Truth be told, that's how Grace, too, had always regarded it. But this year it seemed different. This year it had had the aspect of a thorough but gentle purging of her system, the kind that leaves a person rejuvenated and feeling healthier.

But on another level, neither Rosh Hashanah nor Yom Kippur really did the trick for Grace. The God of her people was still a God of harsh judgments and of promises of communal rewards that always remained unfulfilled. Her people were a people who, despite their reputation, were a community of amazing warmth. But their faith itself – not their culture, but their faith, their theology – left her cold. She knew that it wasn't supposed to leave her cold, knew that for many observant Jews it was a faith of joy and hope. But, despite two surprisingly good experiences at these September Holy Days, the faith didn't yet give her warmth or fill her void.

It certainly didn't unnerve her and inspire her and frighten her just a tad in the good way of boosting her adrenaline a little, the way that Mad's lines quoted in the newspaper had unnerved and inspired her several months earlier. She still had that newspaper article she had clipped out, the one that quoted Mad saying: "Go out and love God today, because in the course of loving we find small but wonderful redemptions along the way." She still didn't quite comprehend what "redemption" really meant. But in her own way, Grace had vowed to find out. One day. When she had time. When it would be easier for her to think about.

Four and a half months later, she still hadn't found time. And she had experienced four horrible days in a row and was playing hooky from work and sulking in bed with the TV on. It was early afternoon, and she decided to check out that "Winifred" show that she had heard so much about but had never been able to watch. Winifred was the universally known one-name moniker of the host whose classy TV talk show made her perhaps the most widely respected black woman in the country.

When Winifred opened that day's show with her usual recitation of who and what would be that day's guests and topics, Grace gasped so hard it made her chest hurt. She hadn't expected this:

"And we're thrilled to have the author of a great new book that's climbing high on all the country's best-seller lists," said Winifred to the camera. "When we return from this commercial, please welcome Mad Jones to talk about his book of spiritual rejuvenation, *Mad Religion*."

For his part, Mad was exceedingly nervous about appearing on the "Winifred" show. In the aftermath of his retreat two weeks earlier, he had at least temporarily found an equilibrium and a humble confidence that he had not known since Claire's death. The book tour had resumed with ever-larger crowds that were ever-more insistent on getting Mad to comment on the Senate's trial of Bill Clinton – but Mad had become ever-more adept at avoiding politics and keeping the focus on his now more sharply honed theological message(s). More and more, Mad got the sense that people were leaving his book-signing/speaking sessions with a new openness to faith and a renewed sense or purpose. Shiloh agreed. He said that at the beginning of each event he had his hands full with making sure the crowds did not become unruly, but that by the end of virtually every session he had the sense that people were paying respectful and even rapt attention to Mad's words.

But Winifred was the big-time. Winifred had clout. If Mad screwed up on her show, or if she baited him or put him on the hot seat in front of millions and millions of people, he was afraid he could easily lose his newfound inner peace. Mad actually had the sense that he would like Winifred, but he didn't trust that sense. His experiences with national media so far had been anything but pleasant.

His fears turned out to be unfounded. What Grace and millions of other viewers saw was an attractive, compelling young man with a cogent, interesting, and even inspiring message, conversing pleasantly with an informed, empathetic interviewer. Winifred had done her homework; she took Mad and his writings on their own terms, and asked questions designed neither to embarrass nor to entrap Mad but rather to entice him into elucidating his theology in an approachable, comprehensible manner. The cameras, the lights and the audience quickly seemed to recede into the background, and Mad felt as if he were engaged in a coffee-table conversation at a cosmopolitan sidewalk bistro.

"Mad, please stop me if this gets too personal for you," Winifred said at one point. "But, knowing your story, I was struck by how raw the emotions seemed to be in your theses numbered 16 through 19. They seemed to me to contain the very heart of your complaints against, and anger at, God. And the depth of their pain makes it even more remarkable that you found such strong resolve to return to God in spite of the agony you went through. Let me read those theses, or parts of them, out loud:

"'The words of Jesus to the crowd of wailing women as Jesus was led on his march of death to Golgotha: Daughters of Jerusalem, weep not for me, but weep for yourselves, and for your children. For behold, the days are coming, in which they shall say, Blessed are the barren and the wombs that never bore and the breasts that never gave suck. Luke, Chapter 23.' And then you write: 'What kind of God, except a fallible God who is a jerk, would curse innocent women whose wombs become with child.' And then you quote several verses from the letter to the Romans, 'For we know that the whole creation groaneth and travaileth in pain together,' and 'For thy sake we are killed all the day long; we are accounted as sheep for the slaughter.'

"Mad, that's pretty grim stuff. And as I understand, you wrote it in a hospital bed where you had gone for some R&R after suffering a horrible triple-tragedy, with your wife and unborn child dying of a hemorrhage and your mother-in-law perishing in a car crash. In other words, there you were grieving about your wife whose womb was full, whose very pregnancy cost her her life, and you are quoting Jesus saying that it would one day seem that only the barren are blessed, because they at least would not know that kind of pain.

"Okay, I don't mean to make this a monologue, but am I right in thinking these theses grew directly and explicitly out of your own agony?"

The camera focused tight on Mad's face. Looking stoic, he merely nodded while silently mouthing the words "Yes, that's right."

"Okay," Winifred continued. "And yet you somehow found the strength to turn all that around. Instead of being sheep for the slaughter, you quickly become an advocate of being lionhearted on God's behalf. You write that 'Christ calls us all to be lions.' And you quote the letter to Hebrews saying that *'we are made partakers of Christ, if we hold the begin-*

ning of our confidence stedfast unto the end.' And so on and so on, you keep meeting pain with strength, and overcoming disaster with confidence and even hope, and now in the last four or five months you've gone beyond that even to preaching about God's joy.

"So here's my question: How did you do it? Where did you find a way to overcome the pain of the whole earth travailing and groaning? And, more important for those of us in today's self-centered world who always want to apply everything to our selves, where and how do we who read your book, or who listen to you preach, where do *we* find that strength? Can all of us, Mad, find a way to overcome adversity as impressively as you have?"

"That's very kind of you, Winifred," Mad answered. "At the risk of seeming really self-absorbed by quoting myself, there's a poem I wrote just two weeks ago – and two lines from the poem are the crux of the matter:

"'The limelight shines not *on* me, but *through* me,

To **God**, who works in me and for me, despite me.'

"You see, Winifred, just as I blamed God for my pain, I have to give Him credit for the strength I found to overcome that pain. I know it sounds like a paradox, Winifred, but the best way to become strong is through submission. The best way to triumph is by letting life come to you and accepting what it gives you. I'm not saying something stupid like you win by losing – not by a long shot – but I am saying that we win by being willing to lose, and by accepting losses if they come our way and not regarding them as final. And the God we put our faith in is a God who never stops offering love; even when He allows us to be ripped by pain, He still offers love – and so the credit is His, not ours, when we accept that love and use it to find strength and to triumph.

"And, to close the circle, the most important step toward finding the glory of joy is to give the glory to God rather than taking it for ourselves. I miss my wife Claire every day, Winifred, but I am humbled by the knowledge that she is secure in God's love. That's the true glory, and my small job is to bear witness to it."

Another camera focused tight on Winifred's face as she wiped a single, genuinely heartfelt tear from her eye. And all across America, people watching the show were crying. And Grace was crying, too, and vowing to herself that she would keep searching to understand and to find the love that Mad was talking about.

A full half-hour of that day's "Winifred" show was devoted to Mad and his theses and his book. By the end of it, Mad seemed a heroic figure. By the end of it, more than a hundred thousand Americans who had forsaken faith, Americans who were Catholics and mainline Protestants, evangelical Protestants and Jews and atheists, vowed to return to churches or temples or synagogues and give faith another chance. They were vows that many actually kept.

"Madison Jones, may God be with you," Winifred said in conclusion.

"Thank you so much, Winifred," he said. "No thanks to me, I think He already is."

* * *

A few weeks later, the MMW Corp. board gathered in Mobile for its semi-annual meeting. Becky announced with pride that, after salaries and expenses, MMW already had accumulated $76,427 to distribute for charitable purposes. Moreover, it was a near certainty that earnings during the next six months would dwarf that sum. For a company less than a year old, it was a stunning achievement. Nevertheless, Becky as an executive was still a tightwad: She berated both Buzz and Mary for each having the gall to make reservations, on the corporate account, at the most expensive hotel in town. "Hey, little lady, cut us some slack," Buzz responded. "You can write it all off on our corporate taxes, anyway." Across the table, Mary shot a knowing look (and an approving one) at Buzz, while Mad (playing peacemaker) suggested the group just move on to more important matters.

The board decided to set aside $25,000 as the corpus of a new, permanent foundation fund (for as-yet unspecified purposes) and used the rest of the available revenues for grants to a wide array of causes across the country. In Mobile, MMW gave a grant to a program called G.R.O.W.T.H. (Girls Reaching Our Womanhood Through Healing), a new program for at-risk minor offenders; and (at Peter Vignelli's request) to Catholic Charities. In New Orleans, a beneficiary was the Trinity Educational Enrichment Program, a hugely successful summer educational project run by the Episcopal Church Mad had liked so much during his visit there the previous month. In St. Louis, MMW gave a grant to a women's shelter; in Houston, to an inner-city grocery co-op that was a favorite cause of some oil executives. A soup kitchen in Washington, D.C. also benefited, as did a prison ministries program in New York. In all, 11 organizations earned grants ranging from $1,200 to $12,000. Justin was upset that he couldn't convince the others to become one of the major sponsors for a local 10-kilometer road race for charity, but everybody else seemed more than satisfied with the selections.

But the biggest decision ratified by the board of directors involved a major change in event-planning strategy. The "Winifred" appearance had been such a success that the publishing house had cancelled the remainder of the book tour (with the exception of one more major appearance each in New York and in Los Angeles), on the quite reasonable grounds that *Mad Religion* was selling so spectacularly that it didn't need any more boosts from Mad's appearances at bookstores. Moreover, Mad's celebrity and popularity were now so great that Becky, Mad and Shiloh all figured that Mad could easily fill far larger venues than before. Henceforth, Mad would speak at only one major event every other weekend, at paid-admission forums as large as mid-sized college basketball arenas. Mad's speaking engagements still wouldn't be events as large as, say, the Billy Graham Crusade, but on a smaller scale Mad would begin to follow the Graham model.

An added advantage of this approach was that it would keep Shiloh at home far more often. LaShauna had begun to complain vociferously about Shiloh being away so regularly from her and their toddler, and under the new arrangement Shiloh would begin helping Becky with administrative and other duties around the MMW Mobile office when he and Mad were not on the road. Between that, and his still-part-time "backup" status with the Mobile Police Department, and one night class that he was now taking as his first stab at college, Shiloh would be a busy man indeed. But at least he would be able to be at home enough to maintain marital harmony. Well, *sort of.*

"You know, Shiloh," LaShauna had said to him, "I actually agree with what Mad says about religion more than you do, and I admit that he seems to be treating you well. But I just don't trust a white man like that; he's using you for his own reasons, I'm sure, even though I don't know what those reasons are. You just better damn well be careful, cuz I don't want my baby's daddy to get screwed over and ruin my baby's future because his daddy was too dumb to be suspicious enough of some whiteface Yuppie."

Home wasn't the only place where Shiloh was still catching grief for working for Mad. When Shiloh reported to the police headquarters once while Officer Williams was also there, his former partner sidled up to him to give him some hell. "You better come back full-time to the Force soon, Jones-y," he said. "You know that religious freak-ass you work fer is gonna start gettin' a big head with all his celebrity, dontcha? Pretty soon, young freak-ass is gonna figure he's important enough so he don't need no Negro around no more to make him look acceptable to the Yankee Jewboys who run the media. Yer gonna be out on yer ass then, Jones-y, and don't try to say I didn't tell ya so."

Shiloh somehow found the graciousness to laugh at Williams' remarks as if Shiloh were the willing brunt of a big joke. "Well, Buster, it's a good thing I've got you watching my back," he said. "It's a good thing I've got a mentor on the Force who's got enough horse sense for the both of us."

Speaking of mentors, Peter Vignelli, along with both Shiloh and LaShauna, joined the five board members for a celebratory dinner at the elegant downtown restaurant Justine's – and it was a good thing that he did. The Jesuit had a way of defusing tension, and there was indeed tension to defuse. At the board meeting earlier, there had been a constant undercurrent of friction between Becky and Mary. For one thing, Becky and Mary had clashed about the new dual check-signing system they had set up after the incident with Preacher McGee. Becky had to admit that the system had operated well – Mad still didn't quite understand the concept or how it worked – but the truth was that she just didn't like any situation where she wasn't in total control. Anyway, Father Vignelli effortlessly used his wiles to guide the dinner conversation in such a way that Mary and Becky found themselves on the same side of a discussion of the merits of various movies. As for Justin and Buzz (and to Buzz's surprise) the two of them found much in common in their mutual (but quiet) denigration of a few "chick flicks" that the two young women adored. Somehow, the dynamic worked so well that, later on, Mary, Becky, Buzz and Justin found themselves all happily out drinking after dinner at a neighborhood dive called "The Garage," long after all the rest of the crew had gone home.

LaShauna and Mad, meanwhile, soon were engaged in a side conversation about how even God can, and does, make mistakes. As Shiloh drove home later that night, LaShauna rested her head on her husband's shoulder. "You may be right, honey," she said, contentedly. "I think Mad really might be an okay guy, especially for a white man. You keep being careful, honey, but I think you might really be in a good situation after all."

In all, by weekend's end everything looked rosy indeed for all the principals of Mad's accidental enterprise.

* * *

Time whizzed by. Mad passed the one-year anniversary of Claire's death without sinking back into depression or hopelessness or other pathology. With his lighter travel schedule, he began putting more time and thought into the responses he wrote for his syndicated advice column, and into more carefully crafting his remarks for the big "Mad Religion" rallies that Becky scheduled for him around the country twice a month. He also began auditing a theology course at Spring Hill College, and haphazardly (but not infrequently) doing volunteer work around town at a soup kitchen, at Habitat for Humanity houses, and other social service agencies.

Becky finally began, haltingly, to find a life in Mobile outside of MMW. She went on a few dates, joined a running club, and when there was nothing better to do, she more readily accepted Justin's entreaties to join him at various excursions around town. "Hey, Pal," she would say when she recognized his funny-sounding voice on the phone. "Whatcha got goin'?"

The little guy, meanwhile, was feeling like a rising tycoon. His "Justin Time" holistic training business was going so well that he had to hire a personal secretary and still had enough money left over that, by late April, he was able to make the down payment on a Lamborghini.

As for Shiloh, he earned a B- in his first mid-term exam at the University of South Alabama, and a C+ on his first mini-essay and a B- on his second one. Not a bad start.

MMW Corp. began running like clockwork. Mad drew large crowds and inspired them while avoiding gaffes and negative publicity. His column now was running in 86 papers. The web site was getting so many hits that advertisers were in a virtual bidding war for the right to appear on it. The book kept selling like hotcakes after a week-long fast. Two of the three traditional network morning shows had Mad on as a guest, and both were friendly and intellectually unchallenging in a way that helped Made appear almost preternaturally compelling and charismatic. (The network for which Laura worked on "Acute Vision" had also been ready to issue him an invitation for its morning show, but its bigwig Spike Walters of "Hour of Truth" got word of the plans and quashed them.)

As the whole Clinton impeachment/trial imbroglio faded remarkably quickly from public consciousness, so did the tendency of political actors from both the Right and the Left to use comments from Mad (or others) as pretexts for verbal assaults. But several of the more liberal congressmen did not forget Mad's few critical comments about the president, nor did they forget how useful a foil he turned out to be for their never-ending quest to denigrate their opponents as right-wing haters. On the other hand, neither the Revs. Rob Patterson nor Larry Falstaff nor Bill White forgot how, when Mad left himself open to the Left's attacks, he was used as a prop for an attack on the three of them and their politico-ministries as well. Even on the rare occasions when they kept *their* heads low, this young creep let himself be used as a pretext for calumnies on the Religious Right. Moreover, what particularly galled Patterson was that many of his own followers had ignored his denunciations of Mad, and had ignored the reports about what he called Mad's "unforgivable sexual licentiousness," and instead had rallied around Mad the more the Left attacked. Patterson considered Mad not only a charlatan but also a rival.

Finally, Spike Walters also didn't forget. He despised the whole lot of what he thought of as "those hypocritical Christian troublemakers," and he had in his head the idea that Mad, with his youth and attractiveness, was the gravest new threat from that source. The "Hour of Truth" hit piece on Mad had been put on hold, but it had been anything but buried.

But for now, none of that mattered. All of that was hovering underneath radar. For all anybody else (including Mad and his associates) could see, the ministry of MMW had left all political controversies in its wake and now was skyrocketing in popularity, without any obvious remaining enemies. With Winifred's imprimatur, combined with Mad's new sunny disposition and palpable inner calm, there seemed little reason to expect anything but a continuing growth in pop stardom and respect. Mad's audiences and his readers alike were overwhelmingly receptive to Mad's messages, not to mention inspired by them.

Seemingly unchallenged pop stardom also carried with it certain rewards – or at least what some people might consider to be rewards. Mad had survived the tabloid report that presented him as an out-of-control satyr, and in truth his subsequent night with Mindy had revived his old tendency toward satyriasis. In short, every time Mad traveled he turned into a horn-dog. As always, it was easy for him: first the eye contact, then the virtual contract sealed with merely a nod of the head or the surreptitious hand exchange of a phone number, and then, after Shiloh had retired to his own room without suspecting a thing, the final assignation and its attendant cheap-won passion. For Mad there was no real emotion involved, but merely release. And because he took these pleasures only while on the road, there was no opportunity for the awkwardness of follow-up chance meetings. In Mobile Mad remained perfectly chaste, and thus perfectly unhindered by complications or guilt.

In fact, the only continuing troubles that seemed to plague Mad were the now-regularly reappearing "trances" of the sort that plagued him that day on the golf course and the day with the blackberries and the night Shiloh found him with a glazed expression by the ice machine in Atlanta. Almost invariably, the episodes occurred on his first or second day back from his bi-weekly travels. But because Mad worked mostly from home, he was always alone when the episodes returned. There Mad would be, writing or reading or studying, or maybe lost in thought while on an evening run. And, without warning, there he would find himself 45 minutes or an hour later, having no idea where the time had gone. Mad would emerge from his daze (sometimes with a clammy forehead and elevated heart rate) and find new phone messages on his machine or random ink scrawls on his papers or books, or (if he had been running when the episodes attacked) perhaps find himself sitting heavily against some old oak tree well off his intended course.

The episodes puzzled Mad, but he tried not to worry about them too much.

* * *

The chat room remained a never-ending source of entertainment, enlightenment, and almost enraging idiocy, each aspect randomly distributed throughout the room's pages and pages of cyber-comment. There were probably about 60 or 70 regular contributors now, along with literally thousands who found reason at least once to put in their own two cents worth. In truth, there was no way Mad could possible review all the entries each day before chiming in with his own daily comment. Although Mad tried to avoid paying undue attention to the "regulars" who had been with the site almost from the start, he still was naturally drawn to a closer reading of their wisdom and wisecracks than he was to the remarks of even the more active "regulars" of more recent vintage. When Affirmed or Cowardly Lion or D Thom or Ever Faithful or Defender joined the conversation, Mad almost always read every word. And he kept a special eye out, without much satisfaction, for any word at all from Jezebel? or M. Magdalene.

Not often, yet less and less infrequently as time went by, Mark Mariasson also took part. His handle (which he had told Mad) was "No Dice," in reference to Einstein's comment about how God interacted with His universe. One day in late May of 1999, No Dice wrote that he very respectfully disagreed with a recent bit of Mad's newspaper-column advice. A letter-writer had asked Mad whether God was complicit in the death of her son by way of a lightning bolt that struck him the summer before, when his sailboat had been caught in a sudden squall. "Only in the sense that God did not intervene to stop the lightning bolt," Mad had written, before launching into some boilerplate (he had been lazy while writing that column) about how what now mattered was not how much loss the woman still felt but rather how she chose, with God's help, to work through the loss.

"Mad's usually right, but he's wrong this time," wrote No Dice. "Of course God is complicit in ways other than a mere failure to intervene. God is a God of science, too, and it was God who created the natural processes that cause lightning. And God knew when he created lightning that lightning could be deadly, and that lightning would kill people like this woman's son. God does not play dice with the universe. His universe is a purposive universe, a universe always working its way towards a loving goal that God has set for it. And as a purposive universe, it is a universe whose every instant and whose every occurrence is continually used by God, through the natural laws He Himself created, to achieve an ultimate purpose that is His alone to comprehend. So, yes, God IS to blame for her son's death by lightning, even if only by mistake, and Mad's own other writings teach us that our role is to accept God's complicity and yet still love God and work with Him in the furtherance of a better creation."

"Hmmmm….," wrote D Thom. "No Dice is making some sense here, I think. I think he has applied Mad's own theology better than Mad himself did in this morning's column."

"Balderdash!" wrote Ever Faithful. "The pain this woman is feeling, due to her son's death, is a manifestation of the work of the Evil One. God never causes pain; He only causes joy. But Satan takes advantage of man's own sinfulness to unleash evil and pain on the world. All of these other theories, whether they come from Mad's idiotic brain or from you other New Age nincompoops, is nothing but pseudo-religion. Why don't y'all spend less time reading Mad's claptrap and more time reading the Bible?"

"You're *all* wrong," opined Cowardly Lion. "The lady's son hasn't suffered evil; he's been blessed. And it wasn't a mistake by God; it was a deliberate act as surely as God meant to send that tornado that took Dorothy to Oz. The lady's son is in the everlasting Emerald City now, and that's cause for celebration!"

Mad enjoyed the debate. For his daily entry, he typed: "First, I must say that I am awed by the Lion's never-ending ability, day after day, to find Oz-related metaphors. Frank Baum would be proud of you, my courage-seeking friend. But, more seriously, I stand corrected. My good friend No Dice is correct (as is D Thom's concurrence): The logical conclusion from everything I've been saying since my wife Claire died is that God IS complicit and yet that He still merits our love. I think I must've just been lazy when I wrote this morning's column. I'll issue a corrected answer in my column in the next few weeks.

"As for Ever Faithful, I should have said this long ago: You and your cyber-pal Defender have my utmost respect. Here you are in total disagreement with my whole theological outlook, and yet you continue consistently to engage in the dialogue on my web site. That kind of persistence is commendable, and it adds immeasurably to the richness of these chat-room conversations. Please keep it up!

"G'night, y'all!"

Chapter Two

Chet Matthews was livid. That S.O.B. Spike Walters had really done a job on him. Or to be more accurate, Walters had demonized a small, privately held oil company whose majority owners were close associates of Chet's. Chet himself owned 20 percent of the company, and Chet knew from a recent geological survey that one of its oilfield leases was soon to produce a fair-sized jackpot. Chet already had plans to take his share of the earnings and leverage it for an even bigger deal he was putting together with a subsidiary of a major oil company. And what nobody else knew was that if all the pieces fell into place – and for the astute Chet Matthews, the financial pieces *always* fit together – then Chet eventually wanted to parlay his riches into a self-financed run for high political office. Not that Chet wasn't already plenty rich, mind you. Yet all of Chet's other holdings were tied up in long-term enterprises. Only with this side deal he had working could Chet find the short-term liquidity he needed to fund the political race on his own, without having to ask others for contributions. And that was the only way Chet would attempt the race, because Chet Matthews would never allow himself to be beholden to anybody. Just like his daughter Becky, Chet liked to be in control.

But now the "Hour of Truth" had come in and done a real number on the little oil company that was the key to Chet's plans.

There had been a little environmental mishap. It was small in scope, but at least temporarily disastrous for a small nearby Indian reservation. Spike and his gang had gotten wind of the story, and by the time they finished massaging it into yet another of their stock morality plays, the small oil company came out looking like a corporate version of Pol Pot. The core of the report, of course, was true: The mishap had indeed occurred, and the Indians did suffer. But the truth was that the mini-disaster was entirely an accident: A worker had mistakenly left some valve open when he rushed off to the hospital after hearing that his wife had gone into premature labor. The company had offered a more-than-generous settlement to the Indians, a huge majority of whom accepted the offer with alacrity. Nevertheless, "Hour of Truth" found one victim who wasn't satisfied – a victim who retained the services of a rich plaintiffs' attorney married to the daughter of the CFO of one of the biggest sponsors of "Hour of Truth."

The little oil company's goose was torched. None of the mitigating circumstances were aired. Interview tapes were spliced in such a way that Chet's associates, in reality rather decent corporate citizens, came out looking heartless and even deliberately cruel. Within a week after the show aired, credit lines had been pulled right and left, and eco-freak activists had overrun the company's major oil field and used their bodies as human shields to block production. Within another two weeks, the company filed a preliminary motion in bankruptcy court.

And Chet Matthews' secret political plans were effectively aborted.

* * *

In her Mobile office, Becky Matthews pored over the latest numbers. It was late June, and she was preparing for MMW Corp.'s semi-annual board meeting that would be held two weeks hence. In one sense, the numbers looked spectacular. Royalties from the "Mad Religion" book had been pouring in, and paid attendance at Mad's speaking engagements around the country had exceeded all earlier expectations. On July 1, the 99th, 100th and 101st newspapers would begin running Mad's daily spiritual advice columns. It looked as if the corporation would be able to distribute close to $400,000 to charities this go-round.

But Becky had inherited her business acumen from her father. She saw things in the numbers that others would not notice. She saw the numbers beginning to flatten. Book sales, still strong, were nevertheless beginning to drop. While attendance at Mad's last two rallies – most recently in Madison, Wisconsin, and before that in Berkeley – had been substantial, it had not quite reached the newly heightened expectations. And Shiloh reported that Mad's speeches (or, as Shiloh called it, Mad's "preaching") were becoming more and more intellectual and even esoteric. The preaching also had lost much of its edginess. No longer was Mad saying that in the long run it didn't matter that God could sometimes be a jerk; now he had begun leaving out all mention of God's jerkiness. The speeches were all joy with little anger or sorrow, all redemption with almost no suffering to be redeemed. The tone was verging on the vanilla of elevator music, but the concepts sometimes became as abstruse as avant-garde jazz. Mad's charisma still helped keep his audiences enthralled, but they were no longer responding as viscerally as they once had.

"I wrote down some of the words he's been using," Shiloh told her. "He's using words like 'noosphere,' whatever that means, and 'cosmogenesis,' and quoting some guy named Teilhard de Chardin. It's like he thinks he's Confucius or something. Sometimes nobody even knows what he's talking about. But then he cracks a joke, or tells some really moving story about Claire, or something like that, and so the audience can relate again, if you know what I mean. So he still thinks he's doing just great."

Becky figured that Mad, and the non-profit company she had built around him, could coast along for a while. But because Mad was still so new on the national scene, he had not had enough time to be an iconic figure so enmeshed in the popular heart and mind that his name alone could command attention. A little controversy every so often – as long as it didn't get out of hand – might actually be desirable. Otherwise Mad risked fading like so many other flashes in the pan.

Just as Becky mulled over these things, her secretary put through a call. "There's a woman on the line, name of Martina Beritzky," said the secretary. "Says she's calling on behalf of Spike Walters of 'Hour of Truth.' Sounds important."

* * *

Spike Walters wasn't one to rest on his laurels. Three weeks before Beritzky's phone call to Becky, Spike had ended the 1998-99 TV season with a splash by crucifying a couple of those asinine oil barons who were despoiling the environment and making poor people sick. But he was already thinking ahead to how his show would open its 22nd season in September. He knew the show's staff would come up with a hot current topic for one of the three segments, and some other corporate villain for another. But for the third segment, *his* segment, he wanted something unique. He wanted to expose hypocrisy, pop somebody's balloon, nip some noxious weed in the bud. He had just returned from San Francisco, where he picked up yet another "public service" award from yet another foundation, and he had seen a small article in the paper there about an appearance at Berkeley by this Mad Jones creep. Walters still regretted that he had not found a good enough reason to spank that young jackass on the air. And now, according to the news article, Mad was going great guns in front of a crowd of 4,300, talking about how the upcoming millennial celebration really shouldn't be seen as important at all.

"First of all," Mad was quoted as saying, "the real millennium, mathematically, won't happen until 2001 — and chronologically, if you date it from Jesus' real birth date of approximately 4 B.C., the millennium actually has passed already. And nothing much happened.

"People, don't you see that God isn't bound by human time? Don't you see that in the greater scheme of things, the cosmogenesis that is occurring all around us will not be the slightest bit affected just because a human calendar changes to a number with three zeros at the end? What we should be talking about here is the ultimate will of God, not some dumb computer bug and not how many women's shoes full of champagne you can drink from around midnight on December 31."

"Cosmogenesis?" Walters had thought to himself. "What is this flake talking about?"

Walters had put the article aside an hour ago. This Mad Jones kid might be a fruitcake, but Walters didn't see how "Hour of Truth" could develop a storyline about him that would grab the public's attention. Jones had briefly become a moderate pop phenomenon, but Walters had bigger fish to fry.

But then his aide, Al Bobbitt, poked his head in to say that the Rev. Rob Patterson was on the phone demanding to speak to Walters. This should be interesting. Spike Walters actually was in Patterson's debt. Two years earlier, "Hour of Truth" had done a hit piece on Patterson but had demonstrably screwed up the facts on a major allegation. Not only that, but Patterson somehow had assumed possession of a recording that could be embarrassing to Walters. The tape featured a stray comment of Walters' that a boom microphone picked up, at one of those black-tie dinners Spike always was emceeing. "I hate those Christian assholes," Walters had said to the dinner's host, during a private side conversation about an anti-abortion demonstration in that day's news, "And I'll do whatever it takes to hang them from their own holier-than-thou cross."

In short, Patterson held in hand some reasonably good materials for a high-profile libel suit.

To Walters' surprise, Patterson had been willing to cut a deal. If "Hour of Truth" ran a retraction of some of the disputed "facts" from its report, *and* if Walters promised that Patterson could call in a chit one day, then Patterson would hold off from a messy libel suit. But if Walters failed to do a return favor for Patterson whenever the televangelist called in his chit, Patterson would release the damning audiotape of Walters seeming to slander all Christians.

"Hiya, Spike," Patterson said on the phone now, his voice oozing false sincerity. "I got a story I want you to do, yes indeed I do. Time for both of us to settle old scores, both with each other and with a piddly upstart who's blaspheming his way to the top."

"Do tell," Walters said, his curiosity piqued.

The truth, which Patterson didn't mention, was that the preacher feared his empire might be falling apart. His TV show was having trouble finding enough advertisers. Dues-paying membership of his organization was well down from its peak. Sales of videotapes and religious-themed lapel pins and bumper stickers were declining. And Patterson's big investment of time and money into millennial-themed merchandise was not paying dividends. He thought that, especially with the Y2K bug scaring everybody, he would be able to attract a flood of new converts to his version of that old-time religion. But for some reason it just wasn't working out that way. And since the Rev. Patterson couldn't figure out anybody else to blame, he blamed Mad. Mad's blasphemous messages were proving popular. And last year's attacks against Mad from the lefties in Congress had made Mad a hero among Patterson's natural constituency. Good people of the Lord always rallied to the defense of whomever was under assault from the enemy. Patterson had always taught that the enemy of our enemy is our friend. Now, that teaching was coming back to haunt him.

Not only that, but Mad was now going around the country belittling the importance of the millennium. Mad was saying that despite the millennium, God's ultimate judgment was not necessarily at hand. Even worse, that idiotic Rev. Hebert down in Louisiana kept giving Mad cover by vouching for Mad's *bona fides* to any Evangelical Christian who would listen.

Hence, Patterson's call to his former nemesis, Spike Walters. If anybody had the power to destroy the young upstart, it was Spike.

On the phone, of course, Patterson didn't mention any of his empire's weaknesses. Instead, he focused on how horribly worried he was that a blasphemer, a heretic, was leading his flock astray. "He's one of those 'false prophets' the Bible warns about," he said to Walters, "and he needs to be crushed. It took Winifred to make him a hero; now you can make him back into the villain he really is. I need you to find the dirt on him and bury him with it by year's end, Spike, or else I'll…. well, you know what I mean, my good friend. I need a favor, if you know what I mean. Mad Jones says that God is a jerk; I need you to show the world who the jerk really is!"

Spike Walters really hadn't paid much attention to Mad's past preaching. He had only skimmed through the voluminous dossier that Al Bobbitt and Martina Beritzky had prepared for him. All he knew was that Mad had criticized the president and arranged for some guy dressed as Lewinsky to give him a mock blow job, plus what Walters had read in *The Zodiac*'s big hit piece (which had *not* mentioned Mad's earlier infamy for calling God a jerk).

"What do you mean that Jones called God a jerk?" Walters asked. "Did he really say that? If I play that remark right, that's enough to rip him to shreds right there! None of you preacher guys can survive by cursing God, can you?"

Patterson tried to explain that just about everybody who knew anything about Mad knew that Mad had called God a jerk, but Walters was not to be deterred. In his mind, that was red meat to exploit.

"Not only that, but you're in luck totally aside from that," he told the televangelist. "I've already got a file going on this guy. We'll nail him to a tree, mark my words. If you're sure that us nailing this little shithead will make you and I all even, then it's a go. You sure this is the favor you want? Promise me it'll make bygones by bygones?"

So the deal was sealed, and Walters told Bobbitt and Beritzky to make the Mad Jones file active again, *pronto*, and within two weeks his team was ready to roll.

* * *

As for Becky, she was delighted to receive Martina Beritzky's call. What a lucky break! Here she was, just now thinking that Mad needed a new burst of publicity to give him (and *her* nonprofit company) some oomph, and lo and behold, somebody calls from the most popular TV news magazine in the country. Bingo!

Becky's guard was down. Ever since Winifred gave Mad such a sympathetic hearing, it seemed like nobody much was out to tear Mad down anymore. And with the new peacefulness Mad had shown since their January retreat with Father Vignelli, Mad seemed far less prone to major foot-in-mouth-itis. Even when the mime showed up, which was far less frequently, the mysterious silent actor also behaved himself.

So Becky saw no downside to the interest from "Hour of Truth." She figured that if they played their cards right, MMW Corp. could jack up the admission prices for Mad's "rallies" *and* hold out for an ever bigger advance than the substantial sum the publisher was already offering for a second book deal. Besides, didn't the great Spike Walters have a reputation for always siding with the underdog? He was probably tickled pink that a young guy like Mad had made good in response to personal tragedy, and that Mad was shaking up the worlds of all the holy rollers who posed as evangelists.

Martina Beritzky played right into Becky's preconceptions. Martina was well practiced in the misdirectional arts of a TV news magazine producer. Most subjects, she had found, were so awed by the interest of a celebrity such as Spike Walters that Spike's name was all the bait needed to hook them right through the gills and reel them in.

"Yeah, Spike wants to do a segment on Mr. Jones," she said, as friendly as could be. "He thinks Mr. Jones is a breath of fresh air on the religious scene. He wants to get into Mad's – can I call him Mad, instead of Mr. Jones? – anyway, to get into Mad's theology, and even to give Mad a chance to put to rest all that controversy last year about the impeachment stuff. D'ya think we can set up an interview?"

"That sounds cool to me," Becky said. "Could we do it down here in Mobile? I'd love to meet Mr. Walters; it seems like I've been watching him all my life."

Martina was more than agreeable. "Oh, and one more thing," she said. "Mr. Walters will probably want to interview a bunch of people who have known Mad for a long time, maybe see some of his college records, talk to the professors who taught him theology, that kind of stuff. We usually find that people are more than willing to talk for a friendly interview if they know that the subject of the story doesn't mind. Any problem with signing one of our standard blanket-waivers to give everybody permission to help us, so we won't have to bother you every time somebody balks at helping us out without your specific go-ahead?"

Becky, usually so practical, had stars in her eyes. Her mind was racing ahead triumphantly. Sure, Mad had been a hit with Winifred, but to businessmen such as her father that was just "women's stuff." Once Mad got a boost from Spike Walters and "Hour of Truth," she could really rub her success in her daddy's face.

Because she avoided talking to her father, she was unaware of her father's own animus against that particular TV show.

"Sure, just fax the waiver to us and I'll sign it and send it back," Becky said. "I know it'll be okay with Mad, and he's already given me power of attorney to handle these kinds of details for him. When do y'all wanna come down for the interview?"

* * *

Four days later, it was Becky's birthday. As usual, her mother had a family flunkie send Becky another pair of pearl earrings. As usual, her father deposited more stock options in Becky's account. And as usual, her father also called her on the phone to wish his little girl a Happy Birthday.

"Yeah, daddy, I've gone another year without nabbing you a son-in-law you can talk football with in the hunting blind," Becky sneered as soon as she heard his voice. "Don't even pretend that's not the real reason you're calling, so you can make me feel guilty for screwing up for another whole year."

Chet Matthews sighed. Why couldn't he have a decent relationship with his little girl?

Becky continued: "But I'm doing you one better this year, Daddy Dearest. We're gonna be featured on the show of 'Hour of Truth.' I know you thought your stupid little girl was wasting her time on this religion business, but we're raking in money hand over fist and now we're gonna really hit the big-time. Spike Walters' producer called me just a few days ago; I'm gonna leave you and your oil business in the dust."

Chet nearly gagged. He smelled disaster.

He tried to tell Becky the story of how Walters had cheap-shotted and killed the little oil company in which he owned the 20 percent interest. He tried to tell her that Walters didn't play fair. He tried to warn her that she was being set up for a kill. All of which, of course, only made her resentful. She thought he was competing with her, belittling her, refusing to give her the credit she was due. Nothing was ever good enough for him, she thought. Nothing.

Voices were raised. Old wounds were rubbed raw. Stilettos slashed along hundreds of miles of fiber-optic phone lines. But before hanging up, Chet Matthews tried one more time to make his point clear and set things right.

"Dammit, Becky, you never listen to me! But if you ever calm down, remember this: I want to help. At some point you're gonna realize that Spike Walters has an agenda to make you look bad. I guarantee it. And when you realize it, if it's not too late, call me. I've got some folks here who want revenge on that SOB, and I want to keep you from getting hurt. Call me, and we'll figure out some way to beat this bastard."

"As if I'm gonna run to *you* for help!" she said. "You just can't stand the thought that I'm a success without you. Just go blow, Daddy, just go blow."

* * *

Mad wasn't so sure that cooperating with "Hour of Truth" was a good idea. Yes, "Winifred" had gone well, but she specialized in human-interest stuff. Laura's intermittent kindnesses notwithstanding, he had learned to distrust these big-time national media folks. He saw Spike Walters as a "gotcha journalist," always out to make somebody look bad. Yes, Becky said that this Beritzky woman sounded friendly on the phone, but Mad still had a hard time believing the program would open its fall season with a story complimentary to *anybody*. As he saw it, "Hour of Truth" lived for controversy and for taking scalps. He wanted his own scalp protected.

On the other hand, he didn't see how they could back out now. Becky had promised that Mad would do an interview, and a lack of cooperation now would surely just invite trouble. The interview was scheduled for late July, at the studios of the network's Mobile affiliate. Between now and then, Mad had plenty of time to prepare. Besides, the MMW board's next semi-annual meeting would take place in just over a week, and he felt sure his friends would be good at advising him about how to put his best foot forward.

For now, Mad was most worried about his recurring episodes of spaciness. Another had happened again just last week, the day he returned from Madison. The night before that, he had enjoyed the company of one of those pretty, fair-skinned, healthy Teutonic Midwestern girls. She had had lots of energy. She was one of those young women intent on discovering "how many times it could happen in one night." Mad had done his best to help her find the answer.

But the next day, back home in Mobile, he had fallen into his longest trance yet. More than three hours just disappeared. He didn't understand what was happening, and it was starting to bother him. A few more trances, he told himself, and maybe he really should see a doctor.

Then again, maybe not. He otherwise felt perfectly fine. And life was good: Nobody was hounding him, audiences seemed to love him, young women swooned, and he had a pleasant routine at home and friends of enough varying ages, interests, and outlooks to keep things interesting. He still missed Claire, of course, and deeply, but other than that he had no complaints. Maybe Candide's Dr. Pangloss wasn't too far off: If this wasn't "the best of all possible worlds," then at least it was a pretty darned good one.

* * *

From St. Louis, Mary was due to fly into Mobile on a Friday night for Saturday's board meeting. Buzz was due to arrive from D.C. at about the same time. Don't bother picking them up, they told Becky; they would share a rental car to the (this time inexpensive) motel where Becky had insisted they both stay. As it turned out, it was a good thing that nobody had to pick them up. Becky probably would have forgotten. She was dealing with a crisis.

Late that afternoon, a certain Dr. Theodore Theodore had called the MMW offices in West Mobile. He was distraught. He thought that Mad ought to know what was happening. Just that morning, he had been interviewed by phone by Martina Beritzky. And he had the overwhelming feeling that she was up to no good.

Ted Theodore was the sympathetic psychiatrist who *The Zodiac* had identified as the one who signed the papers 16 months earlier that released Mad from the psych ward. He said he had tried to avoid Ms. Beritzky for days, but that she had faxed him the waiver Becky had signed. Among other things (in a clause Becky had not noticed), the waiver released all medical and legal personnel from confidentiality requirements concerning Mad. The producer also had left phone messages for Dr. Theodore at his home, sounding sweet as honey, explaining that *of course* Mad wanted him to talk to them, because the doctor obviously had been impressed enough with Mad to let him out of the hospital.

But Dr. Theodore still avoided her calls until once, just as he was arriving home, he heard the phone ringing and raced to pick it up before his machine kicked in. He had been a second too late – and then had to let the machine run as he spoke to Ms. Beritzky (for the first time, a real dialogue, rather than just machine messages), to try to get her off his back. His interrogator, though, seemed to think he had turned the machine off when he picked up the phone.

"Did you really think Mr. Jones was, you know, *all together*, if you know what I mean," she had asked, "or did you just think that even if he was a little loopy he was no threat to himself or others, and thus could not be kept in the hospital against his will? I mean, letting somebody go is different from pronouncing him totally sane, isn't it?"

"I thought he was a nice young man having a perfectly understandable reaction to tragedy," Dr. Theodore had said. "Tell the truth, I was very impressed with him. Frankly, I thought Dr. Roberts, who had seen him earlier in the week, had been too hard on him."

"But what about all those nurses who he made inappropriate advances to?" she had asked. "I mean, from what I've heard, the guy could act like a total menace. I mean, seems to me you'd look awfully good if you could say how reluctant you were to let him leave the hospital. You could be an advocate for reforming the whole system if you explain how little choice doctors really have when dealing with self-admitted patients. Our show could really give you a megaphone for reform. You'd be famous."

"Look, I don't care about any old confidentiality waiver," he had responded. "I'm not talking about a patient to an outsider."

But before Ms. Beritzky had hung up, she had wheedled out of Dr. Theodore the fact that Dr. Richard Roberts now was practicing in Tallahassee, and she left the distinct impression she soon would be following up with Dr. Roberts – *very* soon.

"I got the overwhelming sensation she was trying to find ways to make Madison Jones look bad," Dr. Theodore said to Becky. "I mean, you can just hear it in the tone of her voice. I've played the tape over again to listen, and it's obvious she's up to no good."

"So you've still got the tape?" Becky asked.

"Yep. And it's all yours, if you want it," he said.

Becky said yes, please, she'd like the tape. But it didn't give her any comfort. If this doctor was right, she had made a *huge* mistake. Not only that, but it would mean her father had been right, and she wrong: a thought that made her nearly apoplectic. If "Hour of Truth" was able to destroy Mad and the non-profit company she had built around him, her father would, for the rest of her life, be able to remind her about how much wiser she would be to just take advice (or orders) from him.

And tomorrow she would have to tell the board that she might have made a mistake so grievous that it could obliterate all the company's gains. This was an utter disaster.

It was a disaster Becky couldn't figure out how to fix. So, despite some of the personal strides she had made since the retreat with Father Vignelli, Becky reverted to her usual method of dealing with looming failure that she couldn't control. She rushed home, opened an extra-large bottle of wine, and started guzzling it like grape juice.

* * *

The next day, Becky ran the board meeting with a fierce hangover. The others couldn't figure out why she seemed so unenthusiastic, so lifeless, when the numbers she reported all looked so good. Together the board enjoyed deciding which charities would be the most worthy recipients of the $397,438 that MMW had available for distribution. ("This just rocks, dudes, this absolutely rocks!" enthused Justin.) But they didn't understand why Becky refused to accept a pay raise that Mad offered her as he gave her ample and eloquent credit for the company's successes. "Stupid slut-whores don't deserve any more pay," she replied in a dead voice, as the rest of the board tried to figure if she was somehow attempting to sound facetious. After not too much longer, Becky's odd, downbeat mood began to wear on them.

Finally, Buzz could stand it no longer: "Lookit, what in God's name is eating you?!"

Becky sighed. And steeled herself. And then she finally launched into an explanation of Spike Walters' interest in Mad, and her own signing of the confidentiality waiver (Mad blanched), and her father's warning, and Dr. Theodore's report of Martina Beritzky's apparently unfriendly agenda. "And now Spike Walters is due down here to interview Mad in 11 days," Becky said, "and if Walters is out to get you, you're pretty much a goner."

Becky said this while staring relentlessly down at the table-top in front of her and rubbing her palms repeatedly across her temples and down around the back of her neck. Her strawberry-blonde hair, usually so lustrous, had taken on an aspect of wilted hay. She was taking this as hard as if her whole self-worth were tied up in her immunity from bad decisions concerning the corporation. She looked positively ill.

As usual, Mary was the implacable one. As she had done at other meetings, she quietly took charge.

"Now Becky, what's that you said about your father wanting 'revenge' on Spike Walters?" Mary asked. "He's got lots of money and power; why don't we see what *he* can do to bail us out?"

"I'd rather die," said Becky, without much conviction.

But the others all warmed to the suggestion.

"Look, Becky, even though I've been against this 'Hour of Truth' thing ever since you mentioned it to me, I don't think it's the disaster you're making it out to be," Mad finally said. "I think I can handle Spike Walters okay. I'll take whatever he dishes out. But what's the harm in us calling your dad and seeing what he can do to make it easier on us? Hell, I'll be glad to call him myself and tell him what a wonderful job you're doing and how incredibly talented you are. I'll make it so that asking him for help here won't sound like some kind of panic move, but like – oh, I don't know, like a mutually beneficial business deal or something. How's that sound, Beck? I promise you won't be embarrassed."

In the end, Becky gave in. That day, she didn't have much fight in her to start with, anyway. She tracked down her father coming home from his favorite Houston golf course and put him on speaker-phone so all five board members could kibitz.

"That sumbitch Walters is always up to no good!" Chet exclaimed when he was apprised of the situation. "He's a nasty, cheap-shot artist sumbitch and the turd of all turds. We need to flush him down the crapper, and flush him *but good*!"

Becky wasn't up for saying much, so Mad jumped in: "Becky said, Mr. Matthews, that you might have some ideas about how to block Walters. Said that you knew some people who could hurt him, or something like that?"

"No specific ideas, son, but just me and some other bidnessmen with a desire to slap that sumbitch so silly that he thinks he's Jerry Lewis. But I'll tell you what: How reliable do you think that doctor is, the one who warned you about the tone of that interview? Do you think he'd be believable on camera if he said that the producer-lady was clearly out to nail your hide?"

"Hey, Daddy, it's me again," Becky said into the speaker. "I was the one who spoke to the doctor, and he sounded like a good guy. But nobody would have to just take his word for it; he says he's got the whole thing on tape. His answering machine recorded the whole conversation. He dropped the tape off to me this morning. I haven't had time to listen to it yet, but I've got it right here in my purse."

"Hot damn, little girl, you got game! Mr. Hidden Microphone gets caught by a hidden microphone! This is bee-you-tiful! This gives us sumthin' good to start with: That's my girl! Let's hear this tape right now. You got a machine can play it for us?"

Never mind that Becky had lucked into the tape: Chet Matthews was giving his daughter the credit as if she herself had deliberately sucked Walters (or, actually, Martina Beritzky) into a ruse.

Everybody assembled listened intently to the tape of Beritzky's voice: "Letting somebody go is a different thing from pronouncing him totally sane, isn't it?... From what I've heard, the guy could act like a total menace..."

"That sure as hell ain't no objective reporter," Chet said from his car phone. "If we could get Walters himself sounding so biased ahead of time, maybe we'd have a fightin' chance to put his sorry ass in a noose." (Chet Matthews didn't mind mixing metaphors.)

This time it was Buzz who spoke up. "You know, my friend Steve Matheson doesn't like Spike Walters, either. Steve's an up-front guy; he doesn't like all those hidden agendas and 'gotcha journalism' stuff with edited remarks and all that. He said over a beer one night that he'd like to put a hidden camera on Walters the way Walters does to everybody else – and, come to think of it, the same way that doctor in effect had a hidden microphone taping the phone call with that producer lady. Wouldn't that be pretty sweet? I bet I could even get Steve to play it on his show if we caught Ol' Spike on camera deliberately screwing us over."

"Cool, Dude!" chimed in Justin, high-pitched voice climbing even more than normal. "Screw the screwer and make him the screw-ee instead! A sting operation! Redford and Newman stuff! That'd be just the coolest!"

Both Buzz's and Justin's voices were unfamiliar to Chet, and Justin's threw him off a little. But Chet warmed very quickly to the idea.

"I tell you what, folks. Why don't we just set a trap for this turd? No reason we can't pull off a hidden camera. How much time we got before he interviews you, Madison?"

"Eleven days from now, Daddy – but I don't see how we can set up a camera," Becky said. "The interview is at the local network studio. They'll be totally in control."

"Christ, little girl, that's what negotiatin' is for! Come up with some reason – any cockamamie excuse'll do – for insisting that the interview be conducted there in your offices, or at Madison's house, or someplace like that. Don't take no for an answer! And between now and then, I'll pay for whatever technician you hire to go set up a camera in a wall or in a bookshelf or, or, uh, through a mirror, or however the crap these things are done. But damn, if we get him on camera doing somethin' crooked in the interview, we'll have some damn good leverage. We can figure out what to do with the film later, but the first step is catching this bastard in the first place. Just go to it, girl, and send me the bill! I'll be damned if Ol' Spike is gonna mess with my daughter. Before I let him bust up your business, Becky, I'll stick that turd where the sun don't shine!"

Mr. Matthews' take-no-prisoners attitude was so infectious that even Becky forgot for a moment to keep hating him. She resented his "little girl"ing her, but when she thought back on the conversation later she would find herself touched by the fact that, however much of an ogre she tried to make him, Chet seemed to genuinely care what happened to her. As for the rest of the board, by the time Chet hung up, they were ready for battle.

* * *

As it turned out, Spike Walters was delighted with the invitation to film at the MMW offices. "As we're going in, be on the lookout for any good little details," he told Martina. "You know: anything that shows ostentatious wealth that makes him look like one of those people using religion to make a quick buck, or anything that shows him to have a big ego, like pictures of him with celebrities … that kind of thing. Get that stuff on video, and we'll show what a fraud he is."

"Oh, we'll have no trouble blowing him out of the water," said the producer. "The shrink in Tallahassee, Dr. Roberts, gave us all kinds of good stuff to use. He said this Jones kid showed a hostile streak a mile wide, and some severe sexual hang-ups. As a matter of fact, when he saw Jones on the news just a few days after the other doctor let Jones out of the hospital, he Xeroxed the written records of his analyses of Jones. As long as we don't say that we got the records from him, we're free to use them however we want. For a little fee, of course."

Walters chuckled. "Good, good, good. But don't stop there. Any good pics we can take of his house or office, to make him look like the profiteer charlatan he is, don't hold back. I'll never forget seeing that little pissant pretending to be President Clinton getting a blow job! If we don't pick off these right-wing jackasses one by one, they'll be taking over the country. But not while Spike Walters can do anything about it! I'll tell you that: not while Spike's around."

* * *

Five days before the interview, Laura Green called Mad on his cell phone. It was the first time they had spoken since their "canoodling" (and its aftermath) the previous November.

"Hey, sweetheart," she said. "I wish I were calling for something fun like a rendez-vous or something, but there's no time for that right now. Mad, I've just found out that you're up shit's creek. Word around the network offices up here is that Spike Walters is out to castrate you. I don't know what you did to get on his bad side, but he's aiming to make you his first big scalp of the news season. Or not a scalp, actually, but a eunuch. He's going after your balls, Mad. This is serious."

Since her mini-flurry of publicity last fall, Laura had continued to attract a high enough percentage of male TV viewers that "Acute Vision" had again been renewed for at least the first half of another season. That moderate success, combined with Laura's talent for internal politics, had kept her near the top of the network's short list of rising young stars. In addition to her main duties with "Acute Vision" and an infrequent cameo on the nightly news, she now was slated for one segment of "Hour of Truth" (subject yet to be determined) in the coming season, so the network brass could see if she could handle the Big-Time.

The only problem was that she and Martina Beritzky flat-out didn't like each other. It was one of those situations where, when young women clash, they *really* clash. In the network's pecking order, they were approximately equal: Laura had a leg up because she was on-air "talent," but Martina had the plum assignment of working for the network's only perennial, money-in-the-bank, Nielsen-ratings heavyweight. Laura had an added advantage in that her hot-shot network boyfriend had hinted that a marriage proposal would finally be in the offing by summer's end. But Martina wasn't far behind: She slept with a high-profile, artsy-social A-list "consumer advocate" attorney.

In short, Laura wanted Martina to fail. And when she heard the talk about *Mad* being the target of Spike and Martina (and Spike's creepy assistant, Al Bobbitt), she had even more reason for wanting to see a project blow up in Martina's face.

Hence, the phone call.

For the most part, Mad now trusted Laura. He still had a tiny spot of doubt about her in the back of his mind, but he made a spur-of-moment decision to bring her at least partly into his confidence on this. After all, she was being kind enough to call, out of the blue, with this warning.

Mad told Laura about the answering-machine tape of Martina Beritzky's call to Dr. Theodore, and about how he and his friends were now aware that Spike Walters meant them harm. (He did not yet tell her about their plans to install a secret camera in his office.)

"God, it's good to hear from you, Laura!" he concluded.

Laura asked Mad if there was anything she could do (very quietly, obviously) to help.

"I dunno, Laura. Thanks for offering. I guess if there's any way to find out exactly how he intends to hit me, what kinds of questions he's gonna try to trip me up with… that'd help. In fact, any intelligence you can give us about his plans. The more we know, the better. For that matter, I don't even know why he's after me. What did I ever do to Spike Walters?"

"Dunno," Laura said. "But this producer Beritzky is a bitch and a half. I have no idea what else exactly I can learn for you, but anything I find out I'll be glad to pass along. But sweetheart…?"

"Yeah?"

"Please be careful. These people can really ruin you if you give them the slightest opening."

"Believe me, Laura, I'm not taking this lightly. But you're really sweet to call, and anything else you can find out, please lemme know… But anyway, girl, how've you been doing? You're looking mighty good on your show when I get a chance to check you out."

So the two of them talked pleasantries for about seven or eight minutes more, and then Laura again promised to keep an ear to the ground for him. And after they hung up, Mad called Becky to give her the news.

* * *

Two days before the interview, The Colonel called. He said he had received word that that some lowlifes named Bobbitt and Bitchkey had been snooping around the University of Virginia, asking questions about the Crazy Eights. "They won't find anything bad about us, of course, or at least nothing bad that's true," he said, "cuz there's nothin' bad to find, I say, there's nothin' bad there to find. But I say, Son, I say, I just want to ask you that whatever's going on, you keep your nose clean and watch the Society's back. We're all behind you, Son, I say, we're all behind you. You been keeping your nose clean and staying out of controversy, and our wives are all saying you come across as a nice young man. But now these reporter creeps from some highfalutin' TV show are asking lotsa questions, and we don't want either you, or us, to get hurt."

The Colonel paused for breath. "Now what the heck's going on with these snoops, anyway? You got any idea what they're up to?"

The Colonel always made Mad nervous. Mad always suspected that because The Colonel was part of a secret society, he had a hidden agenda as well. But because Mad's father and great-uncle had been members, and because Daddy Lee had been loosely affiliated with the group, Mad always gave the Eights the benefit of the doubt. He filled in The Colonel on everything he knew about Spike Walters' agenda, and about the plans the MMW board (and Chet) had cooked up to surreptitiously videotape the interview. What they would do with the tape, Mad still didn't know.

"That's rich, Son, I say, that's really rich! Videotape the videotapers! I love it! And you say Chet Matthews is involved? I've heard of him before. Tough-as-nails businessman, he is. But honest, I've heard. He'll run you over like he's a tank, but no dirty deals. He'll always have an angle, but he'll never cheat. Or so I've heard. Maybe I can have some of my people get in touch with him. Maybe together we can teach a lesson to old Spike Walters. I say, Son, maybe we can make old Spike lose his toupee – and that lump the toupee's attached to, if you know what I mean, Son."

Abruptly as always, the line went dead.

* * *

The day before the interview was scheduled, the technicians finished installing the hidden videotaping system in the MMW offices, and taught Shiloh how to operate it from inside a closet. (Becky would be sitting in the interview room, off camera, but close enough to provide any factual assistance needed.) That night, Shiloh and LaShauna (their toddler in tow) joined Mad and Father Vignelli at a little chapel on the Spring Hill campus.

"Let us pray," said the Jesuit. "Tonight, Lord, we pray for wisdom and courage, for patience and for insight. Tomorrow our friend Madison will be accosted by people who mean to do him harm. Tomorrow Madison will be tested. Tomorrow, Madison's very ministry may be at stake. It is not an orthodox ministry, Lord, and his is not a theology fully consonant with the One True Faith to which I have devoted my life – but Mad is nevertheless bringing sheep back into the fold, Lord. Mad is bringing people back to you who have long utterly rejected you. I have seen them come back to you, Lord, and I have seen their lives transformed in your love because of his ministry. Madison Jones is doing good work, Lord, and we pray tonight that his work not be destroyed. So, therefore, in tomorrow's interview, we pray that you give him the mental acuity and the spiritual grace to turn an intended attack into an opportunity. Whatever happens tomorrow will be part of a broadcast seen by 25 million Americans, Lord. Please let Madison parry whatever thrusts come his way, not with anger but with love. Please let him be a vessel for your love, and let his words be a vessel for your truth, so that those 25 million Americans are, not enraged by Madison's weaknesses, but inspired by his ultimate dedication to you and by the redemptions he has found despite his pain.

"And Lord, finally we pray that those who interview Mad tomorrow will themselves have their hearts transformed, so that when they craft their story for broadcast, they will be moved to fairly and responsibly and sympathetically represent our friend Madison Jones. All of this we pray, Lord, in the name of and through your Son, our Savior, Jesus Christ, and through the Holy Ghost. Amen."

"Amen," said the other three, in unison. "Amen!" merrily shouted the nearly two-year-old Gloria Jones from a hiding place underneath a pew. Shiloh had begun to add a "Praise the Lord," but instead began chuckling at his daughter's timing.

"Thanks, y'all," said Mad. "I'm really nervous about tomorrow. This little session has helped. Really. Thanks. Have a good night. And Shiloh, I'll see you in the morning."

* * *

As scheduled, the "Hour of Truth" crew arrived at the MMW offices at 9 a.m. sharp to begin setting up. Shiloh, equipped with some water and even a small makeshift pissoir, already was ensconced in the hidden closet. Martina Beritzky and Al Bobbitt acted oh-so-benevolently, as if their highest calling were to give a positive forum to a young, unordained preacher. And Becky and Mad (and MMW's grandmotherly secretary) all acted slightly starstruck, as if they were honored and thrilled that "Hour of Truth" found them worthy of attention. (Justin, too, was there, having taken the morning off, and he kept flitting around nervously, getting in the way.) The technical crew, seven people strong, unraveled lots of electrical cord, and moved chairs around and moved them around again, and fiddled with their huge light stands, and whispered back and forth to Martina in conspiratorial tones. But one cameraman, a bearded Hispanic in his 30s, did find the opportunity to pull Mad aside and whisper, apropos of apparently nothing: "I don't care what my bosses think; I think you're onto something. No matter what happens, don't give up, okay?"

As for Spike Walters, he didn't arrive until nearly 10:30. He was muttering some complaint, inaudible to Becky, about the lack of some amenity or other in "this pathetic little burgh" of Mobile. (Oddly, Becky bristled when she heard this, even though she had until recently considered Mobile with the same contempt.) Crankily, he ignored Becky as somebody wholly unimportant. But, as if turning on his personality with the flick of a switch, he immediately assumed an ingratiating manner when he was introduced to Mad.

"You're all the rage, young man," Spike said, so convincingly jovial that Mad might not have noticed the smarm if his antenna hadn't already been attuned for it. "Here you are, just beginning your little career, and already you've made a wave or two. Well, Spike here is gonna make you a household name beyond your wildest imaginations, young man. Yes, Spike here knows what power is, and believe me, Spike can guarantee that Mr. and Mrs. Sixpack will be talking about you once Spike's done making you famous."

Mad made sure to beam like an ingénue. "You're awfully kind to come down here, sir," he said. "I'm incredibly flattered that you are interested in anything I have to say."

So all appeared to be sweetness and lucency as the two men, following Martina's stage directions, took their respective seats. And when the camera lights finally shone red, Spike Walters had the inquisitive smile on his face of an ever-reasonable interlocutor.

"So, you've got yourself a wonderfully redemptive story, Mr. Jones, don't you?"

"Well, sir…"

"No need to 'sir' me, we're all friends here."

"Well, sir, I mean not 'sir,' but you know, anyway, I don't know if anybody should see *me* as some redemptive examples, or anything like that. I mean, I'd rather not have had the dire straits in the first place that you're saying I was redeemed from. The important thing is…"

Again, Walters interrupted. He was a master at this business of pretending to be so kind that looked like the 'good guy' on camera at the same time he threw his interviewees off their message by cutting them off just before they made the point they wanted made.

"Those dire straits you mention, (…)" he said, "I guess anybody would sympathize, now wouldn't they? There you were with a beautiful young wife, still newlyweds, and she was pregnant, and then, mysteriously, she died alone next to you in your bloody bed. It would make anybody just sick with grief, now, wouldn't it?"

"Oh, I can't even begin to tell you," Mad said. "I mean, the shock of that is just so great that you have trouble even thinking straight, and …"

(Becky blanched. She saw that Mad had given Walters a perfect set-up line.)

"Thinking straight is really the nub of it, isn't it, Mr. Jones? There you were, grief-stricken, and so you ended up in a psychiatric ward. Tell us about that, Mr. Jones."

Walters still had empathy painted all over his face. Mad knew that even with advance warning, he already had stepped right into quicksand he had been determined to avoid. It was one thing to go into an interview expecting to be set up; it was a far tougher thing, even when supposedly prepared, to actually keep one's wits when being interviewed by such a master.

In the closet next door, Shiloh watched his tiny video feed and felt the pit of his stomach become queasy.

The good news was that Mad knew this topic would come up and had prepared extensively for it. The bad news was that Spike Walters somehow was already in total control of the interview. Mad had a prop ready in his pocket – a prop he had not intended on relying upon quite so soon – but, feeling defensive, he pulled it out now.

"Well, I want to make clear that this was always a matter of my own choice, of me just wanting a place to hide from the world, not of me being 'committed,' or anything like that. I checked myself in of my own free will, and when I was ready to leave, this is what the doctor wrote…." Mad looked down as if to begin reading from his prop, which was Dr. Theodore's exit evaluation of him that, among other things, called Mad "grieving, but well-adjusted. A thoroughly charming young man, bereaved but neither beaten nor bereft of his full faculties." But Mad never got to read it. Spike Walters, reading from a similar hospital evaluation form that magically appeared in his hand, said:

"Oh, yes, the doctor. Here's what the attending physician wrote, man by the name of Dr. Richard Roberts. He wrote that you were 'belligerent.' He also wrote, and I quote, that you were 'full of unresolved sexual angst, even to the point of obsessing about bestiality, and full of rage, and highly emotionally unstable.' Now some would say this suggests that you…."

This time it was Mad who interrupted.

"Wrong doctor, Mr. Walters. That's not fair! What Dr. Theodore wrote was…."

"This is all part of the record, Mr. Jones. If you'll just calm down… [Walters smiled reassuringly for the camera] … you'll see how we're just establishing a context for you that lets you explain your unique religious views. We're trying to understand you, Mr. Jones, trying to be genderous to you. …."

Walters screwed up his face and turned to Martina. "Damn, that came out 'genderous' instead of 'generous.' Cut that; let's do it over."

Mad, incredulous, watched as the camera light went off, and then Walters caught a breath, and then Walters nodded to the cameraman and the light went on again. As if it was part of an uninterrupted train of thought, Walters repeated: "We're trying to understand you, Mr. Jones, just trying to be as generous to you as we can be."

"But Mr. Walters! I…."

"Context is everything in your line of work, isn't it, Mr. Jones? That's why we want to give you the benefit of every doubt. Mental illness these days isn't as much of a stigma as it once was, so we want to let you establish your prior mental illness in case you need it to explain anything else we cover. For instance, in the light of this bit about bestiality, it's almost a relief to know that, if other published reports are right, that you're a rather randy young ladies' man. Now isn't that right?"

The rout was on.

If Mad left an obvious opening, Spike dived in. If Mad seemed to have a good answer prepared, Spike interrupted and changed the subject. If Spike messed up, they stopped the tape and re-started it. If Mad said something that sounded the least bit charismatic or wise, Spike found a way to turn the statement on its head.

For instance, in talking about the Crazy Eights (of which Mad said, truthfully, he was not a member), Mad said this: "I know nothing about how they operate, but I've heard they are famous for giving anonymous gifts to their university. You're wrong to condemn them for secrecy, because they are merely following the advice of Christ himself. Jesus said that when you give alms, do it in secret, and beware of practicing piety in front of men, but do it in secret instead, so that you'll be doing good deeds for the sake of the good itself and not for the sake of having others praise you for your generosity."

It was one of the longest uninterrupted statements Mad had been allowed to make all morning, partly because Spike had been sipping a glass of water. But Spike's mind had not a bit of the slowness of some of his septuagenarian contemporaries. He came right back at Mad by pulling out of thin air a biblical quote, even though he himself disdained most religion.

"But didn't Jesus also say something about how you shouldn't hide your light under a bushel?" Spike asked. "Any clever young Bible-thumper can quote the Good Book out of context to justify all sorts of nefarious action, now isn't that true? That's been the favorite trick of evil men throughout the centuries, to quote the Bible wrongly when cornered by their own immorality."

Spike was taking Mad apart, piece by piece. He covered the gamut, from Mad's reported Clinton-bashing to his supposed anti-Catholic bias (based on the old press release from Gladys Phillpott). "You've even been condemned by the national office of your own Episcopal Church," he noted. All that was left was the subject that Spike thought was his ace in the hole. ("That's old hat, and we've got enough to hang him with, anyway," Martina had told Spike the day before, but Walters wouldn't listen.) This was what he thought would most permanently drive a wedge between Mad and everybody who was the slightest bit devout. "For one final topic," he said to Mad, "I bet a lot of your newest followers don't know this about you, because you haven't stressed it much all year from what I can tell. But you are on record multiple times as saying that 'God is a jerk.' You can't deny you've said that. Isn't that an obnoxious position to take, and an arrogant one, and one that throws into doubt whether you are a man of God at all?"

Mad had had enough.

"Well, God's nowhere near as much of a jerk as you are, Spike. And the other difference is that God really *is* God, while you just like to *pretend* that *you* are."

Walters' face turned red. He was so used to rolling over people that the last thing he expected, this late in an interview in which he had so repeatedly worn down his subject's defenses, was for his subject to come back at him with an insult.

"*Cut!*" he yelled at Martina. "Cut this crap right now!" And then, with the camera off, he said to Mad: "You think you're very clever, don't you, you nutcake son of a bitch? You must not know who you're dealing with. This is Spike Walters you're talking to. I have the power to make you a hero or to ruin your life, whichever I choose. And you just signed your own death warrant."

Spike took a deep breath, and then took a few swallows of water. Then, to Mad: "Okay, cocksucker, let's try this again."

Mad, smiling nervously, nodded.

"For a final topic, here's your own words coming back to haunt you. I bet a lot of your newer followers don't know that you spent time last year babbling that God is a jerk. Doesn't that throw into question the very idea that you're somehow a man of God?"

"You must not have done your homework, Spike. I've answered that question a million times, and in the context of all of the religious theses I published, you'd have to admit that my message is one of both thanks and praise to God."

"So you're denying that you said God is a jerk?"

"Holy cow, you're thickheaded! Of course I don't deny it. Can't your pea-brain get around the fact that thinking can evolve? Can't you see that me writing about God being a jerk was, quite openly, just one stage of a longer process of understanding God?"

"The fact is, then, that you've said God is a jerk. In fact, you've gone even farther than that: You've also said that God is, quote, a 'flawed SOB.' Whose side are you on, anyway: God's, or the devil's?"

"Spike, old man, you must have never taken a class in formal logic. If you start with a hypothesis at step one, and by step 59 you're reached an entirely different conclusion, then the hypothesis no longer stands. My hypothesis was that God is a flawed SOB. That was thesis number one. My conclusion is that…"

"Oh, cut the crap! You know you're cornered, Mr. Jones. Do you or do you not believe that God is a jerk?"

"If you would stop interrupting me, Spike, my man…"

"Don't 'Spike my man' me, you cocksucker. I can cut this videotape any place I want it. Nobody'll ever see anything but me giving you all the time in the world to answer a reasonable question. Now give me an answer: Is God a jerk?"

"Not according to my final thesis, Mr. Walters, and I quote: 'God's love has been poured into our hearts through the Holy Spirit which has been given to us.' What's important, Mr. Walters, is the redemption."

"So you're denying that you've said God is a jerk? How can you deny what you yourself put down on paper?"

"The same way you can edit the videotape so that nobody will see you using the word 'cocksucker,' Mr. Walters."

"Mr. Jones, do you realize the trouble you're in now? Do you even know what you're getting into?"

"I don't know, Mr. Walters. I can't rightly remember. You may have mentioned that to me a few moments ago." Mad's voice was full of disdain and sarcasm.

Spike Walters turned to Martina and the technicians: "It's a wrap. Let's go home and crucify this bastard."

The interview, including all the stops and starts, had lasted more than an hour. And it would prove to be more than an hour of truth.

* * *

"Jesus Christ, we're screwed," said Becky once the TV crew had left. "What the hell was that 'bestiality' stuff?"

Mad explained how, when Dr. Roberts had accused him of a sexual obsession with his mother-in-law, he had shot back an angry, sarcastic line about giving blow jobs to rhinoceri. Dr. Theodore had even asked him about the reference, in Dr. Roberts' report, to that outburst, and had chuckled appreciatively when Mad told him why he said it.

Becky didn't think it was funny. Again, she said: "Jesus, we're screwed."

But Justin, bless his heart, always saw the positive side of things. "We're not screwed! We're all set! We got all we need to blow them outta the water! Don't you see? We have our own videotape. We've got a tape of him saying 'cocksucker.' We've got a tape of him bragging about how powerful he is. We've got a tape of him being totally unfair. He's the one gonna get screwed, not us!"

Becky had for months been far kinder to Justin, but this time she couldn't hold back. "I don't care what we have, you stupid little shit," she snapped. "They've got a report saying Mad was into bestiality. There's nothing we can do to overcome that!"

"And we've got Dr. Theodore on our side," countered Justin, trying to hide the hurt over Becky calling him a 'little shit.' "He'll tell the truth! He'll explain it!"

Becky started arguing back, but Mad wasn't saying anything. He was looking through his copy of Dr. Theodore's report. As it turned out, Dr. Theodore had filed an addendum with an unusually thorough explanation for his decision to release Mad from the hospital, on the off chance that Dr. Roberts, as the prior attending physician, ever asked for a formal review of the dismissal.

"Here it is," he said suddenly, and then began to quote from the paper. "Mr. Jones also complained that Dr. Roberts accused him, for no reason, of a sexual attraction to his mother-in-law. Said he responded sarcastically with a joke about also lusting after a rhinoceros. Said he wished he could file a formal complaint about Dr. Roberts' conduct. Said it with good humor, though. Seemed pretty funny to me. No problem there at all."

"What good does that do us?" Becky said. "Spike Walters never let you say anything about that on the air. We can't even prove that he has a copy of that addendum from Dr. Theodore. And even if we have the videotape of how unfair Walters was, what good does that do us? What are we ever gonna do with the videotape that can possibly match the 30 million people who'll see the version that runs on 'Hour of Truth'?"

And there matters stood for about 12 days, spilling into August. Chet Matthews called several times to discuss how to respond to the September airing of the show, and The Colonel called Mad at odd hours of the night for the same reason. Indeed, Chet reported that some guy named "The Colonel" also called him in Houston, out of the blue, to say he wanted to help.

"Guy won't say exactly who he is or what his connection is to you, Madison," said Chet on the phone. "But said he and some mysterious colleagues had some money to spend, and that they are hatching a plan. He says he knows how to pull lots of strings. And I've got some money to spend, too. Some of my oil buddies, guys on the board of a big conglomerate that often advertises on 'Hour of Truth,' they hate Walters as much as I do. Seems ol' Spike has made a habit of making some oilmen look bad. We're all up for hitting back at this asshole, if we can only figure out how."

* * *

"Sweetheart, it's Laura! I'm so excited, sweetheart, I've got big news!"

Laura reported that she had been given access to the videotape library of "Hour of Truth." She said the network execs wanted her to study old shows, to get a perfect feel for the formula the show used in crafting its reports. "It's a highly evolved reporting style," she said. "They just keep using the same tricks of the trade, and the same story-telling techniques, over and over again. They said that once I master their techniques, they'll give me an assignment on a segment to air right after New Year's."

Mad wasn't catching on. "That's great Laura; so you get to watch a lot of old shows," he said. "And you'll be on the air with those same shitheads who are out to destroy me. I guess I'm happy for you, but right now I'm about to get my scalp taken off."

"Mad, don't you see? I have unrestricted access to their library and their offices! I can make copies of tapes! As long as I put the original tape back where it goes, I'm sure I can get away with smuggling out a copy without anybody knowing."

Mad still didn't see the point.

"C'mon Mad!" Laura said. "It's so obvious! They'll have their report on you ready to go probably ten full days before it airs. But if I smuggle a copy out to you, you'll know in advance exactly what they're gonna do and you can have a response all prepared."

Laura smelled Martina Beritzky's blood in the water. If a Beritzky project blew up in Walters' face, Laura knew that somehow the blame would be foisted onto her rival.

That night, Becky arranged a five-way conference call with her father at one end, The Colonel dialing in from an undisclosed location, Buzz calling from D.C., Mary phoning from St. Louis; and she, Mad, Justin, Shiloh, and a highly cooperative Dr. Theodore at the MMW offices in Mobile. For once, everything came together in a wonderful synthesis. Together, the conspirators hatched a superbly clever plan.

Chapter Three

Two days later, Shiloh and Dr. Theodore flew together to New York, with tickets paid for by The Colonel. Shiloh had called ahead, from the Mobile police headquarters to a private parking lot at network headquarters in New York, for advance permission to enter the lot with an amateur video camera and a partner. One of those "hush hush" drug investigations, dontcha know? Trying to nail the New York source for a Mobile drug runner, he said. Won't even have a firearm, he said. Just need about a half-hour of surveillance.

At the expected time, a limo driver pulled into the lot and Spike Walters emerged from the back seat. "Excuse me, Mr. Walters," said Dr. Theodore, emerging from the shadows. "Sorry to bother you like this; I just want you to have these papers. They'll clear up something about that young guy in Mobile, Madison Jones. I know you're after him; this'll help."

Startled, but reassured by Dr. Theodore's friendly manner, Walters took the papers. He never saw Shiloh, sitting quietly in a nearby car with the video rolling. Dr. Theodore then turned and began walking away, full of nonchalance. Spike Walters went on up to his office, and Shiloh caught up with the doctor a while later.

* * *

During the editing sessions to prepare the final version of Spike's report, Walters was as meticulous as ever. Even when he seemed to have gotten the best of Mad, Spike wanted to look better still. "See that bit where I pull out the line about a 'light under a bushel'?" he said to Martina and the technician. "I sound a little like I'm guessing, because I said Jesus said '*something like*' not hiding our light. Why don't you insert in there one of those scenes we have of the Jones kid looking like he's been caught in a lie, one of those stricken looks we caught him in, and let me do a voiceover there before I resume my question? I looked it up: the bushel bullshit in the Bible came *right before*, just a few verses before, the crap he quoted about giving alms in secret. So let's record my voiceover citing the exact location of that passage in the book of Matthew. It'll emphasize that even a layman like me knows more about the Bible than this faker."

On that, and on everything else in the report, what Walters wanted, Walters got.

* * *

The night arrived for the season opener of "Hour of Truth." With a big football game as a lead-in, the national audience was particularly large. The first two segments did not disappoint them. And then came the final story, reported by the venerable Spike Walters. As an unparalleled morality play, it was boffo. Here was a young high school history teacher who in just a year and a half had conned an entire country into thinking he was a religious sage. But the charlatan did not entirely refute the evidence of a connection to a shadowy secret cabal at a university that once was a bastion of Southern white-hood. And he had taken cheap shots at President Clinton. And he was certifiably a psychiatric case, so messed up that he fantasized about bestiality. And not only that, but his theology, such as it was, amounted at heart to a rant against God. God was both a jerk and a flawed SOB, he had said. And when asked point blank, "Whose side are you on, anyway: God's or the devil's?" Mad's apparent answer (with tape expertly and cleverly spliced on Spike Walters' orders) was this: "I don't know, Mr. Walters. I can't rightly remember."

All throughout, Spike Walters looked like he was doing his level best to be "generous" with Mad. "We want to give you the benefit of every doubt," Spike told him quite clearly. "We're trying to understand you, Mr. Jones."

And every time, Mad was forced to admit, uncomfortably, that Spike was right. "The shock of that is just so great that you have trouble even thinking straight," Mad said, in acknowledging that he was a nutcase. "My hypothesis was that God is a flawed SOB," he confirmed.

The Accidental Prophet | 445

Spike also culled the usual outside sources. Charles Pringle, the radical Episcopalian bishop who denied the divinity of Christ but whom nevertheless was always held up by the media as a bulwark of mainstream Christianity, said that Mad obviously didn't know what he was talking about. Pringle said God is not a jerk, but rather pure love which forgives all sins and is comfortable with all lifestyle choices. Rabbi Ehud Heintz added that because Bill Clinton obviously was a King David-like figure, the president could have as many women as he wanted and that Mad had thus been small-minded to criticize him. (Left on the cutting room floor, of course, were Mad's protestations that, first, he had never made a habit of criticizing the president and, second, his rare comments on the situation had focused less on sex than on obstruction of justice.) Finally, to hurt Mad with more conservative viewers, Spike Walters quoted the Rev. Patterson (off camera) as saying that Mad was "a dangerous charlatan and a false prophet."

By the time the report was over, there seemed no doubt that Mad was utterly finished, destroyed, *kaput*. Nobody could survive such a thrashing.

And yet... *And yet*. Something funny happened right after the report ended, when "Hour of Truth" cut to its last commercial break before returning to advertise the topics of the next week's show. The commercial began with the familiar figure of the executive for a corporate conglomerate that often advertised on "Hour of Truth." The executive had a folksy manner and had excelled as a TV pitchman as well as a brass-knuckles corporate czar. But it wasn't the same commercial. A new one had somehow been smuggled in.

"By now, you out there in American TV-land are probably used to seeing my ugly mug," said the executive. "But I'm just here in this ad to introduce my friend Madison Jones."

Then the camera panned back far enough to see Mad sitting next to the exec.

"The show you just saw was entirely fraudulent," Mad said to the camera. "If you'll now turn to the 'American Heritage Network' on most of your cable systems, you'll not only see the real Madison Jones, but also the real Spike Walters. We have caught him red-handed, with proof that he's a scam artist. Go ahead, change the channel now. You'll never think the same way again about Spike Walters."

And then Mad was gone from the screen.

The American Heritage Network was a fairly new outfit that had only recently negotiated a spot on most of the nation's cable lineups. Advertising on it was still relatively inexpensive. And between Chet and his oil friends, and the mysterious Colonel and his ability to "pull lots of strings," Mad's team had arranged to buy an entire half hour of airtime.

The effect was devastating. With the videotape that Laura had smuggled out, Mad and his team (including some Mobile-area film editors hired by Chet) had interspersed segments from Spike's report with sections of the wide-angle, uncut recording of the interview that Shiloh had secretly taped.

"There are lots of serious breaches of trust in the 'Hour of Truth,'" Mad said at the beginning. "But first, let's take a silly little example to show the kinds of techniques that Spike Walters used throughout. Watch how Mr. Walters is so vain that he even does a new 'take' to hide that he mispronounced the word 'generous.'"

He then played, from Shiloh's version, this uncut portion of the interview:

> "This is all part of the record, Mr. Jones. If you'll just calm down… [Walters smiled reassuringly for the camera] … you'll see how we're just establishing a context for you that lets you explain your unique religious views. We're trying to understand you, Mr. Jones, trying to be genderous to you. …."
>
> Walters screwed up his face and turned to Martina. "Damn, that came out 'genderous' instead of 'generous.' Cut that; let's do it over."
>
> Walters caught a breath, and then Walters nodded to the cameraman and the light went on again. As if it was part of an uninterrupted train of thought, Walters repeated: "We're trying to understand you, Mr. Jones, just trying to be as generous to you as we can be."

Mad continued: "Now here's an even sillier example. Note how Mr. Walters actually does a voice-over, added later, to make it look as if he, purely from his own knowledge, had come up with the reference to the Gospel of Matthew."

Mad then showed Shiloh's unedited version of this full exchange, beginning with Mad speaking:

> "Jesus said that when you give alms, do it in secret, and beware of practicing piety in front of men, but do it in secret instead, so that you'll be doing good deeds for the sake of the good itself and not for the sake of having others praise you for your generosity."
>
> "But didn't Jesus also say something about how you shouldn't hide your light under a bushel?" Spike asked. "Any clever young Bible-thumper can quote the Good Book out of context to justify all sorts of nefarious action, now isn't that true?"

Then came the final version from the just-completed airing of the show, in which, between "bushel" and "Any clever...," Spike was heard saying: "Matter of fact, if memory serves, the bit about not hiding your light was in the Gospel of Matthew – and it was just a *few verses* before the passage about giving alms in secret that you just quoted out of context."

Mad now looked at the camera: "Let's watch that again. First, here's the original interview." (Again the scene with the Matthew-less dialogue.) "Now, here's the part with a voice-over added later, to make it appear that Mr. Walters knew the Gospel of Matthews off the top of his head." (Again the voice-over with a close-up of Mad looking stricken.)

Mad again to the camera: "Now if Spike Walters will go to all that trouble on a relatively unimportant point, imagine how dishonest the rest of the report was."

The rest of the MMW-produced half-hour was a series of comparisons between the original interview's reality and the Spike-edited version. Particularly damaging to Spike was this exchange from the actual interview, at a point where a discomfited Mad had begun trying to talk tough to make up for being so obviously cornered:

"The fact is, then, that you've said God is a jerk. In fact, you've gone even farther than that: You've also said that God is, quote, a 'flawed SOB.' Whose side are you on, anyway: God's, or the devil's?"

"Spike, old man, you must have never taken a class in formal logic. If you start with a hypothesis at step one, and by step 59 you're reached an entirely different conclusion, then the hypothesis no longer stands. My hypothesis was that God is a flawed SOB. That was thesis number one. My conclusion is that…"

"Oh, cut the crap! You know you're cornered, Mr. Jones. Do you or do you not believe that God is a jerk?"

"If you would stop interrupting me, Spike, my man…"

"Don't 'Spike my man' me, you cocksucker. I can cut this videotape any place I want it. Nobody'll ever see anything but me giving you all the time in the world to answer a reasonable question. Now give me an answer: Is God a jerk?"

"Not according to my final thesis, Mr. Walters, and I quote: 'God's love has been poured into our hearts through the Holy Spirit which has been given to us.' What's important, Mr. Walters, is the redemption."

"So you're denying that you've said God is a jerk? How can you deny what you yourself put down on paper?"

"The same way you can edit the videotape so that nobody will see you using the word 'cocksucker,' Mr. Walters."

Of that, of course, the only part that had made it onto "Hour of Truth" was the question about whose side Mad was on, God's or the devil's. It was followed on "Hour of Truth" by Mad's later comment that "*I don't know, Mr. Walters. I can't rightly remember.*"

Now, to the camera, Mad said: "My comment about not remembering something had nothing to do with God or the devil. It came from an entirely later section of the original interview."

Mad continued: "But the worst distortion of reality, the single slimiest and sleaziest, was that Mr. Walters effectively accused me of bestiality. Here's the tape."

Mad then ran the appropriate segment from "Hour of Truth", with Spike talking:

> "Here's what the attending physician wrote, man by the name of Dr. Richard Roberts. He wrote that you were 'belligerent.' He also wrote, and I quote, that you were 'full of unresolved sexual angst, even to the point of obsessing about bestiality, and full of rage, and highly emotionally unstable'."

Mad again: "To explain not just how unfair that was, but how Spike Walters knew that it was unfair, here's Dr. Ted Theodore, the physician who did my exit interview at the hospital where I had checked myself in, *by my own choice*, as a way for me to grieve the death of my wife and unborn child without interruption."

Dr. Theodore came onto the screen. He showed a video clip of Mad trying to quote from his exit analysis, but with Spike not letting Mad do so. He then read from his own glowing analysis of Mad. He then explained that Mad himself had told him about the "rhinoceros" remark, and its context, and that he thought it was a humorous and perfectly appropriate response to an out-of-line comment from the other doctor.

"What's worse," Dr. Theodore said, "was that from the very start, it was obvious that 'Hour of Truth' was biased against young Mr. Jones. Here's a tape from my answering machine at home, with Spike Walters' producer, Martina Beritzky, weeks before Mr. Walters even interviewed Mr. Jones, showing clearly what their agenda was:

> "Letting somebody go is a different thing from pronouncing him totally sane, isn't it? … From what I've heard, the guy could act like a total menace…"

"My report on Mr. Jones refuted all their charges, specifically including the rhinoceros part," the psychiatrist continued. "And what's amazing is that Spike Walters himself had my report in his hand, but he ignored it."

He then ran the videotape from the parking lot of him personally handing the report to Walters.

"I'm appalled," said the doctor to the camera. "Spike Walters knew that Mad Jones is a bright, engaging, and perfectly sane young man, but he deliberately made Mr. Jones out to be some sort of wacko. In his hands was my contemporary analysis that Mr. Jones was 'grieving, but well-adjusted. A thoroughly charming young man.' But Spike Walters bent the truth to his own will. And that's despicable."

Mad came on camera again:

"To this day, I don't know why Spike Walters decided to do a hatchet job on me. I don't know what he has against me. But it's clear that he detests me, and that his entire goal was to distort reality in whatever way he could, solely to make me look bad. As my final proof, here are two more exchanges from the actual interview. For obvious reasons, Mr. Walters never put these verbal exchanges onto TV."

Then Mad played a segment from Shiloh's tape beginning with Spike talking:

> "'God is a jerk.' You can't deny you've said that. Isn't that an obnoxious position to take, and an arrogant one, and one that throws into doubt whether you are a man of God at all?"
>
> Mad: "Well, God's nowhere near as much of a jerk as you are, Spike. And the other difference is that God really is God, while you just like to pretend that you are."
>
> Walters' face turned red: "Cut!!" he yelled at Martina. "Cut this crap right now!" And then, with the camera off, he said to Mad: "You think you're very clever, don't you, you nutcake son of a bitch? You must not know who you're dealing with. This is Spike Walters you're talking to. I have the power to make you a hero or to ruin your life, whichever I choose. And you just signed your own death warrant."

Then came this segment:

> "Mr. Jones, do you realize the trouble you're in now? Do you even know what you're getting into?"

"I don't know, Mr. Walters. I can't rightly remember. You may have mentioned that to me a few moments ago." Mad's voice was full of disdain and sarcasm.

Spike Walters turned to Martina and the technicians: "It's a wrap. Let's go home and crucify this bastard."

Mad, again to the TV audience: "Let's play that again."

"Let's go home and crucify this bastard." And again: "Let's go home and crucify this bastard."

Mad spoke one more time to the TV audience: "Well, my friends, I'm still standing. No crucifixion here; not even a cross. But if Spike Walters even *had* a conscience, then his utterly dishonest and unfair treatment of me tonight would be an incredibly heavy cross for *his* conscience to bear for the rest of his life. As for me, I'll stick with the same message of redemption and hope that is my 59th and final thesis, a thesis that Mr. Walters would not let me say on his show. It's a direct quotation from the letter of St. Paul to the Romans. I quote: 'Suffering produces endurance, and endurance produces character, and character produces hope, and hope does not disappoint us, because God's love has been poured into our hearts through the Holy Spirit which has been given to us.'

"Thank you very much for watching."

* * *

The fallout from Mad's "sting" operation was immediate. The very next night, Steve Matheson finally featured Mad (not just Buzz) as a guest on his show, and for a full half-hour at that. Matheson's criticism of "Hour of Truth" was withering. The late-night TV comedians all made fun of Spike Walters all week, and one of them even shoehorned Mad into the show's schedule for the Monday a week later. Cable-TV and the two other traditional networks all had field days with the story. Newspaper columnists, especially conservative ones, went bonkers. Editorial boards weighed in, almost uniformly lambasting "Hour of Truth." (The one exception was *The Metropolitan Daily* [self-styled motto: "The newspaper of record"], which cluck-clucked awhile about Walters' ethical lapses before arguing that this one episode shouldn't obscure Walters' "distinguished record of journalistic service," especially considering that "Madison Jones is, after all, a brazenly cheeky young hothead with a flair for self-promotion but not a single relevant academic degree. Almost anybody could be excused for finding Mr. Jones distasteful; Mr. Walters' sole error was succumbing to the understandable temptation to dramatize Mr. Jones' obvious shortcomings.")

Republican politicians jumped eagerly on the anti-Walters bandwagon. "He's a perfect example of why the scourge of the left-wing media must be destroyed," said one. "The evil underbelly of the liberal New York media has been exposed," said another.

Not to be tarred with the same brush, the unctuous Democratic "Gentleman from Michigan" said that "Spike Walters has shown that when you wrestle with dogs you get fleas. Rather than wasting time on a right-wing hater, Mr. Walters should be examining why so many of our citizens don't have health care and why the Republicans have kept the minimum wage so low."

At "Hour of Truth," network execs made Martina Beritzky the primary scapegoat. She was easy to blame for supposedly being careless with the show's videotape: She was the only one who had signed out a copy before it aired, and the assumption was that somehow, somebody had "borrowed" it from her when she wasn't looking. (Laura, of course, had been careful to smuggle her copy out under separate cover. Besides, she had spent the better part of a year denigrating Mad for having had the gall to try to kiss her that night in New Orleans, thus almost ruining her career. Everybody at the network thought that she legitimately despised him.) Walters blamed Martina, too, for doing the "flawed" research that misled him into a "poor understanding" of Mad's ideas. He also claimed that when Dr. Theodore handed him Mad's medical file, he had merely passed it on to Martina without examining it himself. Clearly, he said, it was her fault that they misrepresented "the bestiality stuff." Result: Martina Beritzky found herself out of a job.

Network execs also put out a statement noting the "stress" Walters had been under because of high blood pressure combined with the recent diagnosis that his wife "might" be suffering the early stages of Parkinson's disease. The statement said that Walters had "magnanimously" tried to assume some of the blame that belonged at Martina's feet, and that because of all these factors combined, the network would "regretfully" accept the "venerably newsman's offer" to take a one-year leave of absence from full-time duty with "Hour of Truth."

* * *

The chat room, of course, went nuts. D Thom pronounced himself again to be FD (Formerly Doubting) Thom, and firmly in Mad's camp. New participants wrote that Mad was "an inspiration" and "a hero." Even usual critics Ever Faithful and Defender wrote that Mad had been unfairly treated.

And Affirmed was over-the-top: "Spike Walters is like the Roman emperors and Mad like the Christian martyrs fed to the lions for sport! Mad is surely now a candidate for sainthood. He should be canonized while he's still alive!"

Amazingly, M. Magdalene also broke her silence. "This episode clearly shows that programs like Hour of Truth need new blood. It's a credit to Mad, both his guile and his essential decency, that he survived. But others may not be so lucky. So let's everybody pay tribute to Mad, but agitate for change from the networks!"

* * *

Mad was now a certifiable superstar. His bi-monthly rallies began attracting up to 20,000 attendees per event. He signed a hugely lucrative contract for another book, with a small part of the advance going to him and to Becky personally (she had insisted on the former, he on the latter) in the form of tax-protected personal savings accounts, rather than to MMW Corp. He signed a deal to do a weekly national radio call-in show (an hour each Sunday), to begin just after the New Year. And by November 1 the list of newspapers subscribing to his daily column grew from 101 to 153, and the column's allowable length, 300 words on weekdays, was expanded to 400 words for Sundays.

And through all that autumn's hoopla, Mad tried (not always successfully) to keep a level head and tried to keep his focus on refining his theological message.

Later in November, he chose as his column's subject letter one that was written to him by a "G.F. Martin." (He did not recognize the name.) "Dear Madison," it began. "In the Christmas story, as read in 'Charlie Brown' by Linus, there is a great line about shepherds being 'sore afraid.' That captures my own feelings perfectly, although for a different reason. I'm a Jew by birth, but always more of an atheist than anything. And recently, largely because of what I've read and seen from you, I've been recognizing a big void in my life and trying to see if God can fill it. I just don't 'get' Christianity, though, and my own Jewish tradition leaves me cold. I'm haunted by a God who has abandoned his promise and allowed the Holocaust to happen, and I don't see any real hope in 'God' no matter how hard I look. That's why I'm sore afraid – afraid that this emptiness inside will never leave me. In my situation, what do you think I should do?"

"Dear G.F.," Mad answered. "I wrote in my theses that those who keep the Jewish rules of Leviticus 'are to be honored,' and that 'all, of all faiths, should honor the Jews.' You belong to a faith tradition that is an inspiration to all people of good will. While I myself am a Christian because I believe that God's redemptive promise has been made incarnate, along with God's very being, in the person of Jesus Christ, I am always eager to reassure Jews that even without Christ, God's redemptive kindness, and promise for more of the same, is manifest throughout the history of your people. At the end of Second Chronicles, and again repeated almost word for word in the beginning of Ezra, there's the story of what happens after Jerusalem has been destroyed and its people butchered in what for those days was a holocaust. But the Lord did not forsake his people. He raised up a Gentile king, Cyrus, and moved his heart to compassion. And Cyrus ordered that a new house, a new temple, be rebuilt for 'the Lord, the God of Israel. … And let each survivor, in whatever place he sojourns, be assisted by the men of his place with silver and gold.'

"God does not forsake you, G.F. I urge you to try again to understand Christianity, but if not that, take pride and take heart and find your spiritual center in your Jewish heritage, which is noble and good. May God be with you."

Lamentations

Chapter One

In those days a decree went out from Washington that all America should be enrolled in a census. But also in those days would be an end of an age, a millennium, and the apocalyptic visions of Daniel and John made people sore afraid. For not only was the enrollment threatened, but all the machines that kept track of the enrollment and of all the rest of life as well, yea, all such machines were threatened, according to the curse of the end of the millennium. For the mark of the Beast took the form of a Y2K, and the Y2K was a sign to many that the end was near. And the preachers of the Word preached about the end of the millennium and the mark of the Beast, and the believers took heed and stocked up on canned goods and shotgun shells. For Y2K was coming, and the destruction it would bring would be so vast that only the truly righteous would be saved. For the only census that would matter would be the book of the Lord in which the names of the righteous were written. And while the righteous awaited the judgment of the Lord, with their shotgun shells a-ready, the unrighteous planned to party like it was 1999. But the righteous knew that woe betide the ones who would party like it was 1999, and woe be to all those who did not stand ready to build the New Jerusalem, because the Lord's judgment would be a consuming rage. Surely this godless age would pass away – perhaps in a flood of champagne, or perhaps in the fires that would light the night sky in all the great capitals of the world….

But none of this hoopla, none of these fears or hopes and none of these compulsions toward raucous celebration, stirred in the soul of one Madison Lee Jones of Mobile, Alabama. Mad Jones, superstar preacher and slayer of the Spike, was content to sit at the lunch-and-coffee counter in the middle of an art gallery co-op, eating chicken salad and drinking a smoothie and gossiping with Tucker and Diane, the two women who were responsible for the delectables. The rest of the world could prepare to party, or obsess about Y2K, but Mad was above all that nonsense. It was early December 1999, and Mad Jones was as untouchable as Elliott Ness.

The kind-faced local reporter was due shortly at the Kaffé Cathedral art gallery/café, to interview Mad about his take on the upcoming millennium celebration. Mad, not wanting to eat while he answered her questions, had arrived early enough to order and finish his lunch before she came. Chicken salad sandwich, plus a scrumptious dessert. Chocolate-chess walnut pie. Justin was always telling Mad that he needed to watch his diet if he wanted to stay in shape, but Mad was untouchable. He felt especially exalted because Tucker had queued up a Leslie Smith CD while she worked the counter. Mad was a superstar, life was easy, dozens of brightly colored paintings adorned the walls around him to create an aesthetic feast, and worries didn't exist.

As it turned out, the kind-faced reporter asked good, probing questions. She noted that Rob Patterson and Larry Falstaff both were busily preaching that their flocks should prepare for the millennium. She noted that even mainline Protestant clergy were using Y2K as a subject for sermons and for their little essays in their churches' weekly newsletters. But she had noticed that Mad's recent writings and speeches were not even touching on the topic. "Do you believe," she asked, "that there's just no theological aspect at all to the observance of the millennium?"

"Well, even setting aside the fact that Jesus Himself was surely born several years B.C.," Mad said with a hint of arrogance in his voice, "intelligent people who can count know that the so-called new millennium doesn't even begin until 2001. So why should I bother preaching about it *now*? And not only that, but where in the Bible does it say the Day of Judgment will occur on a nice, round human number? Nowhere, that's where. People need to get a grip on reality. Somebody's gotta be pretty dumb to make a bigger deal about this New Year's than about any other."

"Okay, let's posit that there's no biblically literalistic reason to believe that this New Year's is going to be the Day of Judgment or anything like that," said the reporter. "Still, aren't there at least any good symbolic reasons to use this as an occasion to take stock of one's life? Or maybe to take stock of our lives together as the corporate body of Christ? Isn't this as good a time as any to begin working together to create what the Bible calls a 'New Jerusalem'?"

"How very idealistic of you," said Mad, intending to sound complimentary but instead sounding a bit condescending. "But why now? Shouldn't we *always* be trying to build the New Jerusalem?"

"A lot of mainline traditions would indeed say that," she said. "But ever since you stumbled into the Clinton-Lewinsky controversy, you've specifically refused to involve yourself not just in politics, but in any broad-based social advocacy of any kind. How do you build a new Jerusalem without preaching the 'social Gospel,' especially if you refuse to use even a tailor-made occasion like the new millennium as an opportunity to mobilize the faithful for the task?"

"Social Gospel, my rear end," Mad said. "The Gospel exhorts us to bear witness to the Lord, to live righteous lives, and to work individually and through the church to feed the hungry, house the homeless, clothe the naked, and all that. But that's as 'social' as the Gospel gets. There's a theologian named Troeltsch who I think was right on target when he wrote that 'the message of Jesus is not a programme of social reform.'"

Mad stopped to sip from a cup of coffee but put up a hand to stop her from asking another question.

"Wait, I'm not finished," he said. "Here's the problem with all this misuse of apocalyptic stuff. The right-wingers all want to hijack the millennium to separate themselves from the rest of the supposedly sinful world, because they say the judgment of the Lord is at hand and they therefore need to disassociate themselves from all the sinners. What a crock! Jesus came into the world to save everybody who will accept God's grace, and to exhort us toward *greater* communion with, and forgiveness of, each other.

"But the left-wingers, meanwhile, want to use the millennium as yet another occasion to get *too* involved in everybody else's life by using the state, or international bodies, to compel people to support the left-wing agenda of higher taxes, more regulations, etcetera, etcetera, all in the name of helping the poor or saving the spotted owl or some other trendy cause. And they want to claim the moral authority of their churches in support of their agendas.

"Well, I say they're all full of it. I say everybody else has it wrong. Every day of our lives, we should be serving as vessels for God's love to be shared with the world, by witness and by individual and community action – undertaken voluntarily without compulsion or force or law – to create the conditions around us that will allow more people the chance to be open to God's saving love. But we shouldn't be so arrogant as to think that we have all the answers so down pat that we can cite church authority to take political positions, or to otherwise browbeat others into changing their behavior."

"We're getting sort of far away from a millennium discussion here," said the kind-faced reporter, "but let's just keep going. It sounds to me like you're making a rather radical critique here of virtually all the Christian denominations. I mean, let's leave aside the conservative churches that, you say, are preaching separatism from everybody else. That alone is a rough charge you're making against them, but let's leave it aside. Because the other thing you're claiming, if I understand you right, is that all the other denominations are becoming too involved with earthly power. People make that charge all the time against, for instance, the Christian Coalition, but not against Catholics or mainline Protestants. But it sounds like you are saying that it's even wrong for the Catholic bishops, for instance, to issue position papers on the economy. Or for the Episcopalian or Lutheran or Methodist Church as a corporate whole to take a position against welfare reform, or for environmental causes, or what-have-you."

(Mad nodded his head affirmatively.)

"In 1996," she continued, "I remember a host of top clergy, including the Presiding Bishop of your own Episcopal Church, put out a statement criticizing legislative efforts to outlaw abortion," the reporter continued. "Are you saying they have no right to issue their opinions, not even on a moral issue like that one? No right to use their faiths to inform the public arena? And if that's what you're saying, doesn't that put you in the position of saying that the only people who don't have free speech are people who are religious?"

"That's not exactly it," Mad said, "but before I get directly to your question, let me get this straight: Are you saying that the previous presiding bishop actually came down in favor of legalized abortion?"

"If I remember right," she answered.

"What a pathetic commentary on how wacko my church has gone!" Mad said. "I mean, I can easily see abortion as a gray area, a tough call, an issue that I'm still struggling with myself – but to actually put the weight of an entire national church *in favor of* killing babies, as if being pro-abortion is the only proper position of the faithful, that blows my mind. That bishop always was a creep. Same guy who let his secretary steal all that money, or whatever. My national church is a friggin' embarrassment. Nothing but left-wing politics where the church shouldn't be in politics at all, or else big fights about sex between moralists and 'politically correct' libertines. Ridiculous!!"

The reporter pressed Mad to get back on track. What about the broader issue of churches lobbying for certain government policies?

"Well, you've only characterized my position partly correctly," Mad said. "Of course everybody has free speech rights, especially as individuals. And nobody's talking about denying the same rights to communities speaking together in a unified fashion. But what I'm saying is that the church denominations themselves, or their leaders, shouldn't be putting the collective authority of the church behind a particular political position – unless, of course, it's such an overriding case of an unambiguous moral evil, like Nazism, for instance, that the issue is, normatively, black-and-white. What do the bishops know about economics? Where do church elders find the authority in Scripture, much less the scientific expertise, to take a stand on whether certain technologies contribute to global warming, and on which particular regulations or incentives are the wisest ones to use to keep pollution down? What does any of that have to do with religious faith? And where do bishops or other clergy find the right to claim, as part of their institutional authority, that there is an approved Catholic or Presbyterian or Greek Orthodox position on tax cuts or missile defense or whatever else these idiots are spouting off about? Who made them God, anyway?"

"Well, then, what *is* their role?" the reporter asked.

"Their role is in the spiritual preparation of their church members. Their role is internal: to facilitate their clergy, and through them the individual members, in their searches for God. And to set an example of charity, of good works by individuals and by the corporate body of their own churches, to feed the hungry and house the homeless. But they should render to Caesar that which is Caesar's, not tell Caesar how to choose between Keynesian economists and supply-siders."

"Would you offer the same critique of church leaders if they took political positions that matched yours?" she asked.

"Damn straight I would," he said. "I'm a Jack Kemp-type tax cutter myself, but I would feel awfully uncomfortable if my presiding bishop were out there giving the impression that God is in favor of a flat tax or a capital gains tax cut. The way I see it, if God had a position on government reform, then Jesus would have joined the zealots to overthrow Rome. How many times must the Scriptural Jesus emphasize that the Kingdom of God is within us, and not a matter of state authority, before these politicized church leaders – these Pharisees and hypocrites, these chief priests and their scribes – start paying attention?"

Mad took the last few swallows from his coffee cup, and then caught Tucker's attention. "Hey, can I have another piece of that pie?"

And lo, Mad Jones felt invincible, like a prophet favored by God, and neither earthly powers nor fattening foods, nor Y2Ks nor census takers nor TV bigwigs, could slow down his ministry of lion-hearted, science-accepting, God-forgiving truth.

* * *

Truth was, something within Mad had changed. And not for the better. Although his case was relatively mild, Mad was developing what Cornell psychiatry professor Robert Millman would dub "acquired situational narcissism." It's what happens all too often when people suddenly become celebrities. One day they are merely popular with the people who know them; the next day they are superstars adored by multitudes. They are no longer normal; they're better than that. And while Mad would remain basically a kind and considerate person – one still not overly prone to self-delusional grandeur – he did begin to lose the necessary sense of his own fallibility. After all, Spike Walters had put him through the "Hour of Truth," and it had turned out that *Mad* was The Truth, while Spike wasn't.

A few others were losing their sense of proportion as well. The mime, for instance, showed up at an event dressed in an old-style political campaign styrofoam hat decked out in red, white and blue, holding aloft a sign saying "Mad for President!" But chief among the overenthusiasts was Affirmed, who in a year and three-quarters had yet to find a single thing about Mad that he didn't like. As December wore on, more and more of the messages on Mad's web site were, naturally, related to Christmas. But one from Affirmed, characteristically exuberant, stood out.

"O come, o come, E-Mad-uel!" it read. "Am I getting punny, or what? Anyway, I'm still about a year away from knowing this for sure, but I'm working on a new theory about what Mad's real place is in the greater scheme of things. How could I have been so blind as to think he is just another Martin Luther? His message is one of glad tidings of great joy! How fortunate we are to be able to hear his trumpet! Merry Christmas, everybody!"

Mad, reading this aloud on the phone to Shiloh, couldn't help but laugh. "First he said I was Luther, and then Moses and Lord-knows-who-else. But this takes the cake! Looks to me he's about to claim I'm the angel Gabriel! Can you *believe* this guy? I mean, next thing you know, he's gonna expect me to find a virgin and tell her she's pregnant with the Second Coming or something!"

But Shiloh wasn't laughing. "I don't think that's funny," he said. "Even just joking about something like that sounds sorta, what's that word, not-religious, uh, un-sacred... umm... oh yeah, *sacrilegious*. I mean, you've got a pretty good message and all – a lot better than when you started, a lot more respectful of God – but you've gotta let people know not to go overboard with this stuff."

Mad chuckled some more. "Don't worry, Shiloh," he said. "I know I'm not Luther or Gabriel. I'm perfectly happy being just an ordinary super-stud!"

Shiloh didn't think that was funny either, but Mad hung up thinking he had been pretty clever.

* * *

The kind-faced reporter did an excellent job with her story on Mad. So good, in fact, that it was picked up by a national religious newswire. By this time, just about anything Mad said had the potential to be treated as serious news, and this story also boasted a high quotability factor because Mad had referred to church leaders as "these Pharisees and hypocrites, these chief priests and their scribes." Predictably, a host of church leaders, of several denominations, took umbrage at Mad's comments. Bishop Pringle said that "Mad Jones' denigration of the Social Gospel, his obvious antipathy to the just concerns of the poor, the dispossessed, and the differently gendered, gives ample evidence of a bent towards fascism. Frankly, I think the man is a menace."

"The Rev," appalled as could be that somebody he had initially praised had turned out to be so "reactionary," had this to say: "Our hands were extended, but Mad Jones has offended. For the poor who want a hand up, he gives only the back of his hand. To women's reproductive rights he offers only a blight, of coat hangers and back alleys for every Sue, Jane, or Sally. His Southern white man's hegemony needs to undergo an epiphany. But he, too, shall be overcome. We shall overcome. We shall overcome."

And from the national office of the Episcopal Church of the United States, there was this statement, again without a specific name attached, as if disembodied: "It is with great sadness that we observe the ignorant pseudo-theologizing of one who, at least nominally, claims to be of our own Episcopal flock. His cramped understanding of the Social Gospel is testimony to his un-Christian viewpoint. We repeat our position made clear some time ago, that Madison Jones speaks and acts with no ecclesiastical authority, and that he is unworthy of respect as a theologian, preacher, or religious sage. He is therefore deserving of no further comment. As for the Episcopal Church, we will continue our mission of outreach and advocacy to serve all God's children and to improve the polity of these flawed United States. As Christ commanded, we will not rest until the least of our brethren are afforded the sustenance and dignity that is their due."

Privately, Mad scoffed at these predictable reactions. After all, he was untouchable.

Not only that, but he figured he was making new friends as well. Through the grapevine he heard that even Gladys Phillpott, the old-line conservative Catholic, had said some kind words (at some forum or other) about his comments. He even tried calling her to thank her, but she never returned his call.

What Mad didn't know, and what certainly would have hurt his feelings, was that a couple of dozen activists at Mad's own church in Mobile took the national church's statement and ran with it. They used it as grounds to take to the parish vestry a request that Mad be respectfully asked to find another house of worship. The vestry said it would take the request under advisement at its January meeting.

* * *

Christmas went fine, even though the Rev. Bill White took a shot at Mad from the right in his special Christmas radio broadcast. "It is true," he said, "that nobody knows the exact time of the judgment of the Lord. But it is also true that the Bible tells us explicitly that we are always to be prepared for the final judgment, because it will come like a thief in the night. And the Bible also tells us what signs to look for, signs that will portend the day of the Lord's judgment, and in this sinful world today the signs are abundant. So do not believe those who tell us not to be prepared. Do not believe those who accuse us of being separatists just because we have the commitment to prepare ourselves spiritually for the Second Coming. In this Christmas season, when we celebrate the arrival of our Lord Jesus Christ, it is not just our right but our duty to prepare for His coming again. And those who say otherwise are either speaking the Devil's words, or else they are mad. Yes, they are mad. Mad Smiths, mad Johnsons, and definitely Mad Jones. Do not let these false prophets, especially one whose very name advertises his madness, do not let them lead you astray. The millennium is coming, and the Lord Jesus Christ himself might be coming again as well. That is our expectation, that is our hope, and such will be our deepest joy."

Nevertheless, unless most people somehow missed it, there was no Rapture when the clock struck midnight and the calendar turned to the year 2000. Rapture of a different sort, though, came to Becky, for the first time in nearly two years. For Becky thought she finally had found herself a man, a young businessman from an old Mobile family. That New Year's celebration was only their second date, but the fireworks over the river were as nothing compared to those in her condo bedroom afterwards. And she both saw and felt that it was good, and then she rested.

Justin, meanwhile, celebrated the countdown by himself, in his health club, pumping iron in rhythm with the "10-9-8-7-6-5-4-3-2-1" of an overly breathless TV announcer. Justin thought Becky had agreed to accompany him for the evening, but somehow she had avoided ever making an explicit commitment – and then when she met her new man, she had made a great but unsuccessful effort to let Justin down as gently as possible. Justin compensated by telling himself he just hadn't yet proven to be man enough to satisfy Becky's libido, so with every optimistic ounce of his body he worked out even harder and told himself even more fervently that he would make himself worthy to be Becky's guy.

As for Mad, he turned down every single invitation for New Year's festivities. By now, his denigration of all the millennium foofaraw had gone beyond a conviction and become a conceit. Not only was everybody wrong for celebrating the millennium a year too early, but in his mind the whole world was acting downright stupidly. He, Madison Jones, knew better, and he would demonstrate that he knew better by refusing to celebrate at all. He stayed at home and watched some sports on TV and read a book and even tried to go to bed an hour before the clock struck 12. He wanted to be fast asleep by midnight, in silent protest of everybody else's stupidity.

Oddly, though, he couldn't sleep at all. The more he tried to will himself to sleep, the more he tossed and turned. The more he tossed and turned, the more he sweated. For some reason, he found his heart racing, beating lickety-split like a thoroughbred's hooves at the Derby, and the more he tried to calm down the more nervously his heart thumped its rhythms. At 11:55, he jumped out of bed, muttered darkly to himself, and turned on his downstairs TV to a movie channel. When he heard, in the distance, the crackling of fireworks, he tried to ignore them. But something strange was happening. He couldn't concentrate on the movie. He couldn't concentrate on anything but his heartbeat. And, without really falling asleep, Mad fell into yet another of his trance-like states, staring blankly at the screen with eyes wide open but mind mostly blank.

It was 3 a.m. before he realized that the movie now playing was not the one he had been watching. And that his forehead was clammy. And that he didn't know where the last three hours had gone.

And that he really, really, really should go see a doctor.

* * *

One other person whose "millennium" celebration left something to be desired was Grace Feinstein Martin. She had taken heart at Mad's response, in his newspaper column, to her letter – but it didn't last long. Her kids, as much as she loved them, still acted like brats. Her ex-husband was a constant thorn in her side, on all number of issues, and her job was a pain in the neck. Hanukkah came and went, and much as she tried – as Mad had suggested – to take pride in her heritage, the celebration for her fell flat. She then had tried the Christmas service at the grand old St. Louis Cathedral, but the whole Catholic bit made her feel distinctly uncomfortable. All she could think about was the Catholic stance on abortion, and how she once had cavalierly obtained one herself. And she felt condemned as a sinner and bothered by the instructions that those not baptized Catholic were not welcome to partake of the Eucharist. Not that the thought of communion appealed to her; she actually was repelled by all the talk about eating Jesus' flesh and drinking his blood. Still, she was rankled by the exclusivity of the invitation to communion.

So, although Grace kept Mad's column folded up in her purse, and frequently consulted it and took momentary solace from it, she nevertheless felt, mostly, just as lost as ever.

And then the New Year came, and her kids announced to her that at ages 8 (nearly 9) and 7 (nearly 8) respectively, they were fully old enough to stay up and join all the celebrating. She knew better, of course, because she knew their behavior always deteriorated when they were tired. But they whined and the wheedled and spluttered and stomped until she gave in. And sure enough, somehow her son managed to come up with some firecrackers, and when Grace wasn't looking, he set them off right at his sister's feet. One of them exploded right into the little girl's calf, which hurt like the dickens and scared her even more. And while, when all was said and done, the injury turned out to be far less serious than it appeared, the upshot was that Grace and her kids spent the first several hours of the year 2000 at a hospital emergency room waiting to get the wound dressed.

And Grace just didn't see how she could take any more. She thought life sucked, and if there was a God, He clearly and most definitely was a jerk.

Chapter Two

Mad's growing arrogance was not serving him well. Even as his public stardom grew and his popular following grew ever more devoted to him, the list of his enemies also continued to expand. And it wasn't only public figures who were becoming annoyed. The semi-annual MMW board meeting in January of 2000 featured at least a mildly unpleasant undercurrent from the very start. For one thing, Becky announced that there was a small discrepancy in the financial numbers that she just couldn't figure out. Sure, MMW would again be able to donate hundreds of thousands of dollars to charities, but somehow it seemed there should have been about $25,000 more. Both Buzz and Mary gave Becky some grief for "losing track" of such a sum; and because Mad didn't make the slightest move to defend her, Justin took offense on her behalf. Matters weren't helped when Mad himself chided Justin for going too far afield with the holistic theories he was pushing through his "Justin Time" company.

"I gave you the right to tie in your whole-body health system, or whatever you call it, with my theology," Mad said, "but not to change my theology for your own purposes while still using my name."

Justin said that he had not changed a jot or tittle of his original language about how mind/body/spirit health depended on being "lionhearted," etcetera – but Mad said that Justin had failed to appreciate the "growth" his own preaching had undergone, and that Justin's take on it was now too simplistic.

"No big deal," Mad said dismissively. "Just see to it from now on that you get it right, okay? I mean, you're getting rich off of using my name, so you owe it to me not to corrupt my message by making it sound trite. Got it?"

Buzz chimed in: "Mad's actually right, Justin; but while we're at it, Mad, you make it sound like you've achieved all this success all on your own. Hell, if Mary hadn't done such a good job with the legal work back when you didn't even want to start this company in the first place, and if I hadn't created a friendly audience for you through my ties with Steve Matheson, you would still be a nobody."

Mad just rolled his eyes. He didn't bother to voice the judgment he had come to, namely that while his godfather had been a good friend to his family and was a dependable enough sort, the "obvious" fact of the matter was that Buzz was pretty much a mediocrity in his career and his life in general. Instead, Mad just said, "Yeah, yeah, *whatever*. Look, why don't we just move on to figuring out which charities we'll bestow our riches on this time and get this damned meeting over with."

It wasn't that Mad had lost any of the essential goodness of his heart – or that, when push came to shove on anything really important, he couldn't be counted on to do the right thing – but just that, in person, he was less and less likely to suffer gladly those he considered more foolish than he.

Anyway, it was far from a thoroughly happy crew that joined, almost *pro forma*, for the board's post-meeting dinner at a nice local restaurant. Becky, who truly was the workhorse carrying all the corporation's daily labor on her back, had been bruised by the others' criticism about the $25,000. She was feeling unappreciated, and so she began drinking too heavily again. Justin, hurt by Mad's criticism and unhappy with Becky's new love life, begged off as early as possible. At separate times, Buzz and Mary each pronounced themselves tired from their travels, and vamoosed. And Mad, who might otherwise have been on the road and able to pick up some female fan or other for a one-night stand, was feeling randy. And as he found himself at the restaurant at meal's end with only a tipsy Becky left for company, Mad for the first time in two years allowed his eyes to feast on her. Damn, she really was a hot-looking girl. The strawberry-blonde locks, the to-die-for figure, the obvious willingness to lose inhibitions: All combined to remind him why he had "hooked up" with her during that brief interlude back at Georgetown.

Mad fixed his eyes on hers. "You've drunk too much to drive, Becky," he said, in a way that managed to be empathetic rather than accusatory. "Looks like it'll have to be my pleasure to drive you home."

It had been many, many months since Becky had given up on Mad making a play for her – and now, as of just a few weeks ago, she had a boyfriend. But something about Mad's piercing stare, something about the way he leaned towards her, something about her state of moderate inebriation, something about her bruised ego in need of affirmation, and maybe even something about Mad's scent, combined to bring the old feelings back. As happened with virtually every woman Mad met, Becky felt her knees grow a little weak. By the time they reached her condo door, she was child's play for him. He didn't even wait until they were inside before he started kissing her. And once inside, he didn't wait long at all before ushering her to her bedroom.

He was still there the next morning.

Problem was, Becky's new boyfriend, apprised by her that this Saturday evening was reserved for her board dinner, had not stayed out as late as he had planned on his "night with the boys." Driving home, he only had had to zig just a little off his normal route to pass by Becky's condo, just to see if her car was home yet and, if so, to try to still make a night of it with her. He got there just in time to see Mad kiss her and then, with her rapt encouragement, enter her door. Incredulous, he sat in his car and waited for a while to see if Mad would re-emerge. Of course, Mad stayed. And the next day the would-be boyfriend left a message on Becky's machine calling her a "two-timing slut" who wasn't worth his time.

Two years for Becky to find a boyfriend, and just three weeks for her to lose him.

And, as she soon found out, Mad had no intention of making their tryst into anything more lasting. From the next morning forward, sweetly as could be, Mad reacted obliviously to all Becky's hints and, while constantly finding things to praise her for, never again pursued her romantically. He still had all his road dolls, a constant bevy of little foxes, available for sport on his twice-monthly travels – and that was all he needed.

*   *   *

About five weeks later, in the wee hours of his 27th birthday (two years and a day from when he had first begun writing his theses), Mad had a dream stranger than most. In it, his mother Mel, whom he had never known but of whom he had seen plenty of photographs, semi-laughingly scolded him for his fox hunting. "That's what killed my father, Daddy Lee," she said. "But I guess boys will be boys. And maybe that's a better way to go than is dying from a hemorrhage. My real-life personal Sonny Jurgensen died of a hemorrhaged aneurysm in the barbeque pit. Fox hunts make you hot enough to die from a hemorrhage." And then Mel was climbing on Bishop John Carroll's statued lap at Georgetown, and Mad was falling off his pedestal into Faulkner's woods where Shiloh kept trying to remind him something he just couldn't remember because the plot wasn't written on the walls or the tenement halls where the words of the prophets echoed in the wells of sounds of 3:16-haunted silence where hours disappeared while he sat in a trance. Marcelle told Mad that she had made some soup to cure his mono trance, but only if the doctor heated it up for him.

Mad awoke in a clammy sweat, his heart racing, his head pounding a Mick Fleetwood drum roll. This was getting to be more than he could take. Mad dug up the home number of the long-time family friend who for 15 years had served as his doctor, caught the poor man before he had even drunk his first cup of coffee, and apologized profusely. "It's just that I gotta see you first thing this morning, Doc Kellogg," Mad said. "Please tell me you can work me in."

An hour later, already again feeling perfectly normal, Mad was in the doctor's office telling him about his recurring trances ("blackouts," the doctor renamed them) that sometimes were accompanied by cold sweats, rapid breathing, and a generalized sense of unease. Doc Kellogg's first reaction was to just write off the episodes as being stress-induced, sort of like anxiety attacks. But then he had a second thought. He remembered well the odd way that Ben Jones had died and was aware of Mad's entire family history of early deaths.

"Your blood pressure now is fine and your heart rate is fine," he told Mad. "You've clearly added a few pounds, so I'm gonna run a test to check your cholesterol, but you seem to be in pretty good shape overall. But I'll tell you what: I'm gonna run some other blood tests as well, and if nothing else shows up on the tests but you keep having these blackouts, I may send you to a neurologist or maybe even an endocrinologist just to be on the safe side. Sudden bad luck with health seems to run in your family, so we might as well find out if there's anything mysterious we can nip in the bud before it gets you, too."

As it was, the blood tests turned up basically okay as. But just a week and a half later, the day after returning from another major rally (and another post-rally sexcapade), Mad experienced another short blackout. He informed Doc Kellogg, and the doctor that day called to set him up for appointments with both a neurologist, Dr. Mills, and an endocrinologist, Dr. Monitor.

"I still think it's probably just like a panic attack," Doc Kellogg said. "But better to be safe than sorry."

* * *

As for Becky, she was miserable again. Abandoned by Mad and by her short-lived boyfriend, effectively accused of incompetence by Buzz and Mary, and insulted by her mother during a recent phone call home to Houston, Becky didn't know where to turn. True, she had the solace that her father's respect for her business acumen was now so obvious that even she had to accept it as genuine. And her daddy *really* had come through for her during their collaboration on the "sting" of Spike Walters. But a quarter century of mistrust was not so easily abandoned: The best she could manage so far was an attitude towards Chet of a wary truce. And that wasn't really much comfort to fall back on.

It was a Friday in late March, and Becky had not a single plan for the weekend. Bored and lonely, she couldn't bear the thought of another night without any companionship at all.

She picked up the phone. "Hey Justin," she said. "Wanna go to a movie tonight? My treat? I'm tired and I'll want to go home and sleep right after, but I could use some friendly company for at least a few hours."

Naturally, Justin jumped at the chance. "You've always got a friend here, Becky babe," he said. "What movie do you wanna see?"

* * *

The St. James church vestry had kept trying to put off the issue of whether to disinvite Mad from attending services there. Episcopalians just didn't do that sort of thing. Such a disinvitation wasn't genteel. It sounded too much like the Amish practice of "shunning," or somesuch. But in late March, Mad had been quoted in *The Metropolitan Daily* (out of context, but readers had no way of knowing that) saying that the Episcopal Church "used to be known as 'Catholic without the guilt,' or 'Catholic Lite,' but now it's just plain generic Lite with not only no guilt, but precious little sustenance aside from some politically correct platitudes." Mad had been referring to the national Episcopal Church as a corporate body, specifically in response to a church leader's statement in support of the repatriation of Cuban boy Elian Gonzalez to Castro's admirable "workers' paradise" – but it came across in print as a blanket indictment of all Episcopalians. For the group that had been long-offended by Mad, this was the final hay-bale on top of the camel. Forty-five of their number descended on the April vestry meeting *en masse*. Mad had been asked to come to the meeting as well, but he was on the road making a speech and had forgotten to officially decline the request to attend. He didn't really think the situation was all that serious. He had attended St. James his entire life, and it was his spiritual home. The thought of being ejected from home just seemed absurd.

But the vestry was weak. Four of the 45 agitators happened to be among the congregation's biggest financial contributors. Another six of them had the financial werewithal to vastly increase their pledges. Three of their number ran the altar guild. So, in a close vote, the vestry decided to take the unprecedented action of telling the rector to ask Mad to find another church parish.

When Mad returned to town, he found a message from the rector asking him to join him for a cup of coffee at the church. There, the rector laid it all out.

"Look, Madison, nobody is going to hire a guard to keep you away from our services, or anything like that," he said. "And if I had my choice, much as I disagree with many of your statements, I wouldn't take this step myself. But the vestry has voted, and I think it just would be better for all concerned, and especially far more comfortable for you, if you don't keep coming to a place where, in the eyes of a number of people, you are just not wanted. Personally, I hope you find a place more to your liking. I'm quite fond of you, you know. But this probably really is all for the best."

Truth was, Mad had only intermittently attended church while growing up. Granted, he had made a real effort, ever since writing his theses, to attend more regularly, but because he was traveling every other weekend and often busy when in Mobile, he still made it to Sunday services only about three times every two months. And, other than occasionally volunteering at church-sponsored Habitat for Humanity days, Mad had never become a highly active participant in the church community. In that sense, the rector's words should not have been terribly hard on Mad.

But on the other hand, this was his lifetime church, and its parishioners were mostly families he had grown up with. These were his people. It was bad enough that he had already, two years earlier, been relieved of his teaching job at St. James school. But that was a job; this was his spiritual home.

Mad was devastated.

But he didn't try to argue. Not only was he tired from a typical amorous adventure during his just-completed road trip, but he was both too stunned and, like many men, too unwilling to show how hurt he was. Instead, he just accepted the rector's words in silence punctuated by a few *un-hunh*s and *okay*s, and then shook the rector's hand and exited to the parking lot. He opened the door, sat behind the wheel of his car, put the key in the ignition, wiped away a few tears, and then briefly put his head down on the steering wheel to try to choke back a sob. That's when he had yet another episode. It was more than an hour later that he "came to," realized he was still in the parking lot, and drove home. But for the first time in seven months, it occurred to him he might not be so untouchable after all. This rejection hurt. This rejection seared his psyche. It left a wound.

* * *

Every year during Holy Week, Grace's ex-husband took the kids for eight full days. Even though he was hardly an observant Catholic, he wanted his children to get the full Catholic flavor of the triumph of Palm Sunday, tragedy of Good Friday, and celebration of Easter, rather than being "poisoned" by their mother's Judaism-*cum*-atheism. This year, Grace took the opportunity to accept a longstanding invitation to visit an old New Orleans friend who had moved to Washington, D.C. Easter was late this year, not until April 23, and the cherry blossoms and other flowering plants and trees promised to be in full bloom. Grace had always heard, quite accurately, that springtime in D.C. is a beauteous wonder to behold.

Grace had decided to forego the Passover observance this year. After so many disappointments in her recent quest for religious understanding, she just saw no appeal in a familiar observance of unleavened bread and yet more promises from a God who was either non-existent or else plain jerky.

But her friend, a still-unmarried young woman named Beth, was an active Episcopalian. She attended a church on Capitol Hill, called St. Mark's, that had a reputation for a funky, *sui generis*, lively, creative and somewhat renegade congregation. Word was that its former rector once actually had ridden a motorcycle into the nave itself in order to make some now-long-lost point.

"You'll just *love* this place!" Beth gushed. "It's just perfect for you. This church publicly identifies itself as being particularly welcoming of skeptics and non-believers. Lapsed Catholics, Jewish Christians, former Bible thumpers, atheists: You name it, we've got it. There's more tension and more personal grudges and simmering controversies here than there are three blocks away in the U.S. Capitol building, but when it comes right down to it, everybody here loves each other like there's no tomorrow. It's really cool! You've gotta let me bring you there!"

So far, every one of Beth's suggestions during the week had been right on target. One night they visited the Phillips Collection, a great old art gallery in a tony townhouse near DuPont Circle, and followed it up with a visit to the Brickskellar – a marvelous, catacomb-like bar/eatery featuring the choice of about 587 different beers from around the world. Another night they took in the Tombs (the place where Ben had met Mel), where the Georgetown Chimes, a male *a cappella* singing group, were holding forth. Yet another night was reserved for a play at the Kennedy Center. Also fun and enlightening had been daytime visits to various Smithsonian museums, to the Capitol and the ornate Library of Congress, and way out to James Madison's old Montpelier estate in rural Virginia. By the time Thursday night rolled around, Grace was thus willing to be persuaded to go along to a "Maundy Thursday" dinner that Beth said was a special highlight of the St. Mark's church experience.

Unlike at many other Anglican churches, where jackets and ties for men are the accepted style, the "dress code" at St. Mark's for that service is classy-but-comfortable casual (actually a step up from the almost-anything-goes of Sunday morning services). And the first hour or so takes place in the "Pub," or parish hall, where like at an unstilted cocktail party the libations flow somewhat freely and warm fellowship abounds. During that time, many in the congregation enter the church nave one by one for a ritual foot-washing, re-creating Christ's own insistence on washing the feet of his disciples. (That part seemed too weird to Grace, so she declined.) After that, in the nave itself, the parishioners celebrate a potluck "*agape* meal" at large, brightly candle-lit tables of ten that surround a center altar. Then, right there at the tables, the Eucharist is passed, with "believers and skeptics alike" welcomed to participate. Ritually, the altar is stripped, and then comes a service known as "Tenebre," or the "service of shadows."

Grace found it haunting.

The themes of all the readings were those of sorrow and death. Each reading seemed to bring a darker mood, and at the end of each the figurative darkness was matched by the dousing of yet more candles until only one, the Paschal candle, remains. The key reading is of Psalm 51:

> "Have mercy on me, O God,
> according to thy steadfast love;
> according to thy abundant mercy
> blot out my transgressions.
> Wash me thoroughly from me iniquity,
> And cleanse me from my sin!....
>
> Behold, thou desirest truth in the inward being;

> Therefore teach me wisdom in my secret heart.
> Purge me with hyssop, and I shall be clean;
> wash me, and I shall be whiter than snow....
>
> Create in me a clean heart, O God,
> and put a new and right spirit within me.
> Cast me not away from thy presence,
> and take not thy holy Spirit from me.
> Restore me to the joy of thy salvation,
> and uphold me with a willing spirit....
>
> The sacrifice acceptable to God is a broken spirit;
> a broken and contrite heart, O God, thou wilt not despise.
> Do good to Zion in thy good pleasure;
> rebuild the walls of Jerusalem...."

And then the Paschal candle itself was carried out of the nave, and the church was in utter darkness. Sniffles and muted sobs could be heard throughout the church, and Grace herself was not immune.

And then: **WHAM!** A priest (or somebody so appointed) made a hugely loud banging sound, for final and purgative punctuation. And a dam broke inside of Grace, and the sobs erupted, and somehow all her sorrows, that the service had brought to the surface, overflowed – and, in so doing, broke themselves away from all the hard, dim corners of her soul and scurried, **WHAM!**-scared, into the church's darkness and, at least for a while, disappeared.

And for the first time in her memory, Grace found that tremendous and fascinating *mysterium* so well described by theologians, and felt a longing within her answered not by nothingness but by the presence of an indefinable somethingness. And while she still was confused by the notion that the next day's crucifixion could be described as *Good Friday*, and still turned off by the idea that suffering and sacrifice could be ameliorative, Grace nevertheless discovered the sensation of spirit in a formerly spiritless world, perhaps even the foretaste of faith in a universe where nothing had been worth the effort of belief.

Grace flew home to New Orleans two nights later, because she was due to pick up her kids almost immediately after their Sunday's Easter service and there were no available Sunday morning flights that would get her back early enough. Inspired by the St. Mark's experience, she decided to press her luck and give herself at least the opportunity to finally fathom the puzzle of Easter. St. Mark's was Episcopal, so Grace figured her best bet for Easter would be to stick with the same denomination. Because the few of her Uptown friends who were Episcopalians all raved about Trinity Church on Jackson Avenue, that's the one she tried. Trinity had an excellent reputation.

Once inside, Grace found that about the only thing Trinity shared with St. Mark's was an enveloping spiritual warmth. But where St. Mark's was casual almost to the point of irreverence, Trinity was far more formal, in dress as well as attitude. Where St. Mark's had been almost rambunctious in its liveliness, Trinity managed to exude a lively air despite an almost stately bearing.

The building itself was lovely. Amazingly high arched ceilings; old-style stained-glass windows of an artistic excellence nowadays almost impossible to find; fine wooden pews and spectacular molding; and, as an auditory treat, a pipe organ so grand it almost defied comprehension.

Grace didn't know the hymns but found them beautiful and easily picked up.

> "Jesus Christ is risen today-ay,
> Ah-ah-ah-ah-ah-lay-hey-lu-u-ia!
> Our triumphant holy day-ay,
> Ah-ah-ah-ah-ah-lay-hey-lu-u-ia!
> Who did once upon the cross,
> Ah-ah-ah-ah-ah-lay-hey-lu-u-ia!
> Suffer to redeem our lo-hoss.
> Ah-ah-ah-ah-*ah*-ah-lay-hey-lu-u-ia!"….

And this:

> "Come, ye faithful, raise the strain
> of triumphant gladness;
> God has brought his Israel
> Into joy from sadness;
> Loosed from Pharaoh's bitter yoke
> Jacob's sons and daughters;

> Led them with unmoistened foot
> Through the Red Sea waters
>
> 'Tis the spring of souls to-day;
> Christ hath burst his prison,
> And from three days' sleep in death
> As a sun hath risen….."

The joyfulness abounded. And again and again, in small way after small way, this service, like Thursday's, made clear an unbroken link between what the Christians were celebrating and the common Jewish heritage she shared with them. Thursday had featured the Psalm, so alike to Mad's newspaper response to her letter, concerning the rebuilding of Jerusalem. And this hymn here spoke of a redemption specifically of Israel, "Jacob's sons and daughters." The whole thing made her feel welcome, and surprisingly at home.

Hill Riddle's sermon was good as well: His very first words seemed to pick right up from where the Maundy Thursday service in Washington D.C. had left off. "A familiar line from a Christmas hymn is: 'How silently, how silently the wondrous gift is given.' The same can be said about Easter morning. It all happened so silently and in the dark." Later on in the sermon, he noted: "Then there was more to the message. The young person in the white robe said to the women: 'He goes before you.' Which means He is ahead of you. You will find Him as you move away from here and into the future. … These are the times we need to remember that Jesus goes before us. Easter lets us know that He will be there. We will see Him if we believe in the power and reality of Easter."

And then this: "If we fully believe that Jesus will always be leading us, that He goes before us into our future, then we can face the future with courage and fortitude. It is the silent event of Easter morning that changed the lives of those women. It is this event that can change us and lead us the rest of our lives unafraid."

When the service finally ended, Grace left the church feeling, if nowhere near fully comprehending of the theology involved, at least as inexplicably content as if she herself had been tried, ransomed, and (in a still-difficult concept) at least partially redeemed. She had been through the silence and darkness in Washington, and now in a joyful way she had been told that the Easter offered a way forward out of the darkness. For once, something about a religious message actually rang true.

No, she wouldn't have called herself even a theist yet – much less a Christian – but Grace was finally and indisputably on a journey toward faith.

* * *

That same Easter day, Mad attended services at All Saints Episcopal Church on Government Street. His notoriety earned him a number of questioning looks, but for the most part he was welcomed warmly.

Becky was upset that Mad had refused to do a big local rally for Easter. As a Christian homilist, he should have treated Easter as his big day. But because Mad hadn't been feeling well, and because he had been getting so much flack from his home parish of St. James, and because, truth be told, Mad was getting a little bored with the whole Christian subject matter, Mad had declined. Instead, he merely put out a special Easter newspaper sermonette, and told Becky to leave him otherwise alone.

The day after Easter, Mad was scheduled for more tests arranged by the endocrinologist.

Chapter Three

The day after Easter, Officer Williams ran into Shiloh at police headquarters, where Shiloh was still pulling some part-time desk duty. "Big black buck like you oughtta be bustin' heads on the street," said Officer Williams to him, intending to be complimentary. "Whatchu see in that uppity religious pissant, anyway? He really paying your bills like he promised to?"

What Officer Williams didn't know was that at the very same time he was speaking to Shiloh, his own new patrol partner was filing an official complaint with the police chief alleging that Officer Williams was unfit for duty because of a virulent strain of racism. The partner, a young black man named Clarence Moss, was sensitive to racial connotations of the sort that Shiloh would allow to roll harmlessly off his back. For just one example, it was only the other day that Officer Williams had been trying to be jovial as he and Clarence rode past a young black woman sitting on a stoop while feeding her baby: "I gotta hand it to you people: At least your women don't mind putting a little meat on their butts so you got something to grab onto when you humpin' your poontang." Frankly, Officer Williams was finding it harder and harder to remain so "pleasant" to young Officer Moss, considering that Clarence always seemed to have a chip on his shoulder. He thought Clarence didn't have half enough character to respect his superiors the way Shiloh did. Hell, Shiloh still remembered to give Officer Williams a Christmas card every year, but young Clarence wouldn't even say "Merry Christmas" in person. Maybe Clarence was into that newfangled Kwanzaa crap, or something.

And now, as Buster Williams would discover in the coming days, Clarence had set into motion some proceedings that could be of serious detriment to the retirement benefits that Williams had worked so long for, and which were now less than two years away from being enjoyed.

The internal investigation, and eventually hearings, would go on for months.

* * *

The mime sat in his tiny French Quarter apartment and brooded. Here he was, an immensely talented performance artist who had been plastered all over the cover of a national tabloid, and still no agents nor talent scouts nor philanthropies – not even the National Endowment for the Arts – were offering him sponsorships. Here he was, Madison Jones' foremost adherent, but Mad barely even acknowledged his presence anymore on the occasions when the mime still managed to appear for Mad's events. And here he was, perfectly delighted to rage against God, as Mad had done at the start of Mad's ministry, yet Mad himself seemed to have replaced the rage in his preaching with lots of happy-happy-joy-joy talk.

Not only that, but he had been oh-so-careful with the trust account left to him by his great-grandfather. Thrifty as he was, though, the account wouldn't last much more than a few years longer.

All in all, the multiple unfairnesses were becoming unbearable.

So the mime fumed and brooded and brooded and fumed. And then he smoldered some more.

* * *

"Say, has anyone noticed a change in tone from our young Mad friend?" wrote The Scot in the chat room. "He talks about these high muckety-muck theories beyond my ken, and he seems to have a high-faluting sense of his own religious worth. It's as if he thinks he's invulnerable to hazards. I liked him better when he was scraping around for pars like all us other mortals, but now it's like he expects to float over every burn and bunker like they're not even there. The young man acts like he can get by even on an unfamiliar course by himself, without even a caddy to guide him. What ho, am I right?"

"I've told you all along that he's a nutbag!" wrote Defender. "The one true faith is 2000 years old, and guarded well by the magisterium of the church, but Mad Jones acts as if he is a church unto himself."

"He's a blasphemer, pure and simple," wrote Ever Faithful. "A heretic. Always has been."

What was particularly disturbing was that Mad's longtime detractors were now representing more and more the tenor of the whole chat room. Worse, they weren't reacting to any particular statement or action of Mad's — criticism always flares up during controversies — but instead reflecting what seemed like a deeper, more entrenched, generalized dissatisfaction. And Shiloh felt it, too. He had gone so far as to voice his concerns in private to Father Vignelli, urging Mad's mentor to try to intervene and help Mad rediscover the groundedness Mad had lost.

"I fear you are correct, Shiloh," said Peter. "But it's impossible to force wisdom on someone not ready to receive it."

Meanwhile, in the chat room, at least one fan still was backing Mad without reservation. Perhaps even backing him *too* unguardedly.

"Oh, go rot in purgatory, all ye of little faith!" wrote Affirmed. "How can you be so blind? If Mad acts like a church unto himself, maybe that's because he's unique. How can you miss the truth that's right in front of your eyes? You must heed Mad's word, or else be left behind in perpetual darkness!"

The response to this was blistering. "BS, you goofball idiot!" sneered somebody who ID'd himself as Boz. "Get your head out of Mad's a**, why don't you?"

That comment, in return, brought a surprise re-entry, after many many months of silence, into the discussion. "Oh, calm down everybody," wrote Jezebel?. "Whether Mad is perfect or not, or correct or not, he has us all talking about God. Isn't that accomplishment enough?"

* * *

For the eighth weekend in a row, Becky found herself out at a movie with Justin. She was finding him less and less annoying, more and more endearing (albeit in an oddball way). They had already seen T*he Cider House Rules, Anna and the King, The Sixth Sense, Erin Brockovich, Life is*

Beautiful, Keeping the Faith, and *Any Given Sunday.* The little guy had so well proven his friendship for her by now that he was almost akin to a Linus blanket. This time they went to the quirky *High Fidelity,* starring John Cusack as a used-phonograph-record store proprietor with a habit of listing in rank order his worst dating disasters. It wasn't a great flick, but it was amusing. Justin and Becky were still chuckling about scenes from the movie as they arrived afterwards at The Bakery Café for a drink. One side of The Bakery is a semi-expensive, creatively high-cuisine restaurant; the other is a well-designed bar room with just the right amount of bar-stool space and standing room combined with just enough tables and just the right ratio of light to darkness to accommodate a wide variety of customers. (In the back, connected to the bar, is a fresh food deli-winery, but it was already closed by that time of night.)

"Damn, that John Cusack character even gives *me* a run for my money in the dating-disaster category," Becky laughed, while patting Justin on the arm. "I even had a guy who was all hot for me until just the time I got naked, and then he drooped like limp spaghetti!"

"He was probably so stunned by your beauty that he suddenly feared he'd never be worthy of you, and so he got self-conscious," said Justin, with such obvious sincerity that it didn't sound nearly as cheesy a comment as it might have. By now Becky had become so accustomed to his smitten-ness with her that his devotion had stopped seeming cloying and become almost cute.

"Look, Hot Stuff," he continued earnestly, "You're the crème de la babes, and you shouldn't settle for just any schmuck lawyer with a Jag and a tan."

Becky reached across the table and grabbed one of Justin's hands that had been gesticulating bizarrely as he spoke.

"Justin, honey?" she said.

"Yeah, babe?"

"I've got a favor to ask you. Would you mind not calling me things like 'babe' and 'Hot Stuff'? You sound so forced, like you're reading from a 1970s TV script or something...." (Even in the dim lighting, Becky could see Justin blanch, so she quickly continued.) "I'm not criticizing you; I just don't think it's necessary for you to say them. Can you just call me 'Becky'? That's my name, and I think it sounds just fine to me."

"Sure, Hot Stu--… I mean, sure, Becky," he said, a tad nervously. "I just want to make you feel special, that's all."

Becky realized she had embarrassed Justin. She hadn't meant to do that. He really was so sweet to her. And he was honest, and he worked harder than any man she knew. No less than she, he was an entrepreneur at heart, and an entirely self-made success at his entrepreneurial endeavors. And she felt like she could say absolutely anything to him, without worrying about him judging her conduct or character.

Also, for such a shrimp with such an obvious genetic predisposition against athleticism, he certainly was "ripped" with muscle. Every time he gestured with his oddly off-timed movements, she could see the fabric of his shirt stretched by the sinew underneath. If only he weren't such a weird little character, she might be able to see herself finding him attractive.

Becky finished her glass of wine and ordered another one. Justin was nervously blabbing away again about some dumb topic or other, and she tried to think of something to say. She tuned in again and realized he was saying something about *The Sixth Sense*. Why was Haley Joel Osment like Mary Magdalene?, he was asking. She shook her head without thinking about it.

"I see dead people!" Justin said, trying to imitate the little boy's voice. "That's what she said to the disciples, get it? She saw a dead person!!"

It was an unbelievably dumb joke, but Justin was laughing so infectiously at his own humor that Becky, too, found herself laughing. Strange, dear, sweet little man!

Not quite an hour later, Justin was pulling his Lamborghini up to her condo and, as always, gallantly walking her to the door. She put the key in the lock and turned it, and then pivoted back towards Justin to thank him for his company by means of a little peck on the cheek. But this time as she pecked him, he seemed to be, well, quivering. Suddenly, mongoose-like, he jutted his face forward again and planted his lips on hers and smooshed them together for an insistent, lingering few moments before withdrawing in abject fear.

That's when something odd happened to Becky. It was an oddness growing from a deep fondness that she had finally developed for him. "Come inside for a minute," she said, pulling him by the hand and shutting the door behind them. "Relax, honey. Here, like this."

Tenderly, Becky kissed him until Justin's whole body became more comfortably on alert, in place of the somewhat spasmodic, twitching-like response that was his first reaction. Becky withdrew her mouth and looked at him, and then leaned forward and kissed him again. And, this time, she felt him haltingly getting the hang of it.

She pulled away again, for breath, and with all sincerity said, "Thank you, Justin, for a lovely evening. Thank you for always being there for me. Thank you for being you."

And as she opened the door and guided him out, Becky felt a rich warmth envelop her, the kind of warmth usually reserved for times of peaceful comfort with a soulmate. It was a warmth that caught her off guard, a warmth that soon sent her deep into a pleasantly dreamy sleep.

As for Justin, he drove home in silence. He wasn't sure how to interpret what had just happened. All he knew was that he loved this woman desperately, and that kissing her felt right.

* * *

Buzz Buskirk met Steve Matheson for a beer at The Tombs. It had been months since they got together. Steve just loved military history, and he wanted to pick Buzz' brain about the newest Stephen Ambrose book concerning World War II. Somewhere around their third beer, though, a random remark from Buzz led Matheson to change the subject. "So what's the latest with that godson of yours?" he asked. "He did a damn good job on my show, but other than one short comment I read from him about Elian Gonzalez, he hasn't made much news lately. Is he still kickin' butt at those rallies in front of thousands of people?"

"Yeah, Mad always lands on his feet," Buzz said. "There's always somebody else willing to do all the heavy lifting for him, while he just coasts. He goes along saying whatever the hell pops into his head, and if he gets in trouble there's always somebody who bails him out. Not only that, but from what I understand through the grapevine, I hear he's getting laid every which way from Sunday every time he goes on the road. I hear he just does his nice guy, blond-haired thing and the next thing you know he's in the sack with some little hottie. At least that's the rumor; I couldn't prove it by you, but it would be just like him. He's a good kid at heart, but it wouldn't hurt him if somebody brought him down a peg or two."

Matheson laughed. "More power to him, Buzz, more power to him. You know, I need somebody on my show soon to talk about Bush's proposal to fund faith-based charities. I know he says he's avoiding politics these days, but this has to do with religion. D'ya think he'd do it?"

"Shit, Steve, I dunno. He'll tell you different, but I think at heart he's as much a hound for publicity as he is a hound for getting laid. He'd probably do it if you asked."

Matheson finally noticed something odd about Buzz' tone of voice. Two years ago, Buzz sounded so proud of Mad that he almost sounded like he was talking about his own son. But now there seemed a real air of – what? Resentment? Envy? Disappointment? *Something* wasn't quite right anymore with Buzz' view of his godson. Strange. Matheson filed that away in his memory bank and changed the subject. Matheson was a happily married man, but he always was curious about what life was like for guys his age who were still (or again) single.

"So, Buzz, you getting any tail yourself these days, or what?"

* * *

In St. Louis, Mary McGuire – er, McWyre – looked at the latest pile of checks that Becky had sent her to co-sign. As far as she was concerned, this dual-signing system had been a stroke of genius. And although the partners at Zimlich, Shanahan and Woods gave her as much other legal work (meaning way too much) as most big firms give to their youngest associates, she didn't mind the extra work for MMW. The time was all bill-able, and it didn't require research or other heavy lifting. Mary smiled. She maintained a fairly quiet existence, and nobody really paid all that much attention to her, but she more-or-less liked it that way. As far as she was concerned, her life was developing quite nicely, thank you very much.

* * *

Shiloh had taken two classes this semester at the University of South Alabama instead of one, making it a total of five in the past 16 months. Taking one or two classes per term (including summer sessions), he planned to finish college in just under seven years. In his first three classes, he had earned two final grades of C+ and one B. Perfectly respectable. But, as he walked to the bulletin boards outside the offices of this semester's two professors, where the final grades were to be posted, he thought there might be something different in the offing this time. One of the classes had proved particularly daunting, and that was the one he checked on first. The 'C' listed by his Social Security number actually made him sigh with relief. But it was the next office that really made him nervous. It was for a math class in which, he thought, he had well comprehended the material. And what made him nervous was that his hopes were fairly high. He had worked so dadgummed hard at this class. He had been so diligent. But he just didn't know if his hard work had been enough.

As he approached the appropriate bulletin board, Shiloh slowed down. He really was afraid to look, and he was gratified to see a classmate just leaving the board and coming his way. Shiloh stopped the classmate and shot the breeze for a good six or seven minutes. Shiloh was pleased that most of his classmates seemed to genuinely like him.

Finally, the classmate went on his way, and Shiloh had no other excuse to avoid looking at the posted grades. Slowly, he ran his finger down the list until he found his Social Security number. Shiloh stared hard at the letter marked next to it. He knew what he was seeing, but it still didn't seem real. He blinked his eyes and stared some more.

Finally, he allowed himself to smile. And then he laughed. He was overcome with happiness. LaShauna would be so proud of him. His parents would be so proud of him. The dyslexic kid, whose family had never been able to boast a college student, was now a man with a family and a career – and, in an actual college class, he had earned an 'A.'

As he drove home to LaShauna, he told himself that the Lord had truly blessed him.

* * *

Early June. The office of Dr. Monitor, the endocrinologist. Yet another round of test results were finally in. Mad still didn't know much about what Dr. Monitor was looking for. Dr. Monitor was one of those men who gave out information only on what he considered a need-to-know basis. If the doctor was still more than a little unsure about what the possibilities were, and if there was nothing the patient could do in the meantime in terms of lifestyle changes or medicine that would be certain to help, then the patient didn't need to know what the doctor's hypotheses were. "I'm looking at your endocrine system," Dr. Monitor had told Mad, oh-so-helpfully, when Mad had pressed for more details.

"Yes, but what *about* my endocrine system is it that you are testing?"

"Well, various parts of it," said the doctor. And that was that. This had gone on for a couple of months now. The tests were complicated, the doctor said. The results took a while to show up.

But now the doctor had promised Mad at least a little more elaboration. It was high time for him to do so. The blackouts were driving Mad crazy.

The doctor walked into the examination room. He looked at Mad, and then looked back down at his chart. He flipped a few pages back and forth.

"Well?" said Mad, after an uncomfortable silence.

"Well," said Dr. Monitor, still flipping the pages.

"Well *what*? What in the heck is wrong with me, Doc?"

"Well, I don't think you're gonna die any time soon."

"Okay… that's a start. But what in God's name is gonna happen to me? Do I have anything bad?"

"Hmmm…"

Silence. Then again, "Hmmm…"

Mad rolled his eyes.

Finally, the doctor spoke again. "Frankly, Mr. Jones, I'm still a little baffled. These test results are definitely peculiar."

Mad looked at the doctor, expecting more. The doctor stared back.

"Dammit, doctor, *how* are they peculiar?"

"Well, they're not normal. That's how."

"*What's* not normal?"

"Your *tests* aren't normal." Then, with a sudden grace that very briefly broke through his phlegmatism, Dr. Monitor added: "It's your hormone levels. Various hormones. They don't add up. We know from the neurologist that neurologically you're perfectly sound, so that's why we're checking your endocrine system. ("Well, *duh-hey-now!*" thought Mad.) And we've found that your hormones are a little off. But what we really need to know is where those hormone levels are when you actually have a blackout. Because, when we test you, you're close to normal – not enough to cause a blackout. I need to know what happens when you're blacking out."

It was the longest uninterrupted bit of information-sharing that Dr. Monitor had allowed himself, at least in Mad's presence, in two months. Still, Mad decided to press his luck and ask for more.

"Well, Doctor, which hormones, and what are the possibilities? And how do you want to go about testing me during a blackout?"

"The blackouts? How? That's what I'm trying to figure out. Let me think on that a while. Call me back in a week and I'll see what I can come up with."

And that was that. Mad would just have to wait.

* * *

In exactly a week, Mad called the doctor's office.

"Oh, yes, Dr. Monitor told me to expect your phone call," said the nurse. "He wants to you come back in. But he's all booked up for the next two days, and then he's taking a five-day weekend. We've got an opening a week from Thursday. Can you come at 2 o'clock?"

A week from Thursday at 2 p.m., Mad was ushered back into the examination room. Dr. Monitor entered 15 minutes later. "Do you think you can take your own blood sample?" the doctor asked him. "And I assume you can pee in a jar, so that part'll be easy."

"Huh?"

"I'll write the instructions for the nurse. She'll be in here in a minute." And the doctor left.

Ten minutes later, the nurse entered.

"You seem to have these blackouts most often the day after you return from a trip," she said. "So the doctor said that the next time you return, take this needle and this vial and take a blood sample as soon as you wake up, and pee in this jar at the same time. And then take a second needle and vial, and keep them with you all day, and if you should happen to black out, take another sample of each as soon as you come out of it and realize that your mind has been gone somewhere. Matter of fact, Doctor asked me to give you a number of these jars and vials and needles. If you don't black out, you can just get rid of the samples you've taken that morning and try again the next time you return from a trip. But what Doctor said he needs is endocrine levels from as close before and as close after a blackout as possible. Here, let me show you the best way to take your own blood."

A week and a half later, Mad returned from a trip and, the next morning, took blood and urine samples. But he never blacked out that day. So much for that effort.

Two weeks later, after a 25,000 person rally outside of Las Vegas, topped off by not just one but two young lovelies at the same time, Mad returned home exhausted. The morning after his return, he again took the samples, and then went about his business working on some newspaper columns. Sure enough, sometime in mid-afternoon, he faded away. It was nearly two hours later that he recovered his sense of time and place. It was another ten minutes before he remembered to take the samples. But take them he did, and then called the doctor's office. The nurse said to hustle the samples *in post haste*. He did. She said the doctor (or her) would call when there was anything to tell Mad.

"Bye, now," she said. And then as he was walking away, she finally couldn't help herself any longer. "Hey, Mr. Jones! Did anybody ever tell you that you're really cute?"

* * *

Two days later, on a Thursday, Officer Williams was nervous as could be. The processing of his partner Clarence's complaint had taken its usual slow route through the police bureaucracy. At the regulation-appointed time, Officer Williams had been duly notified about the complaint, and reassigned to desk duty (away from Clarence Moss) for the remainder of the investigation. Buster Williams was furious. How dare that young nigger file a complaint against him! He had gone far, far out of his way to make shithead Clarence feel welcome in his patrol car. And this was the thanks he got! Shithead nigger. Just like one of his kind to be stirring up trouble. And Officer Williams had been extra careful not to discriminate against Clarence or against any other nigger in the whole department. In fact, because he knew those folks weren't smart, he always cut them some extra slack. Again, this was the thanks he got! If this complaint, alleging racist behavior on his part, were found by the review board to have merit, then he, Officer Williams, might even be dishonorably discharged. And *that* would mean a major reduction in the pension that he would get upon leaving the force. After all those years knocking criminal heads! What was the world coming to, anyway?

Now, today, the review board was due to take testimony from Officer Williams' previous patrol mate, Shiloh Jones. Buster Williams had always thought Jones-y was a good boy. But you never knew with niggers. They might even have a pact amongst them, where all the "brothers" had to stick together or something. Maybe there would be too much pressure for Jones-y to bear even if Jones-y didn't want to give Williams the shaft. Anyway, that's the prospect that scared the bejesus out of Buster Williams.

What he didn't know was that the bulk of the pressure was coming not from fellow black officers, but from LaShauna. "You always told me that Williams was a fat racist pig," she told her husband. "All you'll have to do is tell that to the review board, and he'll get exactly what's coming to him!"

"Yeah, LaShauna, he's a good ol' boy redneck straight outta the George Wallace playbook," Shiloh said. "But you gotta understand, honey, Mr. Williams never meant any harm. He would say racist things all the time without even realizing how racist they sounded. But he never treated me badly, and he didn't treat black suspects any worse than he treated white suspects. He saw all lawbreakers as scum – not just black ones. I can't hang a man for dumb attitudes, honey. I gotta tell the truth, which is that he was obnoxious, but he always did a good job. I didn't like him, honey, but he's not really a bad man. Ignorant and hard and dumb, but not truly bad. That's the truth, honey, and that's what I'm gonna tell the board."

LaShauna was furious. Her husband always looked for the good in people, even when there was no good to be found. If this Williams guy was a redneck racist, he should suffer the consequences. Shiloh had told her too many stories about Williams' racist remarks for her to forgive the fat pig, no matter whether Shiloh forgave him or not.

"Damn it, Shiloh, when are you going to realize that you're a *black* man and that you've got to do battle against all those white guys who want to hold you down?!? Have some *pride*, damn you: Have some pride!"

Shiloh didn't sleep well at all before the night of the testimony. He never slept well when LaShauna was mad at him.

So when he entered the police headquarters that Thursday morning, Shiloh was in what for him was a rare, foul mood. Just about the first person he saw was Buster Williams, pacing around nervously. And when Officer Williams saw Shiloh, he made a beeline towards his old partner even though rules forbade any contact between them before Shiloh testified. Officer Williams didn't want to put pressure on Shiloh; he wanted to beg him for mercy.

For once, Shiloh's foul mood got the better of him. As Officer Williams' walrus-waddle took him within close earshot of Shiloh, the younger officer snarled at him in a low-but-clear voice. "Get away from me, you redneck bastard! You know damn well we're not supposed to talk!"

Officer Williams was stunned. Even Jones-y had turned against him. Damn niggers! He watched Shiloh's retreating back as Shiloh kept right on walking into the hearing room. And Officer Williams thought Shiloh's back told him all he needed to know: that his whole career had come to shit, less than two years before the comfortable retirement for which he had worked so long.

Officer Williams was a tough man, but this was too much for him to take. He waddled over to a bathroom, entered a stall where nobody could see, and then started shaking like a blubbery hippo with pneumonia. For the first time he could ever remember, Officer Williams cried.

And cried. And cried some more. In the stink of the john, Officer Williams cried until he couldn't cry any more. And just as he finished crying, the stink overwhelmed him, and he vomited.

In the hearing room, though, Shiloh said exactly what he had told LaShauna he would say. He told the examiners about all the racially insensitive things Officer Williams he had heard Officer Williams say. He told of how the older officer seemed to always assume that Shiloh was dumb.

But he also told them that Officer Williams was a good cop nonetheless. That Williams respected the law. That his attitudes towards black people didn't interfere with how he performed his duties. And Shiloh reminded them of the time Officer Williams had come upon a young white guy, sort of a skinhead type, kicking an old black bum who was partially underneath a blanket beneath the raised portion of Interstate 10. Officer Williams never hesitated: He jumped out of his car, gun raised, and lumbered toward the skinhead while bellowing like an enraged rhino. "Don't you dare run or I'll shoot-cher-ass like it's target practice!!!" The skinhead had taken Buster at his word and did not try to escape. And Williams brought him in and booked him for assault. Williams didn't realize that Shiloh had been within earshot when Williams said to another white officer: "Yeah, those shiftless nigger bums are a blight around here, but not even a shiftless nigger deserves to be beat up for no reason."

"I understand why Clarence, I mean why Officer Moss, filed his complaint," Shiloh said. "But I ask for some lenience. Officer Williams has some major flaws, but just considering the job he does, he's a good cop and a dying breed. He'll be off the force soon anyway; I urge you not to discharge him dishonorably. Just don't partner him with any more black officers. That's all."

"Thank you for your testimony, Officer Jones," said the chief examiner. "We'll consider all the evidence you've presented."

Chapter Four

The next day would be the start of a long, long weekend for Mad. It was again time for the company's semi-annual meeting, and he could tell Becky was really nervous about something. She had asked him to be in the office all day long on Friday, for several unspecified reasons. "C'mon, Mad, please don't ask a lot of questions; just take my word for it that I need you in here, okay?"

Mad really didn't want to think about the business. He woke up Friday morning sweating, and he finally had to acknowledge to himself that he was becoming more and more nervous while waiting for his medical test results. Despite his blackout earlier that week, he had tried to tell himself that there was really nothing to worry about. Obviously, though, he had been deluding himself. He had been told the results would not be in until Monday or even Tuesday; and the truth was that, in those deep recesses of the mind where fears reside, the burden of the unknown was growing. And to have a board meeting in the midst of waiting seemed too much to bear. Mad didn't know why the board meetings were becoming increasingly contentious, but something told him again to expect an unpleasant experience. Mad's "flight-or-fight" response to pressure, or to disagreeable circumstances, definitely tended more towards flight. So a whole day in the office with Becky, preparing for the potential unpleasantness, seemed like a horrible idea.

But Mad had been in the office less than five minutes when he was confronted with yet another unpleasantness. Officer Williams, eyes bulging with nervous energy, steamrolled his way right past the elderly secretary and into the mini-kitchen where Mad was using a coffee percolator as a stalling device. (The longer it took to produce its brew, the longer he could avoid sitting down with Becky.)

"Mr. Jones, Mr. Jones, I gotta talk to you!" The officer was trying to sound like he was giving orders, but it came out like a plea. "You gotta help me with something. You gotta help me with something *right now!*"

Mad immediately knew what this was about. The previous afternoon, Shiloh had told him about the whole thing. But he didn't know why Officer Williams would come to him to help. He thought the officer despised him.

"You're a man of God, you're a man of forgiveness," said the officer to him after it became clear that Mad was familiar with the situation at the police department. "And you're a white man: You know how the deck is stacked against us. I think your man Jones-y done screwed me over, Mr. Jones. He wouldn't even look at me before the hearing, and then he called me a bastard. After all I done for him, he called me a bastard! I think he probably talked some real shit to that hearing board, and it's gonna ruin me! I know you and I ain't always seen things the same way, but I need your help now, Mr. Jones. You're a man of God; you got clout. You gotta step in and keep me from bein' done dirty, Mr. Jones. You just gotta!"

Again, Mad wanted nothing but flight. Mad tried to tell the officer it was none of Mad's business. "Besides, the police board doesn't care what I say. I barely even know you, Officer."

"But you pay Jones-y's salary, Mr. Jones! If you won't talk to the hearing board, you can at least talk to Jones-y! Get him to change his testimony. Get him to go back to the board and say he reconsidered, or something. Get him to tell them that he's now remembering all the good things I done'im. Tell Jones-y that God wants him on my side. He'll listen to you; he thinks you got a direct pipeline to Jesus or somethin'. You gotta do this for me, Mr. Jones!"

"But why would he change his testimony, Officer Williams? He told me he asked the board to be lenient on you."

Officer Williams was stunned. "*What's that?!?* You mean Jones-y *didn't* sell me out?"

"Not from what he told me, Officer. He told me that he agreed with part of the complaint against you, but not all of it. Frankly, Officer, Shiloh told me he testified that you've got a racist mouth and that you are always assuming he's dumb just because he's black." Williams scowled.

"And God knows I've seen that from you myself, Officer. You've made *me* angry with some of the things you've said. But Shiloh also told me that he testified you were a good cop. He said he told them there's a difference between you pissing him off and you being a bad cop. He said that even though your attitudes are racist, that you don't act any differently to black suspects than to white ones. He said you do your job okay. He said he asked the board not to fire you, but to just keep you away from black partners from now on. He didn't screw you over; he bailed you out."

Officer Williams couldn't help himself. He started blubbering. And, as the whole conversation had taken place in the mini-kitchen, where the officer's bulk had kept Mad penned in, the blubbering occurred in such close proximity to Mad that it felt almost aggressive, and certainly disgusting. Mad closed his eyes and shrunk back against the refrigerator. But to no avail. The corpulent cop advanced the last two steps and put his head on Mad's shoulder and leaned into Mad for support. The officer reeked, and his weight against Mad was almost suffocating.

Mad summoned all his athletic strength and pushed the officer away.

"Officer, I'm gonna forget I ever saw you like this. I don't know what the police board is going to do, but I know that whatever happens, you can't blame Shiloh. Now I've got a meeting to go to, so I'm going to have to ask you to leave."

He looked at the officer's fat, tear-smudged face. It was vile. But something in its vulnerability suddenly touched a vein of compassion. Mad spoke again:

"But I'll tell you what, Officer. I'll say a prayer for you. I'll ask God to move the hearing board to leniency. I'm not a priest or anything, Officer, but for what it's worth, I'll pray for you."

Officer Williams tried to fight off another gusher of tears. "Will you do that fer me, Mr. Jones? Will you really do that? That'd be really good of you, Mr. Jones. I don't think I ever done anything to get on the bad side of God, but if you've got stroke with Him, I'd sure be happy if you'd use it for me. I can't afford to be disson-able discharged, not this close to retirement I can't."

So Mad reiterated his promise to pray, and the officer finally allowed himself to be escorted out. And, in a way, Mad kept his promise. As soon as Mad was alone in his seldom-used private office, he did pray: "God, please take care of that idiot cop. Please let him not have his retirement affected. Maybe he'll learn a lesson from all this, but please don't let the idiot be punished just for being an ignorant slob. Thanks, God, Amen."

Mad was already exhausted, and he hadn't even sat down yet with Becky.

* * *

Oddly, though, it was Becky rather than Mad who kept procrastinating. It wasn't until lunchtime that she said she was ready to meet with him. "We can talk over lunch," she said. As it turned out, what Becky was so nervous about were more financial anomalies. She said she wanted Mad to know, before she reported to the whole board the next day, that another sizeable chunk of change was missing. She just couldn't understand it; this kind of situation was precisely what they had been trying to avoid by setting up the dual check-signing system with Mary. But somehow, random checks written to MMW cleared the bank but never showed up in the corporate accounts. (Mad didn't understand any of this – and frankly, he didn't want to.) The total missing for the past six months was more than $54,000.

Becky said she would be reporting lots of good news, too. The $54,000 would be a drop in the bucket compared with the hundreds of thousands of dollars of "profits" again to be distributed by the board to charities, not to mention the huge sums expected to be generated by the book *Mad Religion II*, due out on Labor Day. In all, she would report that their enterprise remained tremendously strong, Mad's fan base still immense. But the $54,000, she knew, would get all of the attention. Buzz and Mary had been so nasty to her back in January about the $25,000 that she expected this new discrepancy to be the cause of immensely harsh comment. But, no matter how hard Becky tried, she just couldn't reconcile the books.

"Aw, hell, Becky, don't worry too much," Mad said. "We'll get it figured out. I know you've been working your butt off. If they give you any grief, I'll just tell them to stuff it. Okay?"

Thus reassured, Becky had one more major item on the agenda for her and Mad that day. She wanted to spend a good chunk of the afternoon monitoring the "Mad Religion" chat room along with Mad, so they could interact together with Mad's fans and also so she could lighten up Saturday's board meeting with a lengthy transcript and report on the the lively site.

"Well, Becky, I'll be glad to do this with you, but it might not be so positive," Mad said sheepishly. "For some reason there seem to be a lot more negative comments out there about me than there used to be. Lots and lots of people still seem to hang on every word I say, but now the detractors are more vociferous. And my backers, they seem less enthusiastic."

Mad hadn't wanted to admit this reality even to himself, but now that he voiced it to Becky, he knew that it was true. Nonetheless, the two went ahead with Becky's plan when they returned to their offices.

"Mad has been my savior," wrote somebody calling himself "Lazarus," whom Mad had never before noticed in the chat room. "It was a year and a half ago, at the Maple Street Book Shop in New Orleans, where Mad was doing a book signing. And he told this really touching story about how his late wife had talked some girl down off a roof at college, and then how his wife claimed it wasn't her own wisdom that worked with the girl, but God using her as a vessel for His love. And I said that was all just so sweet and so nice, but that it left behind all of us who think God is a jerk. I was in a bad, bad way that day, so bad that if I were the killing kind, I might have even killed somebody.

"But then Mad said that just because all of us acted jerky sometimes, that it didn't mean we ourselves are incapable of love. Mad said that God is like that, too: that He could be a jerk, and then recognize His own jerk-ness, and make up for it with even more love than we humans can possibly imagine.

"Somehow, that got through to me. In fact, it changed my world. It changed my whole outlook on life. And ever since then, I've been at much greater peace with the world. So as I read all of you out there criticizing Mad, I ask you to think again. Mad is a force for good, and you should cut him some slack."

Mad was blown away. He remembered the young man on Maple Street. He didn't know he had had such a good impact on the guy. Testimony such as this made Mad feel that his efforts were indeed worthwhile – a proposition he had lately begun to doubt.

The semi-euphoria was short-lived, though. Ever Faithful and Defender both quickly chimed in with caustic comments telling Lazarus that he had merely succumbed to feel-good modern psychologizing, and that Mad was a heretic unworthy of respect. Somebody named "Colorado" agreed. Somebody named "Ravenmaster" went farther, saying that he, Ravenmaster, was a proud denizen of the "dark realm," and that he recognized Mad as a kindred spirit who was doing the work of a "Mr. B.L. Zeeboob."

Affirmed was nowhere to be found, nor were Jezebel?, M. Magdalene, Cowardly Lion or FD Thom. About a dozen other detractors chimed in. To Mad, who had avoided saying anything terribly controversial for months now, some of them seemed angry just for the sake of being angry, without anything specific from him as their leaping-off point.

Some lady named "Priscilla" tried, rather meekly, to defend Mad, but she gave up rather quickly. Ever Faithful again wrote that Mad was a heretic, and added that "God is by definition perfect, and because Mad says otherwise, he obviously is doing the work of Satan even if he intends to be doing good."

Becky was appalled. She had never spent much time monitoring the web site, except to make sure that Mad was still writing his required daily messages. Somehow, she had been under the impression that it was a hotbed of pro-Mad fervor, with merely a few dissenters. Desperately, she waited for Lazarus to write something else to put the detractors in their place again. But Lazarus didn't comply.

Just when the whole thing was becoming too depressing for Mad and Becky to continue monitoring, however, somebody named "Phoebe" piped up. "You guys are all so mean! Isn't this the same reaction Paul got from the Pharisees when he started preaching to the Gentiles? Just like Paul did, Mad is bringing in converts. Don't get hung up in all the particulars! Look at the big picture! Mad is bringing people to God, so what's wrong with that?"

Becky copied the comments of Lazarus, Ravenmaster, Ever Faithful and Phoebe, to be included with the semi-annual report presented to the other three board members on Saturday. And at day's end, Mad asked if he could treat her to dinner in order to relieve her stress a bit – but she said she had other plans.

So Mad spent the night alone, trying to avoid thinking about his medical tests.

* * *

The board meeting began at 9 a.m. Mad had asked Father Vignelli to attend, even though the Jesuit wasn't on the board. Mad figured that the priest's wise counsel and calming influence would help the proceedings go more smoothly, with less unpleasantness.

For a while, he was right. Peter's opening prayer asked God's help in keeping the board members "mindful that our two purposes here are to serve God and, through the good works of charity, to serve His world with an active and abiding love."

Becky's excerpts from the chat room also helped. The other three board members were impressed by the testimony of Lazarus and, in juxtaposition with that, they found the words of Ravenmaster humorous rather than disturbing. ("Shouldn't it be *Mrs.* Zeboob rather than *Mr.*?" Buzz joked. "And shouldn't zere be two of zee boobs razzer zan only von?") And the comment from Phoebe, that the mere fact of spurring people to talk about God was a worthy achievement, seemed to sum up the entire purpose of their enterprise. ("Just a few weeks ago another of my longtime supporters, calling herself 'Jezebel,' used similar words in that exact same context," Mad said. "She wrote that making people think about God was 'accomplishment enough.'")

But despite Peter Vignelli's presence, the good will began dissipating once Becky began describing the particulars of the financial report.

She tried to do it backwards: to announce the total amount available for charitable donations and to vote first on how to divvy it up, before going into specifics about the "details" of accounts receivable, expenses, and the touchy subject of the mysteriously missing $54,000. She tried to steal everybody else's thunder (and their questions) with a bold new proposal: that rather than continuing to merely donate to other charities, MMW ought to consider founding and running its own faith-based social program. "Surely, Mad, there must be a cause so dear to your heart that you want to make sure you put your own stamp on it … *right?*" she asked. And although Justin immediately chimed in with high praise for the idea (Justin, of course, praised *every* idea of Becky's), the others were not as quick to respond well. Mad, for one, felt blindsided. Why had Becky not discussed this idea with him in advance? She was doing a terrific job, he said, but as the person around whom the entire enterprise revolved, he said he should be the one presenting major ideas such as this one.

Mary's countenance expressed disapproval of the idea, but she kept her own counsel. Instead, she shot Buzz a look that spurred him to take up a cudgel against the idea. "Hey, Becky, somebody always has to rein you in," he said. "Things are going well; why rock the boat?"

Buzz' tone was a bit accusatory, so Father Vignelli stepped in.

"If I may?" he asked.

"That's why you're here," Mad said. "You may not be a voting board member – yet – but in all other respects I want you to act as if you are indeed one. I always want your guidance, Father."

"Mad, again, will you *please* call me 'Peter'? Anyway, I think Becky should be applauded for her other-directed ambition, and for thinking big. But I've been around the block more than a few times with charitable endeavors. Starting one ourselves would require a much bigger enterprise, a much bigger staff, and an expertise that none of us directly possesses. The way we're going now seems to work so well: Mad attracts people to think and talk about God, and the company serves as a conduit to give money to people who already have the staffing and expertise to accomplish the social services that we think are important. I applaud the initiative Becky is showing, but to me it sounds a little too much like re-inventing the wheel."

Truth be told, Becky wasn't terribly upset to see her idea go nowhere. She still thought it was a good idea, but she never really thought it would fly with the rest of them. What it *did* accomplish, though, was to succeed in reversing the normal order of business. From the starting point of her idea, it only seemed natural to consider the relative merits of the charities applying for grants, rather than first to delve into financial minutia.

In other words, the unpleasantness of the $54,000 would go unreported until closer to the meeting's end. That would allow the other business to be disposed of with less discord.

It was an innocent enough maneuver. But many months later, it would briefly look far from innocent.

The board had so many grant proposals that they didn't finish doling out their money until after lunch. Disputes, of course, arose as to which organizations would receive grants, but Father Vignelli helped keep tensions down. Still, though, the priest picked up on some bad blood between Buzz and Becky. It was as if Buzz was just waiting to pounce.

Sure enough, that's what happened when Becky finally got around to reporting the $54,000 discrepancy.

"Dammit, girl, you're supposed to be the business genius," he scolded. "How the hell could this be happening? Are you just incompetent, or is it something worse?"

It was Justin who took more offense at this than Becky herself did. "That's enough from you, Mr. Perfect!" Justin actually was shouting, and his poorly cut red hair was bouncing on his head as if it had reverse static cling. "You sit up there at your university doing Jack Shit for the company but hobnobbing with Washington TV pundits like you're not Jack Shit but Hot Shit instead! You couldn't do all the great work that Becky's done even if you had five other ivory tower eggheads to help show you the way!"

Father Vignelli was unable to stem the tide. Something within the group had gone rotten, and he was powerless to stop it. And Mad made matters only worse. In his heart, he knew that Buzz was the one who was less "on board" with the rest of them (Mad thought it might be a generational thing), but Justin was the one whose histrionics were most easily assailed. Besides, Mad remained unhappy that Justin's spin-off "holistic health" company still had not noticeably updated the "spiritual" part of its package to more closely reflect Mad's current message. Here Justin was, the only one making a financial killing through his association with Mad, and Justin wouldn't do what Mad asked. And now Justin was flying off the handle at Buzz. Result: Mad jumped on Buzz' side and, as tempers flared, he said that he "ordered" Justin to incorporate Mad's now "improved" theological thinking into Justin's training materials, or else to cease advertising any link between the "Justin Time" company and MMW. Going overboard, he even brought up the spectre of legal action if Justin didn't comply.

"Madison!" Peter Vignelli was appalled at all of them. But he thought it was up to Mad to provide better leadership. "Mad, how can you get up there and make speeches about the need for *us* to forgive *God* for being a 'jerk' – as if that's not disrespectful enough – and about how we need to nevertheless be vessels for the love that God intends us to feel … when all of you at this table are yourselves acting like jerks? Buzz, you're supposed to provide more mature leadership, and the rest of you, please grow up! This ill will is disgusting."

Mad and Becky, who knew the Jesuit the best and respected him the most, were duly chastened. Justin, so hurt by Mad that he was almost shaking, quieted down but fidgeted profusely. Buzz merely rolled his eyes, like he was bored. And Mary, who had been mostly quiet anyway, characteristically remained so.

The meeting ended with most feathers still ruffled. Neither Buzz nor Justin nor Mad had much stomach for the traditional post-meeting dinner. (Mad did, however, call Shiloh and LaShauna and arrange to take them out to dinner anyway, just with him, because they had already made plans to join the board that night.) But Mary had other ideas. She had sensed that there was more information to glean. Knowing Becky's fondness, under stress, for alcohol, she suggested that "just us girls" go out by themselves for a bite and a bottle of wine at a different restaurant in town.

Of that bottle, Mary drank only a glass and a half. And then she insisted that the two of them hit the downtown nightspot "Haley's" for some more libations. "I'm driving my rental car," she said to Becky, "so I'll go slow. But you go wild, girl, cuz you deserve it."

They were out late. At one point, the bar crowd thinned out. That's when Mary asked the question.

"So, Becky, I noticed that Justin is still taking up for you at every opportunity, and now with even more passion," she said. "You used to roll your eyes when he did that; now you look at him like you're grateful. Have you finally gotten accustomed to the little guy, or what?"

"Mmmmm…mmmm," Becky said. And then she laughed.

"Well?" said Mary again. "What's the scoop, girlfriend?"

Becky, drunk, smiled like a feline surrounded by catnip. "You're not gonna believe this, Mary, but that 'little guy' is *good*!!!"

Mary couldn't quite believe what she was hearing. "You mean….? The two of you? Not, like, doing the nasty, huh?"

Becky grinned again.

Mary: "N'*WAY*, girl! Get out!"

Becky: "Yep." She grinned again. And then the floodgates opened, and she couldn't shut up. "For about a month now. And he gets better every week. It's not the size of the dog in the fight, and all that stuff. You just wouldn't believe him, Mary! He's short, but he's in better shape than any man I've ever been with. And anything I want, I get." By now, Becky was giggling after every phrase. "He just goes and goes and goes like the Energizer Bunny. I'm like setting a new record for the number of times I, you know, well, anyway, it's like every week he gets me there more times than he did the week before! I mean, like, Wow!"

Mary kept punching buttons, and details kept flowing. Finally, Becky stopped herself. "But Mary, you GOTTA promise me sumthin' okay? Nobody's supposed to know. Especially Mad. He thinks Justin's just a little buddy of mine. Please don't tell anybody."

"Lips are sealed, girl," Mary said. "Lips are sealed."

* * *

Mad's test results did not come in on Monday, much to his dismay. So he played hooky from his reading and writing chores for MMW and played golf instead at the Spring Hill College course. But he had the damnedest time reading the greens, and his putting woes frustrated him so much that he ended his round more keyed up than when he began it.

The way Mad saw things, he hadn't done much of anything wrong. Everybody had told him that he had a calling to bring God to the skeptical and the angry, and he had done so. Just about anything he was asked to do, he did. And every time some muckracker tried to entrap him, Mad's essential goodwill and decency had won the day.

So why had things begun to go so wrong? Why were so many more chat room denizens against him? Why was his board so fractious when they all started out as his friends? And why did he keep having these damned space-out episodes? Just when life had finally begun to make some sense and his personal tragedies began to recede into a spot where their memory didn't cause searing pain, everything seemed to be falling apart – not from any particular disastrous event, but almost as if through sheer entropy.

Entropy: Where the heck had that word come from? How had it popped into his brain?

Oh... that's right. Now he remembered. It was a favorite word of Mark Mariasson's. It came from the Second Law of Thermodynamics, according to which energy tends on its own to dissipate into an inert uniformity. In essence, entropy is a measure of disorder: Unfocused energy tends to spin itself out of control until it dissolves into a sort of nothingness. Or something like that. Mad decided to pull out his books by Teilhard de Chardin when he got home.

Which he did. He found again that Teilhard wrote that the universe is home to two contrasting impulses: entropy, and life. That which is not evolving is devolving into chaos. The way Teilhard saw it, in effect, was that the evolution of life was towards higher consciousness, with the highest consciousness being God. And in that sense, entropy was the prime obstacle to, perhaps even the enemy of, faith.

Maybe he was on to something. He decided to call Mark up in Oxford to talk about it further.

But Mark wasn't there. (Further disorder, dammit!) So Mad left a message. And then he called the nurse at Dr. Monitor's office, just before she left for the day, to check one more time on whether the results were in.

"I'll tell you what, Cutie Pie," she said. "Why don't I just put you down for an appointment at 3 tomorrow – I'll work you in, no matter what it takes – and if the results aren't in by, say, 1:30, I'll call you and re-schedule again? But I'm sure they'll be here by then. And I want to see my Cutie Pie again as soon as possible!"

Cutie Pie? Why did all these women always want to become so familiar with him?

Anyway, Mad said that sounded fine.

And with nothing else to do, Mad called a pizza place and ordered a delivery, and then started checking the TV listings for sports.

* * *

The nurse never called (nor, for that matter, had Mark yet called back, either), so Mad arrived at the doctor's at 3 o'clock sharp. As soon as the nurse saw him, her eyelashes went all aflutter and she started shamelessly flirting. So much so that she ignored other patients until they complained. The waiting room was already backed up.

Somehow, though, the nurse pulled a fast one and ushered Mad into an examination room within ten minutes of his arrival. And then she lingered, fussing around the room as if she had some real business to attend to. She was a mousey-haired girl in her early 30s, sort of chunky and overripe, but with a cute smile. Mad knew she was his for the taking. But he avoided pressing his advantage. He told her that another of the patients in the waiting room had looked really ill, and suggested she go attend to that other patient instead. Reluctantly, as if she were a First Grader forced to stand in the corner, she did.

Not long after she left, Dr. Monitor entered. He was phlegmatic, as usual. "Fascinating," he said. "Looks unique."

Asked by Mad to elaborate, he said simply: "Androzestione." Pressed further, he said: "Very high."

Eventually the doctor handed Mad a Xeroxed copy of a recent article in a medical journal. "This'll explain it," he said. "And the doctor in the article: I want you to see him. He's the one who knows about this. Can you get to Washington, D.C.?"

By now Mad had lost just about all patience with the doctor. Didn't the man know how to talk, fergodsakes? But before Mad could say anything else, the doctor said: "Other patients waiting. Work with Myrna to set up appointment in Washington. If can't, I'll be back in here in half hour. But hope I don't. Very busy. G'luck." And the doctor was gone from the room, white lab coat waving like an aft-side spinnaker behind him.

Mad gathered that Myrna was the mousey nurse. He made his way to the front desk to find her. There she was, busily compiling some notes Dr. Monitor had dictated into one of those hand-held doohickeys that translates spoken words into written ones, along with a few hand-written scribbles on a scrap of paper and a copy of the same article he had given Mad, this one with several passages highlighted with that yellow transparent ink.

"Hey Cutie Pie," she said. "It'll take me a minute to put this all together."

Two minutes later: "Oh, I see what he wants."

Long story short, Myrna explained that the tests indicated a slight hormonal imbalance on a number of fronts, but that the post-blackout readings showed an especially suspiciously high level of androzestione, a newly discovered hormone about which a doctor at the Georgetown University School of Medicine was the nation's recognized expert. Dr. Vikas Raj had a reputation as an oddball genius, some of whose theories bordered on quackery, but whose groundbreaking research on the three-way interplay between androzestione, pulse, and brain endorphin levels had just that February been fully confirmed through extensive peer review.

Dr. Monitor wanted Mad to consult with Dr. Raj.

"I'm actually scheduled to speak at Georgetown, which is my old *alma mater*, for the student Lecture Fund in October," Mad said. "There, and at the University of Virginia as well. Maybe I can see this Raj guy then."

So that's how they left it. Mad would get back to Myrna to tell her the exact dates of his D.C. trip, and she and Dr. Monitor would arrange an appointment with Dr. Raj.

"But what if something bad happens before then?" Mad asked. "I mean, how serious is my condition? Is it life-threatening or anything like that?"

"I don't think Dr. Monitor would let you wait until October if he thought you were gonna die, Cutie Pie," she said. "But I'll ask. Meanwhile, if you feel one of those nasty blackouts coming on, why don't you call me and I'll rush right over to hold your hand?"

Myrna's voice sounded light and breezy, but Mad thought her face looked flushed.

Chapter Five

Mark Mariasson didn't call back until Wednesday night. But he said he was thrilled that Mad wanted to talk about entropy. He launched right in to a highly scientific explanation, with lots of references to both Einstein and Newton and some other guys named Clausius and Blotzmann, and to logarithms and stone-a-rhythms and all kinds of other jazz that left Mad totally lost in space.

"Slow down, Mark, slow down!" he said. "For a while I was into all this stuff, but I let it slip, and I'm not sure I really understand the science of it. I mean, all this 'Process Theology' stuff and 'cosmogenesis,' it all makes reference to entropy and the Second Law of Thermodynamics and all this other crap you're trying to explain. But I just can't get a handle on it, exactly, and then I was thinking about how everything *I'm* doing suddenly seems to be subject to a type of entropy as well, and I'm just trying to figure if I'm onto something. Whaddya think?"

"Okay, let me take this slowly," Mark said. "But first, yes, I do think you're onto something. But it's nothing new; all those scientist/theologians I turned you onto have been positing this for years. But you've got the audience to take these ideas to the general public, and that's what's really so exciting about this."

"Go on," said Mad.

"Well, here's the deal," Mark said. "You've already been talking about how God is 'purposive' – how God means good for us, and means us to experience love and joy, even when in the short run God acts in ways, or sets in motion the scientific processes that causes events to happen in ways, that makes God seem like a jerk. I know you follow me so far, because you've been preaching this now for well over a year.

"Anyway, the whole upshot of God having a purpose, and of His working through history to help this world evolve towards that purpose, is that we and the whole world are becoming more and more organized towards greater consciousness and greater love and greater eventual joy. And in scientific terms, whether you are talking quarks or quasars, atoms or galaxies, what's happening when things evolve and become better organized is that energy is transformed again and again into higher and higher forms."

"I think I follow you," Mad said.

Mark: "But think about what happens if you organize something. Let's say you're organizing your desk. It gets neater and neater and the papers get stacked in appropriate piles and you eventually reach a point where, because you're organized, you become much more efficient. But here's the catch: When you organize, part of the process is that you throw things out. And what's thrown out doesn't disappear; it just gets carted off somewhere else and dumped. It has no more use and no more meaning, but it's still there. And the unused or discarded material is like the dissipated energy that results from entropy. It's landfill – but somewhere or other, landfill gets in the way.

"On the other hand, if you gather material together to organize it, but then you *don't* actually organize it, then all that paper conglomerates on your desk and becomes a big immovable lump that gets higher and higher and more and more daunting, and thus more and more enervating. So in that case, what was intended for organization is itself a source of entropy, but not in some landfill, but right there on your desk instead.

"Either way, the result of progress, or attempted progress, or attempted movement towards higher consciousness, is that entropy and disorder grow as well. The evolution and entropy, one towards something higher and one towards chaos, parallel each other and gain a sort of reverse momentum from each other – sort of like putting the wrong ends two magnets together, where the magnetic fields push them away from each other the more you try to push them close.

"In other words, the entropy and the evolution feed off each other. And the only question is whether you are going to let the entropy occur on your desk, or whether you want the work on your desk to evolve, in which case the entropy is shunted off somewhere else, which in this case is the landfill."

Mad's head was spinning, but he thought he followed the gist of Mark's theory. But then he realized that his main question still wasn't answered:

"Okay, then, even saying that I understand exactly what you are saying – which I sort of do, but not fully – that still leaves the question of what any of this has to do with faith or with God."

"Don't you see?" Mark asked. "If God's world is purposive, but if the waste products from purposive evolution work the other way, into chaos, then the choice that's left for us is whether we want to join with the purpose or instead get swept into the chaos. It's one or the other. We organize our desks, or else we let them become unmanageable. We take control of our lives and work to make those lives consonant with God's purposes, or else our lives get taken in the other direction. And by 'taken in the other direction,' I mean either of two things. Either we succumb to various evils, or else what's more likely for well-meaning people, we refuse to do or fail to do much of anything at all, and thus risk becoming so flaccid that we ourselves aren't worth much more than the refuse that gets thrown away."

"But isn't that what I've been saying anyway, just in different words?" Mad asked. "I mean, from the very beginning I've been saying that God loves those who try and those who win and those who show courage and those who act even despite all the bad things that happen. In other words, God wants us to act, not to sit back and suffer. And that's the same thing you're saying: that either we get with the program, or else we fall into chaos."

"Bingo!" said Mark. "And then the question becomes, are you just saying those things, or are you actually living them? If you think that entropy has set into your world, could it be that you're allowing it in by just coasting along? Are you really organizing your desk, are you really running your own life, or are you waiting for somebody else to organize it for you?"

Mad was struck by just how far Mark had come, how much more assertive (in a good way) Mark had become, in the 23 months since they had first met. And he realized Mark was right: Mad himself needed to become more assertive. Things had gone so well for him that he had been coasting – and in the vacuum created, the less noble sides of his friends had found room to grow. Everybody had parts of themselves that were less admirable than others, even if they were basically good people. But Mad had created opportunity, and then let it slide. He had begun to organize, but not kept at the job. Either evolution, or entropy: Once the process starts, you get one or the other. He had started the process, but not finished, and so entropy was winning.

It was almost assuredly the right lesson. The question was whether he would apply the lesson wisely and well.

* * *

The presidential election season was beginning to heat up. When Al Gore chose Sen. Joe Lieberman as his running mate on the Democratic ticket, the media angle *du jour* became the supposedly sudden growth in popularity of a faith-based politics.

When the Christian Coalition had become a political force years earlier, the media treated that group's unabashed religiosity as a mortal threat to the First Amendment's supposed "wall of separation" between church and state. Down that road, the pundits all said, lay theocracy and the rise of an American ayatollah.

But when Sen. Lieberman became the Democratic nominee, the pundits treated his unapologetic devotion to his Jewish faith as a refreshing and welcome addition to the political scene. It was suddenly cool to be kosher.

The media dutifully ran around to every religious leader they could find, asking for comment on this new phenomenon. The more enterprising of them noticed the praise Mad had offered in his theses for Jews such as Lieberman who adhered strictly to all the rules of Jewish orthodoxy. In short order, Mad was besieged with requests for comment on the Lieberman phenomenon. As had been his practice for well over a year now, Mad tried to decline comment. Again and again he put out a simple blanket statement: "I choose not to comment on politics." But when a TV newsie at one of Mad's rallies (near Pittsburgh) followed up by asking "why not?", Mad made the mistake of saying: "I've found that mixing faith and politics only leads to trouble." In context, it was obvious that he was referring to his own experience. But what went out on the air that night, and thence to the news wires, was the more abbreviated statement that "mixing faith and politics only leads to trouble" – as if Mad were somehow criticizing Sen. Lieberman with a blanket denunciation of anyone in politics who dared admit to a strong faith.

In short order, the unctuous Democratic "Gentleman from Michigan" again jumped on Mad's case. "These Republican hypocrites have no shame!" said the unctuous one. "When it's a Democratic president with private failings, Mad Jones slings his religiosity around like cow chips and says that true religion condemns such a man as our president from even being on the political stage. But when a Democrat is a good and honest man unafraid about acknowledging his faith, such as Joe Lieberman, then Mr. Jones becomes a critic of mixing politics with religion. The truth is that right-wingers like Mad Jones are happy as long as their judgmental religion rules the day, but they can't abide the idea of an observant Jew on a national ticket. Methinks I smell here a whiff of Goebbels!"

More chaos ensued. Entropy accelerated. A new media frenzy threatened to spin Mad's world out of control.

That's when Mad thought back to his conversation with Mark Mariasson. In his mind, he again heard Mark asking: "Are you really organizing your desk, are you really running your own life, or are you waiting for somebody else to organize it for you?" Mad's silence, his avoidance of the issue at hand, had left a vacuum for others to fill with misinterpretations and misrepresentations. If he didn't make his own message clear, then somebody else would define his own purported message for him. In short, it was time for Mad to take control.

But how to do so? What forum could Mad trust?

At the MMW offices, Mad thumbed through the stack of media requests that Becky had laid on his desk. Brokaw? Too liberal. Rather? Too damned weird. Imus? Way too unpredictable.

Oh. Of course. Steve Matheson. Matheson might interrupt Mad a gazillion times, but at least he wouldn't misrepresent Mad's position or try to entrap him unfairly. And during political season, Matheson had high ratings. Mad would have to be alert and forceful to get his two cents in without being overwhelmed by Matheson's hyperactive verbosity, but at least he'd get a fair shake. So he picked up the phone and dialed the number on the message sheet. Yes, he told Matheson's producer: For Mad, it was 'Gut Check' time again.

Mad did the show by remote (from a Mobile TV studio) in the latter half of August. Buzz, of course, took credit for lining up the appearance, but became a little miffed when Mad showed little interest in Buzz' advice for how to approach the interview. For one thing, Buzz wanted Mad to use the occasion to blast the Democratic ticket. (Unlike Mad, who truly was only slight right of center, Buzz was a rock-ribbed conservative.) "This is your chance to throw the hypocrisy charge right back in their faces!" Buzz argued. "After years of trying to kill all religion in the public square, now all of a sudden they're advertising their faith! I mean, I think Joe Lieberman is sincere and he's a good man, but all the Democratic strategists and handlers, all those atheists and New Agers, they're just cravenly running to where the votes are. Blast'em all to Kingdom Come, Mad, blast their asses hard!"

Mad didn't feel anywhere near so strongly about it, but he did feel that Buzz had a point. Still, he wanted to do just the opposite: to extricate himself again from politics, not to become publicly partisan.

Problem was, Buzz had primed Steve Matheson for the assault he wanted to see Mad launch. Matheson was a little surprised; he thought he understood that Mad had developed an aversion to politics. But if Mad's own godfather said Mad was ready to let'er rip, then Matheson the showman was delighted to goad him into it.

"So, now we have one of my favorite guests, Mad Jones of Mobile Alabama," Steve told his TV audience by way of introduction. "He's a primo preacher, a gutty gunslinger in the media wars who has humbled myriads of us media mavens, not the least of which was the time he spanked Spike Walters right off the air for the first time in two decades. Welcome, Mad!"

"Hi, Steve."

"Look, Mad, you know why you're on tonight: It's all this Lieberman as man-of-faith stuff. You're a religious lecturer who once was burned by a few random political comments, and for ages now you've avoided political controversy. But now, here's what you said a few weeks ago in Pittsburgh."

(Videotape of Mad saying that "mixing faith and politics only leads to trouble.")

"And here's the response from one of the leading Democrats in Congress." (Videotape of the Michigander comparing Mad to Goebbels.) "So now I understand you're ready to take the gloves off. It's Gut Check time again, Mad, and we're ready for you to blast away!"

"Well, Steve, the only people I'm here to blast are those who throw around false accusations and cheap shots like that reference to Goebbels. Fact is, the context for that clip you showed of me was me *declining* to make a political comment, because every time I do it only leads *me* to trouble. I wasn't referring to Sen. Lieberman at…"

"But you're for Gov. Bush, aren't you?"

"I'm not interested in endorsing anybody for…"

"But c'mon, Mad, doesn't it make you angry to see somebody compare you to Goebbels? Doesn't that make you want to blast away at everybody on that guy's side?"

"Steve, that's not where I'm coming from. I think it's terrific that Sen. Lieberman is an observant Jew. What I'm more interested in is…"

"So you like Lieberman?"

"I think he seems like an ethical man. I think the White House needs some ethics again. But what I'm …"

"Oooh, a shot at the current occupant, no doubt? More ethics in the White House? That's a great euphemism! I guess it's pretty hard to see Joe Lieberman borrowing the Oval Office from Al Gore and asking an intern to bring him a pizza and cigar!"

Mad didn't like where that was going. But when he tried to cut back into the conversation, Matheson's hot-wired brain made another connection, this time to his barroom conversation with Buzz three months earlier:

"Not that you begrudge a man his amorous pursuits, eh, Mad? I mean a single man like you, word is you're quite the Lothario. Chickadees in every city in the country, from what I hear. Where's the line where private morality and the public interest intersects?"

Steve Matheson wasn't trying to embarrass Mad. He was just being a showman and having fun with the conversation just the way he'd have fun with a buddy out for a beer. When push came to shove, he wanted Mad to come out of the show looking like a sharp and fun young guy. But Mad had been taken way off guard. This interview wasn't going at all as he had planned, and it seemed as if Matheson had him cornered.

"Look, Steve, I'm not here to talk about my sex life. What I'm…"

"Neither am I, Mad," Matheson interjected. "That's not the point of my question. But I thought you had a real critique to make about how the Democrats use religion when it suits them but reject it as a threat when it doesn't. C'mon, Mad, take off the gloves!"

"Dammit, Steve, I'm not here to take off the gloves. What I want to talk about isn't fighting; it's our need to evolve. We've got to take control, in public life and private, of the evolutionary process of us reaching a higher union with God. What I mean is…"

"Evolution? What's this, a return to the Scopes Trial? You're always so unpredictable, I just love it! Love ya', man, I just luv ya'. Look, stick around and we'll come back to you right after this commercial break."

Matheson was having a high old time. He loved guests who didn't stick to a boring set of talking points. During the commercial break, off air, he said to Mad through their ear-plug connection: "Hey, Mad, buddy, you're doing great! Sorry about that crack about your love life; it just popped out. But damn, you're lotsa fun!"

"But Steve, look, can we please…"

"Wait, Mad, gotta go: My producer is saying something to me. We'll be back on in about 45 seconds. Hang tight."

Forty-five seconds later, back on the air, Matheson jumped right in: "Okay, I think I've been jumping the gun on my guest, religious lecturer Mad Jones of Mobile. I've been kidding with him a little, but I think he really has a serious point to make. Hey, Mad, you got a good sound bite I can use?"

Mad was too flustered to have a sound bite. "Well, Steve, it's just that this whole topic has gotten out of hand. I don't think faith should be a political commodity, Steve. But not because faith is going to somehow pollute politics, but because politics will provide a temptation to pollute one's faith. I think most of the press is going overboard in their focus on Sen. Lieberman's observation of Jewish orthodoxy, and I think the Gorgeous Georgians of the world who are running the Democratic war rooms are just using Sen. Lieberman's faithfulness for cynical purposes. What I'd really like to see is…"

"Ooohhh, he lands a hard right hook to the chops! So the Democrats are cynics! Now we're finally reaching some good Gut Check stuff! I think you're my favorite guest, Mad-oh my friend, because you always swing from the heels. Nothing fake about you, no sirree!"

Mad was panicky now. He still hadn't been able to say what his main point was, which was that if everybody turned down the volume a bit and grappled with God in private, rather than using God in public to grapple with each other, then the end result would be a higher plane of both private *and* public conversation without all the cheap shots and rancor.

But all he had the chance to say was: "I'm not trying to throw punches here, Steve. What I'm trying to say is that the private sphere of religion is much more profound than the public sphere that the media always bollixes up. What I'm saying…"

"That's great, Mad, that's great, it's a perfect lead-in to my next guest, from the liberal media watchdog group, Fairness and Accuracy In Reporting, or FAIR. I think he has a different take on it. Mad, I'm told our satellite window with Mobile is due to expire in a second. Thanks so much for being on. You're always so much fun!"

Mad seeming to blast Clinton again for the Lewinsky mess. Mad as an oversexed Lothario. Mad re-opening the Scopes Trial. Mad attacking Carney James (the Democratic consultant known as the Gorgeous Georgian). Mad attacking the media.

There was enough grist from his appearance to gin up enemies galore. More entropy. More chaos.

* * *

Jock, the ace reporter for *The Zodiac*, picked up on Steve Matheson's comments about Mad's sex life. A week later, the tabloid ran an "I had Mad sex" issue, with four of Mad's recent conquests all fessing up.

Gladys Phillpott said that Mad was "a dangerously loose cannon." She said it wouldn't do for a prominent critic of the Democrats to be living such a libertine lifestyle.

Carney James ignored the sex. He called Mad "a member of the right-wing hate squad that threatens to throw the United States back to the Dark Ages."

The Revs. Larry Falstaff, Rob Patterson and Bill White all blasted Mad for what Falstaff called "this New Age psychobabble about evolution." Outside of New Orleans, the Rev. Hebert sorrowfully admitted (against his wife's wishes, because she still thought Mad was "a nice young man") that he had been wrong about Mad all along. As a leader in the movement to force "creationism" to be taught in Louisiana's public schools in place of, or at least alongside, evolution, the Rev. Hebert was appalled that Mad would suggest that God created man not in God's own image but in the image of an ape.

The Rev. Patterson added that "Mad Jones has yet to refute the rumors that he is a rampant fornicator, so we must assume the rumors are true. He shouldn't be preaching; he should be praying for forgiveness."

On the left, The Rev took on the same issue. "Mad Jones is not led by Jesus but by his weak disciple, Peter. He's an example of the 'peter principle.' He follows his peter until the cock crows."

On one of the cable news political shoutfest shows, one of the liberal panelists said that Mad's "attempt to smear the Gore-Lieberman ticket" with his "crack about Clintonian sexual ethics" earned Mad's comments the choice as "outrage of the week."

And an officious, supercilious spokesman for the Bush campaign told reporters that the Texas governor had never met Mad Jones and did "not welcome such a divisive figure as an ally."

* * *

Mad's second book came out on Labor Day weekend, so September was devoted to a grueling book tour akin to the one two years earlier. But this time all the book reviews were sour. "What was new two years ago is no longer new," wrote one critic. "*Mad Religion II* not only plows no new ground, but it waters down Madison Jones' earlier message into a thin New Age gruel."

"Mad Jones is an act that has suddenly gotten old," wrote another. "He moves back and forth between, on one hand, Generation X-type whining that 'God is a jerk,' and on the other hand, a content-less happy-talk about God's essence being 'joy.' In the 1960s, there was 'God is love.' Jones' 'joy' appears to be no more than love on a diet."

But the reviewers saved their sharpest insults for the introductory essay that was one of the few wholly original parts of the book. (As in the first book, this one consisted largely of reprints of Mad's newspaper columns.) One reviewer called the intro "impenetrable." Another called it "highly confused, and thus confusing." A third wrote that it was "tedious and tendentious."

For whatever reason, Mad and his publishers had missed their mark.

Mad's introduction had used as a starting point his 45th thesis, "Do all such good works as the Lord hast prepared for us to walk in." In essence, it allowed him to carry forward the themes of his dispute with the national Episcopal church. When the disagreement had become public the previous spring, a former theology professor of Claire's had written Mad a thoughtful, personal letter asking Mad for clarification of his position.

"On the one hand," she wrote, "it seems that you simply mean to argue that the mainline churches have overstepped the bounds of authority in making policy recommendations about economic affairs and the like. This would be a fairly limited (though telling) sort of claim. On the other hand, you give evidence of having a more radical critique in mind – perhaps a belief that churches ought not to be giving specific moral guidance at all. Or perhaps you want to say that some sorts of moral guidance are okay, but that other sorts are not. Now if this is what you want to argue, you have to do the hard work of figuring out what sorts of pronouncements are legitimate (and why) and what sorts are not (and why not). In the absence of such an effort, you seem to be advocating the paradoxical (and unhelpful) view that all Christians ought to 'labor' in 'good works,' but that no one should make any effort to say what constitutes 'good works.'"

With that challenge in mind, Mad had decided to elaborate further on how a Christian could identify the "good works that God has prepared for us to walk in."

> "So that my readers will not misunderstand me, I am not saying that individual or voluntary collective attempts to prepare the way for the Kingdom of God are rejected in the Gospels, but only that Jesus consciously refused every opportunity to create such a Kingdom through any means other than the Word which produced an inner faith. There is not only no authority for clergy to create a 'Christian social program,' but no convincing reason why clergy should claim any authority to delve into economics or politics at all. A bishop who is also a student of economics has every right to express his personal beliefs on the proper way to manage a political economy to achieve the desired ends of a sort of 'shadow Kingdom' of God on Earth, but he must make clear that he is doing so not in his role as bishop but in his role as a studied economist. I see a particular danger, for both the church and the world served by that church, in claiming too much authority, lest a backlash threaten even the general recognition of the church's primary spiritual mission.
>
> "The clergy's role, therefore, lies in the *spiritual* preparation of the laity so that the laity is able to carry out its own private good works and to act in its social and political communities to attempt to achieve the greatest good possible.
>
> "And for all of us who are not clergy, then, our proper role is indeed private good works such as the donation of time, talent, and money to those in need. And if we choose to do it in an organized fashion – in other words, in community with each other – so much the better. Clothe the naked. Feed the hungry. House the homeless. Provide medical care for the infirm, and a steady shoulder and open heart for those in distress. But God forbid that we should make the claim that we know, with 100 percent certainty, that what we are doing is God's will. All we can know is that we as individuals are trying mightily to discern and act on God's will, and then to act boldly with the thought that God shall forgive us if

we have discerned incorrectly. The good works that God has prepared for us to walk in amount to an active and prayerful loving of our neighbors, but with a humility that requires us to constantly question our own motivations and constantly try to ground our behavior within the perceived will of God. And a good sign that we have acted in the right spirit is if we are able to do so joyfully. If the good works feel like a burden, then we have not become one with God's purpose, even if those works themselves are indeed worthwhile.

"So go love thy neighbor, and do so joyfully and with courage. Amen.

Mad Jones"

In a liberal weekly magazine, the reviewer of *Mad Religion II* had this to say about that introductory essay: "Obviously, beneath the pitifully thin veneer of an apolitical lay preacher lies the stone-cold heart of an anti-government conservative who believes that no mandatory collective effort is required in order to take care of social ills. Fix all ills with private charity, he says, but when the 'push' of social needs too overwhelming for the private sector comes to the 'shove' of government action (and taxation) which is the only real cure for those needs, Mad Jones would accept the push, and its attendant pathologies, without a second thought. His is a cramped and ungenerous view of our duty to be good Samaritans, and such a cramped view is what makes Mad Jones a menace."

Reading the review over the phone to Chet Matthews (who ever since the "Hour of Truth" episode had taken to calling Mad about once a month "just to shoot the bull"), Mad sneered: "Those limousine liberals! It's a wonder they have time for all their social engineering in between mouthfuls of their Chablis and brie."

Chet laughed. "Hot damn, young cowboy, we're gonna make a conservative activist outta you yet! You starting to sound like a young Ronald Reagan!"

But as the book tour was showing, Mad didn't have Reagan's unerring sense of the mood of a crowd. At every stop on the tour, the audience sizes were at least slightly smaller than expected. And at every stop, the numbers at the end of Mad's remarks were less than when Mad began.

Not even the bad reviews had cured Mad of his serious bout of esoterica, and the crowds were getting bored.

* * *

"I say, Son, I say, I'll be interested to see what you say at my beloved university next week." The Colonel had woken Mad up at 1:08 a.m. with his phone call. "Evruh time I think I got a handle on what you're all about, you up and suh-prise me, I say, you suh-prise my old bones somethin' fierce. One minute you're attacking the pantywaists who've hijacked my beloved Episcopal Church, and I think you're a great young fella, and then the next moment – the very next moment, I say – you go and get into some kinda deal where you're not being discrete enough about your tom-catting around, and so the talk is all about sex. And then you go and talk about some freako Jesuit named Tie-hard My Garden, or whatever, and about noogiespheres or some kinda weird newfangled nonsense word. Why can't you stay disciplined, boy, why can't you keep your focus?"

Mad had been in deep REM sleep, and he was still trying to shake the fog from his mind. "Well, Sir, I don't always control the topic. I mean, people ask me questions I don't want to be asked. I'm sorry, Sir. But as for that Jesuit you referred to, Teilhard de Chardin, I've gotta talk about him. None of what I say holds together without Teilhard. But, Sir, I really…."

"I say, Son, I'm no theelogeyan, I say, so I don't rightly know about all that. But evruh time you start talking about ol' Tay-Yard, I think people's eyes are glazin' over. Anyway, that's not why I called, Son, I say, that's not why I called. I called to talk about your speech at the University of Virginia. You know somebody's gonna ask you about us, don't you? I say, it's bound to happen that somebody asks you about us."

By now Mad was fully awake – and at this hour, he resented it. Resented it so much that for once he lost the deferential tone he usually used with The Colonel.

"Mr. Colonel, Sir, I'll tell you exactly what I'm gonna do. If they ask me about the Eights, I'm gonna tell'em the truth." (An audible gasp came from the other end of the line.) "And not only that, but I'm gonna tell'em the truth in a way that makes you proud. So, Mr. Colonel, I don't ever mean to be rude to you, but I'm tired and I want to go back to sleep. So I thank you for calling, but that's all I have to say. Good night."

* * *

Two days later, the chat room was polluted six different times by an anonymous message that said, simply, "Mad muss die."

The good news was that even Mad's harshest critics longtime critics, Defender and Ever Faithful, quickly wrote in with condemnations for the message. "Whoever you are, Sicko, you're not funny or clever," wrote Defender. "Somebody needs to lock you up."

The bad news was that the next day, the sicko returned three more times with the same message. Every time, the word "must" was misspelled as "muss."

* * *

"I'm worried about Mad." Shiloh was sitting with Father Peter Vignelli in the back room of Carpe Diem.

"You mean about those threats on the web site?" the priest asked. "I saw those, too. You never really know, but for now I wouldn't really worry about them. Probably somebody just blowing off steam."

Shiloh hadn't been checking the web site, and so was unaware of the messages. But, after Father Vignelli described them to Shiloh, the bodyguard agreed with the priest's assessment.

"Anyway, Father, that's not what I'm worried about," he said. "I worried about something else. What I'm worried about...."

The Jesuit interrupted: "I am, too, Shiloh; I am, too. Oh, sorry to interrupt. I was anticipating you were going to say you were worried about Mad's perspective, about his focus, about his lifestyle, even about his mental health. Is that what you were going to say?"

"Yes, Father. You've seen it, too?"

"Yes, Shiloh. It's been bothering me more and more for months. I mean, if all these tabloid reports are true, then it's obvious he's using cheap sex as a way to detach himself from any kind of more meaningful human interaction. And I gather that he's losing touch with his audience, and he seems more distant to me, and it's clear that the interactions on the company's board are toxic. I think his heart is still in the right place, but it's as if he's let his celebrity, maybe combined with all that sex, serve as a substitute for any *real* connection with other people or even with his own feelings. And also… Oh, I don't know, Shiloh, there's so much else that worries me. But he's stopped calling me for coffee or tennis or golf or whatever; he's just been pulling away."

"Father, I've gotta tell you, I had no idea for the longest time about the sex. He always goes back to whatever motel we're staying at and goes right into his room when I go into mine. But then, just a couple of months ago, I left my room to go to the ice machine at the end of the hall, and when I looked back I saw him leading some little redhead into his room. I think all those stories about him may be true. And it bothers me, Father, it really bothers me. I wasn't a saint when I was single, Father, but I really think a man needs to make an effort at least not to give in to all that temptation. It just seems wrong to me, Father, it just seems wrong."

"I think that's just a symptom, my friend," said the priest. "It's just a symptom of something else not right. Have you noticed anything at his rallies, anything different about how he's acting? I get the impression that he's all over the map and over-intellectualized. Am I right?"

"That's exactly it, Father," said Shiloh. "Half the time I can't really follow what he's talking about, and I've heard variations of most of it time and time again."

After a pregnant pause, Shiloh added: "And, Father, there's one thing more. There are times when he seems to go into weird trances, as if his mind isn't even turned on even though his eyes are wide open. It's almost like he's not even there."

Peter Vignelli sat back in his chair and turned his head to stare into the empty fireplace. He pulled up his hand and started massaging his chin, as if deep in thought. The two men were silent.

Finally, after a few minutes of this, the Jesuit spoke again. "I'll try to talk to him, Shiloh. I really do think he's off track. I'll see what I can do…. Now, let's forget about Madison for a while. How are *you* doing, my friend? And how are LaShauna and that smart little daughter of yours?"

* * *

Officer Williams sat behind a desk at police headquarters. The disciplinary board had made its ruling five weeks earlier: The fat white officer would not be discharged dishonorably and would suffer no reprisals concerning finances or rank. But he was taken off patrol duty, put behind a desk, and told he would be "asked" to retire in exactly one year, with full pension benefits. The only times he would be serving on the streets again would be for special events where extra police were needed for crowd control.

In the meantime, Officer Williams was to be considered "on probation," with particular emphasis placed on him remaining respectful to fellow black officers.

On this early October morning, Shiloh made a quick stop into headquarters to take care of some paperwork concerning his part-time police responsibilities, before embarking on his next trip with Mad. Officer Williams saw Shiloh quite clearly. He wanted to say something to Shiloh. But he was afraid to. He didn't understand these young niggers. He couldn't figure out whether his former partner hated him or liked him. And he was afraid that some "innocent" thing he said might be interpreted wrongly. He had just dodged a bullet from the disciplinary board, and he didn't want to risk any more trouble when he was now just a year removed from retirement with full pension.

Buster Williams saw Shiloh notice him. He saw Shiloh start to turn to wave, or nod, or perhaps to just say a quick neutral "hello." Williams, nervous, didn't want any contact with Jones-y. He quickly stared down at some papers on his desk, as if deeply concentrating on some work. Shiloh shrugged and kept walking. And as Officer Williams saw Shiloh's powerful frame retreat from the vicinity, Williams rubbed his forehead with both his meaty palms. Suddenly, Officer Williams had a headache.

* * *

The mime sat at the bar of The Tombs. He was completely out of costume; he wore a simple rugby shirt and blue jeans. He needed a beer to relax. Nothing much had been going right for him. He knew he was a great talent, but no agents ever came calling. And Mad Jones, to whom he was so devoted, never even acknowledged his presence, despite all of the attention the mime had brought Mad's way. The mime's cash was virtually at an end, and he couldn't afford to travel much longer, so he showed up at Mad's rallies only about once every three months or so these days. But the mime figured that Mad's two events up D.C.-way would provide a good forum. He had heard rumors that some media folks were interested in the twin angles of Mad returning to his *alma mater* and of Mad also speaking at U.Va., with all of the rumors of Mad's shadowy alliance with the mysterious Crazy Eights Society.

And now, the night before the first of Mad's two campus appearances, the mime suddenly thought his luck might be changing. Two barstools away, a guy in a panama hat was talking a little too loudly to one of the bartenders.

"You been around this place for a while?" the Panama Hat Guy was saying. "You look like you're the type that knows a lotta fun stuff about all kinds of people."

The bartender laughed. He was an eternal Ph.D. student who had held the part-time bar job at The Tombs for seven years now. If something juicy happened in or around Georgetown, he certainly had heard at least snippets of it. "I hear a lot," he said. "But I don't tell."

Panama Hat just smiled. He was used to this. He stuck out his hand. "Name's Jock," he said. "I'm a reporter. Write for *The Zodiac*. We've got a nice expense account to make information a little more worthwhile to give. All anonymously, of course, if that's what you want."

Out of the corner of his eye, the bartender noticed the mime staring at Jock as if his panama hat was the Ark of the Covenant. The bartender cleared his throat and said, fairly loudly, "Nice to meet you Jock, but I'm like a good Catholic priest: I don't divulge the confessions I hear." The bartender rolled his eyes quickly to indicate to Jock that the mime was listening. Jock caught his drift – glanced at the mime and thought to himself that this guy in the rugby shirt looked vaguely familiar – and then lowered his voice.

"Well, how about another beer?" Jock said.

When the bartender returned with a Rolling Rock, Jock leaned in and spoke quite softly. "Look, man, I'm tracking down more stories about Mad Jones. I already blew the whistle on his Don Juan act when he went to Georgetown, but now that he's coming back here to speak, I have a feeling he'll do something new worth writing about. For some reason my editor is really hot for more Mad stories. Says they always sell papers. Anyway, I know this place used to be his hangout. If you hear or see anything, I was sorta hoping you'd give me a call."

With that, Jock hung his hand over the inside of the bar, as if he were stretching. In his hand was a business card and folded up next to the card was a $50 bill. Trying not to be noticed, the bartender let his hand brush Jock's, and he pocketed the items Jock had offered. "There's more where that came from," Jock said out of the side of his mouth. The bartender nodded. "It's a deal," he whispered.

Not much later, Jock left The Tombs, again glancing at the mime in his rugby shirt. Where *had* he seen that guy before?

What he didn't know was that the mime had extraordinarily good hearing. Despite the efforts of Jock and the bartender, the mime had heard every word. He had been trying to screw up his courage to talk to Jock, but the reporter exited before the mime could find his voice. Finally, the mime spoke.

"Hey, barkeep," he said. "Come'ere." The mime indicated a desire to speak in whispers, so the bartender leaned in. "Look, man, I heard all that. How about I give you a $20 if you let me copy down the phone number on that card the reporter gave you?"

This was the Ph.D. student's lucky night. He had served a total of four beers to these two guys, combined, and was $70 the richer for it. It was no skin off his back to let the mime copy Jock's phone number. Sure. No problem.

And the mime, now short of his next day's lunch money, nevertheless was smiling broadly as he walked up The Tombs' stairs back to the street. Turning right, the mime crossed the street and stood at the top of the Exorcist steps. In a low voice that only he heard – speaking to the empty stairwell where, 75 steps down, a fictional young Jesuit had met his death after saving Linda Blair's soul – the mime said with an air of defiance: "You can't touch me, Devil. I'm not falling down those stairs.

Hell ain't gonna get me now. You keep on torturing me, but I'm gonna win, and you're gonna lose."

* * *

Sure enough, Mad entered The Tombs a little later that night. He and Shiloh had arrived in D.C. a couple of hours before, and Shiloh already had turned in for the night. But Mad was keyed up about his appointment the next day with Dr. Raj – more worried about that, in fact, than about his speech in Georgetown's Gaston Hall the next night or his visit to the University of Virginia the day after that. The frequency of Mad's trance-like spells had actually increased during the previous month as Mad's travel schedule had sharply increased during the book tour. And whereas most of his "blackouts" previously had occurred when he was by himself at home, two of them in the previous month had been interrupted by Shiloh literally shaking him back into mental focus – once when it was time for them to de-plane in Kansas City, and once when Shiloh (driving both of them home from the Mobile airport) was trying to drop Mad off at Mad's own house.

Anyway, the stress of not knowing what was wrong with him was becoming unbearable. And the best way Mad knew to relieve stress was to drink a beer and find a woman. Sure, he had been enraged by the tabloid coverage of his sex life, but he was after all a widowed man, and he wouldn't let some sleazebag reporters keep him from living his life as he wanted.

Ten minutes after walking down the steps to The Tombs, while sitting at the bar, Mad spotted a thin, six-foot tall blonde with long straight hair, sitting with two friends at one of the restaurant tables. With practiced ease, Mad went to work.

The bartender watched all this for about a half hour. Asking the other bartender to "hold the fort" for just a minute, he retreated to a private back stairwell where he could hear a phone conversation better. He called Jock. "Hey, if I've got something for you, how do I know you're good for the other 50 bucks?" he asked.

Jock was already in bed, but he said: "I'll be right over."

Less than a half hour later, Jock was hurrying down 36th Street on foot when he spied Mad, accompanied by the tall blonde, emerging from the stairwell of The Tombs. Like a practiced gumshoe, Jock followed at a distance during a walk of about five blocks. He saw Mad and the blonde enter an "N" Street townhouse. He saw an upstairs light go on, and then, fairly quickly, off again. There was a tall tree outside the townhouse. It was an Indian Summer October night, so the temperature was a comfortable 65 degrees. An upstairs window, right next to a tree limb, was open, and some thin curtains occasionally flapped out in a slight breeze.

Jock climbed the tree, carefully making sure to protect his camera as he did so.

Most of the time he couldn't see inside. But when the curtains flapped, he caught glimpses of amorous activity. If he only timed it right....

There! A gust of wind, a curtain funneling open wider than usual, an unobstructed if quick view of two white upper torsos – and Click! went Jock's camera, accompanied by a white flash that neither Mad nor the blonde were inclined to pay any attention to.

Jock had his money shot.

And speaking of money, the bartender never saw the other $50. After all, Jock had spied Mad without needing to enter the restaurant again. Why pay for what you can get for free?

* * *

The next morning, at the Georgetown medical center, Mad was ushered into the office of Dr. Raj. He was immediately struck with the certainty that Dr. Raj was brilliant. The doctor's British-Indian accent was combined with a precise vocabulary and acutely analytical (and unerring) leaps of logic. But something about Raj's eyes was a little bit wild, a little unsettling.

"I've been looking forward to seeing you," said the doctor. "You may just be the patient I've been looking for. A perfect specimen, perhaps." A funny half-smile, ever-so-briefly, shot across one side of his face. "I have all your charts; I know your earlier hormone measurements. But I need more blood for an updated test: Here, stick out your arm."

The doctor also took Mad's blood pressure, gave him a tiny little pill, and then said: "We have the technology to expedite the results, since you're a special case. I'll be back in two hours. But if you don't mind, there's a little camera in the corner. We'll be watching you, just in case something goes wrong. And wear this device to monitor your heartbeat. The pill is a usually harmless isotope that will let us perform our next test, but there's about a one-in-250-thousand chance it could cause your head to swell up like a pumpkin. Meanwhile, you'll see a host of very good magazines in that drawer. I hope that you'll find something that will keep these two hours from boring you."

Dr. Raj bustled off.

Slightly more than an hour later, though, the nurse in the outer office was startled by a beep on her machine that was attached, through wall wiring, to the heartbeat monitor in Mad's examination room. Mad's heart rate (per minute) had slowed to about 35. The nurse looked at the closed-circuit TV screen and saw that Mad's head, while not swollen, was fixed in an oddly rigid posture.

"Dr. Raj!" she said into an intercom. "Dr. Raj! I think Madison Jones needs your attention!"

Dr. Raj, trailed by the nurse, bustled into Mad's room and discovered his patient in the midst of one of his trances.

"Eureka!" said the doctor under his breath. "Stick him with a needle and take some more blood! We have lucked into a blackout in progress!"

The needle, of course, brought Mad back to full consciousness.

"What the….!"

"You were blacked out!" said Dr. Raj. "I'll bet this blood has an extremely high level of androzestione! And quick, spit into this device! Your saliva may hold the telltale signs of an endorphin imbalance."

Mad, trying to shake off cobwebs, did what he was told.

"But, Doctor, what does this all mean?" he finally asked.

"Mr. Jones, you must be honest here; I know this must be true: Confirm for me, please, that you had intercourse last night."

* * *

After two hours of waiting for the blood test results, Dr. Raj confirmed for Mad what the doctor suspected: Mad had a rare hereditary syndrome involving a very strange mix of hormones marked especially by high levels of androzestione (ADZ). Moreover, the androzestione tended to spike even higher within 12-to-24 hours of sex. A spike in ADZ in turn caused a lower heart rate, combined with a marked shift in the normal mix of several brain chemicals (including endomorphins). Result: Mad's "trances," his "blackouts," or as Dr. Raj suggested they henceforth be called, his "ADZ sleep." (High levels of stress, or distress, could also cause the same phenomenon.) Whenever the ADZ sleep ended, the hormone's levels retreated within hours to what for Mad was "normal" – still far higher than in most people, but lower than during the ADZ sleep. (That's why Mad's tests with Dr. Monitor had shown high ADZ initially, rising ADZ the morning after a tryst, and higher-still ADZ an hour after emerging from a trance. But since Dr. Raj had been able to take Mad's blood right in the midst of ADZ sleep, he had been able to find the ADZ levels so high as to be virtually off the charts.) The trances were not in themselves dangerous, the doctor explained. In fact, in the midst of the trance Mad was probably like a healthy hibernating bear, perfectly safe. It was just that the trances were a symptom of a larger syndrome that could, on the whole, be quite worrisome.

For one thing, Dr. Raj explained, there was this: ADZ and heart rate tended to move in opposite directions. For a man whose body was accustomed to high ADZ accompanied by occasionally higher-still ADZ-level "spikes" after sex, a long-term lack of sex could be one of several scenarios that was highly dangerous. If "stasis" was a heart rate of, say, 65, and ADZ of, say, 1,500, then if ADZ dropped to, say, 800, then the heart rate (and blood pressure) might be prone itself to a random, huge burst in the opposite direction up to life-threatening levels of 150 or more. Dr. Raj theorized that such an occurrence might have been what killed Ben Jones – and, for that matter, what killed *Ben's* own father, who died too young for Mad to even know him.

"Now, is there any chance you can come back in two more days?" the doctor asked. "I have one more test to run, and one more theory to check out after analyzing these specimens and the data I have from you. Only after that can I tell you what, if anything, you can do about your syndrome."

Mad was due to fly out of Reagan National Airport two mornings from then, but he was certain he could find a late afternoon flight instead.

"Sure," he said, not sounding sure at all. He was both intrigued and frightened by these findings. The one thing he knew immediately, though, was that he felt utterly compelled to find out as much information as he could, as soon as he could. Uncertainty about his prognosis was torture. If flying out half a day later could help end the uncertainty, then that's exactly what he'd do.

As Dr. Raj started to leave, Mad stopped him with one more question.

"So, tell me, Doc: Am I gonna die?"

Dr. Raj got a vexed expression on his face. He looked genuinely perturbed. "You better not die on me!" he said sternly, as if he were a drill sergeant giving an order. "If you die, it will disprove my most important theory, and set my research back at least a year! For you to die would be exceedingly inconsiderate! So don't you dare!"

* * *

That night in Georgetown's tastefully and impressively ornate Gaston Hall on the third and fourth floors of the stately Healy Building, Mad should have felt like he was experiencing a moment of triumph. How many men at age 27 were already welcomed back to their *alma mater*s as featured speakers and honored guests? And especially in such a magnificent setting! The hall held perhaps 500 people, with a balcony in back. The lighting and decor somehow made the room seem emotionally warm. (Mad wasn't a particularly visual person, so he couldn't say exactly why this was so, but he felt it to his bones.) And all around the walls, at one level, were the crests of other Catholic colleges. At another height, the walls were adorned with marvelous quotations from the world's greatest sages. Plutarch. Socrates. Vergil. Aquinas.

But Mad was shaken. He had been told he had the same syndrome that almost certainly killed both his father and his grandfather. He had a doctor who was brilliant but also perhaps an oddball, one who seemed more interested in him as a specimen for research than as a patient to be nurtured.

And somehow it was all tied in with sex, a subject that was proving increasingly problematic. For him, sex and guilt had never been part of the same universe. He always had enjoyed himself to the fullest extent possible, with only two rules: First, as a single man, always use protection; second, in a marriage, remain faithful. During marriage, faithfulness was part and parcel of a sacrament. Even as libertine as he was, Mad always took seriously the Ten Commandments, and he considered adultery a grievous sin.

Claire had been his only committed relationship, and then his wife. With Claire alive and part of his life, he had never been tempted by anybody else. He had loved her so deeply that he gladly honored her commitment to stay pure until marriage, and within marriage their wholesome passion had never waned.

But now, even though he was widowed and uncommitted to anybody in particular, the tabloids were treating him as some kind of sleazebag. Then, today, Dr. Raj told him his weird blackouts – his "*ADZ sleep*" – also were a by-product of sex. For Mad, ever since his first experience with Grace, sex (except with Claire) had always been a crutch, a balm that required little emotion from him but that soothed him by reassuring him of his desirability and thus, in some sense, of his own worth.

And his book was getting bad reviews and its sales were mediocre, and his friends on the MMW board were at least partly estranged, and almost all sides of the political and religious spectrum (not to mention some creeps in the media) were taking potshots at him. Nothing much seemed to be going right, and so the thought of an appearance in Gaston Hall seemed not triumphant, but daunting.

Thusly disturbed, Mad felt exceedingly nervous until he suddenly found solace as, led by Shiloh and by his university hosts, he entered the auditorium from a rear hallway to avoid what he'd been told was a throng outside the main entrance. He noticed on the wall a couple of the quotations, and as he walked to the stage, he tried to remember one that had always inspired him, that he remembered as being somewhere towards the back of the hall.

Oh yeah: Now he remembered. It was a line from Dante. "Stand firm as the tow'r that never shakes it top, whatever wind may blow."

Yes, Mad thought, he just needed to stand firm. He just needed to keep his wits and his faith. If he did that, he'd do just fine.

Mad's resolve was tested quickly, however. As it turned out, his return to campus had caused great controversy – more so with outside agitators than with Georgetown students themselves. Some wacked out protest group or other – something like "Male Feminists Against Global Warming Economic Rape of Universal Health Care Rights" – had held its "Million Word March" on the Capitol the previous weekend, with hundreds or at least dozens of demonstrators daring to face the hegemonic powers of tens of thousands of bored Washington commuters. As many as 50 or 60 of the protesters hadn't yet been able to borrow money for bus fare back to their global villages. With nothing better to do, they had congregated at Mad's speech at Georgetown in order to protest his rumored habit of cavalier assaults against female dignity and his infamous attacks against Clintonian village-building. None of them had tickets to the Gaston Hall event, so they milled around the foyer and the great stone stairwell, complaining about the lack of closed-circuit monitors and chanting slogans against abuse of differently cultured sensibilities. Universally gaunt, goateed, and in baggy olive drab, they made for quite a sight.

The primary influence of the protesters, at least at first, was to raise the nervous-energy level (and the barely-post-adolescent excitement level) of the ticketed students inside Gaston Hall. In a good-natured sort of way, a number of the student Hoyas were, if not actually rowdy, at least guilty of somewhat rambunctious lèse majesté.

Mad delivered a well-crafted, if overly erudite, speech that wove his major themes around some kind words for Georgetown professor Jack Haught, the favorite of Mark Mariasson's, and Thomas King, S.J., who is the nation's premier scholar of Teilhard de Chardin. To give Mad credit, his speech went over fairly well with the majority of the audience. But with the nervous energy in the auditorium, combined with the fact that Mad himself was still almost young enough to still be a grad student, erudition didn't stand much of a chance of winning the day. In the Q&A part of the event that followed Mad's speech, the very first student questioner – a real smart-ass probably trying to impress his girlfriend with his risqué wit – went straight to the collegians' always-favorite topic of sex.

"Mad – I mean Mr. Jones – you spoke a lot tonight about the theology of evolution, and creativity in what you call the noosphere, or whatever that word is," the student said, trying to sound serious while not-quite-successfully hiding a smirk. "Well, as all of us know, you can't have creative evolution without procreation, and you can't have procreation without sex … [a few guffaws from fellow students] … and as we all know, the tabloids have reported at length upon your rumored exploits in that regard.… [more guffaws] …. So since you're such a ladies' man, and since you supposedly were such a stud back when you were a student here, I was wondering if you could give us guys some advice on where are the best places on campus to 'score,' and how to get girls to go there?"

Near bedlam. Students gasping for breath amidst their laughter. Stricken looks from both the student host for the event and the faculty sponsor, both heretofore looking and acting very officious up on stage. And Mad, sex already on his mind in the context of a potentially deadly hormonal imbalance, feeling suddenly like the guy being pinned to the wall by a circus' knife-thrower.

Still, Mad tried to maintain control. Waving the two event hosts off with an "I'll handle this" hand motion, Mad took the microphone. "Maybe there's a serious question in there somewhere," he said. "You know, my philosophy has always been that sex lives should remain private. … [then, trying to get the audience on his side with a resort to collegiate humor:] …. And besides, even if I were such a Don Juan, I'd never answer that question. If all of us ladies' men revealed our secrets, how could we maintain our advantage?"

A few guys in the audience began whooping and hollering. A campus security audience outside the hall opened the doors a few inches to see what was causing all the racket. The raggedy demonstrators, sensing a chance to hear what was going on inside, crowded closer to the doors.

The next person at the Q&A microphone, one of those earnest girls to whom all issues are intensely moral, tried to bring the discussion to a more serious plane.

"Okay, well, I was going to ask something else, but, well, seeing as how the topic is sex, well, in the midst of all the smirking from the last questioner there really is a serious issue," she said, long-windedly. "What I mean is that this isn't all a joke. Some of us think that making love is a serious moral issue. How can you, who supposedly are a religious leader, ever expect to be an influence for a disciplined faith when you so obviously can't be disciplined yourself in your sex life? I mean, even if you acknowledge that it's tough to avoid sex before marriage, shouldn't there at least be an attempt to keep it within a somewhat committed relationship?"

(More hooting from some of the less mature audience members. "You can commit to my eight inches, baby!" yelled one guy.)

Mad, sweating, tried to answer the girl with respect. "You know," he said, "I think too many people talk way too much about sex and religion, as if all of religion boils down to whether and with whom somebody has sexual relations. I think there's only one thing clear, at least for Christians and Jews, about when sex is definitely not kosher. 'Thou shalt not commit adultery.' That's very clear. If you're married, and you stray, you have sinned. But I can't find anything in the Bible that tells us, or at least that specifically says to *men*, because there are Biblical double standards for women unfortunately, nothing that tells men that you shall not get laid before marriage or after you are widowed or after your wife has divorced you against your will. I'll respect everybody that abstains, but if I choose not to abstain, that's nobody's business but mine."

More hooting and hollering. An angry murmur from the mostly male feminists outside at the mention of double standards for men and women. Shiloh, previously standing placidly at the base of the stage, now straightened nervously as he sensed trouble outside.

The girl at the microphone wouldn't move aside but insisted on asking a follow-up question: "You almost sound like you think women are just there to be used and discarded, without any regard to moral considerations. Are you saying that the Bible says that men can do whatever they want?"

This was a weakness in Mad's moral universe. Ben had been distracted and offered little explicit guidance; and Daddy Lee, Mad's role model, had been the prototypical tomcatting cavalier. And now he had a doctor who was telling him his own sex drive was a health risk, or somesuch. What he said to answer the girl came out in a way he had not intended.

"Well, no, we can't do whatever we want. We can't just screw around until it kills us." (More bedlam, and some angrier murmurs from outside the door.) "And it's also not like women are victims in all of this. It's not like all sex is rape; and, for that matter…."

The feminists outside could take it no longer. Already a grumpy lot because their weekend march had earned almost no media notice, they now were being afflicted with an obviously patriarchal troglodyte. "HEY EVERYBODY!" yelled one to his scraggly compatriots. "LET'S GO INSIDE!"

With that, he rushed the door as if he were wired on too many Ritalins chased with too much cappuccino. The security guard stopped him with a perfectly executed forearm shiver. At the sight of the violence, about a dozen others charged the door, and the others, needing to release their pent-up earth-loving frustrations, followed like angry lemmings. They overwhelmed the security guard and burst through the doors, where three more were felled by a flying tackle from an alert Shiloh. But the others just jumped right over the top of the Shiloh pile and, not knowing what else to do, rushed the stage.

Mad's "flight-or-fight" mechanism told him to flee. But the stage-rushers came from his right, on a line that cut off his access to the official back exit. No matter: Mad knew another way. Behind the piano at the back of the stage risers, to his left (and the audience's right), a secret doorway opened onto one of the narrowest, spookiest, darkest winding stairwells anybody could imagine. A friend from the campus service fraternity, Alpha Phi Omega, had shown him the secret stairway back during his student days. Mad turned and ran four steps, dove under the piano, kicked open the almost-hidden door, and dropped down into the stairwell, closing the door behind him. To most of the confused and riled-up audience, it seemed as if Mad had virtually vanished into thin air.

In the back of the auditorium, Jock clicked away on his camera for all he was worth, as did two student photojournalists. Also writing notes at a rapid clip was an on-campus stringer for the *Washington Post*.

Less than 30 seconds later, a dust-covered Mad emerged two floors below onto the blocked-off street that ran beside the Healy Building. Heart pounding, still in full flight, he ran for all he was worth across Healy Circle, through the campus gates, and down 'O' Street, not stopping for breath until about five blocks later. His hotel was only another three blocks after that, and Mad kept walking briskly until he was all the way back in his room. There, still in his business suit, he sat in the tub and turned on the shower to a lukewarm temperature. Almost as if flashing back to his week in the psych ward, he curled up into a fetal position. Within 15 minutes, water still beating down, he slept.

Chapter Six

Most of the male feminist goofballs managed eventually to melt away into the night, although six of them were detained and turned over to metro police. Shiloh emerged from the bedlam in Gaston Hall mostly unscathed, but furious and confused by Mad's disappearing act. Back at the hotel, he convinced the manager on duty that there might be a medical emergency, and so was able to be let into Mad's room. Relieved beyond measure when he was able to rouse Mad from the shower, Shiloh took a stern tone once Mad dried off and emerged from the bathroom.

"Mad, my friend, you have some real problems," Shiloh said. "When we get home from this trip, I'm gonna insist that you take one major big vacation. You're losing control, Mad, losing control. And although you won't tell me what's going on with this doctor-guy you saw today, I don't think it's just your health, Mad. You're losing touch with the Lord, Mad. I think you oughtta have a long talk with Father Vignelli. I really do, my friend. You're in bad shape."

* * *

The next day, Mad's frame of mind improved as he reverted to a practice he had enjoyed immensely during college: tour guide. Leaving their D.C. hotel early in the morning, he and Shiloh first drove out to Orange, Virginia to James Madison's old home, Montpelier. "My father was a devotee of Madison," he told Shiloh. "That's where I got my name. His 250th birthday is coming up in March, and I've heard the folks who run this place are doing a great job getting the old mansion back in tip-top shape."

He had heard correctly.

From Montpelier, he and Shiloh drove to Monticello, where Thomas Jefferson's genius emanated from every nook and cranny.

"Here's what gets me," Shiloh said, after marveling at the dumb waiter and the letter-copying machine and the rest of Jefferson's inventions. "To listen to all of the black leaders these days, all of us black people are supposed to despise Madison and Jefferson and all those guys because they all owned slaves. But I can't despise them. I respect them. After all, look what they created. They founded a country, the first one in the world, whose very existence was based on freedom and equality. These guys may not have been strong enough to apply their own ideals to black people, but by founding a country specifically based on those ideals, they set the stage for us all to be free. With no Jefferson, no Madison, no Declaration, no Constitution, there would have been no independent union for Lincoln to preserve, no ideals he could call on to free the slaves. These men founded the nation I love. They did the best they could, and what they did is better than just about anywhere on Earth. These guys are heroes in my book. They were flawed heroes, but still heroes. After all, the Good Book tells us that all of us are sinners. Who am I to judge them for the good they failed to do? Far as I'm concerned, I should praise them for the good they did do, with the good Lord's blessing and surely His guidance as well, and I'll let the Lord worry about the rest."

* * *

Speaking at the University of Virginia that evening, Mad was ready to spring a long-planned surprise. This is how he began his speech:

"In Wisconsin folks tell of Vince Lombardi, Bart Starr, and frozen endzones. The British talk of the days of blood, toil, tears and sweat, or, among the truly romantic ones, of a round table and a Holy Grail. Somewhere within each of these tales lies historical truth, but also within them lie truths that have little or nothing to do with what the intelligentsia call history. The communities that remember these stories and pass them on to succeeding generations do so less to preserve the facts (though that is a consideration) than to communicate feeling and meaning. The events of the memories possess importance in themselves, but also beyond themselves. For a community to exist, it must have a common memory, a shared history which originally drew it together; to continue as a community it must ascribe some ongoing meaning to that collective past which still has meaning in the present. Otherwise, the community becomes something else altogether – a collectivity without anything other than material bonds.

"The Christian community, which is what I have spent the last two and a half years speaking and writing about, has a familiar and sacred common memory. It is a memory of a story, and an ongoing reality, that stresses sacrifice and redemption, life springing from death, hope from despair. It is a memory and a message that is renewed in each generation, and that will always be renewed as long as we act with courage and an acceptance of joy and a willingness to evolve within the guidance of God's will.

"And there will be plenty more to say, including tonight, about that Christian community, about Christian beliefs and Christian imperatives for action. When I finish talking tonight, I'll gladly take questions on my views on all those matters.

"**But!** – Yes, there is a 'But.' The 'But' tonight is that I have a message that is only tangentially related to these concerns of faith. It is related only in this sense: It is related in that part of the Judeo-Christian ethic is the importance of giving something back to the communities which spawned us, the communities that have given us – just as the Lombardi Packers gave to Green Bay – a memory and a meaning beyond ourselves.

"Tonight, I come to repay an obligation.

"As you all know, my first name is Madison. My father named me after James Madison, who was for decades the closest political confidant of, and indeed at times the co-planner of this very university with Thomas Jefferson, whose vision and love created this very University of Virginia to be a cradle of learning. My father named me Madison because, as a graduate student at Jefferson's university, he devoted his Ph.D.

dissertation to the political thought of James Madison. You cannot know Madison without knowing Jefferson, and you cannot know Jefferson without knowing Madison. And, most importantly, you cannot fully appreciate and celebrate being an American without appreciating and celebrating the work that Jefferson and Madison did to found the American nation.

"As a nation, our memory and our meaning is and always must be suffused with a sense of who Jefferson was and who Madison was, and of the ideals that animated them.

"For me, personally, I owe a great debt to this university of Jefferson's, almost as great a debt as I owe to my *alma mater* Georgetown, whose charter was signed by then-President Madison. Not only did the University of Virginia provide a place of learning for my late father, but it provided for my education and development as well.

"You all have heard the rumors, and I'm here to tell you tonight that in part, and only in part, the rumors are true: After my father's death, and in my father's honor, my immediate financial well-being was secured through the efforts of some gentlemen of U.Va. My impression is that they are among the most honorable of men, but I know very little more about them than any of you do. You know them as the 'Crazy Eights' society, and my impression is that they give and give and give to this university community in ways always designed to preserve the memory and meaning of Jefferson's vision...."

With that mention of the "Eights," the mime made the appearance he had been planning for. Dressed as a black 8-ball, he rolled out on stage just in front of Mad's podium, as if to indicate (or so he planned) that this topic of Eights would put Mad "behind the Eight-ball." Jock, standing off to the side of the front row, panama hat perched on his head, was quick enough with his camera to snap a photo at just the right angle and moment. But security personnel for the event were not amused, and they rapidly cornered the mime and led him from the hall to the sound of great laughter.

Mad couldn't help laughing, too. When order was finally restored, he looked down at his text and said, "Aw, hell, this is too damned ponderous. So let me get to the point: I don't know who the members of the Crazy Eights are, so I cannot repay them directly for their past kindness. But now that my non-profit corporation is earning lots of money to give to charities, I prevailed upon my board to make a contribution to this place of memory and meaning called U.Va."

From his suit pocket, Mad withdrew a bank check.

"As of this moment, I begin endowing a scholarship for a graduate student here at the University of Virginia, one every two years, whose chosen course of study involves research with the aim of explicating, in at least a mostly positive light, the political thought of James Madison. At Jefferson's university, homage should be paid to Jefferson's greatest friend and ally. This check is written to the university in the sum of 108 thousand dollars."

Watching on closed-circuit TV from a special campus hideaway, a very surprised "Colonel" began to weep. He wept so joyfully that he lost his breath, and his heart started rebelling. Fortunately, The Colonel had his heart pills with him. The nitroglycerine nipped the heart attack in the bud. But, as a precaution, he spent the rest of the night in the hospital.

* * *

The next morning, as Shiloh nervously read a magazine in the waiting room, Mad was ushered back into the inner sanctum of Dr. Raj's office. The doctor was rubbing his hands together gleefully. "I am so glad you came to me, young Mr. Jones, so very glad to find you. All my tests have confirmed that you have just the problem I need for my research! You are a wonderful freak of nature!"

This was hardly reassuring to Mad. He wanted to be cured, not be a curiosity.

"Here's what you are to do," continued Dr. Raj excitedly. "In a few minutes, the nurse will be in to hook you up to lots of wonderful tubes and monitors. Very good monitors. And we have secured a young volunteer to sit across from you and be connected to other devices. She does not know why she is there. She will be in the room with you for an hour. You may talk with her, you may read, you may do whatever you want, but you may not make sexual advances towards her. You may not make romance with her. You are to be friendly, but not *friendly*, if you know what I mean."

"But, Doctor, what's the point of all this?" asked Mad.

"I will gladly explain it all as soon as the experiment is over!" exclaimed the doctor, again rubbing his hands with anticipation as he exited the room.

Sure enough, a few minutes later an elderly nurse escorted into the examination room a rather heavyset, plain-faced college student named Jackie. Mad and Jackie were dutifully introduced, and then each placed in comfortable armchairs about ten feet apart. As they made some small talk, the nurse bustled around, poking and prodding them and hooking up a series of high-tech-looking machines. Finally, turning a few final knobs, the nurse said the doctor would be back in about an hour – and she left.

"So what's this all about?" asked Jackie brightly.

"Damned if I know," said Mad, a trifle frustratedly.

For some reason, Jackie found Mad's pique attractive. She found herself shifting her weight so she could lean forward towards him.

"Say….," she said. "You look familiar. Haven't I seen you somewhere before? Or maybe at least seen your picture? You're some kinda guy in the news, aren't you?"

For the next hour, Jackie did her damnedest to keep Mad engaged in conversation. Mad had seen this all before: the widened pupils, the tilt of the head, the distracted playing with her hair. To be polite, he did the best he could to seem interested in Jackie and her yammering. But he found her tiresome, ignorant, and shallow. It was with great relief that he heard Dr. Raj's footsteps outside the door and then the door handle turning.

"Yes, very good, very good indeed, oh yes, this is wonderful," the doctor kept repeating as he went about unhooking the two patients from their "tubes and monitors." Turning to Jackie, he said, "Young miss, I thank you very much. The nurse will have your check for you for serving as my guinea pig this morning. Yes, thank you; you have been a very good specimen indeed!"

Long story short, Dr. Raj explained to Mad that these final tests confirmed the doctor's hypotheses. Mad's hormonal imbalance was acute, and it was quite rare. Over the long term, it could be deadly – but probably not in the next few years. In the meantime, what was worrisome was not the ADZ sleep itself, but the transition back into full consciousness. Mad didn't fully understand the doctor's explanation, but he latched onto the simple advice offered: "Always take two aspirin – no, make that three aspirin – the morning after you have sex," he said. "That will thin your blood, and so your heart-rate rising again when you come out of your trance will be less likely to do the damage of which I have spoken!"

But the doctor insisted on remaining mysterious about the point of Jackie's presence in the testing room.

"There are two things you must understand," he said. "One is that I must run six more months of drug-testing on my laboratory rats before I can test it on humans. If you so desire, and if you so sign the release papers, I want you to be my first human subject for my wonderful new drug. That will be in six months, I assure you – plenty of time to head off the accumulated dangers of your syndrome.

"The second thing you must understand is that there is a related phenomenon which involves how the women respond to you. Nobody else knows about this phenomenon. I cannot tell you about it yet, because you may spill the beans! Some other scientist might steal my thunder! Somebody else may steal my patents! Somebody else might cheat me out of my rightful credit and my rightful money that comes from my discovery!

"Also in six months, just about the time I can begin testing my drug on you, my paper on this related phenomenon will come out in a prestigious medical journal. My paper has already been tentatively accepted; this test today with Miss Jackie is my final proof. Once the journal is ready to publish, then I can tell you the import of this related phenomenon! Only six months. It will not be long!"

Try as he might, Mad could not get Dr. Raj to divulge anything more.

But before the scientist dismissed Mad for good, Mad insisted that he answer one other question that in the previous two days had been weighing on his mind. "You know how you said that my high-ADZ syndrome probably killed my father and my grandfather?"

"Yes," said Dr. Raj.

"Well, it occurs to me, what about my mother?" Mad asked. "And my wife? Could this have anything to do with them dying while pregnant or giving birth?"

Dr. Raj was uncharacteristically gentle.

"I'm afraid so, Madison. You see, if the baby inherits this high level of ADZ, and the woman is not accustomed to such high levels in her own system, then I can theorize that it would be highly possible that a sudden burst of ADZ *from* the baby, through the umbilical chord, *to* the mother, could shock her system so much that she has a hemorrhage."

Mad was crushed. Inwardly inconsolable, in fact. Finally, with all the paperwork signed, he was allowed to leave the offices to where a nervous Shiloh paced around the waiting room.

"Well, my friend?" Shiloh asked, noticing that Mad looked horribly pale.

"I killed my own mother," Mad said. "Shiloh, I killed my own mother, and then I killed Claire!"

* * *

In the next week, Mad was all over the headlines again. The protesters' stage-rush at Georgetown (coupled with Mad's mysterious vanishing act), the mime's rolling 8-ball at Virginia, the donation to U.Va. in the context of paying homage to a secret society (which, by conventional media wisdom, *must* by its very nature be racist, sexist, elitist and homophobic, not to mention proto-fascist and just plain icky): All made for good, off-beat copy to relieve the monotony of reporting on Al Gore's "lockbox" and George W. Bush's "fuzzy math."

Then, of course, these stories were topped off by Jock's new article in the weekly *Zodiac*: not only a highly creative re-telling of the college-speech controversies, but also a shocking photograph through a window of two bare and apparently writhing upper torsos, with Mad's profile clearly recognizable. "PREACHER CAUGHT IN FLAGRANTE!" screamed the headline. "*Mad passion reigns!*" read the subhead.

To make matters worse, the day after *The Zodiac* hit the supermarkets checkout aisles, the web site was struck four more times by the anonymous message that "Mad muss die."

Mad felt like cornered quarry, with a flock of vultures circling above, a precipice ahead and, in his soul and behind his back, nothing but seas of quicksand.

He also felt tremendously let down. He expected gratitude for his donation to U.Va., especially from The Colonel. Instead, his gift had been met only with silence.

Result: Not since his days in the psych ward had Mad been so depressed, so world-blackeningly distressed, so empty. Bouts of self-pity alternated for several days with episodes of rage. His mood only worsened on October 13, 2000, a Friday. Mad *hated* Fridays the 13th. So when he read in *The Metropolitan Daily* that a House Republican leader, whose two political bases were the religious right and a group of multi-national corporations, had complained that the media were always "tarring conservatives with the same brush used for charlatans like Madison Jones," Mad tracked down the reporter to vent. A small story in the next day's paper dutifully reported Mad's retort that the congressman in question was undeserving of respect because the congressman "worshipped nothing but the Mammon of corporate whoredom." The remark had the element of truth, but all it served to do was to alienate yet another powerful group of public actors.

"Mad, son, you're in a bad way," said Father Vignelli when Mad reluctantly picked up the phone at his house. "Don't even try to argue with me; I'm coming over there within the hour. You know as well as I do that we need to talk."

"Yeah, whatever," said Mad. "Everybody else is yelling at me; you might as well come here and yell at me too."

* * *

"Our Father, Who art in heaven, hallowed be Thy name...." began the Jesuit, kneeling in Mad's living room with the hand of a likewise kneeling Mad gripped in his own. "Thy kingdom come, Thy will be done, on earth as it is in heaven...."

Upon arrival at Mad's house, Father Vignelli had insisted that before either one of them said anything else, they ought to begin with a prayer. "No matter how bad your life may seem to be going," the priest said, "the crux of everything is still the necessity of a right relationship with God."

Mad stifled the urge to say something smart-assed such as *"Yeah, well, what about God's duty to work at maintaining a right relationship with me?"*

"Mad, young friend," said Peter once the Lord's Prayer was completed, "I'm afraid that we're losing you. Or, what's worse, I'm afraid that you are losing yourself. And your friends are afraid of the same thing. They've spoken to me about this, Mad. They're worried about you. They're afraid you're about to implode."

Mad looked, somewhat fearfully, into the Jesuit's face.

"Peter," he said. Mad swallowed hard. He tried to say something else, but instead merely swallowed hard again. Finally, in a sudden blurt: "Peter, I killed Claire."

Haltingly, Mad explained what Dr. Raj had told him – or at least Mad's interpretation thereof. And despite all of the priest's efforts at logic ("Mad, *you're* not responsible for the effects of a genetic abnormality"), Mad held tightly to the notion that if he hadn't been born, his mother would still be alive, and that if he hadn't wooed Claire, then Claire would still be happily brightening the atmosphere of every life she touched.

"Don't you see?" he said to Peter. "If it's hereditary, then it's the sins of the fathers being visited upon the sons. But within that whole concept of sins repeated throughout the generations is the notion that the sons themselves are somehow culpable as well by virtue of themselves becoming fathers and passing the sins onto new generations still. It's up to me to break the chain, and instead all I did was keep the chain of death alive." (Mad was too distraught to realize how oxymoronic that sounded.) "That's why everything I do gets twisted and misinterpreted and turns to harm rather than to good: because I'm cursed with sin and haven't had the humility to admit it. I keep blathering about being courageous enough to transcend a jerky God, when instead it's I who am the Jerk! That's why everybody turns against me: because I don't deserve to be liked, because I'm a carrier of rottenness!"

Father Vignelli recognized this as the voice of a severe depression, the reason-twisted cry of a soul-sick man. So intent was Mad on self-blame, on turning anger inward, that no compliment and no reason would be able to penetrate his self-loathing cocoon. But Peter also knew that somewhere, somehow he had to prevent the cocoon from calcifying, had to at least open some cracks in the cocoon's shell – because, as a wise older Jesuit had once told him, "God works in the cracks."

"Madison," he said to the far younger man. "Listen to me. Whatever else you are or have been wrong about, there is one thing you are right about. There is one part of your message that not even you at your most mule-headed can deny. It is a part of your preaching that is utterly sound, straight out of Holy Scripture. It's that part where you said that God wants us to be courageous. He wants us to be strong and of good courage. He wants us never to give up. Giving up is a sin. Suffering produces endurance, and endurance produces character and then hope, and hope WILL NOT disappoint us, not in the long run. Whether or not God is a jerk – which I say He most certainly is not – and whether or not Madison Jones is a jerk, the fact remains that Jesus suffered and died and was redeemed so that all of us who are willing to follow His cross may find the courage and the faith ourselves to accept God's ultimate, redemptive grace. Go ahead and blame yourself for what's not your fault, if that's what you want. But don't you dare compound the sin by making yourself so weak that God can't find the strength in you, so weak that He can't find the courage in you, to help you lift yourself through His grace to His everlasting love."

Even for Mad, who had been immersed in all these themes now for 2½ years, the density of all this theologically tinged language was dizzying. He wanted to argue with Father Vignelli, but his depression-racked brain was unable to make the intellectual effort required. The result was that Peter's words went unchallenged, and thus never effectively refuted. Instead, the unchallenged words just latched onto Mad's cocoon and started eating away at it, creating tiny little cracks through which both right reason and faith might somehow find a way inside. Mad didn't know it at the time, but those words and those cracks held the promise, or at least the remote possibility, of his salvation.

"Peter," Mad said finally. "I'm exhausted. I just want the world to go away. I need some time off. I need to cancel all my obligations."

Mad was surprised to see Peter nod his head. "I do believe you're right, Mad. I'll talk to Becky; I'll handle everything. You just take it easy, maybe make a reservation for the Bahamas or something. As Mary Magdalene said in Jesus Christ Superstar, 'let the world turn without you tonight.' Let it turn without you for a whole month, maybe even 40 days. If you won't trust God to make things come out right, at least trust me to keep them from totally falling apart. Then, maybe, we'll see where we can go from there."

Albeit with a dull and pained expression, Mad nodded in the affirmative. Mary Magdalene had been right about Jesus, and Father Vignelli was right about Mad: Let the world turn without him for a while.

Chapter Seven

M. Magdalene, however, wasn't at all happy. Writing in the chat room for the first time in more than a year, she said she was outraged by Mad's promiscuity. "I'm no prude," she wrote, "not in the slightest. But there's a difference between even casual sex based on strong mutual attraction and the kind of rapacious, serial, utterly self-indulgent sex that it now is clear that Mad engages in. Mad uses women and throws them away; he objectifies them in a way that shows an obnoxious disrespect. For those who don't recognize my moniker because I haven't been on site very often, you all should know that I was one of Mad's biggest and earliest boosters from the very start, within a day or so after this chat room started. And I used to laugh at reports of Mad's romantic adventures. He's a single man, I thought, so why is this anybody else's business? But now that it's clear what his m.o. is, and just what a woman-using slimeball he is, I've had it with him. And now I hear an announcement that he's gonna run and hide from all his bad publicity and cancel all his public appearances for 40 days. What a coward!"

Reading this, Mad was crushed. Even though she was far from a frequent contributor, the anonymous M. Magdalene had for the better part of three years been a tremendous emotional comfort for Mad. He felt reassured just by knowing that there was some woman out there who, based apparently on his words alone, had been so strongly attracted to his ideas that she supported him unwaveringly. (His idealization of M. Magdalene almost assuredly also had much to do with the fact that her first words of support had come when he was at his lowest ebb, less than a couple of weeks after Claire's death. Unexpected comfort always means more when it comes at a time of greatest need.) Now, just when life seemed bleaker than it had since the tragedies of 1998, the attack from such a formerly staunch ally cut all the more deeply and painfully.

"Be silenced, Whore!" wrote back Affirmed in a fury, obviously falling prey to the unbiblical myth that wrongly conflated the real Mary Magdalene with the woman Jesus famously saved from a stoning. "I am only weeks away from revealing the final blessed truth about Mad Jones and lack only one final piece for proving the puzzle. Ye who desert him now will be all the more damned because you are rejecting him just when the time of testing is almost at hand!"

Mad didn't know what Affirmed was talking about and took little comfort in his message. By now, Mad had pretty much concluded that Affirmed, whoever he might be, was a little cracked.

What was worse was that Affirmed's voice in support of Mad represented an increasingly minority position. It seemed as if only about one in every six or seven entries in the chat room were messages in Mad's favor. FD Thom again had dropped the "F" (for "Formerly") to become, this time seemingly permanently, Doubting Thom. "I want to give credit where it's due, and Mad does deserve credit for the last few years of raising some important issues and leading us to re-examine aspects of faith," wrote D Thom. "But all along I've been going back and forth as to whether Mad's leadership could be fully trusted. Now it's clear, unfortunately, that even if his motivations are generally good, he's too flawed a character, too volatile and too personally undisciplined, to lead a faith-centered movement."

Somebody named "Bingomaster" chimed in with: "Well, *Duh*! When are you crackers going to figure out that ALL faith is a crock of shit?!"

At this affront, Defender was outraged. "I wonder if you'll still feel that way when you're roasting in Hell?" he wrote. "How dare you denigrate our faith. How dare you denigrate the Lord? The truth is that D Thom is right this time, or at least mostly so. There ARE serious problems with Mad's message, but the biggest problem is the messenger. Mad Jones has always been off base. He's always been too flawed. I almost feel sorry for him. He actually seems to mean well, but he's just a confused young man. Why did anybody ever take him seriously?"

* * *

Becky was furious with both Mad and Peter Vignelli. Mad's sudden decision to take more than a month off meant that she had to cancel three big planned speaking engagements, one each in Chicago, Detroit, and Minneapolis. By now, every event Mad did was planned down to the nth detail. And not only did the cancellations mean that a heck of a lot less money would be coming into MMW coffers, but it also meant a huge outlay of unrecoverable costs. Contracts had to be broken (and in a few cases bought out), fees still had to be paid and pre-paid tickets refunded. Contract-breaking also required more work by Mary's law firm, and those fees were far from inconsiderable.

Moreover, the bad publicity was adversely affecting Justin. Because the "spiritual" part of his "holistic" health program relied so heavily on Mad's theses, and was so advertised, Mad's fall in public favor had the effect of driving way down the market for Justin's offerings. It had already been bad enough that Mad had been pressuring Justin to alter Justin Time's program to keep up with Mad's ever-evolving theological message (and even, despite all of Justin's loyalty to him, threatening to withdraw permission for Justin to advertise any link between them at all). But now Mad's lack of emotional stability was harming the business that Justin had so painstakingly built. In short, Mad was hurting the man Becky loved.

For reasons of their own, Becky and Justin had remained discreet about their romance (Mad still had no clue about its existence), and the secrecy somehow had the effect of intensifying Becky's feelings for the little guy. It had taken her so long to appreciate Justin – how loyal he was, how sweet, how kind, how true – that something within her felt guilty for failing to more quickly reciprocate his devotion. She therefore was even more uncommonly sensitive to others' slights (or what she perceived as slights) of her boyfriend. Anything that hurt Justin infuriated her. Despite Peter's entreaties, therefore, Becky's emotional distance from Mad kept growing wider.

In order to keep the entire MMW enterprise from imploding, Becky did insist that whatever else Mad reneged on during his sudden sabbatical, he must continue doing the newspaper advice column. Fail in the commitment to the newspapers (and their readers), and Mad would lose all legitimacy whatsoever.

What Becky didn't know was that Peter now was helping Mad with the columns. The Jesuit also was spending plenty of time with Mad on the tennis court and especially on the golf course, carrying on subtly spiritual conversations between shots. The priest's goal was twofold: both spiritual rejuvenation for his young friend *and* theological refinement for Mad, almost surreptitiously, as well. In Peter's view, every theological phase Mad had gone through in the past few years had been exaggerated. Early on, the anger, the bitterness, and the rebellion in the theses had been overdone. Later, so too had been the insistence on an earthly joyfulness. And then had come the overkill of what at base were some useful ideas, namely the compatibility of science with religion and the whole "evolutionary, purposive universe" schtick of Pierre Teilhard de Chardin and other similar theorists and theologians. In all of this, even in Mad's original anger at God and his re-casting of Christ's role as "mediator," Father Vignelli found at least a bit of merit. But some of it truly was, in his mind, heresy. The "one true Catholic faith" demanded of him, a Jesuit, the continuing effort to save souls by drawing them back to God's revealed truth as passed down through His one true church by means of grace and apostolic succession.

In short, on essentials at least, Father Peter Vignelli was nudging Mad back towards orthodoxy.

"Great shot, old man!" said Mad on the day of Election Eve as he followed the flight of one of Peter's five irons towards the flag. And then, in what these days for him was a rare moment of levity: "Are you *sure* God doesn't give you a perfect golf swing as some kind of *quid pro quo* for all the other worldly pleasures you give up as a Jesuit?"

"Convert to Catholicism, Mad, and maybe the secret will be revealed!" laughed the priest.

* * *

Thanksgiving Day fell exactly 40 days after Mad's Vignelli-inspired decision to take a lengthy unscheduled vacation, and Becky and Mad had long planned a major patriotic rally at a high school football stadium in Baldwin County, Alabama, just on the other side of Mobile Bay. Mad's publisher had worked out a deal with the American Heritage Network for a live national broadcast of the rally, and a Vignelli-rejuvenated Mad actually felt real excitement, plus some nervousness, about the event.

Ever since his preparations for his early October trip to Washington, Mad had been on a patriotic kick inspired by the ideals of Madison and Jefferson and their fellow founders, and by his late father's devotion to the same. And now, with controversy raging about which presidential candidate, Al Gore Jr. or George W. Bush, had actually won the state of Florida and thus the whole election, Mad sensed a special need to strike up themes of praise for the American political system and reassurance about its ultimate workability. And all of this, naturally, he would try to accomplish with reference to the gifts bestowed on the country by divine providence.

Despite the Jesuit's spiritual ministrations, though, a psychologically improved Mad was still a Mad who was slightly blue and not quite fully confident. He was thus delighted, the night before the event, to see in the chat room a rare message from Jezebel?. "Hey, everybody, I just think it's great that Mad is going back in public tomorrow, and if he's reading this, I wish him the best!" she wrote. "He's come under a lot of fire in the past few months, but people should not forget all the good he's done in bringing skeptics and disaffected people back to God, not to mention all the money he's raised for charities. He certainly has had a big influence on my life for the better, and one of my biggest thanksgivings tomorrow will be to thank God for Mad's ministry."

"Wow!" Mad thought to himself. "Laura comes through for me again!"

Sure by now that Laura and Jezebel? were one and the same, Mad was not only touched but deeply moved. Every time he had needed a boost for the past three years, Laura or Jezebel had been there. At the Pontchartrain Hotel in New Orleans. Singing Counting Crows songs to him in his house. On "Acute Vision" when, in retrospect, she had treated his message just right even though he had at the time thought he wanted her to make the whole story go away. Definitely at his time of great peril when he had been in Spike Walters' cross hairs. And time and again, not super-often but always perfectly timed, in his chat room with Jezebel?'s comforting words.

Mad even thought to himself that maybe his intended new, post-Claire soul mate had been there right from the start. He determined to give Laura a call up in New York sometime real soon, perhaps even the upcoming weekend. Meanwhile, with Jezebel?'s encouragement, he felt far, far better about the next day's Thanksgiving rally.

* * *

Whatever Laura Green thought of Mad these days, though, she thought far more often and with far greater concentration about other things, with her career being Item Number 1. For the most part, it was going well. Now a semi-regular on "Hour of Truth," she was earning solid but unspectacular reviews from audiences, focus groups and, most importantly, the network brass. Her position at the network, therefore, wasn't tenuous, but it was also far from untouchable. It wasn't as strong, for instance, as that of the hotshot reporter she had dated so long whom she had finally married in June. She knew the network execs still considered him to have more star power than she did.

Which was a shame, because after all this time she had determined that he was an egotistical jerk. Ever since their wedding, she had become more and more put off by what she considered his interminable arrogance. Then again, she now considered that to be par for the course. Truth was, an overarching groupthink raged at the television network (and at several other networks as well). The orthodoxy was liberal, feminist, politically correct, multiculturalist. One of its tenets, subscribed to (at least for public consumption) even by the men, was that men generally were vermin unless their attitudes were regularly leavened by reproaches from women.

Laura had always been adept at adapting herself to the prevailing ethos of whatever culture she found herself in, and by now she had effortlessly adopted the requisite viewpoints to keep herself in step at the network. Problem was, because her personal vermin outranked her, she couldn't afford to ditch him right yet. The result was that most days now found her in a rather sour mood.

* * *

Eight thousand people turned out for Mad's event in Baldwin County. (Shiloh had been worried that the crowd might contain dangerous elements, but nothing disturbing occurred. Even the mime, who was in attendance wearing a turkey suit, behaved himself well.) Nielsen ratings would later show that another million people tuned into the small cable network to watch on TV. Mad did not disappoint. "George Washington first proclaimed Thanksgiving as a national holiday," Mad told everybody. "The man whose namesake I am, James Madison, was Washington's close ally in calling the constitutional convention and in pushing Washington's policies through the first-ever Congress. While neither one was particularly pious, both of them agreed that without divine providence, this great nation they had founded would never last. And both founders felt confident that providence had been and would continue to be forthcoming. Both felt that a strong United States would further God's purposes for mankind.

"Now, for many of you who have followed my speeches and writings for these past several years, you will recognize my assertion that, while God can be a jerk, he ultimately means to do, and will indeed, do good by us if we have faith, because his purposes are ultimately loving. This is a purposive universe, and we are all God's people.

"I'm here to tell you today that I believe with every fiber of my being that when God created this great land, and when he people it with freedom-loving leaders of great character such as Washington and Madison, God was acting out of His best self – or, in the vernacular, He was as far from being 'jerky' as a good and loving God can be. The creation of America was an example of God at his most perfect self acting through men who, though imperfect, were nevertheless far-more-than-usually enlightened.

"And what's going on with the presidential election right now isn't an example of those men's failure, but of their genius. There are no major riots in the street. There is confidence among the people that no matter who is finally declared the victor, this nation and its governmental system will continue without major upheavals. In short, there is a deep, if unverbalized, civic faith that prevails in our land, a faith born of more than two centuries of practicing the constitutional system that our forbears laid out.

"And those same founders, who knew well what they were doing, gave credit to God for our blessings and for His guidance. They knew that America could and would serve God's most loving purposes, and they gave thanks for it and declared the practice of Thanksgiving to be a national priority...."

And so, in fifteen more minutes of this kind of talk, did Mad meld his theses and his theological studies and his deep, abiding patriotism. He closed with a personal note: "Now as you probably know, this is my first event after more than a month off. My time off was, in effect, a sabbatical. During that month, I renewed myself spiritually, under the guidance of my friend, Father Peter Vignelli of the Society of Jesus. With his guidance, and your kind welcome today, I feel refreshed and renewed after a trying time. And if such renewal can happen for me, it can happen for this country for which we give thanks today. This election controversy is a time of trial, but it also can be time of renewal as we enter the *real* mathematical beginning, Year 2001, of a new millennium. Thanking God in advance for helping us make it such a time of renewal, let us move forward with purpose and with hope and with courage, as one nation under a God whom we never forget to thank."

Even Mad's most vociferous critics pronounced his words and performance a big and deserving success. And, basking in applause, Mad at least momentarily thought he had turned another corner and put the worst behind him. That weekend, he tried to call Laura in New York. He got a machine, and left a message, confident that she soon would call him back.

* * *

A week and a half later, on the first Sunday in Advent, December 3 of 2000, Affirmed posted a curious message in the Mad Religion chat room.

"Prepare ye the way!" he wrote. "Prepare ye the way, for The Word is coming!

"One year ago I wrote that a year from then – which means now – I would reveal the secret toward which my research and my faith were leading me. Today I am here to tell you that every piece of my hypothesis, with the sole exception of one, had fallen into place in the intervening year. Then, blessedly, the last piece came into place on Thanksgiving Day. The piece I had been missing was provided by Mad himself, by his own words, after his 40 Days away from the crowds.

"But now that all the pieces are in place, I realize that my secret revelation is too important to waste in a random chat room comment without advance fanfare. This new knowledge is too important to hide its light under a bushel. Let me say, too, to those who doubt: THIS IS BIG! It is the most important truth you will ever learn! Because it is so important, I have decided to set up an entire new web site dedicated to this truth, a web site with all the evidence and all the proof, a web site worthy of such important news. I mean no disrespect to this MMW web site, which is holy indeed, but it is clear that for this truth to be self-promulgated on Mad's own site would be inappropriate. It is for someone else, in this case me, to proclaim the ultimate truth that all of us on this site have been missing despite it being right before our eyes. And I want to put together the site in just the right way, with great care.

"So, therefore, I announce right now that on March 1 of 2001, a new web site will be launched, a web site that contains the ultimate truth while still paying homage to this MMW web site as the new site's progenitor. The new site's name will be taken from thesis 28: 'And God said: Yes.' In other words, God said: Affirmative. My name is Affirmed, and the site is affirmative, and it is inspired by Mad. As this current site is called 'Mad Religion,' my new site will be called 'Mad Affirmative.'

"So again, I announce: On March 1 of 2001, open your eyes to the new truth! Open your eyes to a web site that will announce the truth. Open your eyes to Mad Affirmative, and be enlightened, and thus be saved!"

Ever Faithful's response was brief and caustic. "Hey, Affirmed," he wrote, "you're a nutcase!"

* * *

Two weeks after that, the sicko returned to the chat room. "Mad muss die!" "Mad muss die!" "Mad muss die!" Eight different times during the course of one day, the message was repeated. All the web site's regulars, fans of Mad and critics alike, denounced the message, but it just kept coming. And it put a serious damper on what for a few weeks now had seemed to Mad to be a brightening outlook. Book sales, although nowhere near what they were for Mad's first effort two years earlier, had nevertheless picked up during the Christmas season. Crowds at Mad's two public appearances since Thanksgiving had been large and enthusiastic. Scandal and controversy again seemed to have left Mad and his ministry without any mortal wounds. And, although Laura still had not returned Mad's call, he felt sure in his bones that the two of them had a future together. So sure, in fact, that on his last two trips he had avoided his usual habit of picking up on a starry-eyed road groupie for some nighttime recreation. (As if to confirm Dr. Raj's diagnosis, Mad returned from his two sex-less trips without suffering ADZ-sleep incidents either time.)

On top of all that, the U.S. Supreme Court had finally ruled that the Florida Supreme Court had grossly exceeded *its* authority and, therefore, that all vote "recounts" must stop. In short, George W. Bush would be the next president – and, despite the unkind words about Mad several months earlier from the mouth of an officious Bush sokesman, Mad still had voted for Bush and was comfortable that Bush, Cheney, Powell, Rice and company would lead the country well.

In short, circumstances seemed to be lining up well to make Mad rather content. But then came the sicko with his threatening message, and it somewhat hobbled Mad's Christmas spirit.

* * *

Becky felt internally conflicted, greatly so, as Christmas rolled around. Her father had gotten it into his head that, tabloid tales of Mad's sex-capades notwithstanding, Becky and Mad were romantically attached. It was a prospect that gave him great pleasure. He had taken a shine to Mad; Mad's athleticism and charisma, even if a trifle offbeat, made him appear to Chet to be a real "man's man." Becky's ice-like mother, meanwhile, considered it a character flaw of Becky's that at nearly age 28 she remained unmarried, when so many lawyers and rich businessmen would obviously be thrilled to show off a wife with Becky's tremendous physical assets.

Yet Becky, to her own great surprise, had truly and deeply fallen in love with Justin. Justin treated her with respect and thoughtfulness, and a kindness so profound that it gave ample evidence of an abiding love. Not only that, but despite his small stature he was in better shape than any man she had ever known. There was a kinetic physicality about Justin that Becky had come to cherish.

Problem was, Becky was sure that neither of her parents would approve of Justin. He was too short, too quirky, too unrefined, too frenetic. Yet these were things she could not adequately explain to Justin. They had been together for more than half a year, and he wanted to meet her family, but she dreaded the introductions.

Not only that, but their "couple-hood" was still, quite awkwardly, a secret even to Mad and virtually everybody else they knew as well. They had kept it a secret for several reasons. Especially early on, when they were unsure (or at least Becky was) that their odd coupling would last, they thought it better to keep it under wraps so as not to raise expectations among those around them. They thought that Mad, particularly, would be so happy at their pairing that he might go overboard in trying, as it were, to help it along. And if Mad found out, and then they split up, it might send him back into a funk. Later, they together began to resent it when Mad threatened to disallow Justin from affiliating his successful holistic training program with Mad's "ministry." Justin still had trouble acknowledging to himself that Mad was anything other than perfect, but he deferred to Becky's judgment on the matter.

At first Justin had found the "cloak-and-dagger" nature of their romance a great game. Now, though, it was starting to gnaw at him. He wanted to show the world what a terrific woman he had won.

Result: Justin was deeply hurt when Becky did not invite him back to Houston for the holidays. She gave all kinds of excuses about how she was "on the outs" with, and embarrassed by the lack of warmth in, her family. She promised that within a few months she would introduce him. She said, though, that Christmas was just too stressful back home for her to be comfortable with him there. Christmas was always a disaster, she said, and she didn't want Justin to be "scared away from her" because of it.

So off Becky went, back to a mother who called her a slut and a loving but (unintentionally) overbearing father who was upset she hadn't brought Mad with her.

Finally, what Becky also didn't tell Justin (or anybody else) was that there were more problems with MMW's financial records. She couldn't understand what was going on, and she hoped to use her Houston sojourn, unpleasant as it might be, to figure a solution.

* * *

In his newspaper column and on his web site, Mad proclaimed a "special message for the last Christmas of the millennium." He wrote: "The millennium, the year 2001, is an arbitrary mathematical construct, without any religious significance. Apocalyptic visions now, just as they were last year, are misguided. God does not act on a human time schedule. Instead, what is important is what we commemorate today, namely the entering into our world, in human form, of the divine Word made flesh, the mediator and living sacrifice, Jesus Christ. The sufferings of Jesus would redeem us, and mutually redeem our relationship with God, so that we would have the courage and fortitude to bear our crosses for the ultimate glory God offers us through his grace. That offering comes again and again, and will come again for time immemorial, regardless of any trick of humanity's calendar. It is up to us to be lionhearted enough to accept that grace, knowing as we do that accepting grace without strings attached requires of us the humility, and the strength of character, to admit that grace is unearned. Yet, without this babe in the manger who always must be King in our hearts, that grace which is our salvation would remain ever unattainable, ever unavailable for our mortal souls. Unto us a child is born; unto us a king is given; and unto us a sacred mystery unfolds and evolves through time, beckoning us to follow its leads along that path which ends in the ultimate, all-enveloping love of God."

Responding in the chat room, though, M. Magdalene wrote: "Yeah, *right*. As if Mad Jones was interested in any path which leads anywhere other than to another piece of a$$!"

Chapter Eight

All the eights, and all the aces, were no longer available to grace the hands of The Colonel. The doctor told The Colonel that he had no more tricks up his sleeve. The Colonel's ticker, said the doctor, wouldn't hold out much longer. It was time for The Colonel to get his chips in order, because odds were he'd be cashing out soon. He might only have another eight weeks, or perhaps eight weeks and eight days; he almost certainly would not see another eight months. The Colonel was, after all, almost 80 years old, and he had enjoyed a blessed and happy life.

* * *

During an unpleasant time in Houston, Becky had come up with a plan to give herself time to solve the mystery of the disappearing funds. Henceforth, if everybody else agreed, the MMW board would meet only once per year instead of twice – and the meeting would be timed for the last weekend in April, to coincide with New Orleans' Jazz and Heritage Festival, only two hours away from Mobile. The Jazz Fest would give everybody a fun option either right before or right after the board meetings, and perhaps improve attitudes as well. Also, the weather would be nicer than it is on the Gulf Coast in either January or July, when the semi-annual board meetings were formerly held. She also told everybody that by doling out grants to charitable causes only every 12 months rather than every six, the total disbursements would be (obviously) twice as large – and thus twice as impressive when announced. It would provide an excellent PR bonanza. The more that MMW Corp.

could boast about its good works, the more support it would continue to attract for Mad's ministry.

What Becky didn't say, of course, was that by delaying the meeting until May, she also would have time to track the missing monies. The sums kept getting larger and larger, and she told Justin she was desperately concerned.

* * *

In early January, after Mad had left a half-dozen messages for her, Laura Green finally returned Mad's calls. She was married now (albeit not happily); and as for Mad, he had proven himself just another sex-hound on the make. Besides, she didn't see any new way he could further her career. Despite Mad's conviction that she was a stalwart friend and perhaps even in love with him, the truth was otherwise. Sure, Mad had been fun for a couple of nights, and he might vaguely mean well – and his non-profit business had raised a ton of loot for good causes – but really, that's about all there was to him. He was just another male. She had helped him, and he had helped her, and they had had a good time, and the equation was in balance with neither owing the other anything else.

What really galled her, though, was that Mad had left his messages *at her office*. Didn't the stupid bastard know that he wasn't exactly a favorite person around her network, and especially around the offices of "Hour of Truth"? Back when she had helped Mad set the trap for Spike Walters, she had cleverly and successfully foisted blame onto Martina Beritzky. But if word got anywhere beyond the phone operator that Mad was calling her, it might raise suspicions about their relationship. After she had worked so hard to climb the network ladder, the idiot in Mobile might topple the ladder from underneath her. So when she finally picked up the phone to call Mad, she was fuming.

Mad's cell phone wasn't on when she called. "Mad," she said, "this is Laura returning your calls. Look, Mad, I gotta tell you, you're sorta making me angry. Don't you know any better than to call me at work? Don't you know that you're a pariah around there? If you give somebody there the impression that we're friends, I'm up shit's creek! So don't call me there any more, okay? Whatever you want, please call my cell phone, not my office. If I can talk then, I'll tell you; if I can't, I'll call you back. But Jesus, Mad, use some common sense, okay?"

With that, Laura dictated her cell phone number and hung up.

When Mad retrieved her message, he was more than a little surprised by its tone. This sure didn't sound like the fresh-voiced Laura who had shown such devotion to him. Okay, so maybe he had screwed up by calling her at work. But where was the friendship, much less any sign of romantic inclinations? Mad was confused. He'd have to think on things some more before he tried her again.

* * *

Late January, a trip to Asheville, North Carolina. Right in the heart of Billy Graham country. Also, though, the home of a massive number of Bohemian young adults drawn to the area's mountains and rivers, or to the university community of UNC-Asheville. Plenty of ripe pickings if Mad were inclined to revert to old habits. He told himself he wouldn't do so – but then he spied a thin brunette with a runner's build, whose looks reminded him remarkably of Laura's, who obviously was vying for his attention. He told himself later that he really couldn't have resisted even if he had tried. Truth was, he hadn't tried very hard. As he had with so many other young women, he ended up with her that night.

Sure enough, after deplaning in Mobile the next day and returning to his house, Mad soon fell into another of his trances, his ADZ-sleeps, and this was perhaps his deepest one yet. More than three hours passed that for the life of him he just couldn't account for. Obviously, Dr. Raj was right – but damn the doctor anyway. This syndrome of Mad's was really getting worrisome. Why the hell should Mad wait another few months before the doctor provided him the experimental drug, or whatever it was? And what was Dr. Raj's other mysterious hypothesis? Mad wanted to know right now. Patience was not Mad's virtue.

* * *

The mime had made the journey to Asheville, but nobody paid the slightest bit of attention to him. He couldn't last like this much longer. Public acclaim for his artistry continued to elude him. He was growing increasingly bitter, and increasingly distrustful of the world at large.

What he knew he should do was something that he had trouble forcing himself to attempt. He knew, in his heart, that his salvation lay in his very possession, in the form of the business card of Jock from *The Zodiac*. But calling Jock would require that the mime talk. And as a mime, talking wasn't his strong suit. So the mime continued to fume, and continued to rehearse what he would say to Jock if he ever found the courage to call.

* * *

Peter Vignelli was becoming frustrated. He had grown so fond of Mad, so very fond of him, and he felt that his mentorship was doing Mad some good. Yet no matter how hard he tried, he couldn't quite bring Mad around to a recognition that the path to salvation lay in the One True Faith of the Catholic Church. What kind of Jesuit was he if he could be so obviously respected by his young charge, yet so unable to get him over the hump? Mad's theology was still too unorthodox, his sinfulness still too frequent, his penitence still too rare. Maybe, Peter thought, he might make some headway once Lent began. Maybe that penitent season would foment in Mad the kind of inner reflections that would lead him to make what Peter regarded as the final, essential leap of faith. Ash Wednesday was still more than three weeks off, on February 28. The Jesuit prayed that God would give him patience.

* * *

In early February, the sicko struck again. "Mad muss die." Seven times in the course of three days. Shiloh, whose job it was to protect Mad from the crowds, was becoming more and more concerned. "You've *got* to have this looked into!" he told Mad. "After so many of these messages, you have to consider this a real threat. I know you don't want me to do this, but it's my duty as a policeman to report threats like these to the authorities. Threats like these are a crime. It's time for the crime to be investigated. Mad, I'm going to tell the police chief, and I think he'll probably have to call in the FBI."

Mad thought Shiloh was overreacting, but he didn't try to stop his friend. Mad had other things on his mind. Valentine's Day was coming up, and he again was feeling Claire's absence like a deadly weight around his neck. He knew, in his heart, that Claire would want him to move on emotionally, to find himself a new love. But he remembered, so strongly, the love he had poured into the poem he wrote for Claire three Valentine's Days ago, and he remembered how wonderful it had been that night when he first felt his child move in Claire's belly. The pangs of his loss were coming back full force.

Even so, in the back of his mind Mad had an oddly insistent feeling that he and Laura were meant to be together. Ever since Laura's unexpectedly scolding phone message, Mad had avoided calling her back. But he still was convinced that her scolding tone was an aberration. Surely, he thought, she had proven time and again that she loved him.

Now that Mad was again missing Claire so fiercely, he was momentarily loath to contact Laura again. But "after Valentine's," he told himself. "After Valentine's, and before the 28th, I'll try Laura again. I think that's what Claire wants me to do."

The significance of the 28th was that it was the third anniversary of that awful early morning when Mad had awakened to a bed full of blood. Somehow, Mad felt it would be appropriate to explore this thing with Laura after the commemoration of Mad's highest high of Valentine's, but before the anniversary of his lowest low. In those two weeks, three years ago, Mad had been full of the sense of, full of the hope of, new beginnings. If Laura was indeed intended to be his new beginning, that two-week window would be the time period when Mad should start to find out.

* * *

But on February 15, a blue Mad became bluer still after he finally reached Laura on her cell phone. For one thing, she sounded far from warm towards him. More importantly, she told him she was married. He hadn't known that. Ever since the Thanksgiving message from Jezebel?, Mad had worked up a whole construct in his mind whereby Laura would be his personal angel whose support for him never wavered, whose insouciant sexual play with him masked a deeper love. How could she be married? And how could she sound so much less warm in person than she sounded in the chat room?

When a depressed person builds a psychic scaffolding to prop himself up, and the scaffolding collapses, the underlying depression can suddenly return full force. After only a few minutes on the phone with Laura, that's what began to happen to Mad.

But Laura, self-absorbed as she was, still wasn't really a witch. At some point in the conversation, she heard the plaintive sound in his voice and recognized its pain. Therefore, although she wasn't genuinely interested in whatever was going on in Mad's world then, she rallied her humanity enough to feign interest. ("Ever since I've known this poor schmuck," she told herself, "he's really been pretty damned weak underneath his sex appeal and charisma.") Searching for a topic to keep him on the phone long enough to ease the blow of her earlier coldness, she swiveled in her chair to face out her window, with her back to her open office door. Her quick mind soon came up with a subject.

"Wait, Mad, don't hang up yet," she said. "It just occurred to me that I haven't seen any announcements this winter about which charities your ministry is donating to. Don't you usually dole out a bunch of money in late January? I remember being impressed in the past by how much good y'all have been doing."

Mad explained to her that, at Becky's suggestion, they had determined to move to an annual board meeting rather than a semi-annual one, so their choices of charities wouldn't be announced until May.

Instinctively, Laura fell into an old strategem for talking with people who seemed gloomy. Pretend, in what is obviously a good-natured way, to tease them about something, in a way that makes them laugh; at least some of their gloom might momentarily lift. So Laura – also thinking that since Mad still *was* after all, a newsmaker, she might as well stay on his good side – proceeded to do just that. "Gee, sweetheart, if I were wearing my suspicious reporter's hat, I'd start grilling you right now about whether this schedule change is a dodge, a way to hide less-than-stellar results. The tough-chick reporter in me wants to know if your ministry is foundering. Tell me true, sweetheart, are you spending all that money you're making on a bunch of other women when you should be giving it away to the Little Sisters of Charity?"

Laura's words sounded accusatory, but her tone was anything but. Instead, her tone was that of a friend needling another friend in a bantering way. "C'mon, sweetheart, I was counting on you donating all that loot to the 'Make Laura My Superstar Mistress Fund.'"

Mad's head reeled. One moment Laura seemed cold and distant, and now she was teasing him like an old buddy. Maybe, he decided, what he had thought was coolness had been his own imagination after being stunned at news of Laura's marital status. Off balance, grasping at Laura's friendliness like a lifeline, Mad fell into a confessional mode. "Truth is, Laura, I wish it were that simple. Becky doesn't know it, but I suspect that she actually might be using the delay in our board meeting as a time for her to figure out the books. She has a good business sense, but for some reason she has a real hard time with making accounting numbers balance. And you know me: When it comes to the business, I just do what I'm told."

"Gee, Mad: Cooked books! Sounds like a real scandal to me!" Laura still had a jocular, needling tone. "I'm really gonna have to look into this. If I crack this case, it'll surely boost my ratings!"

Laura glanced at her watch, and realized she was late for a meeting. "Oh, gee, Mad, I'm late for something. Gotta run. But it was great catching up with you after all this time!"

Both of them hung up the phone on a friendly note. But what Mad didn't know was that when Laura swiveled her chair back around, she found herself, unexpectedly, staring straight into the eyes of Spike Walters standing in her doorway. Spike's "leave of absence" had ended a month ago, and he was now back at the reigns of "Hour of Truth" fulltime. He had obviously heard a good bit of Laura's end of the conversation.

"Damn, girl, you're good!" Spike said. "Please tell me that was Mad Jones on the line?! Are you onto some kinda scandal involving that fraudulent young pissant? Sounds to me like you were playing him like a violin!"

Laura didn't know what to do. She knew Spike hated Mad with a passion. And Spike had built up so much clout over the years that he had not been killed off professionally by Mad's counter-hit-job on him 17 months earlier. Spike was back full force as the power at "Hour of Truth" who could make or break Laura's career. She tried, therefore, to sound nonchalant.

"Oh, well, it seems that Mr. Jones is waiting until May to make his numbers add up. I was just, uh, just …"

Spike interrupted her. "Just moving in on a story you know will make old Spike really, really happy! You can't fool me, Laura Green, your reputation is too entrenched. You're ambitious and you're smart: What better way to impress old Spike and make your career than to dig up dirt on just the guy I want dirt on more than anybody else! Way to go, little girl, way to go!"

Laura was appalled but was too self-controlled to show it. For now, she would just have to play along.

And that was how Spike Walters decided to launch another investigation of Mad Jones, this time hiring a financial analyst to unearth any discrepancies in the tax filings of the MMW Corporation. Nobody got away with embarrassing Spike Walters. *Nobody*.

* * *

At 3:16 a.m. on Ash Wednesday, Feb. 28, 2001, Mad awoke with a start and turned on his bedside lamp. There was blood on his pillow. *Godalmightysonofabitchingcrap*! It couldn't be happening again! It just couldn't!

When Mad calmed down a little, he was able to determine that the volume of blood wasn't high. He had some almost-dried blood caking at the base of his right nostril. Something had given him a nosebleed, but it didn't appear to be serious. Maybe it had something to do with how much he had drunk the day before. Just as New Orleans did, Mobile held a full-fledged Mardi Gras season. In fact, the Mardi Gras tradition as is known in North America actually started in Mobile in the mid-19th Century before some Mobilians transported it to New Orleans – which, as is that city's wont, soon did it far bigger and more wildly than Mobile ever could. Still, Mobile's celebration wasn't negligible, and it was striving these days to catch up in exuberance (if not in bawdiness) with the Crescent City's. Anyway, Mad had indulged to a far greater extent than usual. He had been thrown off stride by his talk with Laura, and on Mardi Gras Day he overcompensated. So, he thought, maybe the nosebleed was alcohol-related.

Whatever caused the noseblood, though, what it accomplished – as if Mad needed any reminders anyway – was to make him even more aware of the tragedy that had happened three years before, to the very minute.

For the past two weeks, since his conversation with Laura, Mad had been struggling to avoid the pit of depression. He was bored again, overwhelmingly bored, with his ministry. He hadn't chosen this vocation, dammit; it had been thrust upon him. What he really wanted was to go back to teaching high-school history and coaching baseball. And now, this! This exact-minute reminder of his gut-wrenching loss. Here, after all this time, was God being a total jerk again. Mad tossed and turned again for the rest of the night, trying to fight off visions of dead Claires and dead babies and dead Dads and dead Daddy Lees. He never again that night drifted fully off to sleep.

It was, therefore, an extremely sour-mooded Mad (and, what was rare, a hung-over one) who met that morning with Peter Vignelli, S.J. Peter had been insistent upon meeting for coffee and muffins at Carpe Diem. Mad didn't know what Peter wanted, but he knew it had something to do with Ash Wednesday. Whatever it was, Mad was in no frame of mind for it.

"Mad, I'd like you to consider something very important," Peter was saying once they had begun sipping their coffee. "I know you've been out of sorts; I know you've been struggling. I sense that you've reached a spiritual cul-de-sac. I sense you feel like there's no way forward. Am I right?"

"Yeah," Mad said tiredly. His head was pounding. "Or whatever. Not that I care a rat's ass about it."

"That's the thing, Mad," said the priest. "You've *got* to care. You have a gift, and you've been called. Like it or not, you've been commissioned to bring people to God. You've been commissioned to find the lost sheep, the skeptics and unbelievers, and guide them back to God's flock. Nobody ever said the shepherd's job was an easy one. But as the Bible says, it's a job that must be done. … Listen to me, Mad! Your own theses tell you the way. God loves those with the courage to carry on."

Mad was peevish. "Then let Him love somebody else. There's an Episcopal hymn that's right on target: 'The peace of God, it is no peace, but strife closed in the sod.' Screw that. I'm tired of the strife. I've tried for three years. It seems like 30. That's enough, and enough is enough, and enough is too much."

The Jesuit fixed Mad with an unyielding gaze. "I know that hymn, Mad. You left out the next line. The peace of God, yes, is strife closed in the sod. 'Yet brothers, pray for just one thing: the marvelous peace of God.'"

"Okay, so you can quote a hymn at me, Peter. Big whoop."

Peter Vignelli recognized a broken spirit. And he knew that broken spirits also are spirits most susceptible to being put back together in a new and better way. Peter recognized his duty, and he stepped up to it. Mad's "big whoop" was the invitation for Peter's salvific intervention.

This was Ash Wednesday, Peter explained. This was the ultimate day of penitence. And penitence was the ultimate means of transfiguration. Penitence is a state of openness to grace. Lent is an opportunity. And opportunities are to be seized.

"Mad, the way out of your dead end is to retrace your steps," he said. "You are moving in the right direction, but you went up a blind alley. Go back, Mad, go back. Go back to first principles. Go back to first faith. Go back to the first church. Mad, all that's left for you to do is to take your passion and your charisma and your ideas, put them in a slightly different light, a slightly more disciplined light. Put them in the light of the Holy Catholic Church, Mad. That which is catholic is universal. The universe is open to you, my son. Mad, it's time you became a Catholic."

Father Vignelli had spoken from the heart. But Mad's heart was not in position to hear it. Mad reacted with a cold fury.

"Dammit, Peter, no offense, but don't give me that crap! I don't believe in transubstantiation. I don't believe in veneration of a quadrillion different saints. I don't believe that Mary, too, was immaculately conceived, nor do I pray to her. I'm not big on formal confessions. I don't get into praying the rosary. I don't believe any Pope can ever be infallible on any doctrine, even though I think the current Pope is wonderful. I'm not into church hierarchy. I'm not into works-righteousness. I don't believe that the Catholic Church is the only route to salvation, and I resent the Catholic exclusivity that says, in effect, that members of all other Christian denominations cannot know redemption unless they convert . I'm not a Catholic, Peter, and I never will be. And I'm damn sure not gonna waste my time today listening to a conversion speech. Claire and Marcelle and my baby died today, Peter, and I just don't want to hear your crap. Peter, I love you, but you're way the hell off base."

With that, Mad swallowed the remainder of his coffee, pushed back his chair, and clodded out of the coffee shop through its back hallway. Behind him, Peter Vignelli rubbed a weary forehead. Peter wasn't accustomed to failure. The priest was not accustomed to comeuppance. With a sick feeling in the pit of his stomach, the priest had nothing left to do but pray.

Chapter Nine

The next morning, a new web site appeared on the Internet. Called "Mad Affirmative," it was the long-promised explication of the world according to Affirmed. It also was truly mad. Obnoxiously, sacrilegiously so.

The home page featured a representation of Jesus Christ on the cross. But it wasn't a steady picture. Over about ten seconds, the torso of the Christ figure morphed into a photo of Madison Jones, and then it slowly morphed back again. In the lower right corner was another photo, much smaller, of a burly, bearded man standing next to a baptismal font. Underneath his photo was the name "John Batiste." Up the left-hand side of the page ran the usual list of sub-pages with headings such as "Theses," "Quotes," "Media Coverage," "Chronology," "Photos," and a few others. Larger than the others, right at the top, was this: "The Truth." Site visitors who clicked on the cross figure, on the burly man, or on "The Truth" all were sent to the same page. In big letters on that page was the larger headline of "The Truth and its Proof."

Here's how the text read (minus a raft-full of picayune footnotes):

> "Know the truth, and the truth shall set you free. The truth is this:
>
> Madison Jones is the Second Coming!
>
> My name is Paul John Batiste. I have always been known by my middle name of John. All my life I have felt a special calling, but I did not know to what end. All my life, my spirit has been moved, but I did not know whither it was that my spirit blew.

Now I know. My name has always been an obvious clue, but I did not recognize it. But my destiny always lay in my name. I am a new John the Baptist, and I now Affirm that I have come to bear witness to the truth.

Everything in this text below is taken from direct personal observation or from public records (including from Mad's own recollections in various of his speeches/testimonies during the last three years). Everything not already commonly known is footnoted.

Three years ago today, Madison Jones began the week-long creative process that would produce the theses, the ultimate wisdom, to which so many of us have pledged our troth. Just as James Madison was the Father of his country, our Madison (the son) is the progenitor of our faith. And like God the Father, Mad Jones worked hard (in the hospital) for six days, and on the Seventh Day, he rested.

What was it that brought him into the hospital in the first place? It was, Mad has said, at 3:16 a.m. that he awoke to find his wife and unborn son dead. What is the significance of 3:16? John 3:16, of course (Thesis 55): 'For God so loved the world, that he gave his only begotten Son, that whosoever believeth in him should not perish, but have everlasting life.'

And what did Mad say happened in that hospital, what revelatory experience turned his outlook around? He said he was angry at God, but that God laughed. He said in one of his homilies, and I quote, 'God laughed through me. He laughed not at me, but from somewhere deep inside of me.' Now, I say to you, how can God laugh through and from inside of somebody who isn't Himself divine?

And how long was it, after Mad began writing the theses, before the doctor signed his release papers? Exactly 111 hours. That's the numeral '1' three times. Three in one. The Father, Son, and Holy Ghost.

And when he drove to New Orleans the night he posted his theses, what route did he take into the French Quarter? Elysian Fields. He took the route of heaven.

When he left New Orleans, (Mad told us in a humorous metaphorical aside in a homily on May 5, 2000), he made a stop along the roadside, where he encountered a serpent. And he called the serpent 'Satan,' and told the serpent to get away from him. And what time period was that in? It was during the 40 days (yes, exactly 40 days) between the time he entered the hospital and the day of his big inaugural sermon, on Good Friday, at Apostles of the Word Church outside of New Orleans. Forty days until Good Friday. Telling Satan to get behind him. All pretty obvious, don't you think so?

Once back in Mobile, he was greeted with accusations that he was a heretic, just as Jesus was rejected at home. (A prophet is without honor in his home country.) Then he went to play golf. What's the big-selling golf book called? Golf in the Kingdom, that's what. And he called the golf course his sanctuary, and he drove the bad guys off the course just like Jesus drove the bad guys out of the temple. (Then he did something that put me off track for a while. He told the media guys they would have a plague on their houses, and both indeed soon experienced plagues, and that's what made me think for a while that Mad was Moses, just as at other times I have mistakenly thought Mad was Luther or Elijah, etc. But it was just a red herring that I fell for, looking for the wrong truth and missing the real one. None are so blind as those who cannot see.)

By the way, what was Mad's old job in Mobile? He was a teacher, that's what. And what was it that Jesus' follower sometimes called him? They called him Rabbi, Teacher. Just like Mad.

Once the 'Mad Religion' web site went up, who was one of Mad's earliest boosters? M. Magdalene, that's who. And another of his earliest disciples took the name Doubting Thomas. There's a reason why all those seeming coincidences kept happening.

Also, Mad comes from Alabama, which still calls itself the 'Heart of Dixie.' He's from the Old Confederacy, in other words. Go into some parts of Alabama, and they still consider themselves to be occupied by a foreign power. Mad came to deliver a message to a subjugated people, but it was not a political message, not the message of rebellion that they wanted to hear. Just like Jesus Christ.

Then there was the reaction to Mad, which still goes on today, from Rob Patterson and Larry Falstaff, who surely are our modern-day Pharisees. They want his ministry dead. They see him as a threat to their empires. They want to stomp Mad down. Just like the Sanhedrin did.

Then there is the media. Everybody has always seemed to be against Mad – except for Steve Matheson, who was the first guy to treat Mad fairly. Steve Matheson was Mad's apologist and defender. Steve Matheson went against the reigning media orthodoxy, against the anti-religionists' own secular leanings. And why is this significant? Because his name is Stephen. And who was the first important martyr for the new Christian religion? Stephen, of course. (That's what makes me nervous on Matheson's behalf: I hope that his basic friendliness towards Mad doesn't lead somebody to hurt him.)

It all begins to add up: John the Baptist… progenitor of faith… rest on the 7th Day … 3:16… 3 in 1… Satan behind him during the 40 Days… prophet without honor… anger at interlopers in his sanctuary… rabbi/teacher… Magdalene, Doubting Thomas, and Stephen.

But wait: There's more!

What is Mad's message? It's a totally new understanding of God's relationship with man. Just like the Gospels were. In short, it's a New Testament.…"

Reading this, Mad rubbed his eyes in disbelief. This was horrible! It wasn't true, and it was crazy, and it was sacrilegious. But Mad knew the media well enough by now to be sure that somebody would report all this as if Mad himself was the one claiming he was the Second Coming. This was a disaster. With a sick feeling growing ever worse in the pit of his stomach, Mad kept reading.…

"…. New Testament. And think about it this way: Who else but the Second Coming of Christ would give us a new testament that is so Christo-centric? When Christ first came into the world, it was to focus attention back on God the Father. But now too many men have let their lives stray from the proper attention to Jesus Christ, and too many focus so much on Jesus' humanity that they forget his divinity. (The so-called 'Jesus Seminar,' anyone?) So, Mad Jones, who isn't Jesus but is the Christ, gives us theses that re-explain, and re-focus the necessary attention on, Jesus Christ's role as mediator and advocate. As Jesus re-focused us on God the Father, Mad re-focuses us on God the Son.

And just as Jesus warned us that false prophets would seize false opportunities to warn of the end of the world, so too did all the Pattersons and Falstaffs preach that the new millennium, which they called New Year's Day of 2000, would be the long-awaited Rapture or Armageddon or whatever. And it was up to Mad, the Second Coming, to tell us to ignore the false prophets, and even to point out that they were a full year ahead of the mathematical millennium. Only the prophet, the Second Coming, the *real deal*, could have so clearly warned us of the false prophets' error.

I could go on (and on and on). The proofs of Mad's Second Coming-ness are legion. But here's the kicker. Here's the final, most important proof of all, especially considering everything else I have described and explained so far. Look at all the people closest to Mad. Who are they; what are their names?

Becky **Matthews** runs his non-profit corporation. **Mark** Mariasson created his web site. Justin **Luke** is his childhood friend who is the only person allowed to officially affiliate his business with Mad's, with Mad's own theses forming the spiritual basis of Mr. Luke's holistic health training system. And Mad's bodyguard and (more importantly) by most accounts, his good friend, is Shiloh **Jones**.

Matthews, Mark, Luke and Jones. How obvious can it be? And then there is his attorney, who by all accounts is the mother (legally speaking) of MMW's corporate design. Her name is **Mary** McWyre. And then there is Mad's godfather, named Buzz. He represents all the rest of the disciples. This baffled me a little, at first, until I re-listened to Jesus Christ Superstar and heard all the apostles repeatedly concern themselves with 'what's the *Buzz*, tell me what's a-happenin'?' By Mad's choosing a godfather in this way, with the clue being hidden not in the Bible but in a modern rock-opera about Jesus' life, Mad shows just what a sly sense of humor he has. It's an important theological message, just as it was when Mad said God laughed through him in the hospital. The message is that we've all missed the importance, for the salvational process, of humor and laughter.

I must admit that the Jones thing threw me off a little, too. Why not John? Why a mere semi-homonym? It made me doubt my whole theory. I prayed to God that, if I was right, He should send me a sign. Right after praying, I opened a New Oxford Annotated RSV Bible, and looked at the first page of the Gospel of Mark, 'commonly thought to have been the first written of the Gospels.' There it hit me: The RSV annotations explain that the author of the Gospel of Mark is actually thought to be a man named 'John Mark.' And it refers the reader to Acts 12:12 to see who John Mark is, and it says in Acts that he is the son of a woman named Mary. Now look at the name of our modern-day Mark: Mark Mariasson. *Mark, Maria's son.* Mark, son of Mary. It all fits together. And again, the fact that Mad chose a Jones, a mere near-homonym of 'John,' again shows his playfulness, his sense of humor, which is such an important part of his new New Testament.

So now almost everything was in place. This was by advent of the year 1999. Only one thing was missing. What I asked myself was, how could there be a Second Coming, especially one so designed that it had a Matthew, Mark, Luke, John (Jones), Mary, John the Baptist, and Stephen, and yet *not* include a Peter? For a full year I held off publishing my witness, because I could not find a Peter to ice my case. (And it couldn't be any old Peter; it had to be one who is truly significant to Mad.)

But then came Mad's Thanksgiving message this year – after another period, so typical of the Bible, of Mad taking a *40-day* break, in the wilderness as it were, away from the public, away from the crowds – and it all came clear. How I missed it, I don't know, but I guess Mad had just never mentioned this man publicly before. But in that message, Mad credited his close friend and mentor, Father **Peter** Vignelli. And he identified his Peter not just by the vernacular name of Jesuit, but as a member of the Society of **Jesus**.

Which is why there now can be no doubt that Mad Jones is the Second Coming. That is the truth I proclaim. It is the truth to which I bear witness. I, John Batiste – I, John the Baptist – bear witness to this truth. Chop off my head if you want, but you cannot chop up the truth that I have now revealed.

The truth is especially important now, because it has now been exactly three years since Mad began his ministry. Three years. That's exactly how long Jesus the Lord himself spread his own ministry before he was betrayed and crucified. That's why it is now, especially, important that I proclaim, that we all proclaim, the most important truth we will ever know:

THE WORD is with us again, just as it was in the beginning, and as it ever shall be, world without end, Amen."

Finally, mercifully, the screed was complete. It was the work of a highly disturbed individual. But Mad knew it would cause no end of trouble.

* * *

Mad was right. Sparked by a carelessly written wire story that did not make it clear early enough that this "Second Coming" claim came from somebody with no direct connection to Mad, a number of harried desk editors at newspapers across the country came up with headlines like "Mad claim: Jones is Christ," "Jones Affirmed as Second Coming?," and "Web site sights Christ." A few cable networks and tabloids went nuts with the story. (One or two cable networks did handle it well, but that didn't lessen the sting Mad felt.) All of the "big three" networks also mentioned the story, two of them as end-of-newscast curiosity (one of those markedly snidely), the third as a longer piece that treated Mad as a religious fanatic. Only the cable networks (and at that, not all of them) bothered to track down John Batiste, *aka* Affirmed, to interview him. Batiste was a burly, middle-aged, former day laborer living on pension- and disability-income (plagued hatby an old back injury) near Bismarck, North Dakota. He was an unmarried loner with a sort of wild-eyed countenance. In the interview, he spoke way too loudly. But, like the wire story, one of the cable networks that interviewed him failed to make clear that Batiste/Affirmed was acting on his own, unaffiliated with Mad in any way.

Mad and Becky had, predictably, quickly arranged for a press release disassociating Mad from Batiste's web site. "I categorically deny these claims," Mad said. "I am flattered to have fans, but I want to make it clear that I in no way encourage anybody to elevate my importance above that of a simple lecturer, in pursuit of public discourse about a God who is a wonderful mystery to all of us."

The interviewers in North Dakota who did the job right also asked Batiste to respond to Mad's statement. Batiste did not seem angry to be contradicted by his hero, unless (like Shiloh) one were inclined to read malice between the lines. "That's okay," Batiste shouted into the camera. "It would be unseemly for Mad to claim divinity before my truth is more widely accepted. But I'm sure that at some point soon he'll step in to validate my message. I wouldn't expect him to let me hang out to dry. Gods do not forsake their true believers."

Reaction from all the usual quarters was swift. Rob Patterson and Larry Falstaff blasted Mad, Patterson in shrill tones, Falstaff in self-consciously sober cadences. The Rev rhymed a few outraged insults. A few publicity-seeking congressmen from both the right and the left piped up to say they were horrified.

Dozens of demonstrators showed up outside of Mad's door and outside of the MMW offices. Shiloh of course kept close watch from the porch, but the regular police force also showed up to help provide crowd control. Even the lady with the bonneted iguana came over from New Orleans to make an appearance for the first time since that very first day in the French Quarter. In essence, the whole carnival freak show had returned.

* * *

As the frenetic phantasmagoria continued to unfold, Mad also was shaken by a visit from the FBI. A police investigation of the threatening chat room messages had determined them to be at least potentially serious, and a week earlier the FBI had begun trying electronically to trace the source. Now, however, the FBI was reporting a singular lack of success. Somehow, the messages had been so ingeniously coded and masked that even sophisticated tracking techniques had run into a cyber wall. The FBI therefore wanted to work at the problem from the other end – first, by asking Mad if he knew of anyone who might have reason to despise him; second, by asking if he knew the real identities of any of the chat room "regulars"; and third, by tracing all the regulars' own cyber signatures and seeing if, by working backwards on them, they might find some kind of match with the electronic footprint of the threat-maker. (The psychological profile they had worked up indicated a likelihood that whoever wrote "Mad muss die" was probably somebody already neck deep in Mad-mania.)

They did say they had already determined that Affirmed, or John Batiste, was not the one who made the threats, nor did they consider him dangerous. He seemed a little off his rocker, they said, but gentle as a lamb.

Mad told them of his conviction that Laura Green and Jezebel? were one and the same. (He avoided telling them the full story of why he so believed.) He said he did not know who any of the other "regulars" were, but that he truly missed the commentary of Perdicaris ever since Perd had signed off in a huff over Mad's anti-Clinton remarks. He noted that M. Magdalene seemed to have turned against him, but not so badly that he could ever conceive of her making threats. And he said he didn't know of anybody else with any reason to wish him harm.

"We do believe you could be in serious danger," said one of the G-men. "Nobody would have gone to so much trouble, and used such high-level electronic ingenuity, to mask the sources of these threats unless he had some serious intentions."

* * *

Spike Walters smelled blood, and lots of it. Not only was he directing a crack team of researchers who were analyzing the MMW Corp.'s financial reports, but now he had this Mad-is-Christ foolishness to hang around Mad's neck. He knew that any report he did against Mad must, by virtue of Spike's earlier embarrassment, overcome a large credibility gap. But he was Spike Walters, dammit! Nobody got away with messing around with him. Spike had lost very few battles in his time, and even then he had never lost a whole war. Damn the little "moral thermometers" (a phrase of George Will's) who might question any report Spike did on Mad. Damn the asinine conservative media watchdog groups such as the Media Research Center, who would attack Spike unmercifully. Damn all the idiotic followers of Mad who might be upset. Damn the torpedoes: Full speed ahead!

* * *

Friday, March 16 of 2001 was James Madison's 250th birthday. Mad Jones, reeling from all of his own controversy, had in the past six months grasped onto his father's hero (not to mention the man whose namesake Mad was) as an object of fascination, veneration, and private study, and as a way to think about something other than the theology that had turned Mad's life into one of near-constant uproar. He was proud, therefore, when he was asked to give the (lay) benediction at one of the events commemorating James Madison's quarter-millennium celebration, and Becky had found a way to combine it (the following afternoon) with a small MMW-fund-generating speech in Daddy Lee's own Shenandoah territory. But angry protesters ("Christ is not Mad!" and "Neither Madison nor Christ!") greeted Mad at every turn. Despite his own better judgment, then, as well as against Shiloh's warnings, Mad looked for the only type of solace he knew he never had difficulty in finding. At the Shenandoah event he spotted a girl he had met several times as a teenager. The granddaughter of one of Daddy Lee's many old flames, Brooke was a wild-eyed lass whom he remembered as always having a quirkily flamboyant air about her. With only the briefest of eye contact, Mad knew she was his for the taking.

By now, Shiloh was finally on to Mad's m.o. (and definitely disapproved), but right now Mad didn't care. When Shiloh made a restroom visit, Mad escaped and made his assignation in a back room of the lecture hall where his speech had so recently concluded. Mad had intended then only to make arrangements with Brooke for an engagement later in the evening, but Brooke couldn't wait. Before he knew it, she was pulling him into a large broom closet.

Just 20 minutes later, with a few audience members still milling around out front (and Shiloh feverishly searching the premises), Brooke went running across the lawn clad in little more than a grin, right out in front of God and everybody. Dowagers clutched at faux pearls, and at least one elderly man tipped his hat at her, grinning right back.

Shiloh, furious, found Mad waiting shame-faced in their rental car out back, and they sped off as a few rural reporters ran, too late, for their own vehicles of would-be pursuit.

The next day, back in Mobile, Mad had another bad episode of ADZ sleep. When he regained full consciousness, he dialed up Dr. Raj's office and angrily demanded some answers. "Two more weeks," said a curiously gleeful Dr. Raj. "Just two more weeks, and all will be clear and all will be well. Yes indeedy-dee. Do not fret: I, Dr. Raj, make no mistakes!"

With that, he hung up, leaving Mad still spluttering on the other end of the line.

* * *

A day after that, the FBI agents returned to report on their findings so far. They still had been unable to crack the threat-maker's code, but they had had far more success in tracing the identities of other chat room participants. Privacy laws, they said, precluded their sharing their findings with Mad (unless they had the permission of the person identified, which in most cases they didn't). Mad was disappointed to learn that he could not find out who Defender was, or who Perdicaris and the weird-but-funny Cowardly Lion were, but the agents wouldn't budge. The agents, though, could and did tell him that nobody, whether familiar regular or a more infrequent participant, had an electronic signature that came close to matching the threatening messages. And nobody traced so far seemed to represent even the glimmer of danger to Mad.

Mad didn't know whether to be relieved or worried. On one hand, it was reassuring that the FBI had yet found no credible threat among the dozens of leads they had pursued. On the other hand, it was sort of scary that the identity of the "Mad muss die" author was still a mystery.

Then, however, came the news that to Mad was the greatest shock. "Hey, guys," he said to the agents as they made moves to gather up their papers. "Can you at least confirm for me that Jezebel is Laura Green? I mean, since I guessed it already and all that, and since she's a public figure anyway, can't you make an exception to the privacy rules in her case?"

The two agents looked at each other in a way that indicated they had a prior agreement. One of them stood up and pivoted in the direction of the door. The other one, who was no fan of the media in general, said, softly, "We sort of thought you would want to know that. But even public figures have the right to privacy. Miss Green is no exception … But, uh, I guess I can tell you who she's *not*. I can categorically deny that Laura Green and this character Jezebel? are one and the same." As his partner reached and opened the front door, the agent shuffled his papers some more, and tried to look perplexed. He cleared his throat, meaningfully. "Aww, you know what, I seem to have lost one of my file folders somewhere around this table. Dammit, my boss always is on my case about being a klutz with paperwork. … Well, darn it, I must've left it in the car. I'll tell you what, though: If you should find it, I trust you'll, ah, not peek inside, but will get it back to me next time I visit – *right*? I mean, if you should happen to see what it says, it'd be a shame, and all that."

The two agents left (to the sound of a few protesters chanting that Mad was a heretic and a megalogomaniac). Under the last agent's chair, in fairly plain view, was a manila folder labeled "M. Magdalene." Mad picked it up and looked inside.

"Every one of the messages self-styled 'M. Magdalene' traced back to the same personal e-mail account," began the brief report. "The very first such message was sent on the date of Thursday, March 12, 1998, via remote phone, the call originating in Mobile, Alabama. It began as follows: 'Oh, ye of little understanding! These are NOT the end times. It's only the end of the line for you morons who think the whole world's history has been building toward the opportunity for you to prove yourself holier than the rest of us….' Unlike the remote phone location in Mobile, the account through which the message was sent was registered in New Orleans, Louisiana. The account, still active, belongs to one Laura Green, now of New York, New York."

Mad's eyes began to blur. It was all there: It was Laura who had used the alias M. Magdalene to boost both Mad's profile and her own audience. "Make it sound like a real grassroots uprising of interest," Laura had written to the other chat room denizens early on. After her "Acute Vision" profile of Mad, she had written that Mad's "most important ideas were highlighted superbly by reporter Laura Green. She has a real future and TV journalism needs more bright and balanced reporters like her." And so on and so forth. Entry after entry had seemed complimentary of Mad, some of them expressing simple and apparently genuine concern – but time and again, M. Magdalene had worked in praise for Laura Green, and time and again (although not always) the compliments for Mad had arrived at a time when Laura stood to benefit from attention focused Mad's way.

Laura/M. Magdalene had only, or at least regularly, been using Mad for her own purposes, and Mad had been too much in her thrall to see it. Sure, Laura had come through in the biggest way possible by smuggling the "Hour of Truth" videotape away from the network studio, so maybe she really did care for Mad on some level. Even then, though, she had benefited by the removal of a rival from the "Hour of Truth" team.

And then there was the horribly nasty message the previous autumn that had so shocked and hurt Mad's feelings. She had written of "the kind of rapacious, serial, utterly self-indulgent sex that it now is clear that Mad engages in. Mad uses women and throws them away; he objectifies them in a way that shows an obnoxious disrespect." And she had called Mad a "coward."

Had she hated him all along? Mad didn't know about Laura's newfound feminist anger; all he knew was that she/M. Magdalene had seemed to turn on him viciously. And this was the woman he had recently convinced himself would be his new love, his salvation! How could he have been so wrong? Was his discernment really *that* pathetically off-base? And if he had been so wrong about Laura, what else was he badly wrong about? Everywhere Mad turned, the foundations of his view of his world were being shaken or even crumbling. One nutcase said he was Christ, another was threatening to kill him, a bunch of others were protesting him as if he himself had made the claim to be the Second Coming, and his relationships with all his friends were at least a little strained. And now he found that he was wrong about Laura as well! What had he done to deserve such pain and confusion?

* * *

Mad again was certifiably depressed. He asked Becky to cancel his remaining two scheduled major rallies between then and the board meeting now scheduled for the end of April. Afraid to roil the protesters who had turned his block into a permanent freak show ever since Affirmed posted his "Second Coming" thesis, Mad holed up in his house even more than usual. His neighbors complained about the protesters, but there was nothing he could do. The police department would no longer guaranty security for Mad, so Shiloh took to sitting watch on Mad's covered porch during nighttime hours, and Becky used MMW funds to hire for cheap a poor excuse for another (uniformed) security guard during the day.

And then, four days after his return from the Shenandoah, Becky and Justin rocked Mad's world even further. They had asked if they could come to his house, pizza and beer in tow, for a chat. He was sure they wanted to talk about what the controversy and his depression were doing to the MMW business, and to him personally, and he really didn't want to "go there." But he was in no mood to argue, especially about a visit from friends who, even if flawed, always seemed to have his best interests at heart.

But that's not what the two wanted to discuss. Instead, they were finally ready, after all these months, to enlighten Mad about their relationship. They had chosen this moment because they just had made plans to visit Chet and Ginger Matthews in a few weeks, to introduce Justin to the parents. (Chet had been stunned and disappointed to learn that Becky and Mad were not an item. But he was nevertheless eager to see his daughter's beau.)

At Mad's house, Becky and Justin started with small talk. They waited until each was on his (or her) second slice of pizza before breaking the news.

"We're sorry to have hidden this from you for all this time, ol'Buddy-ol'Pal," Justin said in his curiously juvenile phraseology that Becky had not yet weaned him of. "But we didn't want you to feel caught in the middle if it didn't work."

"Yeah, Mad," Becky broke in, reaching for Justin's hand. "But now we're pretty sure it's gonna keep on working for us, and we want you to be part of our happiness."

Becky was beaming. There was, finally, the semblance of a peace in her countenance that she had always lacked before. But Mad, in his depression, was blind to such subtleties. And while he actually would be happy for both of his friends, that's not the emotion that hit him first. What Mad first felt was guilt: guilt that he had been so blind as to fail to see the romance blossoming under his nose; guilt that he was so out of touch with people who long befriended him that he missed the signs of their growing joy; guilt that he had been so self-centered as to assume that Becky still pined for him and that Justin's oddities would forever relegate the little guy to second-fiddle status beneath Mad's shadow.

Depression, all the psychology textbooks say, is anger improperly directed inward, and a depressed person can perceive almost any occurrence as an occasion for more self-anger and guilt. (Modern medicine now knows, of course, that brain-chemical changes play a prominent role in such circumstances, but the basic psychological insights about the predilection toward guilt remain mostly true.) Plus there was the self-imposed guilt of wondering where he had failed as a friend so that Becky and Justin had felt they had to hide their romance from him.

Finally, there was this: As fond as he was of Justin, he had never really taken Justin seriously – had always considered him the way a golden lab must consider a friendly, yapping little terrier, as not quite his own equal. And always, somewhere in his subconscious, it had fed his ego that he, Mad, had so easily held sway over the desires of a beautiful woman like Becky. But if Becky was winnable even by friendly little oddball Justin – a nice guy but, on the desirability scale, to all eyes a second-rater – then that meant that Becky's own standards maybe weren't so high, and, by logical extension, that her earlier desire for Mad didn't necessarily say anything good about Mad's own stature. (Syllogism: If "A" desires only a person who ranks high [Premise 1], then he who "A" desires must necessarily rank high [Conclusion 1]. But if "A" desires somebody who demonstrably does *not* rank high, then that destroys Premise 1, and so Conclusion 1 is undermined and no conclusion at all, on known facts alone, can be reached about previous persons desired by "A.") Mad didn't think all this through, of course, and never would, but on a subconscious level it further weakened his own sense of worth.

Mad made all the right noises about being so happy for his friends (and on one level it was certainly true), but what stayed with him most, after they left his house, was a feeling that his assumptions about the normal order of the world had been further shaken at a time when he himself already felt more than shaky enough.

* * *

Jock the reporter was on site in Mobile when his cell phone rang. "Hi: You don't know me, but you've seen me a bunch of times," said the voice on the other end. "I'm the mime who made Mad Jones famous."

Jock smelled a story. Maybe the mime knew something about Mad that hadn't been reported yet, something that could titillate readers in the checkout lines. Just the week before, *The Zodiac* had for the first time been out-sensationalized on a Mad-related story by another supermarket tabloid. The other tab had notched big sales by running on its cover a banner headline proclaiming: "Evidence in: Mad really *is* Messiah!" Inside, a doctored photo showed a halo above Mad's head as he preached in front of a cross.

The mime and Jock met at the bar in the Admiral Semmes Hotel in downtown Mobile. Over glasses of Jack Daniels, the mime kept reeling Jock in by hinting at big revelations to come. In truth, though, the mime himself was just as interested in information and publicity as Jock was. The mime wanted, first, to impress Jock with the conviction that he was a talented artist worthy of fame. Second, he wanted to find out who it was who had called him a "nutball" immediately after his Lewinsky impersonation at the Hebert's church. In the mime's mind, it was that "nutball" comment which had put an almost insurmountable barrier in the way of him reaching fame and fortune.

The mime was a bit confused about who Jock was. It was in *The Investigator*, not in Jock's *The Zodiac*, that an anonymous observer had said "that mime is obviously just a nutball," and in which "sources" had said "that proof will soon be forthcoming that the White House made him a nutball for hire."

But Jock was helpful anyway. Jock was plugged into all the right gossip lines. Jock knew, from another reporter who got it straight from *The Investigator*'s reporter, that the source for both comments was Mad's old press secretary, Don. "How does this press secretary stuff work, anyway?" the mime asked. "Do press secretaries usually speak just for themselves, or do they only put out statements approved by their bosses?"

Jock explained that his experience was that some press secretaries freelanced a little, but that on most important remarks the words were almost certainly vetted by the public figure whom the press secretary served. "As far as we reporters go," Jock said, "we treat a press secretary's words as being virtually the equivalent of being words straight from the horse's mouth – or maybe that's the 'horse's ass' mouth,' because most public figures are horse's asses."

The mime was crushed. Crushed and furious. He had done nothing but try to serve Mad's interests for three years now, and it turned out that Mad was responsible for the mime's reputation as a "nutball."

The mime became too agitated to be of any more use to Jock. The mime decided he would have to stew on this information in private. The mime, muttering fierce imprecations, a frighteningly angry look on his face, abruptly left the hotel bar – and Jock finished his Jack Daniels alone and angry at himself for having wasted his time trying to get a scoop from a guy with a serious screw loose.

* * *

Shiloh and LaShauna had had another argument. Shiloh was shaken, truly shaken, by events of the past few weeks. All along, he had had mixed feelings about Mad's theology – mixed feelings that for three years were overcome by his sense of Mad's good heart, by Mad's earnestness, and by the way Mad's faith-reaffirming final theses had such a demonstrable effect of leading skeptics and non-believers back into a relationship with God. But Shiloh also had real misgivings about Mad's lack of orthodoxy. And Shiloh disapproved of Mad's promiscuity. At first he had excused it as just a phase of Mad's grief over losing Claire, but now it was clear that it was a compulsion of Mad's that was so strong that not even loads of adverse publicity could make Mad stop it. Shiloh felt that Mad's activities put Shiloh in the role of an "enabler," a cover-up artist.

And now there was this "Second Coming" stuff. To Shiloh, it was patently offensive. He knew that Mad was not intentionally responsible for it, indeed that Mad was appalled by it. But Shiloh nevertheless blamed Mad, at least in part, for letting things get out of hand. The constant controversy, with the hint of blasphemy, was getting to be too much for Shiloh. He had decided that he wanted to resign from Mad's employ and return to the police force full-time. He still wanted Mad to be his friend, but not his boss.

LaShauna felt otherwise. She liked Mad's theology. She liked its tinge of anger and rebellion. Her only doubts about Mad involved his skin color, a lack of pigmentation that she had grown up mistrusting. But those doubts, and all other factors, were outweighed in her mind by the material benefits that were accruing for her family while Shiloh worked as Mad's bodyguard. Mad paid Shiloh a good salary. Mad paid tuition for Shiloh's part-time college classes, all of which continued to go fairly decently. Mad, far more than the police force, promised Shiloh and her family a brighter material future.

Confronted with Shiloh's concerns, LaShauna predictably became volatile. The more that Shiloh tried to discuss the matter in reasonable tones, the more enraged she became. She finally insisted that Shiloh spend the night alone on their sofa. And it took three days for them to reach an accommodation: that Shiloh would hang tight until the board meeting now scheduled for late April, at which time it was becoming obvious that the whole MMW enterprise would need to be re-focused, at the very least, anyway.

For Shiloh, though, the next month promised to be quite uncomfortable.

Chapter Ten

Chet Matthews had insisted on meeting Becky and Justin at the airport. It was Saturday, March 31, and it was finally time for Becky to introduce her boyfriend to her family. Chet was both excited and nervous. His disappointment that Becky and Mad weren't an "item" had dissipated when it finally became clear that the stories of Mad's promiscuity were true. And because he knew his own daughter was no saint in that regard, he was thrilled to find out that she seemed to have settled on one "serious" boyfriend and, maybe, into a more stable life. Still, he hoped that he and the new young man would "hit it off" well. He had spent so many years trying to build a relationship with his daughter – one which only recently had begun to thaw – and had secretly been so distraught about their lack of rapport, that he felt he would be walking on eggshells when he met the new guy. As a strapping "man's man," Chet wasn't accustomed to walking on eggshells. In fact, he often trampled on emotional eggshells without any remorse at all. But in this case Chet wanted so strongly for everything, for once, to go smoothly and amicably during one of Becky's infrequent visits. He loved his daughter deeply, and he wanted her to love him back.

Chet, unaccompanied by icy wife Ginger, stood in the airport terminal with a huge bouquet of roses for Becky and a beefy handshake waiting for Justin. What he didn't expect was a short, unruly-orange-haired, squeaky-voiced bundle of nerves who wore an ill-fitting green sport jacket. Becky had told her father that Justin was an athletic trainer, but the jacket hid Justin's well-muscled physique and somehow emphasized only his shortness. And his over-exuberant "Gee, Mr. Matthews, it's just so *cool* to meet you," combined with a goofy grin, did nothing to help the first impressions. Becky had warned Justin to be calm, but his nervousness overcame him and made him act his usual part of the eager-to-please puppy.

Houston oilmen do not like bouncy, squeaky puppies.

Chet swallowed his shock and tried to act as warmly as he could. His warmth, as always, came across like aggression. Within 15 minutes, Becky was having difficulty hiding all her old resentments, all the old misplaced anger she had long directed at Chet.

It was an inauspicious start.

"So, Daddy Dearest," she said as he wove his Mercedes through traffic, "what kind of shindigs have you got planned this weekend so you can show off your daughter like a Barbie doll?"

"You're not a Barbie doll, darling," he said, trying to placate her. "I've just got a few friends coming to see what a wonderful success my intelligent, beautiful girl has made of her life."

For once, Becky stifled another Pavlovian, sarcastic response. She had matured in the past few years, and although something about her father still pushed all her wrong buttons, she recognized, just in time, his earnestness. But the entire next day and a half would prove a struggle for civility, especially in light of the huge personality differences between her father and Justin.

And that was the least of the problems. Ginger, of course, acted beastly to both her daughter and her daughter's beau. "This must be your idea of a sick joke," she said to Becky through clenched teeth at the first opportunity. "With all the tall, dark lawyers you've screwed, you expect me to believe that this little carrot-top floats your boat?"

Try as he might to fit in, Justin remained way out of his element. Chet recoiled, as if hit, when Justin turned down an offer of Jack-on-the-rocks in favor of some carrot juice. Chet trembled, as if physically shaken, when Justin ate only two ounces of beef but loaded up on the broccoli. And Ginger blanched, as if mortally offended, when Justin enthused about the salutary health benefits of sweat.

For Becky's emotional state, this weekend was crucial. It had taken her so long to even begin to build a relationship with her father, and her slow-developing love for Justin had now taken such deep root, and her frustration with all the controversy surrounding Mad had reached such a boiling point, and her confusion about the problems balancing the company accounts had reached such a crescendo, that all her hard-won psychological maturation hung in the balance. She wanted her father's approval *so* much, and so desperately desired Justin to fit into her world, that each obvious misconnection between Justin and her parents took on an increasingly distressing importance to her.

Affairs reached a head at an "intimate" brunch for 20 at the Matthews home on Sunday. Chet and three of his business partners had retired to the billiard room for a quick game of 8-ball. Becky approached the room bearing a message from Ginger "ordering" the four men back into the "main" living room for some special, ceremonial kind of post-brunch libation. (Ginger had some ulterior social motive in mind, but as it turned out, she never would get the chance to put it into effect.) As Becky reached within earshot, however, she overheard a snippet of conversation that would make her see red.

"… He comes across like a little faggot…" Chet was saying to another oilman. "For the life of me, it's hard to understand what Becky sees in him, and at first I thought he might be part of an elaborate April Fool's joke…."

Becky turned on her heels, beet-faced, and marched into the living room where Justin was holding court about the virtues of self-denial. "I need you, *right now!*" she said to her boyfriend, and then pulled him away from the startled guests and through the house to the guest cottage where both were staying.

What Becky had not heard was the rest of Chet's conversation. "… But I'll tell you what, I trust my girl's judgment, and I'm gonna keep trying to get to know Justin Luke until I see the good Becky sees. I know he's turned his business into a big success, and I know he treats Becky like a princess, so I'm gonna have to learn to like him. And I'll tell you what I admire: For a guy as little as he is, he sure doesn't back down from life. I think he's got guts, and that goes a long way!"

If Becky had heard those comments, her reaction surely would have been different. As it was, though, they were the proverbial straw – actually, the whole bale of hay – on the overworked back of her heightened sensitivities. Twenty minutes later, without explanation, she and Justin were speeding off in her father's Lexus (Chet had given them use of his second car for the weekend), toward the Houston airport. Within a few hours they were on a flight to Las Vegas. A few hours after that they were married, and they spent most of the next day with Justin attempting to satisfy the manic desires of a new wife trying desperately to mask her pain.

The next day, a Tuesday, found them on a plane to the Cayman Islands for a honeymoon Becky's money arranged in the course of just four hours. Nobody, including a confused Mad back in Mobile, knew where they were.

* * *

In St. Louis on Monday morning, Mary McWyre pulled out two checkbooks. It would be the final time she pulled this particular maneuver. One checkbook was hers, personally. Her official signature emphasized her capitalized letters so heavily that only the barest squiggles interrupted the large "*MMW*" that covered the check's bottom-right line. MMW: **M**ary **M**c**W**yre.

The second checkbook was for the account of the Mad Mad World Corporation. Outgoing checks were co-signed by her and by Becky. Incoming checks, though, were simply made out to "*MMW*."

It was a perfect scam. And her boyfriend of nearly three years, now – one Myron "Buzz" Buskirk – was in on the scheme. They both were tired of always being overlooked. They both were tired of lives as second fiddles. And they both thought it absurd for Mad to pay company directors such small stipends (Mary, of course, was also paid for her legal work) when the non-profit company was bringing in so damned much money. Hell, if it weren't for those two, there would be no company. It was Buzz who had handled everything for Mad when Mad went AWOL; it was Buzz who arranged the good rapport with Steve Matheson, the first national media guy to give Mad an even break. Without Matheson, Mad's enterprise would soon have disappeared. And without Buzz, no Matheson. Or so Buzz told himself. As for Mary, she grudgingly credited Becky for all her day-to-day business acumen. But it had been Mary who first devised the idea of a ministry for Mad, and Mary who had drawn up the legal papers and cajoled Mad into signing them when Mad was still acting goofy and unable to decide even which direction to loop his shoe knots. What the two secret lovers were doing, they told themselves, was no more than they had earned. Now it was their time to finally grab for the gusto of an exotic new life in which they would play second fiddle to no one.

For one last time, Mary stopped by the bank and asked to meet privately with a diffident, fat mid-level executive who no women paid attention to. For one last time, Mary flirted with him and let her hand rub dangerously high on his thigh. For one last time, she cajoled him into performing a complicated wire transfer of what had slowly become increasingly large sums. The money would eventually wind up in an account in the Cayman Islands. Within 24 hours, that's where Mary and Buzz would both end up as well. If they played their cards right, and if Buzz grew his hair and a bushy beard, and if Mary cut her hair short and dyed it blonde, and if they managed their funds cleverly… well, if all that happened, the two of them could enjoy lives in paradise for years to come.

* * *

That same morning, April 2, Mad was on the phone with Dr. Raj. The doctor was tremendously excited. That very morning, the expected approval had come from the Food and Drug Administration that would allow him to begin experimental testing of a drug he had developed to control ADZ levels. That drug, he promised, would be shipped to Mad that very afternoon, with all instructions clearly printed inside.

In that afternoon's mail, meanwhile, subscribers to an elite scientific journal would receive the issue that contained Dr. Raj's scholarly article on the aspect of Mad's syndrome that the doctor had for so long kept mysterious.

"This is a wonderful discovery I have made, Madison!" yelled the doctor through the phone line. "It explains everything! It explains the reason why women find you so irresistible! They just can't help themselves, Madison: All they do is follow their nose!"

An incredulous Mad listened as the doctor explained. For years, he said, he had been involved in research on pheromones, the subconscious scents that have long been theorized to play a large role in sexual attraction. Different people respond differently to different levels of different variations of pheromones, said Dr. Raj – but all women seemed to respond impulsively to elevated levels of one particular pheromone on which the doctor had focused his research. The name of the pheromone didn't register with Mad, but the doctor kept referring to it as "the love molecule." And this love molecule, the doctor's research had gone a long way towards proving, increased in direct proportion to levels of ADZ. The hormone triggered the pheromone, and the pheromone made women's knees grow weak.

"If the women bother you too much, Madison, just take my drug and you'll be ordinary in no time!" said Dr. Raj. "In fact, you may even have to work as hard as all the rest of us to get a date!"

For some reason, Dr. Raj found that thought exciting.

For Mad, however, the news came as a severe blow to his ego. Depressed as he had become, he still had been able to take pride in his romantic prowess. But now this oddball doctor was telling him – if Mad understood correctly – that it wasn't Mad's looks, it wasn't his wit, it wasn't his charm or his body language or his eye contact or his innate confidence that made him attractive to women. No, it was just some dumb chemical he had inherited, one which he had not earned, that was doing the work. He wasn't singularly attractive; he just smelled good.

That's the message Mad took away from the conversation. He was a freak of nature, a lucky freak, and he deserved no credit for his freakiness. His conquests were ones not due to his personality or his spirit; mere biological determinism was at work.

Soul didn't matter; only matter counted.

Within hours after hanging up with Dr. Raj, Mad found himself profoundly dispirited. He had no wife, no family, and now apparently no charm. He had become at least partially estranged from his friends; his ministry was suffering; his name was a scandal; and his false public profile (at least to those who only glanced at headlines) was that of a megalomaniac posing as the Second Coming of Christ. Some sicko on his web site wanted him dead, and now it appeared that nobody loved him: They just loved his smell.

* * *

Not only did Becky fail to show up at the office that week, but she also failed to call to let anybody know where she was. The office secretary called Mad in a panic, wondering what to do. An already distraught Mad spent two full days burning up the phone lines, to no avail. Chet told Mad that Becky and Justin had vamoosed from his house without any warning, and for no known reason. By early Tuesday afternoon he had discovered that his Lexus was sitting in the long-term lot at the Houston airport. By early that evening, using all the clout Chet's money could buy, he had traced the couple's movements first to Las Vegas and then to Grand Cayman. But the trail ended there. The discoveries left Chet baffled, hurt, angry, and frantic with worry.

Mad called Father Peter Vignelli, to see if he had heard anything from Becky. He had not. Tuesday night Mad tried reaching Mary in St. Louis and Buzz in Washington to tell them that something seemed terribly amiss. Neither one, of course, was home.

LaShauna suggested to Shiloh that Becky and Justin had decided on a spur-of-the-moment wedding and honeymoon. Impulsive behavior was something LaShauna understood. In this case, of course, she was correct. But to everybody else, that explanation seemed too facile. Except for her tendency a few times a year to go on one-night drinking binges, Becky always seemed to be so in control, her life so meticulously businesslike and planned out, that such a bender from her seemed unlikely. And Justin... well, Justin was as loyal as they came. Sure, he loved Becky and would follow her lead – but he was so devoted to Mad that neither Mad nor Shiloh could envision Justin knowingly leaving Mad in the lurch.

Shiloh, meanwhile, was already so uncomfortable with the state of affairs at MMW that this added confusion made him start unconsciously grinding his teeth. By Tuesday night, the grinding was so audible that it was driving LaShauna crazy. "Here, Shiloh, stick a big wad of gum in your mouth and chew on it instead of on your own teeth," she said, "and don't you dare go without any gum until you're able to stop those big ol' teeth of yours from soundin' like a grindstone in heat!"

For his part, Mad was so disturbed that he thrashed around in bed all that night, unable to sleep more than a few slim minutes at a time. He had nightmares about Justin and Becky running across the brick "Red

Square" on Georgetown University's campus, disappearing around the building into a red-blood-soaked bed, leaving him alone in all the world.

He was finally aroused from bed for good the next morning at 7 a.m. when Laura Green, of all people, called him at home. He was so groggy that he never exactly understood what she was calling about. Everything seemed so topsy-turvy to Mad that he no longer knew who was friend and who was foe. He now knew that Laura was M. Magdalene, who had turned on him so harshly. But she was wearing her "trust in me" voice that had worked such wonders on him three years earlier (and ever since). And Mad was desperate for somebody to tell him everything was okay. Result: Mad couldn't help but blurt out all the details of the strange disappearance of Becky and Justin.

* * *

Laura already was in a quandary. Her career meant just about everything to her, and she would do almost anything it took to advance her career even further. She was a schemer. But she also meant no harm to anybody who was not necessarily in her way. She did have a conscience, albeit a limited one. And she had profoundly mixed feelings about Mad. She had indeed felt something for him sexually, something strong. And she recognized in him, or at least thought she recognized, a basically innocent heart. Yet she also considered him to be a bit of a fool, in effect a naïf, and she didn't suffer fools gladly. Then there was his womanizing, which deep down made her jealous (though she wouldn't admit it even to herself), and which offended her new feminist sensibilities.

Then Spike Walters enlisted her in his project to blow Mad away once and for all. Professionally, she could not afford to blow off Spike Walters. With deep misgivings, then, and with what conscience she had being burdened with guilt, she had called Mad that morning both to pump him for one last bit of information and to ascertain, seemingly quite casually, where he might be at what time of day. Mad didn't know it, but Spike and a camera crew were at that very moment in Mobile.

* * *

"But Mr. Walters, don't you see?" said Laura, plaintively, into the phone. "It all adds up: Mad Jones doesn't know anything about the disappearing money, because he had nothing to do with it, because it's obviously embezzlement by this Becky girl who now has run off to the Caymans, where she can keep her bank accounts secret. It's not fair to ambush Mad Jones today. He's not the guilty party. If you just hold off on your story, you can get to the bottom of the embezzlement and nail the real crooks in this affair."

"Oh, come now, little Laura," said Spike condescendingly. "I know you feel territorial about Jones, because he was your first ticket to stardom. But old Spike here is ready to rumble, and you know that once matters get this down and dirty, only old Spike knows how to rumble and win. Let Spike handle this, little girl – and don't worry: I promise your name will run prominently in the credits when we blast this faker to Kingdom Come. I promise, and old Spike here never forgets a promise!"

No matter what arguments Laura used, Spike Walters would not be swayed. He was ready to make the kill, and he would do it today. Mad was toast.

By the time Laura hung up the phone, her troubled conscience had grown, like the Grinch's heart, three sizes in a very short time. Poor Mad. Laura had betrayed him. She put her head on her desk and cried. She had taken the moniker of Mary Magdalene, but she felt like a female Judas.

* * *

Mad was at his office at 10:30, poring over financial records and helping the secretary man the phones. Shiloh was in the next room, doing likewise. Becky had always handled everything, and handled it so efficiently, that Mad was almost wholly unfamiliar with the myriad day-to-day details of how MMW Corporation was run. He looked haggard, and he had a pounding headache.

That's when the door burst open and Spike Walters, trailed by two different cameras, strode over the threshold like a conquering marauder.

"Mr. Jones, Mr. Jones, I have evidence here of serious financial fraud related to your supposedly charitable company!" Spike's voice was at a near-screaming decibel level. "My investigation has indicated that MMW Corporation already had a discrepancy of more than $80,000 between its net income, after salaries and expenses, and its disbursements to various charities. And that information does not take into account the fact that your company failed to file the required quarterly estimate this past January 15. And new information indicates a possible connection to the Cayman Islands, which is a nefarious banking haven for modern-day pirates. What are you hiding, Mr. Jones? Do you plead guilty, or do you take the Fifth?"

Mad's hair was disheveled. He had circles under his eyes. He was wearing a faded Oxford shirt with a visible stain on the collar. Utterly surprised by Spike's entrance, he looked like a shady con-man caught red-handed. He said the first thing that popped into his head. It was the wrong thing to say.

"What the…?! How did you know about any of this?"

"That sounds like an admission to me, Mr. Jones!" said Spike moving within feet of Mad so that one of the cameras could catch the confrontation in a close-up frame. "So you acknowledge there's something you don't want me to know about? You admit there's money missing, and that there's a Cayman connection?"

"I, uh, no – I mean, uh, what do you know about the Caymans? No, wait! I mean, I don't have anything to say to you. Who let you in here?"

The more Mad talked, the bigger the hole he dug. Spike followed with a barrage of other questions, and Mad retreated from the front room towards a private back office. Shiloh, having heard the commotion, emerged from yet a third little office and apprised the situation. His protective instincts kicking in, he made a beeline toward Spike and the cameras and physically tried to block their way while reaching to try to cover the lenses with his hands.

The whole scene made for perfect "Hour of Truth" TV viewing, even before selective editing would make it look more dramatic still. There was the cornered rat retreating toward his lair. There was the bulky black guy trying to manhandle the journalists. And there was Spike, representing justice and the American way, exposing corruption and expressing the appropriate universal outrage of offended sensibilities.

Spike had the triumphal air of a man who knew that vengeance would soon be his. Nobody got away with embarrassing Spike Walters. *Nobody*!

Spike's ambush completed in just a few minutes, he and his cameras exited Mad's offices. That very night, on the nightly news of Spike's network, the anchorman showed a clip of the confrontation and reported that famed lay minister Mad Jones had been confronted with alleged financial improprieties of a serious nature. "Rarely does this newscast do promos for 'Hour of Truth,' which has its own independent news team," said the anchor portentously, "but it's worth noting that the full details of this breaking story will air this Sunday night, April the 8th, in the normal time slot for 'Hour of Truth.'"

Watching the newscast that night, and seeing Mad's haunted, hunted appearance, Laura Green became physically ill. Her arrogant husband was on special assignment in the Middle East that night, and she was alone.

The next morning, via home fax, Laura tendered her resignation from 'Hour of Truth' and, in effect, from the network as well. She did so even though she thought it meant her meteoric TV career would be at an end. Leaving a cryptic note for her husband on their penthouse dining room table, Laura took a cab towards LaGuardia, rented a car, and began a long, slow, and meandering drive home to New Orleans.

* * *

In a tiny little private cabana on the smaller of the Cayman Islands, Becky and Justin knew none of this. They were deliberately without phone, without TV, without any modern communication device. Justin wanted very much to contact Mad to tell him where they were, and why, but his heart belonged even more to his new wife Becky, and she insisted that they leave the whole world behind them for a week. She felt she had no family, no real home other than the place she occupied in the heart of this funny little orange-haired man with surprisingly rippling muscles who treated her like a princess and loved her with all his soul. Yes, let the world turn without them for a week. She would set things right once they finally returned to Mobile – but not a moment sooner.

* * *

For the rest of the week, Mad was helpless. He knew that "Hour of Truth" was about to send his world even further into Hell, but there was nothing he could do. Chet was too busy trying to track down his daughter (he hired a private eye on Wednesday afternoon) to worry about what Spike Walters would say about Mad Jones. The Colonel had been incommunicado for months. Mary's law firm said that Mary had gone on vacation to parts unknown, and that only she knew enough of MMW's legal and financial affairs to be able to prepare a defense against Spike's upcoming assault. Buzz was, oddly, also nowhere to be found. And while Peter Vignelli made himself available for spiritual counseling, there was nothing he could do to help avert the coming catastrophe.

And catastrophe was exactly what it became. Sunday night's show was the "hit piece" of all journalistic hit pieces. The numbers were laid out in excruciating detail. Over the past few years, MMW Corporation had increasingly built up a discrepancy in its financial accounts. And what looked likely to be, by far, the largest discrepancy of all was hidden by a failure to file the most recent quarterly report. Sources said that on Friday the IRS had mailed an audit notice to the MMW offices. Not only did this guy Jones give rise to the claim that he was Christ, but he seemed to have his hand in the till as well. Also, Jimmy Swaggart-like, he couldn't keep his fly zipped up. He had a bunch of followers who were kooks, and an equally rabid group of protesters against him. As a gratuitous topper, Spike put on camera a glossy "conservative" young congressman from near New Orleans who lit into Mad as an affront to all things truly godly and good. (For the ambitious politician, it was the perfect opportunity to get his face before a larger audience.)

In short, Mad was portrayed, quite devastatingly, as a scam artist and a megalomaniac of the first order – and one kept from escaping only because Spike Jones had exposed his scheme just before Mad was likely to split the country. Ever since the newscast Wednesday, though, Mad had been warned by federal agents to not even attempt to leave the USA.

To close the report, Spike Walters looked triumphantly into the camera. "For three years now, Mad Jones has sold a cleverly packaged religious rant as if it were a vehicle for putting charities first. But while many charities certainly have profited, it seems as if Mr. Jones or his compatriots have put a little extra cash aside, for who knows what fun and games. Eighty thousand dollars as of six months ago, perhaps well over a hundred thousand dollars by now: That's not pocket change. Mr. Jones may consider it to be mere 'Mad money,' but the tax authorities may yet show him that trying to get away with loot of that amount is just plain crazy."

* * *

Mad had insisted on being alone as he watched the show. He wanted to suffer in seclusion. He was convinced this was the end of the line. Today was Palm Sunday, and Mad felt as if he were the ass.

But Shiloh and LaShauna had other ideas. This time, the two were on the exact same page. Just weeks earlier, Shiloh had been ready to abandon ship. But as he watched Spike Walters perform the televised hit job, Shiloh felt his bile rising. Mad had flaws, but he was a well-meaning man with the best of intentions. Shiloh knew that Mad was wholly innocent of any financial shenanigans. Shiloh considered Mad a friend, and friends don't abandon friends in times of trouble. Ten minutes after "Hour of Truth" ended its report, Shiloh showed up unannounced at Mad's front door. When Mad didn't answer the bell, Shiloh used a spare key Mad had given him. He found Mad back at his kitchen counter, glassy-eyed, staring into space.

"I'm with you, Mad," Shiloh said softly. He shifted the gum around in his mouth to make his enunciation even clearer. "We're gonna fight this thing and rescue your good name. No matter how long it takes, friend, I'll be right by your side."

Chapter Eleven

The chat room was overloaded with messages. They ran as much as nine-to-one against Mad. He was labeled a "crook," a "criminal," and a "shyster," in addition to all the usual charges of him being a blasphemer and a heretic. "It is now long past time for somebody to put Mad's so-called 'ministry' out of its, and our, misery," wrote Defender. "All he is, is a money-grubbing televangelist without the TV," wrote somebody calling himself "Ontario." And so distressingly on, with only the odd "Hang in there, Mad!" to break the run of vituperation.

But in the midst of all the anger and epithets, a wholly unexpected series of notes were introduced. Not once, not twice, not thrice, but a full dozen times, the message came in that "Mad muss live!" And none of the previous death messages were anywhere in sight.

The "muss" notes were little solace to Mad, however. For one thing, he had never been particularly concerned when they said "die" instead of "live." Just some nut on the Internet, he thought – "that's all." For another thing, there was no way to know if the author of the "live" messages was even the same person, or group, who had earlier written that he "muss die." Finally, Mad's depression was such that it shut out any positive input. In fact, his depression was so great that virtually all his anger was turned inward, with almost no anger left over to direct at Spike Walters. The one exception to this trend was his fury at Becky and Justin, who by now he had finally decided were the real culprits in the financial improprieties. Father Vignelli warned Mad not to jump to conclusions, but in Mad's mind it all made too much sense: Becky and Justin both might have reason to resent Mad – for taking them for granted, for failing to be the friend to them that they had been to him, and in particular for him riding Justin so hard about Justin's failure to update his holistic health program to reflect the maturation of mad's theology. "They must have convinced themselves that they've earned this money anyway," he told Peter. "They must resent me so much that they've justified their crookedness in their own minds and blamed it on me instead. Well, they can go to hell! I may have been a jerk, but it's not me they're robbing; it's the charities that otherwise would get the money!"

"Mad, I just don't believe that," responded the priest. "They have proven to be your friends come hell or high water. And friends don't do things like that to their friends. For that matter, friends don't accuse friends of such bad faith before all the facts are in."

Father Vignelli was correct, but Mad's mind was too troubled for him to recognize the wisdom.

"If only Mary weren't on vacation!" he thought. "She's the legal expert; she'll surely know what legal recourse we have to recover our assets."

At that moment, though, a dyed-blonde Mary with a false passport was lying on a Cayman beach next to her quarter-century-older boyfriend. By secretly selling all their assets, cashing in early all their insurance policies and pension plans, and combining all that with their carefully embezzled lucre, the two together had laid away far more than $300,000. Eventually, they figured, they might have to get part-time jobs selling fruit drinks on the beach. But if they lived simply and with some fiscal discipline in this tropical paradise, they figured their loot (with interest, once they laundered their money into regular bank accounts) might last for 15, 20, even 25 years.

* * *

By Tuesday afternoon (as Newsweek magazine hit the stands with a photo of Mad next to the headline of "Fallen Prophet"), Chet's private eye was reporting that he expected to find Becky and Justin within the next 24 hours. He said he had found a hotel where they had stayed during their first night on the island. To Mad, who was sitting in the MMW offices, this was great news. Shiloh and LaShauna had convinced Mad that he should try to fight back, should try to get the truth out and correct Spike's insinuations that Mad himself was some kind of scam artist. Mad thought that if somebody was able to track down Becky and

Justin and keel-haul them, he might be able to get the real facts out in a major press conference.

Thus, the very last thing Mad expected when his cell phone rang was Justin's voice, cheery and open as ever, sounding as if there were nothing at all to be guilty about. He and Becky had finally returned to the less remote Grand Cayman Island, where they could again use modern communications.

"Hey ol'buddy ol'pal, yernotgonnabelieve it ol'buddy, and I'm so sorry we felt we had to do it on the quick and that we haven't called you before now ol'buddy, but Becky and I are married!" Justin could barely contain his excitement. "Her dad didn't like me, and so she flew me off to Vegas and...."

"You son of a bitch!" Mad wasn't listening. In his hurt and anger, he was almost beyond reason. "You actually have the gall to call me and gloat about your, uh, your sonuvabitching crooked-ass escape to paradise! And to think I trusted you! Well, don't think you're beyond the law there, you little shit, because we're on to you. We'll do what it takes to extradite your ass and bring you here to face the music!"

Dead silence on the other end of the line. Silence, and then the gurgling sound of somebody gasping for breath. Poor Justin had no idea what Mad was talking about. But here was the one person he had always looked up to, always considered to be his one stalwart friend, accusing him of something that sounded terribly like a crime.

Mad was too worked up to notice. He sounded like he was becoming almost unhinged: "I mean I know I've been a jerk these past couple of years, but that doesn't excuse this, this abomination. How'd Becky talk you into this, you little jackass? Don't you know that money should have gone to charity?"

All Justin could do was to splutter. The joy he had been so eager to share with his friend had been yanked away by something so painful he could not even name it. Mad was accusing him of something awful, but Justin still didn't know what. He had been out of touch with the real world for more than a week, and he felt like the world to which he returned was some kind of evil "twilight zone."

Justin's confusion and pain would only grow. Before he could find out what in God's name Mad was talking about, Justin heard a commotion through the phone line, followed by an audible expletive, followed by the sound of a cell phone clattering on the floor. A second later, the line went dead.

What had happened was that Shiloh, full of excitement, fury and triumph, had burst into Mad's private office. His colleagues at the police department had passed on to him a piece of big news: Buzz Buskirk had officially been reported "missing" by his college history department. Investigations showed a series of odd financial transactions in the previous two weeks, with every single asset Buzz owned having been turned into cold cash or else wired to one "Mary McWyre" in St. Louis. On further investigation, it had been discovered that Ms. McWyre had similarly engaged in a purging of all her financial assets. She was supposedly on vacation, but had left no word as to where, and had not been in touch with anyone at her law firm in the meantime. Beyond that, the trail so far was cold. Both of them seemed to have disappeared without a trace.

The shock of the preliminary news had been so great that Mad had dropped his cell phone. It would be days before he and Justin, or he and Becky, would speak to each other again. Mad would be full of remorse about the accusations he leveled at his friends, and they would be full of bitter pain at being so suspected.

* * *

The next afternoon brought odd and unexpected news of a different sort. It came from the FBI agents who had been investigating the threatening web site messages. The "Mad muss live" notes had been sent without any of the clever codes that masked the origins of the earlier ones that told him to die. But once they were traced, which was a simple matter, they turned out to all come from the same sources as the threats. And it turned out that the threats weren't threats at all.

What the FBI explained to Mad all involved complicated techno-stuff that made Mad's head spin. But the gist of it was that the techno-messengers were a small group of 12-year-old computer geeks playing a highly original, highly complex mathematical game in a numerical code of their own creation. The key was the word "muss" instead of "must." If the letter "A" corresponds to the number "1," the FBI agents explained, and if "B" stood for "2" and "C" for "3," and so on, then the act of adding up the letters of "muss" produced a sum of 72. And 72 is a number easily divisible by a host of smaller numbers: 2, 3, 4, 6, 8, 9, 12, 18, 24, and 36. The letter-numerals in the words "Mad" and "die" both add up to 18, which also is a divisor of 72. The geeks had used Mad's chat room as a mere means to the end of a cyber-game that amounted to something along the lines of "Dungeons and Dragons"-meets-Sherlock Holmes-meets-*A Beautiful Mind*. And the months-long game had ended only earlier that week, with the victory signal being "live" instead of "die." Why "live"? Because its letters added up to 48, which is the next highest number below 72 that is divisible by each of 72's first five divisors.

Mad didn't even pretend to understand it all. Nor, really, did these two particular FBI agents. What it meant, though, was that Mad had never been in any danger. His chat room had merely been a convenient site for the kids' cyber-play. As far as the FBI could tell, nobody disliked Mad enough to want to kill him. The kids would be given a stern warning, and maybe even a fine if some cyber-law could be used against them – but otherwise it was a case of "no harm, no foul."

For the first time in weeks, Mad's mood began, ever so slightly, to lift. If nothing else went right, at least he was physically safe.

* * *

By that time, Becky and Justin were landing back in Mobile, to be met at the airport by Father Peter Vignelli, who would bring them fully up to date on everything they had missed during their sudden honeymoon. Chet Matthews wanted to be there, too, but on the Jesuit's advice he had stayed away. The priest said that, over time, he would run interference for Chet and try to mediate between him and his daughter. Peter assured Chet that he wouldn't rest until, somehow, the father and daughter – and son-in-law, for that matter – had developed the loving relationship that Chet had always wanted.

The returning couple would find, when they reached their abodes, a lengthy letter of deep remorse, highly self-critical, from Mad. He had been a fool and a rotten friend, he said. He didn't expect them ever to forgive him, because he could never forgive himself for suspecting them, but he wanted them to know how deeply he had cherished their friendship and support over the years. "I don't deserve your friendship," he concluded. "But I am willing to spend the whole rest of my life trying, as hard as I possibly can, to earn it back." Reading it, Becky felt spent. Impulsively, she ripped it in half and threw it in a trash can before going to unpack her clothes.

An exceedingly morose Justin stared at the two pieces of paper sticking up from the trash can's edge. Finally, crying softly, he picked the letter out of the can and put the pieces together so as to read it one more time. And then he read it yet another time. He put his head in one hand, rubbing his red eyebrows with his thumb and his newly adorned ring finger. After a while, still silent and uncharacteristically listless, Justin folded the letter neatly and put it in his pocket.

* * *

The next day, Maundy Thursday, would see a swarm of activity at the MMW offices. Law enforcement personnel of several different stripes were in and out all day, as were auditors from the IRS. In Washington and St. Louis, analysts were feverishly trying to track the paper trail (and, more importantly, the e-trails) of Mary and Buzz. The grandmotherly secretary bustled around non-stop. All the principles were there, too. Mad monitored developments in one room. Becky and Justin worked some phone lines in another room. Those two weren't ready to speak to Mad directly, so Father Vignelli ran messages back and forth. Shiloh made himself useful in numerous ways.

A local PR person came in and out. And Mark Mariasson, amazingly, had shown up unannounced after a six-hour drive from Ole Miss. With the PR guy and Mark, Mad intermittently worked at drafting what began as a brief announcement and grew into a lengthier statement and metamorphosed again into a substantive speech that he hoped, against all his depressed hopes, would leave a strong, noble, and lasting impression.

Somebody monitoring the chat room brought to Mad's attention an entry from "Lazarus," the young man who once had challenged Mad outside the Maple Street Book Shop in New Orleans. "All you naysayers are vultures! I refuse to believe that Mad Jones embezzled any money. Time and the legal authorities will determine that. But, people, why can't you see the truth in front of your noses? Mad brought me back to God; he brought a lot of people back to God, and while doing so he raised, what, probably hundreds of thousands of dollars for charity. Not only is he innocent until proven guilty, but I say he is in some ways saintly until proven otherwise. For me he has been a vessel of God's love, and I will not forsake him."

* * *

Laura Green found herself on Interstate 65 about two hours south of Montgomery, Alabama. The past eight days had been an aimless odyssey for her, but now her hometown of New Orleans was less than three hours away. Her self-absorbed husband had cursed her on the phone when he found out she had resigned from "Hour of Truth," and she told him she considered themselves officially separated from each other, with divorce a definite option.

New Orleans was forefront in her mind, but the road sign announcing a mere 30 miles to Mobile made her reconsider. She figured that Mad now would hate her for life, but she wanted to look him in the face, apologize for playing a role in his destruction, and tell him that she had, belatedly, listened to her conscience and resigned from the character-assassination outfit that called itself a TV news magazine. So Laura decided to zig into Mobile, to the MMW offices, on the off-chance Mad would consent even to see her.

What she discovered there was a sight similar to one she had beheld three years earlier. Outside the building, a dozen protesters, kept at bay by police, chanted angry slogans. A TV camera, having received word of more frenetic activity at the offices, surveyed the scene in case something interesting happened. And law enforcement vehicles were parked out front in "No Parking" zones.

The policeman outside the offices had no idea who Laura was and wouldn't let her through. Laura used her cell phone to try to call Mad's. She was surprised when he answered.

"Mad, this is Laura. I'm here by myself. I don't know what to say. This is personal, not job-related. Can I please come up and talk to you?"

"Oh, right: Laura Magdalene, isn't that your name? And what personal business could you possibly have with… what did you call me, wasn't it a 'womanizing slimeball'? And what's the deal this time? Has old Spike Walters put a hidden camera in your brassiere?"

"No, Mad, I promise. I *promise*. Mad, I'm all by myself, and Spike doesn't know I'm here, and I really really really really need to see you. Please, Mad. *Please*."

Inside the building, Mad figured that there was nothing more Laura could do to him that would cause any more harm than had already been done. He had a sudden urge to look her in the eye for himself and try to figure out why she had forsaken him. He sent Shiloh outside to escort her in.

A half hour, long explanations, and many tears later, Mad did the most grace-filled thing he had done in quite some time. He forgave Laura Green. He was moved that, career-oriented as she always had been, she had resigned just at the moment when she had proven herself invaluable to the leading power for the leading TV news magazine in the country. Her contrition was palpable, her concern for him quite real.

"You know, Laura, you and I are different breeds," Mad said to her. "You always have all the angles covered; I just try to avoid the sharp angles altogether. For the longest time I thought, deep in my heart, that you and I were meant for each other. But that's not the case at all. We're not meant for each other – but I think we may be meant to help each other. How would you like it if I gave you an exclusive? Do you still have good relations with the network affiliate in New Orleans? Do you think your old station would want you back? How about if *I* play the angles for once, so that you and I can come full circle?"

It somehow didn't matter that Mad's sentence made no sense, geometrically speaking. Laura quickly understood what he meant.

That conversation occurred just before 4 p.m. It was followed by several "background" conversations Mad arranged for Laura to have with some of the law enforcement personnel. It was followed by a quick session with Becky – who, albeit with great skepticism, performed a crash course for Laura on MMW's financial records. And that in turn was followed by a phone conversation with a skeptical New Orleans TV producer, who eventually was impressed when an FBI agent (on background) confirmed the gist of Laura's tale.

At 5:15, Laura was reporting live, via phone, to her old New Orleans affiliate. "Renowned lay minister Mad Jones has been exonerated by federal agents of all charges in connection with the disappearance of more than $100,000 from his non-profit corporation," she reported. "The young man who began his ministry with a set of religious proclamations affixed to the door of New Orleans' own St. Louis Cathedral now will have a major announcement tomorrow at 11:30 a.m., probably at the Mobile Civic Center – an announcement which promises to be every bit as dramatic as the assertion that 'God is a jerk' with which he first gained prominence. This is Laura Green, reporting live from Mobile."

The report worked like a charm, as just the news "teaser" it was intended to be. Word would travel overnight up and down the national media grapevine. The fact that the report was broken in a city different from the origin of the news made the story seem more noteworthy. The cryptic nature of the reported facts gave just enough information to raise interest, but not enough information to answer the most relevant questions. In short, the stage was now set for a command performance.

And Mad, depressed as he still was, was sure he saw a dim ray of daylight through his tunnel of doubt.

Chapter Twelve

Inside a small room of the Mobile Civic Center, a bank of TV cameras, photographers and inky wretches of the print media crowded towards a podium. Outside, more than 400 protesters, supporters, and curious onlookers stood in a small courtyard across the street, watching and listening to the proceedings via a large video screen set up for the purpose. The throng was kept at bay by about a dozen of Mobile's finest – including Officer Williams, looking more like an albino hippo than ever, who was relieved from desk duty only at times like these when extra manpower was needed on the streets for crowd control. He was in a good mood. Life was working out for him better than expected. Thanks in large part to Shiloh, he had been spared a disciplinary action; and he was finding that he liked the change of pace of not being in the patrol car all day. A decent retirement would be coming very soon. When Mad, Shiloh and Father Vignelli arrived at the Civic Center (the local PR guy, Mark Mariasson and a still-angry Becky and Justin already were there making sure that everything was set up properly), Officer Williams tried to smile and catch their eye and wave. But Mad and Shiloh were too intent on other matters to see him.

Earlier that morning, those two and Father Vignelli had asked permission to use the chapel of Mad's new Episcopal Church, All Saints, for some moments of silent prayer. Despite Peter's Catholicism, Mad had wanted this day to begin at a sacred place of his own denomination, where he would feel most at home. He prayed for calm; he prayed for wisdom; he prayed for guidance. He prayed for God's blessing in the course he had chosen. It was the morning of Good Friday; it was the morning of the day when darkness fell so that the world could better receive the light.

But in the midst of his somber and sincere prayers, Mad could not force from his mind a stupid, piddling superstition. This Good Friday also fell on April 13. And Mad hated, absolutely hated, Fridays the Thirteenth.

All of which helps explain why, although his mood had lifted some the night before, Mad again was feeling unsettled, even taciturn. It explains why he had tunnel vision, too wrapped up in his own drama to notice clearly what was occurring around him, including that Officer Williams smiled at him and that some other familiar faces dotted the crowd outside the Civic Center.

Once inside, Mad strode to the podium. He held up his hands for silence and, after some last-second buzz from the media died down, Mad began to read.

"Just over three years ago, on another Friday the Thirteenth, I gave an interview for a TV news magazine in which I tried to downplay the list of religious theses I had written in the previous few weeks, and in which I asked for the public spotlight to leave me. After it was edited, though, the interview only served to help thrust me further into the limelight.

Also about three years ago, on Good Friday of 1998, I made my very first speaking appearance under the auspices of a new, non-ordained ministry that a number of my friends urged me to launch. I was late for that particular engagement – but every time I tried to apologize for my lateness, the audience assumed I was speaking in parables. My words took on a meaning I did not intend, but the unintended meaning proved popular, and I let myself be swept along by that popularity.

Today, on what is both a Friday the Thirteenth and a Good Friday, I realize I again am late in doing what I should have done long ago. Therefore, at the end of this statement, I will make an announcement that I sincerely hope will prove to be better late than never."

("I wish he'd cut all this elliptical bullshit and get to the friggin' point!" whispered one reporter, too audibly, to another.)

"I preface this announcement with a lengthy introduction," Mad continued, "in order to emphasize the ways in which life always seems to come full circle. Life always begins and ends with the magical mystery of God, and with our constant quest to understand and respond appropriately to His will for us. God is the Alpha and the Omega, the beginning and end, the whole and sum of every part and the cause and effect of everything we do. And though each circle comes back to its own starting point, the circle also yet moves forward, just as a wheel can roll ahead and yet rest on the very part of itself which originally bore its weight."

("The **point**, dammit, get to the **point**!" said the particularly impatient reporter.)

Mad: "I myself began this ministry at a time when I considered my life, or whatever was worth living for, to be at an end. You know the story by now, of how I lost my grandfather, my final blood relative, in an accident, and then how six weeks later, within 24 hours, I lost my wife, my unborn child, and my mother-in-law who had become to me like the mother I never had. But from that ending, or rather that conglomeration of endings, from a grief and pain that was akin to madness, sprang my odd ministry of sorts which leveled the worst of charges at God and yet still maintained that He should be loved and worshipped.

In essence, the message was that, just as God offers us his redemptive grace – a grace far greater than we deserve and far beyond our power to understand, much less earn – we, too, weak humans though we are, must have the grace to forgive God for all the great big, great sick jokes He seems to play on us. Our grace may be as a thimble compared to God's vast oceans of grace, but it nevertheless is our duty, and it should be our joy, to offer our full thimbleful.

It is only through forgiving that we may be forgiven.

And it is only with a load of courage that we can find the strength it takes for us to forgive. As the lesson, paraphrased, says: From suffering comes character comes endurance comes hope comes the recognition of the wonder of God's love.

For whatever reason, hundreds of thousands, even millions, of people seemed to respond affirmatively to that message.

That response, it must be said, was seductive. I was seduced by that affirmative response. I was seduced into believing, at least at times, that the response was an approving reaction to me, personally, rather than to the message I had the honor to carry. Some of my behavior shows, perhaps, that the seduction went to my head.

But if it went to my head, I still don't think it went to my heart. I took pride, maybe too much pride, in the fact that while I could have made myself very wealthy indeed through my ministry, I instead devoted the vast bulk of the earnings to charitable endeavors. To date, my nonprofit MMW Corporation has donated $892,350 to various charities. At our next board meeting, scheduled two weeks hence, we will allocate approximately another $170,000 to good, needy causes.

To give credit where it's due, the money that MMW has given away is not attributable to my own good sense. All I do is serve as a vessel for the message. The rewards the message has garnered for charity are due, overwhelmingly, to the business acumen and the good wills and good, laborious works of my colleagues and friends, the recently married Becky and Justin Luke. Becky, especially, who has made this her life for three years, day in and day out, deserves the credit, and I thank her from the very depths of my soul. More than that, I thank them both for their friendship.

As you all must be aware, however, our charitable endeavors would have been yet greater had there not been a glitch in our system. Last Sunday, a televised report outlined the dimensions of that glitch: Through last Fall, more than $70,000 raised by MMW, and not accounted for by legitimate overhead expenses and audited salaries, had disappeared. Our best estimates are that upwards of $40,000 more has disappeared since then. All told, the discrepancy has meant that our donations to charity could have been, indeed should have been, a full ten percent higher than they will end up being. For that, I am truly sorry.

But I tell you here today that I am not responsible for the disappearing money. I have been authorized, by federal authorities, to make this announcement, which they will confirm immediately after I am finished talking. The announcement is that the culprits have been identified, by means of overwhelming evidence. Two former colleagues of mine, who are the culprits, have disappeared. With them have disappeared the embezzled funds. I am cooperating fully with the authorities in their efforts to find and apprehend my former colleagues, and the authorities have privately, and will publicly, clear me of all suspicion of wrongdoing in this matter.

Though I am freed from suspicion, however, I cannot be free from a sense of guilt. All along, for three years now, I have been a little out of control. I was out of control, legally innocently but still in some senses morally culpably, of the finances of my non-profit business. I have been out of control of my personal life. I have been out of control of my own theology at times, evolving perhaps too rapidly and with too little grounding. And, in my example of a slightly reckless personality, I have somehow, without meaning to do so, encouraged recklessness in others. I have inspired anger where I meant to build understanding. I have become controversial when I meant to be unifying. I have come across as political when I meant to speak of things far more important than politics.

Some oddball people have taken up my cause, and I have apparently done too little to dissuade them. These oddballs wear various costumes, at least figuratively speaking, but what they mask is an almost dangerous restlessness that seems to have fed off of me rather than be soothed by me.

One fan of mine, this very minute, continues to run a web site making the ludicrous claim that I am the Second Coming. I denounce his claim as absurd.

But in many ways the damage has been done. I hope that, through my seat-of-the-pants ministry that I never originally intended to start, some or even many good people may have found their way to God. I don't know if that is the case. I pray that it is. But I do know that I should long ago have recognized that my own persona, my own flaws, have been dragging down the worth of my message so that I today am doing almost as much harm as good. Or at least that's what it feels like from where I stand.

In sum: God is good. Mad is weak. God rectifies mistakes in the long run. Mad Jones compounds his own errors.

So it's time for me to get out of God's way. It's time for me, having come full circle, to get off of the merry-go-round I set in motion three years ago from a hospital bed.

It is time for me to end my ministry. If a good school will have me, it is time for me to go back to teaching high school history.

I therefore announce that, as of our board meeting two weeks hence, the Mad Mad World Corporation will distribute the remainder of its applicable funds to charities, and then it will cease and desist. This is not a Mad world after all; as I have said in numerous speeches and homilies over the past couple of years, this is a very purposive universe. May all of us always be open to God's purposes, and willing to be vessels of His love."

With that, Mad turned on his heels and, taking no questions, left the room via a side passageway. With the door shut behind them, Mad Jones embraced Shiloh Jones and Peter Vignelli, and slowly the three made their way through a private corridor away from the paparazzi.

Outside, the sky darkened as if about to rain.

The three men had parked their car a good several blocks from the civic center. Mad had wanted to walk through the fresh morning air to clear his head before his speech. Now it was time to find a side exit so they could return to their car in peace.

They found, however, that three different side exits all were locked. Their only recourse was the way they had entered, right through the front doors of the Civic Center, past whatever crowds still remained behind the police line manned, among others, by Officer Buster Williams.

By the time they reached the exit, a few – a very few – in the crowd had left the scene, melting into their cars or onto the pretty, oak-lined streets of the Church Street East historic district.

Also by the time they reached the exit, something seemingly wonderful had happened. There had been major tears in the anteroom as the three men embraced after Mad's speech. But as they wandered around the big building looking to make a private getaway, something about the situation – the situation of having left the stage, only to find they still were trapped – seemed absurd in a funny way, and they had begun to laugh. Shiloh even allowed himself the pleasure of blowing a bubble with the big wad of gum that LaShauna insisted he keep in his mouth. As they laughed, the realization hit Mad that he no longer would have to carry the burden of the public eye, no longer would be asked to be a spiritual mentor to thousands of strangers, no longer would be asked to be an authority on a faith whose ultimate answers eluded him still.

Although the feeling might be characterized as trite, Mad truly did feel as if a great weight had fallen from his shoulders.

So, as the men walked out of the front door of the Civic Center, the still-milling crowds behind the barricade seemed fun like a carnival, not invasive like a bevy of parasites. "You know what?" Mad said to his two friends. "Now that I know that nobody actually thinks that I 'muss die,' that throng doesn't look even a tenth as threatening as it did just a week ago."

The three walked past Officer Williams, who smiled at them a big old friendly ugly hippopotamus smile and waved. At a corner of a side street, a small Toyota was stopped and the driver was yelling something. The passenger-side window was towards Mad, and it was open. Through the window, Mad thought he recognized the face. It was pretty. Framed by blonde hair. A face from his past. "Mad! Mad! Over here! Mad: Do you remember me?"

As Mad pivoted towards the Toyota, and bent down towards the open window, Shiloh scanned the crowd. Even now, he was doing his bodyguard duty, making sure Mad was safe. Father Vignelli followed Shiloh's gaze.

"Hey, guys, look at that," said the Jesuit. "There's our old friend the mime again. I wonder what his point is this time?"

Both of the other men looked, too. This time the mime was dressed and painted in a full military camouflage disguise. His get-up was so good it struck them all as stunningly artistic.

"Damn, he doesn't miss a detail," Mad said as the mime stepped to the very edge of the barricade line, only some 15 yards away. "The guy's actually pretty good. Even that gun he has looks absolutely, military-issue real!" All three men were laughing lightly at the sight.

Then, in an instant, all holy godforsaken hell broke loose. A slo-mo video camera would have caught the action like this:

1) "My God, it IS real!" shouted Shiloh.

2) The mime suddenly extended the gun at full arm's length.

3) Shiloh pushed Mad aside with one arm and dove in the direction of the mime.

4) A deafening blast sounded, and then another, as smoke rose from the gun barrel.

5) "Mad, jump in!" yelled the blonde from the Toyota.

6) In accordance with Mad's usual "flight" instinct when confronted with a "fight or flight" situation, Mad began to dive headfirst through the open passenger window.

7) Shiloh simultaneously hit the ground at full-length sprawl as Office Williams thrust his hulking weight into a full body-block against the mime while a third blast sounded.

As bedlam continued on the street and sidewalk, the Toyota sped off in the direction of Canal Street, Mad's legs still waving from its window.

Revelation

There are times when faith stands, undiminished but momentarily unable to act, amidst events occurring too fast for its human host to comprehend.

The Rev. Peter Vignelli, S.J. stood for an instant in the middle of the street, Toyota speeding off in one direction, Shiloh sprawled flat five paces away, mime crushed under the weight of Officer Williams another two paces beyond him. He then watched as several other police sprang to the mime's position, holding him down as he gasped painfully for breath, while Officer Williams crawled away on shaky, lubbery hands and knees. For once, Father Vignelli was in no control of any aspect of a situation, and he remained rooted to his spot. Like the poets in the Springsteen song, all he could do was "just stand back and let it all be."

Sometimes humans must act without waiting for God's guidance. Sometimes a crisis will free a soul from its shackles and force the soul to express its most essential nature, whether it be for good or ill. If necessity is the mother of invention, then emergency can be the mother of either courage or cowardice, virtue or ignobility.

Officer Williams had no time to think of such considerations. The reason the fat officer crawled away from the mime once his fellow policemen jumped in to help was that he saw Shiloh Jones sprawled flat on his back on the asphalt, just a few feet away. Blood streamed from beneath Shiloh's upper left back, and his dark black face featured a pained, breathless expression.

"*Jones-y!*" yelled his former partner. "Jones-y, are you okay?!?"

Shiloh's eyelids were scrunched shut, but even through closed lids it appeared as if his eyeballs had rolled back into his head.

"Don't die on me, Jones-y!" yelled the fat cop. "Jones-y, please don't die!"

Saliva drooled and spat from Williams' mouth and sweat poured from his brows. Gingerly at first, he tried to shake Shiloh awake. Around him, bedlam reigned.

Crying, yelling at his former partner, Officer Williams leaned over Shiloh and gasped for breath. A sob welled up from his huge gut, and snot dripped from his nostrils. Again he yelled, "Don't die!"

From somewhere in his brain, the fat policeman's training kicked in. This was human-to-human, not white-to-black. Pinching Shiloh's nose, Buster Williams leaned down and put his mouth on the black man's mouth. Tremblingly, he exhaled, and then again.

No real response.

All this had happened in less than 20 seconds since Shiloh fell. Peter Vignelli finally came out of his trance and sprang to the two officers' sides, grabbing Shiloh's hands and beginning to pray.

Buster Williams tried once again to revive Shiloh mouth-to-mouth, and thought he heard a gurgle. Frantic, he leveraged his massive weight above his comrade and, pressing the heel of his palm to Shiloh's sternum, pushed down. With a great spluttering cough, Shiloh expelled a large wadded-up chunk of gum and, with loud labor, began again to breathe. The gum landed right on Buster Williams' beefy forehead and fell down the collar of his sweat-soaked shirt. It was of no moment to the officer. "Stay with me, please, Jones-y, you gotta stay with me! C'mon you beautiful nigger, please don't die!"

Shiloh's breaths began coming with less labor, and he found the strength to squeeze Father Vignelli's hand. The priest continued to pray. "Heavenly Father, save this thy son Shiloh. Heavenly Father, please save this thy son."

A minute passed.

"Are you gonna be okay, Jones-y?" cried Officer Williams. "Please be okay!"

"My shoulder," said Shiloh. "I think I hurt my shoulder."

A burn mark and a blood-soaked hole marred a spot just under Shiloh's left collarbone. Blood still seeped from underneath. Some sirens sounded; the mime was manhandled into a squad car; somebody claiming to be a medic came up and pushed Officer Williams aside. Within another minute or two an ambulance roared up. A stretcher appeared; Shiloh was loaded onto it. "I'm coming with him," said the Jesuit, and nobody argued. As the stretcher was loaded into the ambulance, Officer Williams also trailed behind it until a medic stopped him from going farther.

"Buster!" Shiloh spoke more loudly than one would have expected him to be able. "Thanks, Buster. Thanks."

Medics, Shiloh, and the Jesuit disappeared inside the vehicle and its rear doors closed. Siren blaring, it sped away. Watching it go, Buster Williams allowed tears to run unashamedly down his face. "Hang on for me, Jones-y," he whispered, to nobody that could hear him. "Just hang on, Jones-y; just hang on."

* * *

Grace Feinstein Martin was not very familiar with Mobile's streets, but she remembered the way back to Interstate 10. Neither she nor Mad could find any words to say during the three minutes to the highway, even after Mad had wriggled the rest of the way through the window into the front seat. Both were too stunned by events.

"I, uh,… Mad, uh, it's me, uh, Grace Martin. Grace Feinstein," she said, finally.

Mad had figured out by then who it was. It had been almost 15 years since he had laid eyes on her. Her face was fuller, part and parcel of the 20 pounds she had added to her short frame since college. But she was still pretty – older, obviously, with a tiredness to her eyes, yet with a clearly remaining aspect of sexiness. Her breasts strained against the shoulder harness of a seat belt.

"What are you doing here?" he finally said, not terribly brightly.

Turning to look at him in order to try to answer, she noticed a red liquid pooling on the floor of the passenger side. "My God, Mad, you've been hit!"

Mad had noticed a numbness in his right foot. He followed Grace's gaze. The little-toe area of his right loafer was blown full off. A bit of mangled flesh poked out.

"Jesus, Mad, where's the nearest hospital?" Grace asked.

Less than fifteen minutes later, their conversation having consisted of little more than street directions, the two of them pulled into the emergency entrance of Mobile Infirmary, just behind the ambulance carrying Shiloh.

* * *

As it turned out, the third bullet fired by the mime had taken off just the tip of Mad's little toe as he dove into Grace's Toyota. But the national cable news networks would report for hours that both Madison Jones and his bodyguard, Shiloh Jones, had been hit by fire from a would-be assassin, with much confusion as to how bad the injuries were. "At least one of the two," said one network, "is reported to be in serious condition."

In truth, Mad's wound was painful and would force him to make some substantial changes in his future athletic pursuits (a small toe is surprisingly important for balance), but it was of the sort that allowed him to be discharged from the hospital with a pronounced limp within about five hours.

Shiloh was another matter. One of the first two bullets had ripped underneath his collarbone and out his back, taking an edge of his back left shoulder blade with it. (Apparently the second bullet hit nobody.) For two days he would be listed in "serious-but-stable" condition. Hospital staff insisted that, aside from LaShauna and the Jesuit, nobody would be allowed to see Shiloh until Monday at the earliest. Although he seemed in no life-threatening danger, he had lost a lot of blood and would also be on serious painkillers for many days.

In the hospital before his discharge, Mad was nearly catatonic. He did not respond well to stress or crisis or bad news. Although he asked after Shiloh and was told only that his friend "should eventually be okay," Mad accepted with docility the edict against visitors. Grace, who didn't know Shiloh from Adam, told Mad the best thing to do would be to jot a note down and send it via a friendly nurse to LaShauna. Mad dutifully obliged. But he seemed to be in shock, or something like it. He kept grabbing Grace's hand, almost like a small child would hold a teacher's hand to cross a street.

Eventually the two of them left the hospital, with an orderly's help, through a little-used side exit, in order to avoid a bank of cameras stationed outside the hospital entrance. Grace retrieved her car, drove around the side to pick Mad up, and whisked him off into the late afternoon.

* * *

For the rest of that Easter weekend, the network news shows were full of the story of the attempted assassination of the young religious leader who had just ended his ministry, of the bodyguard hospitalized with a hole near his shoulder, and, soon most of all, of the mystery of the whereabouts of Madison Lee Jones. Mad was right that life keeps working in circles: The days before he posted his theses and unknowingly started a ministry, he had mysteriously hidden away from the world; now in the days just after his enterprise ended, he again was a hideaway unable to be found.

Grace Martin had driven Mad eastward, past Destin, Fla., to a secluded house another ten miles east of the place where Peter Vignelli had taken Mad and Becky on their private retreat. That's where Grace had been planning to travel anyway, just for a four-day weekend while her kids were with their father, before she had found reason to stop in Mobile *en route*. In Easter weekend traffic, the drive from Mobile took well over three hours – three remarkably silent hours, hours in which Grace's repeated efforts to speak with Mad were rebuffed, not unkindly but rather vacantly, with monosyllabic responses or vague non sequiturs.

Once they reached the tiny cottage Grace had rented, Grace walked a hobbling Mad into the single bedroom, helped him remove his shirt and blood-spattered trousers, and tucked him into bed in his underwear like a babysitter would tuck in a small but mindful child. The difference was that Grace (after brushing her teeth and washing her face) climbed in beside him and held him from behind. There was nothing sexual about the arrangement; it was just that Grace sensed that Mad needed to be encircled, or as close as possible to it, with a kindly human touch. Wordlessly, Mad eventually drifted off to what would prove a nightmare-filled sleep.

* * *

In the year since the previous Easter, Grace Martin had circumnavigated her own spiritual globe. She also had tunneled through the center of her psyche. She had leapt from Everest-heights of doubt, without a bungee cord, into a frighteningly deep ravine called faith. To her surprise, she found that faith held her aloft; she had not hit bottom.

Easter week the previous year had made a profound impression on her. The doorway to her spirit, which Mad had forced ajar, had been pulled further open during that week, and continued to swing more widely ever since. All manner of new thoughts and feelings and confusions and convictions had taken the opportunity to rush in.

If she had to categorize her current state of belief, she would have said she was a Jewish Christian, or maybe a Christian Jew. And she saw nothing oxymoronic in that position.

On one hand – or, rather, on one side of a hand – her profound new openness to God had suddenly infused with tremendous meaning all of the observances, celebrations and rituals of her Jewish heritage. Yom Kippur, Rosh Hashanah, Hanukkah, Passover: All became suffused with significance, even wonder, for the first time in Grace's life. The struggles of her people, their hardiness and Covenant-centered refusal to lose their identity or to forswear their heritage, amidst centuries of diasporas and pogroms and Holocaust, now inspired her with an awe so fierce it often shocked her. And because Christianity grew so directly from Judaism and considered Jesus Christ to be God's very redemption of the Jewish Covenant, Grace did not understand why Christians do not themselves take more pride in their Jewish heritage. Why should Christians *not* celebrate Yom Kippur, or Passover, or the others? The way Grace looked at it, most Jews obviously weren't Christians, but all Christians should still be first and foremost Jews. A celebration of Jesus without celebrating his Jewishness seemed to her the equivalent of celebrating New Year's Day without recourse to a calendar – only on a much more profound level. (For that matter, she thought that to be simultaneously Christian *and* antisemitic was akin to being an American patriot but hating the Constitution: At least subconsciously, it amounted to a belief system that was both nonsensical and self-loathing.) Anybody who believes that Jesus is the Messiah must, by purely logical extension, believe in the faith to which Jesus himself adhered and which Jesus the Christ was believed to have redeemed.

Certainly there is a difference between not being bound by every particular of the Jewish Law – *pace* the Evangelist Paul – and renouncing the entirety of the Jewish heritage from which Jesus and His Twelve Disciples sprang. Jesus may have been a light also to the Gentiles, but His light was supposed to attract Gentiles also to His Jewishness.

On the other side of the same hand, those were the same reasons why Grace believed she could remain a Jew while becoming a Christian. She could still be fully a Jew while believing that, yes, Jesus was indeed the promised Messiah and Son of God for whom the Jews of the Old Testament had waited for so many centuries. Jesus *was* the redemption of her people's Covenant – but her belief therein did not, in any way, remove her from her Jewishness. She now believed that those who are Jews without being Christians have, in the vernacular, "missed the boat" so to speak, but not that they are therefore doomed. The event that for Christians would be seen as the Second Coming would for Jews be seen as the first redemption for their millennia of suffering – but for both peoples it would be equally salvific. (And even if Christians believe Jesus' injunction that "no one comes to the Father except through me," their belief that "Christ will come again" means that Jews still will have another chance to accept Christ as their Messiah.) The only difference between her and her fellow Jews was that she believed that Jesus of Nazareth was the First Coming, and would come again, while they believed he was merely an important prophet still foretelling a coming Messiah. First Coming, Second Coming: What does it matter, as long as He will indeed come in the future?

Grace therefore had surprised and delighted her family by eagerly and devoutly taking part in all of the traditional Jewish observances during the previous year, and by occasionally showing up to services at the synagogue. What her parents didn't know was that, in weeks in which she did not observe the Jewish Sabbath, she usually attended Trinity

Episcopal Church instead. She secretly was taking an adult inquirer's class there as well and hoped to be baptized within the next year.

This weekend, she had arranged for her ex-husband to keep their kids for one more day than his usual allotment, so she could relax in Florida and reflect on all of her spiritual ferment without having to fight the Easter Day traffic back to New Orleans. Before agreeing to rent the cottage she chose, she made sure that there was a Christian church nearby at which she could celebrate Easter.

Grace had planned to leave early Friday morning. Thursday evening, however, she had been watching the local newscast and had seen Laura Green's phoned-in report. She heard Laura report that Mad would make a major announcement at the Mobile Civic Center on Friday. After her long spiritual journey that began with news of the posting of Mad's theses, Grace felt a compelling need to see, in person, what Mad had to say in the face of all the horrible allegations against him – and, if possible, to show her support. She did not believe for a minute that Mad was a crook. Mad deserved for the whole world to know it, and to see that Mad still had strong supporters.

Mobile is right on the way to Florida. It would all be so easy, Grace thought. Just stop off in Mobile, find the Civic Center, and go cheer Mad on.

She hadn't known that the public would be kept at bay behind the barricades. She hadn't known that Mad would announce the end of his ministry. She hadn't known that that same stupid mime, the mime from the Apostles of the Word church, would be in the same barricaded crowds, watching Mad's announcement on a large-screen TV and plotting to kill Mad immediately thereafter.

And she certainly didn't know, when she left the crowd to get her car right after Mad finished speaking, that she would be driving past the scene, along the side street, just as Mad would emerge and just as the mime would fire.

* * *

Becky and Justin and Mark Mariasson had set up an information nerve center at the MMW offices. Frustrated that they couldn't visit Shiloh, depressed that they had seen no solution other than to shut down and thoughtful and well-intentioned as Mad's would have been worth my time to point out its errors. If he truly closes down the MMW Corporation, I will miss the debate with a more-than-worthy adversary. Mostly, though, I wish Mad good health and a fruitful and rewarding life as a teacher, or on whatever path he chooses. And to his bodyguard Shiloh Jones, who proved himself a hero of all heroes for taking a bullet for his friend, I send my prayers and the deepest admiration of my soul. May God be ever with them both."

And in the Cayman Islands on Saturday afternoon, Buzz perused a morning paper. "Holy shit, Mary, Shiloh took a bullet!" he yelled. He and Mary, both still perfecting their disguises for their new lives of leisure, had become crooks but were far from lacking human feeling. Eventually they decided to launder about $1,000 of their ill-won loot into well-worn $20 bills and, whenever they next found themselves on a side trip away from the Caymans (so their location couldn't be traced), they would Fed-Ex the cash to Shiloh with no return address.

But not just yet. It was still too important that they not blow their cover. Maybe six months from then, if the search for them had grown cold....

* * *

Late that afternoon, during one of Shiloh's more lucid moments amidst the fog of painkillers, a weeping LaShauna, with Peter Vignelli still at her side, read out loud a hand-scrawled note to her husband.

> "Shiloh – I'm here at the hospital, but they won't let me see you. I'm scared, but they tell me you'll be okay. That's good. All I know is that I admire you more than anybody I know, and that your friendship means more to me than any friendship I have ever experienced. When it comes to getting well soon, please Carpe Diem. Love, Mad."

Shiloh nodded, and smiled faintly, and used his uninjured hand to wipe a tiny tear from one eye. He was a strong man. With friends and family such as these, he knew that eventually he'd be just fine. A college degree awaited, and he had a wonderful little daughter to raise.

* * *

Mad, unaware of the sympathy and kind wishes flowing his way, remained in his oddly near-catatonic state all day Saturday. So much, so much that was bad, had happened so fast, that it all spurred flashbacks to that time three years earlier when his whole life had fallen apart, rapid-fire, without warning. And as someone who always had skated through, or rather above, life, with what for most people would have seemed a blessed effortlessness, Mad was unequipped for crisis. Mad's theses called for courage, but Mad himself was weak. Good-hearted, intelligent, well-meaning, but weak. Truth was, he always had been so.

Besides that, his family were all dead. His ministry was ended. He had no known definite job prospects. His friends were either hospitalized or, he thought, probably estranged for life. His home church congregation had kicked him out. The national Episcopal Church office hated him. Millions of people thought, based on Spike Walters' reporting, that he was a crook. His attractiveness to women, which had always been his crutch, was no credit to him but a mere freak of scent. His hormonal imbalance had killed his own mother, wife, and child: Their deaths, in his mind, were his fault.

And now he had become so hated that somebody had tried to kill him. *Kill him!* Somebody actually wanted him dead – and as a result of Mad's ability to inspire such hatred, his best friend had been almost killed and may well be physically handicapped for life. That, too, Mad told himself, was all his fault.

Then, as a sort of bizarre reproach to top it all off, he had been saved, out of the blue, by the woman with whom he first had, well… *sinned*. Yes, that was it: It must have been a sin. The religious traditionalists must have been right all along. He had fornicated, and done so at a very young age, and everything that had happened since was God's way of punishing him for it. That's why Grace had shown up: To make the message oh-so-clear that all the misfortune was all his fault, all a punishment for his own lustful sins!

And now, surely, Grace would want him to sin again. He had not yet begun to take the pills that Dr. Raj had sent him; his pheromones would still be strong, and Grace would surely want him.

Being already damned beyond redemption, Mad thought, he might as well oblige. He would oblige, and God would punish him more, and he would oblige someone else, and God would punish him again and again, world without end, Amen.

That's what Mad thought to himself on that Saturday afternoon. Ignoring all orthodox theology and all his own theology as well, that's exactly what Mad thought.

But he didn't tell Grace this. He didn't tell Grace much of anything. No matter how hard Grace tried to engage him, Mad barely would talk at all.

His mind was scrambled. For the time being, at least, Mad indeed was mad.

And Grace, poor Grace, felt sorrow for Mad deep in her bones, and knew not what to do.

* * *

Mad wouldn't even walk on the beach with her. He wouldn't read the Bible she offered. He wouldn't do much of anything.

At least Mad consented to eat when Grace gave him food. She had come to Florida well prepared with rations. But he wouldn't say much, not even over dinner, and he kept looking at her oddly – as if she were a ghost. Then again, after 15 years – 15 years after their unexpected tryst followed by her guilt-induced withdrawal from his adolescent life – she figured that as far as Mad was concerned, she might as well be a ghost. The ghost of trysts-that-passed.

This was not the short vacation Grace had bargained for. But she felt somehow responsible for this handsome, wounded young man. He looked like a dreamboat – but he acted childlike, and fragile, and defeated. It wasn't lust that drew Grace to Mad now; it was simply human kindness.

Wordlessly, the two of them watched TV after dinner. As early as about 8:30, Mad began to nod off.

"Honey, why don't you go to bed now?" Grace suggested. "Tomorrow's Easter. It'll be a better day. That's God's promise to you, to all of us: On Easter, he will raise us up. Sleep now, Mad, and let Easter come to raise you up.

Mad didn't argue much. After a few minutes he did indeed wander off to bed.

A half hour later, Grace checked in on him. Mad was already asleep. Grace grabbed a spare blanket and closed the door softly. Tonight, she would sleep on the couch.

First, though, she would try to figure out whom to contact to let them know Mad was okay. She didn't know how, but she knew she would have to try.

Mad's personal effects, keys and the like, had been piled onto a coffee table. Among them was his cell phone. Grace turned it on.

Its screen indicated that 14 messages were stored in its voice mail. Grace didn't know Mad's code. But she fiddled around and found a list of the phone numbers of incoming calls. She didn't know whose numbers they were, but she figured that whichever number showed up most would probably be somebody important in Mad's life. Grace picked that number and pushed the "return call button."

It rang only twice before Becky Matthews Luke picked up. "You don't know me, but...," Grace began. The two women talked for something like 80 minutes. Grace took copious notes. At times, both of them were weeping. And at the end, Grace promised to deliver Mad back to Mobile, safe and sound, on Monday evening. Before that, though, Grace had some thinking to do, and would endure, on the couch, a fitful sleep.

* * *

"For I long to see you, that I may impart to you some spiritual gift to strengthen you, that is, that we may be mutually encouraged by each other's faith, both yours and mine." – *Romans, 1:11-12*.

* * *

The earliest bright morning sunlight streamed through the windows of the Florida cottage. It would be a glorious day.

Grace, awakening, gathered up all her notes from her conversation with Becky and tiptoed into the bedroom. Mad's eyes were wide open. "Hi, Grace," he said. He sounded a bit more focused, but still a little shaky. "I think I'm feeling a little better. But I still don't know what you're doing here. Why were you in Mobile when I was shot? How did you know I needed saving?"

Grace sat down, next to Mad, on the edge of the bed. In fits and starts, with laughter and tears, she told him the whole story. How she had been mortified at what happened between them when he was still so young. How she had been married, and then how the jerk had left her. How she loved her kids but couldn't control them. How she felt like a failed parent. How her boss was a slimeball. How she had been an only nominally Jewish atheist. How she had felt uncentered, unrooted, unfulfilled. Empty.

She told him how she had seen the first TV reports about his theses and about the deaths of Claire and the rest of his family. How she had felt pangs of pain on his behalf. She told how she had followed the progress of his ministry. How she had shown up at his appearances at Apostles of the Word, and how weird the experiences were for her – and yet, how oddly galvanizing. How somehow, something had awoken in her a yearning to understand all this God business. Not just something, but him, Mad. He and his theses and his preaching and his own odyssey had been a useful burr under her spiritual saddle.

She told Mad that she, Grace Feinstein Martin, was "Jezebel?."

"No way!" he said.

"Yes, way. I'm Jezebel, with a question mark, because my own knowledge of the Bible was so dim that I wasn't sure the particulars of who Jezebel was. I just had it in my mind that she was an evil woman. I felt like an evil woman. Evil for robbing you from the cradle. Evil for not being good at raising my kids. Evil for my promiscuity as an adolescent and young woman, and evil for being so lacking in faith. And I put a question mark because I wasn't sure if that made me an apt parallel for Jezebel. And I also put the question mark there, I think, because I didn't want to be Jezebel forever, and had a question as to whether that would be my name, be my fate, for all time."

"Jezebel? encouraged my faith," Mad said. "*You* encouraged my faith. When I had doubts, there you were on the web site, giving me hope that I was on the right track."

Then a puzzled expression crossed his face, and then his countenance darkened. The thought of a wounded Shiloh again had pierced his mind.

"Your kindness was much appreciated," he said. "Too bad it was wasted on somebody like me who was doing everything wrong."

Grace protested, but Mad wouldn't hear her. Struggling to climb out of his pit of despair, he had slipped and fallen partway back down again. His whole ministry, he said, had been a failure. People hated him, and he was a heretic, and Shiloh had nearly been killed.

"Mad, would you believe me if I proved to you that you're wrong?" she asked. "Would you believe that you've actually done some good?"

Mad shook his head in the negative. He even began to retreat into a fetal position, or at least a semblance of one. Kind as Grace was, he wouldn't let her keep his self-loathing from condemning his soul.

That's when Grace pulled out her notes. She explained that she had tracked down Becky last night. She said that Becky was worried sick about him, and that Becky and Justin said they forgave him, and that they loved him. She said that thousands and thousands of messages had come in, all wishing him well. Thousands and thousands of people he had touched. Thousands and thousands who loved him.

By this time, Grace had curled next to him on the bed, almost spooning him while propping herself on one elbow so she could read her notes. At times, she stroked his arms. She stroked his arms and told him people loved him.

The very thought, the thought that somebody could love him when he was so down on himself, came at Mad as a threat – a threat to his current self-image. It didn't accord with what he was feeling, and he reacted against it. He fell back on his crutch. People loved him, she said. With a bastardization of the same word, he responded:

"People love me: *Right*. And next you'll say that women love me. So what's next, Grace? Is it time for me to make love to you? I'll make love to you if that's what you want. I know that's what you want. [Mad fixed his eyes on hers.] You know, I really could make you feel *loved*."

Grace felt a familiar thrill run down her spine. She didn't know it, but Mad was still emitting pheromones like pollen from a fertile oak. Even in his pitiful state, Mad still had it. Whatever "it" was, Grace thought, Mad had it.

But she ignored the feeling. She caught her breath. It wouldn't be right. She had come to the conclusion, sometime during divorced parenthood and during her journey of faith, that there actually was something sacred about the conjoining of man and woman. Or at least that there should be. There actually was morality involved, and ethics, and something else even deeper that she couldn't quite find words for. She knew, finally knew, that sex was not meant to be taken lightly.

"No, Mad," she said. "That's not what this is about."

Mad was stunned. He knew she was feeling something for him. He could see it in her posture. "You don't fool me," he said, kindly but firmly. "I know you want to sleep with me."

Grace took a deep breath. "No, Mad," she said again, and then began to say something else. That's when some Robert Frost lines oddly entered her head – not that she identified them at the time as Robert Frost's, but just as odd lines she had heard somewhere or other – and, riffing off of them, she said:

"We have promises to make and keep, and miles to go before we sleep together. Miles to go, before we sleep."

Mad looked confused.

"Promises to make, and keep," she repeated. "It may not be with you, but I may need a vow. But certainly not now, Mad. Not here. Not now."

Even without taking the pills from Dr. Raj, Mad concluded he apparently no longer had his crutch of sex. Not even his sex-appeal worked any more! For at least a few minutes, that discovery would send him further back into a funk.

Grace, wanting to get back on subject, continued to read him more messages. The one from Steve Matheson, she had taken down word for word. Likewise the one from stern old Gladys Phillpott. The chat room entry from Defender.

Mad still seemed unimpressed.

"Would you really believe all these people are wrong about you?" she asked. Mad merely shrugged.

"Okay, here's another one," she said. "This one is long. But your friend Becky said to be sure you saw it. I'll read it word for word:

"Dear Madison,

You won't recognize my name, because, as far as I know, you never even knew my husband's name. He wanted it that way. You knew my husband as The Colonel. I understand that he called you often.

Madison, I don't know if you realize this, but my husband had grown very fond of you. At first he was quite wary of your penchant for generating publicity, but the more he saw of you, the more he saw your grandfather's – I believe you called him 'Daddy Lee' – your grandfather's cavalier spirit. And as your grandfather was one of his dearest friends, that made him able to get over his wariness about you.

So my husband had grown fond of you anyway. That was even before your speech at his wonderful *alma mater*, the institution to which he devoted his life, the University of Virginia. What you did that day, by beginning to endow a scholarship for the study of James Madison, touched my husband's heart in a way I don't think anybody outside of our immediate family has ever touched it. Not only that, but it made him very proud. Furthermore, it was a very very good thing you did, on its own merits, completely apart from my husband's approval.

You didn't know this, Madison, but the Colonel had become ill. His heart had begun to grow weak. He knew he was running out of time. In fact, he had one of his heart attacks the very night of your speech. It was a small one, but it signaled the beginning of the end. That's why you haven't heard from him in so many months. The Colonel was dying. Two months ago, on February 8, on his 80th birthday, The Colonel passed away.

He did not do so, however, without remembering you. I have not told you this until now, because I was waiting for all the legal affairs of the estate to be straightened out, something that still hasn't fully happened yet. But when I saw the news that you had been shot, I thought it would cheer you up to know this. Fine print be damned, as my husband would say, this is going to happen, and hopefully by this coming fall. In his will, my husband left a bequest, and directed that the Crazy Eights match the personal amount of his bequest, to the effect of fully endowing the Madison scholarship at the university. Between your donation, and his donation, and the Eights' donation, the James Madison scholarship you created will now be funded in perpetuity.

When all the fine print is worked out, a personal letter from The Colonel to you will also be delivered.

My dear young Madison, I wish you the speediest of recoveries, the best of health, and the best of fortune in your future endeavors. Wishing to honor The Colonel's request to remain anonymous, I am very sincerely yours,

> The Colonel's Wife

Something good began to stir inside Madison Lee Jones, but his pain and confusion were so great that the stir was barely noticeable. He was moved, though. Deeply moved. Moved just enough to recognize how much more he needed to be moved.

He reached for Grace's arm. He didn't want to conquer her, but he desperately wanted to lie with her. He needed the comfort only a woman could provide.

Again, she rebuffed him. Again, he was stunned.

"Mad, I can't do that," Grace said, herself struggling with her feelings. "It's not that I don't like you. I do. And I feel a real chemistry between us. Even more than that, though, Mad, I think you are something special. It was you – your theses, your newspaper advice column, your preaching – that helped me find myself for the first time in my life.

You even answered a letter of mine in your column, a letter I signed G.F. Martin. I don't know if you knew who I was. But what you said meant a lot to me Mad, and what is inside you means a lot to me. It has nothing to do with how I feel for you physically, Mad. This isn't some kind of biological determinism. I've felt attracted to you these past few years without even being near you. It's what *inside* you that means so much. And because it means so much, I don't want to sleep with you. Even though I desire you, I will not sleep with you now. Because what you have done for me is too important for casual sex, Mad. It's too important. Would you please believe that I want to know you as a person before I 'know' you in the biblical sense? Would you believe that, Mad?"

Mad just stared at her. Then: "I'm a loser," he said. "I guess I did one thing right, with that scholarship, but everything else I've done is pathetic. And God knows I'm pathetic. I'm not Job; I'm one of those who think they are so high that God must strike them low."

"No, Mad, that's not true," she said. "People love you, Mad. Your friends, they love you. And all those people who you've re-introduced to God, they love you, too. Would you believe that all those people love you?"

No answer.

"Would you believe that I might grow to love you?"

No answer.

"Would you believe that without you, and without your ministry, my life would still be miserable? Would you believe that in the last year I've begun to find God, and with it my own better self, because of the journey that you, Mad Jones, started me on?"

Still no answer... but a flicker of calm amidst Mad's heretofore pained expression.

"Mad, would you believe that God doesn't want you to suffer? Would you believe that He wants you to know joy? That's what you've preached, Mad: that God wants you to know joy."

Mad nodded in recognition of his own words. Grace pressed on.

"Would you believe that you've done great good in the world, Mad? Would you believe that just by talking about God, by beginning the conversation in a meaningful and thoughtful and original way, you have done God's work by opening thousands, maybe millions of people to a new consideration of God?

"Would you believe that God is good? Would you believe that He loves us all if only we accept his love? Would you believe that God so loved the world that He gave His son for its sake? Would you please believe that if you go to God when you are heavy laden, He will refresh you?"

Something more powerful began to stir in Mad's breast. He could feel it now. He wanted to be numb, but Grace's words were making him feel.

"Come *on*, Mad… *Please*?!" Grace couldn't see what was happening inside Mad's spirit. All she saw was his blank expression. His blankness scared her. Why couldn't she get through to him? She tried one more time.

"Mad, please believe that we're all in this together? Would you please believe that much at least? You and I and your friends and all of us in this crazy world, all of us together with God, God with us, all struggling, all striving, all learning from each other, all trying to find the way to share God's love? Would you believe that God is struggling, too? Would you believe that in our struggles we endure, and that endurance creates hope and all that other good stuff you like to quote all the time?"

Silence from Mad – but an almost imperceptible beginning of a look of clarity.

"Come on, Mad, would you believe that God loves you? Would you believe that this life we live is a gift of God's love? Would you believe that we can all find God's love together? Come on, Mad:

"Would you believe?"

"Yes.

"Dammit… *yes*."

Acknowledgements for *The Accidental Prophet*

This book took a long, long road to publication. Along the way, so many people have helped me hone it, have given me encouragement, and have consoled me when hope seemed lost, that I am sure I will forget someone who should be on this list.

But I must especially acknowledge these six (of the seven) people who did the most to help along the way. For my friend and superb public servant Bob Livingston, who invested in my effort from the very start, I cannot express enough gratitude. And for my lifelong friend Hugh Russell and my aunts and uncles Carter and Pat Hillyer and Alex and Kippy Comfort, who read the whole book and gave me extremely helpful, constructive criticism, I am more thankful than they will ever know.

My brother-in-law Murray Robinson offered superbly incisive analysis. My longtime agent Kathryn Helmers finally gave up after several years of trying, but she truly "got it" in terms of what I was trying to accomplish, and gave me highly valuable advice along the way. Quinn Todd Fitzpatrick provided early, wise editing assistance.

Novelists Nancy Lemann, Roy Hoffman, and Winston Groom offered suggestions and encouragement. Friends Bill Black and Jennifer Markley Hed gave me a very early boost before even two chapters were finished—and before that, Kenya Brunson insisted that I write a novel, even before I had an idea for one, and she gave me a little book in which to start hand-writing it.

For other advice and encouragement, I thank Deroy Murdock, Gary McElroy, and Nan Tolbert; Tom Tripp and Jameson Campaigne; my brother Haywood Hillyer IV and my mom Brenda Hillyer, along with my late father Haywood Hillyer III; my godfather Ben C. Toledano, and Margaret Toledano; Cendra Lynn of GriefNet.org; Jon and Adrienne Gray; and Craig Shirley. For spiritual inspiration, I thank The Right Reverend Duncan Gray III. For intellectual inspiration and for spurring my interest in Martin Luther, I credit Georgetown Professor Dianne Yeager.

My editor at Liberty Island, David Swindle, rescued Mad Jones from oblivion. My thanks to him for resurrecting Mad are boundless. Ditto, and then some, to Jamie Wilson, who has republished this in a single volume.

***

When this book was originally published in three volumes, each volume was dedicated individually as follows:

Heretic:

In memory of William Hillyer, Richard Livingston, Julie Hollahan, Brett Watson, Christopher Thomas, Michael Beauchamp, and Chiggy Rhodes, all of whom slipped away far too young—but not before leaving an indelible, wonderful imprint on our lives.

Hero:

In loving memory of Haywood H. Hillyer III and Haywood H. Hillyer IV.

Agonistes:

In memory of Gary McElroy, the most literate friend I've ever known, a heart that defied science, and the first friend with whom I celebrated finishing this novel. October 27, 1948-March 4, 2018.

***

And, last and most, to the person who read through, lovingly critiqued, lived with the unpublished novel for 14 years, comforted me in the course of all the stops and starts and false hopes involving this novel—my wife Tresy—I can only say "Wow." She is a trooper, a helpmate, and the love of my universe. Thank you, Tresy.

Appendix A

Theses

By

Mad Jones

Would you believe …

1. God is a flawed sonuvabitch, just like the humans he created.

2. "So God created man in his own image, in the image of God created He him; male and female created He them." Genesis 1:27

3. "I, the Lord thy God, am a jealous God, visiting the iniquity of the fathers upon the children unto the third and fourth generation." Exodus 20:5

   "For the Lord thy God is a consuming fire, even a jealous God." Deuteronomy 4:24

4. "For thus saith the Lord God of Israel unto me: 'Take from my hand this cup filled with the wine of my wrath, and cause all the nations, to whom I send thee, to drink it. And they shall drink, and be moved, and be mad, because of the sword that I will send among them." Jeremiah 25:15-16

5. God is arrogant, and mad with power, as when he tortures Job. God says: "Who then is able to stand before me? Who hath prevented me, that I should repay him? Whatsoever is under the whole heaven is mine." Job 41:10-11

6. Christ said: "And his lord was wroth, and delivered him to the tormentors, till he should pay all that was due unto him. So likewise shall my heavenly Father do also unto you, if ye from

your hearts forgive not every one his brother their trespasses." Matthew 18:34-35

7. 7. It therefore follows that when God created man in God's image, or "likeness" (Genesis 5:1), it was a spiritual and emotional likeness — an interior image — intended, not a physical likeness (which is abundantly made clear throughout the Bible). So we see that God is jealous and wrathful and unfair (as He was to Job), and arrogant and prone to going mad with His own power, and that He punishes mankind overly harshly, even unto torture, when man acts imperfectly, even though it was He, God, who created man as an imperfect being because man is in God's own image — which, of necessity, means that God Himself is imperfect. QED.

8. As God is imperfect, therefore He is inconsistent — yea, even mercurial.

9. As God is mercurial, therefore His mercy, at least here on earth, is dependent on God's mood swings, or, i.e., contingent rather than unconditional.

10. As God's mercy is contingent, and as God is imperfect, so therefore may His mercy be contingent on something other than man's own merit, but rather, at times, on circumstances beyond the ken of man.

11. God's mercy is therefore entirely unpredictable and unreliable, at least within man's temporal existence.

12. For all intents and purposes, then, to man's way of knowing, God Is A Jerk.

13. Because God is a jerk, mankind cannot count on God for comfort during this life.

14. Therefore, men and women must rely on other men and women for comfort on earth. (For what it's worth, safe sex can be heap big comfort.)

15. When human turns to human for comfort, which man often does because God cannot be counted on to provide it, God may become jealous (for He is a jealous God), and in His jealousy God may deliberately cause discomfort to man – for no good reason, not even for good reason according to the unknowable lights of God.

16. This reality helps explain the words of Jesus to the crowd of wailing women, as Jesus was led on his march of death to Golgotha: "Daughters of Jerusalem, weep not for me, but weep for yourselves, and for your children. For behold, the days are coming in which they shall say, Blessed are the barren, and the wombs that never bore and the breasts which never gave suck." Luke 23:28-29

17. Yea, verily do I ask of you: What kind of God, except a fallible God who is a jerk, would curse innocent women whose wombs become with child according to the life-creating union sanctified by God himself through Holy Matrimony?

18. "For we know that the whole creation groaneth and travaileth in pain together until now." Romans 8:22

19. "As it is written, For thy sake we are killed all the day long; we are accounted as sheep for the slaughter." Romans 8:36

20. If we are in pain, and are counted as sheep for the slaughter, shall we then bleat like sheep? Nay, we are sheep only insofar as we acquiesce to sheep-hood.

21. To acquiesce in sheep-hood is to sin greatly, for it puts us in the position of trying to become Christ, who is the only Lamb of God. Christ Himself commanded us, not to be lambs, but rather to consume Him, the only Lamb, by partaking of the Eucharist. Lambs do not eat Lamb; lions do.

22. Therefore, Christ calls us all to be lions.

23. No wonder, then, that the first of God's worshipful seraphim was like a lion (Revelation 4:7) and that the being found worthy

to open the book of God was "the Lion of the tribe of Judah" (Revelation 5:5).

24. As we are called to be lions, and to honor the Lamb by consuming the Lamb, therefore let us also devour life with both reverence and gusto, or else God's great but imperfect creation will devour us who are unworthy, timid souls whose existence rebukes God by reminding Him that what He created can be weak.

25. "For we are made partakers of Christ, if we hold the beginning of our confidence steadfast unto the end." Hebrews 3:1

26. "Cast not away therefore your confidence, which hath great recompense of reward… but if any man draw back, my soul shall have no pleasure in him. But we are not of them who draw back unto perdition, but of them that believe to the saving of the soul." Hebrews 10:35, 38-39.

27. "The Lord loves winners." Gene Hackman, in The Poseidon Adventure.

28. Winners and lions. The Wind and the Lion. Perdicaris alive. And God said: Yes, we can survive even in the desert of our souls. Yes.

29. Jesus survived the wilderness of the desert for 40 days, and withstood the temptations of Satan, all on God's account; yet God repaid Jesus' loyalty by requiring that Jesus suffer on the cross. Jesus did not forsake God, yet Jesus on the cross was moved to ask, and ask rightly, "Eloi, Eloi, lama sabachthani?" – which means "My God, my God, why have you forsaken me?" (Matthew 27:46; Mark 15:34) They were his last words.

30. Christ, God the Son, was forsaken by God the Father. It is said that Christ suffered in order to take upon himself the sins of the world – but God the Father created the world, and created it flawed, so the world had sin. Therefore, God is the original author of the sins of the world, sins which we, mankind, who

are not omnipotent, have therefore not only committed but also suffered from due to the sins not of our own commission, but of God's.

31. As in: "Hath not the potter power over the clay, of the same lump to make one vessel unto honour, and another unto dishonour?" Romans 9:21

32. Christ's suffering therefore not only redeemed us, for our sins against God, but also redeemed God for his sins against we humans who mightily suffer.

33. Christ died, and was raised through the ultimate grace and glory of God, to save sinners; so, therefore, Christ died to save God, whose mercy grew in strength because Christ allowed Himself to be forsaken and thus gave God a new birth in man's hearts just as he gave man a new birth in the Holy Spirit.

34. In prayer we call Jesus Christ "our only mediator and advocate." A mediator, by nature, mediates between two (or more) entities, and so therefore both entities are equally beneficiaries of the mediation. God, therefore, is a beneficiary of Christ's mediation with us just as we are beneficiaries of Christ's mediation with God.

35. "As it is written, There is none righteous, no not one." Romans 3:10

36. God, too, is among those who aren't righteous. Jesus withstood Satan's temptation, but God did not withstand Satan's temptation when Satan challenged God to prove His power over Job. "Then Satan answered the Lord, and said, Doth Job fear God for nought?" Job 1:9

37. God also cruelly tested Abraham: "And He said, Take now thine only son Isaac, whom thou lovest, and … offer him thee for a burnt offering." Genesis 22:2

38. What kind of God is it who requires that his chosen patriarch be willing to sacrifice the son who is most dear to him, and that

his righteous follower Job suffer, and that His only Son be crucified, all to demonstrate His own power and glory (Amen)?

39. Yes, until Christ Jesus transcended the Law so that man might be justified by faith in God's grace, God was consistently a jerk – and He continues frequently in such jerkiness, which is part of His flawed nature, with the distinction that, post-Christ, God allows us eventual union with God's better self, by means of our spiritual resurrection after death, which is given us through our faith by means of God's grace.

40. Because God sent Christ to redeem man to God and God to man, and because God's ultimate will is grace (even when his temporal will is inconstant and jealous and wrathful, and causes us to suffer for no good reason); therefore "whatsoever ye do, do all to the glory of God (Corinthians 10:31)."

Q: How, then, does one do glory to a fallible, jealous, and wrathful God who nevertheless wills to us, by way of his better self, a merciful life everlasting?

Would you believe?

41. Abide by the Ten Commandments, as Christ explained.

42. Abide by the two Great Commandments identified by Christ Jesus. (Love the Lord with all thy heart, etc., and the second is like unto it, etc.)

43. Ignore (if you must) all those other rules in Leviticus, which were for a particular people at a particular time, for Paul said (in effect) that the Law was superseded by Christ – although those who keep the rules still are to be honored for keeping their faith through the centuries.

44. All, of all faiths, should honor the Jews, "chiefly, because that unto them were committed the oracles of God." Romans 3:2

45. Do all such good works as the Lord hast prepared for us to walk in.

46. It is very meet, right, and our bounden duty that we should at all times, and in all places, give thanks unto… Everlasting God.

47. Yet the greatest thanks we can give God is our honesty, which means we should curse him mightily (though fearfully and with love-not-hate) when he does us wrong.

48. God respects and ultimately blesses those who wrestle with him honestly, as Jacob did at Penuel. Wrestle with God for that which is good, however, not to give license for sin.

49. The Twelve Commandments are to be observed because they are right and just and good in and of themselves, not because we want to gain God's favor.

50. Just as the Law (12 Commandments) condemns us when we break it (though we are not eternally condemned if we accept God's grace), so too does the Law condemn God when we faithfully observe the Law and God does not reward us in this life for our doing so.

51. God is condemned by the Saints who He allows or forces to suffer even though they abide by the 12 Commandments.

52. God is redeemed by offering the grace of eternal life in propitiation for the sins He and we commit against each other.

53. There is a special place in Heaven for the saints, who become Guardian Angels and thus find the special joys of helping future generations abide and find some triumph over the pains of earthly life. (For reference, see angels throughout the Bible.)

54. "Blessed are they that do his commandments, that they may have right to the tree of life." Revelation 22:14

55. Despite his temporal jerkiness, "For God so loved the world, that he gave his only begotten Son, that whosoever believeth in him should not perish, but have everlasting life." John 3:16

56. Said Jesus Christ: "Come unto me, all ye that travail and are heavy laden, and I will refresh you." Matthew 11:28

57. Forgive God the Father, take comfort and joy in God the Son, and honor both by striving to be lions and winners.

58. Therefore, hold fast to that which is good; be strong and of good courage.

59. As Paul wrote (Romans 5:3-4): "Suffering produces endurance, and endurance produces character, and character produces hope, and hope does not disappoint us, because God's love has been poured into our hearts through the Holy Spirit which has been given to us."

Amen.

Here I shout; I cannot do otherwise.

Madison Lee Jones

Made in United States
Orlando, FL
10 January 2024